Ovid
Metamorphoses

Translated
by
Ian Johnston
Vancouver Island University
Nanaimo, British Columbia
Canada

Richer Resources Publications
Arlington, Virginia
USA

Ovid
Metamorphoses

Copyright 2012 by Richer Resources Publications
All rights reserved

Cover art by Ian Crowe

No part of this book may be reproduced in whole or in part without express permission from the publisher except for brief excerpts in review.

Reprint requests and requests for additional copies of this book should be addressed to

Richer Resources Publications
1926 N. Woodrow Street
Arlington, Virginia 22207

or via our web sit at www.RicherResourcesPublications.com.

ISBN 978-1-935238-58-4
Library of Congress Control Number 2011943134

Published by Richer Resources Publications
Arlington, Virginia
Printed in the United States of America

Once again, for Colleen

OVID
THE METAMORPHOSES

TABLE OF CONTENTS
[For more specific details of the contents of a particular book, consult the summary provided at the opening of that book]

Translator's Note 6

A Note on Ovid 6

Book 1 9
[Invocation; Creation; Four Ages, War of the Giants; Lycaon; the Flood; Deucalion and Pyrrha; creation of new life; Apollo and Pytho; Apollo and Daphne; Jupiter, Io, and Juno; Argus, Io, and Mercury; Pan and Syrinx; Phaëton and Clymene]

Book 2 42
[Phaëton and Apollo; Daughters of the Sun; Cycnus; Callisto, Jupiter, and Juno; Callisto and Arcas; Raven and Crow; Coronis and Apollo; Ocyrhoë; Battus and Mercury; Mercury and Herse; Aglauros, Juno, and Mercury; Europa and Jupiter]

Book 3 78
[Cadmus and the Serpent; Actaeon and Diana; Semele, Jupiter, and Juno; birth of Bacchus; Juno, Jupiter, and Teiresias; Echo and Narcissus; Pentheus, Acoetes, and Bacchus]

Book 4 110
[The Daughters of Minyas; Pyramus and Thisbe; Mars and Venus; the Sun, Leucothea, and Clytië; Salmacis and Hermaphroditus; Athamas and Ino; Cadmus and Harmonia, Perseus and Atlas; Perseus and Andromeda]

Book 5 143
[Perseus and Phineus; the Muses and Minerva; the Daughters of Pierus and the Muses; Typhoëus and the Gods; Pluto and Proserpine; Ceres and Cyane; Ceres and Arethusa; the Sirens; Arethusa and Alpheus; Triptolemus and Lyncus]

Book 6 173
[Arachne and Minerva; Niobe and Latona; Latona and the Lycians; Marsyas; Tereus, Philomela, and Procne; Orithyïa and Boreas]

Book 7 206
[Jason and Medea; Medea and Aeson; Medea and Pelias; Cycnus and Hyrië; Medea and Aegeus; Medea and Theseus; Minos and Aeacus; Cephalus and Aeacus; Plague in Aegina; Laelaps; Aeacus and the Myrmidons, Cephalus and Procris]

Book 8 244
[Minos and Scylla, Minos and the Minotaur; Daedalus and the Labyrinth; Theseus and Ariadne; Daedalus and Icarus; Daedalus and Perdix; Calydonian Boar Hunt; Althaea and Meleager; Perimele and Acheloüs; Baucis and Philemon; Ceres, Erysichthon, Hunger, and Maestra]

Book 9 283
[Hercules and Acheloüs, Nessus and Hercules; Death of Hercules; Alcmene and Galanthis; Iole and Dryope; Byblis and Caunus, Iphis and Iänthe]

Book 10 320
[Orpheus and Eurydice; Cyparissus; Jupiter and Ganymede; Hyacinthus and Apollo; the Cerastes; the daughters of Propoetus; Pygmalion; Myrrha and Cinyras; Adonis and Venus; Atalanta and Hippomenes]

Book 11 352
[Death of Orpheus; Midas and Silenus; Midas and Bacchus; Pan and Apollo; Apollo, Neptune, and Hercules; Peleus and Thetis; Peleus and Ceyx; Chione and Daedalion; Peleus and Psamathe; Ceyx and Alcyone; Morpheus and Alcyone; Aesacus and Hesperië]

Book 12 385
[Agamemnon at Aulis; Iphigeneia; Home of Rumour; Cycnus and Achilles; Caeneus; Centaurs and Lapiths; Theseus and the Centaurs; Cyllarus and Hylonome; Caeneus and Latreus; Nestor, Hercules, and Periclymenes; Neptune, Apollo, and Achilles]

Book 13 413
[Ajax and Ulysses, Destruction of Troy, Achilles and Polyxena; Hecuba and Polymestor; Aurora and Memnon; Aeneas and Anius; Voyage of Aeneas; Acis, Galatea, and Polyphemus; Scylla and Glaucus]

Book 14 456
[Glaucus, Scylla, and Circe; Aeneas and Dido; The Cercopes; Aeneas and the Sibyl; Aeneas in the Underworld; Apollo and the Sibyl; Achaemenides and Polyphemus; Macareus and Ulysses; Ulysses and Circe; Picus, Canens, and Circe; Diomedes in Italy; Aeneas in Latium; the fall of Ardea; Aeneas becomes a god; kings of Alba; Vertumnus and Pomona; Iphis and Anaxarete; Venus saves Rome; Romulus becomes a god]

Book 15 493
[Numa; Myscelus and Crotona; Pythagoras; Egeria, Hippolytus, and Diana; Tages; Romulus' spear; Cipus; Aesculapius; Julius Caesar; Augustus Caesar; Envoi]

Glossary and Index 530

The Transformations 550

Acknowledgments 555

Note on the Translator 556

Translator's Note

In this translation, the numbers in square brackets refer to the lineation in Ovid's Latin text, the numbers without brackets refer to the English text. In the latter, partial lines are counted together in the reckoning, so that two or three short lines are equivalent to one full line.

The explanatory footnotes, the headings at the right-hand margins, and the summaries at the start of each book have been added by the translator.

Following common conventions, I have used a dieresis over a vowel to indicate that it is pronounced as a separate syllable (e.g., Phaëton has three syllables, Prothoënor has four). Final vowels in names are usually pronounced by themselves, unless the name is fairly common in English (e.g., Hyrie, Hecate, and Cybele have three syllables each; whereas, Crete, Rome, Nile, and Rhone have only one). For help with the pronunciation of names, consult the section at the start of the Glossary and Index (on page 530).

Ovid frequently changes tenses from past to present and back again, often in the same passage. While this practice is not uncommon in colloquial English, it is relatively rare in formal poetry. Following the example of a number of others, I have retained Ovid's practice of shifting tenses, but have done so in a way that is, I hope, less abrupt than in the Latin text.

Another minor difficult with Ovid's text is his habit of having speeches within speeches. To avoid the cumbersome punctuation involved with this stylistic feature, especially with a speech within a speech within a speech, I have used double quotation marks for direct speech and single quotation marks for all indirect speech and have indented the left margin to indicate that a particular speech is part of what someone else says.

A Note on Ovid

Publius Ovidus Naso was born in 43 BC in Sulmo, a town in central Italy. After an education preparing him for the practice of law, he became a full-time poet and produced three collections of erotic poetry and his best known work, *The Metamorphoses*, in addition to other poems and a dramatic tragedy, *Medea* (now lost). In AD 8 he was banished by Emperor Augustus to Tomis on the Black Sea where he died in AD 17. The reasons for his exile are unknown.

The Metamorphoses is one of the most famous and long-lasting works in our traditions. It has exerted a decisive influence on the development of Western culture almost since its first appearance, not merely in literature but also in painting and sculpture, and that influence continues to the present day. For hundreds of years it was the principal source of material about Classical mythology, and the poem decisively shaped the work of countless poets, dramatists, artists, and sculptors.

Ovid is particularly celebrated for his sophisticated style. His stories, most of which involve physical changes of human beings, nymphs, and gods into different forms, are not presented as a mere catalogue but are seamlessly linked by subtle transitions and narrative techniques which make different stories part of continuing series of dramatic events. Hence, the poem maintains a rapid forward momentum, with no sense of constantly stopping and starting over.

Ovid will often trace the origin of a story back to the psychological motives which launched it (the anger or lust of the gods, the confused feeling of a young girl in love, for example), so that the story is not merely a succession of events but an unfolding drama with an acute sense of the emotional complexities of the participants.

Ovid's visual imagination is also remarkable. His poem creates extraordinarily graphic images, often with the insertion of a single detail. This quality he frequently uses to inject a cozy eroticism, a moving pathos, or an unexpectedly brutal detail into his descriptions. It is no accident that this poem has always been a fecund resource for visual artists.

But the most famous and complex aspect of the poem emerges from the narrator's attitude to his own work, one important source of Ovid's famous "wit." For while the narrator is a master storyteller and clearly enjoys delivering yet another well known traditional tale, he is also constantly mocking belief in the truth of the stories. Unlike most of his predecessors, he refuses to take the myths seriously, except as artistic fictions. The result is that the stories are celebrated, first and foremost, as poetic creations, rather than as essential embodiments of a system of belief. The technique is risky, of course, for there's a danger of undercutting the emotional effects of the story by calling attention to its absurdity, but Ovid's narrative tone is so masterfully controlled that we find both the stories and the narrator's attitude delightful.

This element of the style, of course, helps to explain why this thoroughly pagan poem was so popular in Medieval Christian cultures, because, unlike other Classical epics, the poem itself does not take the divine figures particularly seriously as objects of veneration. One can enjoy their adventures as wonderful stories, without disturbing orthodox Christian beliefs or, alternatively, interpret the stories as delightful allegorical depictions of Christian teachings.

In addition Ovid is very aware of his most illustrious predecessors, particularly Homer, Lucretius, and Virgil, and his text is always reminding us of their earlier works. Here again, the style is often elusive—in part a tribute to his great ancestors, in part a gentle satire on them, and in part a reminder that the poet of the *Metamorphoses* can match their efforts when it comes to a traditional epic or dramatic set piece, like a battle in a banquet hall, a storm at sea, an urban plague, a dangerous hunt, a philosophical disquisition, a formal argument, and so on.

For a more detailed introduction to Ovid's poem prepared by the translator, please consult the following internet site:

http://records.viu.ca/~johnstoi/introser/ovid.htm.

Book One

I

[Invocation; Primal Chaos; formation of Earth; regions of Earth; distribution of winds; creation of life; Prometheus makes human beings; the Golden Age; the Silver Age; the Bronze and Iron Ages; war of the Giants; Jupiter's anger at the human race; the story of Lycaon; the Deluge; Deucalion and Pyrrha restore the human race; the creation of other life; Apollo kills Pytho; Apollo and Daphne; Daphne is transformed; Inachus and Io; Jupiter has sex with Io, changes her into a cow, and gives her to Juno; Juno sets Argus to guard Io; Io reveals herself to Inachus; the story of Syrinx; Mercury kills Argus; Juno ends Io's torments; the story of Phaëton begins.]

My spirit drives me now to sing about
the forms of things changed into new bodies.
Since you gods caused these transformations, too,
inspire what I am going to write about,
and bring forth an uninterrupted song,
from the primal origins of the world
down to this present age.

                   Before the sea,   PRIMAL CHAOS
land, and heavens, which cover everything,
the entire world of nature looked the same.
They called it Chaos, a crude, confused mass,
nothing but lifeless stuff and scattered seeds
of matter not yet properly combined,
all piled up in the same place together.
There was no Titan yet providing light
to the world, Phoebe did not grow larger
and renew her crescent horns, nor did Earth
remain hanging in the surrounding air,
balanced by her own weight.[1] Amphitrite
had not yet pushed her arms through long margins
of the coastal shores, and where there was land
there was also sea and air, but the ground
was not solid, the water was not fit
for swimming, and the air lacked any light.[2]
No matter retained its own proper shape—
one thing would keep obstructing something else,
for in one body cold things fought with hot,
wet with dry, soft with hard, and heavy things
with those which had no weight.

---

[1] In Greek mythology, the Titans were the immediate divine descendants of the first two gods Gaia and Ouranos. Phoebe (from the Greek for *shining*) was one of the original Titans and became synonymous with the moon, while the Titan who provided light from the sun was Hyperion or Hyperion's son, Helios. Ovid usually identifies the sun god as Apollo.

[2] Amphitrite, wife of Neptune, god of the sea, here stands for the sea generally.

Book One

                  This conflict   FORMATION OF THE EARTH
god and more favourable nature stopped.
For he cut land off from sky, and water   30
from land, and separated the bright heavens
from heavy air. Then, once he had drawn off
these elements and taken them away
from the confused mass, he set them apart,
fixing them in place in harmonious peace.
The fiery might of vaulted, weightless sky
pushed out, creating for itself a place
in the loftiest heights. Closest to it
in lightness and location was the air.
The Earth, denser than these two, attracted   40
the larger elements and was pressed down   [30]
by its own weight. Water flowing round it
took possession of the furthest regions
and enclosed the solid sphere completely.

After the god—whichever god it was—   REGIONS OF EARTH
had divided Chaos and arranged it
in this way, forcefully dividing it
in sections, first of all he shaped the land
in the form of a large sphere, to make sure
it was the same on every side, and then   50
he commanded seas to be spread around
and swell with blustery winds, encircling
shore lands of the places they surrounded.
He added springs, huge pools, and lakes, and set
sloping banks to contain descending streams.
These differ in different locations—
some the earth itself absorbs, while others   [40]
reach the sea and, entering the expanse
of open water, beat against the coasts
instead of riverbanks. He also ordered   60
plains to be extended, valleys to sink,
leaves to cover trees, and stony mountains
to rise up. And just as heavens are split,   CLIMATES ON EARTH
with two zones in the north, two in the south,
and a fifth zone hotter than each of these,
so the god was careful to distinguish
the enclosed matter with the same number
and on earth marked out as many climates.
Of these, the one in the centre is too hot
to live in, and two are covered in deep snow.   70   [50]

Book One

Between these areas he placed two more,
assigning them a temperate climate,
mixing heat and cold. Over these hangs air,
heavier than fire, to the same extent
that earth is heavier than water.[1]

There he also ordered clouds to gather   DISTRIBUTION OF WINDS
and vapours, too, and thunder which so stirs
the minds of human beings, as well as
winds producing lightning bolts and flashes.
The maker of the world did not permit   80
these winds to take possession of the air
indiscriminately. It is, even now,
difficult to stop them ripping the world
to pieces, though each of them directs his blasts
at different places, so great is the strife   [60]
among the brothers.[2] Eurus moved away
towards Aurora, to Nabath's kingdom,
to Persia and the heights lying underneath
the rays of morning sunlight.[3] Zephyrus
is closest to the evening star and shores   90
warmed by the setting sun. Cold Boreas
invaded Scythia and northern lands.[4]
And rain-filled Auster with his constant clouds
soaks regions lying on the facing side.[5]
Over these he placed bright, weightless aether,
without a trace of earth's impurities.

Scarcely had he separated all things   CREATION OF LIFE
within specific limits in this way,
when the stars, which had remained long hidden,   [70]

---

[1] The heavens had been divided up by astronomers with five parallel circles: the equinox (in the centre), the two tropics (Cancer and Capricorn), and two polar circles. These verses indicate that the god marked out the climates on the earth's surface in a similar numerical pattern: the hot zone is between the tropics, the temperate zones are between the tropics and the polar circles, and the frigid zones are beyond the polar circles. The Latin uses the terms *right* and *left*; following many others, I have substituted *north* and *south*.

[2] The winds were the sons of Astraeus and Aurora and thus brothers. The idea here is that the creator of the world controlled the ferocity of the winds by having them blow in different directions (or from different places) rather than all together in the same direction.

[3] Eurus was the east wind (i.e., blowing from the east). It comes from Aurora (meaning dawn). Nabath was a name associated with regions in the Middle East, especially Arabia.

[4] Scythia refers generally to northern territories.

[5] Zephyrus was the west wind, Boreas the north wind, and Auster the south wind.

buried in thick mist, began to blaze forth
through the entire sky. And to make sure
no place would lack its forms of living things,
the stars and forms of gods inhabited
the floor of heaven. Then waters yielded
to let glittering fish live there, the land
took in wild beasts, the gusting air took birds.
What was still missing was an animal
more spiritual than these, more capable
of higher thinking, which would be able
to dominate the others. Man was born—
either that creator of things, the source
of a better world, made him from divine seed,
or the Earth, newly formed and divided
only recently from lofty aether
still held seeds related to the heavens,
which Prometheus, Iapetus' son, mixed
with river water and made an image
of the gods who rule all things.[1] Other creatures
keep their heads bent and gaze upon the ground,
but he gave man a face which could look up
and ordered him to gaze into the sky
and, standing erect, raise his countenance
towards the stars. Thus, what had been crude earth
and formless, was transformed and then took on
the shapes of human life, unknown till then.

First the Golden Age was born. It fostered
faith and right all on its own, without laws
and without revenge. Fear and punishment
did not exist. There were no threatening words
etched in brass and set up for men to read,
nor were a crowd of suppliants afraid
of the looks of men who judged them.[2] They lived
in safety, with no one there to punish.
No chopped-down pine tree had yet descended
down its mountain slope into the flowing waves,

---

[1] Iapetus and his son Prometheus were Titans, members of the family of ruling gods before Jupiter overthrew his father, Saturn, and imprisoned him. Jupiter and the major gods around him are called Olympians, because they are associated with Mount Olympus in northern Greece.

[2] The Romans inscribed their laws on brass and placed the tablets in a public place for people to see.

so it might travel to a foreign world,
and mortals were familiar with no shores
except their own.[1] There were no deep ditches
enclosing towns, no straight trumpets of war
or horns of curving brass, no swords or helmets.   140
People passed the time in gentle leisure
and security, with no need for troops.   [100]
The earth itself, also free and untouched
by hoes, not yet carved up by any ploughs,
produced all things spontaneously, and men,
content with food which grew without duress,
gathered arbutus fruits, mountain berries,
cornels, berries clinging to harsh brambles,
and fallen acorns from the spreading tree
of Jupiter.[2] It was always springtime,   150
and gentle breezes of warm air caressed
flowers which did not grow from any seeds.
Soon unploughed earth brought forth her crops, as well,
and the land, without being refreshed, grew white   [110]
with heavy ears of grain. Rivers of milk
would sometimes flow. Sometimes streams of nectar
and yellow honey dripped from green oak trees.

Once Saturn was cast in gloomy Tartarus,   THE SILVER AGE
Jupiter ruled the world. A Silver Age
then followed, less favourable than gold,   160
but still more valuable than yellow bronze.[3]
Jupiter shortened the previous springtime
and split each year into different seasons,
with winter, summer, changeable autumn,
and short-lived spring. Then, for the first time,
air glowed white, scorched with blazing arid heat,
and ice hung down, congealed by wind. Then men   [120]
first moved to houses. Their homes were caverns,
dense thickets, and brushwood bound with bark.
Then they began to bury Ceres' seeds   170

---

[1] The reference here is to chopping trees down on mountain slopes in order to construct ships from timber.

[2] The tree of Jupiter was the oak.

[3] The first family of gods, led by Saturn, was overthrown by Jupiter, and most of them were confined deep underground. Tartarus was the lowest point of the underworld.

in lengthy furrows, and young bullocks groaned,
straining at the yoke.[1]

                      After these two ages,   THE BRONZE AND IRON AGES
a bronze race followed, with fiercer natures,
more inclined to wage horrific war,
but not to act without due piety.
Finally came the brutal Age of Iron.
During this era of debased desires,
every form of crime broke out, and honour,
truth, and faith ran off. In their place appeared   [130]
cheating, treachery, deceit, viciousness,   180
and criminal cravings for possessions.
Men set sails to catch the winds, though sailors
at this point did not understand them well,
and ships' keels, which for a long time had stood
high in the hills, scudded through unknown seas.
Careful surveyors marked long boundaries
on lands as common to men earlier
as air and sunlight. And the fertile soil
no longer was required to provide
just crops and food it was obliged to give,   190
for men went to the bowels of the earth
and dug for ores, which spurred them on to vice.   [140]
These the earth had hidden and moved away
to Stygian shades.[2] Now harmful iron emerged
and gold, which brings more injuries than iron.
Then war, which fights with both, comes on the scene,
brandishing and rattling weapons in hands
all stained with blood. Plunder becomes a way of life.
Guests are not safe from those who welcome them,
nor is the father from his son-in-law.   200
Love of brothers is also rare. Men hope
their wives will die, and wives all feel the same
about their husbands. Dreadful stepmothers
mix lethal poisons, and sons keep asking
about their father's age before his time.
Piety lies conquered, and virgin Astraea,

---

[1] Ceres was the goddess responsible for food and grain crops.

[2] The Stygian shades were associated with the river Styx, one of the main rivers of the Underworld. Thus, iron and gold are deep in the earth, close to Hades.

the last celestial being, abandoned Earth [150]
now soaked in blood.¹

              And to make the lofty aether   WAR OF THE GIANTS
no more safe than Earth, they say that Giants
tried to overrun the realms of heaven,   210
by piling one mountain on another,
up to the soaring stars. Then Jupiter,
the all-powerful father of the gods,
hurled down his lightning bolt, smashed Olympus,
and split Ossa away from Pelion
lying underneath.² When those frightful Giants
lay buried in the structure they had made,
men claim that Earth, drenched with great quantities
of her children's blood, grew damp, then gave life
to the warm gore, and changed it to the form   220
of human beings, so that some monuments
of that ferocious race might still remain.
But those progeny, scorning gods above,   [160]
were violent—eager, before all else,
to keep on killing. You could well conceive
that they were born from blood.

              When Saturn's son,   JUPITER SUMMONS THE GODS
father of the gods, sees what is going on
from his loftiest citadel, he groans,
and, recalling the polluted banquet
at Lycaon's table, as yet unknown,   230
because it is so recent, in his mind
senses an enormous rage, a feeling
befitting Jupiter.³ He calls a meeting.
Those summoned are not tempted to delay.

There is high in the heavens a pathway
conspicuous for its very whiteness
and visible when skies are clear. This track
men call the Milky Way. For gods above
the road leads to the halls and royal home   [170]
of the great Thunderer. To left and right   240

---

¹Astraea, daughter of Jupiter, was goddess of justice.

²Olympus, Ossa, and Pelion were all mountains in northern Greece. The Giants, children of Earth, piled them on top of each other in order to attack heaven.

³The story of Lycaon is told below, lines 1.283 ff.

stand crowded throngs beside the open gates
of homes belonging to the nobler gods.[1]
Common gods inhabit various places,
but here the powerful and famous ones
who live in heaven make their dwelling place.
If I might be allowed a bold expression,
this is a place I should not hesitate
to call great heaven's imperial palace.[2]
And so, when the gods above are seated
in the marble inner room, Jupiter,   250
sitting high above them all and leaning
on his ivory sceptre, shakes his head
three or four times, tossing that fearful hair
which sets the earth, sea, and stars in motion,   [180]
then opens his mouth, and speaks these words,
stating his indignation:

                 "My worries
about the earthly realm were no greater
when each of those serpent-footed Giants
was ready to throw his one hundred arms
around the captured sky, for even though   260
the enemy was savage, still that war
hung on one group and had a single cause.
Now I must wipe out the race of mortals
over the entire world, in all places
where Nereus roars.[3] I swear I'll do it,
by all the infernal rivers flowing
through Stygian groves underneath the earth![4]
We have already tried all other options,
but a wound beyond all cure must be removed,   [190]
sliced off with a knife, so that healthy parts   270
are not corrupted, too. My subjects
include demi-gods, rustic deities,

---

[1] The great Thunderer is, of course, Jupiter himself. The nobler gods correspond, more or less, to the twelve Olympian gods of Greek mythology. They are Jupiter, Juno, Vesta, Minerva, Ceres, Diana, Venus, Mars, Mercury, Neptune, Vulcan, and Apollo. Pluto, brother of Jupiter and Neptune, lives in the Underworld.

[2] The expression might be considered "bold" because it involves an implicit comparison of Jupiter and Augustus Caesar.

[3] Nereus was an ancient sea god. Here the name stands for the sea generally.

[4] The gods commonly swore their most solemn oaths on the river Styx, a major river of the Underworld. Such oaths cannot be broken.

nymphs, fauns, satyrs, and wood-dwelling spirits
in the mountains. These we do not yet think
worthy of a place in heaven—but still,
we may surely let them live on in those lands
we have assigned to them. Do you believe,
you gods above, that they will be quite safe,
when Lycaon, famous for his cruelty,
sets traps for me, the god who governs you   280
and has the lightning bolt at his command?"

All the gods respond. With great passion
they demand punishment for the person
who has dared such things. It was like the time
an impious gang were burning to snuff out
the Roman name with the blood of Caesar.
The sudden terror of so great a fall
stunned the human race, and the entire globe
shook with horror.[1] The people's loyalty
was no less pleasing to you, Augustus,   290
than those gods' feelings were to Jupiter.
When he has spoken out and raised his hand
to check the noise, all the gods stop talking.
Once stifled by that royal authority,
the murmuring dies down, and Jupiter
breaks the silence once again by saying:

"You need not worry. That man Lycaon   LYCAON
has been punished. But I will inform you   [210]
what he did and tell you his penalty.
Reports of that bad time had reached our ears.   300
I hoped that they were false, so I slipped down
from the top of Mount Olympus and moved
across the earth, a god in human form.
It would take too long to describe in full
how much evil I discovered everywhere.
The report itself was less disturbing
than the truth. I had passed by Maenalus,
a dreadful place where wild beasts have their lairs,
Lycaeus with its ice-cold groves of pine,
and Mount Cyllene.[2] From there, just as   310

---

[1] It is not clear whether these lines are a reference to the murder of Julius Caesar or to a conspiracy against Emperor Augustus.

[2] Maenalus, Lycaeus, and Cyllene were mountains in Arcadia, in the Peloponnese.

late twilight is dragging in the night,
I reach the realm of the Arcadian king
and his inhospitable home. I signal [220]
a god has just arrived, and common folk
have started praying. At first, Lycaon
ridicules their pious vows. Then he says:

> 'Using an obvious test, I will confirm
> whether this man is mortal or a god,
> and there will be no doubt about the truth.'

He is prepared to kill me in the night 320
without warning, when I am fast asleep.
He finds that way of testing for the truth
amusing. And not satisfied with that,
he takes a sword and slices open the throat
of a hostage sent from the Molossians,
makes some of the half-dead limbs more tender
in boiling water, and roasts the rest of him
above an open fire.[1] When he sets this flesh
on dining tables, with avenging fire [230]
I bring the roof down on his household gods, 330
who are worthy of their master. He runs off
quite terrified, and then, once he reaches   LYCAON IS TRANSFORMED
the quiet countryside, begins to howl,
trying without success to speak. His mouth
gathers up the fury he holds inside,
and his bloodlust for habitual slaughter
turns him against herd beasts, so even now
he delights in blood. His clothes have disappeared,
changed to hair, his arms to legs. He is now
a wolf and still retains some vestiges 340
of his old form—the same grey colouring,
the same violence in his expression,
the same glare in his eyes, the same savagery
in his appearance.

                Thus, one house collapsed,
but more than one deserves to be destroyed. [240]
Wherever Earth lies open, the Furies
exercise their sway.[2] You might well believe

---

[1] The Molossians lived in north-west Greece, near Epirus.

[2] The Furies were goddess of blood revenge, particularly within the family. If they are everywhere on earth, then people must be very wicked.

that men had sworn to act as criminals.
Let them all quickly pay the penalty
they richly merit! So stands my judgment." 350

Some of the gods speak up, endorsing
what Jupiter has said, spurring him on
and encouraging his rage, while others
play their parts with silent affirmation.
But still, for all of them the destruction
of the human race is something grievous.
They ask about the future of the world.
How will Earth look if she lacks human life?
Who will now place incense on the altars?
Is Jupiter prepared to let all things 360
be preyed upon by savage animals?
The king of the gods commands them not to ask
such questions and, to relieve their worries, [250]
tells them he will take care of everything.
He promises a race of beings unlike
the previous ones and says their origin
will be a wonder.

              And now Jupiter   THE FLOOD
is about to scatter his lightning bolts
on every country, but he is afraid
the sacred aether, by some accident, 370
may be set on fire from so many flames
and distant polar regions may burn up.
Then, too, he remembers that Fate decrees
there will come a time when the sea and land,
as well as all the palaces of heaven,
will be attacked by flames and set alight,
and Earth's mass, produced with so much effort,
will be in danger.¹ So he sets aside
those weapons forged by hands of Cyclopes
and approves a different punishment— 380 [260]
he will send rains down from the entire sky
and wipe out mortal men beneath the waves.²
So he immediately locks up North Wind
in Aeolus' caves, along with any blasts

---

¹An ancient Roman prophecy predicted the world would end in fire.
²The Cyclopes (singular Cyclops) were huge, one-eyed monsters. They worked for Vulcan, god of the forge.

which scatter clouds collecting overhead,
and sends out South Wind, flying on sodden wings,
his dreadful face veiled in pitch-black darkness,
his beard heavy with rain, water flowing
from his hoary locks, mists sitting on his forehead,
his flowing robes and feathers dripping dew.[1]   390
When Jupiter stretches his hand and strikes
the hanging clouds, heavy, crashing rainstorms
start pouring down from heaven. Iris,
Juno's messenger, dressed in various colours,   [270]
gathers the water up and brings it back
to keeps clouds well supplied.[2] Crops are flattened,
fond hopes of grieving farmers overthrown,
their long year's work now wasted and in vain.
And Jupiter's rage does not confine itself
to his own sky. For Neptune, his brother,   400
god of the azure sea, provides him help
with flooding which adds to the pouring rain.
He summons the rivers to a meeting
and, after they have entered their king's home,
says to them:

                "This is not now the moment
for a long speech from me. What we require
is for you to discharge all your power.
Open your homes, remove all barriers,
and let your currents have free rein to flow."   [280]

Neptune gave his orders, and the rivers   410
return, relax the mouths of all their springs,
and race down unobstructed to the sea.
Neptune himself with his trident strikes the land.
Earth trembles and with the tremor lays bare
the sources of her water. Streams spread out
and charge through open plains, sweeping away—
all at once—groves, planted fields, cattle herds,
men, and homes, along with sacred buildings
and their holy things. If any house remains
still standing and is able to resist   420
such a huge catastrophe, nonetheless,
waves higher than the house cover the roof,

---

[1] Aeolus was the god in charge of all the winds.

[2] Iris, as well as being a messenger for the major deities, was also the goddess of the rainbow.

and its towers, under pressure, collapse [290]
beneath the surge. And now the land and sea
are not distinct—all things have turned into
a boundless sea which has no ocean shore.
Some men sit on hill tops, others in boats,
pulling oars here and there, above the fields
which they just ploughed not long before. One man
now sails above his crops or over roofs   430
of sunken villas, another catches fish
from high up in an elm. Sometimes, by chance,
an anchor bites into green meadowland,
or a curved keel scrapes against a vineyard
submerged beneath the sea. And in those places
where slender she-goats have grazed on grasses,
misshapen sea calves let their bodies rest. [300]
Nereïds are astonished at the groves,
cities, and homes lying beneath the waves.[1]
Dolphins have taken over in the woods,   440
racing through lofty branches and bumping
into swaying oaks. Wolves swim among sheep.
Waves carry tawny lions and tigers.
The forceful, mighty power of the boar
is no help at all, nor are the swift legs
of the stag, once they are swept into the sea.
The wandering bird, after a long search
for some place to land, its wings exhausted,
falls down in the sea. The unchecked movement
of the oceans has overwhelmed the hills,   450
and waters beat against the mountain tops. [310]
The deluge carries off most living things.
Those whom it spares, because food is so scarce,
are overcome by gradual starvation.

The fertile territory of Phocis,   DEUCALION AND PYRRHA
while still land, separates Aonia
from Oeta, but when that flood took place
was still part of the sea, a wide expanse
of water which had suddenly appeared.
In that place there is a soaring mountain   460
which has two peaks striving to reach the stars.[2]
Its summit rises high above the clouds.

---

[1] Nereïds, daughters of Nereus and Doris, were nymphs of the sea.
[2] Aeonia was part of Boeotia. The mountain in question is Parnassus, near Delphi.

Deucalion lands here in his small boat,
with the wife who shares his bed, for the sea
now covers every other place. They revere
Corycian nymphs and mountain deities [320]
and prophetic Themis, too, the goddess
who at that time controlled the oracle.¹
No man was finer than Deucalion,
no man loved justice more, and no woman   470
had more reverence for gods than Pyrrha.
When Jupiter observes the earth submerged
in flowing water, with only one man left
from many thousands not so long before
and sees one woman from so many thousands
a short while earlier, both innocent,
both worshippers of the gods, he scatters
the clouds, and once North Wind has blown away
the rain, he makes land open to the sky
and heaven to the earth. And the sea's rage   480   [330]
does not persist. The lord of the ocean
sets down his three-pronged weapon, calms the seas,
and summons dark-blue Triton standing there
above the ocean depths, his shoulders covered
by native shells, and orders him to blow
his echoing horn and with that signal
summon back the flooding waters and the sea.²
Triton raised his hollow shell, whose spirals   TRITON
grow as they curl up from the base—that horn,
when filled with air in the middle of the waves,   490
makes coastlines under east and western suns
echo its voice—and thus, once the god's lips,
dew dripping from his soaking beard, touched it,
and, by blowing, sounded out the order   [340]
to retreat, all the waters heard the call,
on land and in the sea. They listened to it,
and all of them pulled back. And so the sea
had a shore once more, full-flowing rivers
remained within their banks, floods subsided,

---

¹The Corycian Nymphs were naiads (nymphs living in fresh water lakes and rivers) inhabiting the springs on Mount Parnassus. The goddess Themis was, according to Greek legends, in charge of the oracles at Delphi before Apollo.

²Triton was the son of Neptune and Amphitrite (although there are other lesser sea deities called by that name). His famous horn was made from a conch shell.

hills appeared, land rose up, and dry places
grew in size as the waters ebbed away.
After a long time, exposed tops of trees
revealed themselves, their foliage covered
in layers of mud. The world had been restored.
When Deucalion sees that earth is empty   CREATION OF LIFE ANEW
and observes the solemn silence over
devastated lands, with tears in his eyes   [350]
he speaks to Pyrrha:

           "O wife and sister,
the only woman alive, linked to me
by common race and family origin,   510
then by marriage, and by these dangers now,
we two are the total population
of the entire world, every place spied out
by the setting and rising sun.[1] The sea
has taken all the others. Even now,
there is nothing secure about our lives,
nothing to give us sufficient confidence.
Those heavy clouds still terrify my mind.
O you for whom I have so much compassion,
how would you feel now, if you had been saved   520
from death without me? How could you endure
the fear all by yourself? Who would console   [360]
your grief? For if the sea had taken you,
dear wife, I would follow you, believe me,
and the sea would have me, too. How I wish
I could use my father's skill to replace
those people and infuse a living soul
in moulded forms of earth. The human race
lives now in the two of us. Gods above
thought this appropriate, and we remain   530
the sole examples left of human beings."

Deucalion said this, and they wept. They thought
it best to pray to the celestial god
and to seek help from sacred oracles.
Without delay they set off together
to the stream of Cephisus, whose waters
were not yet clear but by now were flowing   [370]

---

[1] Deucalion, son of Prometheus, and Pyrrha, daughter of Epimetheus, are first cousins (the children of brothers) as well as husband and wife.

within their customary river banks.[1] And there,
once they have sprinkled their heads and garments
with libations, they approach the temples   540
of the sacred goddess, whose pediments
are stained with filthy moss and whose altars
stand without a fire. As they touch the steps
before the shrine, they both fall on the ground,
and kiss the cold stone, in fear and trembling.
Then they speak these words:

              "O Themis, if gods
may be overcome with righteous prayers
and change their minds and if their anger
may be averted, reveal to us the art
by which destruction of the human race   550
may be repaired and, most gentle goddess,   [380]
assist our drowned condition."

                          The goddess
is moved and through the oracle speaks out:

"Leave the temple. Cover your head, and loosen
the garments gathered around you. Then throw
behind your backs the bones of your great parent."

For a long time they are both astonished.
Pyrrha's voice is the first to break the silence,
refusing to act on what the goddess said.
Her mouth trembling, Pyrrha asks the goddess   560
to grant her pardon, for she is afraid
to offend her mother's shade by throwing
her bones away. Meanwhile, they both review
the obscure dark riddle in the language
of the oracle they have been given,
examining the words between themselves.
And then the son of Prometheus consoles   [390]
Epimetheus' daughter with these words
to reassure her:

              "Either we have here
some subtle falsehood, or, since oracles   570
respect the gods and do not recommend
impious acts, our great mother is the Earth
and, I assume, what people call her bones

---

[1]Cephisus was a river which rose on Mount Parnassus and flowed near Delphi.

are those rocks in the body of the earth.
These stones are what we have been commanded
to throw behind our backs."

                Although the way
Deucalion has interpreted the words
encourages the Titan's daughter, their hopes
are plagued by fears—that's how much both of them
have doubts about the heavenly command.
But then what harm will there be in trying?
They go down, cover their heads, unfasten
their tunics, and, as they have been ordered,
throw stones behind where they are standing.
The stones—and who would ever think this true,
if old traditions did not confirm it?—
began to lose rigidity and hardness.
Gradually they softened, and then, once soft,
they took on a new shape. They grew larger
and before long acquired a gentler nature.
One could make out a certain human form,
but indistinctly, like the beginnings
of marble carvings not yet completed,
crude statues. But still, those pieces of them
which were earthy and damp from any moisture
were changed into essential body parts.
What was solid and inflexible changed
to bones, and what just a few moments before
had been veins remained, keeping the same name.
Soon, with the help of gods above, the stones
which the man's hand had thrown took on the form
of men, and the stones the woman had cast
changed into women. That's why human beings
are a tough race—we know about hard work
and provide the proof of those origins
from which we first arose.

                The Earth brought forth   CREATION OF OTHER LIFE
the other animals spontaneously
in various forms. After the moisture
which had been there earlier had grown warm
from the sun's fire and wet swamps and marshes
had swelled up from the heat, the fertile seeds
of matter, nourished in quickening soil,
as in their mother's womb, increased in size
and, over time, took on a certain shape.

When the Nile with its seven river mouths
leaves the sodden fields and sends its waters
down their old channels and the brand new mud
grows hot from the aetherial sun, farmers,
as they turn the soil, find many animals.
Of these creatures, some are just beginning,   620
at the moment of being born. Men see
some which are incomplete and lacking limbs.
Often in the same body one section
is alive, while another is crude earth.
And so it's true that when heat and moisture   [430]
reach a certain temperature, they give birth,
and from these two things all beings spring up.
Fire may be the enemy of water,
and yet moist heat produces everything—
this discordant concord is appropriate   630
for conceiving living things. And therefore,
when Earth, still muddy from the recent flood,
grew warm again from penetrating heat
of the aetherial sun, she then brought forth
countless forms of life, in part restoring
ancient species and in part creating
new monstrosities.

          Though it was something   APOLLO AND PYTHO
Earth did not desire to do, at that time
she also created you, great Pytho,
serpent no one had ever known before.   640
You took up so much space on mountain lands,   [440]
you terrified those creatures newly made.
The archer god, who before this had not used
his lethal weapons, except to bring down
fallow deer and fleeing goats, killed the snake,
by shooting a thousand arrows into it,
until his quiver was almost empty
and poison poured out from the snake's black wounds.[1]
And to guarantee that the passing years
could not erase the fame of that great deed,   650
he set up sacred games, celebrated
for their competition, called the Pythia,
after the snake which he had overcome.

---

[1] The Archer God is Apollo, son of Jupiter and Latona.

Book One

In these games any young man who prevailed
in boxing, running, or in chariot racing
received the honour of an oak leaf crown.[1]
There was no laurel yet, and so Phoebus [450]
adorned his graceful temples and long hair
with leaves from any tree.[2]

                Apollo's first love   APOLLO AND DAPHNE
was Daphne, the daughter of Peneus.[3]   660
It was not blind chance which made him love her,
but Cupid's savage rage. The Delian god,
proud of his recent conquest of the snake,
saw Cupid flexing his bow, pulling back
the string, and said to him:[4]

                    "Impudent boy,
why play with weapons which are made for men?
Carrying that bow suits shoulders like my own,
since I can shoot wild beasts and never miss
and wound my enemy. I am the one
who with my countless arrows has just killed   670
that swollen Pytho, whose venomous gut   [460]
covered such vast tracts of ground. Stay content
kindling any kind of love you fancy
with that torch of yours, but do not pre-empt
those praises due to me."

                    The son of Venus
then replied to him:[5]

                "O Phoebus, your bow
may strike all things, but mine can strike at you.
Just as all animals are less than gods,
so, to the very same extent, your fame
is less than mine."

---

[1] The Pythian Games were one of four Panhellenic athletic competitions. They were held every four years at Apollo's shrine in Delphi.

[2] Phoebus was another name for Apollo. He is usually associated with a laurel wreath for reasons which emerge in the next section of the poem.

[3] Peneus was a river god.

[4] Apollo was sometimes called the Delian god because he and his twin sister, Diana, were born on the island of Delos.

[5] Cupid was the son of Venus, goddess of love, and Mars, god of war.

                    Cupid spoke. Keen to act,   680
he struck the air with beating wings and stood
on the shady peak of Mount Parnassus.
He pulled out two arrows from his quiver,
each with a different force. One of them
makes love run off, the other brings it on.
The arrow which arouses love is gold,   [470]
with a sharp, glittering head, while the arrow
which inhibits love is blunt and has lead
below the shaft. With this second arrow
the god hit the daughter of Peneus,   690
but with the first he struck Apollo's bones,
piercing right through them, into the marrow.
He is immediately in love, but she
runs away from the very name of love,
delighting in deep places in the woods
and skins of the wild beasts she chases down,
emulating virgin Phoebe.[1] A ribbon
holds her tousled hair in place. Many men
court her, but she dislikes all suitors.
And so, rejecting men, knowing nothing   700
of them, she roams the pathless forest glades,
without a care for Hymen, love, or marriage.[2]   [480]
Her father often said:

                    "Daughter, you owe me
    a son-in-law."

                    And often he complained:

    "Daughter, you owe me grandchildren."

                    But Daphne,
despising the bridal torch as something
criminal, with a modest blush, would wrap
her loving arms around her father's neck
and say:

        "My dearest father, allow me
    to enjoy virginity for ever.   710
    Diana's father did that earlier."[3]

---

[1] Phoebe was a name often given to Diana, the hunter goddess.

[2] Hymen was one of the gods of marriage.

[3] Diana was the virgin goddess of the hunt. Her father was Jupiter.

Her father does, in fact, grant her request,
but your beauty, Daphne, is an obstacle
to what you so desire. The way you look
makes sure your prayers will not be answered.
For Phoebus glimpses Daphne and falls in love.
He wants to marry her, and what he seeks
he hopes to get. But his own oracles
deceive him. Just as light straw catches fire
once grain is harvested, and hedges blaze
from torches which some traveller by chance
has brought too near or else left there at dawn,
that's how Phoebus is changed then into flames.
That's how his whole chest burns, and by hoping,
he feeds a love that is in vain. He sees
the tangled hair hanging around her neck
and says:

>   "What would that hair of hers look like,
> if only it were beautifully arranged."

He observes her eyes, like bright fiery stars,
gazes at her lips—but the sight of them
is not enough—and praises fingers, hands,
her arms, and shoulders (more than half exposed!),
imagining those parts which lie concealed
are even lovelier. She runs away,
swifter than a soft breeze, and does not stop
when he calls her, crying these words:

>   "O nymph,
> daughter of Peneus, stay! I beg you.
> I do not chase you as an enemy.
> Nymph, stop! This is the way a lamb runs off,
> fleeing a wolf, or a deer a lion,
> or a dove on quivering wings takes flight
> to escape an eagle—each one of them
> racing from its enemy. But the reason
> I run after you is love. Alas for me!
> I feel so wretched—you might fall headfirst,
> or brambles scratch your legs (which don't deserve
> the slightest injury)—and I might be
> the one who brings you pain. You rush ahead
> through rugged places. Set a slower pace,
> I beg you, and restrain your flight. I, too,
> will follow you more slowly. At least ask

who it is that finds you so delightful.
I am no shepherd or mountain dweller,
or some uncouth local custodian
of herds or flocks. You have no idea,
you thoughtless girl, you do not know the man
you're running from. That's why you scamper off.
The Delphic lands, Claros, and Tenedos,
the palace of Pataraea—all serve me.[1]
Jupiter is my father, and through me
what has been and what is and what will be
are each made known. Through me songs and strings
resound in harmony. True, my arrows
always find their mark, but there's an arrow,
with truer aim than mine, which has transfixed
my uncommitted heart. The healing arts
are my invention, and throughout the world
I am called the Helper. The power of herbs
is under my control. But my love now,
alas, cannot be cured by herbs, and arts
which aid all people are no help at all
to their own master."

                The daughter of Peneus
with timid steps ran off, away from him,
as he was on the point of saying more.
Though his speech was not yet over, she left,
and he was by himself. And even then
she seemed so beautiful. The winds revealed
her body, as the opposing breezes
blowing against her clothing made it flutter,
and light gusts teased her freely flowing hair.
She looked even lovelier as she fled.
The youthful god can endure no longer
wasting his flattery. Love drives him on.
With increasing speed, he chases after her.
Just as a greyhound, once it spies a hare
in an open field, dashes for its prey,
and the hare, feet racing, runs for cover—
one looking now as if he is about
to clutch her and already full of hope
he has her in his grip, his outstretched face

---

[1] Claros refers to a city in Asia Minor or to an island. Tenedos was an island near Troy. Pataraea was a city in Lycia, in Asia Minor.

brushing against her heels, while she, not sure
whether she has been caught, evades his jaws,
and runs away, his mouth still touching her,
that's how the god and virgin race off then,
he driven on by hope and she by fear.
But the one who follows, who has the help [540]
of Cupid's wings, is faster. He gives her
no rest and hangs above her fleeing back,
panting on the hair across her shoulders.
She grows pale as her strength fails, exhausted   800
by the strain of running away so fast.
Gazing at the waters of Peneus,
she cries out:

       "Father, help me! If you streams
have heavenly power, change me! Destroy
my beauty which has brought too much delight!"[1]

Scarcely has she made this plea, when she feels
a heavy numbness move across her limbs,
her soft breasts are enclosed by slender bark,
her hair is changed to leaves, her arms to branches, [550]
her feet, so swift a moment before, stick fast   810
in sluggish roots, a covering of foliage
spreads across her face. All that remains of her
is her shining beauty.

                Phoebus loved her
in this form, as well. He set his right hand
on her trunk, and felt her heart still trembling
under the new bark and with his own arms
hugged the branches, as if they were her limbs.
He kissed the wood, but it shrank from his kiss.
The god spoke:

       "Since you cannot be my wife,
you shall surely be my tree. O laurel,   820
I shall forever have you in my hair,
on my lyre and quiver. You will be there
with Roman chieftains when joyful voices [560]
sing out their triumphs and long processions

---

[1] Along with many other translators I omit line 547 in the Latin ("which is the reason why I suffer harm").

march up within sight of the Capitol.¹
And you, as the most faithful guardian
of Augustus' gates, will be on his door,
and protect the oak leaves in the centre.²
And just as my untrimmed hair keeps my head
forever young, so you must always wear 830
eternal honours in your leaves."

                Paean finished.³
The laurel branches, newly made, nodded
in agreement, and the top appeared to move,
as if it were a head.

                In Haemonia   INACHUS AND IO
there is a grove enclosed on every side
by steep and hilly woods. Men call it Tempe.
Through here Peneus pours his roiling stream   [570]
from the foot of Pindus.⁴ His heavy fall
gathers up mists and drives them on, like fumes,
drenching the tops of trees with spray. Places 840
both near and far grow weary of his roar.
This is the house and home, the inner heart,
of the great river. Seated in a cave
carved out in the rocks, he sets down laws
for the flowing rivers and nymphs who live
within those streams. There the native waters
of that country first assemble, unsure
whether to congratulate or console
Daphne's father—the restless Enipeus,
poplar-growing Spercheus, Aeas, 850
old Apidanus, gentle Amphrysus,   [580]
and not long afterwards other rivers
taking exhausted waters to the sea,
weary from meandering here and there,
wherever their stream's force has carried them.⁵
Only Inachus is absent. Hidden

---

¹The Capitol was one of the seven hills of classical Rome, an important site in the city.

²On the gates of Augustus Caesar's home, there was a crown of oak leaves, with laurel branches on either side.

³Paean was a name commonly given to Apollo as a healer of sickness.

⁴Haemonia was an old name for Thessaly, a region of northern Greece. Tempe was a valley through which the Peneus flowed. Pindus was a mountain in the area.

⁵The names indicate rivers in Thessaly.

deep inside a cave, he is increasing
the volume of his water with his tears,
in total sorrow, grieving for Io,
his missing daughter. He has no idea   860
if she is enjoying life or sitting
among the shades. Since he is unable
to locate her anywhere, he believes
she must be nowhere and so in his heart
fears for the worst. Jupiter had glimpsed her   JUPITER AND IO
returning from her father, the river,
and had said:

      "Virgin, worthy of Jupiter
and about to make some man or other
happy in your bed, while it is so hot,   [590]
with the sun in the middle of his path,   870
at his highest point, move into the shade
of the deep woods."

          Jupiter pointed to
some shadowy groves.

          "If you are afraid
to go all by yourself into places
where wild beasts lurk, you can safely enter
the deepest parts of any grove at all
with a god to guard you—no common god,
but me who holds the heavenly sceptre
in my powerful fist and who flings down
wandering thunderbolts. Do not fly from me!"   880

She was already fleeing and by now
had gone past Lerna's pastures and the trees
planted in Lyrcaean fields.[1] Then Jupiter,
spread darkness and concealed earth far and wide.
He caught her as she was running away
and forced her to have sex against her will.   [600]

Meanwhile Juno looks down on middle Argos,   JUNO, JUPITER, AND IO
curious why swift clouds in bright daylight
have brought on what looks like night. She knows
they have not come from rivers, nor been sent   890
from the moist earth, and looks around to see
where Jupiter might be, knowing already

---

[1] Lerna was a swampy area in Argolis. Lyrcaea was a region in the Peloponnese near Arcadia.

her husband's tricks, for he has been caught out
so often. Not finding him in heaven,
she says:

              "Either I am quite mistaken,
or I am being wronged."

                       She glides down
from the lofty aether, stands on the earth,
and commands the clouds to go away.
Jupiter has foreseen his wife's arrival   [610]
and has changed the daughter of Inachus   900
so she resembles a sleek heifer. Even so,
transformed into a cow, she is lovely.
Juno, Saturn's daughter, reluctantly
approves of the fine-looking cow and asks
who it belongs to, what herd it comes from,
as if she is quite ignorant of the truth.
Jupiter lies. In order to forestall
any questions about parents, he claims
the cow was born from earth. Juno then asks
to have it as a gift. What can he do?   910
To hand over his own love is cruel,
not to hand her over is suspicious.
Shame insists he should surrender Io,
but then love insists he should refuse.
Love would have conquered shame, except for this—
if he refused the partner of his bed   [620]
and his own sister such a trifling gift,
the cow might seem to be no cow at all.[1]
He gave the girl to Juno.

                   The goddess   ARGUS AND IO
did not set aside all her fears at once.   920
She was not sure she trusted Jupiter
and worried about his devious tricks,
until she handed Io on to Argus,
son of Arestor, to keep watch on her.
Around his head Argus had a hundred eyes,
and these would take a rest, two at a time,
while the others stayed awake and remained
on guard. No matter where he placed himself,
he could see Io. When he turned his back,

---

[1] Jupiter and Juno were husband and wife and brother and sister, both children of Saturn.

Io was still there, right before his eyes. 930 [630]
He lets her graze by day. Once the sun sets
below the earth, he puts her in a pen
and ties a rope around her innocent neck.
She eats arbutus leaves and bitter herbs.
In her sad state, she lies upon the ground,
often on bare earth where there is no grass,
instead of in her bed, and takes a drink
from muddy streams. Then, too, when she wishes
to hold those arms of hers in supplication
out to Argus, she has no arms to stretch, 940
and when she tries to utter a complaint,
her mouth just makes a lowing sound. The noise
makes her alarmed and scared of her own voice.
She goes to riverbanks where in the past
she often used to play by Inachus.
But when she sees her new horns in the stream, [640]
she draws back from herself, amazed and fearful.
The naiads have no idea who she might be,
and even Inachus himself is unaware.
But she walks behind her father and trails 950
her sisters, allowing them to touch her,
and approaching them for their approval.
Old Inachus pulls herbs and holds them out.
She licks his hands, kisses her father's palm,
and does not hold back her tears. If only
words would come out with them, she would declare
her name, describe her troubles, and ask for help.
Instead of words, her hoof draws in the dust
letters which convey the wretched story [650]
of how her body changed. Old Inachus, 960
her father, hanging on the horns and neck
of the snow-white heifer, groans and cries out:

"I feel so sad"

              And then he groans again.

"I feel so wretched! Are you the daughter
I have been searching for in every land?
When you were missing, there was less sorrow
than there is now, after we have found you.
You cannot speak or answer what I say,
but only give out sighs from your deep chest.
The only way you can converse with me 970

    is with lowing sounds. In my ignorance,
I was getting marriage and a bridal bed
prepared for you. My first hope was to have
a son-in-law and then some grandchildren.
But now you will have to have a husband
from the herd, and then offspring from the herd.   [660]
And this great grief of mine I cannot end
by dying. It is painful being a god.
Since the gate of death is closed, our sorrows
are dragged out into everlasting time."   980

While Inachus is grieving for his daughter,
bright-eyed Argus takes Io from her father
and leads her away to different pastures.
He himself sits on a high mountain peak,
some distance off, where from his position
he can keep watch in all directions.

The ruler of the gods cannot endure   MERCURY AND ARGUS
that the granddaughter of Phoroneus
suffer such misery a moment longer.[1]
He calls his son whom the bright Pleiad bore   990
and orders him to put Argus to death.[2]   [670]
Mercury does not delay for long. He ties
wings on his feet, his strong hand grips that rod
which brings on sleep, and he covers his head.[3]
This done, the son of Jupiter leaps down
from his father's citadel to the earth.
There he takes off his cap and wings. The rod
is the only thing he keeps, and with it,
looking like a shepherd, he drives she goats,
which he has stolen as he walks along,   1000
through trackless countryside, playing a song
on reeds he tied together. Juno's guard,
enchanted with the sound of this new art,
speaks out:

        "Whoever you are, you can sit
with me here on this rock. There's nowhere else

---

[1] Phoroneus was the father of Inachus.

[2] The Pleiad who gave birth to Mercury was Maia, one of the seven daughters of Atlas. They became the Pleiades when they were placed among the stars.

[3] Mercury carried a rod or staff which could rouse people from sleep or put them to sleep or summon shades of the dead.

where there is better grazing for your flock.
As you see, this shade well suits a shepherd."

The grandson of Atlas sat down and spent
the passing day in conversation, talking
of many things and playing melodies   1010
on reeds he stuck together, attempting
to overpower Argus' watchful eyes.

But Argus fights to keep soft sleep at bay,   SYRINX
and though some of his eyes doze off, others
stay awake. He asks how the shepherd's pipe,
something invented only recently,
has been developed. Mercury replies:

"On the icy mountains of Arcadia
among the hamadryads of Nonacris   [690]
the most celebrated was a naiad—   1020
nymphs called her Syrinx.[1] She had eluded
many times the satyrs who pursued her,
as well as those gods who inhabited
the shady woods and fertile countryside.
She worshipped the Ortygian goddess
in her actions and remained a virgin.[2]
She tied up her dress just like Diana
and could have been confused with Leto's child,
except her bow was made of cornel wood,
while Diana's was of gold. Even so,   1030
her appearance was deceptive. Once Pan,
with a wreath of pine around his head, spied her
on her way back from Mount Lycaeus
and spoke to her."[3]

                    Now Mercury had to give   [700]
more details—how the nymph then ran away,
despising his pleas, through pathless regions,
until she came to the gentle waters
of the sandy Ladon stream and how here,
with water hindering her way, she begged
her sisters of the stream to change her shape,   1040
how Pan, just when he thought he had Syrinx

---

[1] Hamadryads were tree nymphs. Nonacris was a mountain in the Peloponnese.

[2] The Ortygian goddess was Diana. The word is a reference to the island Delos.

[3] Pan was the god of shepherds and a common presence in mountain forests.

in his arms at last, was holding marsh reeds
instead of the nymph's body, and then how,
as he sighed there, wind passing through the reeds
had made a subtle, plaintive sound, and Pan,
captivated by the new art's sweet voice,
had said:

       "This way of conversing with you   [710]
will remain with me."

              And by using wax
to join together reeds of different lengths,
he had immortalized the young girl's name.   1050

The Cyllenean god, about to speak   DEATH OF ARGUS
of these events, sees all of Argus' eyes
have closed, their bright lights overcome by sleep.[1]
He lowers his voice at once and touches
the drowsy eyes with his magical rod,
forcing them to doze more soundly. And then,
with his hooked sword he quickly hacks away
the nodding head from where it joins the neck,
throws it, covered in gore, down from the rock,
and stains steep cliffs with blood.

            "Lie there, Argus.   1060
The light you had in all those eyes of yours
has been extinguished, and a single night
now sits inside your hundred orbs."

              Then Juno,
Saturn's daughter, picked up those eyes, set them
in her own bird's feathers, and filled its tail
with starry gems.[2] Immediately enraged,
she made no attempt to hide her anger.
To the eyes and mind of that Argive girl
she sent out a terrifying Fury,
pierced her breast with hidden stings, and drove her   1070
through the whole world in wandering terror.

And you, O Nile, remained the final stage
of Io's measureless pain. She reached you,
fell onto her knees at the river's edge,   [730]

---

[1] The Cyllenean god is Mercury, who is associated with Mount Cyllene in Arcadia.

[2] Juno's bird is the peacock.

BOOK ONE

threw her neck back, lifted her face high up
towards the stars—that was the only thing
that she could do—and by her groans and tears
and sad lowing seemed to be complaining
to Jupiter and praying for an end
to her distress. Jupiter throws his arms 1080
around Juno's neck and asks her to end
her punishment. He says:

        "Set your fears aside.
In future she will never cause you grief."

And he commands the Stygian waters
to witness what he says. Once the goddess   IO IS RESTORED
has calmed down, Io regains those features
she possessed before and becomes the nymph
she was in earlier days. The stiff hair
leaves her body, the two horns shrink away,   [740]
her eyes contract, the bones inside her jaw   1090
decrease in size, her arms and hands come back,
and her hooves vanish, changing to five nails.
So Io now looks nothing like the cow,
except for her still beautiful appearance.
Happy to have the use of her two feet,
the nymph stands up, but is afraid to speak,
in case she should utter lowing noises,
just like a heifer. Timidly she tries
once more to use the words she has stopped using.
Now she is a very famous goddess,   1100
worshipped by large multitudes of people
dressed in linen. In time, Io bore a son,
Epaphus, who came, so it is believed,
from the seed of almighty Jupiter.
With Io he now guards our civic shrines.

Phaëton, child of the sun, was the same age   PHAËTON AND CLYMENE
as Epaphus and equalled him in spirit.   [750]
At some point, Phaëton boasted aloud
that Phoebus was his father. He was proud
and would not back down, something Epaphus,   1110
grandson of Inachus, could not endure.
So he said:

        "You are mad if you believe
everything your mother tells you and then

puff yourself up with the fancy image
of a fictitious father."

     Phaëton blushed—
shame checked his anger—and took the rebuke
of Epaphus to Clymene, his mother,
saying to her:

    "To grieve you even more,
mother, I was silent, though I am free
and bold. These insults make me feel ashamed.   1120
I hear them said without being able
to speak against them. If I originate   [760]
from a family of gods, show me some sign
of a lofty birth and confirm for me
I come from heaven."

     He spoke and then wrapped
his arms around his mother's neck and begged,
by his own head and the head of Merops,
her husband, and by the wedding torches
of his sisters, that she would offer him
some proof of his true parent. Clymene   1130
was moved—but one could never say for certain
whether that came from Phaëton's pleading
or from her resentment of the charges
made against her. She stretched out both her arms,
looked up to the sun's light, and cried:

       "My son,
I now swear to you by this radiant light,
marked by brilliant rays, which hears and sees us,
that you are the child of this very sun
which you are looking at. You are from him,
the controller of the world. If my words   1140 [770]
are false, let Sun himself remove from me
my power of seeing him. Let that light
be the last to reach my eyes. And for you,
it is not difficult to learn about
your father's home. The house where he rises
lies in land beside our own. If your mind
has any inclination, then go there,
and put your questions to the god himself."

After his mother says this, Phaëton,
overjoyed, at once runs off, seizing hold   1150

of heaven in his mind. He travels past
his own Ethiopians and India,
located under fiery stars, eagerly
rushing to where his father rises.[1]

---

[1] Merops, husband of Clymene, Phaëton's mother, was king of the Ethiopians, traditionally close to the land where the sun rises. In identifying Apollo with the sun, Ovid is breaking with Greek mythological traditions which make the Titan Helios or Hyperion god of the Sun. In later books Ovid sometimes reverts to this older tradition.

Book Two

II

[The palace of the Sun; Phaëton asks to drive his father's chariot; Apollo reluctantly agrees; Apollo instructs Phaëton how to drive the chariot; Phaëton sets out but loses control; the Earth catches fire; springs and rivers dry up; the Earth appeals to Jupiter; Jupiter destroys Phaëton; Phaëton's family laments; the daughters of the Sun are turned into trees; Cycnus is transformed into a swan; the Sun reacts to Phaëton's death; Jupiter seduces Callisto; Diana rejects Callisto; Juno punishes Callisto by turning her into a bear; Arcas meets his mother Callisto as a bear; Jupiter sets Arcas and Callisto in the constellations; Juno visits Tethys and Oceanus; the Raven and the Crow; the daughters of Cecrops; Minerva punishes the Crow; how the daughter of Coroneus became a crow; the Raven tells Apollo about Coronis; Apollo kills Coronis but rescues his child from the womb and gives him to Chiron; Apollo punishes the Raven; Ocyrhoë is turned into a horse; Mercury turns Battus to stone; Mercury and Herse; Minerva visits Envy; Envy poisons Aglauros; Mercury turns Aglauros to stone; Jupiter and Europa; Jupiter abducts Europa]

PALACE OF THE SUN

The palace of the Sun, high in the sky,
has soaring pillars, bright with gleaming gold
and fiery bronze, the highest pinnacles
are of white ivory, and double doors
give off a silver light. Their artistry
is even finer than the materials,
for on them Mulciber has carved the seas
encircling lands lying in the centre,
the globe of Earth, and heaven suspended
above that globe.¹ The waves hold sea-green gods—   10   [10]
echoing Triton, shifty Proteus,
Aegaeon with arms pressing the huge backs
of whales, along with Doris and her daughters
(some seem to be swimming, others sitting
on the shore, drying their green hair, and some
being carried on a fish—in appearance
all look different and yet somehow the same,
as sisters ought to).² The Earth has cities,
human beings, woods, wild beasts, rivers, nymphs,
and other rural deities. Above these   20
is placed the image of a brilliant sky,
six constellations on the right-hand doors
and the same number on the left-hand side.³

---

¹Mulciber was another name for Vulcan, the divine artisan.

²Triton, as we have seen in Book I, had a conch shell whose noise resounded around the world. Proteus was a sea god who could change his shape at will. Aegaeon was a sea monster with a hundred arms. Doris was a sea nymph, daughter of Oceanus and Tethys and wife of Nereus.

³The constellations are the signs of zodiac.

Book Two

After Phaëton, Clymene's son, came   PHAËTON AND PHOEBUS
up the steep path and went inside the home
of the father he was not sure about,   [20]
he instantly set out to make his way
into his father's presence, but then stopped
some distance off. He could not continue
moving any closer to that brilliant light.
Wrapped in purple robes, Phoebus was sitting
on a throne sparkling with bright emeralds.[1]
To his right and left stood Day, Month, and Year,
Ages and Hours, spaced equally apart,
with the new Spring encircled by a crown
of flowers. And naked Summer stood there,
carrying garlands of wheat, Autumn, too,
stained with trodden grapes, and icy Winter
with untidy snow-white hair. Then the Sun,   [30]
placed in the middle of them all, with eyes
which perceive all things, noticed the young man
trembling at the strangeness of the palace
and said:

    "What has led you to travel here?
What are you seeking in my citadel,
Phaëton, child no parent should disown?"

Phaëton said:

                "O universal light
of the enormous world, Phoebus, father—
if I use that name with your permission
and if Clymene is not concealing
some crime under a deceitful picture—
give me a token, father, so that men
will believe I am a true child of yours.
Erase the doubts in my own mind."

                             He spoke.
His father set aside the beams gleaming   [40]
all around his head and told Phaëton

---

[1]Ovid here and elsewhere calls the sun god Phoebus, from the Greek word for "shining." The name is most commonly associated with Apollo, whose identification as the god of the sun is not normally found in earlier Greek mythology, where the god involved with the sun is usually a Titan, not one of the Olympians. Elsewhere in the poem Ovid sometimes makes the god of the sun a Titan (the son of Hyperion).

to come closer. Then he embraced the lad
and said:

        "You are a worthy son of mine—
that cannot be denied—and Clymene
has stated your true origin. Now ask
for any gift you like which will relieve   60
the doubts you feel, so I may offer it
and you receive it. Let Stygian pools,
which my eyes have not yet seen and which gods
swear by, be present here as witnesses
to what I promise."[1]

        He had scarcely finished,
when Phaëton asked for his father's chariot,
the right to drive his wing-footed horses
for one day. Phoebus regretted the oath
he had just sworn. He shook his splendid head
two or three times and said:

        "Those words of yours   70   [50]
have made my words too reckless. I wish I could
take back what I have promised! I confess
this is the one thing, son, I would refuse.
Still, I can try to talk you out of it.
What you want is not safe, Phaëton. You've made
a huge request for a gift not suited
to your strength or youth. Your fate is mortal,
but what you wish is not for mortal men.
In your ignorance, you are aspiring
for more than what is lawful to be done,   80
even with gods above. Each deity
is allowed to follow his own pleasure,
but no one, except myself, is able
to stand upon the fire-bearing axle.
Even the one who governs vast Olympus,   [60]
whose terrible right hand hurls thunderbolts,
does not drive this chariot. And what is there
more powerful than Jupiter? The track
is steep at the beginning—fresh horses
in the morning can hardly make the climb.   90
The highest part is in the middle of the sky,
where looking down upon the sea and land

---

[1] When gods swear a promise by the river Styx, the promise cannot be withdrawn or changed.

BOOK TWO

is often frightening, even for me,
and giddy terror makes my heart tremble.
The final section of the path slopes down.
It requires a steady hand. Moreover,
Tethys herself, whose waters down below
receive me, has a constant fear I'll fall
too quickly.[1] Then, too, the sky rushes past   [70]
in a never-ending whirl, dragging stars   100
high up, spinning them in rapid circles.
I drive in the opposite direction,
but its force, which overpowers all things,
does not overpower me, as I move
against its rapid orbit. But suppose
you get the chariot. How would you manage?
Will you be able to make way against
the whirling heavens, so their swift motion
does not carry you away? Perhaps your mind
imagines there are groves up there, cities,   110
homes, and temples richly endowed with gifts.
The road passes through dangers and visions
of wild beasts. Even if you keep on course
and are not drawn astray, still you must move
through the opposing horns of that bull Taurus,   [80]
the bow of Haemonian Sagittarius,
the maw of the fierce Lion, on one side
the savage claws of Scorpio bending
in a sweeping arc and, on the other,
the curved claws of the Crab.[2] And those horses—   120
you will not find them easy to control,
those spirited beasts, whose mouths and nostrils
snort out the fires blazing in their chests.
They have trouble following my commands
when their fierce hearts are hot. Their necks fight back
against the reins. My son, you must take care
I don't become the giver of a gift
which kills you. While conditions still permit,
change what you want. Of course, you still desire
sure evidence which will help you to believe   130   [90]

---

[1] Tethys was a goddess of the sea and a Titan, daughter of the original gods Ouranos and Gaia.

[2] Haemonian also means Thessalian. This is a reference to the centaur (half horse, half human being) Chiron, who, according to a number of writers, was placed in the zodiac as Sagittarius.

Book Two

you are born of my own blood. But I provide
firm proof by fearing for you, and I show
I am your father by a father's worries.
Look at my face! I wish you could insert
those eyes of yours into my heart and sense
my fatherly anxiety in there!
Finally, look around at whatever
the rich world contains and ask for something
great and good out of heaven, earth, and sea.
There are so many! I will not refuse. 140
This is the only thing I'm asking you
not to take, and, in truth, it should be called
a punishment rather than an honour.
Phaëton, you're asking for a penalty
and not a gift. Why, in your ignorance,
my boy, do you put your arms around my neck [100]
to win me over? Do not have any doubt—
I shall give whatever you have chosen,
for I swore by the waters of the Styx.
But you must make a wiser choice."

                    Phoebus 150
ends his words of warning, but Phaëton
rejects his father's words and, all aflame
with desire to guide the chariot, holds out
for what he's asked for. And so his father,
having delayed as long as possible,
leads the young man to the soaring chariot,
a gift from Vulcan. The axle is gold,
as is the pole and the curved outer rims
running around the wheels. The rows of spokes
are made of silver, while along the yoke 160
chrysolites and gems set in a pattern
cast their dazzling light back onto Phoebus. [110]
While bold Phaëton is admiring these,
gazing at the artistry, lo and behold,
watchful Aurora from the shining east
opens up the purple doors to the hall
crammed full of roses. The stars all vanish,
their cohorts driven off by Lucifer,
the last to leave his celestial station.[1]
When the Titan sees him go, as the earth 170

[1] Lucifer was the morning star, which appeared just before the dawn.

and world are growing redder and the horns
on the crescent moon appear to vanish,
he tells the swift Hours to yoke the horses.[1]
Those quick goddesses obey his orders.
They lead the horses out from lofty stalls—
the beasts, filled with ambrosial nourishment, [120]
are snorting fire!—and then attach to them
the jingling harnesses. Next, the father
rubs divine ointment on his young son's face,
making it invulnerable to searing flames. 180
He sets his rays in his son's hair, heaving
sighs from an anxious heart prophesying
disaster, and says:

          "My boy, if you can
at least listen to your father's warnings,
spare the whip, and hold the reins more strongly.
These horses charge ahead all on their own.
What's hard is holding them with their consent.
And do not be tempted by the pathway
directly through the five celestial zones.
There is a track carved out at an angle 190
in a wide curve contained inside three zones. [130]
Avoid the Arctic and the southern poles,
and the Bear linked to the north.[2] Make your trip
along this route. You will see certain tracks
left by my wheels. And so heaven and earth
get equal heat, do not guide the chariot
too low or drive it through the upper sky.
If you go too high, you'll burn up heaven's roof,
and if too low, the earth. The safest course
to take is through the middle. Do not let 200
the right wheel make you turn aside towards
the twisted Snake or the left one lead you
to the low down Altar.[3] Maintain your course

---

[1] Ovid here calls Phoebus a Titan. The Greek sun god was usually the Titan Helios, son of Hyperion, but Apollo is an Olympian god, not a Titan.

[2] For a description of the earth's five zones, see 1.63 ff. This advice appears to be warning Phaeton not to take a direct route across the five zones and crossing the poles, but to follow the sun's usual path. The Bear (now often called the Plough or the Big Dipper) is a constellation close to the North Star.

[3] The Snake and the Altar are constellations. The former is high in the northern sky, the latter very low in the southern sky. Since the Sun's path is from east to west, the north will be to the right of the chariot.

between the two. All that remains I leave [140]
to Fortune, who I pray will help you out
and take better care of you than you do.
While I tell you all this, damp Night has touched
the boundaries placed on the western shore.
We do not have the freedom to delay.
We have been summoned! Bright Aurora shines, 210
and the darkness has been driven away.
Your hands must seize the reins, or if your mind
has changed, take my advice, not my chariot,
while you still can, while you still have your feet
on solid ground, and while you are not yet
acting on your unfortunate desires
and, with no experience, standing there
inside the chariot. Let me provide the earth
with daylight, while you look on in safety."

Phaëton, with his young body, takes his place 220 [150]
in the light chariot and waits there, happy
to have the reins now resting in his hands.
He thanks his reluctant father. Meanwhile,
the swift horses of the sun—Pyroeis,
Eoüs, Aethon, and the fourth one, Phlegon—
keep whinnying. They fill the air with flames
and strike the barriers with their hooves. Tethys,
who does not know her grandson's destiny,
throws back the gates and offers those horses
the freedom of the boundless universe. 230
They race off on their journey, hooves speeding PHAËTON'S JOURNEY
through the air, slicing the opposing clouds.
Lifted on wings, they outstrip the eastern wind [160]
rising from the same regions of the sky.
But for the horses of the sun the weight
is much too light, for they no longer pull
their customary load. Just as curved ships
without a proper ballast toss around,
for their lack of weight makes them unstable,
as they move through the sea, so that chariot, 240
without its usual freight, leaps through the air
and is tossed up high, like something empty.
As soon as the four-horse team observes this,
they charge ahead, leaving the beaten track,
not running the same path they used before.
Phaëton, alarmed, unsure how to use

the reins entrusted to him, does not know
where the path might be, and even if he did, [170]
he would still lack the strength to guide his team.
Then, for the first time, the cold Triones   250
were warmed by the sun's rays and tried in vain
to dip down in the forbidden ocean.[1]
The Serpent, closest to the frozen pole,
who earlier was sluggish with the cold
and not a threat to anyone, warmed up
and grew more frightening from the heat.[2] They say
you, too, Boötes ran away confused,
though you were slow and held up by the Plough.[3]
But when unfortunate Phaëton looked
from high in the aether down on the earth   260
lying far, far underneath him, he turned pale.
His knees shook with sudden fear, and his eyes, [180]
in such a powerful light, were obscured
by darkness. And now he would have preferred
never to have touched his father's horses.
Now he is sorry he confirmed his birth
and managed to get what he requested.
Now he desires to be called Merops' son,
as he is carried like a ship driven
by North Wind's blasts, whose captain has let go   270
the useless rudder and turned things over
to praying and the gods. What can he do?
A large part of the sky lies behind him,
but even more is there before his eyes.
In his mind he surveys them both, sometimes
glancing ahead towards the west, which Fate
will ensure he does not reach, and sometimes
looking back towards the east. Stupefied, [190]
not knowing what to do, he is unable
to let go the reins or keep gripping them.   280
He does not even know the horses' names.
He trembles to see astonishing things

---

[1] The Triones, meaning ploughing oxen, are the Great Bear and the Little Bear constellations. The stars look something like a wagon with oxen attached. These stars, at the latitude of the Mediterranean, do not disappear below the horizon (i.e., are forbidden to dip into the sea). For the story of these constellations see the section on Callisto below (2.584 ff.).

[2] The Serpent (also called Draco and Anguis) is a constellation in the northern sky.

[3] Boötes (from the Greek word for ox driver) is a northern constellation.

and images of huge wild beasts scattered
in various places throughout the sky.
There is a place where Scorpio curves his claws
in two arcs and, with his tail and pincers
bending on either side, stretches his limbs
across the space of twin constellations.
When the boy sees this beast, moistened with sweat
from pitch black poison, threatening to attack   290
with his curved sting, cold terror numbs his mind,   [200]
and he lets go the reins. Once they drop down
and touch the horses' backs along the top,
the team then swerves off course and runs ahead
without restraint, through regions of the air
unknown to them. Wherever their instincts
drive them, they race forward, with no control,
and charge at stars fixed high in lofty space,
hurtling the chariot through trackless places.
At times, they head for the highest regions,   300
and then at times are carried headlong down,
on a path much closer to the earth. Moon
is astounded that her brother's horses
are racing on below her own. Scorched clouds
give off smoke. In all the highest places,   [210]
the land goes up in flames, then splits apart
into yawning cracks, and with its moisture
drawn away, dries up. All the grass turns white,
trees and leaves catch fire, and parched harvest crops
supply the fuel for their own destruction.   310

But these complaints are insignificant.
Great cities perish, walls and all. The flames
turn whole countries and their populations
into ash. Woods and mountains are consumed.
Athos burns, as do Cilician Taurus,
Tmolus, Oeta, Ida (once famous
for its springs but now dried out), Helicon
(home of the Muses), Haemus (not yet linked
to Oeagrus). Aetna is on fire, too,   [220]
a tremendous blaze with redoubled flames,   320
along with twin-peaked Parnassus, Eryx,
Cynthus, Othrys, Rhodope (now at last
about to lose its snow), Mimas, Dindyma,
Mycale, and Cithaeron (which was made
for sacred rituals). Even Scythia

BOOK TWO

gets no protection from its icy cold.
Caucasus is on fire, as are Ossa,
Pindus, Olympus (greater than either one),
towering Alps, and cloud-capped Apennines.[1]
Then Phaëton sees all parts of the world 330
ablaze and cannot bear the intense heat.
His mouth inhales the scorching air, as if
from some deep furnace. He feels his chariot [230]
get hot. He can no longer tolerate
the ash and sparks thrown up. On every side
he is surrounded by hot smoke. Darkness
swallows him up, and he has no idea
where he should go or where he is, carried
by the will of his swift horses. Men think
that at that time the Ethiopians 340
had their blood drawn to the body surface
and turned black, while Libya was transformed
to an arid desert, all its moisture
drawn off by the heat. Back then, too, the nymphs,
their hair dishevelled, wept for springs and lakes.
Boeotia looks for Dirce's liquid springs,
Argos for Amymone's fountain stream,
and Ephyre for Pirene's waters.[2] [240]
And even rivers held in place by banks
spaced far apart are not safe—the Tanaïs 350
(its waters in the middle give off steam!),
old Peneus, Teuthrantian Caïcus,
quick Ismenus, Phocean Erymanthus,
Xanthus (about to burn a second time),
yellow Lycormas and Maeander, too,
(whose waters play as they come twisting back),
Thracian Melas, and Taenarian Eurotas.
The Euphrates in Babylon caught fire,
as did Orontes and swift Thermodon,
the Ganges, Phasis, and the Ister, too. 360

---

[1]This sequence of names refers to well-known mountains and mountain ranges: Athos in northeastern Greece, Taurus in Asia Minor, Tmolus in Lydia, Oeta in Thessaly, Ida outside Troy, Helicon in Boeotia, Haemus in Thrace (where Orpheus, son of Oeagrus, was torn to pieces), Aetna and Eryx in Sicily, Cynthus in Delos, Rhodope in Thrace, Mimas in Ionia, Dindyma near Troy, Myclae in Caria, Cithaeron outside Thebes, Caucasus in Asia, Alps in northern Italy, Apennines in Italy.

[2]These are the names of famous springs in classical Greece: Dirce in Boeotia, Amymone in Argos, and Pyrene in Ephyre (Corinth).

Alpheus boils, banks of Spercheus blaze, [250]
The gold the Tagus carries in its stream
flows by on fire, and river birds whose song
made those shores in Maeonia famous
glow with heat midstream on Caÿster's waves.
Nile flees in fear to earth's most distant place
and hides his head, which still remains concealed.
Its seven mouths fill up with dust and empty,
seven beds without a stream. The same fate
dries up Ismarus, with Hebrus, Strymon,   370
and western rivers, too—Rhine, Rhone, Padus,
and Tiber (which has received a promise
it would rule the world).[1] In every region
the ground breaks up and sunlight penetrates
down through the fissures right to Tartarus,   [260]
alarming the ruler of the Underworld
and his consort, too. The sea gets smaller.
What has recently been water now becomes
a field of arid sand. Mountains covered
by deep seas stand out, raising the number   380
of the scattered Cyclades.[2] Fish swim down
to the lowest depths, and curving dolphins
do not dare to leap above the water
up into the air, as is their custom.
In the sea, seals are on their backs, lying
lifeless on the surface. And men report
even Nereus himself, with Doris
and her daughters, lay hidden in warm caves.
Three times Neptune, looking grim, attempted   [270]
to extend his arms up from the waters.   390
Three times he could not stand the scalding air.
But fecund Earth, surrounded by the sea,   EARTH AND JUPITER
between the ocean waters and the springs,

---

[1] These names list a series of rivers famous in myth and history: Tanais (now called the Don) in the north, Caïcus in Mysia, Ismenus in Boeotia (near Thebes), Erymanthus in Arcadia, Xanthus near Troy (which is set on fire in the *Iliad*, hence the reference to its burning a second time), Lycormas in Aetolia, Maeander in Phrygia (famous for its very winding course), Melas in Thrace, Thessaly, and Asia, Eurotas in Sparta, Thermodon in Cappadocia, Ganges in India, Phasis in Colchis, Ister (now called the Danube) in Europe, Alpheus in Arcadia, Tagus in Spain, Caÿster in Lydia (also called Maeonia), Nile in Egypt, Strymon in Thrace, Rhine in northern Europe, Rhone in France, and Padus (now called Po) and Tiber in Italy. Ismarus is a mountain in Thrace.

[2] The Cyclades are a group of islands in the Aegean Sea.

Book Two

which were all shrinking, burying themselves
in the womb of their dark mother, lifted
her ravaged face, all scorched down to her neck,
set her hand against her forehead, making
all things shake with her powerful tremors,
sunk back a little and was lower down
than her usual level. In a broken voice, 400
she said these words:

           "O ruler of the gods,
if this is what you want, if this treatment
is something I deserve, then why hold back
your lightning? Let the power of your flames [280]
destroy me, let me perish in your fires,
and let the majesty of the author
of this disaster mitigate its pain.
It's hard for me to open up my jaws
to speak these words."

           (And, true enough, the heat
made speaking difficult).

           "Look at my hair— 410
it's scorched—and all these ashes in my eyes,
over my whole face. Is this the reward,
the honour, you pay for my fertility
and service, because I endure the wounds
of the curved plough and harrow and am worked
the entire year, because I provide leaves
and tender nourishment for cattle herds,
grain crops for the human race, and incense
for you gods? Still, suppose I do deserve
to be destroyed, what have the waters done? 420 [290]
Why does your brother deserve such treatment?
Why are those waters which chance committed
to his care shrinking and moving further
from the sky.[1] But if you are not concerned
about me or your brother, have pity
on your own heaven. Take a look around.
Both of the poles are steaming. And if fire
destroys the poles, then your own house will fall.

---

[1] In Greek mythology, the three brothers Zeus (Jupiter), Poseidon (Neptune), and Hades (Pluto) drew lots to determine which of them should rule particular parts of the world. Neptune drew the lot for the sea, Pluto for the Underworld, and Jupiter for the sky.

Book Two

Look! Atlas himself is in great distress!
His shoulders can hardly hold up heaven—
it's so white hot.[1] If the seas, if the earth,
if the celestial palace is destroyed,
we are thrown into primordial chaos.
Snatch from the flames whatever still remains,
and help preserve the safety of the world."

Earth spoke. Then, unable any longer
to endure the heat or keep on talking,
she pulled her face back deep within herself,
into caves closer to the dead below.

But the all-powerful father, calling
gods above (and especially the god
who has loaned the chariot) to bear witness
how a dreadful fate will destroy all things,
if he does not help out, climbs way up high,
to the very heights of heaven, from where
he spreads the clouds across wide earth, stirs up
thunder, and hurls his pulsing lightning bolt.
But at that time he had no clouds to drag
across the land nor any rain to send
down from the heavens. He thunders and hefts
the lightning bolt by his right ear, hurls it
at the charioteer, and, in an instant,
expels him from the chariot and from life.
With his savage fire he puts out the fires.
The horses, in their confusion, all veer
in different directions, pull their necks
free of the yoke, and, with the harness torn,
run off. Reins lie in one spot, the axle,
torn off from the pole, lies in another,
spokes from the broken wheels are somewhere else,
and the remnants of the shattered chariot
are scattered far and wide. But Phaëton,
his golden hair consumed by fire, is thrown
and carried headlong on a long pathway
through the air, just as in a peaceful sky
a star sometimes seems to fall, even though

---

[1] Atlas was a giant son of Iapetus. He was changed into a mountain in North Africa which supported the heavens and kept them apart from earth. For the story of his transformation see below 4.934 ff.

BOOK TWO

it has not really fallen. Far away
from his own land, in a distant region
of the world, Phaëton is taken in
by mighty Eridanus, who cleans off   470
his blackened face.[1] The body, still smouldering
from the three-forked flame, Hesperian naiads
set in a grave and mark the stone with verse:

> Here lies Phaëton, who wished to guide
> his father's chariot. And though he died,
> there was great daring in what he tried.[2]

But his sorrowing father, sick with grief,   PHAËTON'S FAMILY
had concealed his face, and, so people say
(if we can trust their word), one day went by
without the sun. The fires provided light,   480
so that disaster brought some benefits.
But when Clymene had said whatever
needed to be said at such a time of grief,
distracted in her sorrow and tearing
at her breast, she roamed the entire world,
seeking first his lifeless limbs and then his bones.
She found the bones, but they'd been laid to rest
in a foreign riverbank. She sank down
in that place and with her tears bathed the name
she read there in the marble and warmed it   490
against her naked breast. The Heliades,
daughters of the sun, grieving just as much,   [340]
shed tears, vain offerings to Death, their hands
beating against their chests, while night and day
they cry for Phaëton (who will not hear
their sad laments) and lie down on his tomb.

Four times the moon joined up her horns and filled   DAUGHTERS OF THE SUN
her sphere. Those women, as was their custom
(for routine has made their grief a habit),
are offering their laments, when one of them,   500
Phaëthusa, the eldest sister, wishing
to throw herself down on the ground, complains
her feet are growing stiff. Fair Lampetie
then tries to go to her, but is held back,

---

[1] Eridanus was the name of the Po River in northern Italy.

[2] Tradition located the fall of Phaëton in northern Italy (hence, the naiads are from the Hesperides, meaning regions far to the west of Greece).

suddenly rooted to the ground. A third,
trying to tear her hair with both her hands,
plucks out leaves. One cries that a wooden trunk
now holds her legs, another that her arms
are changing to long branches. While they watch,
amazed at what is going on, bark grows
around their groins and, by degrees, surrounds
their bellies, breasts, hands, and shoulders, leaving
uncovered nothing but their mouths calling
for their mother. What can a mother do,
other than run here and there, wherever
the impulse drives her, and kiss their mouths,
while she still can? But that is not enough.
She tries to tear the bodies from the trees
and snaps off tender branches with her hands.
But drops of blood come dripping from the breaks,
as though they were a wound. Whichever child
is injured in this way cries out

     "Stop, mother!
Stop doing that! I'm begging you to stop!
Inside the tree my body is being torn.
Farewell."

    The bark grows over her last words,
and tears flow from the place. Drops of amber,
dripping from the sprouting branches, harden
in the sun. Then clear streams take this amber
and send it to be worn by Latian brides.[1]

Cycnus, son of Sthenelus, was present
at this remarkable event. And though
he was related to you, Phaëton,
by his mother's blood, his feelings for you
made him even closer. He abandoned
his royal power (for he ruled as king
of several cities in Liguria
and governed people there) and filled the banks
and streams of Eridanus with his cries,
and the forest, too, which, with those sisters,
had increased in size.[2] His voice becomes shrill,
white feathers hide his hair, a lengthy neck

CYCNUS

---

[1] Latium was the region in Italy where Rome was situated.
[2] Liguria was a term referring to north Italy. The Eridanus was the Po river.

Book Two

now stretches from his breast, a membrane links
his reddening fingers, wings dress his sides,
his mouth now sprouts a beak without a point.
Cycnus has become a brand new bird—the swan.
He does not trust the sky or Jupiter,
for he remembers fire unjustly sent
from there. So he seeks out wide ponds and pools. [380]
Hating fire, he chooses to live in streams,
the enemies of flame.[1]

        Meanwhile, Phoebus, 550
Phaëton's father, mourning and bereft
of his good looks—the way he tends to be   THE SUN
when in eclipse—despises light, himself,
and the day. His mind gives way to sorrow,
and, adding anger to his grief, denies
the earth his services, saying:

              "My fate
  from the very beginning of the world
  had been disturbed enough. I am weary
  of the tasks I have been carrying out.
  They bring no honour, and they never end. 560
  Let somebody else, anyone you like,
  control that chariot which brings on daylight.
  If no one will do that and all the gods
  acknowledge they cannot guide the chariot,
  let Jupiter do that himself. Then, at least,
  while he is trying out our reins, he may [390]
  for a while set aside those lightning bolts
  which deprive fathers of their sons. Then, too,
  once he has experienced the power
  in that team of horses with hooves of fire, 570
  he will realize that the one who failed
  to guide them well did not deserve to die."

All the gods are standing around the Sun
as he says this, and in pleading voices
they beg him not to act on his desire
to plunge the world in darkness. Jupiter
also makes excuses for hurling fire,
mixing his regrets with regal warnings.

---

[1]Ovid tells three different stories of the transformation of a man called Cycnus into a swan (see also 7.600 and 12.226).

BOOK TWO

Phoebus gathers up the maddened horses,
still trembling with terror. Ill with grieving,   580
he takes stick and whip and turns his rage on them
(for he is still incensed), berating them
and blaming them for Phaëton's death.   [400]

The all-powerful father moves around   JUPITER AND CALLISTO
the mighty walls of heaven, checking them,
to see if any section has been harmed
by the fire's power. After he confirms
they have their old solidity and strength,
he looks out on the earth and works of men.
But taking care of his own Arcadia   590
is his main concern. He restores the springs
and rivers, which have not yet dared to flow,
gives grass to the earth, and leaves to the trees,
and tells the injured woods to grow once more.
As he moves back and forth, he often stops
to gaze at a young girl of Nonacris.
Then passions kindled in his bones would blaze.[1]   [410]
She was not a girl who spent time working
to soften wool by teasing it or played
with stylish new arrangements for her hair.   600
A simple clasp held her dress together,
and ribbons kept her tangled hair in place.
Sometimes she carried a light javelin.
At other times a bow was in her hand,
for she was one of Phoebe's warriors.
No nymph wandering on Mount Maenalus
was more pleasing to the goddess Trivia.[2]
But no power lasts for long.

                               When the sun,
high in the sky, had moved past the mid-point,
the nymph went to a grove which ages past   610
had left untouched. She set down the quiver
on her shoulder, loosed her bow, and lay down   [420]
on the ground in a patch of grass, setting
the painted quiver underneath her neck.

---

[1] Nonacris was a city in Arcadia.

[2] Trivia is an epithet for the goddess Diana, who is also called Phoebe. She was worshipped in places where three roads met. Maenalus was a mountain in Arcadia.

Book Two

Jupiter spied Callisto there, tired out
and with no one to protect her. He said:

> "My wife, I'm sure, won't learn of my deceit.
> And if she does, will that bickering of hers
> really matter all that much?"

                                Without delay,
Jupiter changes face and clothes to look   620
just like Diana and speaks up:

                          "Young girl,
> one of my companions, in what mountains
> did you hunt today?"

                       Rising from the grass,
Callisto says:

                  "Greetings to you, goddess
> greater than Jupiter! I make that claim
> though he himself may hear me!"

                              Jupiter
does hear and laughs, delighted that she thinks
he is greater than himself. He kisses her,   [430]
but not modestly, the way one ought to kiss
a virgin. She is ready to describe   630
where she has just been hunting in the woods,
but he embraces her to halt her story
and, to get what he desires, commits a crime.
She does fight back, as much as women can.
How I wish you had observed them, Juno!
You would have been much kinder to the girl.
But how could a young nymph conquer Jupiter?
Could anyone do that? Once he has his way,
Jupiter ascends to heaven above.
But now Callisto hates the forest   640
(for the trees are aware of what she's done).
As she leaves the place, she almost forgets
to collect her arrows in their quiver   [440]
and the bow suspended there.

                  Lo and behold,   CALLISTO AND DIANA
goddess Diana with her companions,
on her way over lofty Mount Maenalus,
proud of the creatures she had hunted down,
glimpsed Callisto and, having seen the nymph,

called out to her. Callisto fled the call,
afraid at first the goddess might well be 650
Jupiter in disguise. But when she saw
there were nymphs with her as well, she sensed
there was no trick involved and joined their group.
Alas, how difficult it is not to show
one has done wrong by how one looks! She finds
it hard to raise her eyes up from the ground.
She is not tied to the goddess' side,
pre-eminent in that whole company,
the way she was before, but keeps silent,
and by blushing indicates her honour 660 [450]
has been shamed. If Diana had not been
a virgin, she would have learned about her guilt
from a thousand clues. People say the nymphs
all noticed it.

                When the crescent moon
was rising once again, nine orbits later,
the goddess, tired from hunting in the light
of the Sun, her brother, entered a cool grove
where a stream flowed with a rippling murmur,
rolling the fine-grained sand. She praised the spot,
touching the surface waters with her foot. 670
Commending these as well, she then remarked:

  "All witnesses are far away. Let's bathe
our naked bodies in the flowing stream."

Callisto was embarrassed. All the nymphs [460]
took off their clothes. She was the only one
who tried to hold things up. Reluctantly
she took her garment off. When she did that,
her body, now exposed, revealed her shame.
She desperately tried to hide her belly
with her hands. Diana said:

                      "Go away— 680
far from this place. Do not contaminate
the sacred springs."

                    And she commanded her
to leave their company.

                    For some time, Juno,   JUNO AND CALLISTO
the great Thunderer's wife, had known all this,
but was postponing any punishment

until the time was right. And now there seemed
no reason to delay. For Callisto
had already given birth to a young boy,
Arcas. That, too, really angered Juno,
who thought she was a slut. So when she turned
her eye and savage mind onto the child,
she cried:

   "That's the only thing that's missing,
you adulteress! You would be fertile
and publicly proclaim the injury
by giving birth and thus acknowledging
the disgrace to Jupiter, my consort.
You wretched girl, you'll get your punishment.
I'll take away that shape of yours, which gave
you and my husband such delight."

           Juno spoke.
She grabbed Callisto's hair above her forehead
and threw her face down on the ground. The nymph
stretched out her arms in supplication, but then
rough black hair began to sprout on both her arms,
her hands curved inward, changing to bent claws,
and served as feet. Her mouth, which Jupiter
had earlier praised, became distended
and formed a massive jaw. In case her prayers
and passionate words might move his feelings,
Juno takes away her power to speak.
The voice which issues from her raucous throat
is threatening, angry, full of menace.
Her mind still works the way it did before,
though she has now been changed into a bear.
She expresses her grief with constant groans,
raising her hands (such as they are) to heaven,
and even though she cannot speak of it,
she feels great Jupiter's indifference.
O how often she was too afraid to sleep
in the solitary woods and wandered
beside the fields and home that once before
had been her own! How often barking dogs
drove her across the rocks, and the huntress
ran off in terror, fearful of the hunt.
And often, when she saw wild beasts, she hid,
forgetting what she was. She was a bear,
and yet she trembled when she saw a bear

up in the mountains. Wolves made her afraid,
though Lycaon, her father, was among them.[1]

Now, Lycaon's grown up grandson Arcas,   CALLISTO AND ARCAS
almost fifteen years old, was unaware   730
of his own mother. While he was chasing
wild beasts, selecting suitable thickets,
and setting his woven nets to enclose
the Erymanthian woods, he met her.[2]
His mother saw Arcas and stopped, as if   [500]
she recognized him. Not knowing who she was,
he moved back, worried that she kept her eyes,
which never wavered, staring right at him.
When she wished to move in closer to him,
he was about to jab her with his spear,   740
a lethal weapon, but great Jupiter
intervened, by removing both of them
(and the chance a crime might be committed).
Together they were seized and carried off
through empty space by a tremendous wind
and placed in the sky as neighbouring stars.[3]

When Juno saw that girl of Jupiter's   JUNO, TETHYS, AND OCEANUS
shining among the stars, she swelled with rage
and went down into the sea to visit
white-haired Tethys and old Oceanus,   750
a pious couple whom the gods revere.[4]   [510]
When they asked the reason for her journey,
she answered them:

                "You are asking why I,
queen of the gods, leave my celestial home
to come here? Another woman now sits
in heaven in my place. I do not lie!
Once night comes and clothes the world in darkness,
you will observe some recent stars designed
to wound me, honoured by the highest place
in heaven, up there where the most distant   760

---

[1] For the story of Lycaon, see 1.297 ff. above.

[2] Erymanthia was a mountain in Arcadia.

[3] They became the Great Bear and Little Bear constellations.

[4] Tethys and Oceanus were brother and sister, as well as husband and wife. They were children of the original gods, Ouranos and Gaia.

and the smallest circle in space orbits
the furthest pole. But why would anyone
not wish to injure Juno or worry
about offending me—the ones I harm
I only benefit. Just look how much
I have achieved! How vast my powers are!   [520]
I stopped her being human, and she is made
a goddess! That's the sort of punishment
I inflict on evildoers! That shows
my great authority! Let him remove   770
her savage creature's shape and then restore
the way she looked before, just as he did
earlier with Io, that Argive girl.[1]
Why should he now not get rid of Juno,
wed the girl, set her in my marriage bed,
and take Lycaon for his father-in-law?
But if this slur to your scorned foster child
affects you, then make sure the seven stars
of that constellation are kept away
from your dark-blue waters.[2] Repel those stars   780
which have been given a place in heaven
to reward their fornication. Make sure
that whore will never bathe in the pure sea."[3]   [530]

The gods of the sea agreed to her request.   THE RAVEN AND THE CROW
Then Saturn's daughter moves up to clear air,
her light chariot drawn by painted peacocks,
which have only recently been coloured,
at the time that Argus died, that moment
when you, chattering Raven, not long since
had your wings altered suddenly to black,   790
although before that time you were pure white.
Earlier this bird had silver plumage
with snow-white wings, its colour rivalling
spotless doves, yielding nothing to those geese
whose watchful cries would save the Capitol,
or to river-loving swans.[4] But its tongue

[1]For the story of Io see 1.865 ff. above.

[2]Juno was raised by Tethys and Oceanus and was thus their foster child.

[3]At the latitude of the Mediterranean, the stars of the Bear constellations do not disappear below the horizon (i.e., bathe in the sea), but are visible through their whole orbit.

[4]In a famous story from the early history of Rome some geese on the Capitoline Hill heard an enemy army approaching and warned the garrison in time to save the city.

betrayed it—that chattering voice changed things, [540]
so what was white is now white's opposite.

In all Haemonia no one was lovelier
than Coronis of Larissa.[1] For you, 800
god of Delphi, she was, beyond all doubt,
delightful, as long as she was faithful
or unobserved. But that bird of Phoebus,
an inveterate informer, spied out
her infidelity and winged his way
to tell his master of her hidden crime.[2]
The chattering Crow flew after him
on flapping wings, to find out everything,
and once he heard about the Raven's trip,
he said:

        "This journey you are going on 810
will be no use. Do not spurn prophecies [550]
my voice delivers. Think of what I was   CROW AND MINERVA
and what I am. Ask if I deserve it.
You will find that the loyalty I showed
has done me harm. For once upon a time,
Pallas placed Erichthonius (a child
conceived without a mother) in a box
of woven willow twigs from Actaea.[3]
She gave this box to the three virgin girls
of double-natured Cecrops, telling them 820
they were not to snoop into her secret.[4]
I was concealed in the light foliage
of a thick elm, observing what they did.
Two of the girls, Herse and Pandrosus,
did not cheat and followed their instructions.
But Aglauros calls her sisters cowards.
Her hands untie the knots. Inside the box [560]
they see a baby and there beside him
is a snake stretched out. I tell the goddess

---

[1] Larissa was a city in Thessaly (Haemonia).

[2] The bird of Phoebus Apollo was the raven.

[3] Pallas was a common name for Athena or Minerva. Actaea was an early name for Attica, the region around Athens. Erichthonius was born from the soil, when some of Vulcan's sperm dripped onto the ground.

[4] Cecrops, an ancient king of Athens, had two natures because he was part man and part fish (or serpent).

what those girls have done. And for my trouble
this is the thanks I get—I am informed
I no longer have Minerva's patronage.
I am being expelled, and my position
is now below the owl, the bird of night.
My punishment should warn birds to beware
of running into danger when they talk.
In my view, she had come searching for me
all on her own. I was not requesting
any favours from her. You can ask her
all about this. Pallas may be angry,
but even in a rage she won't deny it.
Famous Coroneus was my father
in the land of Phocis (what I'm saying
is well known). I was a royal virgin,
and rich suitors sought my hand in marriage
(so don't belittle me). But my beauty
was my downfall. Once when I was walking
along the sea shore, strolling leisurely
across the sand, the way I used to do,
a sea god noticed me and grew inflamed.
After wasting time with flattering words,
trying to seduce me, he is ready
to use force. He comes at me. I run off,
leaving the firm shore, and exhaust myself,
quite uselessly, in softer sand. From there
I appeal to gods and men, but my voice
does not reach any human ear. And then,
a virgin god was moved to help a virgin.
As I stretched my arms up to the heavens,
those arms started to turn dark, all covered
with light feathers. I tried to shift my robe
down from my shoulders, but it had now become
more feathers, deeply rooted in my skin.
I made an effort to beat my naked breasts
with my own hands, but by this time I had
no hands, nor any naked breasts. I ran,
and the soft sand did not drag at my feet
the way it had before. I was raised up,
above the surface of the ground, and soon
was borne aloft, transported through the air.
I was made an innocent companion
to Minerva. What use is that to me,
if Nyctimene, who became a bird

thanks to her dreadful crime, has now assumed [590]
my honours? Or have you not heard the tale
(it's common knowledge everywhere in Lesbos)
how Nyctimene stained her father's bed?[1]
Yes, she is a bird, but she understands
her guilt and flies away from human eyes.
She conceals her shame in darkness. And now 880
all birds have banished her from all the heavens."

Once the Crow says this, the Raven answers:

"I hope that your attempt to call me back
turns out bad for you. Empty prophecies
are something I despise."

With that, the Raven   APOLLO AND CORONIS
continued on the journey he had started
and told his master he saw Coronis
lying beside a lad from Thessaly.
When Apollo, her lover, heard the charge, [600]
the laurel wreath fell off his head. All at once, 890
the god's face and colour fell—his lyre, too.
Heart seething with swelling anger, he grabbed
his usual weapons. He pulled back on his bow
until the tips were bent and, with a shaft
which never missed its target, pierced those breasts
so often pressed against his own. The girl,
struck by the arrow, groaned. As it was pulled
out of her wound, her fair white limbs were soaked
in scarlet blood. She cried out:

"O Phoebus,
you could have let me give birth to my child 900
before you punished me. Now in one death
two people die."

Those were her last words.
Then her life and blood poured out together, [610]
and icy death crept up her lifeless corpse.

Her lover regrets his ferocious act—
alas, too late!—and then he hates himself
for listening to the tale and growing

---

[1] Nyctimene, daughter of the king of Lesbos, had sex with her father and, in shame, hid in the forest. Minerva pitied her, changed her into an owl, and made the owl her favourite bird.

66

so enraged. He hates the bird that forced him
to find out about the fault and caused his grief.
He hates his hand and bow, and, with that hand, 910
those rash weapons, too, his arrows. He strokes her,
where she collapsed, and with his curing arts
he tries to stave off Fate. But he is too late.
The healing skills he used have no effect.
Once he saw that these attempts were futile
and that a funeral pyre had been prepared
to burn her body in a final blaze, [620]
then indeed Apollo gave out a groan
produced from somewhere deep inside his heart
(for tears are not permitted to flow down 920
celestial faces), a cry of grief and pain
just like a young cow makes when she beholds
the slaughterer raise his murderous axe
to his right ear and, with a splintering sound,
smash in the temples of her suckling calf.
Phoebus reluctantly poured incense out
onto her breast, embraced her, and finished
the rites which were her due, although her death
was far from just. But Phoebus could not bear
that his own child fall in those same ashes. 930
He ripped his son out of his mother's womb,
right from the fire, and took him to the cave [630]
of Chiron, a creature with a double form.[1]
As for the Raven, who was expecting
to get a fine reward, because his tongue
had spoken the truth, Apollo told him
he was no longer to be included
among birds coloured white.

               Meanwhile, Chiron,   CHIRON AND OCYRHOË
half-beast, half-man, pleased with a foster son
whose parent was a god, took great delight 940
in the obligation and the honour.
Then, lo and behold, the centaur's daughter
comes to him, her red hair cascading down
across her shoulders. The nymph Chariclo,
some time past, had named her Ocyrhoë,

---

[1] Chiron was a centaur, with the body and legs of a horse and the torso, head, and arms of a human being. The child's name was Aesculapius. He became a very famous healer. Aesculapius later was also a god in Rome (see below 15.939 ff.).

because she gave birth to the baby girl
beside a swift stream with that name. And now,
not content with knowing her father's arts,
Ocyrhoë sang the secrets of the Fates.
So when, possessed by frenzied prophecies, 950 [640]
her mind had grown hot from the god enclosed
inside her heart, she gazed at the infant child
and cried:

    "Grow up, young boy, bringer of health
to all the world. Mortal men will often
be in your debt, and you will be allowed
to bring back life once it has been removed.
But if you dare to do that even once
against the wishes of the gods, then flames
from your grandfather's lightning bolt will end
your power—you'll not possess it any more— 960
and from being a god you will be turned
into a bloodless corpse, then to a god,
after being, some time before, quite dead,
thus changing your fate twice. You too, dear father,
now immortal and, by those laws set down [650]
when you were born, created to live on
though all the ages, you will want to die
when you are being tormented by the blood
of that dreadful serpent, which you'll absorb
through wounded limbs.[1] The gods will alter you. 970
From an eternal being you will change
to someone who can suffer death, and then,
those three fatal goddesses will cut your thread."

She still has to speak about some details
of their fates. But from the depths of her heart
she sighs, begins to weep, and then the tears
run down her cheeks. She cries out:

                  "The Fates
stand in my way and tell me not to speak
another word—I may not use my voice.
The arts which bring down on me the anger 980
of the gods are not worth much. How I wish
I had never known about the future! [660]

---

[1] The serpent whose blood will make Chiron suffer is the Hydra, a famous monster with many heads. The blood was used as poison on a weapon which injured Chiron.

BOOK TWO

Now my human shape seems to be going.
Now grass delights me as a food, and now
my instinct is to run in the wide fields.
I am being changed into a mare, a shape
linked to my family. But why completely?
For my father is half horse, half human."

She spoke some words like these, but the last part
of her complaint was hard to understand.   990
The words were so confused. And afterwards,
they did not sound like words or horses' neighs,
but like an imitation of a horse.
A short time later, she gave our real neighs,
and her arms moved in the grass. Her fingers
then fused together, and one smooth hoof joined
five finger nails with solid horn. Her mouth   [670]
and neck grew larger. Most of her long cloak
became a tail, and her free-flowing hair
fell on her neck and changed into a mane   1000
on her right side. And then her voice and shape,
were both instantaneously transformed.
As a result of this amazing change,
she also got another name.[1]

             Chiron,   MERCURY AND BATTUS
semi-divine son of Philyra, wept
and called to you, Apollo, for your help.[2]
But you could not overturn the orders
of great Jupiter, and if you could have,
you were not present at the time, but living
in Elis and Messenian lands. Back then,   1010
you wore a shepherd's clothing made of skins,   [680]
with a wild olive stick in your left hand,
and in your right a pipe with seven reeds
of unequal lengths. While that pipe's music
was soothing you and love was on your mind,
your cattle, so the story goes, wandered
unguarded into the land of Pylos.[3]
Mercury, son of Maia, Atlas' daughter,
up to his usual tricks, stole the herd

---

[1] The new name, not mentioned here by Ovid, was Enippe.

[2] Philyra was a nymph. Chiron's father was Saturn, father of Jupiter.

[3] Pylos was a city in the southern Peloponnese.

and hid it in the woods. No one observed
the theft, except for an old man, well known
throughout that land, where, in every region,
men called him Battus. He was a herdsman,
who tended the grassy fields and pastures
of wealthy Neleus, and catered to
his herds of well-bred mares.[1] Now Mercury,
concerned about this man, took him aside
with a flattering hand and said:

              "Stranger,
whoever you are, if, by chance, anyone
should ask about these animals, just say
you haven't seen them. And to make quite sure
you get some recompense for what you've done,
take this glistening heifer as your reward."

Mercury offered him the cow. The stranger
took it, pointed to a stone, and answered:

  "Go on your way, and rest assured. That stone
will talk about your theft before I do."

Jupiter's son pretended he had left,
but came back with an altered shape and voice.
He spoke to Battus:

              "You there, countryman,
if you've caught sight of any cattle here,
along this path, help me. Don't keep quiet
about those stolen beasts. I'll offer you
a cow and her own bull as a reward."

The old man, with the reward now doubled,
answered:

      "The cattle will be over there,
below those hills."

           And that was where they were.
The grandson of Atlas chuckled and said:

  "Liar! Will you betray me to myself,
telling me things to inform against me?"

---

[1] Neleus was king of Pylos.

BOOK TWO

And he changed the perjured chest of Battus
to solid flint, which is called, even now,
the touchstone, and this old disgrace is linked
to stone that has not merited the slur.

The god who carries the caduceus   MERCURY AND HERSE
took himself from this place on matching wings,
and, as he flew, gazed down upon the fields
in Munychia, on land so pleasing
to Minerva, and on the well-tilled groves   [710]
of Mount Lycaeus.[1] On that day, by chance,   1060
chaste young girls, according to their custom,
carried pure, sacred objects on their heads
in baskets crowned with flowers, on their way
to the festive citadel of Pallas.
The winged god sees them coming back from there.
He does not direct his course right at them,
but wheels in circles. And just as a hawk,
swiftest of all birds, when it sees entrails
but is still timid, since the attendants
stand in dense crowds beside the sacrifice,   1070
circles around, not venturing to fly
any further off, and with beating wings
keeps moving greedily around the food
it hopes to seize—that's how the agile god
from Mount Cyllene angles his flight then   [720]
above Actaean heights and circles there
in the same airy breezes. And just as
Lucifer shines brighter than the other stars
and golden Phoebe more than Lucifer,
that how much Herse, as she walked along,   1080
was lovelier than all the virgins girls.
Among her comrades in that procession
she was pre-eminent. Jupiter's son,
astounded by her beauty, hovered there,
in the air, growing hot with love, the way
a lead ball shot from a Balearic sling
warms up as it flies and, below the clouds,

---

[1] Munychia was a small piece of land close to Athens. The caduceus was the special messenger's staff carried by Mercury. It is commonly depicted as having two snakes entwined around it and a pair of wings at the top.

discovers heat it did not have before.¹
He shifts his course, moving down from heaven [730]
and making for the earth, with no attempt 1090
to change the way he looks—he has such faith
in his own beauty. But still, even though
that beauty is complete, he takes the time
to tidy himself up. He smoothes his hair
and tugs his cloak to hang the way it should
to show the fringe and all the golden thread.
In his right hand he holds his magic wand,
with which he brings on sleep or drives it off,
and on the god's trim feet winged sandals gleam.

Deep inside the house were three rooms adorned 1100
with ivory and tortoiseshell. In these,   MERCURY AND AGLAUROS
Pandrosus lived on the right, Aglauros
on the left, and Herse had the middle.
The girl who occupies the left-hand room
sees Mercury first, as he approaches,
and goes to ask the god who he might be
and why he has come there. Answering her,
the grandson of Atlas and Pleione says:

  "I am the one who carries through the air
what my father orders—and my father 1110
is Jupiter himself. I will not lie
about why I am here. Just be willing
to help your sister out and to be called
my young child's aunt. The reason I am here
is Herse. I'm asking you to help out
someone who's in love."

                              Aglauros looks at him
through the same eyes with which, not long ago,
she had pried into the hidden secrets
of golden-haired Minerva, then asks him
to give her, in return for her assistance, 1120 [750]
a heavy weight of gold. In the meantime,
she demands he leave the house.²

---

¹The Balearic Islands were near the coast of Spain. The residents were well known for their use of the sling.

²For the story of Aglauros and Minerva see above 2.815 ff.

Book Two

                    Minerva,
the warrior goddess, turns her fierce eyeballs
on the girl. From deep inside her, she heaves
a sigh with such emotion that her heart
and the aegis resting on her strong chest
both shake.[1] Her mind remembers that this girl
with profane hands has earlier revealed
her secrets when, contravening orders
she had been given, she looked at the child   [1130]
Erichthonius, offspring of the god
who inhabits Lemnos, an infant born
without a mother.[2] And now her sister
and the god will both be grateful to her.
She will be rich, as well, once she receives
the gold demanded by her avarice.

Minerva leaves at once for Envy's home,   [760]
a filthy, black, corrupted place. The house,   MINERVA AND ENVY
crouched in the lowest fissures of a cave,
with no sunlight, closed off from every wind,   [1140]
is depressing and filled with numbing cold,
always lacking fire, always in the dark.
When the fearful warrior goddess gets there,
she stops before the house (for she believes
it is not right to go beneath its roof)
and hammers on the doorpost with her spear.
The doors shake and then fly open. She sees
Envy inside the house eating the flesh
of vipers, which nurtures her corruption.
Minerva looks and turns her eyes away.   [1150]   [770]
But Envy gets up slowly from the ground,
leaving the bodies of half-eaten snakes,
shuffles forward, and peers out at the goddess,
at her lovely shape and splendid weapons.
Her face distorts. Then she groans and gives off
the heaviest sigh. There is a pallor
smeared across her face, her entire body
is gaunt, her eyesight squints at everything,
her teeth are mouldy with decay, her heart

---

[1] The aegis was a special divine shield, which had the power to terrify human beings and make them run away. It was commonly associated with Jupiter and Minerva.

[2] Erichthonius was produced from the sperm of Vulcan, god of the forge, who was associated with Lemnos. His semen fell into the earth, as a result of which Erichthonius was created.

73

is green with bile, and her tongue drips poison. [1160]
She never laughs, except when she responds
to the sight of grieving, and never sleeps,
for gnawing cares keep her awake. She hates
to witness men's success—the sight of it [780]
makes her waste away. She torments others
and, in that very moment, is tormented
and punishes herself. Though Tritonia
hated Envy, she spoke briefly to her,
saying:[1]

    "Infect one of Cecrops' daughters
with your poison. That is a task for you. [1170]
Aglauros is the one."

              With no more words,
she left, pushing her spear into the earth
and springing upward.

              Envy, eyes askew,
saw the goddess rush away, muttered softly,
unhappy that Minerva would succeed,
picked up a staff completely wrapped in thorns,
and, shrouded by black clouds, went on her way. [790]
Wherever she goes, she tramples down fields
full of flowers, burns the grass, plucks the tops
of growing plants, and with her breath pollutes [1180]
cities and homes, entire communities.
At last, Envy sees Tritonia's city,
so rich in intelligence, resources,
and joyful peace.[2] She finds it difficult
to hold back tears because she cannot see
a single thing to cry about. She goes in
the home of Cecrops' daughter and performs
what she's been ordered, touching the girl's breast
with a rust-stained hand and filling her heart
with spiky thorns. She blows in harmful poison, [1190] [800]
spreading black venom through her bones and lungs.
And to make sure the causes of her pain
do not wander far away, she places
before her eyes visions of her sister,

[1] Tritonia is another name for Minerva. It's not clear what it means (perhaps a reference to the place where she is supposed to have been born).

[2] Tritonia's city was Athens.

her sister's happy marriage, and the god
whose outer form is so magnificent,
enlarging every detail. Aglauros,
Cecrops' daughter, tormented by all this,
eaten up by hidden sorrow, groaning,
racked with pain at night and with pain by day,
wasting miserably from slow disease,
like ice melting from uncertain sunlight,
is burned by joyful Herse's happy fate,
just as a fire placed under thorny plants
which emit no flames, burns with a low heat.
Often she wished to die, so that she might
stop watching what was going on, often
to tell everything to her stern father,
as if it were a crime. Then finally,
to keep the god from entering the house,
as he approached, she sat down by the door.
When he spoke flattering words, wished her well,
and used his gentlest tone, she said:

      "Stop that!
I am not going to move myself from here
till you are sent away.

      The swift god
from Cyllene answered:

      "Let us make that
a pact between us."

      With his magic wand
he opened the sculpted doors. Aglauros
attempted to get up but could not move
the parts she bent when she sat down. Her limbs
were numb and sluggish. She really struggled
to raise herself and hold her body straight,
but her knees were locked, and an icy cold
was spreading through her nails. Her veins were pale
and had lost their blood. And just as cancer,
an incurable disease, tends to spread
far and wide and to transport the illness
to undamaged parts, so a lethal chill
by degrees moved to her chest, closing off
her breathing and her vital passageways.
She made no attempt to speak—if she had,
there would have been no channel for her voice.

BOOK TWO

By now stone had seized her neck, and her mouth [830]
grew hard. There she sat, a bloodless statue—
and not white stone, for her mind had stained her.[1]

When the grandson of Atlas has imposed   JUPITER AND EUROPA
this punishment for what Aglauros said
and for her profane mind, he leaves the land
named after Pallas and, spreading his wings,
goes up into the aether. His father   1240
calls him aside and, without revealing
what he wants (because he is in love), declares:

> "My son, faithful servant of my commands,
> do not delay, but with your usual speed,
> glide down, and make for that land which gazes
> at your mother's star from the left hand side.[2]
> The natives call it Sidon. You'll observe   [840]
> a royal herd of cattle grazing there,
> some distance off, on mountain grasses.
> Take those animals towards the seashore."   1250

Jupiter spoke. The herd, by now driven
from the mountains, was moving to the shore,
as Jupiter had bid. There Europa,
daughter of a mighty king, used to play,
accompanied by Tyrian virgins.[3]
Majesty and love do not fit well together
and do not long remain in the same house.
So the father and ruler of the gods,
whose right hand is armed with triple lightning,
who, by nodding his head, can shake the world,   1260
sets aside his weighty sceptre, takes on
the appearance of a bull, and then joins   [850]
that cattle herd. Looking magnificent,
he lows and wanders through the tender grass.
His colour is like snow which no rough foot
has stepped in and left an imprint and which
the watery South Wind has not melted.
Muscles bulge around his neck, his dewlap

---

[1] We learn no more from Ovid about Mercury and Herse. In some traditional myths they had a child, Cephalus, whose story appears later in Ovid's poem (in Book 7).

[2] Mercury's mother, Maia, was one of the seven stars in the constellation of the Pleiades.

[3] Tyre was a coastal city close to Sidon in Asia Minor.

hangs down from his shoulders, his horns are bent,
but you would think they had been made by hand, 1270
brighter than a perfect gem. His forehead
holds no threats, and there is nothing fearful
in his eye. He has a calm expression.
Europa, Agenor's daughter, amazed
he is so lovely and unthreatening,
at first is fearful about touching him, [860]
for all his mildness. But soon she comes up
holding out bunched flowers for his shining mouth.
The lover feels great joy. Until the time
the pleasure he is hoping for arrives, 1280
he kisses her hands. He finds it difficult,
(O so difficult!) to postpone the rest.
Sometimes he plays and runs through the green grass,
and sometimes he sets down his snow-white side
on the yellow sand. Little by little,
Europa's fear subsides. Now he offers
his chest for the virgin's hand to stroke
and now his horns for her to decorate
with fresh-picked flowers. The royal maiden
even attempts to ride astride the bull, 1290
not knowing she is sitting on a god,
who gradually, as he moves from the land [870]
and from the dry seashore, sets the false hooves
on his feet in sea waves by the water's edge.
From there he moves in further, carrying
his prize across the middle of the sea.
Terrified at being abducted, the girl
looks back to the shore she has abandoned,
clutching one of his horns in her right hand
and bracing the other hand along his back.
Winds keep tugging at her trembling garments.

Book Three

III

[Cadmus searches for Europa; he consults Apollo, who tells him to follow a heifer; Cadmus fights and kills the dragon, sows the dragon's teeth; warriors spring up and fight; Cadmus founds Thebes; Actaeon sees Diana naked, is changed into a stag, and ripped apart by his dogs; Juno tricks and kills Semele; birth of Bacchus; Juno and Jupiter argue about sex, agree to consult Teiresias; how Teiresias became a woman and then a man again; Juno blinds Teiresias, Jupiter gives him the gift of prophecy; Narcissus and Echo; Juno punishes Echo; Narcissus rejects Echo; suffering of Echo; Narcissus falls in love with his own image, pines away, dies, and is changed into a flower; Pentheus and Bacchus; the story of Acoetes; Bacchus changes sailors into dolphins; Pentheus is killed.]

By now Jupiter, discarding the form   CADMUS
of a deceiving bull, has revealed himself
and reached the land of Crete. In the meantime,
Europa's father, who has no knowledge
of what has taken place, orders Cadmus
to look for the abducted girl, saying
that he will punish him with banishment
if he does not find her, thus revealing
both his piety and his wickedness
in the selfsame act.[1] So Agenor's son   10
wanders the world (for who can uncover
Jupiter's secret plans?). By running off,
he stays away from his own native land
and his father's rage. As a suppliant,
he seeks advice from Phoebus' oracle
and asks what country he should settle in.
Phoebus says:

    "In uninhabited fields   [10]
a cow will meet you, one that has never
felt the yoke and has no experience
of the curving plough. With her to guide you,   20
choose your path, and wherever she lies down
on the grass, construct walls for your city,
and give that region the name Boeotia."

Cadmus has scarcely gone down from that cave
beside Castalius when he sees a cow
moving slowly without a guard, showing
on her neck no signs of being harnessed.[2]

---

[1]Europa's father was Agenor, king of Sidon, in Asia Minor. Cadmus was her brother.

[2]Castalius was a fountain near Delphi, below Mount Parnassus, in central Greece.

He follows, closely tracking where she goes,
and pays tribute silently to Phoebus,
who instructed him to make this journey.   30
Once he has passed the fords of Cephisus
and fields of Panope, the heifer stops.[1]
Raising her wide forehead and its long horns   [20]
up to the heavens, with her lowing sounds
she makes the air vibrate and, looking back
at her companions following behind,
she lies down on her side and rests there,
on the tender grass. Cadmus then gives thanks,
kissing the foreign soil and saluting
the unknown hills and fields.

               Intending now   40
to offer Jupiter a sacrifice,   CADMUS AND THE SERPENT
he orders servants to bring up water
from a flowing stream for a libation.
An ancient grove stands there, as yet untouched
by any human hand. It has a cave
in the middle, thickly covered with twigs
and willow sticks, creating a low arch   [30]
with the adjoining rocks. A rich supply
of water is there, too. In this cavern
is hidden a serpent sacred to Mars,   50
distinguished by its crests with golden skin.
Its eyes are gleaming fire, its whole body
is puffed with poison, and its three-forked tongue
flickers beside teeth set in triple rows.
When that race of men from Tyre directed
their ill-fated footsteps into this grove
and a jar they set down in the water
made a noise, from deep within the cavern
the dark green serpent stuck its head outside
with a fearful hissing noise. The jars fall   60
out of the men's hands, blood leaves their bodies,
and their astonished limbs immediately   [40]
begin to shake. Twisting its scaly coils
into rolling circles and with one leap
bending itself up in an enormous arc,

---

[1]Cephisus was a river flowing through Boeotia. Panope was a town in Phocis.

Book Three

it raises more than half its body length
up in the air and looks at the whole grove.
Its body, viewed as a totality,
is as huge as that Serpent in the sky
which separates the Great and Little Bears.[1] 70
It does not hesitate but charges out,
straight at those Phoenicians, whether they wish
to fight or flee or whether instant panic
hinders them from both. The beast then slaughters
some with bites, some in prolonged embraces,
and others by breathing deathly poison
which destroys them.

               The sun, now at its height, [50]
had made the shadows small. Agenor's son
wondered what was holding up his comrades.
He set off searching for the men, covered 80
with skins stripped from a lion, carrying
a lance of gleaming iron, a javelin,
and a heart more firm than any weapon.
He went in the grove and saw the corpses
of his butchered men and the enemy,
their conqueror, with its monstrous body,
as its bloody tongue licked their dreadful wounds.
He cried:

      "Either I will avenge your deaths,
my faithful comrades, or I will share it."

With these words, in his right hand he raised up 90
a huge rock and, with tremendous effort, [60]
hurled the massive weight. High walls with towers
would shake under the impact of that stone,
but the dragon was not hurt. Protected
by its scales, which were like a coat of mail,
and by the hardness of its murky hide,
its skin repelled the heavy blow. But still,
that same protective hide cannot prevail
against the javelin which stands firmly fixed
in the centre of its curving, supple spine, 100
with the whole iron point skewering its gut.

---

[1] The Serpent is a constellation in the northern sky.

Book Three

Writhing in pain and twisting its head round
towards its back, the beast looks at the wound
and bites down on the impaled javelin.
Its huge strength loosens it on every side [70]
and then, with a great effort, rips the shaft
out of its back, but the iron point remains
stuck in its bones. And then, when a fresh blow
has really added to its usual rage,
the swollen veins in its throat grow bloated, 110
white foam flecks its man-killing jaws, the earth
echoes from the scraping scales, and the breath
pumping from its black Stygian mouth poisons
the infected air. At times the serpent
coils itself in massive circles, at times
it rears up straighter than a lengthy plank,
and sometimes it charges on relentlessly,
like rivers fully roused by falling rain,
its chest flattening trees which block its way. [80]
Agenor's son backs off a little, blocking 120
the attack with his lion's hide, checking
the menacing jaws by thrusting the spear
in front of him. The serpent, mad with rage,
tries in vain to wound the tempered iron,
but its teeth break on the metal. By now,
from that dragon's poisonous gullet, blood
is already dripping out. Its spatter
stains the grassy turf. But the wound is slight.
It moves back from the blow, pulling away
its wounded throat, and by retreating 130
stops the spear thrust sinking any deeper
and does not let it penetrate too far.
So Agenor's son, always in pursuit, [90]
keeps shoving the iron spear lodged in its throat,
until an oak tree blocks the beast's retreat,
and he can jam the spear right through its neck
into the wood. The beast's enormous weight
bends the tree, which groans as the very tip
of the serpent's tail beats against its trunk.

While the victor was looking at the size 140
of the enemy he had overcome,
suddenly a voice rang out (it was hard

to tell where it was coming from, but still,
Cadmus heard it):

> "Son of Agenor,
> why are you staring at that serpent's corpse?
> You, too, will be a snake men gaze upon."

For a while, Cadmus trembles, his colour
and his confidence are gone, while his hair [100]
in chill terror stands on end. Then, behold,
Pallas is there, the hero's guardian,
after gliding down from the air above.
She orders him to open up the earth
and sow the dragon's teeth into the ground,
to ensure the growth of future people.
He obeys. After he has sunk a plough
into the soil and carved a furrow there,
deep in that earth he sows the dragon's teeth,
the seeds of mortals, as he was ordered.
What happened then was quite beyond belief. EARTH-BORN WARRIORS
Lumps of earth began to move, and spear points
first appeared to rise up from the furrows,
then, a short time later, heads with helmets
and nodding painted crests, then shoulder blades
and chests emerged, as well as limbs weighed down
with weapons. A crop of men armed with shields [110]
sprang up—just as in drama festivals
when curtains are pulled up, the figures there
usually rise, show their faces first,
and then, little by little, other parts,
so every form moves up in peaceful order,
until the lower margin shows their feet.[1]

Cadmus, frightened by a new enemy,
holds his weapons ready, but one of those
created from the earth cries out:

> "Stand back,
> and do not interfere in civil war!"

---

[1] Riley notes that the theatre curtain, which contained designs with human figures on it, was lowered to the floor to start a performance and raised again at the end. The process described here is the gradual raising of the curtain at the end of the play.

That said, in a combat settled hand-to-hand
he runs at one of his earth-born brothers
and strikes him with his cruel sword. But then,
he himself is cut down by a javelin
thrown from far away. The man who killed him 180 [120]
does not survive. He dies, gasping for air,
just moments after he began to breathe.
In the same way, the whole crowd of warriors
is in a frenzy, and these brothers born
a minute ago are being butchered
in their own battle from wounds inflicted
on one another. Now those youthful men,
whom Fate had granted such a short life span,
were hammering at the sorrowful heart
of their bloodstained mother. Five men were left, 190
and one was Echion. On the advice
of the Tritonian deity, he threw
his weapons down on the ground, requesting
and pledging tokens of fraternal peace.[1]
Thus, Cadmus, a foreigner from Sidon,
had these men as his comrades in the work,
when he carried out what Phoebus ordered
and founded his new city. [130]

                Thebes was now built, ACTAEON AND DIANA
and you, Cadmus, would seem to be happy
in your exile: Venus and Mars were now 200
your in-laws, and add to this the family
from such a noble wife, so many sons
and daughters, and those dear assurances
of grandchildren, already youthful men.[2]
But there is no doubt we should always wait
for someone's final day and call no man
content before he's dead and laid to rest.
The first reasons for your sorrow, Cadmus,
in the midst of so much prosperity,
were your grandson, Actaeon, whose forehead 210
had strange horns attached to it and you, too,
his hunting dogs, who gorged yourselves on blood [140]

---

[1] The Tritonian deity was Pallas, i.e., Minerva.
[2] Cadmus' wife was Harmonia, the daughter of Venus and Mars.

from your own master. But if one enquires
with all due care, one finds the blame for that
in chance, not in some wicked act he did.
What crime is there is making a mistake?

There is a mountain, bloody with the slaughter
of various wild beasts. By now shadows
have contracted under the mid-day light
and the sun is at an equal distance   220
from each end of its path, when Actaeon,
the young lad from Hyantia, speaks out
in a friendly way to the companions
in his hunting group, as they make their way
through secluded undergrowth:[1]

                  "Friends, these nets
and spears are dripping with wild creatures' blood.
Our good luck today has been sufficient.
When a new dawn appears on golden wheels   [150]
and brings back daylight, let us continue
the task we have proposed. Right now, Phoebus   230
is poised halfway between the east and west,
and his heat is opening up the fields.
So stop what you are doing, and remove
the knotted nets."[2]

                  His comrades carry out
what he has asked and then rest from their work.

There was a valley men called Gargaphia,
thick with pine and sharp-pointed cypress trees,
sacred to Diana, who wears her tunic
tucked high up on her legs.[3] Deep in this place,
there is a wooded cave, not formed by art,   240
for nature with her own ingenuity
has imitated art, by tracing out
a natural arch of native limestone rock   [160]
and lighter sandstone. A sparkling fountain pool

---

[1] The Hyantes were the original inhabitants of Boeotia, the region in which Thebes was built. Hence, the term is equivalent here to Boeotia.

[2] Nets were commonly used in hunting. The animals would be driven into them, and the hunters would kill them once they became entangled.

[3] Gargaphia was near Plataea, a region in Boeotia.

of limpid water murmurs on the right,
and grassy banks enclose its open streams.
Here the forest goddess, when exhausted
from her hunting, would bathe her virgin limbs
in the clear waters. Once she reached the place,
she would give one of her armed nymphs her spear, 250
quiver, and unstrung bow. Another nymph
held in her arms the robe she'd taken off,
while two undid the sandals on her feet.
Then a Theban girl, Crocale, who was
more skillful than the rest, tied up the hair
tangled across her neck, into a knot,
though she herself kept her hair hanging down. [170]
Nephele, Hyale, Rhanis, Psecas,
and Phiale fetched water in large jars
and poured it out.

        While the Titanian goddess 260
is bathing there in her usual stream,
lo and behold, Cadmus' grandson arrives
at that very spot.[1] He has set aside
his hunting and is wandering around
the unknown wood, uncertain where he is.
The Fates have led him there. Once he enters
the cave watered by those springs, all the nymphs,
naked as they are, once they see a man,
beat their breasts and fill the entire forest
with their sudden cries, rushing to surround 270
and conceal Diana with their bodies. [180]
But the goddess herself, who is taller,
stands there head and shoulders above them all.
Since she was being watched without her clothes,
Diana's face changed colour to the blush
one sees quite commonly when clouds are struck
by sunlight from an opposite direction
or by the purple dawn. And though a crowd
of her companions was standing round her,
she turned sideways and twisted her head back. 280
How she wished she had her arrows with her!

---

[1] The adjective Titanian means "related to the Titans." It is commonly applied to Diana, although she was not a Titan but a daughter of Jupiter.

But she did have water. She scooped some up
and splashed it in Actaeon's face, sprinkling
his hair with her avenging drops, adding [190]
words which prophesied his future ruin:

  "Now you may say you have seen me naked,
  if you still retain the power of speech!"

Without any further threats, she places
the horns of a full-grown stag upon his head
where she has sprinkled. She stretches out his neck,   290
alters his ears so the tops are pointed,
changes his hands to feet, his arms to legs,
and covers his body with dappled hide.
Then, added to that, she makes him timid.
The son of Autonoë runs away,
astonished, as he flees, he is so fast.[1]
Still, when he gazes in the water and sees [200]
his face and horns, he is about to say

  "I feel so wretched."

                        But no voice comes out!
He groans. That is his voice. Tears trickle down   300
a face that is not his. All that remains
from what he was earlier is his mind.
What is he to do? Should he go back home
to the royal palace? Or hide himself
here in the woods? Shame hinders him from one,
fear from the other.

                While he is in doubt,   ACTAEON'S DOGS
his dogs see him. First of all, Melampus
and keen Ichnobates give a signal
by howling (Ichnobates comes from Crete,
Melampus from a Spartan breed) and then   310
all the other hounds run up, more swiftly
than racing winds—Pamphagos, Dorceus,
and Oribasus, all from Arcadia, [210]
brave Nebrophonos and savage Theron,
with Laelaps and swift-footed Pterelas,
keen-nosed Agre, ferocious Hylaeus,

---

[1] Autonoë, mother of Actaeon, was one of Cadmus' daughters.

recently wounded by a boar, Nape,
born from a wolf, Poemenis, trained to work
with cattle, Harpyia, with her two pups,
slender-flanked Sicyonian Ladon, Dromas, 320
Canace, Sticte, Tigris, and Alce,
white-haired Leucon and black Asbolus,
strong-bodied Lacon and fast Aëllo,
Thoüs, swift Lycisca and her brother [220]
Cyprian Harpalus, his black forehead
marked with a white spot in the middle,
Melaneus, Lachne with a shaggy hide,
and two born from a Dictaean father
and a Spartan mother—Agriodos
and Labros—and shrill-barking Hylactor 330
(there were others, too, but the total list
would be too tedious).[1] The pack of hounds
is driven by its eagerness for prey
over remote cliffs, rocks, and pinnacles,
where the going is rough, without a path.
Actaeon flees through places where often
he pursued before. Now, alas, he runs
from his own helpers! He longs to cry out:

"I am Actaeon. Know your own master!" [230]

But he has no words to express that wish. 340
The barking echoes in the upper sky.
Melanchaetes is the first to wound him
along the back, and then Theridamas.
Oresitrophus bites into his shoulder.
These dogs had gone out later but had found
a quicker route by shortcuts through the hills.
They keep their master pinned, as the whole pack
rushes in a mass and buries its teeth
in Actaeon's flesh. By this point no place
on his body remains without a wound. 350
He groans, making sounds which are not human,
but yet not ones a stag could make, and fills
the well-known hills with dismal cries. His knees
are bent, just like a begging suppliant, [240]

---

[1] Most of the names of these dogs come from Greek words associated with characteristics of hunting dogs: "deer killer," "hunter," "tracker," "howler," and so on.

and he moves his silent features here and there,
as he might move his arms.

                His companions,
quite ignorant of who he is, urge on
the ferocious pack with their usual cries,
while their eyes are searching for Actaeon.
They keep calling eagerly,

                "Actaeon!"   360

as if he were not there (he turns his head
when he hears the name). They criticize him
for not being present, for being too tired
to enjoy the spectacle of their prey.
He might well prefer he could be absent,
but he is there. And he might well desire
to see and yet not feel the savage acts
of his own dogs. They stand all around him,
sinking jaws inside his body, ripping
to pieces their own master, whom they see   370   [250]
as the deceiving image of a stag.
Men say quiver-bearing Diana's rage
was not appeased until Actaeon's life,
after countless wounds, finally was gone.

This event is viewed in different ways.   JUNO AND SEMELE
To some, the goddess seems more violent
than just. Others praise her for holding to
her strict virginity. Each point of view
comes up with its own reasons. Only Juno,
Jupiter's wife, says not a word about it,   380
whether she approves or blames the action,
but she rejoices that this calamity
has fallen on Agenor's family,
for she has transferred the hatred in her heart
from that Tyrian rival to her relatives.[1]
And now, following that earlier cause,
she has another reason for her loathing.
She is enraged that Semele is pregnant

---

[1] The Tyrian rival is Europa, daughter of Agenor and sister of Cadmus. For the origin of Juno's hatred of Europa see the story of the seduction and abduction of Europa (1.865 ff).

from the seed of powerful Jupiter.[1] [260]
She loosens her tongue to abuse the girl 390
and cries:

    "All those numerous complaints of mine—
what good have they done me? I must attack
that girl in person. I have to kill her,
if I am rightly called most mighty Juno,
if it is fitting that in my right hand
I hold the jewelled sceptre and am queen,
Jupiter's wife and sister—well, at least
his sister. But, I suppose, if the girl
is happy with a secret love, the harm
done to my marriage bed is trivial. 400
Still, she has conceived—that's all we needed—
carries clear proof of her disgraceful act
in her full womb, and wishes to become
the mother of a child from Jupiter,
something difficult for me to manage.
She has such great faith in her own beauty, [270]
I'll make sure that confidence deceives her.
I am not Saturn's daughter if that girl
does not fall into waters of the Styx,
dumped down in them by Jupiter himself." 410

Having said this, she rises from her throne
and, hidden in tawny clouds, makes her way
to Semele's door. She does not disperse
the clouds until she has disguised herself
as an old woman, seeding her temples
with white hair, ploughing wrinkles in her skin,
keeping her limbs bent, her steps unsteady.
She makes her voice like an old woman's, too.
In fact, she now resembles Semele's nurse,
Beroë, from Epidaurus.[2] And so, 420
when they have a chance to talk together
and have been chatting for a while, the name
Jupiter comes up. Juno sighs and says: [280]

---

[1] Semele was a daughter of Cadmus, thus part of the same family as Europa and Actaeon.

[2] Epidaurus was a city in the Peloponnese.

> "I really hope Jupiter is the one,
> but I have my doubts about all such things.
> Several men, using the names of gods,
> have entered virtuous women's bedrooms.
> It's not enough he says he's Jupiter,
> if indeed that is the truth. Let him give
> some token of his love. You must ask him
> to embrace you with the style and power
> with which he is welcomed by great Juno,
> and before he does that, he should put on
> the symbols of his full magnificence."

Saying words like these, Juno goes to work
on Cadmus' unsuspecting daughter.
When the girl asks Jupiter for a gift,   JUPITER AND SEMELE
without saying what it is, he tells her:

> "Choose something. I shall refuse you nothing.
> To help you have more faith in what I say,
> let the god of the Stygian torrents
> stand as witness, who makes the gods afraid,
> the god of all the gods."

                    Pleased by what was
to be her doom, prevailing too easily,
and about to die because her lover
desires to please her, Semele replies:

> "Present yourself to me in the same form
> in which Saturn's daughter is accustomed
> to embrace you, when you are entering
> sexual union, the act of Venus."

As she was speaking, Jupiter wanted
to close her mouth, but her voice already
had moved into the air. He gave a groan,
for she could not take back what she had wished,
and he could not take back what he had sworn.
And so, with utmost sorrow, he rose up
to lofty heaven and, with a nod, gathered
the clouds that followed him, then added rains,
lightning mixed in with stormy winds, thunder,
and the inevitable lightning bolt.
Still, he tries to minimize his power,
as much as he is able, and refuses

to arm himself with the fire he once used
to bring down hundred-handed Typhoëus—
there was too much destructiveness in that.¹
There is another less forceful lightning,
to which the right hands of the Cyclopes
attach less flame, less savagery and rage.²
Gods call these his second-order weapons.
Jupiter takes some of them and enters   470
Agenor's home. But the mortal body
of Semele cannot withstand the blast
which comes from heaven, and she is consumed
by her fiery marriage gift. The baby,   BIRTH OF BACCHUS
not yet completely formed, is then torn out
from his mother's womb and, still premature,   [310]
is sewn up (if such things can be believed)
in his father's thigh and completes the term
he would have spent inside his mother's belly.
While in the cradle, his maternal aunt,   480
Ino, raises him in secret. After that,
he is given to the nymphs of Nysa
who hide him in their caves and feed him milk.³

While these events are happening on earth   JUPITER, JUNO, AND TEIRESIAS
through laws of Fate and the crib of Bacchus,
twice born, remains secure, the story goes
that Jupiter, who happened to be full
of nectar, shelved his serious concerns
and shared some slight, amusing anecdotes
at ease with Juno. Jupiter remarked: 490

  "To tell the truth, the pleasure women get   [320]
  from sex is greater than what men receive."

Juno denied the claim. They both agreed
to ask wise Teiresias his opinion,
since he had known both male and female love.

---

¹Typhoëus was a monster who fought against Jupiter. He was overthrown and buried deep in the earth, traditionally under Mount Etna, a volcano in Sicily. For further details about Typhoëus, see below 5.510 ff.

²The cyclopes, one-eyed monsters, work in Vulcan's forge and make Jupiter's lightning bolts.

³The child of Semele and Zeus is Bacchus. Ino is a daughter of Cadmus and thus Semele's sister. Nysa was a mountain far to the east. The baby is hidden to prevent Juno from harming him.

Once in the green forest he had used his staff
to strike two massive copulating snakes,
and (amazingly!) he was then transformed
from man to woman. He spent seven years
like that, and in the eighth year came across 500
the selfsame sight once more. And so he said:

> "If the power in the stroke which hits you
> is so immense it can change the gender
> of the person who delivers the blow
> into its opposite, then I will now
> strike at you once more."

      When he hit those snakes, [330]
his previous form returned, and once again
he was a man. And so he is the one
they choose to resolve their playful quarrel,
and he confirms what Jupiter has said. 510
Juno, they say, was seriously displeased,
unjustly so, out of all proportion
to the dispute. So she condemned the eyes
of the one who had pronounced the judgment
to eternal darkness. But Jupiter,
the almighty Father, to mitigate
his loss of sight (since no god is allowed
to reverse the actions of another god),
gave Teiresias the power to see
into the future and with this honour eased 520
his punishment.

      Teiresias' fame   NARCISSUS
was highly acclaimed in every city
of Aonia. When people asked him, [340]
he provided accurate responses.
Dark Liriope was the first to test
and to confirm the truth of what he said.[1]
The winding river Cephisus had once
embraced her, enclosed her in his waters,
and taken her by force. From her full womb
this loveliest of nymphs had given birth 530
to an infant one could fall in love with,

---

[1] Aonia was a region of Boeotia. Liriope was the daughter of Oceanus and Tethys.

even at that age. She called him Narcissus.
When Teiresias was asked about him—
whether the child was destined to pass through
the distant season of mature old age—
the visionary prophet then replied:

   "Only if he never gazes at himself."

For some time the prophet's words seemed worthless.
But what in fact took place—the way the young lad died
and the bizarre nature of his madness—   540 [350]
proved those words were true.

                     The son of Cephisus
was now sixteen—one might consider him
both boy and youth. Many young men and girls
desired him, but in his tender frame
there was such fearful pride that no young men
or girls affected him.

                          The nymph Echo,   NARCISSUS AND ECHO
with the resounding voice, who has not learned
to hold her tongue when someone speaks or else
to speak out first herself, saw Narcissus
driving panicked stags towards his hunting nets.   550
Back then Echo was not just a voice.
She still had a body. But nonetheless,
though she loved to talk, she could only speak   [360]
as she does now. If a person uttered
many words, she could repeat the last ones.
Juno had made her talk this way, because,
when she could have caught out those mountain nymphs
lying beside her husband Jupiter,
Echo would deliberately detain her
with a long chat, until the nymphs had fled.   560
After the goddess realized the trick,
she said:

   "That tongue of yours has swindled me.
   I will give you less power over it,
   the very briefest use of your own voice."

And she made good her threat by what she did.
Echo just repeats the last words spoken,
merely duplicating what she has heard.

Book Three

So when she sees Narcissus wandering [370]
through solitary fields and burns with love,
she tracks him surreptitiously. The more   570
she follows him, the more she is on fire,
just as quick-burning sulphur smeared around
the tops of torches seizes any flames
which approach too close. O how many times
she longed to meet him with flirtatious words,
using soft entreaties! Nature stops her
and does not allow her to begin. But she
is ready for what Nature does permit.
She waits for sounds which her voice can repeat.
Now, it so happens that the boy, enticed   580
away from a group of faithful comrades,
shouts out:

        "Is there anybody here?" [380]

Echo answers:

        "Here!"

           He is astonished.
He casts his eye in all directions and,
in a loud voice, cries:

        "Come over here!"

She calls back to the person calling her.
He looks around and, when no one comes out,
he shouts again:

        "Why run away from me?"

He gets back all the words he has called out.
Narcissus stands there, misled by what seems   590
a voice which answers his, and calls again:

  "Let's meet here together."

        She could not reply
more willingly to any sound, and cried:

  "Meet here together."

           To support her words,
she came out from the woods and ran to him,

to throw her arms around the neck she loved.
He ran away and, as he ran, complained:

"Take your hands off me! Stop these embraces! [390]
I'll die before you have your way with me!"

All she replied was:

"Have your way with me." 600

Now spurned, she conceals herself in forests,
and, in her shame, covers her face with leaves.
From that time on, she lives in lonely caves.
But still her love is there and even grows
from the pain of her rejection. Worries
and lack of sleep waste her wretched body.
Poverty shrinks her skin, and all juices
in her body move out into the air.
Only her voice and bones are left. Her voice
still lives. The story goes her bones were changed 610
to shapes of stone. Since that time, she hides out
in the woods. No one has ever seen her [400]
in the mountains, but she is heard by all.
It is the sound which still lives on in her.

Narcissus scorned her, just as he had scorned NARCISSUS IN LOVE
other nymphs born in the streams and mountains,
and just as he had previously scorned
whole companies of men. Then one of those
Narcissus had rejected raised his hands
up to the sky and prayed:

"Though he may love 620
another in this way, let him not have
what he desires from love."

The prayer was just,
and goddess Nemesis agreed to it.[1]

There was a clear stream, with limpid waters
like silver, as yet untouched by shepherds
or goats and cattle grazing mountain slopes,
undisturbed by any bird, savage beast, [410]

---

[1] Ovid calls the goddess of Retribution Rhamnasia, an alternative name for Nemesis, daughter of Jupiter, who had a temple at Rhamnus, in Athens.

or bough split off a tree. All around it
there was grass fed by adjacent waters
and trees which would not let the pool grow warm 630
from any sun. Here Narcissus, weary
from eager hunting and the heat, lay down,
attracted by the scenery of the place
and by the water springs. And while he tries
to slake his thirst, another thirst begins.
As he is drinking, he sees an image,
the reflection of his face, and falls in love,
desiring a thing which has no substance.
He thinks the shadow must possess a body.
Astonished by himself, he remains there, 640
motionless, wearing the same expression,
like a statue made of Parian marble.
Stretched out along the ground, he contemplates [420]
the double constellation of his eyes,
his hair, which looks suitable for Bacchus
or worthy of Apollo, his beardless cheeks,
his ivory neck, his sensuous mouth,
and the blush mixed in with snowy whiteness,
admiring every feature which makes him
worth admiring. Without a sense of shame, 650
he desires himself. The one approving
is the person being approved, and while
he is pursuing, he is being pursued.
He kindles fire and burns at the same time.
How often he kisses the devious spring
without success! How often he reaches in
to clutch the neck he sees in the centre
of the water, and yet his arms cannot
embrace himself! What he is looking at
he does not recognize, but what he sees 660 [430]
sets him aflame, and the very error
which deceives his eyes excites them. Why then,
you foolish lad, do you keep trying to clutch
that fleeting image? What you are seeking
does not exist. And if you turn away,
you will lose the thing you love. What you see
is the shadow of a mirror image,
which has nothing of its own. It arrives
with you and stays with you and leaves with you,

if you can leave. No need for Ceres' food, 670
no need for rest can take him from the place.
Instead he lies on the thick grass and peers
at the misleading image, for his eyes
can never gaze enough. He lifts himself [440]
a little, holds out his arms, and cries:

"You forest trees, has anyone ever
been more cruelly in love? You should know,
for you have offered useful hiding places
to many lovers. In all those ages
your life has passed, that huge expanse of time, 680
have you known anyone who pined away
like this? I see him, and he pleases me.
But still, what I see and what pleases me
I cannot find. My loving has been caught
in such a huge mistake! To make my grief
more painful still, we are not held apart
by the mighty sea or by some journey,
or by mountains, or walls with bolted gates.
The only thing which keeps us separate
is that tiny pool! He himself desires 690 [450]
to be embraced. Every time I lean down
with my lips to the clear water, he lifts
his upturned face to mine. And you would think
he could be touched. It's such a little thing
that blocks our love. Whoever you may be,
come here! O you extraordinary boy,
why play these tricks with me? When I seek you,
where do you go? You cannot be running
from my shape and youth, and I am someone
who has been loved by nymphs! You promise me, 700
with that loving face of yours, unknown hope.
When I hold out my arms to you, then you
are happy to hold out your own. When I smile,
you smile. Often I have seen you weeping
when I shed tears. And if I nod my head, [460]
you return my gesture. From the motion
of your fair mouth I guess you send back words
which do not reach my ears. I am in you.
I have felt it. I am not being deceived
by my own image. I am burning up 710
with love for my own self. I rouse the flames

and suffer from them, too. What do I do?
Should I be the person asking or being asked?
But what is there to ask for? What I want
is with me. My riches have made me poor.
O how I wish I could divide myself
from my own body! What a novel wish
for someone who's in love, for I desire
to be divided from the one I love.
Now sorrow saps my strength. My time of life   720
will soon run out, and I will pass away   [470]
in the prime of youth. And for me my death
will not be a burden, since, by dying,
I put my pain to rest. I would prefer
the one I love to keep on living longer,
but now the two of us, both in one life,
will die together."

                 Narcissus finished.
Not thinking clearly, he went back again
to the same image and splashed the waters
with his tears. Once he disturbed the surface,   730
the reflection was obscured. When he saw
the image disappearing, he cried out:

"Where are you going? Stay! Do not leave me,
you pitiless boy, the one who loves you!
Let me gaze upon what I cannot touch,
the food I need to feed my wretched madness."

In his grief, he ripped the upper border   [480]
of his clothing and beat his naked chest
with hands as white as marble. As he struck,
his chest turned rosy red, just like apples,   740
in which some parts are usually red
and some are white, or just as unripe grapes
in various bunches commonly possess
a purple colour. Once he saw his image
in the water, he could not endure it
a moment longer, but, as yellow wax
drips in a tiny flame, as morning frost
dissolves in the warm sun, so Narcissus,
wasted by love, gradually melts away,   [490]
consumed by hidden fire. And now his face   750
has no more colour red mixed in with white.

He lacks vitality and strength, those things
which, only recently, gave such delight
to the body Echo earlier had loved.
She was still angry and remembered him,
but when she saw Narcissus, she was sad.
Whenever the poor boy would cry:

        "Alas!"

her echoing voice would then repeat:

        "Alas!"

And when he struck his shoulders with his hands,
she sent him back the same sound as the blow.
His final words as he was looking in
those waters he habitually watched
were these:

        "Alas, my beloved boy, in vain!"   [500]

The place gave every word back in reply.
He cried:

        "Farewell."

        And Echo called:

        "Farewell!"

He set his weary head down on green turf,
and death closed up those eyes which so admired
the beauty of their master. Even then,
after he had been received in houses
of the dead, he would keep gazing into
waters of the Styx. His naiad sisters
wept for Narcissus. They cut off their hair
and laid it out for him. The dryads, too,
lamented, and Echo returned their cries.
Now they were preparing the funeral pyre,
the torches they would brandish, and the bier.
But there was no body. Instead they found
a flower with a central yellow part
surrounded by white petals on all sides.   [510]

When cities in Achaea heard of this
talk about it made Teiresias famous,
and rightly so. His reputation soared.

PENTHEUS AND TEIRESIAS

BOOK THREE

Of all the people, there was only one—
Pentheus, son of Echion, a man
contemptuous of the gods—who scorned him,
ridiculing the old man's prophecies
and mocking his darkness, his loss of sight
(for Juno had removed his power to see).[1]
Shaking his temples covered with white hair,
Teiresias said:

        "How happy you would be   790
if you, too, were deprived of light, so then
you could not witness Bacchus' sacred rites!
For the day is coming—and I predict
it is not far away—when the new god,
Bacchus, son of Semele, will be here.   [520]
If you do not think of him as worthy
of worship in the temples, you will be
torn up, scattered in a thousand places,
and will pollute the forests, your mother,
and her sisters with your blood. So be it!   800
For you will not believe this deity
merits those honours. Then you will complain
that in this darkness I have seen too much."

As Teiresias is muttering these things,
Pentheus dismisses him. But his words
prove true. What the prophet has predicted
comes to pass.

        Bacchus appears. Fields resound   PENTHEUS AND BACCHUS
with festive shouting, crowds rush about—men,
married women, common folk, and leaders,
all mixed up, carried off to unknown rites.   810   [530]
Pentheus shouts:

        "Children of the dragon,
you warlike people, what is this madness
which has seized your minds?[2] Can the clash of brass
against brass, curved-horn pipes, and magic tricks

---

[1] Pentheus was the son of Agave, a daughter of Cadmus, and thus part of the royal family of Thebes. For details about Teiresias' loss of sight, see 3.511 above.

[2] The Thebans are those who came from Tyre with Cadmus as well as the descendents of those who appeared out of the earth when Cadmus sowed the dragon's teeth (3.153 ff.).

have such a powerful effect, that sounds
of women's screams and the insanity
stirred by wine, obscene mobs, and senseless drums
conquer people who were not terrified
of warlike swords, or trumpets, or columns
of drawn steel? You old men, should I be proud   820
that you, who were borne far across the sea
and in this very region set up Tyre
and your once banished household gods, are now
letting them be taken without a fight?   [540]
You young men, whose age is more vigorous,
closer to my own, you are better suited
to bear weapons than to hold a thyrsus,
and to have helmets covering your heads
rather than a bunch of leaves.[1] I beg you
to recall the race of those you come from,   830
and take on the spirit of that dragon.
He was just one, but he slaughtered many.
He died for his spring and pool, and you men,
you should be winning glorious triumphs!
He put brave men to death. You should drive out
these degenerates and guard the honour
of your ancestors. If Fates have decreed
Thebes will not long survive, then how I wish
siege engines and warriors would demolish
the city walls with crashing fire and steel!   840   [550]
We would be sad, but there would be no guilt.
Our fate would be something we could lament,
not something we should hide, and our weeping
would be free from shame. But now Thebes will fall
to an unarmed boy, who does not delight
in war, or weapons, or using horses,
but likes hair doused with myrrh, tender garlands,
purple garments, and gold embroidery.
But if you stand aside, I will force him
quickly to acknowledge that his father   850
is a pretense and his rites are fictions.[2]
If Acrisius has sufficient courage

---

[1] The Bacchic rites involved ecstatic worship out in the countryside, with plenty of group dancing. The thyrsus was a plant stalk, an important symbol in the ritual.

[2] Bacchus, the new god, claims that he is the son of Jupiter.

to slur a worthless deity and shut [560]
the gates of Argos to stop him entering,
should Pentheus, along with all of Thebes,
be conquered by some foreign charlatan?"¹

Pentheus then ordered his attendants:

"Leave quickly. Go and drag him here in chains,
this so-called leader. And with these commands
there must be no slackness, no malingering!" 860

His grandfather, his uncle Athamas,
and all the others in his crowds of friends
tell Pentheus he is wrong, and they try,
without success, to hold him back.² Warnings
increase the fierceness of his rage, which chafes
and grows when it is checked. And the delays
just make things worse. I have seen streams like that.
When no obstruction blocks the water's flow,
it runs down easily, without much noise,
but wherever logs and stones are in the way, 870 [570]
holding back the stream, it grows turbulent
and races from the barrier enraged.

The king's attendants soon return, covered
with blood. Pentheus asks where Bacchus is.
The servants say they have not seen him, adding:

"But we captured one of his companions,
someone who helps him in the sacred rites."

They show the king a prisoner, with his hands   ACOETES AND BACCHUS
tied behind his back, a stranger who has come
from Tyrrhenian people and follows 880
the rituals of Bacchus. Pentheus,
whose rage has made his eyes look horrible,
looks at the man and, though he finds it hard
to delay the time of punishment, says:

"You who are about to die and whose death
will provide a warning to the others,

---

¹Acrisius was king of Argos. He refused to allow the new god Bacchus or his rites in the city. His story is told in Book 4.

²Athamas was married to Ino, sister of Agave, Pentheus' mother. Pentheus' grandfather was Cadmus.

Book Three

tell us your name, the country you come from, [580]
who your parents are, and why you carry on
these newly fashionable rituals."

The stranger, with no sign of fear, replies: 890

"My name is Acoetes, my country
Maeonia, and, as for my parents,
they were humble common folk.[1] My father
left no fields to till with hardy oxen,
no flocks of sheep, or any cattle herds.
He himself was poor. It was his custom
to hunt for leaping fish with line and hook,
using his rod to bring them in. That skill
was all his wealth. When he passed it to me,
he said:

        'Accept the riches I possess.   900
   You are my heir, successor to my work.'

So when he died, he left nothing to me   [590]
but the streams, the only things I can call
my patrimony. Later, to avoid
being always stuck on the same rocks, I learned
to steer a ship, handling the rudder
in my right hand and keeping my eyes fixed
on rainy stars of the Olenian goat,
as well as Taygete and Hyades,
the Bear, the houses of the winds, and harbours   910
suitable for ships.[2] Well, it so happened
while on my way to Delos, I was blown
onto coastal lands of Chios. With oars
we deftly brought the ship up to the shore.
I leapt out quickly, landing on wet sand.
We spent the night there. And when Aurora   [600]
first began to redden, then I get up
and tell the men to bring fresh water on,
pointing out a pathway leading to a stream.

---

[1] Maeonia was a region in the Near East (part of modern Turkey).

[2] These names refer to figures set among the constellations. The Olenian she goat suckled infant Jupiter (as a constellation it was associated with rainstorms). Taygete was one of the daughters of Atlas, set in the Pleiades. The Hyades were the nurses of Bacchus. They had been changed into constellations.

I myself from a high hill look around
to see what the wind is promising me.
After that I call to my companions
and go back to the ship. My chief comrade,
Opheltes, shouts out:

        'See, all of us are here.'

And he leads up across the shore a boy
with all the beauty of a virgin girl.
He found him in an isolated field
and considers him a prize. The young lad,
heavy with wine and sleep, seems to stagger
and has trouble keeping up. I observe
his clothing, his appearance, and his gait.
I see nothing in him which could make me think
he is a mortal being. Sensing this,
I say to my companions:

        'I'm not sure
just what deity is in that body,
but inside that young boy there is a god.
Whoever you may be, be kind to us,
assist our efforts, and forgive these men.'

Dictys, the fastest man at climbing up
the top part of the sails, grabbing a rope,
and sliding down again, speaks up:

        'Stop praying
on our behalf.'

        Libys agrees with him,
as do blond Melanthus, our bow lookout,
Alcimedon, and Epopeus, too,
who shouted out the stroke-beat for the oars,
called for a rest, and kept their spirits up.
The others all agree with him, so blind
is their desire for plunder. I cry out:

        'But I will not let a sacred cargo
violate this ship. And in this matter
by rights the greatest share belongs to me.'

I block their way. The boldest of them all,
Lycabas, is enraged. He'd been banished

from a town in Tuscany, punished
with exile for an appalling murder.
While I hold him, he hits me in the throat
with his young fist and would have thrown me
in the sea, if I had not, though shaken,
been held up by a rope. That ruffian crew
applauds his action. And then, finally, 960
Bacchus (for it is Bacchus), as if the noise [630]
has dispelled his torpor and his senses
are returning from the wine inside his heart,
speaks up:

      'What are you doing? What's this din?
You sailors, tell me how I reached this place?
And where do you propose to carry me?'

Proreus then replied:

          'Don't be afraid.
Tell us the harbours you would like to reach.
We'll take you to the land you're looking for.'

Bacchus said:

      'Then set your course for Naxos. 970
That is my home. The land will welcome you.'

The treacherous men swear by all the gods
and by the sea that that's what they will do
and bid me hoist sail on our painted ship.
Naxos was on the right. As I spread out [640]
the right-hand sails, each one of them in turn
asks me:

      'What are you up to, you idiot?
What madness grips you now, Acoetes?
Steer to the left-hand side.'

      Most of the men
show me what they mean by nodding, and some 980
whisper in my ear what they are after.
I was horrified and said:

      'Someone else
should take the tiller.'

Book Three

     And I moved away,
not taking any part in what they did
or in their crime. Each one of them shouts out
at me. The entire crew is muttering.
One man—Aethalion—says:

       'It's not as if
our entire safety rests on you alone.'

He shifts himself across to my position,
takes on my work, sets a different course,   990
and sails away from Naxos. Then the god,   [650]
in a mocking way, as if only now
he has at last realized their deceit,
looks out on the sea from the curving stern
and, like a man in tears, cries out:

       'You sailors,
these shores are not the ones you promised me,
not the lands I asked for! What have I done
to deserve such punishment? What glory
do you win for yourselves if you mislead
a boy, if many men deceive just one?'   1000

I had been weeping for some time. The crew,
those profane men, just ridicule my tears
and with oars rowing at a rapid rate
keep striking at the sea. Now I swear to you
by the god himself (and there is no god
more powerful than he) that the events
which I describe are every bit as true
as they defy belief. Our ship stops there,   [660]
in the open sea, just as if it sat
in dry dock. The sailors, astonished, keep   1010
pulling on their oars. They unfurl the sails
and try in these two ways to move ahead.
But ivy locks the oars and, creeping up
in winding tendrils, hangs in heavy bunches
from the sail. The god himself, his forehead
wrapped in a wreath of clustered grapes, holds up
a spear decked out with ivy leaves. Round him
lie phantom visions of tigers, lynxes,
and threatening shapes of spotted panthers.
The men, afraid or mad, jump overboard.   1020   [670]

Book Three

Medon is the first whose entire body
turns black and whose spine begins to twist
in a curving arc. Then Lycabas yells:

'What sort of monster are you turning into?'

As he said these words, his jaws expanded,
his nostrils bent, his skin grew hard and scaly.
Then Libys, who was still trying to get
the seized-up oars to move, suddenly saw
his hands were shrinking. Then he had no hands!
They both had changed to fins. Another man   1030
tried to stretch his arms to the twisted ropes,
but he had no arms, and, arching backwards,
his limbless body tumbled in the sea.   [680]
He had a tail, a curving hook like horns
on a partial moon. Dolphins jump around
in all directions, dripping lots of spray.
They jump again and then dive down once more
deep beneath the waves, in a playful group.
They look just like a company of dancers,
throwing their wanton bodies here and there,   1040
and spouting water they have taken in
through open nostrils. Of the twenty men
some moments earlier (that was the crew
we carried on the ship) I alone remained.
I was afraid and cold, my body shook,
with almost no control. The god spoke up
to reassure me:

        'Free your heart from fear,   [690]
and make for Naxos.'

        So I was taken
to his island home, and at altar fires
I supervise the sacred rites of Bacchus."   1050

Pentheus replied:

        "We have leant our ears
to this long story, so that this delay
might mitigate the power of our rage.
You attendants, take this fellow away,
and quickly, too. Tear his body apart

Book Three

with dreadful tortures, and then send it down
to Stygian darkness."

      So Acoetes,
the Tyrrhenian, is at once dragged off
and imprisoned in a solid building.
But while, as ordered, they are preparing   1060
fire and iron, the vicious tools of death,
doors of the prison, so the story goes,
spontaneously open, and the chains,
on their own, with no one loosening them,   [700]
fall off. Echion's son remains unchanged.
But now he does not tell his men to march
to Mount Cithaeron—he goes in person,
right to the place they've chosen to enact
the sacred ritual. The mountain echoes
to the loud songs and shouts of worshippers   1070
celebrating Bacchus. Just as a keen horse
neighs when the warlike trumpeter sends out
his signal with resounding brass and shows
his love of war, so Pentheus is stirred
by a heaven pierced with drawn-out screaming.
As he listened, his anger blazed once more.

Almost in the middle of that mountain   PENTHEUS AND AGAVE
there is a forest, whose edges enclose
a treeless field, open on every side.
Here Pentheus' mother was the first   1080
to see him watching, with his profane eyes,
the sacred rites. She was the very first
roused to rush insanely at him, the first
to hurl her thyrsus stem against her son
and wound him. She cried out:

      "Come here, sisters,
both of you! There's a huge boar wandering
in our fields! I must kill that boar!"

      The crowd,
one common frenzy, all massed together
and charged, attacking frightened Pentheus,
already terrified and speaking words   1090
far less violent, already shouting

BOOK THREE

he was in the wrong and pleading guilty
to a crime. Though wounded, he shouted out:

"Bring help, Autonoë. You are my aunt.
Let Actaeon's spirit move your heart!"

                                         But she
has no sense at all who Actaeon might be.[1]
As he is pleading with her, she rips off
his right arm. Ino, in a frenzy, pulls out
the other one. The poor man has no arms
to hold out to his mother. He shows her   1100
his mutilated body, with its limbs
torn out, and screams:

                "Mother! Look at me!"

Agave looks at him and howls. She turns
her neck, letting her hair toss in the breeze,
then seizes his head in bloodstained fingers,
tears it off, and shouts:

                    "Friends, look over here!
This conquest is our work!"

                        From a high tree
winds do not rip leaves touched by autumn's cold   [730]
and still clinging on precariously
faster than Pentheus' limbs were stripped   1110
by their abominable hands. And so,
warned by such examples, Theban women
take part in the new rites, offer incense,
and worship at Bacchus' sacred altars.

---

[1] Autonoë, sister of Agave, was the mother of Actaeon, whose story is told earlier in this book (3.217 ff).

Book Four

IV

[The daughters of Minyas scorn Bacchus; the first daughter tells the story of Pyramus and Thisbe; the second tells the story of Venus and Mars being trapped by Vulcan while having sex, and then the story of Helios and Leucothoë: how Leucothoë is transformed into a plant and Clytië into a heliotrope; the third sister, Alcithoë, tells the story of Salmacis and Hermaph-roditus; the daughters of Minyas turn into bats; Juno's hatred of Ino; Juno visits the Underworld, sees Tityos, Tantalus, Sisyphus, Ixion, and the Danaïds being punished; she enlists help of Tisiphone; Tisiphone poisons Athamas and Ino, who go mad and kill their children; Ino and her child become sea gods; Juno changes Ino's companions to stone; Cadmus and Harmonia go into exile and become snakes; Perseus visits Atlas; Medusa's head turns Atlas to stone; Perseus rescues Andromeda; Medusa's head hardens seaweed to stone; Perseus and the daughters of Phorcys; Perseus describes the birth of Pegasus and the origin of Medusa's snake-filled hair.]

But Alcithoë, daughter of Minyas   THE DAUGHTERS OF MINYAS
does not believe those divine rituals
should be accepted.[1] Even now the girl
is rash enough to deny that Bacchus
is a child of Jupiter, and she has
sisters who share in her impiety.
The priest had ordered a celebration
of the festival. He told mistresses
and maids who had been excused from duties
to cover their breasts with animal skins,   10
undo the ribbons in their hair, and grip
a leafy thyrsus in their hands. The god,
he prophesied, would be cruelly angry,
if they offended him. Older women
and young wives obeyed him, setting aside   [10]
looms and baskets and tasks not yet complete.
They offered incense and called on Bacchus,
Bromius, Lyaeus, the Fire-Born One,
the Twice Born, the only one who possessed
two mothers.[2] They added God of Nysa,   20
unshorn Thyoneus, with Lenaeus
planter of the joyous grape, Nyctelius,
father Eleleus, Iacchus, Evan,
and the many others names they call you,
Bacchus, throughout all Greece. For your youth

---

[1] Minyas was a ruler of the Boeotians. The rituals in question are those of Bacchus.

[2] These names and titles are alternatives for the name Bacchus. He is called "fire born" because his mother was destroyed by a lightning bolt from Jupiter, who then removed the infant from her womb. Bacchus is twice born because he was delivered prematurely from his mother, Semele, and came to term sewn up in Jupiter's thigh. For the same reason he has "two mothers." See Ovid's version of the story in Book 3 above.

never ends—you are an eternal boy,
looked upon as the most beautiful one
in lofty heaven. When you are standing
without your horns, you have a virgin's look.
The conquered orient belongs to you, 30 [20]
as far as where dark India is washed
by the distant river Ganges. And you,
venerated god, struck down Pentheus
and Lycurgus armed with his two-edged axe,
both blasphemous men, and hurled the bodies
of those Tyrrhenians into the sea.[1]
You harness the proud necks of two lynxes
with coloured reins. Bacchantes and satyrs
all follow you, as does that drunk old man,
Silenus, who holds up his shaking limbs 40
with a staff and hangs on unsteadily
to his sway-backed mule.[2] Wherever you go,
shouts of young men rise, with women's voices,
drums struck by hand, brass cymbals, and long pipes. [30]
Ismenian women call upon the god,

"Be present here—peaceful and kind to us."[3]

And they celebrate the stipulated rites.
But Minyas' daughters stay indoors,
the only ones to disturb the festival
with inappropriate activities, 50
Minerva's work—spinning wool, twisting strands
by hand, remaining seated at their looms
and keeping their servants busy working.
One of those sisters, as her slender thumb
is drawing thread, speaks up:

"While other girls
refuse to work and are celebrating
these so-called sacred rituals, those of us
who serve Pallas, a finer deity,

---

[1] Lycurgus was a king of Thrace who opposed the worship of Bacchus. Pentheus did the same in Thebes. For the stories of Pentheus and of the Tyrrhenians, see Book 3 above.

[2] Bacchantes were the followers of Bacchus. Satyrs in Greek mythology were male companions of Dionysus (Bacchus), associated with wine, pipes, and sexual pleasure in the woods. Silenus was one of the main companions of Bacchus and his tutor. His name is not given in the Latin text, but the description seems clearly to indicate who is being referred to.

[3] The word Ismenian, from the name of a river, is another name for Theban.

should make these useful tasks much easier
by talking of different things, taking turns
to tell a story to entertain us all
and fill our idle ears, so that the time
will pass more quickly."

                      Her sisters agree
with the suggestion and tell her to start
with the first story. She wonders which tale
she should select out of so rich a store
(for she does know an enormous number)
and is not sure whether she should tell them
how you, Babylonian Dercetis,
can live (so those in Palestine believe)
in an altered form in water, with scales
covering your limbs, or how your daughter
acquired wings and in her early years lived
in dove-cotes painted white, or how a naiad
through her song and herbs with too much power
changed young men's bodies into silent fish,
until she suffered the same thing, or else
how the tree which used to bear white berries,
once it was soaked with blood, now bears dark fruit.[1]
This last one pleases her, since the story
is not well known. So as she spins her wool
to thread, she begins the tale, as follows:

    "In the place where they say Semiramis   PYRAMUS AND THISBE
surrounded her high city with brick walls,
Pyramus and Thisbe lived in houses
side by side—the finest looking young lad
and the choicest girl in the entire East.[2]
As neighbours, they got to know each other
and took their first few steps together. In time,
love grew, and they would have been united,
swearing the marriage oath, but their parents
would not permit it. Still, the two of them
burned with love, minds equally committed,
a fiery blaze their parents could not quench.
No one knows about it. They speak with nods

---

[1] Dercetis was a near Eastern goddess, supposedly half fish. Her daughter Semiramis, a legendary Eastern queen, very early in her life lived among doves. The name of the first sister to tell a story is Arsippe. Ovid does not mention her name here.

[2] The city in the story is Babylon.

and signs. The more they try to hide the fire,
the hotter it burns. Their two houses shared
a wall in common, which had been fractured,
leaving a narrow crack. This had happened
earlier when it was built, and no one, 100
in all the many years, had seen the fault.
But what does love not notice? You lovers
were the first to find it, and you made it
a pathway for your voices. Through that crack
the slightest murmurs of your tender words [70]
would safely pass. When they stood beside it,
Thisbe on one side, Pyramus the other,
and each one of them, in turn, had seized on
breath from the other's mouth, they often said:

    'Envious wall, why be an obstacle 110
to lovers? Would it be so difficult
to let us completely join our bodies?
Or if that is too much, you might at least
open up so we can kiss each other.
We are not ungrateful, for we admit
it is thanks to you we have a passage
for words to reach our loving ears.'

                            They spoke
like this in vain, from both sides of the wall.
Night came. They said farewell, and each one gave
his own side kisses, which did not pass through 120 [80]
and reach the other side.

                        One morning later,
when dawn had sent away the stars of night
and sunlight had dried out the frosty grass,
they met at their usual place. First of all,
they complained about their many troubles,
talking there in quiet murmurs. But then,
they decided they would try outwitting
their guardians in the silence of the night,
go outside, and, once they had left the house,
they would also leave the built-up city. 130
So they would not lose their way wandering
across open fields, they agreed to meet
at the tomb of Ninus and hide themselves
in the shadows of a tree. In that place
stood a lofty mulberry loaded down

Book Four

with white fruit, beside an ice-cold fountain.
They thought the plan a good one. When daylight,
which seems to leave so slowly, is cast down
in the waters and from those same waters
night emerges, Thisbe opens the door   140
and steals out through the darkness, deceiving
her own family. Her face veiled, she reaches
the tomb and sits down by the very tree
they talked about. Love makes her bold. But then,
lo and behold, a lioness comes there,
with foaming jaws smeared from a recent kill
of oxen, intending to slake her thirst
in the waters of the near-by fountain.
Babylonian Thisbe sees the creature
from a distance in the moonlight and runs,   150
with trembling steps, into a murky cave.
In her rush, the veil falls off behind her
and remains there. Once the fierce lioness
has drunk her fill, quenched her thirst, and moved
towards the trees, by chance she finds the veil
(without the girl) and rips the silky fabric
in her bloodstained jaws. Pyramus goes out
somewhat later and in the deep dust sees
clear footprints of the savage animal.
His whole face turns pale. When he also sees   160
the garment stained with blood, he cries:

       'One night
will see two lovers perish. Of the two
she was the one who most deserved to live
a lengthy life. My soul has done great harm.
I have been your death, you unhappy girl,
the one who told you to come out at night
to places full of danger and was not
the first to get here. O you fierce lions,
wherever you may live beneath this rock,
tear apart my body, and with sharp teeth   170
devour my wicked heart. But that's the way
a coward acts—to hope that death will come.'

He picks up Thisbe's veil, takes it with him
to the shade of that tree they talked about.
When he has shed his tears into the veil
he knows so well and kissed it, he cries out:

BOOK FOUR

'Now soak yourself in my blood, too.'

Then, without a pause, he plunges the sword
he carries on his belt into his belly
and, as he is dying, pulls the blade out
from the seething wound. He is on the ground,
lying on his back, blood spraying way up high,
just as a pipe made of defective lead
will split and, through the hissing crack, water
shoots in thin streams far away, as its spurts
pulse through the air. On the mulberry tree
the fruits change colour from the sprinkling blood.
They now look black, and as blood soaks the roots,
it stains the hanging mulberries dark purple.

Lo, Thisbe, not yet free from fear, returns,
so she will not disappoint her lover.
Her eyes and heart search for the youth. She yearns
to tell him the great danger she escaped.
She knows the place and outline of the tree,
which she has seen before, but the colour
of the fruit makes her unsure. She wonders
if this is the tree. While still uncertain,
she catches sight of quivering limbs beating
on the bloodstained soil. She draws her foot back,
face paler than boxwood, and then shudders
like the sea which ripples when slight breezes
brush across its surface. She hesitates,
then sees her love, and, with a cry of grief,
she strikes her innocent arms, tears her hair,
embraces the body of the man she loves,
and fills his wounds with tears, mixing their drops
with her lover's blood. She kisses his cold face
and cries:

'O Pyramus, what accident
has taken you from me? O Pyramus,
answer! Your dearest Thisbe calls to you.
Please hear me, and raise your sagging head!'

At Thisbe's name, Pyramus raised his eyes,
already heavy with death, looked at her,
and closed them once again. She saw the veil,
recognized it was her own, then noticed
the ivory scabbard had no sword. She cried:

BOOK FOUR

'Your own hand and your love have finished you,
unhappy man. I, too, have a strong hand—
enough for this one thing. And I have love,
which will give me strength to endure the wounds. 220   [150]
I shall follow you in death, and people
will call me the most unfortunate cause
and companion of your fate. You, alas,
who could be torn from me by death alone,
will not be torn away in death. And yet,
you poor parents, mine and his, I ask you
with words from both of us, in your great grief,
do not forbid those whom true love has joined
in their last hour to be laid together
in a common tomb. And you, O tree, 230
whose branches now cover the sad body
of one of us and will soon cover two,
keep the symbols of our deaths, and always
yield dark fruit appropriate for mourning, [160]
a symbol of the blood we two have shed.'

Thisbe finished. Then setting the sword point
under her breast, she fell upon the blade,
still steaming from the blood of Pyramus.
But her entreaty did affect the gods
and moved her parents. So when fully ripe, 240
the fruit is dark, and what remains of them
after the funeral pyre sits in one urn."

Her story ended. There was a brief pause.
Then Leuconoë started speaking,
while the other sisters all stayed silent.

"Love has even made the Sun his captive,   VENUS AND MARS
the one who with his starry light controls
all things. I'll speak about his love affairs. [170]
First, this god, so people think, once observed
adulterous acts of Mars and Venus 250
(for this god is the first to catch a glimpse
of anything). He was annoyed and told
her husband, Vulcan, a son of Juno,
about the blemish on his marriage bed
and mentioned where the sex taken place.
Vulcan's heart fell, and his skillful right hand
dropped what he was working on. Instantly
he filed slender chains of brass, nets, and snares

which would deceive the eye. The finest thread
could not surpass his handiwork, not even
spider webs hanging from the topmost beams.
He made them sensitive to tiny movements,
the slightest touch, and set them cunningly
in place around the bed. When his wife came
with the adulterer to that same bed,
thanks to her husband's skill and to the chains
forged in this new fashion, they were both stuck,
caught right in the middle of embracing.
Vulcan, god of Lemnos, swiftly opened up
the ivory doors and let in the gods.
The two embarrassed lovers were ashamed.
One of the gods, not the least upset, said:

'Now, that's the way I'd like to be disgraced!'

The gods above all laughed, and for some time
this was the most famous tale in heaven.

HELIOS AND LEUCOTHOË

Cytherea remembers who informed
against her and inflicts a punishment,
and, in her turn, wounds with similar love
the one who harmed her secret love with Mars.[1]
And so, son of Hyperion, what use
to you now are your beauty, your colour,
and your radiant light?[2] You who burn all lands
with your own fires are surely now being burned
with a new fire, and you, who should observe
all things, just gaze at Leucothoë,
fixing on one young girl those eyes of yours
which should be looking at the entire world.
Sometimes you rise in eastern skies too soon,
and sometimes fall into the ocean late.
Whenever you slow down to look at her,
you drag out the winter hours. And sometimes
you go out. Your mind's anxiety affects
your light, and Earth, now hidden in darkness,
terrifies men's hearts. And you do not fade
because the image of the moon, closer

---

[1] Cytherea was another name for Venus, derived from an island off the Peloponnese, where she first came ashore when she rose from the sea.

[2] Here Ovid is identifying the sun with the Greek god, the Titan Helios, son of Hyperion, rather than, as earlier (in Book 2, for example), with Apollo.

to our Earth, has blocked you. No. It is love
that takes your colour. You love only her.
You spend no time with Clymene, Rhodos,
or with Aeaen Circe's lovely mother,
or Clytië, who yearns for your embrace, 300
though you despise her, and at this moment
nurses a deep wound.[1] Leucothoë
makes you forget so many, the young girl
born to Eurynome, the loveliest
of that perfume-making race, but later,
when the girl grew up, she was even finer [210]
than her mother, as much as Eurynome
was more beautiful than all the others.
Her father, Orchamus, governed cities
in Achaemenia, and is reckoned 310
seventh after ancient Belus, founder
of the royal line.[2]

                        The horses of the sun
pasture under western skies. In those fields
they have ambrosia instead of grass,
which, after their daily task, nourishes
their limbs and energizes them once more.
And while these animals are browsing there
on heavenly feed and it is Night's turn
to do her work, the god of the sun goes
in his loved one's room, after he has changed 320
to look just like her mother, Eurynome,
and in the lamplight sees Leucothoë [220]
with twelve servant women, drawing smooth threads
on twirling spindles. The god embraces her,
the way a mother would her well-loved daughter,
and says:

                     'I need to share a secret.
Servants must leave. Don't deprive a mother
of her right to say some things in private.'

---

[1] Rhodos was a daughter of Neptune. Circe's mother was Persa, daughter of Oceanus. Aeaea was a region in Colchis. Clymene, as we see in Book 1, was the mother of Phaëton.

[2] Eurynome was the daughter of Oceanus and Tethys. The perfume-making races are those living in regions of Arabia. Achaemenia is another name for Persia, derived from the name of one of its kings. Belus was, according to legend, the original king.

They obey, and there are no witnesses
inside the room. The god says:

        'I am the one
who measures the long year, who views all things,
and thanks to whom the earth sees anything.
I am the eye of the world. Believe this—
I find you pleasing.'

      The terrified girl
trembles. The distaff and the spindle slip
from her unmoving fingers. But her fear
makes her more lovely, and the god can wait
no longer. He returns to his true shape
and customary splendor, and though the girl
is frightened by the unexpected sight,
she is overwhelmed by his magnificence
and, setting her objections to the side,
lets herself be ravished by the god.

Clytië was jealous (for there is nothing
gentle about the way she loves the Sun)
and, driven by anger at her rival,
she spread the story of the sexual act,
saying bad things about Leucothoë
and telling Orchamus, her father,
a wild, ferocious man. He buried his child
deep in the earth. As she stretched out her hands
towards the sunlight, entreating him, she cried:

 'He took me forcefully against my will!'

But her father still kept piling over her
a mound of heavy sand. Hyperion's son
dispersed this with his rays and offered her
a passageway to show her buried face.
But Leucothoë could not raise her head,
crushed by the weight of earth. She just lay there,
a bloodless corpse. And people say the god
who drives those flying horses had never seen,
not since the fires which took Phaëton's life,
anything more pitiful than that sight.
In fact, he tried to see if his own rays
might bring back living heat to her cold limbs.
But since Fate is against such bold attempts,

he spread sweet-smelling nectar on her corpse
and on the place and, after grieving, said:

  'In spite of this you will reach heaven still.'

Her body, drenched in heavenly nectar,
immediately dissolved. Its sweet fragrance
soaked the ground, and a stem of frankincense
slowly pushed its root out into the soil,
rose up, and with its tip broke through the mound.

Although love could excuse sad Clytië's pain,   CLYTIË
and her pain excuse the way she gossiped,
the giver of light no longer saw her—
his love for her was finished. From that time,
having abused her love so foolishly,
she pined away. With no time for other nymphs,
she sat down on bare earth by night and day
under the sky, bareheaded, dishevelled,
tasting no food or water for nine days,
breaking her fasting only with her tears
and with the dew, not moving from the ground.
She gazed only on the features of the Sun,
turning to face him as he moved around.
They say her limbs grew roots into the earth
and a lurid pallor changed her colour
to a bloodless plant. But one part is red,
and a flower very like a violet
conceals her face. She is held down by roots,
but always turns her face towards her Sun.
Although transformed, she still maintains her love."

Leuconoë ends her tale. Their ears
are captivated by the strange events.
Part of them denies they could have happened,
and part declares that with genuine gods
all things are possible, but Bacchus, of course,
is not among them.

              After the sisters
quiet down, they call on Alcithoë,   SALMACIS AND
who, while running thread through her upright loom   HERMAPHRODITUS
with her weaving shuttle, declares:

              "I will not speak
of the well-known love affairs of Daphnis,
that shepherd boy from Ida, whom some nymph,

angry at a rival, turned into stone
(the grief that burns up lovers is so strong!),
nor will I tell how laws of nature changed
and Sithon's sex became ambiguous,
both male and female.¹ And I'll overlook
you, too, Celmis, once a most loyal friend
to infant Jupiter and now a lump
of adamantine rock. Nor will I tell
how Curetes were born from storms of rain,
or how Crocus changed, along with Smilax,
to tiny flowers. I'll set these tales aside
and charm your mind with something sweet and new.²

You will learn why the spring of Salmacis
is so notorious, why its waters
have such a strong, malevolent effect,
weakening and softening every limb
they touch. This power of theirs is famous,
but the cause is hidden. Below the caves
of Ida, naiad nymphs brought up a boy
born to Hermes and goddess Aphrodite.
In his face one could make out his father
and his mother, and from them he derived
his name, which was Hermaphroditus.³
When he is fifteen years of age, he leaves
his paternal hills, deserting Ida,
where he was raised, and then takes great delight
wandering around in unknown regions
and seeking unfamiliar rivers. His joy
makes travelling easy. He even goes
to Lycian cities and nearby towns
in the neighbouring lands of Caria.⁴
Here he comes across a pool of water
so clear his eyes can see the bottom. It has
no marshy reeds, barren sedge, or rushes

---

¹The details of this person are unknown.

²Celmis was an infant friend of Jupiter's. Juno changed him into stone. The Curetes were attendants on Rhea, Jupiter's mother. Crocus and Smilax were mortal lovers changed into flowers.

³The Greek names for the parents are necessary here in order to understand the derivation of the boy's name. Ovid calls the father Mercury and the mother the Cytherean (which does not clarify the origin of the name). At this stage Ovid does not provide the boy's name, but it appears later in the story. Ida was a mountain near Troy.

⁴Lycia and Caria were regions in Asia Minor.

with spiked tops. The water is transparent,
but the edges of the pool have borders
of fresh turf, and the grass is always green.
A nymph lives there—not one skilled in hunting
or used to bending bows or to competing
in a race—the only naiad unknown
to swift Diana. Men say her sisters
would often tell her:

         "Salmacis, pick up
a javelin or painted quiver, and spend
your idle hours in a vigorous hunt."

But she will not take up a javelin
or painted quiver or use her leisure time
for active hunting. All she does is bathe
her beautiful body in her own pool.
Often with a Cytorian boxwood comb
she fixes her hair and then gazes down
into the water to see what suits her.
Wrapping herself in a transparent robe,
she lies on piles of leaves or tender grass.
She often gathers flowers, and, by chance,
that's what she was doing when she first glimpsed
Hermaphroditus. And once she saw him,
she wanted to possess him. Though eager
to go up to him, she still did not approach,
until she had composed herself, looked at
her dress, arranged her face, and taken care
so he would think her very beautiful.
Only then did she begin to speak:

         'Young man,
most worthy of being thought a deity,
if you are a god, you could be Cupid,
or if a mortal being, then your parents
are blest, your brother happy, your sister,
if you have one, fortunate—happy, too,
the nurse who fed you at her breast. But still,
far, far more powerfully blest than these
is the girl betrothed to you, if you have
a bride already, if there is some girl
you plan to dignify with marriage. If so,
if you do have someone, let's keep my love
a secret. But if no such girl exists,

Book Four

  then let me be your bride. Let's climb together   480
into one common marriage bed.'

         After this,
the nymph was silent. A blush raced across
the young man's face, for he was ignorant
of what she meant by love, but blushing made him   [330]
even more attractive—with a colour
like apples hanging in a sunlit tree,
or painted ivory, or like the moon
during an eclipse, with a reddish tinge
beneath her brightness, while bronze instruments
crash out in vain.¹ The nymph kept asking him   490
to kiss her (she would not stop)—just one kiss,
the way he'd kiss a sister—and by now
had slipped her arms around his ivory neck.
He cried:

     'Stop that! Or shall I go away,
 desert this place and you?'

         Salmacis
was alarmed and answered:

        'I freely leave
 this pool to you, stranger.'

      She turns aside
and pretends that she is going away.
But then, glancing back, she conceals herself,
kneeling down behind a clump of bushes,   500
and staying near the ground. So the young lad,   [340]
thinking he is unobserved, wanders round
here and there on the lonely grass and dips
his toes and then his feet up to the ankles
in the playful pool, and, captivated
by the tempting coolness of the water,
without delay he strips the soft clothes
from his youthful body. Well, Salmacis
is truly thrilled—inflamed now with desire
for his naked flesh. The nymph's eyes burn   510

---

¹Riley observes that during an eclipse of the moon, people often made noises with various instruments to counter the spells of witches and magicians who were, it was supposed, removing the moon from her proper sphere. These efforts are "in vain" because in a full eclipse the moon does momentarily disappear. I have added the phrase "during an eclipse" to make the reference somewhat clearer.

like the bright orb of the most brilliant Sun
when its mirror image is reflected back.
She has trouble remaining where she is,
trouble suppressing her delight. She wants [350]
to embrace him now. She is already
in a frenzy and finds it difficult
to keep herself in check. Hermaphroditus
claps his hollow palms against his body
and nimbly dives down deep into the pool.
As he moves one arm and then the other, 520
he gleams in the clear water, just as if
someone had enclosed an ivory figure
or beautiful white lily in clear glass.
The nymph cries out:

        'I have won! He is mine!'

Then flinging all her clothing to one side,
she jumps into the middle of the pool
and grabs him. He resists. In the struggle,
she steals kisses, and her hands caress him
down below and touch his unwilling breast.
She entwines her body around the youth 530 [360]
first one way, then another. Finally,
while he fights back against her, still hoping
to escape, she enfolds him like a snake
which the royal bird has snatched and carried
high in the air—as it hangs down, it twists
around the eagle's head and feet, its tail
coiling round the spreading wings, or like ivy
winding itself around tall trunks of trees,
or like a squid which grasps the enemy
it catches in the sea by sending out 540
its tentacles and gripping every part.
The descendant of Atlas does not yield
and denies the nymph the joys she longs for.[1]
She persists, pressing her entire body
to his, as if they were glued together.
She cries:

        'You may fight, you obstinate youth, [370]
    but still you won't escape. And so, you gods,

---

[1] Hermaphroditus' father was Hermes (Mercury), whose mother, Maia, was a daughter of the Titan Atlas.

please grant that no day ever comes to take
this youth away from me or me from him.'

Gods hear her prayers. The entwined bodies
of the two of them are joined together
and grow into a single form, just like
when someone looks at branches where the bark
has been cut back to graft them into one,
so they join, grow, and mature together.
In the same way, when their limbs intertwine
in a firm embrace, there are not two of them,
but one single dual form. One could say
they are not male or female. They appear
neither one nor the other—or else both.

When he sees that the clear pool he entered
as a man has made him only half a man
and that in it his limbs have lost their strength,
Hermaphroditus stretches out his arms
and shouts, but in a voice no longer male:

'Father and mother, grant your son this gift—
he carries both your names. Whoever comes
to this pool as a man, let him leave here
half a man, and, once these waters touch him,
let him become effeminate.'

                        Both parents,
moved by this speech from their bi-gendered son,
granted his request, and poisoned the pool
with a pernicious drug."

                Alcithoë
had brought her story to an end. But still,
the daughters of Minyas continued
with their work, rejecting the god Bacchus,
discrediting his festival. And then,
suddenly, harsh noises from hidden drums
broke out, pipes with curving horns resounded,
cymbals clashed, smells of myrrh and saffron spread
through the air, and (something beyond belief!)
their looms started to turn green, the fabric
hanging there grew leaves and looked like ivy.
Some of it came out as vines, and those parts
which were threads before changed into tendrils.
Vine shoots sprouted from the warp, and purple grapes

in clusters took on the splendid colours
of the weaving. By now the day was past.
The hour had come at which one could not say [400]
whether it was dark or light—there was light, 590
but surrounded by uncertain darkness.
All at once, the rooftops shake, the oil lamps
seem to blaze, houses burn with reddish fire,
and phantom images of wild beasts howl.
By now the three sisters have been hiding
for a while in smoky rooms, avoiding
the fire and light in several places.
While they are seeking shadowy corners,
membranes are stretched across their slender limbs,
covering their arms with tenuous wings. 600
The darkness does not let them realize
how they have lost the form they used to have.
They have no feathers to raise them upward, [410]
but lift themselves on their translucent wings,
and when they attempt to speak, they send out
a very tiny noise, to match their shape,
voicing their grievances in minute squeaks.
They live in houses, not the woods. Hating
the light, they fly at night, and take their name,
vespertilio, or bat, from *vesper*, 610
the late hours of evening.[1]

After this,
the divine magnificence of Bacchus
was indeed talked about in all of Thebes, JUNO AND INO
and his mother's sister, Ino, spoke out
everywhere about the mighty power
of this new god. She was the only one
out of all those sisters who had no cause
for sorrow, other than the grief brought on
by what her sisters had endured.[2] Juno
looks at this woman, who is filled with pride 620
that she has sons, is wife to Athamas, [420]

---

[1] In Latin the word for bat is *vespertilio*. I have added the word here and the English word *bat*, to clarify the etymological connection in the English text.

[2] Ino, daughter of Cadmus, had three sisters: Semele was destroyed by a lightning bolt from Jupiter, Agave helped rip her son, Pentheus, to pieces in a Bacchic frenzy, and Autonoe's son, Actaeon, was turned into a stag and torn apart by his own hunting dogs.

and has a foster child who is a god.[1]
Unable to endure it, Juno mutters
to herself:

     "Could that offspring of a slut
change those Maeonian sailors and throw them
in the sea, give the carcass of a son
to his own mother to be torn apart,
and cover those three daughters of Minyas
with new wings, and Juno be unable
to do a thing, except mourn her sorrows   630
without taking revenge?[2] Is this enough
for me? Is this all the power I have?
Bacchus himself has taught me what to do
(one is allowed to learn from enemies).
With the death of Pentheus, he has shown,
more than enough, the power of madness.
Why should Ino not be tormented, too,   [430]
and pass through the stages of that frenzy
shown by her sisters?"

      There is a pathway   THE UNDERWORLD
going downhill, shaded by gloomy yews,   640
which leads through silent, solitary spots
to the world below, where the sluggish Styx
breathes mists. Fresh ghosts of the dead pass this way,
the forms of those who have had full burial rites.
In all directions the place is dreary,
pale, and freezing. New spirits of the dead
are ignorant of the road which takes them
to that city by the Styx, where black Dis
has his grim palace.[3] This roomy city
has a thousand gateways and entrances   650
open on all sides, and just as the sea
absorbs rivers from all around the earth,   [440]
in the same way this place receives all souls.
There is no group for which it is too small,
nor does it notice large crowds when they come.

---

[1] Ino helped raise the infant Bacchus.

[2] The "slut" in question is Semele, the mother of Bacchus, who had an affair with Jupiter (and hence does not rank very high with Juno).

[3] Dis was another name for the god of the dead, who was usually called Pluto or Hades, and for his city in the Underworld.

Bloodless shadows with no bones or bodies
wander around. Some throng the market place,
some the palace of the infernal king,
and some keep busy working various trades,
in imitation of their earlier life,   660
while others suffer punishments to suit
the wicked acts they have committed.[1]

                 Juno,
Saturn's daughter, left her celestial home   JUNO IN THE UNDERWORLD
and forced herself to travel to this city
(that's how much her rage and fury drove her).
As she went in the place, the threshold groaned,
and Cerberus raised up his triple heads,   [450]
then gave out three simultaneous howls.[2]
Juno called to those dreaded deities,
the implacable sisters born from Night.   670
They were sitting down in front of prison doors
sealed up by steel, combing their black snake hair.[3]
As soon as they recognized the goddess
in the murky shadows, the Furies stood.
The place is called the Home of the Accursed.
Here Tityos stretches on nine acres,
offering his entrails to be ripped apart.
You, Tantalus, cannot scoop water up,
and the tree which arches high above your head
eludes you. You, Sisyphus, are always   680   [460]
seeking out or pushing up that boulder,
which will roll down again. Ixion spins,
both following and fleeing from himself,
and the granddaughters of Belus, who dared
to plot death of their own cousins, constantly
fetch water once again, which they will lose.[4]

---

[1] The lines about punishment (line 446 in the Latin) are sometimes omitted.

[2] Cerberus, the dog guarding Hades, had three heads.

[3] These three sisters, children of Night, were the Furies, the ancient goddess of blood revenge, especially within the family.

[4] This is a short catalogue of the best-known names of those punished in Hades. Tityos, a son of Jupiter and a creature of enormous size, attempted to rape Latona and was killed by Apollo. In Hades his liver was constantly devoured by a vulture and kept growing back. Tantalus, another son of Jupiter, offended the gods and was punished by being unable to drink the water from the pool in which he was standing or eat the fruit in a tree overhead. Sisyphus was punished for various crimes. He had to push a large rock uphill, but just as he
[Footnote continues]

Book Four

With a grim scowl Juno gazes at them all,   JUNO AND TISIPHONE
especially at Ixion. She looks
from him once more to stare at Sisyphus
and asks:

      "Why is this man being punished   690
for eternity, whereas his brother,
proud Athamas, has a wealthy palace
and with his wife is always scorning me?"[1]

She explains why she detests that family
and why she has come there. What she desires
is that the house of Cadmus will collapse   [470]
and sister Furies will drag Athamas
into some crime. She asks those goddesses
for help, mixing her commands with promises
and prayers. Once Juno has stated her request,   700
Tisiphone shakes her snow-white hair (which is,
as usual, dishevelled), flinging back
the snakes which block her mouth, and says these words:

      "No need for long and complex explanations.
Those things you ordered—consider them done.
Leave this dreary kingdom, and take yourself
back to the more pleasant air of heaven."

Juno was delighted and returned back home.
As she was moving into heaven, Iris,
Thaumas' daughter, purified the goddess   710 [480]
by sprinkling her with water.

                    Dread Tisiphone   TISIPHONE AND INO
did not delay. She took a blood-soaked torch,
put on a cloak dyed red with dripping gore,
fastened a coiling snake around her waist,
and left the house. She was accompanied
by Grief and Fear and Terror and Madness
(who has an anguished face). She went and stood
right at the gates of Aeolus' home.

---

was about to reach the top, the rock rolled down again. Ixion attempted to seduce Juno and was tied to a wheel which kept him revolving. The granddaughters of Belus (a king of Egypt) are the daughters of Danaus (the Danaïds), who killed their husbands (who were also their cousins) on their wedding night. They were condemned to spending all their time filling jars from which the water quickly leaked out.

[1] Sisyphus and Athamas (Ino's husband) were both sons of Aeolus, god of the winds.

129

Men say the entrance shook, the maple doors
turned pale, and the sun fled from the palace. 720
These ominous signs made Ino fearful,
and her husband, Athamas, was scared, as well.
They tried to leave the house, but Tisiphone,
the menacing Fury, stood in the way [490]
and blocked the door. She stretched out both her arms
wrapped in knots of vipers, and shook her hair.
The snakes hissed with the motion, some coiling
across her shoulders, some around her breast,
making whistling noises, vomiting gore,
and flickering their tongues. Then the Fury 730
pulled two snakes from the middle of her hair.
Her pestilential hand hurled what it seized,
and the two snakes slithered across the chests
of Athamas and Ino, breathing poison
on them. No wounds appeared on any limb.
It was their minds that felt the dreadful blow.
Tisiphone carried with her a vile potion
of venomous fluids—foam from the mouth
of Cerberus, poison from Ecidna,
wandering delusions, the oblivion 740
of a clouded mind, wickedness, weeping,
mad rage, and a love of slaughter, all these
in a compound mix.[1] She had blended them
in fresh blood boiled in hollow bronze and stirred
with a green hemlock stalk. While Athamas
and Ino stood there shaking, Tisiphone
poured this maddening poison on their chests,
infecting the deep centres of the hearts
in both of them. Repeatedly she whirled
a torch in a constant circle and soon 750
enveloped them with fire roused by her flame.
So, having overpowered them and done [510]
what Juno ordered, she made her way back
to the dead realm of mighty Dis and there
took off the snake she'd placed around her waist.

Athamas instantly goes mad, screaming
in the middle of the hall:

---

[1] Echidna was the wife of the monster Typhoëus and the mother of a number of important mythological monsters (the Chimaera, Sphinx, Lernaean Hydra, Cerberus, and others).

Book Four

"Come, my friends,
spread nets across these woods. I have just seen
a lioness with twin cubs."

                              Quite insane,
he tracks the footsteps of his wife, as if   760
she were a savage beast, and he snatches
his own child Learchus from his mother's grasp—
the boy is smiling, waving his small arms—
whirls him around in the air, like a sling,
two or three times, and brutally smashes
his infant skull against a solid rock.
Then the mother is finally roused to act
(whether that is caused by grief or poison   [520]
spread all through her), and runs, tearing her hair
and howling madly. In her naked arms   770
she holds a little boy (that child is you,
Melicertes) and keeps on crying out:

"Evoe! Bacchus!"[1]

                     At the name Bacchus
Juno laughs and says:

                     "May your foster child
bring you benefits like these."

                           Above the sea
there is an overhanging rock, whose base
has been hollowed out by breaking surf.
It shields the waves it shelters from the rain.
The prominent summit extends its brow
out to the open sea. Ino clambers   780
up this pinnacle (madness gives her strength,
and no fear holds her back), then throws herself
and the child she carries down into the sea,
and where she lands the waves turn white with foam.   [530]

But Venus, pitying the afflictions   VENUS AND INO
of her grandchild, who did not deserve them,
pleaded with her uncle, trying to charm him:[2]

'O Neptune, god of the sea, whose power
ranks next to the might of heaven, it's true

---

[1] "Evoe!" was a cry uttered by those celebrating a Bacchic ritual.

[2] Venus was the mother of Harmonia, Ino's mother.

Book Four

I'm asking something great, but take pity 790
on the ones I love. You can see them now
being tossed out in the huge Icarian Sea.
Add them to your company of ocean gods.
I, too, enjoy some favour with the sea,
since I was once created from the foam
in the middle of the deep and still have
my Greek name, Aphrodite or 'foam born,'
from the place where I arose."

                      She begged, and Neptune
nodded his consent. He removed from them
their mortal parts, and in their place he set 800
a sacred majesty. He also changed [540]
their bodies and their names, calling Ino
Leucothoë and the child Palaemon.

Ino's Sidonian companions followed,   INO'S COMPANIONS
as best they could, the imprints of her feet
and saw their final traces at the front edge
of the rock. They believed there was no doubt
the two had died, so they started wailing
for the House of Cadmus, their hands tearing
their hair and clothing. They blamed the goddess. 810
She had not acted justly and had been
too harsh towards her rival. But Juno
would not put up with their complaints and said:

  "I will make you the greatest monuments
to my ferocity."

                      She made the threat [550]
then acted. For one of those companions
who had been very fond of Ino said:

  "I will go with the queen into the sea."

She was about to leap out from the cliff,
but she could not move at all. She was stuck, 820
fixed to the rock. A second companion,
when she tried to beat her breasts in mourning
in the usual way, felt her arms grow stiff,
as she was trying to lift them. And one,
who by chance happened to extend her hand
out above the waves, was turned to stone,
her hands still pointing to those very waves.
You could see the fingers on another,

as they clutched her head and tugged her hair,
suddenly harden in among the strands.
In whatever stance each of them was caught,
there she stayed. Some of those Theban women
were transformed to birds, whose wings, even now,
skim across the surface waters of that gulf.

Cadmus, Agenor's son, is not aware *CADMUS AND HARMONIA*
that his daughter and his infant grandson
are now gods of the sea. Overwhelmed with grief,
by the succession of catastrophes,
and by astonishing events (of which
he's witnessed an enormous number), he leaves
Thebes, the city he has founded, as if
the troubles overwhelming him come from
the place and not from him. Forced to wander
far and wide with his wife, also exiled,
Cadmus reaches the borders of Illyria.
By now worn down by anguish and old age,
they look back on the first fateful events
their house went through, and, in conversations,
review what they have suffered. Cadmus says:

> "Was that serpent which I butchered with my spear
> a sacred creature, back when I set out
> from Sidon and sowed a new kind of seed,
> those dragon's teeth, into the earth? If so,
> if the firm anger of the gods is working
> to avenge that beast, I pray I myself
> may stretch into an elongated snake."[1]

As he speaks, he changes to a serpent
with an extended belly. He senses
scales growing across his hardening skin.
His body is now black, blue-green spots appear
in various places, he falls down prostrate
on his chest, his legs, little by little,
join together into one and thin out
into a tapering point. His arms remain.
What he has left of them he stretches out,
with tears flowing down his still human face,
and says:

---

[1] For Ovid's account of Cadmus and the serpent see 3.40 ff.

Book Four

"O wife, my most unhappy wife,
come here while something of me still remains.
Touch me. Take my hand while it is a hand,
before the snake has taken all of me."

He really wishes to say more, but his tongue
is suddenly divided in two parts.
He desires to speak, but no words come out.
Whenever he tries to utter a complaint,
he makes a hissing sound. This is the voice
Nature has assigned him.

                    His wife, Harmonia,
her hand striking her naked breast, cries out:

"Stay here, Cadmus, you unfortunate man!
Get rid of this atrocious form! Cadmus,
what's going on? Where is your foot, your hands,
shoulders, colour, face? All of you has gone,
while I've been speaking! You heavenly gods,
why not me, too? Why not change me as well
into the same form of snake?"

                            She said this,
and her husband licked her face, then slithered
to his wife's dear breasts, as if he knew them.
He squeezed her, seeking her familiar neck.
Those present (their companions were all there)
were fearful, but she stroked the slippery neck
of the crested snake. And then suddenly
there were two of them gliding along, coiled
together, until they both disappeared
into the shadows of a near-by wood.
Now they do not flee from human beings
or wound and harm them. They are peaceful snakes,
recalling what they were in earlier days.

But even in this changed form, their grandson,   BACCHUS
Bacchus, offered them great consolation.
He conquered India and was worshipped there.
In Achaea throngs of people gather
in temples built for him. Acrisius,
son of Abas, who shares his lineage,
is the only one still left who keeps on
forbidding Bacchus entry through the walls
of his Argive city, and takes up arms

BOOK FOUR

against the god, thinking he does not stem
from Jupiter.[1] And he does not believe [610]
that Perseus, whom Danaë conceived
in a shower of gold, is Jupiter's son.[2]
But soon (so great is the power of truth) 910
Acrisius regrets he harmed the god
and refused to recognize his grandson.

Bacchus had taken his place in heaven,   PERSEUS AND ATLAS
but Perseus was rushing through thin air
on whirring wings, bearing the famous prize
of a snake-haired monster he'd overcome,
soaring over Libyan sands, with blood
dripping down to earth from the Gorgon's head.
The ground soaked up the drops and gave them life
as various snakes (that is the reason 920 [620]
so many snakes infest this land).[3] Later,
Perseus was carried off here and there,
pushed by warring winds, like a cloud of rain.
From high up in the heavens he gazed down
on distant lands. He flew around the globe.
Three times he saw the freezing Bears, three times
the pincers of the Crab, often driven
to the west, and often towards the east.
Now, as light failed, afraid to trust himself
to the dark night, he halted in the west, 930
intending to rest awhile in the realm
of Atlas, until Lucifer announced
Aurora's fire, and Aurora summoned
the chariot of day. [630]

              Now, this Atlas,
son of Iapetus, surpassed all men
in physical size and was the ruler
of the remotest regions of the world
and of the oceans whose waters receive
the panting horses of the Sun and take in
his weary chariot. He has a thousand flocks 940

---

[1]Acrisius was the son of Abas, king of Argos.

[2]Danaë was the daughter of Acrisus. Jupiter, in the form of a shower of gold, had sex with her and Perseus was the result of their union (as Perseus reveals in a speech later in this book).

[3]The Gorgons were three monstrous sisters whose gaze could turn people to stone. In some accounts two of them were immortal; the third, Medusa, was not. Perseus is carrying Medusa's head.

and as many herds, who roam the meadows.
There are no neighbours to disturb his land.
Leaves on his trees glitter with shining gold,
covering golden boughs and golden fruit.
Perseus said:

            "My friend, if the glory
of high birth has some influence with you,
the founder of my clan is Jupiter.   [640]
If you are someone who applauds great deeds,
you will approve of mine. I'm asking you
for hospitality and rest."

                    Atlas
recalled an ancient prophecy given
by Themis at Parnassus:

                    "The time will come,
Atlas, when your trees will be stripped of gold.
A son of Jupiter will be honoured
for acquiring the spoil."

                    Afraid of this,
Atlas built strong walls around his orchard
and placed in there an enormous dragon
as a guard. He also kept all strangers
off his lands. So he said to Perseus:

"Leave here, in case the glory of those deeds
you lie about and Jupiter, as well,
are not there to help."   [650]

                  To these threatening words
Atlas added violence, attempting
with his great hands to push Perseus away.
Perseus holds his ground, combining force
with reassuring words. But Perseus
is not as powerful (for who can match
the strength of Atlas?). So Perseus says:

"Very well, then, since for you my friendship
has no value, take this gift!"

                        He turns away
and with his left hand holds out the foul head
of Medusa, and Atlas is transformed
into a mountain as huge as he was.
His beard and hair turn into forest trees,

his hands and shoulders change to mountain crests.
What was his head before is now the peak.
His bones are turned to rock. All his features
start to grow much larger, and he becomes [660]
something colossal (so you gods ordained),
and all the heavens with their countless stars 980
now rest on him.[1]

                Aeolus had confined   PERSEUS AND ANDROMEDA
the winds to their prison caves on Aetna,
and Lucifer, the brightest of all stars,
who rouses men for work, had risen up
high in the heavens.[2] Perseus put on
his wings again, tying them to his feet.
Then he took his weapon, a curving sword,
and with the movement of his sandals' wings
carved out a passage through the flowing air.
Passing countless nations in lands below 990
on every side, he came to Ethiopia,
observed the people there, and saw the fields
of Cepheus, where Jupiter Ammon [670]
had unjustly ordered that Andromeda,
though innocent, should suffer punishment
for things her mother said.[3] When Perseus,
grandson of Abas, saw the girl, whose arms
were chained to solid rock, he would have thought
she was a marble statue, but her hair
moved in the gentle breezes and warm tears 1000
flowed from her eyes. Before he realized it,
Perseus caught fire. Amazed and smitten
by the image of the girl he saw there,
he almost forgot to keep those wings of his
beating in the air. He came down, stopped, and said:

---

[1] Atlas kept the heavens and earth apart by bearing the weight of heaven on his shoulders.

[2] Aeolus was god of the winds. Aetna was an active volcano in Sicily. Lucifer "rouses men for work" because he was the morning star who announces the coming of Dawn.

[3] Jupiter was worshipped in Libya (under the name Jupiter Ammon), where there was a famous temple and oracle dedicated to him. Andromeda was the daughter of Cepheus, the ruler of the region. Her mother, Cassiope, had boasted about her own beauty, comparing it to the Nereïds (nymphs of the sea, daughters of Nereus). The Nereïds had asked Neptune for a sea monster to attack the Ethiopians, and the oracle had declared that, to avert disaster, Andromeda had to be sacrificed to the monster. So she was tied to a rock washed by the sea (where the monster could attack her).

Book Four

"These are not the chains you should be wearing,
but rather those which link up those in love.
Tell me your name and what your land is called— [680]
I'd like to know—and why you are in chains."

At first the girl said nothing, not daring, 1010
as a virgin, to talk to a strange man.
Her hands would have concealed her modest face,
as well, if she had not been bound. She did
what she could do and let her eyes fill up
with flowing tears. He kept on asking her
repeatedly, and she, so as not to seem
to be confessing that she was at fault
by her unwillingness to say a word,
told him her name, her country, and how much
her mother had believed in her own beauty. 1020

Before she has finished all the details,
the waves roar, and out of the boundless deep
a threatening monster bursts up, covering [690]
a wide surface of the sea. The virgin screams.
Her father and her mother stand close by,
feeling wretched (the mother more justly so).
They bring no help with them, but cries of grief
to suit the moment. They both beat their breasts,
clinging to the body of the chained-up girl.
Then the stranger says:

           "You can shed your tears 1030
for a long time after this, but right now
there is not much time to help. My name
is Perseus, Jupiter's son with Danaë.
Although she was imprisoned, Jupiter
made her pregnant with streams of fertile gold.
Yes, I am Perseus, who overcame
the snake-haired Gorgon and dared to travel
through gusting breezes on these beating wings. [700]
So if I seek this young girl as my wife,
surely as a son-in-law I will rank 1040
ahead of all the rest. And if the gods
will only show me favour, I will try
to add a further service to those things
I have accomplished. Here's my proposal—
if my courage saves her, then she is mine."

BOOK FOUR

Her parents agree to his conditions
(for who would hesitate?). They plead with him
and promise even more. They offer him
their kingdom as a dowry.

                       Then, just as
the sharp prow of a swift ship driven on   1050
by the sweating arms of its youthful crew
cuts through the waves, so the powerful chest
of that sea monster shoves the waves aside.
When its distance from the rock is as far
as a Balearic sling can send its shot   [710]
whirling through the air, Perseus suddenly
sets his feet against the earth, then rises up
high into the clouds. As his shadow falls
across the surface of the sea, the beast
sees it and, enraged, attacks the shadow.   1060
Just as Jupiter's eagle, when it spies
a snake in an open field exposing
its dark back to Phoebus and seizes it
as it turns away, sinking sharp talons
in its scaly neck, in case it twists back
its savage fangs, so Perseus, descendant
of Inachus, swooping down rapidly
through the empty sky, suddenly makes for
the monster's back and, as it roars, buries   [720]
his sword in its right shoulder, all the way   1070
to the curving hilt. The sea beast, now hurt
with a serious wound, sometimes lifts itself
high in the air or sinks beneath the waves,
and sometimes turns at bay, like a fierce boar
surrounded and driven mad by a pack
of yelping hounds. Using his speeding wings,
Perseus eludes the ravenous jaws
and, every time he sees an opening,
strikes with his curved blade—now along its back,
crusted with hollow shells, now at its ribs   1080
along the flanks, now at the thinnest part
of the creature's tail, which tapers like a fish.
The monster's mouth spews out sea water mixed
with purple blood, drenching his sandal wings
and weighing them down. Perseus does not dare   [730]
to trust his soaking wings. He spies a rock
whose topmost point extends above the sea

when it is still but which is covered up
when the waters surge. Standing on that rock,
his left hand braced against the upper edge,
he strikes the monster's side repeatedly,
three or four times, plunging in his sword.

The shores and the high palaces of gods
resound with noisy shouting and applause.
Cassiope and Cepheus, her father,
are delighted. They greet their son-in-law,
acknowledging him as the one who helped
and saved their house. The girl, freed from her chains,
approaches, the cause of all his efforts
and the reward. Perseus himself cleans
his victorious hands in water drawn up
from the sea. Then he makes a bed of leaves
to soften the ground, so as not to harm
the snake head on the solid sand, spreads out
plants born beneath the sea, and sets down there
the head of Medusa, Phorcys' daughter.
The absorbent centres of that seaweed,
still living, soak up the Gorgon's power,
and, at its touch, grow hard. The stems and leaves
take on a new rigidity. Sea nymphs
try out this miracle on several plants,
and when they all grow hard in the same way,
the nymphs rejoice. They repeat the process
by scattering seeds from those rock-hard growths
into the sea. And corals, even now,
retain this property. They petrify
in contact with the air, and what lives on
below the water turns to stone above.

Perseus raises three earth-built altars
to three deities—the one on the left
to Mercury, the right hand one to you,
virgin warrior Minerva, and one
in the middle to Jupiter. He offers
a cow in sacrifice to Minerva,
a calf to Mercury, wing-footed god,
and a bull to Jupiter, who rules the gods.
Perseus quickly claims Andromeda
as his reward for such a great exploit,
without a dowry. In front of both of them
Hymen and Love hold up the marriage torch,

BOOK FOUR

fires are filled with huge amounts of incense,
garlands hang from rooftops, and everywhere [760]
the melodies resound from lyres, pipes and song,
delightful symbols of a happy heart.
All the golden halls lie open, their doors
thrown back, and the Ethiopian leaders
move to a banquet beautifully prepared
and set before them.

                When the banquet ends
and they have filled their hearts with wine, a gift
from munificent Bacchus, Perseus,   1140
descendant of Lynceus, asks about
the culture and the people of the place,
their character and habits.[1] One of those
present at the feast answers his questions
and then says:

        "And now, most brave Perseus,
I beg you to describe the bravery [770]
and skill you used to carry off that head
with snakes for hair."

                Agenor's descendant   DAUGHTERS OF PHORCYS
then tells them how there is a cave below
the icy slopes of Atlas, safely tucked   1150
inside its solid mass. In the entrance
dwelt the daughters of Phorcys, two sisters,
who both shared the use of a single eye.
He had stolen that eye with a deft trick,
by putting out his hand while the sisters
were exchanging it.[2] And then he describes
how he went through distant, hidden places,
hard to reach, and rocks bristling with dense woods,
and reached the Gorgons' homes, how he had seen
everywhere in fields and roadways the forms   1160
of wild beasts and men who, after looking [780]
at Medusa, had changed from what they were
to stone, how he himself had nonetheless
gazed at dread Medusa's shape reflected
in the shining shield he held on his left arm,

---

[1] Lynceus was the great-grandfather of Danaë, Perseus' mother.

[2] During the exchange the sisters could not see, so that the one passing the eye mistook Perseus' hand for her sister's.

how, while she and her snakes were sound asleep,
he had sliced through her neck and seized her head,
how Pegasus, the winged, swift-flying horse,
was born from Medusa's blood—his brother, too.[1]
He tells them of the dangers he went through [1170]
in his long trip (and these were not made up),
the seas and lands he had seen under him
while he was flying up high, and stars he touched
when he spread out his wings. Then he fell silent,
while they were still expecting to hear more. [790]
One of the leaders there spoke out, asking
why Medusa was the only sister
who had snakes tangled in her locks of hair.
Their guest responded:

                     "Since your question
involves a story well worth telling, listen— [1180]
here is the answer to what you just asked.
Medusa was once extremely beautiful,   MEDUSA'S HAIR
the envious hope of many suitors.
Of all her features, none was lovelier
than her hair. I found a man who told me
he had seen it. People say that Neptune,
who rules the sea, attacked her sexually
in Minerva's temple, and the daughter
of Jupiter turned away, concealing
her pure face behind her aegis. And then, [1190]
to make sure the act was not unpunished, [800]
she changed the Gorgon's hair to filthy snakes.
And now, to terrify her enemies,
to stun them all with fear, on her breastplate,
in the front, she wears those snakes she made."[2]

---

[1] The brother of Pegasus was Chrysaor, sometimes depicted as a young man, sometimes as a flying beast or monster.
[2] When Minerva goes into battle, the Gorgon's head is painted on her armour or shield.

Book Five

V

[Phineus interrupts Perseus' wedding feast; an armed conflict ensues; Perseus holds up Medusa's head and turns his enemies to stone, including Phineus; Perseus overcomes Proetus and Polydectes in the same way; Minerva visits the Muses on Mount Helicon; Urania talks of Pyreneus' madness and tells Minerva about the singing contest with the daughters of Pierus: how those daughters sang about the war of the Giants and the cowardice of the Olympians; Urania tells Minerva of Calliope's song about the Rape of Proserpine: how Venus instructed Cupid to shoot an arrow at Pluto, how Pluto abducted Proserpine, how Cyane tried to stop Pluto and was transformed; how Ceres searched for her daughter and, during her travels, changed a boy into a small lizard, how Cyane showed Ceres Proserpine's belt, how Ceres took revenge against all Sicily, how Arethusa appealed to Ceres and told her where Proserpine was, how Ceres complained to Jupiter, how Jupiter mediated the dispute, how Proserpine ate the seeds which kept her part of the year in the Underworld, how the Sirens became birds, how Arethusa became a sacred pool, how Ceres sent Triptolemus to Asia with harvest seed, how Lyncus was changed into a lynx; the Muses are declared winners of the contest; Pierus' daughters are changed to magpies.]

While the heroic son of Danaë   PHINEUS
was talking about these things in the midst
of feasting with the Ethiopians,
a noisy crowd filled the royal palace.
The sound they made was not the merriment
of a wedding feast but one announcing
armed confrontation. The celebration
instantly became a heated quarrel.
You could compare it to a tranquil sea
when the harsh fury of the winds whips up
its moving waters. In this raucous group,
first and foremost was Phineus, the man
who had recklessly begun the conflict.
Brandishing an ash spear with a bronze point,
he cried:

      "Look here! Over here! I have come   [10]
to avenge my stolen bride! Those wings of yours
won't help you get away from me—nor will
Jupiter, even if he is transformed
into showers of false gold."[1]

         As Phineus
was about to hurl his spear, Cepheus
shouted at him:

---

[1]Phineus was the brother of Cepheus, king of the Ethiopians and now Perseus' father-in-law. The mention of "false gold" is a reference to Jupiter's seduction of Danaë, the mother of Perseus, in which Jupiter transformed himself into a shower of gold.

Book Five

"Brother, what are you doing?
What foolishness has made you so enraged
and driven you to this illegal act?
Is this the gratitude a person shows
for such great service? Is this your reward
for the one who saved her life? If you want
to know the truth, it was not Perseus
who took her from you, no, but the stern god
of the nereïds, with that horned Ammon,
Jupiter, and the monster from the sea, 30
who came to glut itself on my own child.
That was the moment she was snatched from you,
when she was going to die—unless that
is just the thing you want, you cruel man, [20]
that she should die, so you can ease your heart
to see me grieving. It's not sufficient,
I suppose, that when she was bound in chains
you just looked on and were no help at all,
and yet you were her uncle and the one
she was to marry! And, besides all this, 40
are you upset because she was set free
by someone else? Will you now take away
his prize? If that reward appears to you
so valuable, you should have sought her out
among those rocks where she was held in chains.
Let the man who did step up to save her,
who spared me an old age without a child,
take what he was promised for his efforts.
Understand this: we did not value him
more than you, but we thought him preferable 50
to certain death."

                          Phineus said nothing
in reply, but kept looking back and forth [30]
at Cepheus and Perseus, unsure
which of the two he should aim his spear at.
After pausing for a moment, he hurled it,
with all the power his anger gave him,
at Perseus. But the throw was wasted.
The spear stuck in a cushion. Perseus
then jumped up from where he was reclining
and, in a fury, threw the spear right back 60
and would have skewered his enemy's chest,

Book Five

if Phineus had not ducked for refuge
behind the altars which (to his great shame)
offered the miserable wretch a shelter.
But the spear point did not miss, for it struck
Rhoetus in the forehead. The man collapsed.
As the iron was pulled out from the bone,
he kept on kicking and spraying his blood [40]
on fully laden tables. At that point,
the crowd could not control its blazing rage. 70
They threw their weapons. There were people there BATTLE IN THE HALL
who said Cepheus and his son-in-law
deserved to die. But Cepheus by now
had left, moving past the palace doorway,
calling on Trust and Justice and the gods
of hospitality as witnesses
that he had given orders to prevent
what was going on. Warlike Pallas came
to protect her brother with her aegis
and give him courage.[1]

    There was a young man 80
from India called Athis. People claim
Limnace, child of the Ganges river,
gave birth to him in its glassy waters.
At just sixteen years of age, his beauty
was outstanding, and he added to it [50]
with expensive clothing. He wore a cloak
of Tyrian purple edged with gold, chains
of gold around his neck, and a curved band
in his perfumed hair. He was an expert
with a javelin, who could throw and hit 90
his target, no matter how far distant,
but his ability to shoot a bow
was even greater still. At that moment,
his hands were flexing the supple horn tips
on his bow, but then Perseus struck him
with a log smouldering on the altar,
crushing his face into his fractured skull.
When the Assyrian Lycabas, who was
Athis' dearest friend and who did not hide [60]
his genuine love, saw him with his face, 100

---

[1]Minerva and Perseus were both children of Jupiter.

Book Five

which people praised so much, rolling in blood,
while he breathed out his life through that harsh wound,
he wept for his companion as he snatched up
the bow Athis had prepared and shouted:

"Now your quarrel is with me! You will not
rejoice for long over a young boy's death,
an act which brings you more disgrace than praise."

Before he had finished saying these words,
he launched a pointed arrow from his bowstring.
Perseus dodged, and the arrow hung up
in a fold in Perseus' clothing.
Acrisius' grandson turned against him
that curved sword already tried and tested
when he killed Medusa and buried it
deep inside his chest. Now in his death throes,
Lycabas, eyes swimming in dark night,
looked round at Athis, fell down beside him,
and carried to the shadows of the dead
the solace that they had died together.

Then Phorbas from Syene, Metion's son,
and Libyan Amphimedon, eager
to join in the fighting, slipped on the blood
warming up the well-drenched earth around them.[1]
They fell down. As they struggled to get up,
Perseus' sword stopped them, striking Phorbas
in the neck, and Amphimedon in the ribs.

Perseus did not use his sword to fight
Erytus, son of Actor, whose weapon
was a double axe. Instead, in both hands
he hoisted up an enormous mixing bowl
with many carved designs in high relief
and very heavy and brought it crashing down
on the man's head. Erytus vomited
red blood and, lying on his back, his head
kept hammering the ground, as he lay dying.
Perseus slaughtered Polydaemon, born
from blood of Semiramis, Abaris
from Caucasus, Lycetus, who came from

---

[1] Syene was a city on the edge of Ethiopia.

lands beside the Spercheus, Helices
with flowing hair, Clytus and Phlegyas. 140
Perseus trampled on the heaped-up piles
of dying men.[1]

              Phineus, not daring
to challenge his enemy hand to hand,
threw a spear which by mistake hit Idas, [90]
who was trying to stay out of the fight
and not help either side, without success.
Glaring angrily at frenzied Phineus
he said:

    "Since you compel me to choose sides,
Phineus, recognize the enemy
you made, and compensate me for this wound 150
with an injury of your own."

                          On the point
of throwing back the spear he had now pulled
out of his body, he collapsed and died.
His limbs were drained of blood.

                  Then Hodites,
the most important noble in the country
after king Cepheus, died on the sword
of Clymenus, Hypseus killed Prothoënor,
and Perseus then cut down Hypseus.

With them was an older man, Emathion, [100]
who believed in justice and feared the gods. 160
Since his great age kept him out of combat,
he battled on with words, moving forward
and denouncing these criminal attacks.
As his trembling hands clung to the altar,
Chromius swung his sword and sliced his head off.
It fell straight down, right on the altar,
where the tongue, still half alive, kept speaking
words of condemnation. Then its spirit,
in the middle of the fire, breathed its last.[2]

---

[1] Spercheus was a river in Thessaly in northern Greece.

[2] The altar would have a fire burning on it.

The two brothers Broteas and Ammon,
who were invincible in boxing, fell
at the hand of Phineus (if only
their boxing gloves could have defeated swords!),
along with Ampycus, priest of Ceres,
who wore white ribbons around his forehead,
and you, too, Lampetides, who should not
have been invited to participate
in such a battle, for you were a man
who did peaceful work, chanting melodies
and playing the lyre. You had been ordered
to attend, bringing music to the feast
and celebration. Pedasus mocked you,
standing there with your unwarlike plectrum.
He cried out:

        "Go sing all your other songs
to Stygian shades!"

        Then he drove his sword
in your left temple. You, Lampetides,
collapsed and, with your dying fingers, tried
to pluck your lyre strings once more and played,
as you sank down, a mournful tune. That death
ferocious Lycormas would not permit
to go unpunished. From the right doorpost
he seized a heavy bar and brought it down
on Pedasus, shattering the middle
of his bony neck. He dropped to the ground,
like a bull at some ritual sacrifice.
Pelates, who lived by the river Cinyps,
went to pull a bar out of the doorpost
on his left, but as he tried to do this,
a spear from Marmarican Corythus
pierced his right hand and pinned it to the wood.[1]
While he was impaled there, Abas struck him
in the side. Pelates did not fall down,
but, as he died, was held up by his hand,
and hung there on the post. And Melaneus,
one of those who supported Perseus,
was also butchered, as was Dorylas,

---

[1] Cinyps was the name of a river in northern Africa. Marmarica is a reference to Africa.

owner of the wealthiest properties
in Nasamonia—so rich in land,
no other man had such extensive fields
or harvested so many heaped-up spices.[1]
A spear thrown from the side stuck in his groin,
a fatal wound. When Halcyoneus
from Bactria, the one who'd thrown the spear,
saw Dorylas rolling his eyes, panting
his last breath, he shouted:

"Of all your lands
keep this small patch of earth on which you lie!"[2]

He left the bloodless corpse. But Perseus,
avenging heir of Abas, pulled the spear
from the hot wound and threw it back again
at Halcyoneus. It hit his face
in the middle of his nose, kept moving,
drove through his neck, and stuck out on both sides.

Fortune kept his hand strong, and Perseus
slaughtered in different ways two men born
from the same mother—Clytius and Clanis.
For an ash spear hurled with his strong arm drove
through both thighs of Clytius, and Clanis
bit down on a spear head driven in his mouth.
Mendesian Celadon was also killed,
and Astreus fell (his mother came from
Palestine, his father was uncertain).[3]
Once skilled in prophesying the future,
Aethion was on this occasion tricked
by a false omen. Thoactes perished,
amour bearer to the king, and so did
Agyrtes, who was disgraced for killing
his own father.

Perseus was weary,
but he had more enemies to deal with,
every one determined to cut him down.
Around him armed groups of conspirators

---

[1] Nasamonia was region of Libya, in northern Africa.

[2] Bactria was a country bordering India on the west.

[3] Mendes was a city in Egypt, near the mouth of the Nile.

were fighting on, in a cause attacking
his own merit and good faith. On his side,
his father-in-law gave loyal support,
but that had no effect, and his new wife
and mother filled the hall with their laments.
But the clash of weapons and dying groans
of fallen men drowned out their cries of grief.
The war goddess Bellona, all the while,
drenched the polluted household gods with blood
and stirred up further conflict.[1]

                        Phineus
and the thousand men still fighting at his side
encircle Perseus, all by himself.
Thicker than winter hail, the spears fly by
on either side of him, past eyes and ears.
He sets his shoulders hard against a pillar,
a large one made of stone, and with his back
protected turns against the hostile throng
and holds them off. On his left, Molpeus,
a Chaonian, moved up to attack,
and on his right Ethemon from Nabataea.[2]
Just as a tiger driven by hunger
hears lowing noises from two cattle herds
in different valleys and has no idea
which way it would prefer to charge ahead
(it even wants to rush both herds at once),
so Perseus pauses. Should he take on
the person to his right or to his left?
He drives off Molpeus, striking a blow
that penetrates his leg and is content
to see him go, for Ethemon gives him
no time to pause, but charges in a rage,
eager to wound him high up on his neck,
slashes at him with reckless violence,
hits the pillar along its outer edge,
and breaks apart his sword. The blade flies off
and sticks in its owner's throat. But the blow
is not severe enough to bring on death.
Ethemon trembles and holds out his hands

---

[1] Bellona was a sister of Mars and a goddess of war.

[2] Chaonia was region in north-west Greece. Nabataea was a region in Arabia.

which hold no weapon, but in vain. Perseus
stabs him with his curved Cyllenian sword.[1]   280

But when Perseus saw the sheer numbers   PERSEUS AND MEDUSA'S HEAD
would overwhelm his courage, he shouted:

> "Since you yourselves are forcing me to it,
> I'll seek help from my enemy. So if
> anyone here is still a friend of mine,
> turn away your face."

                He said this and pulled out   [180]
the Gorgon's head. Thesculus shouted back:

> "Find other men on whom your miracles
> might have some effect!"

                With that, Thesculus
bent his arm to hurl his deadly javelin.   290
But he was frozen in the very act,
like a marble statue. And then Ampyx,
who was standing right next to Thesculus,
thrust out his sword at Perseus' heart,
so filled with his indomitable courage,
but as he did so, his right hand stiffened.
It would not move at all, back or forward.
Then Nileus, who used to falsely claim
he was descended from the river Nile,
with its seven mouths, and who also had   300
its seven branches etched into his shield,
some parts in silver, some in gold, cried out:

> "Look, Perseus! Gaze on the origin   [190]
> of my race. You will take to silent shades
> this consolation for your death—the fact
> that you were killed by such a noble man."

In the last part of his speech, his voice stopped,
choking on its words. You could well believe
his open mouth wanted to keep speaking,
but the words lacked any way of getting out.   310
Eryx criticized the men and shouted:

---

[1] Perseus' sword was a gift from the god Mercury, who was born on Mount Cyllene in Arcadia. The sword was curved, like a scimitar.

Book Five

"Your own cowardice has paralyzed you,
not the Gorgon's force. Join me and attack!
Knock this young man waving magic weapons
down to the ground!"

                                   He was about to charge,
but the ground stopped him in his tracks. He stood,
immobile, and remained there, an armed man,
but now an image made of stone.

                          These men
received the punishment they well deserved,   [200]
but there was a man named Aconteus,   320
a warrior supporting Perseus,
who, while battling there on his behalf, glimpsed
the Gorgon's face, froze, and was turned to stone.
Thinking he was still alive, Astyages
swung his sword and slashed him. The steel rang out
with a noisy clang. While Astyages stood
dumfounded, his nature was transformed as well,
in the same way. The amazed expression
still sat there on his marble face.

                              To list
the names of the common folk who perished   330
would take too long: two hundred men survived
the fight, two hundred bodies turned to stone,
once they saw the Gorgon's head. Phineus
finally regrets the unjust quarrel.   [210]
But what is he to do? He sees the statues
in various attitudes, recognizes
his own friends, calls them by name, asks their help,
and in disbelief touches the bodies
next to him—all marble. He turns aside
and, confessing what he's done, lifts his hands   340
like a suppliant, holds out his arms,
and says:

                      "You win, Perseus! Put away
your monster, that face of yours which changes
men to stone. Get rid of that Medusa,
whoever she may be. I'm begging you—
get rid of her! I was not pushed to fight
out of hatred or a desire to rule.
I reached for weapons to get back my wife.

Book Five

     Your suit had greater merit, but my claim
had precedence. So I am not ashamed
to yield. Bravest of men, give me nothing
except my life. Let all the rest be yours."   [220]
350

As Phineus said this, he did not dare
look at the man to whom he was directing
his appeal. Perseus replied:

                  "Phineus,
you most cowardly of men, I will give
what I can, a great reward for someone
who is so timid. Do not be afraid.
I will not hurt you with my sword. What's more,
I'll even give you a memorial
to last forever, and in the palace 360
of my father-in-law you will be seen
all the time, so my wife can find relief
in the image of the man she was to wed."

Perseus spoke and then shifted the head   [230]
of Phorcys' daughter over to the spot
where Phineus had turned his frightened face.
He tried to avert his gaze, but his neck
grew rigid, and the liquid in his eyes
hardened into stone. But in that marble 370
his timid look and supplicating face
remained, as well as his submissive hands
and abject stance.

             Victorious Perseus
enters Argos, his ancestral city,
with his wife. To protect his grandfather,   PROETUS AND POLYDECTES
Acrisius, and avenge him (even though
he does not deserve his help) he attacks
Proetus, who has launched an armed assault
against Acrisius, who is his brother,
put him to flight, and taken possession 380
of his citadel. But neither his weapons   [240]
nor the fortress he unjustly captured
help him prevail against the glaring eyes
of the snake-haired monster.

                 But Polydectes,
king of tiny Seriphos, you remain

obdurate, for all the young man's courage,
which his numerous exploits have confirmed,
and his suffering. You nurse your hatred,
harsh and unrelenting, and do not check
your unjust anger. You even ridicule 390
the praises he receives when you insist
his claim he killed Medusa is quite false.
Perseus says:

        "I will provide you proof
of what is true. All others, hide your eyes!"

And with Medusa's head, he then transforms
king Polydectes' face to bloodless stone.

Up to now, Tritonian Minerva [250]
had accompanied her brother conceived   MINERVA AND THE MUSES
in a shower of gold. But now, enclosed
in a hollow cloud, she left Seriphos, 400
and moving past Cythnus and Gyarus
on her right, took what seemed the shortest route
across the sea, making her way to Thebes
and to Mount Helicon, the Muses' home.[1]
Once she reached the mountain, she halted there
and addressed the learned sisters, saying:

"The fame of a new spring has reached our ears.
It gushed out when struck by the solid hoof
of that winged Pegasus, Medusa's child.
That is the reason for my journey here. 410
I wish to see this amazing fountain.
I myself saw Pegasus when he sprang
from his mother's blood."

        Urania answered:[2]

"Goddess, whatever reason you may have [260]
for visiting our home, we are most grateful.
Yes, that report is true. Pegasus is
the origin of that fountain."

---

[1] The Muses, the divine patronesses of the arts and sciences, were the daughters of Jupiter and Mnemosyne. There were nine of them. Cynthus was a mountain on Delos, Seriphos and Gyarus islands in the Cyclades group.

[2] Urania, one of the nine Muses, was the patron of astronomy.

Book Five

                            She led
the goddess to the sacred stream. For some time
Minerva stood marvelling at the spring
produced by a blow from the horse's hoof.   420
She gazed around at stands of ancient trees,
caves, and grass adorned with countless flowers.
She commended Mnemosyne's daughters
for their good fortune having such a place
and, equally, for the fine work they did.
One of the sisters answered with these words:

    "Tritonian Pallas, if your own courage
had not carried you to greater actions,
you would have been one of our company.   [270]
What you say is true. You are right to praise   430
our arts and home. We have a happy lot,
if only it were safe. But there's no end
to what wicked men may do, and all things
bring fear to virgin minds. Before my eyes   PYRENEUS AND THE MUSES
spins dreadful Pyreneus, and my mind,
even now, has not been totally restored.
That ferocious man had captured Daulis
and Phocian lands with his Thracian troops
and imposed his unjust rule on places
he now held. We were going to the shrine   440
at Mount Parnassus. As we were passing
in the rain, he saw us there, and knowing
who we were, his face put on a false look
of reverence for our sacred presences,
and he said:

                'Daughters of Mnemosyne,   [280]
stop here. Do not hesitate, I beg you,
to shelter from the storm and heavy rain
under my roof. Gods above have often
gone in more humble dwellings.'

                          Persuaded
by his words and by the rain, we agreed   450
and went in the front part of his palace.
The storm ended, and the clouds were flying
from the sky, once North Wind overpowered
winds from the south and darkness moved away.
We wished to leave, but then Pyreneus

locked up his home and was getting ready
to turn violent. We escaped the place
by taking to our wings. He stood high up,
on the top part of his fortress, as if
he was about to follow us, and cried:

   'Whatever road you take, the selfsame road
will be the one I use.'

                 Then, in his madness,
he threw himself from the very summit
of the tower and fell down on his face,
fracturing his skull. As he lay dying,
he beat the ground stained with his profane blood."

While the Muse said this, in the air they heard
the sound of wings, and voices greeted them
from branches high up in a tree. Minerva
looked up to discover where those voices
were coming from. The talk was so distinct,
she thought a man was speaking. They were birds,
nine magpies, who can copy any sound.
Perched in the foliage, they were moaning
about their fate. Minerva was surprised,
so Urania explained:

              "These creatures
recently were beaten in a contest
and were included in the flocks of birds.
Pierus was their father, a wealthy man
with great estates in Pella. Their mother,
from Paeonia, was called Evippe.
She cried out to powerful Lucina
nine times, for she was nine times in labour.[1]
This group of foolish sisters took great pride
in their number and, when they reached this place,
after journeying through many cities
in Haemonia and Achaea, they launched
a war of words and made the following boast:

   'You Thespian goddesses have to stop
deceiving the stupid common masses
with your sweet, vain songs, and, if you have faith

---

[1] Lucina was the goddess of childbirth.

BOOK FIVE

in your own skill, you should compete with us.[1]
We will not be outmatched in voice or art, [310]
and our numbers equal yours. If you lose,
you will hand over that spring created
by Medusa's child and Aganippe
in Boeotia. If you win, we will leave
the Emathian plains and move away
as far as snowy Macedon. Let nymphs
be judges in our competition.'[2]

       It's true 500
that entering a contest with those sisters
was demeaning, but it seemed even worse
to refuse the challenge. Nymphs were chosen.
They swore by their rivers they would be fair
and then sat down on seats of natural rock.
We did not draw lots. The one who had first
proposed the contest sang about the wars
fought by gods above. She gave false honours [320]
to the Giants and debased the actions
of the mighty gods.[3] She went on to sing 510
how Typhoëus came out of his den
deep down inside the earth and terrorized TYPHOËUS AND THE GODS
those who lived in heaven, how all the gods
turned tail and fled and tired themselves out,
until the land of Egypt and the Nile
with its seven separate mouths took them in.
She sang how Typhoëus had then come
to that land as well and how the gods above
took on deceiving shapes to hide from him,
claiming that Jupiter became a ram, 520
the leader of the flock (that's why, she said,
Ammon, even today, is depicted
with curved horns). Apollo disguised himself
as a crow, Semele's son as a goat,
Phoebus' sister, Diana, as a cat, [330]
Saturn's daughter, Juno, as a white cow,

---

[1]Thespis was traditionally the first actor. The term Thespian generally refers to performing artists, actors in particular.

[2]Aganippe was a fountain in Boeotia. Medusa's child was Pegasus, whose hoof created the spring on Mount Helicon. Emathia is the name of a region Thessaly.

[3]The Giants were attempting to capture heaven. For Ovid's account of the war see 1.208 ff.

Venus as a fish, and the Cyllenian god,
Mercury, as an ibis bearing wings. She sang
as far as this, playing her cithara.
Then we were called upon for our response. 530
But perhaps you have no time at present
and are not free to listen to our songs."

Pallas said:

              "Do not stop. Repeat for me
your songs in the order you performed them."

With that, Minerva sat down in the shade
of a pleasant grove. The Muse continued:

> "We gave the task of representing us   CALLIOPE'S STORY
> in that challenge match to Calliope.[1]
> She got up, with an ivy wreath around
> her flowing hair. With her thumb she tested   540
> the plaintive strings. Then she sang this story,   [340]
> striking chords to accompany her song:
>
>> 'Ceres was the first to break up fertile ground
>> with a curved plough, the first to give earth crops
>> and wholesome food, the first to give us laws.
>> All things are gifts from Ceres, and Ceres
>> is the subject of my story. If only
>> I could sing something worthy of the goddess,
>> for she is surely worthy of a song.
>>
>> The huge island of Sicily is piled   550
>> above a Giant's limbs. Its immense mass   SICILY
>> keeps Typhoëus buried underground,
>> the one who was so bold he set his sights
>> upon the realm of heaven. True, he tries
>> to struggle and often fights to rise again,
>> but his right arm is pinned down underneath   [350]
>> Ausonian Pelorus, and you, Pachynus,
>> hold down his left. Lilybaeum pushes
>> on his legs, and Aetna presses down his head.[2]
>> Below it Typhoëus, flat on his back,   560

---

[1] Calliope was the Muse responsible for heroic poetry.

[2] Pelorus, Pachynus, and Lilybaeum were the three capes defining the triangular shape of Sicily. Aetna (or Etna) was the famous (and still active) volcano in Sicily.

hurls ash from his fierce mouth and vomits fire.
He shifts around, trying to cast aside
that weight of earth, to roll the mighty hills
and cities off his body. Then Earth shakes.
Then even the king of the silent world
is afraid the ground might open up, split
in a wide crack, and daylight might come in
to scare the trembling shadows of the dead.
Fearing such a great disaster, Pluto   PLUTO, VENUS, AND CUPID
had left his shadowy dwelling place and,   570
riding in a chariot with black horses,   [360]
was carefully circling the foundations
of Sicilian lands. After checking these
and satisfying himself that no regions
were unstable, he set aside his fears.
As he moved around, Venus of Eryx
sitting on her mountain, noticed Pluto.[1]
Embracing her winged son, she said:

                            'Cupid,
my son, my weapon, my hands, my power—
take those arrows you use to overwhelm   580
all beings, and shoot your swift-flying dart
into the heart of Pluto, whose lot won
the last of the three kingdoms.[2] Your great might
conquers gods above, even Jupiter,
and makes them subject to you, gods of the sea,
as well, and the one who rules them all.   [370]
Why leave out Tartarus? Why should you not
expand your mother's kingdom and your own?
The stakes are high—a third part of the world!
I patiently endure the way we're scorned,   590
especially in heaven. Love's power
is on the wane, together with my own.
Do you not see how huntress Diana
has abandoned me, along with Pallas, too?
And if we allow it, that child of Ceres
will stay a virgin, too. She wants to live
like those two others. But if the kingdom

---

[1] Eryx was a mountain in Sicily associated with Venus.

[2] The "lot" is a reference to the time when Jupiter, Neptune, and Pluto drew lots to divide up the three realms of the sky, the sea, and the Underworld.

Book Five

we both share in common gives you pleasure,
then make that goddess and her uncle one."¹

Venus spoke. Cupid opened his quiver,   600   [380]
as his mother had instructed, and picked
a single arrow from the thousand there.
None of the other arrows was as sharp
and accurate, or truer to the bow.
He bent the supple tips against his knee,
and his barbed arrow struck Dis in the heart.

Not far from Henna's walls lies a deep lake   PLUTO AND PROSERPINE
named Pergus. Music from its swans matches
songs Caÿster hears on his gliding stream.²
A wood surrounds the lake, enclosing it   610
on every side. Its leaves act as a shield
and ward off rays from Phoebus, the branches
cool the place, and the moist earth produces   [390]
purple flowers. By that pool the season
is an eternal spring. While Proserpine
was playing in this wood, picking violets
and shining lilies, and, like a young girl,
was keen to fill her baskets and her lap,
trying to gather more than anyone
of her own age, Pluto caught sight of her   620
and, in almost the same instant, loved her
and carried her away—that's how rapid
love can be. The frightened goddess shouted
cries of grief to her mother and her friends,
mostly to her mother. She tore her robe
along its upper edge, and the flowers
she had gathered fell from her loosened clothes.
Prosperine was so innocent and young,   [400]
that this loss also brought out virgin tears.
Her abductor drove the chariot ahead,   630
urging on his horses, calling each one
by name, shaking his dark, rust-coloured reins
over their manes and necks, and charging on
through deep lakes and stinking sulphurous pools

---

¹Ceres was a daughter of Saturn and a sister of Jupiter and Pluto (who was thus uncle to Ceres' daughter). The child of Ceres is Proserpine (also called Persephone) whose father is Jupiter.

²Henna was a city in the middle of Sicily. Caÿstros was a river in Lydia, famous for its swans.

of the Palici, which come boiling up
from a fissure in the earth, past the place
where the Bacchiadae, those people born
in Corinth, beside two seas, had laid out
their city with two very different harbours.[1]

Halfway between Pisaean Arethusa
and Cyane there is an enclosed bay
shut in by narrow headlands. Here there lived
the most famous nymph in all of Sicily,
Cyane. From her that stretch of water
took its name. In the middle of the pool
she rose and showed herself down to the waist,
and, recognizing who the goddess was,
called out to Dis:

    'You will go no further!
You cannot be son-in-law to Ceres
against her will. You should have asked the girl,
not carried her away. If I may compare
small things with great, I, too, had a lover,
Anapis, and married him. But he won me
with his entreaties. I was not frightened
into marriage, like this girl.'

        Cyane spoke.
Then she held out her arms on either side
to block his way. Pluto could scarcely hold
his rage. He drove his dreaded horses on,
and his strong arm hurled his royal sceptre,
which sank down to the bottom of the pool.
Struck by the blow, Earth opened up a path
to Tartarus. The chariot hurtled down
right through the middle of the gaping hole.

But Cyane, mourning the abduction
of the goddess and the disrespect shown
for the rights of her own waters, carries

---

[1] The Palici, two brothers born to Jupiter, were hidden in the earth (to escape Juno). They emerged in Sicily and were worshipped as gods associated with two sulphurous lakes there. The Bacchiadae, a family exiled from Corinth, founded Syracuse in Sicily. The city had two harbours of different sizes. Corinth was on the narrow isthmus linking the Peloponnese and mainland Greece, between the Gulf of Corinth (part of the Ionian Sea) to the west and the Saronic Gulf (part of the Aegean Sea) to the east (hence "beside two seas").

Book Five

in her silent heart a wound and cannot
be consoled. She pines away completely
and melts into those streams where earlier
she has been a potent holy presence. 670
You can see her arms and legs get softer,
bones grow flexible, nails lose their hardness. [430]
First, from her whole body the slenderest parts
dissolve—her dark hair, fingers, legs, and feet
(for it is no great change to turn thin limbs
to chilly waters). Then her shoulders, back,
sides, and chest all vanish, flowing away
in light amorphous streams. And finally,
in her collapsing veins pure water moves
instead of living blood. Nothing remains 680
which you can grasp.

        Meanwhile, the girl's mother,   CERES' SEARCH
Ceres, fearing for her daughter, searches
every land and every sea. When the dawn,
Aurora, with her dew-drenched hair, arises [440]
or Hesperus, the Evening Star, appears,
they do not find her resting. Her two hands
hold flaming torches she has lit from fires
on Aetna. In her frantic state of mind,
she bears these through the darkness of the night,
and when kind daylight once more dims the stars, 690
from the time Sun rises until he sets,
she continues searching for her daughter.
Her constant effort made her tired and thirsty,
for she had not wet her lips at any spring.
Then, she caught sight, by chance, of a small hut
with a roof of straw. She knocked at its low door.
An older woman answered. When she saw
the goddess and Ceres had requested
a drink of water, the woman gave her
something sweet. She had made it earlier 700 [450]
from roasted barley grain. While Ceres sipped
what she'd been offered, a rude, bold-faced boy
walked up and, in a mocking voice, called her
a greedy woman. Ceres was annoyed,
and, as the boy was talking, threw the drink
mixed with barley, what was still left of it,
right in his face. His skin soaked up the drink

and then grew spotted. Where his arms had been,
just a moment before, he now had legs.
A tail was added to his altered limbs,   710
and his form shrunk down to something tiny,
the size of a small lizard, even less,
without the strength to injure anyone.
The old woman, astonished and in tears,
tried to touch the monster, but it ran off,
seeking a place to hide. Now it carries   [460]
a name—the speckled lizard—which well suits
its debased condition and its body,
covered with various spots.

                              To list those lands
and waters where goddess Ceres wandered   720
would take too long. She searched the entire world
in vain and then returned to Sicily.
She crossed that island, looking everywhere,   CERES AND CYANE
and reached Cyane, who would have told her
the whole story, if she had not been changed.
She wanted to, but lacked a mouth and tongue.
She had no organs she could use for speech.
But still, she did provide clear evidence
the mother recognized, by displaying
on the surface of her waters the belt   730
Proserpine had worn. It had fallen off,
by accident, into the sacred pool.   [470]
As soon as Ceres saw the belt, she tore
her unkempt hair, her hands beat on her chest,
again and again, as if at last she knew
her daughter had been carried off. As yet,
she did not know where Proserpine might be,
but she condemned all lands, accusing them
of being ungrateful and unworthy
to receive her gift of grain—above all,   740
Sicily, where she had found the traces   CERES AND SICILY
of her loss. And therefore on that island
her cruel hands break ploughs that turn the soil,
and, in her rage, Ceres condemns to death
farmers and cattle working in the fields,
a similar fate for both. She orders
fields to make the harvest crop a failure.   [480]
She spoils the seed. That land's fertility,

so famous far and wide throughout the world,
is finished, merely a made-up story.   750
Crops are laid waste once their first shoots emerge.
Sometimes excessive sunlight ruins them,
sometimes too much rain. Weather and windstorms
harm them, and hungry birds collect the seeds
scattered here and there. Thorns, thistles, and grass
which no one can control, choke off the grain.

Then from her pool, Arethusa of Elis,   CERES AND ARETHUSA
the nymph Alpheus loved, raised up her head,
brushed back the hair dripping on her forehead,
and said to Ceres:[1]

         'Mother of our food   760
and of that virgin girl you're searching for
throughout the entire world, you should give up   [490]
this endless effort and, though you're angry,
suspend that rage against your faithful land.
Earth has done nothing to deserve your rage.
She opened to that rape against her will.
I am not praying for my own country.
I came here a stranger. My native land
is Pisa, and I was born in Elis.[2]
I am a foreigner in Sicily.   770
But this soil is pleasing to me, more so
than any other place. This is my home.
This is where I live. Most gentle goddess,
preserve it. Why I abandoned Elis,
then moved through such a huge expanse of sea
and reached Ortygia—I will find a time
more suitable to recount my story,
when you are free of worries and your face   [500]
has a more cheerful look.[3] But I came here
when cracked Earth opened up a way for me.   780
I was borne far below its deepest caves,
and it was here where I first raised my head

---

[1] Alpheus was a major river in the Peloponnese.

[2] Pisa was a town in Elis, in the western Peloponnese.

[3] Ortygia was part of Sicily, an island off Syracuse.

and glimpsed the unfamiliar stars.¹ Down there,
while I was gliding on the Stygian stream
below the earth, with my own eyes I saw
Proserpine, your daughter. She was grieving,
that is true, and her face showed signs of fear,
but nonetheless, in that world of shadows,
she was queen, the most important woman,
the powerful consort of that tyrant 790
who rules the Underworld!'

                    When she heard this,
Ceres was stunned, as if turned into stone,
and for a long time seemed to be in shock, [510]
until her intense anguish pushed aside
the weight of her bewilderment. She rushed
in her chariot up to heaven, and there,
face clouded in sorrow, hair dishevelled,
she stood in front of Jupiter and spoke   CERES AND JUPITER
in a bitter voice:

                    'I have come to you,
Jupiter, to plead for my own offspring 800
and for yours, as well. If the child's mother
finds no favour with you, let the daughter
influence her father and, I beg you,
do not let your care for her be any less
because she was born from me. Lo, my child
has been found, the one I have been seeking
for so long, if you can call it finding
when one is still more certain she's been lost,
if you call it finding when all one knows
is where she is. I can accept the fact 810 [520]
that she has been abducted, provided
he returns her. A man who steals and rapes,
is no fit husband for a child of yours,
even if the girl were not my daughter.'

Jupiter replied:

                  'That child is our pledge,
our shared responsibility, yours and mine.
But if you wish to give accurate names

---

¹According to legend, the nymph Arethusa was chased along an underground route by the river Alpheus from Elis to Sicily. Her story is told later in this book (5.891 ff).

to things, this is not a criminal act.
The truth is that this is love. And Pluto
would not be a son-in-law who shames us, 820
if you, goddess, would give him your consent.
If Pluto lacked all other qualities,
he would still be great—he is Jove's brother!'[1]
What if he did not lack my qualities
and were not inferior to me at all,
except for the lot he drew?[2] However,
if your desire that those two separate
is so strong, Prosperine may come back here [530]
to heaven, but on one fixed condition—
her lips have not touched any food down there, 830
for this has been established by the Fates
in their decrees.'

               Jupiter had spoken.
Ceres was resolved to save her daughter.
But Fate would not allow it, for the girl
had broken her fast. In her innocence,
while she was in the cultivated garden,
wandering round, she had picked purple fruit
from a bent-over pomegranate tree,
taken seven seeds from its yellow rind
and pressed them in her mouth.[3] Of all those there, 840
only one observed her, Ascalaphus,   ASCALAPHUS
who, so people say, was born to Orphne,
not the least-known of the Avernian nymphs, [540]
and her own Acheron, in the dark woods.[4]
He saw her, revealed that she had eaten,
and cruelly prevented her return.
The queen of Erebus, in her dismay,
transformed the one who had informed on her

---

[1] Jove is another name for Jupiter.

[2] This is a reference to the previously mentioned lottery which assigned Jupiter the sky, Neptune the sea, and Pluto the Underworld. Jupiter's point is that he is superior to Pluto only because he was lucky and chance favoured him.

[3] Ovid's text does not state specifically that the fruit was from a pomegranate tree, but long-standing traditions and rituals associated with Ceres for centuries identified the "purple fruit" as a pomegranate. The number of seeds varies from one account to another.

[4] Avernus was a poisonous lake in Italy, where, people claimed, birds never flew. It was believed to be near the Underworld. Acheron is one of the main rivers of the Underworld.

to an ill-omened bird. Sprinkling his head
with Phlegethon's waters, she changes it
into a beak, feathers, and enormous eyes.[1]
With his own shape removed, he is wrapped up
in tawny wings, and his head grows larger.
He finds his nails bent into long talons
and can hardly move the feathers growing
on his sluggish arms. He has now become
a lazy screech owl, that hated bird, which brings
news of approaching grief for mortal men,
a fateful omen.

                Now Ascalaphus
would seem to have deserved his punishment
by telling what he saw, but as for you,
daughters of Acheloüs, why do you
have feet and feathers of a bird, while still
possessing faces of young virgin girls?
The reason is that you sweet-singing Sirens
were there with Proserpine's companions
when she was collecting her spring flowers?[2]
After you had searched the whole world for her
and had no success, you began to wish
that you had beating wings to make your way
above the ocean waves, so they could learn
of your anxiety. You found out the gods
agreed, and suddenly you saw your limbs
were growing yellow feathers. However,
to make sure your songs, born to charm the ear,
and your great vocal gifts would not be lost
if your tongues disappeared, your virgin faces
and human voice remained.

                But Jupiter,
to mediate between his grieving sister
and his brother, divides revolving years
in equal portions. So now the goddess,
Persephone, is common to both realms.[3]

---

[1] Erebus was the deepest pit of the underworld. The queen of Erebus was now Proserpine, consort of Pluto. Phlegethon was one of the rivers of the underworld.

[2] The Sirens were the daughter of the river Acheloüs and one of the Muses.

[3] Persephone is the Greek name for Proserpine. As queen of the Underworld, she is usually called Persephone.

Book Five

The months she spends with Ceres up above
match those she spends with Pluto down below.
Her face and nature change immediately.
For now the way she looks, which seemed so sad
a moment ago, that even Dis himself
would notice it, is joyful, like the sun, [570]
which, hidden earlier by clouds of rain,
conquers those clouds and breaks away from them. 890

Nourishing Ceres, happy that her child
had come back safely, asked Arethusa
why she ran away and why she was now
a sacred spring. The waters grew silent,   ARETHUSA AND ALPHEUS
as Arethusa lifted her head up
from the deep pool and her hands wrung water
out of her green hair. Then she spoke of love,
an old tale of the Elean river.

   'I was a nymph, one of a company
inhabiting Achaea. None of them 900
was more eager to roam the forest glades,
none was keener to set our hunting nets.
Though I was spirited and never tried [580]
to become admired for my appearance,
I was called beautiful. But my good looks,
so often praised, were no great joy to me.
Those physical gifts which other young girls
usually delight in made me turn red,
like a country simpleton, and I thought
it wicked to win praises just for that. 910
I remember I was on my way back
from the Stymphalian woods and very tired.[1]
It was hot, and hard work had made the heat
just that much worse. But then I reached a stream
flowing without a ripple or a sound.
You could see right to the bottom and count
each small stone in the depths. You would have thought
it hardly moved at all. Silver willows
and poplar trees, nourished by its waters, [590]
provided, all on their own, natural shadows 920
on its sloping banks. I approached the stream

---

[1] Stymphalus was a city and a region in Arcadia.

Book Five

and, to start with, put my feet in, and then
my legs up to the knees. Not content with that,
I undressed, took my soft clothes and hung them
in a curving willow, and, quite naked,
jumped in the stream. While I struck the water
and drew it to me, gliding around there
in a thousand ways, pushing out my arms
and stretching them, I heard a kind of noise,
a murmur in the middle of the stream
underneath the surface. I was afraid
and leapt out on the nearest river bank.

'Where are you running to, Arethusa?'

It was Alpheus calling from his stream.
He spoke to me again in a harsh voice:

'Why move off so quickly?'

                           I ran away
just as I was, not wearing any clothes.
I'd left them on the other riverbank.
He was all the keener to chase me down.
He was on fire, and, since I was naked,
I seemed to him much easier to win.
So I fled, and he pursued me wildly,
as doves with trembling wings fly from a hawk,
and as a hawk will chase a trembling dove.
All the way past Orchomenus, Psophis,
and Mount Cyllene I kept on running,
past the ridges of Maenalus, then past
cold Erymanthus and Elis.[1] Alpheus
could not outrun me, but my endurance
did not match his. I could not keep moving
at that pace for long, but he was able
to continue a long and tiring chase.
Still, I raced on through fields, over mountains
covered in trees, over rocks, too, and crags,
and through places where there was no pathway.
The sun was at my back. I saw long shadows
stretched out before my feet, unless my fear
imagined them, but I was truly scared

---

[1] The place names refer to locations in Arcadia.

of the sound made by his feet. The deep breaths
coming from his panting mouth stirred ribbons   960
in my hair. Exhausted by the effort
of trying to run away, I cried:

                              'Help me!
I will be captured! Diana, please help
your armour bearer, whom you often gave
your bow to carry and your quiver, too,   [620]
with all its arrows!'

                    The goddess was moved.
She took a thick cloud and threw it round me.
I was shielded by the dark. Alpheus,
the river god, moved around me, searching,
in his confusion, through the hollow fog.   970
Without being aware of it, he walked twice
right past where the goddess had concealed me,
and twice he called out:

                    'O Arethusa!
Arethusa!'

            What was I feeling then,
in such desperate straits? What a lamb feels,
perhaps, when it listens to howling wolves
around the high sheep fold, or when a hare
hidden in a thicket sees the muzzles
of the ravenous dogs and does not dare
make a single movement with its body.   980
But he did not leave, for he could not see   [630]
any further traces of my footprints.
He kept watching the place, eyeing the cloud.
Cold sweat covered my trapped limbs, and dark drops
fell from my whole body. When my foot moved,
a pool collected there, moisture dripped down
from my hair, and faster than I can now
tell you the tale, I changed into a stream.
But then the river god could recognize
the water that he loved. Casting aside   990
the human shape he had assumed, he switched
to his own liquid form so he might mix
himself with me. But the Delian goddess,
Diana, split the ground apart. I plunged
through hidden caverns and reached Ortygia.   [640]

BOOK FIVE

This place delights me, for it bears the name
of my own goddess.¹ Here I first emerged
into the upper air.'

                Arethusa
finished her story here. And so Ceres,
goddess of the fertile fields, then harnessed   1000
two dragons to her chariot, curbed their mouths
with bits, and moved off, through the middle air,
between the earth and heaven. When she reached
Tritonia's city, Athens, she handed
her light chariot over to Triptolemus.²   TRIPTOLEMUS AND LYNCUS
She gave him seed and then instructed him
to scatter it, some on untilled soil, some
on lands which, after a long period
of lying fallow, were being restored.
The youth was carried high above the lands   1010
of Europe and of Asia, and then turned
towards the realm of Scythia, a place
where Lyncus ruled. There Triptolemus
went into the royal palace and stood   [650]
before the king's own household gods. When asked
where he had come from, why he had come there,
what his name and country were, he answered:

'My native country is famous Athens,
my name Triptolemus. I did not come
by ship across the seas or overland   1020
on foot. For me the unobstructed sky
opened a road. I bring gifts from Ceres.
If you will scatter these on your wide fields,
they will give back bountiful harvest crops
of nourishing food.'

                The barbarian king,
Lyncus, was jealous. Wishing to make himself
bringer of such a noble gift, he welcomed
Triptolemus as a guest, but then at night,
when he was sleeping soundly, attacked him
with a sword. As he tried to stab his chest,   1030

---

¹Ortygia, as well as being the name of an island off Syracuse, was also another name for the island of Delos, where Diana was born (hence, she is sometimes called "the Delian goddess").

²Triptolemus was son of Celeus, king of Eleusis.

BOOK FIVE

Ceres changed Lyncus to a lynx and told [660]
the Athenian youth to keep on moving
in her sacred chariot through the air.'

Here Calliope, our finest singer,
ended her song, and the nymphs, with one voice,
declared the goddesses who inhabited
Mount Helicon the winners.[1] Those sisters,
who had lost the contest, yelled out abuse,
so I remarked:

'Since you all well deserve
a punishment for your challenge to us   1040
and now to that offense you add these insults,
and since our patience is not limitless,
we will move to sentence you, following
where our anger leads.'

The Emathian sisters
laughed and ridiculed our threatening words.
But as they tried to speak and menace us   [670]
by screaming and by brandishing their fists,
they saw feathers growing out of their nails
and plumage covering their arms. They looked
at one another and saw their faces   1050
harden into rigid beaks and new birds
being added to the woods. And when they tried
to beat their breasts in grief, their moving arms
lifted them up. They hovered in the air,
as magpies, the gossipers in the trees.
Even now, as birds, that love of talking
they had before remains, their harsh chatter
and their inordinate desire to speak."

---

[1] Here Calliope's story, which begins at 5.543 ends. The speaker is still Urania, who begins her story describing the contest between the Muses and the daughters of Pierus at 5.537.

BOOK SIX

VI

[Minerva hears about Arachne and responds to her challenge; Minerva's weaves scenes of herself and Neptune competing for Athens; Arachne's weaves scenes of divine sexual assaults; Minerva turns Arachne into a spider; Niobe boasts she is better than Latona; Niobe's sons are killed; Niobe's husband commits suicide; Niobe's daughters are killed; Niobe is turned to stone; the story of Latona and the Lycian peasants; Apollo flays Marsyas; Pelops' ivory shoulder; Procne and Tereus; Tereus and Philomela; Tereus rapes and mutilates Philomela; Philomela informs Procne; Procne rescues Philomela; Procne and Philomela kill Itys and serve him as food to his father; Procne, Philomela, and Tereus are changed into birds; Boreas and Orithyïa; Calaïs and Zethes.]

When Minerva had listened to these tales   MINERVA AND ARACHNE
from the Aonian Muses, she commended
their singing and their justified resentment.
Then she told herself:

        "To praise someone else
is not enough. Let me be praised, as well,
and not allow my presence to be scorned
without some punishment."

        She turned her mind
to the fortunes of a Maeonian girl,
Arachne, who, she heard, was being praised
as much as she was for her artistry   10
in spinning wool.[1] It was not lofty rank
or family origins which had made
Arachne so well known. It was her skill.
Her father Idmon, who came from Colophon,
coloured absorbent wool with purple dye
from Phocaean shell fish.[2] Her mother was dead,
but she, too, was produced from common stock,   [10]
and her husband was the same. Nonetheless,
although Arachne's home was very small
and she lived in a tiny town, Hypaepae,   20
she had acquired a fine reputation
throughout the Lydian cities.[3] Often
nymphs would abandon their vine-covered slopes
on Tmolus mountain or leave their waters
on the Pactolus river, to inspect

---

[1] Maeonia was a region in Lydia, in Asia Minor.

[2] Colophon was a city in Lydia, Phocaea a coastal city in Asia Minor, famous for its dye.

[3] Hypaepae was a small town in Lydia.

Arachne's astonishing workmanship.
They loved to see, not just the finished clothes,
but also the way they were created.
She added so much beauty to her skill,
whether she began by winding rough yarn
into new balls of wool or was working
the fibres with her fingers, softening
fleecy clouds of wool over and over,
drawing them out in one long equal thread,
or was using her dexterous thumb to turn
her slender spindle, or embroidering
with her needle. You could easily see
she had been taught by Pallas. But she claimed
that was not the case. She was offended
with the notion she had had a teacher,
even such a great one, and she remarked:

"Let Pallas compete with me. If I lose,
I don't care what she does."

So Pallas changed
into an old woman, adding white hair
to her temples, giving herself weak limbs,
and holding up her body with a stick.
Then she began speaking to Arachne,
with these words:

"We ought not to run away
from all the things which accompany old age.
Advancing years bring us experience.
Do not spurn what I advise. Seek your fame
as the greatest woman working with wool
among mortal beings, but give first place
to the goddess, and, you rash girl, ask her
in a humble voice to grant forgiveness
for the things you said. She will pardon you,
if you ask her."

With a scowl, Arachne glared
at the old woman. She left the weaving
she had started. Her face was very angry,
and she could hardly keep her hands in check.
She said the following words to Pallas
(who was still disguised):

Book Six

"You come in here
worn out by extreme old age, with a mind
which is now feeble. You have lived too long—
that's your trouble. Let your daughter-in-law
or daughter, if you have one, pay attention
to what you have to say. What I believe
is good enough for me. So don't assume [40]
that your advice has any influence.
My views remain the same. As for the goddess, 70
why can't she show up in person? Why shirk
my challenge?"

Then, throwing off her disguise
as the old woman, Minerva cries out:

"She has come!"

And Pallas reveals herself.
The nymphs and women of Mygdonia
treat her divinity with reverent awe.
Arachne is the only one who stands there
unafraid.[1] However, she does turn red.
Against her will a sudden blush appears
across her face and goes away again, 80
just as the sky usually grows crimson
when Aurora begins to move, and then,
a short time later, once the sun moves up,
turns white. She insists on going ahead [50]
with what she started, and, eager to win
a foolish prize, she rushes to her fate.
For Jupiter's daughter does not back down,
or warn her any further, or postpone
the contest. They waste no time, but set up
their positions in two different places, 90
stretch slender threads along the looms, attach
the frame and crossbeam, then with a heddle
separate the woolen fibres in the warp,
interweave the cross-threads in the middle
with pointed shuttles their fingers have prepared,
and, after they have pulled thread through the warp,
press it in place with blows from a notched comb

---

[1] Mygdonia was a region in Asia Minor near Lydia.

with a row of teeth.[1] They both work quickly,
tucking their garments underneath their breasts,
so their skilled arms can move with greater speed. 100
They are so keen to work, they feel as if [60]
it is not work at all. Sometimes, they weave
with purple threads dyed in Tyrian vats,
subtly different shades, hard to tell apart,
just as, after a shower, a rainbow,
when its enormous arc is struck by sunlight,
will often tint a large expanse of sky,
and a thousand different colours shine there,
yet when one looks at it, one cannot see
transitions from one shade to another, 110
so much so that bands which are adjacent
all look the same, but yet the outer bands
are very different. In other places
they also weave in pliant threads of gold.

Each tapestry depicts an ancient story. MINERVA'S WEAVING
Minerva's scene portrays the rock of Mars [70]
on the citadel of Cecrops' city
and the old argument about what name
the country should be called.[2] Twelve gods sit there,
on lofty thrones in solemn majesty, 120
with Jupiter in the middle. She shows
each god with his own particular face.
Jupiter's image has royal presence.
And she pictures Neptune, god of the sea,
standing there, as well, striking a rough stone
with his long trident, and from that boulder
the sea is pouring through an open crack,
the token by which he claims the city.
For herself she provides a shield and spear

---

[1] In weaving, the warp is the series of parallel threads (in most traditional looms these are vertical) held apart under tension by a device called the heddle. The shuttle contains the wool which the weaver moves between the threads of the warp. When a line of thread from the shuttle has been passed through all the individual threads of the warp, it is pushed down against the already woven material with a comb, to make the finished product thick.

[2] Cecrops was a traditional king of Athens. Minerva and Neptune each laid claim to the new city. To resolve their quarrel they were each invited to give one gift to the city, and Cecrops would choose a winner. Neptune provided water, but it was salty sea water, and Minerva provided the olive tree. Cecrops chose Minerva as winner.

with a pointed tip. On top of her head
she puts a helmet. The aegis guards her chest.
She also shows the earth struck by her spear
growing a pale olive shoot with berries,
while gods look on amazed. Her final touch
completes the work, the form of Victory.
But then, so that her rival for great praise
may from her illustrations understand
what sort of prize she can look forward to
for her extremely rash audacity,
Minerva includes four scenes of contests,
one in each of the four corners, showing
figures in brightly coloured miniature.
One corner depicts Rhodope from Thrace
and Haemus, who once had mortal bodies,
but are cold mountains now. They gave themselves
names of the most important gods above.[1]
Another corner shows the wretched fate
of the Pygmy queen, whom Juno conquered
in a contest, then turned into a crane
and ordered to wage war on her own race.[2]
And she pictures Antigone, who once
dared challenge the wife of mighty Jupiter.
Queen Juno had her changed into a bird,
and neither her father, Laomedon,
nor her city, Ilion, were any help.
She turned into a stork, growing white wings,
and with a chattering beak gives herself
incessant praise.[3] The only corner left
shows Cinyras when he lost his children.
He is seen shedding tears, lying on stone,
embracing temple steps that used to be

---

[1] Rhodope, daughter of the river god Strymon, married Haemus, son of the North Wind. They dedicated a cult to themselves and called themselves Zeus and Hera.

[2] The queen of the Pygmies scorned the traditional gods and, as a result, was changed into a bird, the crane. People claimed cranes regularly attacked the Pygmies, who were small people living to the east or north of Greece.

[3] Antigone, daughter of Laomedon of Troy, claimed she was more beautiful than Juno.

his daughters' limbs.[1] Around the outer edge,
Minerva then puts olives, signs of peace.
Her work is now complete. With her own tree
she finishes off and ends her weaving.

Arachne weaves an image of Europa,   ARACHNE'S WEAVING
when Jupiter, transformed into a bull,
abducted her.[2] You could well imagine
the bull was real, the sea waves genuine.
Europa is depicted looking back   170
at the land now left behind, calling out
to her companions, afraid of contact
with the surging waters, and pulling up
her timid feet. She shows Asterië
in the struggling eagle's grip, and pictures
Leda lying prone underneath the swan.
She then adds scenes of Jupiter disguised—
first as a satyr, when he filled the womb   [110]
of beautiful Antiope with twins,
then as Amphitryon, when he took you,   180
Alcmene, a girl from Tiryns, and then
when he tricked Danaë as a shower
of gold, Aegina, child of Asopus,
as a flame, Mnemosyne as a shepherd,
and Deöis as a spotted serpent.[3]
She also pictures you, Neptune, transformed
to a young bull, when you desired to mate
with Aeolus' virgin daughter Canace.
Looking like the river Enipeus,
you fathered twin sons, the Aloïdae,   190
while, as a ram, you tricked Theophane,
daughter of Bisaltus, and as a horse,
you had sex with the gentlest of them all,

---

[1] Cinyras was a king of Assyria. His daughters were changed into temple steps because they claimed they were lovelier than Juno. Cinyras himself was transformed to stone as he lay at the temple grieving their loss.

[2] For Ovid's story about Europa and Jupiter see 2.1236 ff above.

[3] Asterië was a sister of Latona. Jupiter's deceptions and forcible abductions for sex produced a number of famous children (for example, Leda, whom Jupiter assaulted in the form of a swan, was the mother of Helen of Troy, Alcmene the mother of Hercules, Mnemosyne of the nine Muses, and Danaë of Perseus). Deöis was another name for Proserpine, daughter of Ceres and Jupiter.

Book Six

golden-haired Ceres, mother of our crops.
The snake-haired mother of the flying horse
knew you as a bird, and for Melantho [120]
you assumed a dolphin's form. Arachne
pictures all of these, giving each image
appropriate faces and locations.
Phoebus is there, in a scene showing him   200
in rustic clothing. She weaves how he wore,
on one occasion, a hawk's wings, but then,
on another, a lion's skin, and how
in his shepherd's clothes he misled Issa,
Macareus' daughter. She includes
how Bacchus tricked Erigone, using
a false bunch of grapes, and then how Saturn
turned himself into a horse and fathered
Chiron, who was half horse, half mortal man.[1]
The outer part of the design, surrounded   210
by a narrow border, has woven flowers
intertwined with clustering strands of ivy.

Neither Envy nor Minerva could fault
Arachne's work. Enraged by her success,
the goddess with the yellow hair ripped up   [130]
the woven scenes of those criminal acts
committed by the gods, held up her shuttle
(it was made of boxwood from Cytorus),
and battered Arachne, Idmon's daughter,
three or four times across her head.[2] The girl,   220
now desperate, could not endure the blows,
and, in a burst of courage, fixed a noose
around her neck. As she was dangling there,
Pallas took pity, lifted her up, and said:

"You may go on living, insolent girl,
but you must hang suspended. To make sure

---

[1] In the form of the river Enipeus, Neptune forced sex on Iphimedeia, who had two sons, the Giants Otus and Ephialtes. As a ram, Neptune had sex with Theophane (changed into a sheep), who gave birth to the ram with the Golden Fleece. The mother of the winged horse was Medusa, but Pegasus was born from her blood, not from Neptune's seed. Melantho was the daughter of Deucalion. Erigone was the daughter of Icarius, a follower of Bacchus. Bacchus deceived Erigone by disguising himself as a cluster of grapes. Chiron's mother was Phillyra.

[2] Cytorus was a mountain on the southern shores of the Black Sea, famous for its boxwood.

you do not grow negligent in future,
let the same decree which punishes you
be pronounced as well against your family,
the entire line of your posterity." 230

After that, as she was leaving, Pallas
sprinkled Arachne with a potion made
from Hecate's herbs.¹ Touched by this harsh drug, [140]
her hair fell out at once, her nose and ears
were also gone, her head grew very small,
her whole form shrivelled to a tiny shape,
her slender fingers stuck to her sides as legs,
and the rest of her was belly. And yet,
she sent out a fibre from that belly
and, as a spider, continued weaving, 240
the way she used to do in earlier days.

All Lydia was upset by these events. NIOBE AND LATONA
News of what had happened travelled around
through towns in Phrygia, and the wide world
was full of people spreading the report.
Niobe, before her marriage, had known
Arachne. She had been a young girl then,
living in Maeonia and Sipylus,
but though she came from the same native land,
she did not take Arachne's punishment 250 [150]
as a warning she should give precedence
to gods above and speak more modestly.²
Many factors made her proud, but it was not
her husband's skill, or the fine ancestry
they both shared, or their powerful kingdom
which gave her a sense of satisfaction
(although she was delighted with them all)
so much as her own children.³ And people
would have called Niobe the happiest
of mothers, if she had not held that view 260
herself.

¹Hecate was the divine daughter of the original gods Gaia and Ouranos. She was associated with magic, witchcraft, and childbearing.

²Sipylus was a city and a mountain in Lydia.

³Niobe's husband was Amphion, who was a wonderfully skilled musician. They were king and queen of Thebes.

Book Six

      Now, Teiresias' daughter,
Manto, who could see into the future,
moved by an impulse from the gods, wandered
through the middle of the city crying out
in prophecy:

      "You women of Thebes, crown
  your hair with laurel, and go, all of you
  in one large gathering, and offer incense
  and holy prayers honouring Latona
  and her children, Apollo and Diana.
  Through these lips of mine, Latona is now   270   [160]
  proclaiming her commands."

                          All Theban women
do what the goddess has announced. They wreathe
their heads with laurel, as she has ordered,
and offer incense and words of prayer
to the sacred flames. Then, lo and behold,
Niobe arrives—and with her a crowd,
an enormous throng, of her attendants.
She is a splendid sight in Phrygian clothing
interwoven with gold, as beautiful
as her anger will allow. She stands there,   280
tossing her lovely head, shaking the hair
along both shoulders. With a haughty gaze,
her proud eyes sweep around her, and she says:

  "What madness it is to prefer the gods   [170]
  in heaven, whom you only hear about,
  over those that you can see. Why worship
  Latona at these altars built for her,
  when my divinity still lacks incense?
  Tantalus was my father, the only man
  allowed to touch the tables of the gods.   290
  My mother is sister to the Pleiades,
  and her father is the mighty Atlas,
  on whose shoulders rests the weight of heaven.[1]
  My other grandfather is Jupiter,

---

[1] Tantalus, a son of Zeus, was a king in Lydia. He stole from the gods and offered up his son Pelops for them to eat. As a result, he was condemned to the Underworld (for Ovid's mention of him there see 4.578). Niobe's mother, in some accounts, was Taygete, one of the Pleiades (daughters of Atlas, who were set in the sky as stars in a constellation).

and I can also boast about the fact
he is my father-in-law.[1] In Phrygia
people fear me. I rule the royal house
of Cadmus. My husband's power and mine
govern the people and the walls of Thebes,
built by the music of my husband's lyre.[2]   300   [180]
Wherever I turn my eyes inside my home
I see enormous wealth. Then add to that
my beauty, which is worthy of a goddess.
Include with this my children—seven sons
and just as many daughters, and soon
sons-in-law and daughters-in-law, as well!
Now ask if I have reason to be proud,
and then have the presumption to prefer
Latona over me. Why, she was born
to Titan Coeus (whoever he is),   310
and the great Earth once refused to give her
a tiny scrap of ground where she could lie
and give birth to her children. Your goddess
was not welcome in heaven or on earth
or in the sea. She was exiled from the world,
until Delos felt some pity for her,
as she wandered here and there, and gave her
an unstable resting place. He told her:

   'You roam the earth a stranger, the same way   [190]
   I move around the sea.'

                      There she became   320
the mother of two children.[3] But I have
seven times that number, all born from me.
I am fortunate (who can deny it?),
and my good fortune will remain with me.
Can anyone doubt that? Prosperity
has made me safe. Fortune cannot harm me—

---

[1] Jupiter was the father of Niobe's husband, Amphion.

[2] Amphion and his twin brother Zethos, sons of Lycos, built the walls of Thebes. Zethos had to work manually, but Amphion's musical skill was so great that when he played the rocks moved on their own and set themselves in place.

[3] Because of the anger of Juno, pregnant Latona could find no place to give birth, until Delos, a wandering island, offered her space. There Latona gave birth to Apollo and Diana. As a result, the island became fixed in place. Apollo and Diana were often called the Delian gods.

I am too great. Though she could take away
many things from me, she would still leave us
a great deal more. The fine things I possess
outweigh whatever I may have to fear. 330
Suppose some of my numerous children
could be removed from me. I would be sad,
but I would not be left with just those two
Latona has. With a family that size,
how far is she from having none at all? [200]
Go home! Enough of holy sacrifice!
And get those laurel wreaths out of your hair."

The women remove the laurel wreaths and leave,
without finishing the ritual sacrifice,
except by worshipping the deity 340
with silent murmuring, as is their right.

Latona was outraged. On the summit
of Mount Cynthus she spoke to her two twins,
Diana and Apollo, with these words:[1]

"Look, children, I am your mother and proud
to have produced you. There is no goddess,
except for Juno, whom I defer to.
But unless you help me, people will doubt
I am divine and will drive me away
from those altars consecrated to me 350
for all ages yet to come. This is not
my only grief. Tantalus' daughter
has added insults to her profane acts, [210]
by daring to proclaim her family
outranks you both and to assert that I
am childless. May that claim of hers rebound
on her own head! It is quite clear her tongue
is every bit as nasty as her father's."[2]

To what she had already said, Latona
was going to add her own entreaties, 360
but Apollo cried:

---

[1] Mount Cynthus was on the island of Delos.

[2] Tantalus was a notorious deceiver and liar, even to the gods.

Book Six

"Stop! A long complaint
merely delays her punishment!"

Diana
said the same. So the two of them, hidden
by the clouds, swooped down through the air and reached
the royal citadel of Thebes.

Near the walls
there is a wide expanse of level ground
always used for horses. These animals
have trampled down the earth, and many wheels
and solid hooves have softened up the turf. [220]
Some of Amphion's seven sons are there, 370
mounted on spirited horses, sitting
firmly on their backs, all dressed in garments
of Tyrian purple and holding reins
weighted down with gold. Among those riders,
Ismenus, first of all the children born
from Niobe's womb, while guiding his horse
through a perfect circle and pulling back
on the foaming bit, screams out:

"I've been hit!"

In the centre of his chest an arrow
is sticking out. His dying hands let go 380
the reins, and he gradually falls sideways,
over the right shoulder of his horse. Next,
Sipylus, who is right beside him, hears
sounds from a quiver through the empty air. [230]
He gives his horse free rein, just as a helmsman,
sensing an impending storm, scurries off,
once he sees the clouds, and hoists up all his sails,
so he will not lose the slightest breath of air.
Though Sipylus has let the reins go slack,
he is caught by an unerring arrow, 390
and the quivering shaft sticks in his neck,
at the top, while from his throat protrudes
the naked iron tip. Leaning forward
where he is, he falls on his horse's mane,
rolls through the racing hooves, and stains the ground
with his warm blood. Unlucky Phaedimus
and Tantalus (who has inherited

his grandfather's name), once they are finished [240]
their usual training, move to wrestling,
a young man's sport, and, glistening with oil,
are now entangled in a hold, grappling
chest against chest. Then an arrow, speeding
from a taut bowstring, pierces both of them,
as they are locked together. They both groan
and fall together, both at once, their limbs
convulsed with pain. The two of them lie there,
gaze at the sunlight for the final time,
and in one breath both brothers breathe their last.
Alphenor sees them there. Beating his breast
and tearing at his skin, he rushes up,
to lift their icy limbs up in his arms.
While he is doing this pious duty,
he, too, is killed, for the Delian god [250]
strikes him with a deadly iron arrow
deep in his diaphragm, and once the shaft
is pulled out from his flesh, part of his lung
is drawn out with the barbs. His blood and life
escape into the open air together.
But long-haired Damasicthon is not struck
by just one wound. He is hit in the leg,
where the shin begins and sinews of the knee
have a soft spot in between. While he tries
to pull the lethal arrow out by hand,
another drives itself into his throat,
up to the feathers. Flowing blood forces
the arrow out and gushes up in spurts,
piercing the air, shooting in a high arc [260]
a long, long way. Then Ilioneus,
the only son remaining, lifts his arms
in a vain gesture of supplication,
and cries:

   "O, all you company of gods,
 spare me!"

   He said this, for he did not know
there was no need to ask them all. Apollo,
the archer god, was moved, but at that point
the weapon could not be recalled. However,
the young lad died from the tiniest of wounds,

for the arrow was not driven all that far
inside his heart.

     News of this disaster,
popular grief, and her own family's tears
confirmed for Niobe what had gone on   440
in this sudden catastrophe. Amazed
they could have done it, she became enraged
that the gods above had so much power   [270]
and had dared to use it. For Amphion,
the father, had driven an iron sword
into his chest, and, by dying, ended
in one blow both his sorrow and his life.
Alas! How different this Niobe is
from the Niobe who only recently
forced her people from Latona's altars   450
and strolled through the middle of the city,
proud head held high, envied by everyone.
Now she is a woman to be pitied
even by enemies! She collapses
on the frigid bodies and randomly
gives each one of her sons a final kiss.
She turns from them and, raising her bruised arms
up to the sky, cries:

     "Eat your fill, Latona,   [280]
of my sorrow. Cram your chest to bursting
with my pain, and may these seven murders   460
bring satisfaction to your savage heart!
It's over for me. Enjoy the triumph
of the victor over her enemy!
But how are you the winner? I may be
wretched, but I still have more children left
than you do, in spite of your good fortune.
Even after so many sons have died,
I still outnumber you!"

     As Niobe spoke,
a twang from a taut bowstring made a sound
which filled all the people there with terror,   470
except for Niobe—her wretchedness
had made her rash.

Book Six

                      The sisters, dressed in black
hair loose across their shoulders, are standing
by their brother's corpses. Then an arrow
strikes one in the stomach. She pulls it out
and, as she is about to die, faints away
and falls face down on her brother's body.
Another sister trying to console
her grieving mother suddenly goes limp
and doubles over from some unseen wound.
She clamps her mouth shut, but her living soul
has left already. One tries to run away,
but without success. She falls. Another
crumples on her sister. One hides herself,
and you can see one standing there, shaking.
Six sisters are now dead from various wounds.
One last one remains. With her whole body
and her clothes, Niobe protects the girl,
screaming:

        "At least leave me one! The youngest!
Just one out of so many! I beg you!
My youngest!"

                  But while she is crying this,
the child she is pleading for is slaughtered.
Now she has no children. She sits down there,
among her dead husband, sons, and daughters,
rigid with grief. The breezes do not move
her hair, the colour in her cheeks lacks blood,
in her sad face the eyes stand motionless.
There is no sign of life in her at all.
Inwardly, as well, her tongue is frozen
to her hardened palate. Her veins have lost
their power to throb. She cannot bend her neck,
or shift her arms, or move her feet around.
Her inner organs, too, have turned to stone.
And yet she weeps. Then a mighty whirlwind
encircles her and carries her from there
to her own land. Set on a mountain top,
she wastes away, and, even now, the tears
flow down her marble face.

           All men and women
truly fear the anger of that goddess,

Book Six

now it stands revealed. Every one of them 510
pays more respect in ritual worship
to the power of her divinity,
the mother of the twins. As usual,
given recent facts, people once again
recount old stories. One of them begins:

"Long ago in Lycia's fertile fields   THE LYCIAN PEASANTS
the peasants there also spurned the goddess
and paid for it. Now, it's true the story
is not well known, because the men involved
were common folk. Still, it is still amazing. 520
Once I went past the place and saw the lake [320]
those miraculous events made famous.
Since my father, who was getting older,
could not make the trip, he instructed me
to bring back from there some special cattle.
As I was setting out, he offered me
a guide, someone native to the region.
Well, while this man and I were travelling
across the fields, we saw an ancient altar,
black with sacrificial ashes, standing 530
in the middle of a lake, surrounded
by quivering reeds. My guide stopped and said
in a timid whisper:

       'Be kind to me.'

So I did the same and muttered:

       'Be kind.'

But when I asked him if the altar stood there
in honour of the naiads, or Faunus,
or some native god, the stranger gave me [330]
the following reply:[1]

       'No, my lad, there is
no mountain spirit in this altar here.
The goddess who can call this place her own 540
is the one the queen of heaven banished
from the world and who was later rescued
by roaming Delos, still a light island

---

[1] Faunus was the Roman god of the forest, equivalent to the Greek god Pan.

floating in the sea. With great reluctance
he welcomed her, in answer to her prayers.
And on that island, Latona then gave birth
to her twins, leaning up against a palm
and an olive tree from Pallas, thwarting
their stepmother's wishes.[1] But people say   550
that, even after she had given birth,
she left this place, as well, fleeing Juno,
and holding her two children, both divine,
against her breast. Then she crossed the border
into Lycia, the Chimaera's home,
where the burning sun had scorched the pastures.[2]
Weary from her lengthy struggles and parched   [340]
by summer heat, Latona needed water
(her famished children also had devoured
all her breast milk). Then, she happened to see
a smallish lake in a valley bottom,   560
where country folk were gathering rushes,
as well as bushy osiers and the sedge
which flourished in those marshes. The goddess
went up, bent her knees, knelt down on the ground,
and tried to drink some of that cool water.
But the crowd of peasants would not let her.
They pulled her back. And so the goddess said:

> 'Why deny me water? It is put there
> for common use. Nature has not made sun,
> air, or running water the property   570   [350]
> of individuals. I have come here
> to a place which benefits all people.
> And yet I ask you as a suppliant
> to let me use it. I am not going
> to bathe my body or my weary limbs
> here in the lake, but merely quench my thirst.
> Even as I speak, my mouth lacks moisture,
> and my jaws are dry. I can hardly find
> a channel for my voice to pass through them.
> A drink of water will be nectar to me,   580

[1] The stepmother of the newly born twins was Juno, the wife of their father, Jupiter.

[2] The Chimaera was a fabulous monster made up of three different animals (a lion's head, a goat's body, and a snake's tail).

Book Six

and, at the same time, it will save my life.
That I will acknowledge—with the water
you will offer me my life. Take pity
on these children, too, here at my bosom,
stretching out their tiny arms towards you.'

And, as it so happened, the infant twins
are holding out their arms. Who can resist [360]
Latona's moving plea? But those peasants,
no matter what she says, keep her away
and threaten her about what they will do 590
if she does not move further off, adding
insults, too. That is not enough for them.
With their hands and feet they stir up the lake,
purely for spite, and jump around the pool,
to churn up soft mud at the very bottom.
The daughter of Coeus, in her fierce rage,
forgets her thirst and now no longer tries
to plead with such undeserving wretches.
She can no longer bear to utter words
demeaning to a goddess. With hands raised 600
up to the sky, she cries:

          'Live forever
  in that pond of yours.'

             The goddess' wish
has its effect. Those Lycian peasants
are seized by an urge to leap in water. [370]
Sometimes they immerse their entire bodies
in the deep parts of the lake, and sometimes
raise their heads or swim across the surface.
Often they squat on banks beside the pool,
and often hop back in the cooling water.
But even now they use their filthy tongues 610
to quarrel and without a sense of shame
keep trying to shout out their abuse,
even when they are swimming underwater.
Their voices now are rough, their swollen necks
inflated, and the insults they croak out
make their wide mouths even wider. Their heads
rest on their backs—it looks as if their necks
have been removed. Their backs are coloured green,
and their bodies' largest part, the belly, [380]

is coloured white. And now, as new-made frogs,
they hop around there in their muddy pool.'"

When the storyteller, whoever he was,
had finished his account of the downfall
of those men from Lycia, someone else
remembered the story of that satyr,
Marsyas, whom Latona's son, Apollo,
had defeated in a competition
with a reed pipe, the instrument invented
by Minerva, and on whom he later
inflicted punishment.[1] Marsyas cried:

"Why are you tearing parts of me away!"

And he kept screaming:

"Aiii! I'm sorry!
The flute is not worth this much agony!"

As his screams ring out, his skin is sliced off
the surface of his limbs, and he becomes
one huge wound, with blood flowing everywhere.
His bare sinews lie exposed, and his veins
quiver and throb with no skin over them.
You can count his pulsing inner organs,
and fibres of his lungs are clearly visible
inside his chest. The woodland deities
and the fauns living in the countryside
weep for him, as do his brother satyrs
(among them is Olympus, even then
a dear friend of his), the nymphs, and all those
who graze flocks of sheep or herds of cattle
in those mountains.[2] The fertile earth is drenched.
The saturated soil takes in those tears,
absorbing them into its deepest veins,
and transforms them to a stream of water,
which it sends out into the open air.

APOLLO AND MARSYAS

[390]

---

[1] Minerva invented the reed pipe, but threw it away when she found out that playing the instrument made her cheeks bulge. Marsyas picked it up and became an expert on the flute. He challenged Apollo to a musical contest: his flute playing against Apollo's skill with the lyre. The winner could do whatever he wanted to the loser. The Muses were the judges. When they declared Apollo the winner, he flayed Marsyas alive.

[2] Olympus was a satyr, a brother of Marsyas and his pupil.

Book Six

From there it quickly flows down to the sea
between steep riverbanks, the clearest stream   [400]
in Phrygia, named after Marsyas.

Having heard these sorts of stories, people
quickly turned back to present things and mourned
the death of Amphion and his children.
They blamed the mother, although even then
one man, they say, shed tears for her, as well,
her brother Pelops. Tearing his tunic   660
from his chest, he exposed the ivory
in his left shoulder. When Pelops was born,   PELOPS
this shoulder was made of flesh and coloured
just like his shoulder on the right. But then,
soon after birth, he was sliced up in pieces
at his father's hands, and, so people say,
the gods, once they collected all the parts,
put Pelops back together. But one piece
between his upper arm and neck was missing.
So they used some ivory to replace   670   [410]
the part they could not find, and in this way
they reconstructed all of Pelops' body.[1]

The leading men of regions close to Thebes
assembled there, and the near-by cities
urged their rulers to go and offer Thebes
their sympathies—Argos and Mycenae,
the home of Pelops' family, Sparta,
Calydon (before it became despised
by harsh Diana), lush Orchomenus,
Corinth (well known for bronze), fierce Messene,   680
Patrae, low-lying Cleonae, Pylos
(the city of Neleus), and Troezen
(before king Pittheus was in control),
and all the other cities which are closed off
by the Isthmus with seas on either side,
as well as cities which are seen to lie   [420]

---

[1] In Greek mythology, Pelops' father, Tantalus, chopped him up to make a dinner offering to the gods. The gods, however, sensed the plot and restored the boy. However, Demeter had already eaten a missing part. Hence, it had to be replaced with a piece of ivory fashioned by Hephaestus.

beyond the confines of those narrow coasts.[1]
How could anyone believe that Athens
was the only place which did not respond?
War hindered her from doing her duty, 690
for barbarian hordes had come by sea
and were terrorizing the city's walls.
Then Tereus from Thrace with his army
of auxiliaries beat those barbarians
and gained a great name for his victory.

Now, Tereus was an important man, PROCNE AND TEREUS
with wealth and power, who traced his descent
from mighty Mars himself, so Pandion,
king of Athens, gave his daughter Procne
to him in marriage. But neither the Graces 700
nor Hymen was present at the wedding,
nor was Juno, who blesses married brides.
The Furies held up the wedding torches,
which they had taken from a funeral, [430]
and they prepared the marriage bed, as well,
while the ominous screech owl hovered high
above the house and settled on the roof
above their chamber.[2] Such were the omens
when Procne and Tereus were married,
such the omens, too, when they had a child. 710
It's true that Thrace congratulated them,
and they themselves gave thanks to all the gods.
They commanded that the day when Procne,
Pandion's daughter, and Thrace's famous king
were married, as well as the day on which
their son, Itys, was born, should be declared
a public holiday. That shows how much
what really matters lies concealed from us.

---

[1] They were offering sympathy for the destruction of Amphion, Niobe, and their family (the royal house of Thebes). The Isthmus (of Corinth) is the narrow stretch of land joining the Peloponnese to mainland Greece. The two seas are the Aegean and the Ionian seas, on either side. The first group of cities named are south of the Isthmus (i.e., in the Peloponnese). Those beyond the Isthmus would be in mainland Greece (i.e., northeast of the Isthmus). Calydon became despised by Diana because king Oeneus neglected to dedicate the first fruits of his orchard to the goddess (for Ovid's treatment of the story see 8.429 ff.). Pittheus was a son of Pelops and king of Troezen.

[2] The Furies, as goddesses of blood revenge, especially within the family, were hardly the appropriate deities to preside over a wedding.

Now the Titan Sun had drawn the seasons
of the revolving year through five autumns,
when Procne, trying to coax her husband,
said to him:

        "If you feel anything for me,
either let me go to see my sister,
or let my sister come to visit us.
You can promise my father she'll be back
before too long. If you could arrange things
so I can see my sister Philomela,
you'd be giving me a truly lovely gift."

Tereus told his men to launch a ship,
and, using sails and oars, he made the trip
to the port of Cecrops' city, landing
at Piraeus.[1] There, as soon as he met
his father-in-law, they linked right hands,
and Tereus offered his best wishes.
He had started to explain the reason
for his arrival and his wife's request,
promising that if her sister visited,
she would come back soon, when, lo and behold,
Philomela arrived, looking gorgeous
in her rich garments, but even richer
in her own loveliness. She looked just like
what we so often hear about in stories
of the naiads and the dryads who roam
around the middle of the woods, if only
they possessed her refinement and her dress.
Tereus saw the girl and was on fire,
just as if someone were to place a flame
under dry ears of grain or set a torch
to piles of leaves or hay stacked in a barn.
Her beauty, it's true, deserved such feelings,
but he was driven on by natural lust,
and people from his country tend to have
strong sexual passions.[2] So he caught fire
thanks to his country's vices and his own.

TEREUS AND PHILOMELA

[1]Cecrops' city is Athens, and Pireus was (and still is) the port adjacent to it.

[2]Tereus was from Thrace in northern Greece and would therefore be considered far less civilized than the Athenians or the Greeks generally.

Book Six

His desire wishes to corrupt the care
of her attendants and her nurse's trust,
to tempt the girl herself with immense gifts,
whatever his whole kingdom can afford,
or carry her off and defend the rape
with savage warfare. He is so consumed 760
with unbridled passion, there is nothing
he will not dare, for he has no power
to repress the fires blazing in his chest.
And now he cannot cope with a delay.
His eager mouth returns to the request
from Procne, and beneath her very words
he states what he himself desires. His feelings
make him eloquent. When he keeps asking
beyond what is polite, he makes it clear [470]
that this is what Procne has requested. 770
He even adds his tears, as well, as though
she has instructed him to use those, too.
By gods above, how much hidden darkness
the human heart contains! The very things
Tereus does to promote his evil scheme
make them believe he is compassionate.
The people praise him for his evil deeds.
Philomela desires the same thing, too.
With her arms around her father's shoulders,
she coaxes him to let her travel there, 780
to visit her sister. She urges him
for her own well being, though what she seeks
will work against her. Tereus looks on,
and, as he gazes at her, imagines
he is holding her already. He sees
her kiss her father, putting both her arms
around his neck, and he absorbs it all
as an incitement, adding food and fuel [480]
to his frenetic lust. And every time
she holds her father to her, he desires 790
to be that father—although if he were,
his feelings would be no less abhorrent.
Pandion gives way to the entreaties
from both of them. Philomela rejoices,
thanks her father, and thinks, unlucky girl,
she and her sister have now won the day,

195

when that success will bring on both of them
enormous grief.

               The work of sun god Phoebus
by now was almost done. His horses' hooves
were drumming on the slopes of western skies.   800
A royal feast had been set out on tables
with wine in golden cups. They ate their fill
and then retired to have a peaceful sleep.
But although Tereus, the Thracian king,   [490]
went to bed, he burned for Philomela,
recalling her face, her hands, her movements,
imagining those parts he had not seen
to be just as he would want them. He fed
the fires within him and grew so restless
he could not sleep. Dawn came. As Tereus   810
was leaving, Pandion clasped the right hand
of his son-in-law and, with tears running
down his cheeks, implored him to look after
his daughter Philomela:

               "My dear son,
because affection compels me to it,
and both my daughters wish it, and you, too,
Tereus, have said this is what you want,
I entrust her to your care. I beg you,
by your honour, by our united hearts,
and by gods above, to take care of her   820
with a father's love and to send her back
as soon as possible, this sweet comfort   [500]
in my worrisome old age. Any delay
will be too long for me. And Philomela,
if you have any affection for me,
come back to me as quickly as you can.
It's enough your sister is so far away."

He gave these instructions to his daughter
and kissed her. As he issued his orders,
he wept quiet tears. Then he asked them both,   830
as a pledge of faith, for their two right hands.
These he took and joined, and then he told them
to remember to greet on his behalf
his absent child and grandson. His voice choked.
Convulsed with sobs, he could hardly manage

a last farewell. His mind was so afraid, [510]
filled with an ominous sense of trouble.

As soon as Philomela was on board
and the painted ship moved away from land,
as oar blades churned the sea, Tereus cries:

"I have triumphed! I am taking with me
just what I desire!"

                    The barbarian king
is overjoyed. He has trouble putting off
the pleasures his mind conjures up. His eyes
never turn away from her, just as an eagle,
Jupiter's swift bird of prey, sets a hare,
gripped in its hooked claws, inside its lofty nest,
and the prisoner has no place to flee,
while the predator keeps gazing at its prey.

And now the trip is over. Once they reach
Tereus' land, they leave the sea-worn ship,
and the king hauls Pandion's daughter off [520]
to a high-walled building, hidden away
in an ancient forest, and locks her in.
Philomela, pale, trembling, and in tears,
afraid of everything about the place,
keeps asking where her sister is. The king
reveals his criminal desire, and then
his force overpowers the lonely girl,
who often screams in vain to her father,
often to her sister, and above all,
to the mighty gods. She trembles with fear,
like a terrified lamb wounded by the jaws
of a grey wolf and later cast aside,
which does not realize it is now safe,
or like a dove with its feathers soaking
in its own blood, panic stricken, afraid
of the ravenous claws which snatched it up. [530]
Soon, when she regains her senses, she tears
her dishevelled hair, like someone mourning,
scratches her arms, beats them against her breast,
stretches out her hands, and screams:

                    "You barbarian!
Think of what you have done, you savage beast!

Are you quite unmoved by what my father
asked of you with such affectionate tears,
or by any feelings for my sister,
or my innocence, or your marriage vow?
You have confounded everything! I am
now forced to be my sister's substitute
and you the partner of the two of us!
Procne will have to be my enemy.
Why did you not rip out this life of mine,
you traitor? Then your crime would be complete!
I wish you'd killed me before committing
this abominable rape. Then my shade
would have been free of shame. But if the gods
observe these things, if celestial powers
have any influence, if everything
is not destroyed along with me, then you
will pay me for this someday. I myself
will throw away all sense of shame and shout
what you have done. And if I get the chance,
I'll move among your people with the story.
If I'm kept a prisoner in the woods,
I'll fill the forest with my voice and move
the rocks, which know how you have ruined me!
Let heaven hear these things—and gods, as well,
if any gods live there!"

      Philomela's words
enraged the king and also roused his fear.
Spurred by both emotions, he pulled the sword
he carried out of its scabbard, grabbed her
by the hair, forced her arms behind her back,
and tied her up. Once she saw his sword,
Philomela fully believed and hoped
she would be killed and offered him her throat.
But as she struggled to speak and pour forth
her anger, calling out her father's name
repeatedly, Tereus seized her tongue
with pincers, and using his savage blade
he sliced it out. The bottom of her tongue
still quivered in place, but the tongue itself
lay trembling on the dark earth, muttering.
It wriggled about (the same way a tail
from a snake will commonly keep moving

when it has been cut off), as if, in dying,
it was seeking some trace of its mistress.   [560]
They say (though this I hardly dare believe)
that even after this abhorrent crime
Tereus, in his lust, violated
her mutilated body many times.   920

After committing these atrocities,
Tereus calms down and returns to Procne,
who, as soon as she sees her husband, asks
about her sister. He pretends to sigh
and tells a made-up story of her death.
The tears he sheds make her believe his lies.
From her shoulders Procne tears her splendid robes
richly woven with gold and clothes herself
in black. She builds an empty burial vault,
where she makes sacrifices for a ghost   930
who does not exist and laments the fate
of a sister for whom death chants like that   [570]
are not appropriate.

      The sun god circles
through twelve constellations. A year goes by.
What can Philomela do? There is a guard
to keep her from escaping, and the walls
of the place where she is held are thick,
made out of solid rock. Her speechless lips
can provide no details of what happened.
But pain promotes great ingenuity,   940
and when times are bad one grows resourceful.
With great skill she pulls thread into a warp
on a barbarian loom, and, by weaving
patterns of purple on a white background,
she depicts the crime. Once she is finished,
she entrusts the weaving to a servant,
asking her with gestures to present it
to the queen, her mistress, and the servant,
as requested, carries it to Procne,
not knowing what the woven work contains.   950   [580]
The wife of the savage tyrant unfolds
the tapestry and, looking at it, reads
her sister's dreadful fate. She says nothing.
It is amazing she can keep so quiet,

but grief prevents her speech. Her tongue seeks out
words which might be adequate to express
her murderous rage, but cannot find them.
With no time to weep, she rushes ahead,
so totally intent on her revenge,
she no longer separates right from wrong. 960

It was now time for young Thracian women   PROCNE AND PHILOMELA
to celebrate the Bacchic festival
which, following their traditions, is held
at three-year intervals. These rites take place
at night, when Mount Rhodope re-echoes
to sounds of clashing brass.[1] In the darkness,
the queen leaves home, dressed to participate [590]
in sacred rituals and holding weapons
for the ecstatic ceremonial rites,
vine leaves wrapped around her head and deerskin 970
hanging down one side, with a slender spear
across her shoulder. Procne runs ahead
with throngs of her companions through the woods,
instilling terror. She keeps pretending
that you, Bacchus, have inspired her frenzy,
but she is driven on by frantic grief.
At length, rushing through the trackless forest,
she arrives at Philomela's building.
Procne, screaming and howling Bacchic cries,
shatters the doors and seizes her sister. 980
She dresses her in ritual garments
as one of the god's enraptured worshippers,
concealing her face with leaves of ivy,
drags the terrified girl away from there, [600]
and leads her back inside the palace walls.

When Philomela saw that she had come
to that dreadful home, the bewildered girl
trembled with horror, and her face grew pale.
But Procne, once in the house, took away
the symbols of the Bacchic ritual, 990
uncovering her wretched sister's face,
and tried to hug her. But Philomela,
filled with shame, could not bear to raise her eyes.

[1] Rhodope is a mountain in Thrace.

Book Six

She saw herself as a whore who had been false
to her own sister. So she kept her gaze
fixed on the ground. She wished to take an oath,
with the gods as witnesses, that her shame
was forced upon her, and she tried to use
her hands to show it, for she had no voice.
But Procne was ablaze—she could not check   1000   [610]
her rage—and stopped her sister's tears, saying:

    "No weeping now. This is a time for swords,
or something else more powerful than steel,
if you have such a thing available.
Sister, I am prepared for any crime.
I could set the royal palace on fire
with torches, hurl that treacherous Tereus
in the middle of the flames, or with a sword
slice out his tongue, eyes, or the sexual parts
he used to shame you, or I could expel   1010
his guilty soul out through a thousand wounds!
I am prepared for a tremendous act—
but what that act will be, I'm still not sure."

As Procne said this, her young son Itys   PROCNE AND ITYS
came to his mother, and she sensed from him
what she could do. While watching him, her eyes
grew cold, and she muttered:

               "How much you look
  just like your father!"

                    That was all she said.
Then, seething with silent rage, she began
to hatch her ghastly plan. But when the boy   1020
ran to greet his mother, placed his small arms
around her neck, kissed her, and then added
some childish words of love, his mother
was truly shaken, her anger wavered.
Against her will her eyes filled up with tears.
But as soon as she felt too much emotion
eroding her resolve, she glanced away
and looked back at her sister's face. Gazing   [630]
at each of them in turn, she asked:

               "Why is it
  that one of them speaks of his affection   1030

and the other has had her tongue removed
and does not talk? He can call me mother.
Why can she not call me sister? Just look,
daughter of Pandion, at your husband,
the man you married. You are not worthy
of your race. In someone married to Tereus
showing affection is a filthy crime!"

She did not pause, but dragged Itys away
to a distant room in the lofty home,
just like a tigress on the Ganges' banks 1040
hauling a baby fawn through shady trees.
Already sensing what his fate might be,
the child stretched out his hands and cried,

                    "Mother!
Mother!"

           He tried to reach around her neck, [640]
but Procne plunged her sword into his side,
close to his heart. She did not look away.
That one blow was enough to kill him,
but Philomela then took up the sword
and cut his throat, and while the limbs were warm,
still showing signs of life, they sliced him up 1050
and set some pieces boiling in bronze pots,
as others hissed while roasting there on spits.
The inner chamber dripped with blood and gore.

Procne then invites Tereus, her husband,   TEREUS AND ITYS
who has no idea of what they're doing,
to a feast. She falsely states that the meal
is a sacred ritual of her homeland.
Claiming the only one the law permits
to be there is the husband, she dismisses
his followers and attendants. And thus, 1060
Tereus sits in his high ancestral seat,   [650]
feasting by himself, filling his stomach
with his own flesh and blood, so out of touch
with what is going on, he calls to her:

   "Bring Itys here!"

              Procne cannot conceal
her savage exultation. Eager now

to proclaim the news about the slaughter
she has carried out, she shouts:

"You have him
in there with you—the one you're calling for!"

Tereus looks and asks where Itys is.
While he is searching, calling out again,
Philomela jumps at him, just as she is,
hair soaking from the appalling murder,
and thrusts the head of Itys, dripping blood,
right in his father's face. At that moment,
more so than any other, she wishes
she could speak and proclaim her great delight
in words which match her mood.

The Thracian king
gives a tremendous roar and pushes back
the table, screaming out to the Furies,
those snake-haired sisters from the deep valley
of the Styx. Now, if it were possible,
he would tear his chest apart and disgorge
the dreadful meal of half-digested flesh.
He weeps and calls himself the wretched tomb
of his own son. And then with his sword drawn
he chases after Pandion's daughters.
But you would think those Athenian women
have bodies now held up on feathered wings,
for they are taking flight. One of them flies
into the woods. The other nestles down
up in the eaves, still carrying traces
of that murder on her breast, her feathers
stained with blood. Tereus, swift in his grief
and cravings for revenge, is also turned
into a bird, with a crested head plume
and, instead of his long sword, a huge beak
jutting out in front. This bird, which looks armed,
has a name and is called the hoopoe bird.[1]

The pain of these events sent Pandion
to shades of Tartarus before his time,

BOREAS AND ORITHYÏA

---

[1] Ovid does not here indicate the species of the other two birds, but in the traditional myth Procne becomes a nightingale and Philomela a swallow.

before the final days of his old age.
So then the royal sceptre of Athens
and management of its affairs were passed
to Erectheus, a man whose justice
and power in war no one could dispute.
He had four sons and as many daughters.
Two of the girls were well matched in beauty. [680]
One of them, Procris, had a happy marriage
to Cephalus, grandson of Aeolus. 1110
The other daughter, Orithyïa,
was loved by the god of the northern wind,
Boreas, but for a long time his love
could not attain her—he was hurt by links
to the Thracians and Tereus.[1] He pleaded,
choosing to use persuasion and not force.
But when his pleasant words had no effect,
he bristled with rage—his usual mood
and natural state for most of the time—
and cried out:

        "I'm entitled to my rage! 1120
Why did I abandon my own weapons?
My power and anger, my violence,
my threatening spirit? Why have I turned
to what does not suit me—playing beggar?
My way relies on force. With force I drive off [690]
the menacing storm clouds, whip up the sea,
overturn knotted oaks, harden the snow,
and batter the ground with hail. And then,
when I meet my brothers in the open air
(for that's my battlefield) I fight with them 1130
so fiercely that the middle sky resounds
with our collisions, and fires flash out,
discharged from hollow clouds. And then again,
when I move down to those empty caverns
deep in the earth and fiercely push my back
against the lowest depths, my tremors shake
the entire world, even shadows of the dead.[2]

---

[1] Boreas was from the north, that is, from the regions of Thrace, where Tereus came from (i.e, not a place Athenians would think well of after the recent events).

[2] Some ancient thinkers believed that winds played a major role in causing a wide range of natural phenomena, including lightning and earthquakes.

That is how I should have sought this marriage, [700]
not by begging Erechtheus to become
my father-in-law, but by forcing him."   1140

With these or other equally potent words
Boreas shook out his wings, whose motions
blow winds all through the earth and agitate
broad surface waters of the sea. Trailing
his gloomy cloak across the mountain peaks,
the lover rushed along the ground, concealed
in darkness, and swept Orithyïa,
trembling with fear, up in his tawny wings.
As he flew, the ravisher's fires were stirred
and burned with greater heat. He did not stop   1150
that flight through the air until he reached
the city walls where the Cicones dwell.[1]   [710]
There the girl from Athens became the wife
of the icy tyrant—a mother, too,
producing twins, two brothers, both of whom
were like their mother in every feature,
but for their father's wings. Yet people say
their bodies had no wings when they were born,
and as long as they lacked a beard to match
their golden hair, the boys Calaïs and Zetes,   1160
had no wings at all. But then, once yellow hair   CALAÏS AND ZETHES
began to grow on their two cheeks, feathers
started to appear above both shoulders,
just as in birds. So when their childish years
were finished, they both joined the Argonauts   [720]
and sailed over unknown seas in that first ship
to seek out the glittering Golden Fleece.[2]

---

[1] The Cicones lived in Thrace, to the north of Greece.

[2] Ovid does not here use the adjective "golden," although the fleece he is referring to commonly has that epithet. Nor does Ovid use the term "Argonauts"; he calls the adventurers "Minyans," a name which usually refers to inhabitants of Boeotia. The men who sailed off after the fleece were commonly called the Argonauts (after their ship, the Argo).

BOOK SEVEN

VII

[The Argonauts visit king Aeetes in Colchis; Medea's love for Jason; Medea agrees to help Jason; Jason tames the fire-breathing bulls, sows the dragon's teeth, defeats the earth-born warriors, puts the dragon to sleep, and takes the Golden Fleece; Jason and Medea return to Thessaly; Medea's magic restores Aeson's life; Medea rejuvenates the nymphs who nursed Bacchus; Medea tricks the daughters of Pelias into killing their father; Medea's flight from Thessaly; the transformation of Cycnus into a swan and of Hyrië into a lake; Medea at Corinth; her revenge against Jason; Medea in Athens; Medea's marriage to king Aegeus; Medea's attempt to poison Theseus; Athens celebrates the achievements of Theseus; Minos prepares for war; Minos visits Aegina; Aeacus refuses Minos help; Cephalus asks Aeacus for help; Aeacus describes the plague in Aegina; the Myrmidons appear; Cephalus tells Aeacus' son the story of his wife, Procris, of his abduction by Aurora, of his tests of Procris' fidelity, of her life as a follower of Diana; of his dog Laelaps and the monstrous fox, and of his wife's death; Aeacus gives Cephalus soldiers to assist him against Minos.]

By now, in their ship built at Pagasae, JASON AND MEDEA
the Argonauts were carving their passage
across the sea. They had paid a visit
to Phineas, who was dragging out his life
in helpless, permanently blind old age.
The young sons of Boreas had chased off
the Harpies, those birds with young girl's faces,
from the poor man's island.[1] After meeting
many challenges with famous Jason
in command, they finally made their way   10
to the swift stream of the muddy Phasis.[2]
While they were meeting with king Aeetes,
asking him to return the Golden Fleece
from that ram which had carried Phrixus off,
and while king Aeetes was proposing
his grotesque conditions, which demanded
enormous labours from the Argonauts,
the daughter of the king, Medea, was seized
by fiercely passionate love for Jason.[3]

---

[1]Phineas was punished by Jupiter, who blinded him and placed him on an island where his food was stolen by Harpies, flying monsters with female faces. Boreas is the god of the North Wind; his sons are Calaïs and Zetes, mentioned at the end of Book 6.

[2]The Phasis was a river in Colchis, a region in the western Caucasus (on the eastern shores of the Black Sea). Jason, son of Aeson and a prince of Iolcus (in Thessaly), was seeking to win back his father's kingship by acquiring the Golden Fleece. He assembled a crew of heroic figures to sail with him: Calaïs, Zethes, Hercules, Philoctetes, Peleus, Telamon, Orpheus, Castor, Pollux, Atalanta (the only woman), and Euphemus.

[3]Phrixus had been saved from death by a winged ram with a fleece of gold, which had carried him to Colchis. He sacrificed the ram to Neptune, and Aeetes, king of Colchis, kept the fleece in a grove, where it was guarded by a dragon. Jason is asking Aeetes to return the fleece.

BOOK SEVEN

For a while she tried to fight against it,
but when her reason could not overcome
her feelings, she said:

                "To struggle like this, Medea,
is useless. Some god—I don't know which one—
is going against you. I suppose that this,
or something like it, is what people call
being in love. For why do those demands
my father makes strike me as very harsh?
And, in fact, they are far too harsh! But why
am I afraid this man might come to grief,
when I've only now just seen him? What is it
that makes me so afraid? Unhappy girl,
if you can do it, you must douse these flames
which you have fanned inside your virgin heart!
If I could, I'd act with greater wisdom,
but some new force is pulling me along.
My desire tells me one thing, and my mind
says something else. I see the better way
and want to go there, but I take the worse.
Why, you royal virgin, are you on fire
for a stranger? Why these dreams of marriage
in a foreign land? For this country, too,
can offer you someone to love. The gods
will determine if this man lives or dies.
But let him live! I may make that prayer,
even if I'm not in love. For what crime
is Jason guilty of? Apart from those
with pitiless hearts, who would not be touched
by Jason's youth, noble birth, and courage?
Or if he lacked all other qualities,
who could resist his beauty? For it's true—
he has really moved my heart. And unless
I offer my help, the breath of the bulls
will scorch him, or he will have to battle
against those earth-born enemies sprung up
from seeds which he himself has sown, or else
he will be offered up as cruel prey
to that ravenous snake. If I stand by
and let this happen, I'll be confessing
a tigress was my mother and my heart
is made of iron and stone. Why do I

not watch him die—contaminate my eyes
by looking on? Why do I not incite
the bulls or the ferocious earth-born men,
or the dragon that never sleeps to fight
against him?[1] May the wishes of the gods
bring better things! But I should not just pray
for this to happen. I should do something!
Should I then betray my father's kingdom
and use my power to save a stranger
I don't even know, so that with my help   70   [40]
he may remain unhurt, then sail away
without me, get married to someone else,
leaving Medea here, abandoning her
to face her punishment? If he could do that,
if he could prefer some other woman
to me, then let the thankless wretch perish!
But with that face, nobility of soul,
and handsome form of his, I need not fear
he will deceive me or forget my help.
Besides, he will promise himself to me   80
in advance. I will call upon the gods
to witness what we pledge. Why be afraid,
when you will be quite safe? Prepare yourself,
and do not wait. Jason will forever
be indebted to you. He'll marry you
in a solemn rite, and throngs of women
in Pelasgian cities will honour you   [50]
as the one who saved him.[2] So shall I then
be carried off by winds and leave behind
my country, my sister, brother, father,   90
and my gods, as well? But then my father
is a savage creature, my native land
a barbarous place, and my young brother
still a child. My sister's prayers are with me,
and the greatest god is here inside me!
I will not be leaving what is great behind,
no, I will be pursuing what is great—

---

[1] Medea here is listing the tasks her father, king Aeetes, has set Jason, if he wishes to get back the Golden Fleece.

[2] The term Pelasgian refers to all of Greece. The name is derived from the early inhabitants of the region. At times, however, it denotes a specific area (e.g., Thessaly).

honour for saving these young men of Greece,
a knowledge of finer lands and towns
whose fame is celebrated, even here,
and the arts and culture of those regions.
Then there's Jason, for whom I'd willingly
trade everything the entire world contains.
Once he is my husband, I will be called
a happy woman, well loved by the gods,
and my head will touch the stars. Yes, but then
what of those stories people talk about—
rocks clashing in the middle of the sea,
Charybdis, the enemy of sailors,
who sucks down the sea and then spews it back,
and brutal Scylla with her savage dogs
barking in the deep seas of Sicily?[1]
But as I am carried across the sea
on that long voyage, I will be holding
the man I love, embracing Jason's chest.
In his arms I will have no fears at all,
or, if I do, I will be afraid for him,
only for my husband. But, Medea,
do you really think this is a marriage?
Are you not wrapping crime in lovely names?
Instead of doing that, you should consider
just how great a wrong you are proposing
and, while you can, avoid such treachery."

Medea finished. Her eyes were gazing
at those virtues standing in front of her—
right, piety, and modesty. Cupid,
now overpowered, turned his back on her.

Medea set off for the ancient altars
of Hecate, Perses' daughter, hidden
in a shadowy grove, deep in the woods.
At this point she was firm. Her emotions,
now repressed, had ebbed. But then she saw him,
the son of Aeson, and the dampened fires
burst into flame again. Her cheeks turned red,

---

[1] The clashing rocks were the Symplegades, which threatened ships at the entrance to the Black Sea. Charybdis was a whirlpool and Scylla a six-headed monster. They stood on either side of the straits separating Italy from Sicily.

and her whole face grew hot. Just as a spark
buried in the ashes piled above it [80]
is often fed by winds, grows, and, once stirred,
regains the strength it had before, that's how
her passion (now so dull, you would have thought
by this time it had died) blazed up again, 140
when she observed the young man standing there
in front of her. And, as it so happened,
on that particular day Aeson's son
was looking especially attractive.
Her love would be so easy to forgive!
She gazed at him, her eyes fixed on his face,
as if it was the first time she had seen him,
so disconcerted, she did not believe
the man she was looking at was mortal.
She could not look away. When the stranger 150
reached for her right hand and began to speak, [90]
requesting in a humble voice her help
and promising marriage, Medea burst
into tears and answered:

                "I understand
what I am doing. I am being seduced
by love, not by ignorance of the truth.
I will do what I can to save you, but then,
once you are safe, give me what you promise!"

Jason swore by the sacred rituals
of the three-formed goddess, by the spirit 160
in that grove, by the all-discerning Sun,
father of his future father-in-law,
by his own exploits, and by the dangers,
those immense perils, he would face.[1] His oath
convinced Medea. He received from her
immediately some magic herbs and learned
how to apply them. Then, he made his way
back to the palace, overjoyed.

                The next day,
once Aurora scatters the glittering stars, [100]

---

[1] The three-formed goddess was Hecate, who was commonly depicted with three faces (often of a horse, dog, and snake). The Sun was the father of Aeetes, Medea's father.

people stream to the sacred field of Mars 170
and gather in position on the ridge. JASON AND THE GOLDEN FLEECE
Aeetes himself sits in the middle,
dressed in purple. His ivory sceptre
makes him conspicuous. Then, lo and behold,
bronze-footed bulls are snorting Vulcan's fire
from adamantine nostrils! Their hot breath
scorches the grass and sets the ground alight.
Just as fully stoked flaming forges roar
or limestone baked in earthen furnaces,
as it absorbs the heat, makes a loud hiss 180
when water drops are sprinkled over it,
that's how the chests and parched throats of those bulls
resound, as they pant out the roiling flames
they hold inside. But the son of Aeson [110]
moves out to meet them. As he comes nearer,
the dreadful beasts turn their ferocious heads
and iron-tipped horns towards him, pawing
the dusty earth with cloven hooves, bellowing,
filling the air with smoke. The Argonauts
are stiff with fear. Jason moves to the bulls. 190
He does not feel their fire-laden breath
(such is the power of magic potions!).
His hand boldly strokes their hanging dewlaps
and harnesses the beasts under the yoke.
He forces them to pull the heavy plough
and with its blade carves up the untilled field.
The Colchians are stunned. The Argonauts [120]
shout even louder, spurring Jason on.
Then from a bronze helmet he takes out
the dragon's teeth and scatters them, like seed, 200
across the field he has just ploughed. These seeds
have earlier been soaked in potent venom
and, once implanted in the soil, grow soft.
The sown teeth sprout and then begin to turn
into new bodies. Just as an infant child
acquires its human shape within the womb
of its own mother, forming parts inside,
and does not come out into the open air
before its body is complete, so these men
do not emerge out of the fertile soil 210
until they are full grown inside the womb

Book Seven

of pregnant Earth. Even more amazing,
they are brandishing weapons created
at the same time they are. The Pelasgians
watching these warriors about to hurl
their sharp pointed spears at young Jason's head
are fearful—their faces fall, their spirits
fail them. Even Medea feels afraid,
though she has taken steps to keep him safe.
When she sees the young man all by himself
with so many enemies assailing him,
the blood drains from her face. She sits down,
suddenly chilled and pale. And just in case
the power of the herbs she has provided
is insufficient, she recites a spell
to help him and invokes her secret arts.
Jason picks up a heavy rock and throws it
right in the middle of his enemies
and turns the fight from an attack on him
into a battle where those warriors
go after their own ranks. So those brothers,
created from the earth, wound one another
and die, falling in an internecine fight.
The Achaeans cheer, clutch the winner's hand,
and throw their arms eagerly around him.
And you, barbarian princess, you, too,
would like to hold the victor in your arms,
but your fear of being shamed prevents you.
You would embrace him, but are held in check
by concerns about your reputation.
You do what is appropriate—rejoice
with silent feeling and then offer thanks
to your spells and to the gods who craft them.

Jason still had to use his magic herbs
to put the dragon to sleep. This creature,
distinguished by its crest and triple tongue
and with hooked teeth—a terrifying sight!—
was the custodian of the tree which held
the Golden Fleece. Once Jason had sprinkled
the beast with herbal juices which produce
a Lethean sleep and had three times muttered
the words which bring calm slumbers, using spells
which soothe stormy seas and raging rivers,

BOOK SEVEN

sleep settled on that dragon's sleepless eyes,
and Aeson's heroic son carried off
the Golden Fleece.[1] Proud of what he had won
and taking with him as another prize
the person who had made that possible,
triumphant Jason reached the port of Iolchos
with his wife, Medea.

                     In Thessaly,   260   [160]
mothers and aged fathers offered gifts
for their sons' safe return and in the flames
poured heaps of incense. As they had promised,
they led in and killed a sacrificial beast,
whose horns they had wrapped in gold. But Aeson,   MEDEA AND AESON
Jason's father, did not participate
in their rejoicing, for, worn down by age,
he was now close to death. With this in mind,
Jason spoke about him to Medea:

   "Wife, to you, I admit, I owe my life,   270
   and though you have given me everything
   and the sum total of your services
   is beyond belief, if your enchantments
   can do it (and what can those spells of yours
   not bring about?) then take away some years
   from my own life and add them to my father's."

Jason could not check his tears. Medea
was moved by the love Jason had displayed
in making the request. She thought about
her very different feelings for her father,   280   [170]
king Aeetes, whom she had left behind.
However, that thought did not affect her,
and she said:

             "Husband, what unholy scheme
   has just passed through your lips? Do I look
   as if I can transfer part of your life
   to someone else? Hecate would not approve,
   and what you ask is not appropriate.
   But, Jason, I will try to give a gift

---

[1] Lethe was one of the five rivers of Hades. Its waters had the power of making people forget, of bringing on oblivion, and (in this case) bringing on sleep.

greater than the one you have requested.
Using my arts, I will try to lengthen
your father's life without reducing yours,
if Hecate, the goddess of three forms,
will only give her personal consent
to such an immense and daring action
and lend us her support."

                        It was three nights
before the moon's horns were completely joined
into a sphere. But once the full moon shone
and her whole shape gazed down on earth, Medea
slipped from the palace in loose-fitting robes.
Her feet were bare, and her uncovered hair
hung down across her shoulders. She moved off,
without attendants, through the still silence
of the night. Deep slumbers had brought calm rest
to men and birds and beasts. There was no sound
in any hedgerow. Still leaves were silent,
and silent, too, the dewy air. Nothing moved,
except the quivering stars. Stretching her arms,
Medea turned herself around three times,
sprinkled water taken from a flowing stream
three times above her head, and then three times
her mouth let out a piercing howl. Knees bent,
she knelt down on the solid earth and cried:

> "O Night, most faithful to these sacred rites,   MEDEA'S INCANTATION
> and all you stars who, with the golden moon,
> follow the fiery light of day, and you,
> triple-formed Hecate, who understand
> what we intend and come here eagerly
> to undertake the task of helping us
> with our sorcerer's chants and rituals,
> and you, O Earth, who grows the potent herbs
> enchanters use, and you winds and breezes,
> hills, streams, and lakes, you gods of every grove,
> and all you gods of Night, be present here—
> all those who help me, whenever I wish
> to reverse a river's flow, make it run
> past its astonished banks back to its source,
> and with my magic soothe tempestuous seas
> or stir up tranquil waters, scatter clouds

and bring them on, summon the stormy winds
and have them die away. With spells and chants 330
I break the serpent's jaws, rip living oaks
and boulders from their native soil, move trees,
and order hills to shake and earth to groan
and shadows of the dead to leave their tombs!
And you, O Moon, I also draw you down
in an eclipse, although Temesan brass
is there to ease your pain.[1] And my spells make
the chariot of the Sun, my grandfather,
grow pale, and from my poisons Aurora
loses colour! On my behalf, you cooled 340 [210]
the fire from those bulls and forced their necks
beneath the yoke to pull the curving plough,
a task they could not bear. You made those men
born from dragon's teeth fight one another
in savage battle, and you lulled to sleep
the guardian of the fleece, who never slept,
and by deceiving him, sent that treasure
off to towns in Greece. Now I need the juice
by which old age, once renewed, can revert
to the prime of life, get back youthful years. 350
And that you will provide—that's why those stars
are sparkling, why a chariot is on its way
drawn by the necks of dragons on the wing."

A chariot was there, sent down from heaven,
and once Medea had climbed in, patted [220]
the dragons' harnessed necks, picked up the reins,
and given them a shake, it snatched her off,
up to the sky. Looking down on Tempe,
in Thessaly lying far below her,
she drove the dragons on to certain places, 360
where she inspected herbs they might provide—
to Ossa as well as lofty Pelion
to Othrys, Pindus, and Mount Olympus,
an even higher peak. She took the plants
which pleased her, pulling some out by the roots,
and cutting others with a curved bronze knife.

---

[1] As mentioned in an earlier footnote, people made loud noises with brass instruments to get the moon back during an eclipse. Temese was a city in Italy famous for its copper.

She gathered many from the river banks
of Apidanus and Amphrysus streams,
and, Enipeus, you were not neglected.
The waters of Peneus and Spercheus   370
gave her their herbs, as did the reed-filled shores   [230]
of Boebe's lake. And beside Anthedon,
in Euboea, she picked a long-lived plant,
not yet famous for the transformation
it later brought about in Glaucus' body.[1]

Nine days and nights Medea moved around,
drawn in her chariot by those winged dragons,
examining the fields. Then she came back.
The dragons had not eaten any food.
They had only breathed the odour of those herbs,   380
and yet they had cast off their skins, the mark
of their advancing years. She reached her door,
right at the threshold, but remained outside,
with nothing but the sky above her head.
Shunning the company of men, she built
two altars out of turf—one on the right   [240]
for Hecate, one on the left for Youth.[2]
When she had covered these with sacred boughs
from the forest wilderness, she dug out
two ditches in the earth close by and then   390
performed a holy sacrifice, plunging
her knife in a black ram's throat and soaking
the open ditches with her victim's blood.
Next, she poured goblets of liquid honey
on the blood and, in a second offering,
cups filled with heated milk. As she poured,
she uttered spells, calling on the spirits
of the earth, imploring the king of shades
and his ravished wife not to take the life
still left in the old man's limbs too quickly.   400   [250]

---

[1] Apidanus and Amphrysus were rivers in Thessaly, Boebe a lake in Thessaly, and Anthedon a town in Boeotia. Glaucus ate a certain herb and was changed into a sea god. Ovid tells his story in Book 13.

[2] This goddess, also called Hebe, was a daughter of Juno and the wife of Hercules on Olympus (after Hercules was taken up into the company of gods).

MEDEA AND AESON

When she has appeased the gods with prayers
and lengthy incantations, she orders
Aeson's exhausted body to be brought
into the open air. Then with her spells
she puts him into a deep, death-like sleep
and stretches him on a layer of herbs.
She orders Jason and his attendants
to go away, advising them to take
their profane eyes far from her mysteries.
They disperse, as she has asked. Medea,   410
with her hair dishevelled, circles around
the flaming altars, like a worshipper
of Bacchus. She dips her branching torches
into the dark ditches, stains them with blood,   [260]
and at the altars lights them in the fire.
Next she purifies old Aeson, three times
with flame, three times with water, and three times
with sulphur. Meanwhile, a potent mixture
in a bronze cauldron set over the flames
is boiling, seething white with bubbling froth.   420
In this pot Medea cooks up some roots
she dug from fields in Thessaly, with seeds,
flowers, and black herbal juices, adding
stones gathered from the most distant regions
of the East and sand washed by ebbing seas.
She puts in hoar frost she scraped up at night
by moonlight, the ominous wings and flesh
of a screech owl, and the cut-up entrails
of the ambiguous werewolf, which can change
its bestial visage to a human face.   430   [270]
And she does not forget the scaly skin
from a thin Cinyphian water snake,
and liver from a long-lived stag. With these,
she includes the eggs and head from a crow
which has lived nine human generations.[1]

When the barbarian princess had used these
and a thousand other items to attain
her more than mortal purpose, she stirred up

---

[1] The stag and the crow were supposed to live much longer than human beings. Cinyps was a river in north Africa.

the whole mix with the branch of a mild olive,
long since dried out, blending what was on top 440
with what was underneath. Lo and behold,
in that hot bronze cauldron the old stick changed!
First it turned green and then, soon after that, [280]
sprouted leaves and suddenly was loaded
with a heavy weight of fruit. When the flames
made foam boil over from the hollow bronze
and warm drops hit the earth, the ground turned green!
Soft grass and flowers sprung up from the soil!
When she saw this, Medea drew a knife,
slit open Aeson's throat, let his old blood 450
flow out, and replaced it with her juices.
After the old man had absorbed these fluids,
some passing through his mouth, some through his wound,
at once the colour of his hair and beard
changed from white to black, his skeletal frame
in one heart beat had vanished, his pallor [290]
and debility were gone, compact flesh
smoothed out his hollow wrinkles, and his limbs
grew large and strong. Aeson was astonished,
recalling he had been just like this once, 460
some forty years ago.

     From high above,   MEDEA AND THE NYMPHS
Bacchus witnessed the amazing miracle
of this prodigious feat and realized
Medea could restore the youthful years
of Nysean nymphs who had been his nurses.
So he requested and received this gift
from the royal princess of Colchis.[1]

     And her magic   THE DAUGHTERS OF PELIAS
does not stop there. Medea then pretends
she has had a quarrel with her husband
and, under false pretenses, runs away 470
as a suppliant to Pelias, the king.[2]
Because Pelias is himself worn out
and very old, his daughters welcome her. [300]

---

[1] Bacchus, as a child, had been nursed by the nymphs of Nysea.

[2] Pelias was the brother of Aeson (hence, Jason's uncle). He had deprived Aeson of the kingship of Iochus and had sent Jason on the quest for the Golden Fleece.

By simulating friendship with deceit,
crafty Medea soon makes them her friends,
and when she tells them that of her good deeds
the greatest is the way she has removed
Aeson's frailty and when she lingers
on that tale, in Pelias' daughters
she creates the hope that similar spells 480
could restore the youth of their own father.
They ask Medea to do it, telling her
to name her price. She remains quite silent
for a while and appears to hesitate,
keeping those who are urging the request
in doubt, pretending she is still unsure.
Soon, however, she promises to try.
She tells them:

>   "To give you more confidence
> in this talent of mine, your oldest ram, [310]
> of all your sheep the leader of the flock, 490
> will, through my medicines, become a lamb."

Immediately they lead in a woolly beast,
a feeble creature thoroughly worn out
with innumerable years. Its ancient horns
curl round its shrunken temples. Medea
cuts its scrawny throat with her Thessalian knife,
staining the blade (even though the creature
has hardly any blood), and then she stuffs
the creature's body in a hollow cauldron,
which also holds her potent magic juice. 500
This shrinks its body's limbs and melts the horns,
and with those horns its years dissolve away.
From the middle of the cauldron they can hear
a soft bleating noise, and then, right away,
while they are wondering about the sound, [320]
a lamb jumps out and runs away to play
and find its mother's udder for some milk.
The daughters of Pelias are amazed.
And now Medea's promises have shown
she can be trusted, they encourage her 510
even more eagerly to work her magic.

Phoebus had led his horses from their yoke
three times, after completing their descent

into the Iberian sea.[1] On the fourth night
brilliant stars were shining as Medea,
Aeetes' deceitful daughter, set out
on a blazing fire pure water and herbs
(but ones which had no healing potency).
King Pelias and the guards escorting him
by now were fast asleep, bodies stretched out 520
and relaxed, like corpses. Medea's spells [330]
and magic powers had put them in that state.
The daughters, following her instructions,
accompanied the Colchian sorceress
into the room where Pelias was sleeping
and stood there, grouped around the royal bed.
Medea said:

"Why are you so listless?
Why hold back now? Unsheathe those swords of yours,
let his old fluids out, so I can fill
his empty veins with youthful blood! You hold 530
your father's life and age in your own hands.
If you have any loving feelings for him,
if those hopes which spur you are not empty,
carry out this action for your father.
Use your weapons to chase away old age,
and, with one slash of those swords you hold,
drain his corrupted blood."

Urged on by these words,
both daughters, because they love their father,
for the first time set aside their duty.
In order to avoid irreverence, 540 [340]
they carry out an irreverent act.
Still, neither one can watch the stab she makes.
They avert their eyes, turn their heads away,
and with brutal hands blindly stab their father.
Blood pours from the old man, who lifts himself
up on his elbows, half cut to pieces,
and tries to leave the bed. Stretching pale arms
out into the middle of so many swords,
he cries out:

---

[1] The Iberian Sea is the expanse of water beyond the Mediterranean (i.e., the Atlantic Ocean).

Book Seven

"Daughters, what are you doing?
Why take up arms against your father's life?" 550

Their courage and their strength abandon them.
Pelias is about to speak more words,
but Medea cuts off all further speech.
She slits his throat. His mutilated corpse
she then dumps in the seething cauldron.

Medea would not have escaped punishment, [350]
if she had not moved up into the air   MEDEA FLIES OVER THE ISLANDS
with her winged dragons, flying way up high
over shady Pelion, Chiron's home,
over Othrys, and regions made famous 560
by what had happened to old Cerambus,
who, when solid earth was inundated
by flooding seas, with the nymphs' assistance
flew into the air on wings and was not drowned,
and thus escaped Deucalion's flood.[1] Moving past
Aetolian Pitane on her left,
with its stone replica of a dragon,
and the grove of Ida in which Bacchus,
using the deceptive image of a stag, [360]
once concealed a bullock stolen by his son, 570
she passed the place where Corythus' father
lies interred in shallow sand and those fields
where the eerie sound of Maera's barking
makes men afraid.[2] She travelled on past Cos,
Eurypylus' city, where the women
acquired horns at the time when Hercules
and his soldiers left the island, past Rhodes,
Apollo's city, and the Telchines
of Ialysos, whose eyes polluted
everything they saw. Sickened by their deeds, 580
Jupiter drowned them in his brother's waves.

---

[1] Chiron was a centaur (half man, half horse) famous for his wisdom. Cerambus was changed into beetle and flew to the top of Mount Parnassus to prevent being drowned during the great flood. For Ovid's story of Deucalion and the Flood, see Book 1.

[2] Aetolian Pitane was in Asia Minor. The grove of Ida was near Troy. When Bacchus' son, Thyoneus, stole an ox, Bacchus changed the animal into a stag in order to protect his son from the farmers pursuing him. Corythus' father was Paris of Troy. Maera was a dog, perhaps once a human female, now transformed. Some commentators believe the name refers to Hecuba, queen of Troy, who was changed into a dog (for her story see Book 13).

She moved across the walls of Carthaea
in ancient Ceos, where Alcidamas,
a father, was amazed a gentle dove [370]
could fly up out of his daughter's body.[1]
From there she looked down on Hyrië's lake CYCNUS AND HYRIË
and Cycneian Tempe, which gained its fame
overnight, thanks to a swan. In that spot,
Philius had given some birds to Cycnus,
along with a wild lion he had tamed, 590
as the young lad Cycnus had instructed.
Cycnus then asked him to subdue a bull,
and Philius did so, but was upset
his love had been rebuffed so many times
and refused to give the bull to Cycnus
as his final gift, although he begged him.
Cycnus in his anger cried out to him:

"You're going to wish you'd given me that bull."

Then he jumped down from a towering rock.
They all believed he'd fallen to his death, 600
but he was changed into a swan and soared
on snow-white wings high up into the air.
His mother, Hyrië, who was unaware [380]
he had survived, dissolved in her own tears
and turned into the lake that bears her name.[2]

Pleuron lies adjacent to these places.
Here Combe, Ophis' daughter, had escaped
being hurt by her own sons, by flying away
on trembling wings. After that, Medea
gazed down on Calaurea's fields, sacred 610
to Latona, knowing their king and queen
had once changed into birds.[3] Cyllene lay

---

[1]Eurypylus was a king of Cos, an island in the Aegean sea. The women of Cos were changed into cows when they angered the gods. In one version of the story, the gods were displeased because the women abused Hercules when he drove cattle across the island. The Telchines were the original inhabitants of Rhodes. Ialysos was a town on Rhodes. Jupiter's brother was Neptune, god of the sea. Carthaea was a city on the island of Ceos in the Aegean. Alcidamas had a daughter who gave birth to a dove.

[2]This is the second story involving the transformation of someone called Cycnus into a swan (for the first see 2.530 ff.). A third one occurs at 12.228.

[3]Calaurea was an island close to the Peloponnese.

off to her right, where Menephron one day
would, like a savage animal, have sex
with his own mother. Far away from there
she saw Cephisus mourning his grandson's fate,
changed by Apollo to a bloated seal,
and the house where Eumelus was grieving
for his son, now a creature of the air.[1]   [390]

Finally, with her winged dragons she reached   620
Ephyre, home of the Pirenian spring,
where people in the olden days would claim
that in the earliest ages human bodies
were created out of rain-soaked mushrooms.
Here, after Jason's new bride was consumed   MEDEA'S REVENGE
by Medea's drugs and both seas had seen
the royal palace burning, Medea
profanely bathed her sword in her sons' blood.
After this appalling act of vengeance,
she fled, avoiding Jason's armed response.[2]   630

Borne from there on her Titanic dragons   MEDEA AND AEGEUS
she came to Athens, city of Pallas,
which had once seen you, most worthy Phene,
and you, too, old Periphas, both flying,   [400]
and the granddaughter of Polypemon
bearing herself aloft on strange new wings.[3]
Aegeus took her in (and should be condemned
for that one act alone), but welcoming her
was not enough. He also joined himself
to her, and she became his wife.

                And now   640
Aegeus' son, Theseus, whom his father

---

[1] Eumelus killed his son, but Apollo changed the boy into a bird.

[2] Jason married the daughter of the king of Ephyre (an ancient name for Corinth, which stood on the Isthmus and had seas on either side of its territory). Medea, seeking revenge for his infidelity, sent the new bride a poisoned tiara and dress which ate away her flesh, and she died in agony. The king of Corinth died from the poison, as well, and the palace burned down. Then Medea killed both sons she and Jason had had together.

[3] Phene was the wife of Periphas, a mythological king of Athens who was changed into a bird by Jupiter. The granddaughter of Polypemon, Alcyone, was changed into a kingfisher (for Ovid's treatment of her story see Book 11).

BOOK SEVEN

had never known, reached Athens.[1] His courage
had pacified the Isthmus between both seas.   MEDEA AND THESEUS
Medea, in an attempt to kill him,
mixed a strong poison she had brought with her
from Scythian shores. They say this venom
came from the teeth of Echidna's dog child,
Cerberus.[2] There is a hidden cavern
with a gloomy opening and a trail
leading down to Hades. Along this path   650
Hercules, hero from Tiryns, had dragged   [410]
Cerberus off in adamantine chains.[3]
The beast fought back, twisting his eyes sideways,
away from daylight and the sunshine. Roused
to savage fury, its three throats had howled,
all at once, filling the air with barking
and showering green fields with foam-white drool.
This, so men believe, hardened and, nourished
by fertile and productive soil, acquired
a noxious power. Because it is long lived   660
and springs up on solid rock, country folk
have named it aconite.[4] Through his wife's deceit,
Aegeus, the father, gave his own son   [420]
this poison, as if he were his enemy.
Theseus, suspecting nothing, took the cup
his father offered him in his right hand.
But when Aegeus recognized the signs
of his own family on the ivory hilt
of Theseus' sword, he knocked the poisoned cup
from his son's mouth. Medea fled from death   670
in a mist produced by her enchantments.

Although Aegeus was overjoyed his son   ATHENS CELEBRATES THESEUS
had not been injured, he was still amazed
such a wicked crime could be attempted

---

[1]Before coming to Athens, Aegeus had left his wife pregnant in another city, telling her that if she had a son to send him when the boy was strong enough to lift a certain stone and take out the shoes and sword hidden under it. Hence, he had not yet seen Theseus.

[2]Echidna was a famous monster, who gave birth to a number of other monsters, including Cerberus, the triple-headed dog guarding Hades.

[3]Hercules took the dog from Hades as one of his famous labours.

[4]Aconite (also called Wolfsbane) is a plant which is poisonous to human beings.

and come within a hair's breadth of success.
He lit fires on altars and heaped up gifts
for the gods. His axes struck the brawny necks
of oxen whose horns were bound with ribbon.
People assert that no day ever shone [430]
on Erectheus' city more joyful 680
than that day. Senior men and common folk
maintain the festival. They sing songs, too,
and wine inspires their happy festive mood:

> "O mighty Theseus, praised in Marathon
> for shedding the blood of that bull from Crete,
> for making farmers safe from that wild boar
> when they plough their fields in Cromyon.[1]
> Your actions killed them both. That was your gift.
> And thanks to you, the land of Epidaurus
> saw the club-wielding son of Vulcan fall. 690
> The banks of Cephisus watched you as you killed
> the cruel Procrustes, and Eleusis,
> sacred to Ceres, saw Cercyon die.
> You also did away with Sinis, too,
> whose massive strength committed evil deeds.
> He used to bend pine trees and bring their tops
> down to the ground when he wished to strew
> his victims' corpses far and wide. And the roads
> to where Leleges live in Megara
> are now secure, for you disposed of Scyron, 700
> and earth and sea deny a resting place
> for this robber's scattered bones, which, men say,
> have been for such a long time tossed around,
> old age has hardened them to solid rocks
> which carry Scyron's name.[2] And if we wished
> to count your worthy honours and your years,

---

[1] Marathon was a town near Athens, which was threatened by a bull brought into the region by Hercules. Cromyon was a village near Corinth which had to cope with a destructive wild boar. Theseus killed both beasts.

[2] These are the names of famous robbers whom Theseus killed. Vulcan's son mentioned here was Periphetes, notorious for his club. Procrustes would stretch people out or cut off their extremities so that they fit his bed. Cercyon used to challenge people to wrestle him. He would kill them if they refused or if he beat them. Sinis used to tie victims to pine trees he bent down to earth so that, when he let go, they would be catapulted a long way. Scyron forced people to wash his feet on rocks by the sea. Then he would kick them into the sea, where a tortoise ate their bodies.

your noble deeds would be more numerous.
Bravest of men, for you we offer up
our public prayers. To honour you we drain [450]
our drinks of wine."

                       The royal palace echoed 710
people's shouts and their supporting prayers,
and in the city everyone rejoiced.

But Aegeus' joy at welcoming his son   MINOS
is not complete (for, in fact, no pleasure
ever lasts—some worry always interferes
with our delight). Minos is preparing
to wage war. He has a strong force of troops
and ships, but his most powerful weapon
is a father's anger, for he is seeking,
through this war, a just revenge for the death 720
of his son Androgeus.[1] But first of all,
he gathers allied forces for the fight
and crosses the sea with the rapid fleet [460]
which makes him powerful. Then Anaphe
joins Minos' force, swearing an alliance,
and the realm of Astypalaea, too,
once he has overpowered it in war,
then after that low-lying Myconos,
the chalky island of Cimolus, Scyros
(where thyme grows everywhere), flat Seriphos, 730
and Paros, too, rich in marble, and Siphnos,
which treacherous Arne betrayed to him,
once she was paid in gold to feed her greed.[2]
For that she was transformed into a jackdaw,
a bird with feet and feathers coloured black,
which even now is still obsessed with gold.
But Oliaros, Didyme, Tenos,
Andros, Gyaros, and Peparethos, [470]
where shining olives grow abundantly,
did not assist the Cretan fleet.[3] Minos, 740
moving north from there, made for Oenopia,

[1] Minos was king of Crete. His son Androgeus was killed in Athens because he won every prize at a contest sponsored by Aegeus.

[2] The names here indicate islands close to Crete.

[3] Oliaros, Tenos, Andros, Gyaros are islands in the Aegean Sea.

the Aeacidaean realm. Ancient peoples
called it Oenopia, but Aeacus himself
named it Aegina after his own mother.   MINOS AND AEACUS
A crowd rushes down, keen to see the man
who is so famous. Telamon comes out
to meet him with his brother Peleus
(younger than Telamon) and the third son,
Phocus.[1] Aeacus comes himself, as well,
but slowed down by the weight of his old age,   750
and asks Minos the reason for his visit.
The ruler of one hundred cities sighs,
remembering his sorrow for his son,
and answers him:

        "I'm asking for your help
in a war for the sake of my own son.
You will be part of a pious action.
I'm asking that he have a burial mound,
something that will give me consolation."

The grandson of Asopus said to Minos:

        "Your request is futile. What you require   760
my city cannot do. There is no land
more closely tied to the Athenians
than this one. We ratified a treaty."

Minos was not pleased. He went away, saying:

        "That pact of yours will cost you a great deal."

He thought it more practical to threaten war
than to fight and squander his resources
prematurely in that place.

                      Cretan ships   CEPHALUS AND AEACUS
could still be seen from Aegina's battlements   [490]
when a ship from Athens, all sails flying,   770
came rushing into view and moved inside
the harbor of its ally. She carried
Cephalus, as well as a commission

---

[1] These three brothers are the sons of Aeacus, king of Aegina.

from his native land.[1] Many years had passed
since those sons of Aeacus had seen him,
but they recognized him, clasped his right hand,
and then went with him to their father's house.
The well-known hero, still showing traces
of his earlier beauty, went inside,
with an olive branch he brought from Athens.   780
As an older man, he had beside him,
to his left and right, two more youthful men
Clytos and Butes, both sons of Pallas.[2]   [500]
After some initial conversation,
Cephalus summed up, in brief, the orders
he had received from the Athenians
and asked for help, mentioning the treaty
and the oaths their ancestors had taken
and adding that Minos was intending
to conquer all Achaea. By saying this,   790
his eloquence reinforced the reasons
for the orders he had brought from Athens.
Aeacus, his left hand on the handle
of his shining sceptre, said:

                    "Athenian,
do not ask for our assistance. Help yourself.
Do not hesitate to take the forces
which this island now possesses as your own.
We do not lack resources (may this state
of my affairs continue!). I command
sufficient soldiers and, thanks to the gods,   800 [510]
this is a prosperous moment, no time
to make excuses."

                    Cephalus replied:

"May things remain that way and the number
of your citizens keep growing. Indeed,
just now, as I arrived, I was delighted
to come across so many younger folk,

---

[1] According to some accounts Cephalus was the son of Mercury and Herse, the daughter of Cecrops, king of Athens. Hence, Cecrops was Cephalus' grandfather.

[2] The Pallas mentioned here was a member of the royal family in Athens. The reference is not to Pallas Athena.

all so good looking. And yet I did miss
many of those I once saw earlier,
when I was welcomed here in your city."

Aeacus sighed and in a sombre voice
replied as follows:

"After a bad start   THE PLAGUE IN AEGINA
a better fortune follows. How I wish
I could tell you about just one of them
without the other! But now I'll go through
what happened in the order it occurred
and won't detain you with long-winded chat.   [520]
Those people you remember in your mind
and asked about are now just bones and ash.
A huge part of my resources perished,
when a dreadful plague fell on the people,
brought about by Juno's envious rage.
How she despised a land named for her rival![1]
As long as it looked like human illness
and the harmful cause of so many deaths
was hidden, we used our medical skills
to fight against it. But the destruction
swamped our efforts, which simply did not work,
once we were overwhelmed. When it started,
sky blanketed the earth in a thick fog
and with its clouds held in a stifling heat,
and while the moon joined up her horns four times   [530]
to complete her orb and then four times waned,
reducing her full sphere, hot southern winds
kept blowing lethal blasts. We can confirm
the sickness even reached our springs and lakes.
Thousands of snakes crept over untilled fields,
poisoning our rivers with their venom.
The power of this unexpected plague
first revealed itself to us by killing off
dogs, birds, sheep, cattle, and wild animals.
The wretched ploughman was amazed to see
his sturdy oxen fall down as they toiled,
collapsing in the middle of the furrow,

---

[1] Aegina, the island, was named after the nymph who was carried there by Jupiter. She was the mother of Aeacus. Jupiter was his father.

and while flocks of sheep gave out sickly bleats, [540]
their wool fell off, all on its own, as their bodies
were consumed. The lively horse, once famous
on the track, dishonoured its victories,
forgot its previous triumphs, and, now doomed
to a lingering death, groaned in its stall.
Wild boars lost any sense of their own fury, 850
deer had no confidence in their own speed,
and bears did not attack strong herds of cattle.
They were all listless. Decaying bodies
lay in the woods, fields, and roads, and the air
was putrid with the stench. And what was strange
was that dogs, ravenous birds, and gray wolves
would not touch the corpses. They died and rotted, [550]
while their noxious vapours spread contagion
far and wide. As it grew more destructive,
the fatal illness reached unlucky farmers 860
and in the major cities gained control
inside the walls. First, the inner organs
got very hot. Then these hidden inner flames
produced a reddish skin, and drawing breath
grew difficult. Tongues were rough and swollen,
men's mouths were parched, their breathing shallow.
They lay there, open mouthed, dry throats gasping
poisonous air. The sick could not endure
staying in bed or having covers on.
They lay down with their chests against hard ground. 870
But the earth did not cool off their bodies. [560]
Instead, their bodies heated up the earth.
No one could stop it. Savage destruction
broke out even among physicians, too,
and those who tried to use their healing skills
just harmed themselves. The closer people got
to ailing patients and the more faithfully
they nursed the sick, the sooner they would join
those who had died. And when men lost all hope
for any cure and realized their sickness 880
would end in death, they followed their desires
and were not interested in what might help,
since nothing seemed to work. So everywhere
people abandoned any sense of shame.
They clung to springs, wells, and streams. But drinking

did not quench their thirst, not before their lives
were over. Many of them were so ill, [570]
they could not stand up. They even died there,
right in the water. Then some other patient
would come and drink. The desperately sick
found the beds they hated so unpleasant,
they would get up and, if they lacked the strength
to stand upright, would roll their bodies out
along the ground. And people all ran off,
leaving their household gods, in the belief
their homes were deadly. They had no idea
what brought on the disease, and so they thought
the place must be at fault. You could see some
roaming the streets, half dead, if they still had
strength enough to stand, and others lying
on the earth, weeping, rolling their spent eyes
as they lay there dying. They stretched their arms
to the stars in heaven high above them, [580]
breathing their last here and there, wherever
death had overtaken them.
      How did I feel
throughout all this? What one would expect.
I hated life and wished to be a part
of my own people. Wherever my eyes
would turn to look, there were piles of bodies,
like rotten apples which have fallen down
from moving branches or acorns dropping
from a shaken oak. You see that temple
across from you, on top of those long stairs?
It belongs to Jupiter. Who did not bring
his useless offerings to those altars!
How many times did a husband praying
for his wife or a father for his son [590]
perish at the unavailing altars,
with the unused portion of the incense
still in his hand for anyone to find!
How often did the sacrificial bulls
brought to the temple suddenly fall down
without a wound, while the priest was praying
and pouring unmixed wine between its horns!
When I was personally conducting
a sacrifice to Jupiter for myself,

my three sons, and my country, the victim
gave a wretched groan and unexpectedly
collapsed without receiving any blow.
Its blood left hardly any stains on knives 930
we thrust into its belly. Its entrails,
full of disease, had lost all indications [600]
of the truth and of warnings from the gods.[1]
The deadly working of that pestilence
moved deep within, right to inner organs.
I saw dead bodies by the sacred doors
and at the very altars, thrown down there,
so the deaths were even more offensive.[2]
Some people used a noose to end their lives
and by dying escaped the fear of death, 940
quite willing to bring on their looming fate.
Bodies of the dead were not sent away
with any of the customary rites
(the city gates could not accommodate
the funerals). They lay there on the ground
unburied or were simply thrown away
on lofty burial sites. For by this time
no reverence remained. People quarreled
about the pyres, and dead bodies were burned [610]
in flames prepared for someone else. No one 950
was left to weep, and the souls of children
and parents, of the young and old, wandered
unlamented. Places used for burials
had no space or wood for funeral fires.
Overwhelmed by such a huge storm of despair,
I cried out:

      'O Jupiter, if those stories
about you are not false when people say
Aegina, daughter of Asopus, held you
in her arms and if, O mighty father,
you are not ashamed to be my parent, 960

---

[1] Inspecting the entrails of sacrificial animals for prophetic omens was an important element in many sacrifices.

[2] The gods found dead bodies repugnant. Placing corpses by the temples and altars was thus, one assumes, meant to encourage them to intervene and halt the disease.

> give me back my people, or else put me
> with them in a common burial mound.'

He offered me a sign with flashing lightning   THE MYRMIDONS
and another with his thunder. I said:

> 'I take these omens you have given me   [620]
> as pledges. I accept them, and I pray
> they indicate your favour and signal
> what you mean to do.'

Now, it so happened
that close beside me stood an oak tree
sacred to Jupiter, whose seed had come   970
from his holy temple at Dodona.
Its branches were spread out and thinly spaced.[1]
Here I observed some ants collecting grain
in a long column, carrying big loads
in tiny mouths, and following a track
across the wrinkled bark. I was amazed
how numerous they were, and so I said:

> 'O best of fathers, give me this many
> citizens and restock my empty walls.'

The tall oak trembled, and its branches moved.   980
Although there was no wind, they made a sound.
My limbs were quivering, shaking with fear,   [630]
and my hair stood up on end. But I kissed
the earth and the oak, not yet admitting
there was any hope, and yet it gave me hope.
I kept my cherished wishes in my heart.
Then, as night came on, sleep took possession
of my body, worn out with so much care,
and the same oak tree appeared to be there,
before my eyes, with just as many branches,   990
just as many creatures in those branches,
all quivering the way they did before,
and shaking that row of ants collecting grain
down to the ground below. Then these creatures
suddenly grew, looking larger and larger,

---

[1] Dodona, the site of a major shrine to Zeus, had a famous oak tree which played a major role in the oracle there.

and raised themselves to stand up on the ground,
bodies now erect. They lost their slender shape,
their numerous feet, and their black colour.
Their limbs then altered into human forms.
Sleep left. Once awake, I dismissed the dream,
complaining I had got no help at all
from gods above. But inside the palace
there was a noisy sound of people talking.
It seemed to me I could hear men's voices
(and by this time I was not used to that).
I assumed these sounds were still part of my dream,
as well, but Telamon came running up,
threw open the doors, and shouted:

'Father!
Come outside! There are things to see out here
beyond belief, beyond what you could hope!'
I went outside and there I saw some men
like those I'd seen as images in sleep,
arranged in lines in a similar way,
and one I recognized. They came to me
and hailed me as their king. I carried out
my oath to Jupiter, dividing up
the city and its fields, now quite empty
of farmers who had worked in them before,
among the people who had just arrived.
I called them Myrmidons, which I derived
from *myrmex*, meaning *ant*, a name I chose
because it fit those people's origins.[1]
You have seen their bodies. They still follow
the customs they once had in earlier times
and are a thrifty people, hard working,
striving tenaciously for what they want,
and hanging on to what they get. These men,
whose spirits match their age, will follow you
to war, once that favourable east wind
which brought you here veers to the south."

---

[1] I have added the phrase about the derivation of the name from the Greek word in order to clarify the reason the name suits their origins.

Book Seven

>   And, in fact,
> an eastern wind had helped him reach the place.

With these and other stories the two men   CEPHALUS AND PROCRIS
filled a lengthy day. The last part of the light
they spent feasting, and when night came they slept.
The golden Sun brought forth his light once more,
but East Wind was still blowing, holding back
the ships which meant to sail for home that day.
Pallas' two sons met up with Cephalus,
a more senior man, and the three of them
went to meet the king. But he was still asleep.   1040
Phocus, a son of Aeacus, met them
at the door (Telamon and his brother
were mustering men for war), escorted
the Athenians inside the palace,   [670]
to a beautiful, secluded spot, and there
they sat together. Then Phocus noticed
that Cephalus held in his hand a spear
with a golden point, made out of a wood
he had not seen before. So as they spoke
their first few words, Phocus interrupted   1050
what they were saying to ask about the spear:

> "I have a good knowledge of the forests
> and of hunting animals, but for some time
> I've been curious about what kind of wood
> is in the shaft of that spear you're holding.
> If it were ash, surely it would be brown.
> If made of cornel wood, it would have knots.
> I have no idea where it might come from,
> but my eyes have never seen a weapon   [680]
> more beautifully designed for throwing."   1060

One of the Athenian brothers answered:

> "With this spear you will be more astonished
> by its effectiveness than by its looks.
> No matter where it's aimed, it strikes its target.
> Once it is thrown, no chance affects its path,
> and it flies back on its own, stained with blood.
> No one needs to run and get it."

>   This reply
> made Phocus eager to learn more. He asked

all sorts of questions. Why was the spear like this?
Where did it come from? Who had given him
such a wondrous gift? Cephalus answered
what he asked, but was still ashamed to state
what he had paid for it. He fell silent.
Moved by a sense of grief for his lost wife,
he felt tears welling up and said these words:

> "Son of a goddess, this spear makes me weep
> (who could believe that!), and if Fates grant me
> a lengthy life, this same effect you see
> will be produced for many years to come.
> This weapon finished me and my dear wife.
> How I wish I'd never had this present!
> My wife was Procris, sister of that girl
> who was carried away, Orithyïa.
> Though Orithyïa is one your ears
> are far more likely to have heard about,
> if you wanted to compare the two of them
> for looks and manners, Procris was the one
> more worth abducting.[1] King Erectheus,
> her father, joined her to me in marriage,
> and love linked us, as well. People called me
> a happy man, and I was. But to the gods
> that is not how things appeared. Otherwise
> I would perhaps be happy even now.
> The second month after our marriage rites,
> bright Aurora was chasing off the night
> and caught sight of me from the topmost peak
> of Mount Hymettus, where flowers always bloom,
> while I was putting nets in place to catch
> wild deer with horns.[2] She carried me away
> against my will. By the goddess' grace,
> I may speak the truth. Though she is lovely
> with her rosy face, though she looks after
> border regions of the light and darkness,
> though she feeds herself on liquid nectar,
> I loved Procris. Procris was in my heart.
> Procris was always on my lips. I kept

AURORA AND CEPHALUS

---

[1] For Ovid's treatment of the abduction of Orithyïa by Boreas see above 6.1100 ff.

[2] Mount Hymettus was in Attica.

Book Seven

talking about our sacred marriage couch,
the recent consummation of our love,
our wedding held just a short time before, [710]
and the prior rights of our empty bed.
The goddess grew annoyed and said to me:

> 'Stop your complaining, you ungrateful man.
> Keep your Procris! But if my mind can see
> into the future, you are going to wish
> you did not have her!'

                      Still very angry,
she sent me back to Procris. On my way home,
mulling in my heart what the goddess said,
I began to fear my wife might have betrayed
our marriage vows. Her youth and loveliness
forced me to think of infidelity,
but her virtue told me to place no trust
in thoughts like that. Still, I had been away,
I was returning home from a woman
who exemplified that fault, and lovers
are afraid of everything. So I chose
to explore a thing that might be painful— [720]
to test her faithful chastity with gifts.
Aurora encouraged my anxieties
and changed the way I looked (it seemed to me
I could feel her doing it). I went back
to Athens, city of Pallas—no one
knew who I was—and entered my own home.
In the house itself nothing was amiss.
It showed signs that everyone was faithful
and worried that their master was not there.
It was hard for me to come face to face
with Erectheus' daughter—I had to use
a thousand ploys. But when I did meet her,
I was astonished and almost gave up
my plans to test her constancy. In fact,
I found it difficult to keep myself
from telling her the truth and difficult
not giving her a kiss, as I should have done.
She was grieving (but no woman could be [730]
more beautiful than she was in her grief),
suffering with longing for her husband,

who had been snatched away. Phocus, just think
what sort of beauty that woman possessed
who looked so lovely even in her sorrow!
Why should I describe for you how often   1150
her chaste manners spurned my invitations,
how often she said:

             'I am committed
  to one man alone, wherever he is.
  The pleasure I can give I keep for him.'

What husband in his senses would not find
that test of her fidelity sufficient?
But I was not content. I battled on
to wound myself, until, by promising
to confer a fortune on her for one night
and then increasing the amount, at last   1160 [740]
I forced her to relent. By these false means
I won the day and cried:

               'You evil woman,
  this adultery is merely a pretense!
  You traitor, I am your real husband
  You have been caught, and I have witnessed it!'

She said nothing. Overwhelmed with silent shame,
she ran away from her deceitful home
and her wicked husband. Resenting me,
hating the whole race of men, she wandered
in the mountains, basing her way of life   1170
on the customs of divine Diana.
Now I was alone, and a fiercer flame
burned in my bones. I pleaded for forgiveness,
conceding I was wrong and confessing
I, too, if offered gifts, could have committed
such a fault, if such generous presents   [750]
had been proposed. When I admitted this,
at first she punished me for disrespect,
since I had injured her, and then came back.
We spent sweet years, living in harmony.   1180
As if, in giving herself, she had given
a trifling present, she also offered me
the gift of a dog which she had once received
from her own goddess Cynthia, who said:

Book Seven

'He will surpass all other hounds in running.'
At the same time she offered me this spear,
which, as you can see, my hand is holding.
Would you like to learn about what happened
to the dog, that other gift? Then listen
to an astounding story. You will be stirred [1190]
by the amazing details of the tale.

With his own intelligence, Oedipus,
son of Laius, had deciphered the songs
which no one else had understood before,
and that mysterious prophetess, the Sphinx,
had collapsed and lay there, her riddling words [760]
forgotten.[1] But, of course, nurturing Themis
does not let such things go without revenge.
Immediately she sent another scourge   LAELAPS
against Aonian Thebes. Many farmers [1200]
feared the wild beast would destroy their cattle
and kill them, too.[2] We young men of the town
all came and closed off our extensive fields
inside a cordon. But the quick creature,
with an easy leap, overcame our nets
and moved across the tops of traps we set.
We unleashed the dogs. The wild beast ran off
with the hounds in hot pursuit, but its speed,
no slower than a bird in flight, mocked them. [770]
So then with one loud voice they all begged me [1210]
to untie Laelaps (the name of the dog
my wife had given me). By now this hound
for some time had been pulling at his leash,
straining his neck to shake off all restraints.
As soon as we had sent him on his way,
we could no longer tell where he might be.
He left traces of warm footprints in the dust,
but he himself had vanished from our eyes.
No spear could fly more quickly than that dog,

---

[1] Oedipus solved the riddle of the Sphinx and thus destroyed the Sphinx and saved Thebes from a deadly plague.

[2] Ovid does not indicate precisely what the "scourge" or the "wild beast" was. In traditional accounts of the story it was a monstrous female fox (called the Teumessian fox, after a city in Boeotia, or the Cadmean vixen).

Book Seven

no pellet hurled from any twisted sling,   1220
nor any arrow from a Cretan bow.
A hill stood in the middle of the plain,
the top of which looked down on land below.
I went up there to watch the spectacle   [780]
of this curious race, where at one moment
the wild beast looked as if it had been caught,
and at another seemed to pull away
without a scratch. The crafty animal,
as it raced across the ground, did not keep
to a straight line, but escaped the muzzle   1230
of the pursuing dog by circling round,
so its enemy could not launch a charge.
The dog stayed close, kept up a similar pace,
seemed to catch it, but did not have a grip—
his empty snapping fanned the air in vain.
I turned to use my spear. While hefting it
in my right hand, trying to fit my fingers
in the throwing strap, I turned my eyes away.
Then I brought them back to the selfsame spot.
I looked and saw something incredible—   1240
two statues in the middle of the plain,   [790]
made of marble! You could well imagine
one was running away, the other one
pursuing. It was clear that if some god
was with those animals, he wanted both
of those contestants to remain unbeaten."

Cephalus ended that part of his tale
and said no more. Phocus asked:

              "And that spear—
what has it done wrong?"

              Cephalus then told him
about the crimes committed by the spear: 1250

"Phocus, my sad story begins with joy,
and I will talk of that part first. O son
of Aeacus, I get such great delight
remembering the blessed times we had,
when in our early years I had the luck
to live in such content with my dear wife,
and she was happy with her husband, too.

Book Seven

With love we shared all mutual concerns.
She would not have chosen Jupiter's bed
before my love, and there was no woman
who could capture me, not even Venus,
if she had come in person. Equal fires
burned in both our hearts. Like an eager youth,
it was my custom to go out hunting
just as the sun's first rays shone on the hills.
I would have no servants following me,
no horses, no keen-nosed hunting dogs,
no knotted nets. My safety was my spear.
But after my right hand had had enough
of slaughtering wild beasts, I would go back
into the cool shade where a breeze blew in
from colder valleys. When it was really hot,
I'd seek that soothing breeze or wait for it
as a way of resting after my hard work.
I remember how I used to sing:

                'Aura,'

(that was the name I used to call the breeze)

> 'come, you most pleasurable one, bring me
> your sweet delight, come here into my heart,
> and of your own free will relieve this heat
> which I find so oppressive!'[1]

                And perhaps I'd add
more coaxing words (as my fate led me on),
and I may have grown accustomed to repeat:

> 'You are my great delight. You refresh me,
> cherish me, and make me love the woodlands
> and these solitary places. Your breath
> is always trapped inside these lips of mine.'

Someone overheard me (I don't know who),
misunderstood my ambiguous words,
and assumed the name I called so often

---

[1] In the Latin text, the point of the story which follows depends upon the word *aura*, meaning *breeze*, which, because of its feminine gender and its final vowel, could be confused with a woman's name as soon as Cephalus personifies the breeze and starts talking to it. For that reason, I have retained the Latin word *aura* in some places, rather than using the English word *breeze*. I have added the line in brackets to clarify the point.

belonged to a nymph called Aura. He thought 1290
I was in love with her. This rash witness
to an imagined crime at once went off
to Procris and, in whispers, let her know
what he had heard. Love is a credulous thing.
They told me she collapsed in instant pain
and fainted. A long time later she came to,
said she felt sad about her evil fate,
and complained about my lack of loyalty.
Upset by bad acts which did not take place,
her fears were empty. She dreaded a name 1300 [830]
which had no body. The poor woman grieved
as though she had a genuine rival.
But often she had doubts and, as she grieved,
she entertained the hope that she was wrong,
saying she did not trust the evidence
and would not denounce her husband for a crime,
unless she had witnessed it in person.
The following day, when Aurora's light
had pushed away the darkness, I set off,
heading for the woods. Once I had hunted 1310
with some success, I lay down on the grass
and called:

      'Come, Aura—ease my aching limbs.'

Suddenly, as I was saying these words,
it seemed to me I heard a certain moaning—
I had no idea what it might be—but still
I called:

      'Come here, my most delightful one!'

Fallen leaves lightly rustled in reply. [840]
I thought a wild creature must be in there
and let fly with my spear. It was Procris.
With a wound in the middle of her breast, 1320
she cried:

      'Alas! I'm hurt!'

                  Once I heard
the voice of my loyal wife, I rushed out
and, in a frantic state, charged towards it.
I found her half-alive, her clothes all torn

and stained with blood, and (to my great grief)
she was tugging at the spear stuck in her wound,
the gift she'd given me. In gentle arms
I picked up the body which I cherished
more than my own. I bound the cruel wound
by ripping up the clothing on her chest.   1330
I tried to stanch the flow of blood and begged her
not to abandon me and with her death   [850]
make me a criminal. As she lost strength
and was about to die, she forced herself
to utter these few words:

                'I implore you,
as a suppliant, by our marriage bonds,
by my own household gods and those above,
by any good you owe for what I've done,
and by what has occasioned my own death,
that love which even now, as I lie dying,   1340
still lives, do not marry that nymph Aura!
Do not let her share our marriage bed!'

She ended. Then I finally understood
how Aura's name had led to her mistake.
I told her. But how could informing her
be any help at all? She began to fail.
What little strength she had was leaving her,
as her blood flowed out. While she was able   [860]
to look at anything, she looked at me,
and her unhappy spirit she breathed out   1350
on me and on my lips. But she did seem
to be quite free from worry as she died,
with a more tranquil look upon her face."

The hero shed tears as he told this tale,
and his listeners wept, as well. And then,
lo and behold, king Aeacus arrived
with his two other sons, along with soldiers
they had just gathered, all heavily armed.
These Aeacus then gave to Cephalus.

BOOK EIGHT
VIII

[Cephalus returns to Athens; Minos attacks Megara; Scylla falls in love with Minos; Scylla cuts her father's lock of hair and takes it to Minos; Minos rejects her, conquers the city, and leaves; Scylla is changed into a bird; Minos has Daedalus build the labyrinth for the Minotaur; Theseus kills the Minotaur with Ariadne's help and abandons her on Dia; Bacchus changes Ariadne's crown into a constellation; Daedalus makes wings for himself and Icarus; Icarus falls to his death; Daedalus and Perdix; Perdix is changed into a bird; Diana sends a destructive wild boar against Calydon; Meleager assembles a group of hunters; Atalanta's arrow hits the boar; Meleager kills the boar and awards a prize to Atalanta; Plexippus and Toxeus are killed by Meleager; Althaea avenges the death of her brothers by burning the log that determines Meleager's life; Calydon mourns Meleager; Meleager's sisters are changed to birds; Theseus is entertained by Acheloüs, who tells him the story of the Echinades islands and Perimele; Lelex tells the story of Philemon and Baucis, who welcomed Jupiter and Mercury and were changed to trees; Acheloüs tells the story of Erysichthon, who chopped down Ceres' sacred tree; Ceres' gets Hunger to infect Erysichthon; Erysichthon sells his daughter Maestra, but Neptune transforms her; Erysichthon eats himself.]

NISUS AND SCYLLA

Now, after Lucifer dismissed the night,
unveiling a brilliant day, East Wind died down,
moist clouds blew in, and a welcome South Wind
gave Cephalus and Aeacus' sons
their way of getting back.[1] Thanks to that wind,
which kept them on a favourable course,
they reached the harbour they were heading for
sooner than expected. In the meantime,
Minos was laying waste Lelegian lands
along the coast. Before attempting that, 10
he had tried to test his army's fighting strength
in an attack on Megara, where Nisus ruled.
Now, on top of his illustrious head,
amid the white hairs there, Nisus possessed
a lock distinguished by its purple colour.
The security of his great kingdom [10]
depended on that lock of purple hair.

The horns of the waxing moon had risen
six times, and still the outcome of the war
was hanging in the balance. For a long time 20
Victory hovered between both armies
on uncertain wings. A regal tower
had been built within the musical walls,
where men claimed Apollo, Latona's son,

---

[1]Cephalus is returning to his city, Athens. The sons of Aeacus, residents of Aegina, are accompanying him, to help deal with the threat from Minos (see the end of Book 7).

BOOK EIGHT

had placed his golden lyre and where its sound
was present in the stone.[1] Nisus' daughter,
Scylla, would often go up to that spot
during peacetime and with a small pebble
attempt to get some music from the stones.
During the war she would also go there,   30
and from the tower look out on the struggles   [20]
of unyielding battle. Because that war
kept going on and on, by now she knew
the names of the leading men, their weapons,
horses, styles of dress, and Cretan quivers.
Before all others, she could recognize   SCYLLA AND MINOS
their leader's face—Europa's son, Minos—
whom she knew more about than was required
to know just who he was. For if Minos
wore on his head a helmet with a plume,   40
she thought the helmet made him so attractive,
if he carried his brilliant shield of bronze,
he looked so handsome carrying the shield,
if his taut muscles hurled a heavy spear,
the young girl praised his power and his skill,
and when he placed an arrow on his bow   [30]
and bent the wide arc back, she used to swear
that was just how Phoebus Apollo stood,
with arrows he had chosen for himself.
Whenever Minos took his helmet off   50
to expose his face and, dressed in purple,
sat on the back of his white horse, equipped
with an ornate saddle, directing it
by its foaming bit, Nisus' virgin child
could hardly keep herself under control,
hardly stop her mind from going insane.
She'd call the spear he touched a happy spear,
and happy, too, the reins gripped in his hands.
She had an urge (if only she could do it!)
to lead her virgin steps through hostile ranks,   60
and felt like hurling her body down there,
from the very top part of the tower,   [40]
onto the Cretan camp, or opening

---

[1]When king Alcathoüs repaired the walls of Megara, Apollo helped him, and the god's lyre imparted to the stones some of its musical qualities.

Book Eight

the brass gates to the enemy forces,
or anything else Minos might desire.
As she sat gazing down on the white tents
of the Cretan king, she said:

"I don't know
if I should be miserable or happy
that this appalling war is going on.
I'm sad that Minos is an enemy
of the one who loves him. But if this war
had never broken out, I would not know him!
Still, if he were to take me hostage, he could
end this war. With me as his companion,
he could hold me as a guarantee of peace.
O most beautiful of kings, if the woman
who gave birth to you had a face like yours,
no wonder Jupiter burned with love for her.[1]
O, I would be happy three times over,
if I could travel through the air with wings,
touch down in the camp of the Cretan king,
reveal myself, and show my flaming love!
I would ask him what dowry he would want
to be won over, with this provision—
he would not demand my father's city.
I would sooner my hopes for marriage die
than that I should be able to betray him!
But still, if a peace-loving conqueror
is merciful, he often benefits
many of those he has just overwhelmed.
The war he's fighting for his slaughtered son
is clearly just.[2] His cause and the weapons
which defend that cause are very powerful.
And so it seems to me we will be crushed.
If that is to be our city's destiny,
why should these walls of ours be opened up
by his armed force and not by my own love?
It would be better if he could prevail
without killing or delay or shedding
his own blood. At least then I would not fear

---

[1] Minos was the son of Jupiter and Europa.

[2] Minos was avenging his son who had been killed in Athens.

Book Eight

someone might wound your heart by accident,
Minos, for who would be so pitiless,
he'd dare to aim his cruel spear at you,
unless he did not know you? This notion
pleases me, and I'll stand by my resolve
to give myself to you, with my country
as a dowry, and put an end to war.
But wanting to do this is not enough!
A guard stands watching at the entrance way.
My father has the keys for all the gates. 110 [70]
In my sorry state, he is the only one
I'm scared of, the only one delaying
what I desire. O how I wish the gods
could arrange things so I had no father!
But everyone is really his own god,
and Fortune is the foe of idle prayers.
By this time, another woman aflame
with such great passion would be rejoicing
in the ruin of whatever blocked her love.
Why should any woman have more courage 120
than I do? I would dare to go through fire
and through swords. But this time there is no need
for fires or swords. All I need is that lock
from my father's head. To me that purple lock
is more valuable than gold. With that hair [80]
I will be happy and get what I desire."

As Scylla was saying these words, night came,   SCYLLA AND NISUS
great healer of our cares. With the shadows
her boldness grows. The early hours of rest
have now arrived, when sleep takes possession 130
of hearts weary from their daytime worries.
She creeps softly into her father's room,
and (alas for such a criminal act!)
the daughter steals that fatal lock of hair
from her own father. Once she has taken
her abominable prize she goes out
through the middle of the enemy camp
(she has such confidence in the service
she is performing) and reaches Minos,
who is astonished when she speaks to him, 140
and says:

"Love urged me to commit this crime.　　　　　[90]
I am Scylla, royal child of Nisus,
and I am giving you my household gods
and my native land. I seek no reward,
other than yourself. Take this purple hair
as a pledge of love. And trust me in this—
I am not giving you just a lock of hair,
but my father's head, as well!"

　　　　　　　　　She holds out the gift　　MINOS AND SCYLLA
in her treasonous right hand, but Minos
backs away from what she is offering him.　　150
Shocked by the thought of her unnatural act,
he answers:

　　　　　　　"O you disgrace to this age
in which we live, may the gods banish you
from their world, and may all lands and waters
be denied you! I, at least, will not let
someone so monstrous come into my world,　　[100]
into Crete, land where Jupiter was born."

Minos spoke. Then this most just of rulers,
once he had imposed laws on the people
he had conquered, gave orders to his troops　　160
to loosen the ships' cables, man the oars,
and row the bronze-beaked vessels out to sea.
When Scylla saw the fleet was setting off,
already underway across the waves,
she realized their leader would not give her
anything to reward her treachery.
Since she had no more prayers to offer,
her emotions turned to virulent rage.
Hair dishevelled, she held out both her hands
and, in a frenzy, screamed:

　　　　　　　　　"Where are you running—　　170
discarding the one who brought you your success?
O you, whom I chose before my country,
before my father, where are you fleeing,
you heartless man? I deserve the credit　　　　[110]
for your conquest, which is my crime, as well.
Are you not moved by the gift I gave you,
or by my love for you, or by the fact

BOOK EIGHT

that all my hopes now rest on you alone?
If you abandon me, where shall I go?
To my country? It has been overpowered
and lies conquered. But even if my land
were still intact, it would be closed against me,
thanks to my treachery! To my father,
whom I betrayed to you? The citizens,
for their own good reasons, all despise me,
and neighbours fear me as a bad example.
I have shut myself off from all the world,
so Crete alone would be open to me.
So if you, too, keep me away from you
and leave me here, you man without a heart,
Europa could not have been your mother,
but rather that inhospitable Syrtis,
or some Armenian tigress, or Charybdis,
whipped up by southern winds. And you are not
a son of Jupiter, nor was your mother
led astray by the image of some bull.[1]
That story of your birth is all made up!
Yes, your father was a bull—a wild beast
never tamed by love for any heifer!
O Nisus, my father, come punish me!
And you walls which I betrayed, take pleasure
from my pain! For I deserve your hatred—
I admit that. And I deserve to die.
But let one of those whom my impiety
has harmed destroy me. Why punish my crime,
Minos, when it produced your victory?
My criminal act against my father
and my country was a kindness to you.
You are certainly a worthy husband
for that woman who, with a wooden frame,
tricked that bull into adulterous sex
and in her womb bore a misshapen child.[2]

---

[1] Syrtis was a quicksand near the coast of Africa. The tigers of Armenia were famous for their ferocity. Charybdis was a vicious whirlpool in the sea off Sicily. Jupiter assumed the form of a bull in order to abduct Europa. For Ovid's treatment of the story see 2.1236 above.

[2] Pasiphaë, wife of Minos, overwhelmed with lust for a bull sent by Poseidon, had a wooden frame built in the shape of a cow, so she could conceal herself inside and have sex with the animal. The offspring of the union was the Minotaur, a destructive monster, part human, part bull. For Minos' response see 8.248 below.

Is anything I say reaching your ears,
you ungrateful man, or do the same winds
carrying your fleet away also steal
these useless words of mine? And now, yes, now
I'm not surprised Pasiphaë preferred
that bull to you—you're a more savage brute!
How wretched I am! He's ordering them
to scurry off, and now waves are hissing
to the rhythm of their oars, while my land
and I both fade from view. But that won't work!
Your efforts to forget my services
will not succeed. I'll be following you,
against your will, clutching the curved sternpost
on your ship, dragged far across the ocean."

Her speech is hardly over when she jumps
into the waves and swims after the ships.
Her passion gives her strength to hang on there,
to the Cretan vessel, a companion
who is not welcome. Her father sees her
(he has just been changed to a sea eagle
hovering in the air on tawny wings).
He swoops down to tear her into pieces
with his hooked beak, as she is clinging there.
Scylla, in terror, lets go of the stern,
but as she falls, the gentle breezes seem
to hold her so she does not touch the water.
Feathers are growing up out of her arms,
and she is changed into the bird we call
Ciris, or the shearer, a name she gets
for cutting off her father's lock of hair.[1]

As soon as Minos reached the land of Crete,   MINOS AND THE MINOTAUR
he disembarked. To fulfill a promise
he had made to Jupiter, he sacrificed
one hundred oxen and hung his trophies
in the palace as a decoration.
But he faced a growing family scandal.
The shameful adultery of the queen
was obvious from the bizarre nature

---

[1] It is not clear what bird Ovid is referring to. The name *Ciris* allegedly comes from the Greek work meaning *to cut*.

of her hybrid monster child.[1] Minos
chose to move this disgrace out of his home
and to keep it in a complex structure,
a labyrinth built with blind passages.
Daedalus, a man highly celebrated   DAEDALUS
for his skill in architecture, drew up   [160]
the plans. With confusing direction marks
he led the eye into a wandering maze
of various twisting pathways. Just as
the playful waters of the Maeander   260
keep changing course, as they flow here and there
across the fields in Phrygia and can see
the waves upstream moving down towards them,
while their uncertain currents sometimes flow
to their sources, sometimes to the open sea,
that's how Daedalus designed the pathways,
countless wandering passages in the maze.
The structure was so hard to navigate,
that even Daedalus found it difficult
to find his way back to the entry point.[2]   270

In that labyrinth Minos imprisoned
the monstrous double shape of bull and man.
Twice he fed it blood from young Athenians   [170]
chosen by lot at nine-year intervals.
But the third time he collected tribute,
the monster was overcome, for Theseus,   THESEUS AND ARIADNE
son of Aegeus, with the assistance
of young Ariadne, Minos' daughter,
by following a thread made his way back
on the tricky pathway to the entrance,   280
a trip no one had ever made before.
He immediately set sail for Dia,
taking Ariadne with him, but then
cruelly abandoned his companion

---

[1] The hybrid monster, as mentioned above, is the Minotaur—half bull, half human.

[2] The Maeander river (in Asia Minor) was famous for its many ox-bow curves, in which one section of the river looped around and came very close to an earlier portion of the stream. Thus, the downstream waters could, as it were, observe the water further upstream which would soon occupy their present position. The very curved shape of the river meant that sometimes it looked as if the currents in two adjacent sections were flowing in different directions.

on the shore.¹ The girl, in her isolation,
wept bitter tears, but Bacchus embraced her
and provided help. Taking off the crown
around her head, he set it in the sky,
to make her famous as an eternal star.
Up through the lighter air it soared aloft   290
and, as it moved, its jewels were transformed   [180]
to brilliant fires. They settled into place,
retaining still the outline of a crown,
halfway between the kneeling Hercules
and the serpent held by Ophiuchus.²

Meanwhile, Daedalus had grown frustrated   DAEDALUS AND ICARUS
with Crete and his long exile there. He yearned
for his own land, but was held back by the sea.³
He said:

    "Minos may block off land and sea,
but surely the sky is open to us—   300
and that's the route we'll take. He may control
all things, but he does not control the air."

He spoke and then set his mind to thinking
of inventions as yet unknown, and thus
he changed the course of nature. For he arranged
rows of feathers, taking the smallest first   [190]
and then longer ones laid out in sequence,
so it looked as if they'd grown out on a slope,
like those ancient pipes shepherds used to play,
with different reeds which lengthened gradually.   310
Those in the centre he then joined with thread,
those at the ends with wax. Once the feathers

---

¹After Minos defeated Athens, he demanded several young people from the city be shipped to Crete periodically. These he put into the labyrinth, where they were destroyed by the Minotaur. Theseus was part of the third delegation of victims. Ariadne gave him the idea of unwinding a thread as he moved through the labyrinth, so that he could find his way back again. Theseus went in, killed the Minotaur, and followed the thread back to the entrance. Dia is another name for the island of Naxos, where Theseus abandoned Ariadne.

²Like some other translators, I have supplied the names Hercules and Ophiunchus ("Serpent Bearer") in order to clarify the astrological reference to the position of the new constellation (Corona Borealis). It is not clear from Ovid's account where Ariadne's crown came from.

³Daedalus (who in many legends was an Athenian) had been exiled for murder, and Minos would not let him leave Crete. In some accounts Minos was angry with Daedalus for building the wooden cow which the queen, Pasiphaë, had used to have sex with a bull.

were assembled in this way, he shaped them
into a gentle curve, so they looked like
wings of real birds. His son Icarus
stood beside him, unaware that the things
he touched would put his life in danger.
Sometimes he laughed as he caught the feathers
shifting around in the wandering breeze
or with his thumb softened the yellow wax   320
and with his playful games kept interrupting
his father's miraculous construction.
When Daedalus had put the final touches   [200]
on what he had begun, he raised himself
into the moving air, balancing his body
between a pair of wings. He also gave
the following instructions to his son:

> "I warn you, Icarus—limit your flight
> to the region between heaven and earth.
> If you go too low, then water vapour   330
> will weigh down your wings. If you go too high,
> fire will burn them. So fly between the two.
> And listen. Do not look at Boötes,
> Helice, or the drawn sword of Orion.
> I will guide you. Follow the path I take!"[1]

While Daedalus was telling him the rules
of flying, he adjusted the new wings
on Icarus' shoulders. While he worked
and issued his advice, the old man's cheeks   [210]
were wet, and the father's hands were trembling.   340
He kissed his son (he would not kiss him again),
moved upward on his wings, and flew ahead,
concerned for his companion. Just as a bird
leads her tender chicks out of their high nest
into the air, Daedalus keeps encouraging
his son to follow, as he demonstrates
his skill in the dangerous art of flight.
While moving his own wings, he glances back
at the wings of Icarus behind him.
Those who catch sight of them—a man angling   350

---

[1]Helice was an alternative name for the constellation of the Great Bear. Boötes was the constellation of the Herdsman.

for fish with a trembling rod, a shepherd
leaning on his staff, or a farmer resting
on his plough—are astonished and assume
that people who can travel through the sky
must be divine.

                    By now the island Samos,   [220]
sacred to goddess Juno, was on their left,
while Delos and Paros lay behind them,
with Lebinthus on their right, along with
Calymne, rich in honey.[1] At this point,
Icarus started to enjoy the flight,   360
for all its perils, so he left his guide
and, filled with a desire to reach heaven,
pursued a higher path. His close approach
to the fierce Sun softened the fragrant wax
which held his wings in place. The wax melted.
He flapped his naked arms, but since he had
no oar-like wings, he failed to catch the air.
While his mouth was screaming his father's name,
his cries were drowned out by the sky-blue sea   [230]
which takes its name from him.[2] His sad father,   370
now no more a father, shouted:

                            "Icarus!
Where are you, Icarus? Where should I look
to find out where you are?"

                        He kept on calling
"Icarus!"

                      Then he noticed feathers
in the waves and cursed his own inventive skills.
He buried his son's body in a tomb
in a place whose name became Icaria,
after the young lad who was buried there.

As Daedalus was placing the body   DAEDALUS AND PERDIX
of his unlucky son inside that tomb,   380

---

[1] Samos was an island off the coast of Asia Minor. Lebinthus was in the group of islands called the Cyclades, and Calymne was an island near Rhodes.

[2] That is, the Icarian Sea, the southern part of the Aegean between the Cyclades islands and Asia Minor.

a chattering partridge peering at him
from a muddy ditch flapped its wings and sang
to indicate its great delight. Back then,
it was the single member of its kind,
a bird no one had seen in previous years.
It had been created not long before,
as an enduring symbol of your shame,
Daedalus. For your sister, not knowing
what Fate had in store, sent her son to you,
so you could teach him. He was twelve years old
and had a mind eager for instruction.
He was the one who looked at a fish spine
and, with that as his model, cut iron
to make a solid row of sharpened teeth
and came up with the invention of a saw.
He was the first to join two metal arms
at one central point, so when they were kept
a constant distance from each other, one arm
stayed in place while the other one traced out
a circle. Daedalus, in a jealous fit,
threw the boy headlong from the citadel
sacred to Minerva and falsely claimed
the boy had fallen off. But Minerva,
who likes creative minds, gathered him up
and changed him to a bird, covering him
with feathers in the middle of the air.
The inventive energy he once had
was transferred to his rapid wings and feet,
and he retained the name he had before.[1]
But this bird does not raise its body up
high in the air or make its nest in branches
or in treetops, but flies close to the ground
and lays its eggs in hedges, for it recalls
that earlier drop and fears high places.

Daedalus, now tired out, is living
in the land of Aetna, and Cocalus,
responding to his petition for help,
has taken up arms and thus earned himself

---

[1] In his version of this story Ovid does not give names to the sister or to her son. The latter would, one assumes, be called *Perdix*, after the Latin for *partridge* (the bird he is transformed into). In some versions of the story the sister's name is Perdix and the son's name is Talus.

a noble reputation for his kindness.¹
By now, thanks to what Theseus has done,
Athens no longer pays that mournful tribute,
flowers adorn the temples, and people
call out to warrior Minerva, Jupiter,
and other gods, honouring them with gifts,
sacrificial blood, and chests of incense.²
Roaming Fame has spread the name of Theseus
to every city in Argos, and all those
who live in rich Achaea seek his help
when great dangers threaten. Of these cities,
one is Calydon, which comes to Theseus,
as a suppliant, begging him for aid
with urgent prayers, even though the place
has Meleager on its side.³ Their appeal
is caused by a wild boar sent by Diana,
her servant and avenger. She is angry,
because king Oeneus, so people say,
after fine harvests in a bumper year,
offered the first fruits of his crops to Ceres,
of wine to Bacchus, and of flowing oil
from olives to golden-haired Minerva.
He has paid these ostentatious honours
first of all to the rural deities,
and then to all the gods in heaven above.
The story goes that he forgot the altars
of Latona's daughter, the only ones
he ignored and left without their incense.
Rage has its effect, even on the gods.
Diana cried:

"I will not endure this
without reprisal. I have not been honoured!
They will not say I did not get revenge."

To punish the slur, Diana lets loose
a wild boar on Oeneus' estates,

---

¹Cocalus, king of Sicily, protected Daedalus from Minos, after the former's escape from Crete.

²The "mournful tribute," mentioned previously, was paid to Minos in the form of several young Athenians periodically sent to Crete to be killed by the Minotaur (see line 8.273 above).

³Meleager was the son of Oeneus, king of Calydon, in Aetolia (in western Greece).

Book Eight

a beast so immense that lush Epirus
does not have any bulls that match its size,
larger than boars in fields of Sicily.
Blood and fire burn in its eyes, and its neck
is rough and stiff, with bristles sticking out
like rigid spears, [just like a palisade
of thrust-out pikes].[1] Its grunts are harsh and loud,
and hot foam flows down its massive shoulders.   460
Its tusks are huge, like on an elephant.
Lightning shoots from its mouth, and its breathing
scorches leaves. Sometimes this beast would trample   [290]
tender shoots of growing plants, and sometimes
ravage a farmer's full-grown harvest crops,
mowing down ears of grain, turning his hopes
into despair, while threshing floors and barns
would wait in vain for the promised harvests.
It scatters heavy clusters on the vine,
their budding stems, as well, along with fruit   470
and boughs of always leafy olive trees.
It even savages the cattle herds,
which nothing can protect, not herdsmen, dogs,
or even vicious bulls. Men run away,
thinking they are not safe unless they hide
inside the city walls.

                 Then Meleager
and a handpicked group of warriors assemble,   [300]
eager to win fame: twins sons of Tyndarus   THE BOAR HUNT
(Pollux, celebrated for his boxing,
and Castor, famous for his horsemanship),   480
Jason (first man to build a ship), Theseus
and Pirithoüs (best of friends), two sons
of Thestius, Lynceus and swift Idas
(both sons of Aphareus), Caeneus
(now no longer female), fierce Leucippus,
Acastus (famous for his skill with spears),
Hippothoüs, Phoenix (Amyntor's son),
Dryas, two sons of Actor, and Phyleus
(who comes from Elis). Telamon was there,

---

[1] Line 286 of the Latin is commonly omitted, since it is considered an interpolation. I have placed the English translation between square brackets.

257

and Peleus (father of great Achilles), 490
Admetus (Pheres' son), Iolaüs [310]
(a Boeotian), vigorous Eurytion,
Echion (unsurpassed in running), Lelex
from Locris, Panopeus, Hyleus,
fierce Hippasus, Nestor (still in his prime),
as well as those sent by Hippocoön
from ancient Amyclae, with Laërtes
(Penelope's father-in-law), Ancaeus
from Parrhasia, along with Mopsus
(Ampyx's clever son), Amphiaraüs 500
(son of Oecleus, as yet unharmed
by his wife's treachery), and Atalanta,
from Tegeae, a girl who was the pride
of the Lycaean woods.¹ A polished brooch
is fastened on her garment at the top.
Her hair is plainly styled and gathered up
into a single knot. From her left shoulder
an ivory quiver hangs suspended. [320]
The arrows in it rattle. Her left hand
also holds a bow. From her style of dress 510
and from her face someone could truly say
the boy looked like a virgin girl, or else
the girl looked like a boy. Meleager,
the Calydonian hero, glanced at her
and, in that instant, felt a great desire.
Although the gods would not permit his love,
he swallowed down the hidden flames and said:

"O, whoever she thinks worthy of her
will be a happy man!"

                    Time and decency
did not allow him to say any more. 520
The more essential task of the great hunt
was urging him to act.

---

¹This list includes a number of legendary figures. I have provided some names which Ovid does not mention directly (e.g., Castor, Pollux, Peleus). The sons of Thestius were Toxeus and Plexippus, uncles of Meleager. Caeneus was originally a woman. Ovid tells her story in Book 12 below. The two sons of Actor were Eurytus and Cteatus. Telamon was the father of the greater Ajax. Hippocoön, from Amyclae in Thrace, sent three sons: Alcon, Enaesimus, and Leucippus. Laërtes was the father of Ulysses. Amphiaraüs was betrayed by his wife, Eriphyle, for a gold necklace.

Book Eight

                        Above the plain
rose a forest dense with trees which no one
in ages past had ever cut. It looked down
on the sloping fields. Once the warrior group
came to these woods, some spread out hunting nets,
some unleashed the hounds, while others followed
the deep tracks left by the wild creature's feet,
keen to confront their dangerous quarry.
There was a hollow valley where water
would often flow from rivulets of rain.
In its lower part were bending willows,
smooth sedges, marshy rushes, osiers,
and long bull rushes growing with small reeds.
Driven from this place, the rampaging boar
charges the middle of its enemies.
Like lightning bursting from colliding clouds,
its momentum flattens trees, and the wood,
as it breaks apart, makes a cracking sound.
The hunters raise a shout and keep the spears
in their strong hands stretched out in front of them,
moving the large iron points here and there.
The boar rushes on, scattering the dogs
trying to intercept its furious charge,
and routs the barking pack with glancing blows.
The first spear thrown comes from Echion's arm.
It misses its mark and leaves a slender scratch
in the trunk of a maple tree. The next one,
hurled by Pagasonian Jason, is aimed
at the animal's back and looks as if
it may well stick there. But he throws too hard.
His power makes him overshoot the boar.
Then Mopsus, son of Ampyx, cries:

                        "Phoebus,
  if I have worshipped you and worship still,
  grant what I ask and make this spear of mine
  fly straight and hit its target."

                        Apollo
agrees to what he asks and does his best.
The spear does hit the boar but leaves no wound,
for as it travels through the air, Diana
steals away the iron point, so the shaft

259

hits home without the tip. The impact sparks
the wild boar's fiery rage, now blazing out
with all the fury of a lightning bolt.
Its eyes are burning, and its chest breathes fire.
Just as a rock from a taut catapult
will hurtle off and seek out walls and towers
packed with soldiers, so this ferocious beast
attacks the group with an unerring charge.
It knocks down Pelagon and Hippalmus
protecting the right flank. Their companions
help carry them away from where they lie.
But Hippocoön's son Enaesimus
receives a fatal wound. Trembling with fear,
he begins to turn around, but the boar
slices through his sinews behind both knees.
His legs collapse. And Nestor from Pylos
might have died, years before the Trojan War,
but he plants his spear in the ground and vaults,
with the shaft supporting him, up in a tree
which stands nearby. From that safe vantage point
he peers down on the beast he just escaped.
The destructive monster sharpens its tusks
on the trunk of an oak tree and stands there,
grim and menacing. Fully confident,
now its weapons are sharp again, the boar
stabs with its curving tusk and rips the thigh
of Hippasus. But Castor and Pollux,
the celebrated twins, not yet transformed
to heavenly stars, ride up together
on horses white as snow, and both
hurl javelins through the air—the spear points
shiver as they fly.[1] They would have wounded
the bristly beast if it had not backed off
and moved to a place in the murky woods
where spears and horses could not force their way.
Telamon goes after it but rushes in
too eagerly and, in his carelessness,
is tripped up by a tree root. He falls down,
flat on his face. While Peleus is helping
Telamon get up, the girl from Tegea

---

[1] After they died Castor and Pollux became the constellation Gemini.

sets a swift arrow on her string, bends her bow,
and lets the arrow fly. It grazes the beast
along its upper back, then lodges itself
below the ear, and a thin stream of blood
dyes the bristles red. She is delighted
with the shot, and Meleager is, as well,
even more so. They claim he was the first
to see the blood and, once he noticed that,
the first to point it out to his companions,
saying to the girl:

                  "That courage of yours 610
will bring you the fine tributes you deserve."

The men, red with shame, urge each other on,
shouting encouragement and hurling spears,
but with no sense of order. The confusion
makes throwing difficult and hinders them   [390]
from hitting the target they are aiming at.
Then, Ancaeus of Arcadia, armed
with a twin-edged axe, in a mad fury,
charges in to meet his fate, shouting:

                  "You warriors,
learn how much better a man's weapons are   620
than those a woman uses. Let me in there
to do the job! Though Latona's daughter
with her own arms may be protecting it,
my right hand will still annihilate this beast,
despite Diana."

                He is so stuffed with pride
he says these boastful words, raises his axe
in both his fists and, standing on his toes,
prepares to deliver a downward blow.
As he is making this rash move, the boar
attacks. Both tusks spear him high in the groin,   630   [400]
the quickest way to die. Ancaeus falls.
His inner organs slide out in a heap,
with a great flow of blood, and soak the earth
with gore. Pirithoüs, Ixion's son,
moves in against the boar, brandishing a spear
in his powerful right fist. Theseus,
son of Aegeus, shouts out to him:

"You whom I care about more than myself,
who are part of my soul, keep your distance!
You can be brave without going in too close. 640
It was rash courage that destroyed Ancaeus!"

Theseus called and hurled a heavy spear
of cornel wood tipped with a point of bronze.
He threw it well and would have hit the boar,
but an oak tree's leafy branch got in the way. [410]
Jason, Aeson's son, hurled his spear, as well,
but it swerved by accident, missed the beast,
and killed a harmless dog, hitting its legs
and pinning the animal to the ground.
But the hand of Meleager produced 650
a different result. He threw two spears.
The first one struck the earth, but the other
stuck in the middle of the monster's back.
Meleager did not pause. While the boar
was raging on, wheeling his body round,
hissing and slobbering fresh blood and foam,
the warrior who gave the wound moved in,
rousing his enemy to savage fury,
and then buried his shining hunting spear
in the front part of its shoulder. His comrades 660
gave a happy shout to express their joy [420]
and crowded round to shake the victor's hand.
They gazed in amazement at the huge beast
lying there and covering so much ground.
They still believed it was unsafe to touch,
but they all dipped spears in the wild boar's blood.

Meleager set his foot on the creature's head
and spoke as follows:

"Nymph from Nonacris,
accept this trophy, which is mine by right.
Let some of my glory be shared with you." 670

Meleager spoke these words and offered her,
as her special prize, the wild boar's bristly hide
and its amazing head with those huge tusks.
Atalanta was delighted with the gift [430]
and with the one who offered it to her.
But other men were jealous—all of them

PLEXIPPUS AND TOXEUS

muttered amongst themselves. Then Pelexippus
and Toxeus, sons of Thestius, cried out:[1]

"Come on, woman, set aside those trophies.
Do not make off with honours due to us
or place too much faith in your own beauty,
in case that friend of yours, smitten with love,
is not there to help you."

They took the gifts
away from her and told Meleager
he had no right to give them. But Mars' son
could not endure this—bursting with anger,
he clenched his teeth and cried:[2]

"You warriors
who rob other people of their glory,
learn now how actions matter more than threats!"

He drove his lethal sword into the heart
of Plexippus, who was not expecting
that sort of violence. Toxeus paused,
uncertain what to do. He was eager
to avenge his brother's death and also
feared to meet his fate. But Meleager
gave him little time to think it over.
While his sword was still hot with blood
from one brother, he warmed it up again
with the other brother's blood.

As Althaea,
Meleager's mother, was taking gifts
to the sacred temples to offer thanks
for her son's triumph, she saw the bodies
of her dead brothers being carried back.
She screamed. The sound of her howls of sorrow
filled the city. She beat her breasts and changed
her golden robes to black. But when she learned
who had killed them both, all her grieving stopped.
Her passion changed from mourning to revenge.

ALTHAEA AND MELEAGER

---

[1] Plexippus and Toxeus are uncles of Meleager, his mother's brothers.

[2] The phrase "Mars' son" may simply mean "warlike" or it may imply that Meleager was really the son of Mars, who had had sex with his mother Althaea.

Book Eight

Back when Althaea, daughter of Thestius,
was lying in labour, struggling to give birth   710
to Meleager, the three sister Fates
had placed a wooden log inside the fire
and, as they were spinning their fatal thread,
using their thumbs to hold it down, had said:

> "To you, O new-born child, we will allot
> the same length of life as this piece of wood."[1]

Once the goddesses had made this prophecy,
they left. Althaea pulled the burning log
out of the fire and poured water on it.
For a long time, she had kept it hidden,   720
deep in the house, and, by preserving it,
had protected young Meleager's life.
Now his mother brought it out and ordered   [460]
pine wood and kindling to be set in place.
Once these were piled, she lit the hostile fire.
Then she made four attempts to throw the log
into the flames and four times stopped herself.
The mother and the sister were at war.
The two names pulled her heart in different ways.
Often her cheek paled, as she considered   730
the crime she was about to carry out.
Often her fierce rage made her eyes turn red.
There were times her face resembled someone
making vicious threats, and at other times
you could well think she looked compassionate.
And when the fierce emotions in her soul
had dried up her tears, tears still kept coming.   [470]
Just as a ship seized by both wind and tide,
when these two push in opposite directions,
feels the twin force and moves uncertainly,   740
as it obeys them both, so Althaea
kept being swayed by different feelings.
Sometimes she would set aside her anger,
but, once she was calm, would let it blaze again.
But then the sister started to prevail
against the mother, and so, to appease

---

[1] The Fates were three sisters who determined the life span of human beings. At birth, one spun the thread indicating the years, another measured, and the third one cut.

the shades of her blood relatives with blood,
she proved her piety with an impious act.
For once the destructive fire grew in strength,
she cried:

        "Let this funeral pyre consume
the product of my womb."

                As her cruel hands
gripped the fatal wood, the wretched woman
stood praying by the funeral altars:

"O you Eumenides, three goddesses
of retribution, turn your faces here,
to these savage rites![1] To exact revenge
I must commit a crime. Death must pay for death.
Wrong must be piled on wrong, one funeral
on other funerals. Let this cursed house
perish from its accumulated sins!
Shall joyful Oeneus take great delight
in his victorious son, and Thestius
be childless? Better both of them lament.
And you, my brothers' shadows, you spirits
newly made, take note I do my duty.
Accept the offering I have prepared
at such great cost, the perfidious child
produced from my own womb! Alas for me!
Where am I rushing to? O my brothers,
forgive a mother! My hand cannot complete
what it began. Yes, he deserves to die—
that I will concede—but I cannot bear
that I should be the author of his death.
So shall he go unpunished and live on
in triumph, swollen with his own success,
and take royal power in Calydon,
while you lie there as small heaps of ashes
and icy shadows? That I cannot bear.
Let the killer die and drag down with him
his father's hopes, his kingdom—the ruin
of his native land! Where are those feelings

---

[1] The three sisters are the Furies, goddesses of blood revenge, especially within the family. They were often called the Eumenides ("The Kindly Ones"), a euphemism designed to make them less fearful.

Book Eight

of a mother for her child, the sacred ties
of parents? Where are the troubles I went through
for ten long months? I wish I'd let you burn [500]
in that first fire when you were still a child!
That you have lived—that was my gift to you—
and now you die a death you well deserve!
Take the reward for what you yourself have done,
and give me back the life I gave you twice,
once at birth and once when I took the log,   790
or put me with my brothers in their tomb!
I long to do it, and yet I cannot.
What do I do? Sometimes before my eyes
I see my brothers' wounds and the image
of that brutal slaughter. At other times,
affection and my role as mother break
my resolution. I feel so wretched!
It will be an evil matter, brothers,
if you prevail. But still, you will prevail,
provided I myself may follow you   800 [510]
and the consolation you receive from me."

Althaea spoke, then turned herself away
and, with trembling hands, threw the fatal log
into the middle of the fire. The wood itself
gave out a groan (or seemed to), as it was seized
by the reluctant flames and then consumed.

Some distance off and quite oblivious
to what is going on, Meleager
is burning from those flames. He feels his gut
being scorched with hidden fires. His courage   810
copes with the enormous pain, but still,
he is sad his blood is not being shed
and his death will have no glory. He calls
the wounds Ancaeus got a stroke of luck.[1]
With a groan he summons his old father,
his brothers, loving sisters, the partner   [520]
of his bed, and perhaps his mother, too.[2]
The fire and his pain intensify and then
die down again. Both of them disappear

---

[1] Ancaeus had been killed by the wild boar (see 8.616 above).

[2] Meleager's wife was Cleopatra (who, according to Homer was also called Alcyone).

together, and his spirit slips away,   820
little by little, out into the air,
while, little by little, the bright embers
are buried in white ash.

                 High Calydon
lies prostrate with grief. Young and old men weep,
nobility and common folk lament,
and Calydonian women tear their hair
beside Euenus stream and beat their breasts.¹
Meleager's father, prone on the ground,
stains his white hair and his old face with dirt,
blaming himself for having lived so long.   830   [530]
His mother, aware she has committed
a horrific act, has punished herself,
plunging a sword deep inside her body

SISTERS OF MELEAGER

with her own hand. If god had given me
a hundred mouths and tongues to speak the words,
great genius, and all of Helicon,
I still could not describe the wretched state
of his poor sisters, who, losing all sense
of modesty, beat their breasts black and blue,
and while their brother's body is still there,   840
fondle it and embrace it once again,
kissing the corpse and bier on which it lies.
Once he is burned, they heap up the ashes,
press them against their hearts, and hurl themselves
beside his burial site, clutching the stone   [540]
that bears his name and bathing it with tears.
At length, Diana, Latona's daughter,
has had enough of slaughter in the house
of Parthaon and lifts those sisters up
(except for Gorge and Deïanira,   850
daughter-in-law of noble Alcmene),
on feathers which spring up on their bodies,
stretching extensive wings along their arms
and altering their mouths to horny beaks,
then sends them, once transformed, into the air.²

---

¹Euenus is a river in Aetolia in western Greece.

²According to legend, two of Meleager's sisters were transformed into guinea hens. Ovid does not indicate the species of bird. Deïanira was wife of Hercules.

BOOK EIGHT

Meanwhile, Theseus, having taken part THESEUS AND ACHELOÜS
in the group enterprise to kill the boar,
was going back to Tritonia's city,
the town that Erectheus once had ruled.[1]
But Acheloüs' stream, swollen with rain,   860
stood in his way and delayed his journey.
The river said:

      "Famous Athenian,   [550]
 come beneath my roof. Do not trust yourself
 to my rapacious waves. They have a habit,
 as they roar along, of carrying off
 huge trunks of trees and of turning boulders
 over on their sides. I have seen stables,
 large ones near the river bank, swept away,
 their animals, as well. The cattle's strength
 did not help them, nor did the horses' speed.   870
 And the whirling eddies of this torrent
 have swallowed many bodies of young men,
 when melting snows pour down the mountainside.
 It's safer to stay here until my stream
 runs down in its customary channel
 with a gentle flow of water in its bed."

Aegeus' son agreed and answered:

      "Acheloüs,   [560]
 I will follow your advice and use your home."

And he did both, entering a cave carved
in soft porous stone and rough travertine.   880
The floor was soft damp moss, and the ceiling
alternating rows of conch and murex shells.
By now Hyperion had measured out
two-thirds of the daylight path he travels.
Theseus and his comrades sat on couches.
Pirithoüs, Ixion's son, was there,
on one side of Theseus. On the other side
sat Lelex, a warrior from Troezen,
with sparse white hair already covering
his temples, together with some others   890

---

[1] The city referred to here was Athens. Tritonia was another name for Minerva, and Erectheus was a legendary king of the city.

whom the Arcarnanian river god,
overjoyed to have such a noble guest,
thought worthy of a similar honour.
Barefooted nymphs quickly set up tables,
loaded them with food, and then afterwards,
when the food had been removed, poured out wine
in jeweled cups. At that point, Theseus,
most powerful of heroes, looking down
on the sea stretching out before his eyes,
pointed a finger and asked:

                "What place is that?
Tell me the name people give that island,
although there does not seem to be just one."

The river god replied:

                "What you are looking at
is not one island. There are five of them,
all distinct. But the distance hides that fact.
What happened there will leave you less amazed
at what Diana did when she was scorned.
Those islands once were nymphs who sacrificed
ten bullocks, summoned all the rural gods
to sacred celebrations, and led out
dancing choruses for their festival.
But they neglected me. I swelled with rage
and grew as forceful as I always get
when my full cresting waters reach their peak.
My heart and waves were pitiless. I ripped
trees from trees, fields from fields, and swept those nymphs
and the ground they stood on down into the sea.
At last they thought of me, but far too late.
My waters and the sea divided up
that unbroken piece of ground, carving it
into the many pieces you can see,
those five islands called the Echinades,
out there in the middle of the ocean.
But as you look, even from a distance,
there is one island lying by itself,
far from the rest, an island dear to me.
Sailors call it Perimele. She was a girl
I fell in love with, and because of me
she no longer could be called a virgin.

Her father, Hippodamas, was so angry,
he went to kill her, hurling the body
of his daughter from a cliff into the sea.
I caught her there and, as she swam around,
I held her up and prayed:

     'O great Neptune,
Trident-bearer, whose power ranks second
to the might of heaven, picked by lot to rule
the restless waves, [where we sacred rivers end
and to which we run—approach, O Neptune,
and listen graciously to what I pray.
This girl I am supporting I have harmed.
If her father Hippodamas had been just
and merciful or else less impious,
he would have pitied her and forgiven me.]'[1]
Give us your help. I beg you grant a place
to someone drowned by a father's savagery,
or allow her to become that place herself.
[I will still keep holding her.'

     The ocean king
moved his head, making all the waters shake,
to indicate his own consent. The nymph
was terrified, but she kept on swimming.
As she swam, I could feel her breast throbbing
with a pulsing motion, but while I felt that,
I sensed her entire body growing hard
and her chest being covered up with earth
heaped all around it.] While I was speaking,
fresh land enclosed her body as she swam
and a substantial island grew up there
around her transformed limbs."

    After these words,
the river god was silent. The event
was so astonishing, it stirred them all.
But Pirithoüs, son of Ixion,
ridiculed them for their credulity.

---

[1] The lines in square brackets (lines 597-601 and 604-609 in the Latin) are commonly omitted as spurious insertions.

His arrogant spirit despised the gods,
so he remarked:

> "You tell made-up stories,
> Acheloüs, and grant too much power
> to the gods, if you believe they can give
> and take away the forms of things."

The others were upset by these remarks,
for they did not approve of such ideas.
Before anyone else could speak, Lelex,   970
a man mature in years and understanding,
answered:

> "The power of those in heaven   PHILEMON AND BAUCIS
> cannot be measured—it has no limit.
> Whatever gods above desire takes place.
> To ease your doubts about it, just listen.   [620]
> In the hills of Phrygia, a lime tree
> and an oak tree stand beside each other,
> with a low wall around them. I myself
> have seen the place, for Pittheus sent me
> to that country, where his father, Pelops,   980
> had ruled in earlier days. Not far away
> there is a swamp, once habitable ground,
> whose waters now are home to diving birds
> and coots who love the marshes. Jupiter,
> disguised in human form, came to this place.
> Mercury, Atlas' grandson, who carries
> the caduceus, set aside his wings
> and travelled with his father.[1] The two gods
> went up to a thousand houses, seeking
> a place to rest, but all those thousand homes   990
> were locked and barred against them. Then one house
> took them inside. The place was really small.   [630]
> Its roof was made of marshy reeds and thatch.
> Pious Baucis and her husband, Philemon,
> the same age as her, had been married there
> in younger days and had grown old together
> in that very home. By acknowledging

---

[1] The caduceus is a staff with twin snakes curled around it and (usually) a pair of wings at the top. Mercury also wore wings on his sandals.

their poverty, they made it easier
and bore it without any discontent.
If you asked for servants there or masters, 1000
it made no difference, for the two of them
made up the entire household. The same two
gave out the orders and did what they were told.
So when those gods who live in heaven reached
this tiny home and, stooping down, went in
the humble doorway, the old man set out
a bench, inviting them to rest their limbs.
Baucis took care to spread out a rough blanket [640]
on the bench and stirred the still warm embers
in the hearth, bringing back to life the fire 1010
from the day before by nourishing it
with dry bark and leaves and blowing on it
with her old lungs till she produced a flame.
She pulled down from the roof some branching twigs
and dried out sticks, broke them up in pieces,
and set them under a small pot. She stripped leaves
off vegetables her husband had brought in
from their well-watered garden. Philemon
used a fork with double prongs to lift down
an ancient slab of bacon that was hanging 1020
from the blackened beam, sliced off a portion
of the meat they had been saving for so long,
and cooked the piece he cut in boiling water. [650]
Meanwhile, they kept up a conversation
to pass the intervening time, [so their guests
would have no sense of a delay. They had
a wooden tub, suspended from a hook
by a rough-hewn handle. This they filled
with heated water. Their two visitors
used it to clean up and refresh their limbs. 1030
There was a couch with willow frame and legs
on which was placed a central cushion stuffed
with soft sedge grasses.][1] They shook the cushion
and covered it with cloths, which generally
they did not use at all, except at times
of sacred festivals, but even these

---

[1]Lines 658-9 in the Latin are almost exactly the same as lines 656-7. I have omitted most of line 658 and line 659, to avoid the awkward repetition the same words.

BOOK EIGHT

were old and worn, just like the willow couch.
The gods sat down. Baucis tucked in her dress [660]
and, with her shaky hands, set up a table.
It had three legs, one shorter than the others.   1040
She took a broken tile and made it equal,
shoving it in to even out the slope,
then wiped the level table with fresh mint
and put out some doubly coloured olives
of virtuous Minerva, cornel berries
gathered in autumn and preserved in brine,
endives, radishes, a large piece of cheese,
and eggs gently cooked on cooling embers,
all in dishes made of clay. After this,
she brought a mixing bowl with carved designs,   1050
as lavish as her other tableware,
and goblets made from hollow beech, varnished   [670]
with yellow wax. There was a short delay,
before the hearth provided them hot food,
and then the wine, which was not all that old,
was passed around again and set aside
a while, to make way for a second course
of nuts, a mix of figs and wrinkled dates,
plums, fragrant apples in open baskets,
and grapes collected from the purple vines.   1060
In the centre sat a shining honey comb.
And, above all, there were friendly faces,
with no indifferent or hostile feelings.

Meanwhile, the old couple kept noticing
the mixing bowl, whenever it was empty,
would fill itself again all on its own.   [680]
The wine was being replaced spontaneously.
Amazed at this incredible event,
they grew afraid, and so the two of them
timidly held out their hands in prayer,   1070
begging the gods to forgive the dinner
and their lack of proper preparation.
They had a goose, which was the guardian
of their small dwelling and, as its owners,
were prepared to sacrifice the creature
in honour of the gods who were their guests.
But the goose, with its swift wings, eluded them
for quite some time and wore them out. At last,

273

Book Eight

it seemed to fly off to the gods themselves
for refuge. Those heavenly beings said
they should not kill it and added:

      'We are gods.
This evil neighbourhood will now receive
the punishment it deserves. But you two
will be allowed to escape the ruin.
Just leave your home, and come along with us—
that steep mountain we will climb together.'

They both obey. With staffs supporting them,
they struggle on, keeping their feet moving
up the lengthy slope. When they are near the top,
about a bowshot's distance from the summit,
as they look behind, they see all the land
is drowning in a swamp, except their home,
which is still there. While they look on amazed
and lament their neighbours' fate, their cottage,
a modest home even for two people,
is being transformed into a temple.
Wooden poles are turning into pillars,
the thatch is growing yellow, and the roof
seems to be made of gold, the doors engraved
with carvings, and the ground completely paved
with marble. Jupiter, son of Saturn,
in a calm voice speaks to them, as follows:

 'You excellent old man and you, his wife,
who deserves a husband of such quality,
tell us what you would like.'

      Philemon
takes a moment to confer with Baucis
then tells the gods what both of them desire:

 'We want to serve as priests, as custodians
of your shrine, and, since we have spent our years
in mutual harmony, we two both wish
to be snatched away in the same instant,
so I will never have to see her tomb,
and she will never have to bury me.'

What they wanted was fulfilled. They remained
guardians of the temple all their lives,

and then, worn out by time and their old age,
as they were standing on the sacred steps
and, as it so chanced, talking of their deaths,
Baucis saw Philemon starting to sprout leaves,
and the old man noticed leaves on Baucis, too.
By now the tops of trees began to grow
across their faces. They kept on talking,
as long as they still could, both crying out:

   'Farewell, my spouse.'

               The branches grew around them,
both at the same time, sealing up their mouths.
Those dwelling in Tyana still point out
these trees beside each other, which sprang up
out of their two bodies.[1] I heard this tale
from older men who did not make things up
(there was no reason they would want to lie).
As for me, I noticed hanging garlands
on the boughs, so I put some fresh ones there
and said:

       'Let those who cared about the gods,
be gods themselves, and those who worship gods
be worshipped, too.'

       Lelex finished speaking.
All of them reacted to the story
and the man who told it, above all Theseus,
who was keen to hear the wondrous actions
of the gods. So Acheloüs, river god
of Calydon, spoke to him, as follows:

   "Bravest of men, there are some people who,
once their form is changed, keep their altered shape,
and there are some who possess the power
to pass through many forms—like Proteus,
whose home is in the earth-encircling sea.[2]
O Proteus, at times you have been seen
as a youthful man, sometimes a lion.
One moment you have been a savage boar

---

[1] Tyana was a city in Asia Minor.

[2] Proteus, sometimes called the Old Man of the Sea, was an ancient sea god.

and then a serpent which men feared to touch.
And there were times your horns made you a bull. 1150
Often you have seemed to look like stone,
even a tree, and sometimes you assumed
the form of a flowing stream or river,
sometimes the very opposite of water,
when you turned to flame.

                        Autolycus' wife,
Erysichthon's daughter, had the same power.[1]
Her father was a man who spurned the gods [740]
and did not offer incense on their altars. ERYSICHTHON AND CERES
People claim he even desecrated
a grove of Ceres with an axe, abusing 1160
ancient woods with steel. In among these trees
there stood a massive oak, old and sturdy,
a forest on its own, with wreaths, garlands,
and memorial tablets close beside it,
testaments to prayers which had been granted.
Dryads often held their festive dances
underneath this tree, and often they joined hands,
formed a line, and circled around its trunk,
whose huge circumference was forty feet.[2]
That oak stood taller than the other trees 1170
as much as they were higher than the grass. [750]
But such things did not stop Erysichthon
taking axes to the tree. He told his slaves
to cut down the sacred oak. When he saw
them hesitate to carry out his orders,
the villain grabbed an axe from one of them
and said these words:

                      'If this were not just a tree
the goddess loves but the goddess herself,
its crown of leaves would touch the earth.'

---

[1] The daughter's name, which is not mentioned by Ovid here, was Maestra. Autolycus was the father of Anticleia, the mother of Ulysses.

[2] The measurement is "three times five *ulnas*." The *ulna* (as a unit of measurement) is usually translated as *ell*, an old European unit roughly equivalent to the length of a man's arm (i.e., approximately 30 inches, but the precise length varied from one region to another). Dryads were tree nymphs.

Book Eight

                      As he spoke
and raised the axe to strike a slashing blow,
Ceres' oak tree quivered and gave a groan.
At the same moment, its leaves and acorns
started to turn white, and its long branches
lost their colour. And when his wicked hand
struck the trunk and wounded it, blood flowed
from the split bark, in the same way it spurts
from the severed neck of a big strong bull
when it collapses before the altars
in a sacrifice. They were all amazed.
Out of all those there, one man attempted
to stop the evil deed and block the axe.
Erysichthon looked at him and shouted:

   'Take this as your reward for pious thoughts!'

Turning his axe from the tree to the man,
he sliced his head off and went at the oak
with blow after blow. Then a sound emerged
from the core of the tree, a voice which said:

   'I am a nymph who lives beneath this wood,
the one Ceres most loves. And as I die,
I prophesy to you that punishment
for what you've carried out is close at hand,
and that consoles me as I pass away.'

The wicked scoundrel kept up his attack,
and finally, weakened by countless blows
and tugged with ropes, the sacred tree fell over,
crushing large sections of the forest there.

All her dryad sisters, who were appalled
at what they and the forest grove had lost,
dressed in mourning black and went to Ceres,
begging her to punish Erysichthon.
The loveliest of goddesses agreed.
With a nod of her head she shook the fields
loaded down with bountiful harvest crops,
as she devised a kind of punishment
which men would pity, if his savage deeds
had not placed him beyond their sympathy.
She planned to torture him with deadly Hunger.
But she could not see Hunger on her own

(for the Fates do not permit a meeting
between Hunger and the goddess Ceres),   1220
so she commandeered one of the spirits,
a rustic mountain oread, saying:

> 'There is in far-off frozen Scythia
> a place with barren soil, a sterile land
> with no crops or trees. Here live numbing Cold,
> Pallor, Trembling, and ravening Hunger.   [790]
> Go and tell Hunger she must bury herself
> in that man's evil, sacrilegious heart.
> And Hunger is not to be beaten back
> by rich supplies of food. In any fight   1230
> against my forces, she is to prevail.
> If the enormous distance of the journey
> makes you anxious, you must take my chariot.
> Yes, take my winged dragons, and with these reins
> guide them on high!'

                Ceres handed her the reins.   HUNGER
The oread climbed in and flew away,
up through the air, and came to Scythia.[1]
She landed on a steep mountain summit
(men call it Caucasus). Once she removed
the harness from the dragons' necks, she went   1240
to look for Hunger, whom she discovered
in a field of stones, using her nails and teeth
to scratch up grasses scattered here and there.   [800]
She had coarse hair and hollow eyes. Her face
was pale, her lips were gray with dirt, her throat
was lined with scabby sores. She had rough skin,
through which one could make out her inner organs.
Dry bones protruded from her hollow groin.
She had no stomach, just a place for one.
Her sagging breasts seemed to be hanging down,   1250
with nothing to support them but her spine.
She was so thin her joints appeared enlarged,
with puffed up knee caps and huge ankle bones,
swollen beyond the normal size. The nymph
did not approach too close (she did not dare

---

[1] Ceres was the goddess of crops and food generally and, therefore, incompatible with Hunger. The oreads were nymphs of the mountains (as dryads were nymphs of the trees).

come near). She informed her of the orders
she had brought from Ceres. Though the oread
did not stay long, remained some distance off,
and had arrived just a short time before,
she still seemed to feel an urgent hunger.
And so she turned her team of dragons back
and drove them through the air to Thessaly.

Hunger carries out what Ceres ordered   HUNGER AND ERYSICHTHON
(although the way she always operates
works in opposition to what Ceres does).
Raised by the wind she travels through the air
to the appointed house. She does not pause,
but goes to the room where the wicked wretch
is lying fast asleep (for night has come)
and embraces Erysichthon with both arms.
She breathes herself into the man,
blowing inside his throat, his chest, his lips,
and spreading hunger through his empty veins.
Once she has done what Ceres asked, she leaves
the world of fertile lands and journeys back
to her famished home, her customary caves.

Erysichthon, still soothed by the soft wings
of tender sleep, in his imagination
dreams he desires a feast. He moves his jaws
to no effect and grinds his teeth together.
His throat deceives itself by gulping down
meals that are not there. Instead of banquets,
he wastes his time by swallowing thin air.
But when his rest is done, he is possessed
by a frantic urge to eat—the craving
rules his famished jaws and burning belly.
He wastes no time in calling out for food,
whatever sea and land and air afford.
With fully laden tables set before him,
he complains of hunger, and, while eating,
asks for things to eat. What could satisfy
whole cities or a nation does not suffice
for just one man. The more he stuffs himself,
the more he craves. Just as the sea receives
the rivers from the entire earth and yet
is never full of water, as it drinks up

all streams from distant lands, or as a fire,
in its greed, never turns down any fuel,
but incinerates innumerable trees—
the larger the supply of forest fuel,   1300
the more the fire craves, for food itself
makes it want even more—in the same way
Erysichthon's blasphemous mouth devours   [840]
all his meals and, even as it does so,
keeps demanding more. Every kind of food
becomes for him a reason for more food,
and every time he eats a meal he makes
a gaping void.

             By now his appetite
and the pit of his voracious stomach
have diminished his paternal riches,   1310
but his fierce hunger still remains the same.
His burning need for food has not declined
and is still strong. At length, when he has sent
his whole fortune down into his belly,
his daughter is the only thing still left,   ERYSICHTHON AND MAESTRA
a girl whose father is not worthy of her.
Since he is desperate, he sells her, too.
But the noble girl declines a master.
Stretching her hands out to the near-by sea,
she cries:

    'O you who now possess the prize   1320
of my virginity, snatch me away   [850]
from a life of slavery.'

               The one who took
that prize is Neptune. He does not spurn
her plea. Although the man who bought the girl
has seen her only a moment before
and is coming for her, Neptune transforms
her shape and makes her look just like a male,
with clothing that would suit a fisherman.
Her owner looks at her and says:

          'You there—
you using that fishing rod and hiding   1330
dangling bronze hooks in tiny bits of bait,
I hope you have calm seas. And may the fish

Book Eight

be easily duped and fail to sense the hook,
until you snag them. Tell me where she is,
the girl with shabby clothes and messy hair
who was on the beach a moment ago
(for I saw her here, standing on the shore). [860]
Her footsteps go no further.'

                    The girl sensed
the gift the god had given her was working.
Pleased that he was asking her about herself,   1340
she answered him:

                    'Whoever you are,
forgive me. My eyes have not left this pool
to look around in any other place.
I've been completely busy fishing here.
To ease your doubts—and may the god of the sea
assist me as I ply my skills—no man,
other than myself, has stood here on the shore
for some time now, and no woman has been here.'

The man who owned her trusted what she said.
He turned and walked away across the sand,   1350
cheated of his slave. Then the girl's real shape   [870]
was given back to her. Once Erysichthon
realized that she could change her body,
he sold his daughter Maestra many times
to other masters, and the girl escaped,
sometimes as a horse or bird, and sometimes
as a cow or stag, and with this deceit
she gave her famished father nourishment.
But when the violence of his disease
had used up all provisions, the sickness   1360
needed still more food, so Erysichthon
began to tear and gnaw on his own limbs.
The miserable creature fed his body
by eating it away."

                    Then Acheloüs
continued:

"But why do I spend time on tales
of other people. Young man, I, too, [880]
can often change my shape, although the forms
I can take on are limited. Sometimes

I seem to be as I am now, sometimes
I curl up as a snake, at other times,   1370
I am the lead bull of a cattle herd,
with power in my horns. Yes, I said horns,
for once I did have two. Now, as you see,
one side of my forehead lacks its weapon."[1]

He finished speaking and heaved a sigh.

---

[1] Acheloüs in the form of a bull once fought Hercules over the nymph Deïaneira. Hercules tore off one of his horns. Ovid tells the story at the beginning of Book 9.

Book Nine

IX

[Acheloüs tells Theseus how he and Hercules fought over Deïanira, how he lost one horn, and how that became the Horn of Plenty; Nessus offers to help Hercules and Deïanira, but then tries to abduct her; Hercules kills Nessus; Nessus gives Deïanira a shirt soaked in his blood; Rumour tells Deïanira that Hercules is in love with Iole; Deïanira gets Lichas to take the shirt Nessus gave her to Hercules; Hercules puts on the shirt and the poison eats away his body; Hercules recounts his achievements; Hercules kills Lichas, who turns into a rocky island; Hercules builds his funeral pyre and is cremated; Jupiter makes Hercules a god; Alcmene tells Iole how the birth of Hercules was delayed by Juno, until Galanthis tricked goddess Lucina, who changed Galanthis into a weasel; Iole tells Alcmene the story of her sister Dryope; a rejuvenated Iolaüs appears; Themis prophesies civil war in Thebes, the death of Alcmaeon, and the sudden maturing of his infant sons; the gods complain about not being able to rejuvenate their favourite mortals; Jupiter answers their complaints; Miletus and Cyane produce two children, Byblis and Caunus; Byblis falls in love with Caunus; Caunus rejects her; Byblis goes mad and is transformed; Ligdus tells Telethusa he will have to kill their child if it is a girl; Iphis is born and raised as a boy; Iphis is betrothed to Iänthe; Telethusa prays to Isis for help; Isis transforms Iphis; Isis and Iänthe are married.]

Then warrior Theseus, Neptune's grandson,
asked Acheloüs why he had heaved a sigh
and how his forehead had become so marred.[1]
The Calydonian river god, with reeds
around his tangled hair, replied:

                "Your question
is a painful one to me. For who wishes
to remember battles where he was beaten?
But I will tell you how that came about,
since the honour of having fought outweighs
the shame of being defeated. Besides,   10
I get solace knowing that the winner
was such a famous man.

                Perhaps your ears   ACHELOÜS AND HERCULES
have heard of Deïanira, who was once
a very lovely girl, the jealous hope
of many suitors. I was one of them.[2]   [10]
When we suitors went to her father's house
(the man I wanted as a father-in-law)
I said:

---

[1] Theseus' father, Aegeus, was a son of Neptune. For details of the dramatic setting see the final story in Book 8. Theseus is still being entertained by the river god in Calydon.

[2] Deïanira was a daughter of Oeneus and a sister of Meleager.

Book Nine

'Oeneus, son of Parthaon,
take me as a son-in-law.'

                             Hercules,
from Alceus' line, spoke up as I did,   20
and then the other suitors backed away,
leaving just the two of us. Hercules
said he could offer his bride Jupiter
as a father-in-law and spoke about
his celebrated Labours, the orders
he had succeeded in carrying out
for his step-mother Juno.[1] In reply,
I spoke against him:

                    'It is disgraceful
if a god yields to a mortal.'

                         (Back then
Hercules had not yet been made divine).[2]   30

'In me you see the ruler of those rivers
whose winding waters flow throughout your realm.
I will not be a son-in-law sent here
a stranger from a foreign land, but part
of your own kingdom, one of your people.   [20]
Do not let it harm my case that Juno,
queen of heaven, feels no hatred for me
and that all the punishments she ordered
in those labours were not imposed on me.[3]
As for you, Hercules, Alcmene's son,   40
you boast that Jupiter is your father.
If so, then either that is just not true,
or he is truly guilty of a crime.
Your claim he is your father must involve
adultery by your own mother. So choose
which story you prefer—that Jupiter

---

[1] The Labours of Hercules were a series of twelve very difficult tasks Hercules had to carry out for king Eurystheus, to atone for killing his children in a mad fit brought on by Juno. Juno instructed Eurystheus on what he should get Hercules to do.

[2] Hercules was a mortal son of Zeus. After his death he become a god on Olympus, (as Ovid reveals later in this narrative).

[3] Juno had an ongoing hatred for Hercules, since he was a bastard son of Zeus. She was the source of the events which led to the Labours of Hercules.

is your fictitious father or your birth
springs from a shameful act.'

    While I spoke these words,
his scowling eyes kept glowering at me.
He could not act like a courageous man
and keep his burning rage in check. The words
he spoke in his reply were few:

         'My hand
is stronger than my tongue. You may win out
in argument, so long as I beat you
in fighting.'

    And then that violent man
attacked me. I was too ashamed to yield,
after the grand speech I'd just delivered.
So I threw the green clothes from my body,
held up my arms to fend him off, my hands
curved in against my chest, prepared to fight,
and braced my legs to counter his assault.
Scooping some dust up in his hollow palm,
he threw it at me, and he turned yellow
from contact with the golden sand. And then
he grabbed me by the neck, then by the legs,
then by the crotch, or rather seemed to grab me,
attacking me from every side. But my weight
was my defence, and his assault on me
had no effect, just as a mass of rock
attacked by the full force of roaring floods
remains in place, made safe by its own weight.
We pulled back briefly, then rejoined the fight.
We held our ground, determined not to yield.
Our feet were closely intertwined, so I
leaned forward, pushing at him with my chest,
my fingers locked with his, my forehead pressed
against his forehead. I have seen strong bulls
go at each other in this way, striving
to win a mate, the prize they're fighting for,
the loveliest cow in all the meadow.
The cattle herd looks on, trembling, unsure
which one will claim the triumph and become
lord in his great kingdom. Our gleaming chests
were fused together. Then Hercules tried

three times without success to push me off.
But with his fourth attempt, he broke my grip,
loosening the arms I held around him,
and hit me with his fist—I am resolved,
at all events, to tell the truth—and then
he quickly spun me round and draped himself
across my back. He was a monstrous weight.
Believe me—I am not trying to win
more credit with a made-up story—I felt
I was being flattened by a mountain
dumped on top of me. Though it was difficult,
I pushed out my arms, all dripping with sweat,
and, with a great push, loosened his firm hold
around my chest. I was gasping for breath,
but he pressed forward and prevented me
from getting back my strength, then clutched me
by the neck. Finally my knee was forced
to touch the ground, and my mouth bit the sand.
My strength was not a match for his. So I tried
my magic skills, slipping away from him
by altering my shape to a long snake.
But then, when I twisted my body up
in supple coils and flicked out my forked tongue
with fearful hissing, that man from Tirnys
laughed and ridiculed my magic, saying:[1]

    'In my cradle I used to throttle snakes,
and, Acheloüs, though you have more strength
than other serpents, you are only one.
And how much of the Lernaean Hydra
would you be?[2] If wounded, it reproduced,
and cutting off one of its hundred heads
was dangerous, because it grew two more
to replace what it had lost, thus making
its neck more vicious than before. But still,

---

[1] Tirnys in the Peloponnese was the city where Hercules went after the mad fit in which he killed his wife and children, in order to serve king Eurystheus and carry out the twelve labours.

[2] The infant Hercules had strangled two snakes in his cradle, put there by Juno to kill him. The Hydra was a monster with many snake-like heads. If one was cut off, two new ones replaced it. Hercules destroyed the creature by burning the neck where he had cut off a head, thus preventing the growth of replacements. This event was one of his twelve labours.

though serpents grew like branches from its wounds
and harming it just made the monster larger,
I beat that Hydra and, once it was down,
I slaughtered it. What do you imagine
lies in store for you, now you've changed yourself
into the mere image of a snake, using
weapons which are unfamiliar to you
and hiding in a borrowed shape?'

                                              He spoke.
Then his fingers seized the top part of my neck.
I gagged, as if my throat was being throttled
in a vise, and struggled to pry his thumbs
up from my windpipe. He was beating me
in my serpent shape as well, but I still had
my third form, that of a ferocious bull.
Changing my body to that shape, I fought on.
Attacking from the left, he wrapped his arms
around my brawny neck. As I moved off,
he followed, twisting and pulling at my horns,
until he drove them down into the ground
and forced me to fall over in deep sand.
He did not stop there. Seizing my tough horn
in his merciless fist, he snapped it off
and ripped it from my mutilated head.
But the naiads filled up this horn with fruit
and sweet flowers and consecrated it,
so now the noble Goddess of Abundance
is rich indeed, thanks to that horn of mine."

Acheloüs spoke. One of his attendants,
a nymph dressed like Diana, with her hair
streaming across both shoulders, then came in,
carrying all of Autumn's harvest crops
in the overflowing horn, with tasty fruit
to offer as a second course.

                                    Daylight comes.
As the first rays of sunlight strike the hills,
the young men depart. They will not wait there
until the stream is serene and peaceful
and all the flooding waters have calmed down.
Deep down in the middle of his waters,
Acheloüs hides his rustic features

and his damaged head with one horn missing.
Losing that single horn, taken from him
by Hercules, is his only reason 160
for feeling sad. In all other matters
he is unhurt, and he conceals that loss
with reeds and willow leaves around his head. [100]

But you, fierce Nessus, were fatally hurt   HERCULES AND NESSUS
by passion for that same young virgin girl—
a flying arrow struck you in the back.[1]
For Hercules, a son of Jupiter,
while returning to his native city
with Deïanira, his new wife, reached
the swift stream of the river Euenus. 170
Swollen by winter rains, the water flow
was now above its customary height,
with many whirlpools, and could not be crossed.
Though Hercules had no fear for himself,
he did have some concern about his bride.
Nessus rode up. His limbs were powerful,
and he was well acquainted with the ford.
He said to Hercules:

          "Child of Alceus,
with my help she will be deposited
on that bank over there. You use your strength 180 [110]
for swimming!"[2]

          The hero from Boeotia
hands the Calydonian girl to Nessus.
She is pale with fear of both the river
and the centaur. Hercules throws his club
and his curved bow across to the far bank.
Then, just as he is, weighed down by quiver
and lion's skin, he says:

          "Since I have started,
I must cross this river."

          He does not pause
or search out the calmest stretch of water,

---

[1] Nessus was a centaur, born from Ixion.

[2] Hercules was originally called Alciades ("son of Alceus") after his ancestor Alceus.

for he refuses to be borne across
because the stream has given its consent.
As he climbs the further bank and grabs the bow
he hurled across, he hears his wife cry out.
Sensing that Nessus is now intending
to violate his trust, he shouts at him:

> "Where are you carrying her, you brute beast,
> vainly relying on your rapid hooves?
> I'm talking to you, Nessus, you monster
> with a double form. So listen to me!
> Do not run off with what is rightly mine.
> If respect for me does not restrain you,
> that wheel your father rides might well prevent
> forbidden sexual acts.[1] You won't escape!
> Though you may trust your powers as a horse,
> I'll catch you with an arrow, not my feet."

And then he carried out what he had said.
He shot an arrow at the fleeing back.
The iron barb struck Nessus through the chest.
When he removed the arrow, blood poured out,
mixed with lethal poison of the Hydra,
from both his wounds, one where the arrow hit
and one where it was sticking out.[2] Nessus
sopped up his blood and muttered to himself:

> "I will not die without getting revenge."

And so he soaked his shirt in his warm blood
and gave it to the girl he was abducting,
telling Deïanira it was a gift
which had the power to arouse new love.

Many years go by, and the entire world
is full of the deeds of mighty Hercules
and his step-mother's hatred towards him.
Hercules has captured Oechalia
and is preparing to make sacrifice

---

[1] Ixion, father of Nessus, attempted to rape Juno and was punished by being eternally tied to a wheel deep in Hades.

[2] Hercules put the poisonous blood from the Hydra on the tips of his arrows.

to Jupiter at Cenaeum.[1] But then,
chattering Rumour, who takes great delight
in mixing false things with the truth and grows,
thanks to her lies, from the minutest things,
flies on ahead of him and strikes your ears,
Deïanira, claiming Amphitryon's son,
your husband, is in love with Iole.[2]
Deïanira, who loves Hercules,
believes the story of this new affair
and is alarmed. First, she turns to weeping,
and, feeling miserable, vents her sorrow
with laments. But soon she says:

>DEÏANIRA AND HERCULES

[140]

230

"Why am I crying?
My rival will be happy with these tears.
Since she is coming here, I must prepare
some brand new scheme, while it's still possible,
before that other woman takes control
inside my marriage bed. Should I complain
or keep silent? Go back to Calydon
or remain right here? Should I leave this house,
or, if I can do nothing more, should I
at least make things more difficult for them?
O Meleager, what if I remember
I am your sister and with a brave heart
prepare to carry out a crime and show,
by slitting Iole's throat, how much harm
a woman's grief is able to inflict."

240

[150]

Her mind reviewed the different options,
and of them all she chose to send the shirt
soaked in Nessus' blood, to restore the strength
of her husband's fading love. Unaware
that the shirt would make her miserable,
she gave it to the unsuspecting Lichas.[3]
Using words designed to win him over,

250

---

[1]Cenaeum was on the coast of Euboea. Hercules attacked and captured Oechalia because Eurytus, the king, had earlier reneged on a promise.

[2]Amphitryon was the husband of Hercules' mother, Alcmene, who was impregnated by Zeus before Amphitryon married her. After the marriage, she gave birth to twins, Hercules (a son of Zeus) and Iphicles (a son of Amphitryon). Iole was the daughter of Eurytus.

[3]Lichas was one of Hercules' attendants.

Book Nine

the desperate, unhappy woman told him
to give it to her husband.

                             Hercules,
knowing nothing about the shirt, takes it
and drapes across his shoulders the poison 260
from the Lernaean Hydra. At the time,
he is setting incense, offering prayers
by the initial flames, and pouring wine
from a dish onto the marble altars. [160]
The destructive power in that poison
heated by the flames, softens and dissolves
and spreads itself through Hercules' body.
While he still can, he silences his groans
with his habitual courage. But later,
once his agony has overpowered 270
his resistance, he throws the altars down
and fills the woods of Oeta with his cries.
He wastes no time in trying to rid himself
of the fatal shirt. But where he tears it,
it rips away the skin or—the details
are disgusting to describe—sticks to his flesh,
so all attempts to get it off are futile,
or else it shows his mutilated limbs
and massive bones. His very blood sizzles,
boiling from the searing venom, just like 280
red-hot metal plunged in freezing water. [170]
His pain goes on and on. Voracious flames
suck in his stomach, from his whole body
black sweat keeps oozing out, scorched sinews crack,
and hidden poison liquefies his bones.
Raising his hands, he shouts up to the stars:

   "Daughter of Saturn, feed on my collapse.
Eat your fill, you cruel goddess! Look down
from lofty heaven on this destruction,
and glut your savage heart! Or if my state 290
earns pity even from an enemy—
even from you—then carry off my soul,
my wretched spirit, wracked with searing pain [180]
and born for toil. To me death is a gift,
a fitting present from my step-mother.
Was it for this I threw down Busiris,

who desecrated shrines with strangers' blood?
Was it for this I raised wild Antaeus up,
above his mother Earth, who gave him strength,
or stood my ground before the triple shape
of that Iberian herdsman Geryon,
or faced you, Cerberus, and your three heads?
Was it for this these hands of mine hauled down
the horns of that strong Cretan bull, and worked
at Elis, at the Stymphalian lake,
and in Parthenian woods? Thanks to their strength
did I not fetch that belt engraved with gold
back from the Amazons and those apples
guarded by the dragon that never sleeps?
And were the centaurs able to stand up
to me, or that boar which wrecked such havoc
in Arcadia? And was the Hydra helped
by growing larger from its loss, gaining
redoubled strength? And what about the time
I saw Thracian horses fed human blood,
their stables crammed with mangled bodies,
and, once I'd seen that, overpowered them,
and killed those horses and their master, too?
The huge Nemean lion now lies dead,
killed by these arms of mine, and with this neck
I have held up heaven. Jupiter's cruel wife
may have grown tired of issuing orders—
I am still not tired of carrying them out.
But now I am facing some new disease
which courage, weapons, and power in war
cannot resist. An all-consuming fire
roams deep inside my lungs and feeds itself
on every limb, and yet Eurystheus
is thriving. Are there men who still believe
the gods exist?"[1]

---

[1] Hercules in this speech reviews some of his most famous exploits, most of them from his celebrated twelve labours. Busiris was a king of Egypt who sacrificed foreigners. Hercules, passing through Egypt, was arrested by Busiris but broke free and killed him. Antaeus was a Libyan giant who drew his strength from the earth. He challenged people to wrestle and then killed them. Hercules held Antaeus off the earth, from which he drew his strength, until Antaeus weakened and then Hercules killed him. Geryon was a herdsman with three bodies. Hercules, in his tenth labour, killed him with an arrow and took away his herds. Cerberus was a three-headed dog guarding the entrance to Hades. Hercules in his twelfth labour went

[Footnote continues]

Book Nine

When Hercules had spoken, 330
he wandered across the heights of Oeta,
still ravaged by the poison, like a bull
with a hunting spear stuck in its body
after the man who threw it goes away.
You could have seen him there, often groaning
and grinding his teeth, often attempting,
again and again, to rip off his back
the remnants the shirt, flattening trees,
howling at the mountains, or raising his arms [210]
up to his father's sky.

    Then, lo and behold, 340
he caught sight of Lichas hidden away
in a cavernous rock and terrified. HERCULES AND LICHAS
In his pain, Hercules brought all his rage
to bear on Lichas and yelled at him:

      "Lichas!
Weren't you the man who brought that fatal gift
and gave it to me? Are you not the one
responsible for my death?"

      Lichas trembled,
grew pale, and panicked. Timidly he mentioned
his excuses. But while he was pleading
and trying to reach for Hercules' knee, 350
Alcides grabbed him and spun him around
three or four times, then threw him with more force
than a catapult out over the depths
of Euboea's sea. As he soared upward

down to Hades and dragged him up to earth. In the seventh labour, Hercules brought back to Eurystheus the Cretan bull, which was ravaging Crete. At Elis Hercules completed his fifth labour, cleansing the Augean stables. His sixth labour was to drive birds away from the Stymphalian lake. Parthenium was a mountain in Arcadia where Hercules carried out his third labour, capturing the deer with golden antlers. For his ninth labour Hercules brought back the belt of Hippolyta, queen of the Amazons. In his eleventh labour, Hercules brought back apples from the Hesperides. Capturing the Erymanthian Boar was Hercules' fourth labour, and killing the Lyrnaean Hydra was his second labour. The Thracian horses were the mares of Diomedes, which Hercules captured and brought to Eurystheus in his eighth labour (Ovid's text says he killed them). Hercules' first labour was to bring back the skin of an allegedly invincible lion rampaging around Nemea. Hercules visited Atlas, who supported the heavens on his shoulders, and temporarily relieved him of the burden. Eurystheus, king of Mycenae, was Hercules' great enemy, who, on Juno's instructions, assigned Hercules the different labours.

into the airy breeze, Lichas hardened.
Just as rain, so people say, is frozen [220]
by the icy winds—that's how snow is formed—
and in whirling snow, soft bodies are packed down
and rounded into dense clouds of hailstones,
in the same way, so former ages claim,
once those powerful arms threw Lichas up
into the air, fear drained the man of blood,
and, lacking any moisture in his body,
he was transformed to solid rock. And now,
in the waters off Euboea, there stands
a little reef which juts up from the deep
and keeps the traces of a human form.
Sailors are afraid to walk along that rock,
as if the stone might sense their presence there.
They call it Lichas.

                      Then, famous son
of Jupiter, you cut down trees that grew [230]
on rugged Oeta, built up a funeral pyre,   THE DEATH OF HERCULES
and told Philoctetes, son of Poeas,
to take charge of your bow, your bulky quiver,
and your arrows—destined to see once more
the realm of Troy.[1] And with that same man's help
you lit a flame deep in the pyre. While the pile
was catching fire in the ravenous flames,
you spread the hide of that Nemean lion
on the top part of the wood and lay down,
neck resting on your club, looking just like
a guest with garlands on his head, reclining
in the middle of full cups of wine.

                                By now
the growing flames were crackling and had spread
in all directions. They attacked his limbs,
but his body was serene and scorned them. [240]
The gods grew anxious for this protector

---

[1]Troy, according to the decrees of Fate, could be captured only with the bow and arrows of Hercules, who had been to Troy before when he attacked king Laomedon for his failure to keep a promise. Years later, Philoctetes, now the possessor of the bow, went to Troy to help end the Trojan war.

of the earth, so Jupiter, Saturn's son,   JUPITER AND HERCULES
sensing their mood, spoke reassuring words:[1]

"You gods above, your fear gives me great joy,   390
and I can freely and whole heartedly
congratulate myself for being called
ruler and father of a grateful people
and also for the way your high regard
protects my offspring. For though your concern
pays tribute to this great man's achievements,
I also am obliged you honour him.
But do not let an empty fear affect
your hearts. Think nothing of those fires
on Oeta! He who has overcome all things   400
will overcome those flames you now perceive   [250]
and will have no sense of Vulcan's power,
other than in parts his mother gave him.[2]
What he gets from me is everlasting,
beyond death's reach. It will not be destroyed
or consumed in any fire. Once that part
is done with earth, then I will welcome it
to heavenly regions, and I have faith
that all you gods will find this act of mine
a reason to rejoice. But if perhaps   410
some god—and I mean any god at all—
will grieve when Hercules becomes divine
and is not happy to bestow this gift,
that god should realize we're giving it
because his merit makes him worthy of it,
and should approve, although unwillingly."

The gods agreed, even royal Juno,
Jupiter wife, who, if she looked upset   [260]
with his last words, appearing to resent
that he was making reference to her,   420
seemed to accept the rest of what he said.

Meanwhile, whatever the fire could burn up
Vulcan had consumed, and what now remained
no one would recognize as Hercules,

---

[1]Hercules is a "protector of the earth" because he has helped get rid of so many monsters.

[2]Vulcan, as noted before, was god of fire.

for he bore no traces of those features
he had inherited from his mother
and preserved only those he had received
from Jupiter. And just as a serpent
throws off old age when it casts off its skin
and takes great delight in being renewed   430
with glistening fresh scales, in the same way,
when that Tirynthian hero had lost
his mortal limbs, his better part grew strong,
and he began to look much greater than before—
awe-inspiring, with solemn dignity.   [270]
The omnipotent father carried him
through hollow clouds in his four-horse chariot
and placed him among the glittering stars.
Atlas felt his weight.[1]

            Even after this,
Eurystheus, the son of Sthenelus,   440
maintained the hate he felt for Hercules.
His rage against the father turned itself
against the child. Now, Argive Alcmene   ALCMENE AND IOLE
had led a long life filled with anxious cares,
but she had Iole to confide in
and could talk with her about the worries
of old age. She described for Iole
how hard her life had been and how her son
had carried out his labours, now famous
through the entire world. Her grandson, Hyllus, 450
as ordered by his father, Hercules,
had brought Iole to his marriage bed.
He held her in his heart and had planted
the seed of a noble child inside her womb.[2]   [280]
To her Alcmene said:

            "May gods at least
be kind to you, removing all delays

---

[1] As well as becoming a god on Olympus, Hercules also became a constellation. Since Hercules was now part of the sky, his weight was added to the burden Atlas had to hold up in order to keep heaven and earth apart.

[2] Alcmene was Hercules' mother. Hyllus was Hercules' son by Deïanira, who had killed herself after Hercules was poisoned by the shirt she sent to him. Iole, as mentioned before, was the daughter of king Eurytus of Oechalia, captured and killed by Hercules (see above 9.223).

when you come to bear your child and cry out
for goddess Ilithyia, who cares for
anxious women when they are giving birth.
Thanks to Juno, she made things hard for me.[1]
For when the sun had come to the tenth sign
and it was time for Hercules' birth,
his weight had stretched my womb. What I carried
was so huge, you could tell that Jupiter
was the father of my hidden burden.[2]
By this time I could bear the labour pains
no longer. Even now, as I describe it,
I get freezing tremors in my body.
Part of my sorrow is that memory.
I was in torment seven days and nights,
worn down by pain. I kept stretching my arms
to heaven and screaming, calling out for
Lucina and her divine assistants,
the Nixi.[3] And she did indeed arrive,
but before she reached me, she had been bribed
and was intending to donate my life
to spiteful Juno. When she heard my groans,
she sat down on the altar by the door,
and with her right knee crossed over her left
and fingers interlocked, delayed the birth.
She also muttered spells in a low voice,
incantations which slowed the final stage
once it had begun. I kept struggling on
and in my frantic state shouted complaints
against ungrateful Jove—all quite useless.
I wanted to die. My cries of protest
would have moved hard flint. Those caring for me,
women from Thebes, offered up their prayers
and in my suffering provided comfort.

I had a servant there called Galanthis,
a girl of humble birth with yellow hair,

GALANTHIS AND LUCINA

---

[1] As part of her hostility to Hercules, Juno persuaded Ilithyia (the Greek name for the goddess of childbirth) to delay his birth, so that the child she favoured, Eurystheus, could be born first and become king in Argos.

[2] The tenth sign in the constellations of the zodiac is Capricorn.

[3] Lucina was the Roman goddess of childbirth, and the Nixi were her attendant goddesses.

but prompt in carrying out my orders.
I loved her for her services to me.
She sensed that Juno was up to something
and being unjust. On her frequent trips
in and out the door, she saw the goddess [310]
crouching on the altar, with fingers locked
and arms supported by her knees, and said:

> 'Whoever you are, wish my mistress well.
> Alcmene from Argolis has given birth. 500
> Her wish to have a child has been fulfilled.'

The goddess who looks after pregnancy
leapt up in alarm, loosening her hands,
which had been interlocked. By doing that,
she relaxed the bonds of childbirth and so
I was delivered of my son. They say
Galanthis, when she deceived the goddess,
laughed, but in the middle of her laughter,
the savage goddess grabbed her by the hair
and dragged her to the ground. Galanthis tried 510
to lift her body up, but the goddess
forced her down and changed her arms to forelegs.
She is still as vigorous as before, [320]
and her hair retains its previous colour,
but the shape she used to have has altered.
And because, to help me out in childbirth,
her mouth told lies, now her new-born offspring
issue from her mouth. As in former days,
she is a frequent presence in my home."[1]

Once Alcmene had finished speaking, she sighed, 520
moved by the memory of her old servant girl. DRYOPE
As she grieved, Iole, her daughter-in-law,
spoke up:

> "Mother, you are still affected
> by some young woman not of our own blood,
> whose human form was taken away from her.

---

[1] Ovid does not mention the species of animal Galanthis becomes, but, as other commentators have noted, this curious habit of giving birth to the young through the mouth was attributed to weasels, perhaps because that animal (like many others) carries its young around in its mouth. Weasels were also common house pets.

Book Nine

What if I were to tell you the weird fate
of my own sister, though my pain and grief
hold me back and make speaking difficult?
Dryope was her mother's only child—
my father had me by another wife— 530
and of all the girls in Oechalia
she was the loveliest. The god Apollo,
who governs in Delphi and in Delos,
took Dryope's virginity by force.
Later, though she was no virgin, Andraemon
married her and was considered lucky
to have her as his wife.
                              There is a lake
whose borders slope back, just like the seashore.
Its upper ground is crowned with myrtle groves.
Dryope came here. She had no inkling 540
of what Fates had in store, and to make things
even more difficult to understand,
she was intending to offer garlands
to the nymphs. She carried a sweet burden
on her breast, her son, not yet one year old,
and was nourishing the child with her warm milk.
Close by the lake a water lotus bloomed
whose colours, resembling Tyrian purple,
promised it would soon bear fruit. In this spot,
Dryope picked some blossoms, to give them 550
to her child as playthings. I was there, as well,
about to do the same. But I saw blood
dripping from the blooms, and the branches moved,
as if they were afraid. Apparently,
as people there eventually informed us,
but much too late, the nymph Lotis, running
from lecherous Priapus, had been changed
into this plant. Her features were transformed,
but she still retained her name.[1] My sister,
who knew none of this, grew very fearful. 560
She wanted to go back, to leave that place,
once she had finished worshipping the nymphs,
but her feet were stuck underneath a root.

---

[1] Priapus was a rustic fertility god, best known for his large and permanently erect penis.

BOOK NINE

She tried hard to free them, but nothing moved
except her upper body. Then tough bark
grew upward from her feet and, by degrees,
enveloped everything up to her groin.
As she saw this, she tried to tear her hair,
but her hands were full of leaves, and leaves covered
her whole head. Her infant son Amphissos 570
(his grandfather Eurytus gave him that name)
could feel his mother's breasts becoming hard
and when he sucked, no milky fluid came.
I was there, sister, watching your harsh fate,
and there was nothing I could do to help. [360]
As best I could, I tried slowing down
the growing trunk and branches, holding them
in my embrace, and, I must confess, I wished
I might be buried under that same bark.
Lo and behold, her husband, Andraemon, 580
and her most unhappy father come there,
looking for Dryope. When they ask me
I show them the lotus. They kiss the wood,
which is still warm, and, falling on the ground,
keep clinging to the roots of their own tree.
And by now, dear sister, other than your face,
you were entirely a tree. Your tears
fell on leaves sprouting from your poor body.
While you still could—as long as your mouth
left a passage for your voice—you poured out 590 [370]
laments like these into the air:

                'If you can trust
those who are in pain, I swear by the gods
I have not deserved this unjust treatment.
I did no wrong but am being punished.
My life was innocent. If I am lying,
let me wither and lose the leaves I have
or be chopped down and burned. Take this infant
from his mother's branches, hand him over
to his nurse, and let him often drink milk
and play underneath my tree. And later, 600
when he can speak, make him greet his mother
and, in all sadness, say:

Book Nine

'Inside this tree,
my mother is concealed.'
Let him fear lakes,
pick no flowers from trees, and think all shrubs [380]
have goddesses inside. And now, farewell,
my dearest husband, and you, my sister,
and you, my father! If you care for me,
protect me from the wounds of a sharp axe,
and guard my leaves from browsing cattle herds.
And since I may not now bend down to you, 610
stretch your arms up here, and receive a kiss.
While I still possess a sense of touch, lift up
my little boy. I can't speak any more,
for the soft bark is climbing my white neck.
Its highest sections are enclosing me.
Take your hands from my eyes and let the bark [390]
grow over me and shroud my dying sight,
without you adding any funeral rites.'

After she said this, her mouth stopped speaking,
and in that instant, she also ceased to be. 620
But long after her body had been changed,
those new-formed branches still retained her heat."

While Eurytus' daughter Iole
was recounting this marvellous event
and Alcmene was gently wiping off
the tears from Iole's face, even though
Alcmene was herself in tears as well,
something amazing ended all their grief.
In the lofty doorway stood Iolaüs, IOLAÜS
changed back again to almost a young boy, 630
now looking as he did in earlier years,
a slight trace of hair growing on his cheeks.
This favour he had received from Hebe,
Juno's daughter, who had been persuaded [400]
by the prayers of Hercules, her husband.¹
When Hebe was about to swear an oath THEMIS' PROPHECY
that after this she would never offer

---

¹Iolaüs was the son of Iphicles, Hercules' brother, and thus Hercules' nephew. Hercules took Hebe as his wife when he was made a god.

such a gift to anyone, goddess Themis
would not allow it. She prophesied:

> "Thebes is now moving towards civil war. 640
> Capaneus will not be overthrown
> by anyone except for Jupiter,
> the brothers will slaughter one another,
> and the prophet king, Amphiaraüs,
> as the earth opens up to swallow him,
> will glimpse his own dead shade while still alive.
> His son Alcmaeon will carry out revenge
> and kill his mother for his father's sake,
> a pious act but also criminal.
> Overwhelmed with troubles and forced away 650
> from home, he will lose his mind and be chased
> by Furies' faces and his mother's ghost,   [410]
> until his wife Callirhoë demands
> the fatal golden necklace. When he goes
> to his first father-in-law, Phegeus,
> to get that necklace, Alcmaeon will be killed—
> the sword of Phegeus, plunged in his side,
> will drain a kinsman's blood.[1] And then, at last,
> Acheloüs' daughter Callirhoë
> will ask great Jupiter, as a suppliant,   660
> to add years to the age of her young sons,
> so the death of avenging Alcmaeon
> will not go unavenged. Then Jupiter,
> moved by her plea, will offer in advance
> that special gift which you, his step-daughter

---

[1]Themis is prophesying the future civil war carried on by Eteocles and Polyneices, two sons of Oedipus. They had agreed to alternate as kings of Thebes, after Oedipus ceased to be king, but Eteocles refused to give Polyneices his turn, so Polyneices raised an army and attacked Thebes. Capaneus, a great warrior supporting Polyneices, defied Zeus during the attack and was struck down by a lightning bolt. The two brother, Eteocles and Polyneices, killed each other. Amphiaraüs was persuaded by his wife, Eriphyle, to join Polyneices' forces (Eriphyle had accepted a bribe of a golden necklace to get him to agree to go). Amphiaraüs was a prophet who foresaw his death. While he was being pursued during the battle for Thebes, the earth opened up and swallowed him and his chariot. His son Alcmaeon avenged him by killing Eriphyle, his mother. Alcmaeon then went to the court of Phegeus to expiate the killing. There he married Phegeus' daughter. Later he abandoned the daughter to marry Callirhoë, who asked for the golden necklace. When Alcmaeon went back to Phegeus' court to get the necklace, Phegeus sons' (i.e., Alcmaeon's kinsmen) killed him. I have added a few extra words (in lines 654-6) to clarify Ovid's very compressed style here.

and daughter-in-law, confer—he will change
those boys, while still young infants, into men."[1]

When Themis, who knows what the future holds,   JUPITER AND THE GODS
had uttered these prophetic words, the gods
muttered various complaints, wondering
why the selfsame gift could not be given
to other mortals, too. Goddess Aurora,
daughter of the Titan Pallas, grumbled
about her husband, who was getting old,
gentle Ceres complained that Iasion
now had white hair, Mulciber demanded
a renewal of life for Erichthonius,
and Venus, too, affected by concerns
for what would happen in the future,
wished to bargain over Anchises' life
and make him young again.[2] Every deity
had someone whose case he was advancing,
and the quarrel about their favourites
was growing to a heated argument,
until Jupiter opened his mouth and said:

"If you gods have any respect for me,
tell me where this talk of yours is going.
Do any of you think you are so strong
you can overpower Fate? Thanks to Fate,
the years which Iolaüs had used up
were given back to him. And thanks to Fate,
Callirhoë's sons will be young men
before their time, not through their ambition
or feats of arms. Fate also rules you gods.
To put you in a better frame of mind
about that fact, Fate governs me, as well.

---

[1] In Ovid's account, Hebe, goddess of youth, was Juno's daughter, and she had no father (i.e., she was Jupiter's step-daughter). Since she was married to Hercules in heaven, she was also Jupiter's daughter-in-law. The two sons, Amphiterus and Acarnanus, avenged their father Alcmaeon while still very young.

[2] The Titan Pallas is different from Pallas Athena or Minerva. Aurora's husband, Tithonus, had been a mortal. She promised him eternal life, but not that he would stay forever young, so he kept getting more and more ancient and decrepit. Iasion was the son of Jupiter and Electra. Mulciber was another name for Vulcan, and Erichthonius was his son. Anchises was a mortal lover of Venus. He was destined to escape from Troy, and his son (with Venus), Aeneas, would found the Roman race in Italy (the future events Venus is worried about).

If I had the power to alter Fate,
Aeacus, my son, would not be bowed down
by his extreme old age, Rhadamanthus
would always possess a flowering youth,   700
and so would my son Minos, too, now scorned
because he bears a bitter weight of years.
His rule is not as diligent as before."¹

Jupiter's words convinced the gods. No one
continued to complain when they saw Minos,   [440]
Rhadamanthus, and Aeacus worn down
by their advancing age. For when Minos
was in his prime, his very name alone
would terrify great nations. Now weakened,
he was truly fearful of Miletus,   710
Deione's child, a man who took great pride
in his youthful strength and in his father,
Phoebus.² Minos thought Miletus might rebel
against his rule, but still he did not dare
expel him from his native land. But you,
Miletus, you departed on your own,
carving the waters of the Aegean sea
with your swift ship, and in lands of Asia
built a city which bears its founder's name.³
Here you met Cyane, Maeander's child,   720
while she was following the twisting course   [450]
of her father's river banks, which often
turn back upon themselves.⁴ The girl's body
was extremely beautiful and bore you
two twins, Byblis and her brother, Caunus.

Byblis was seized by passionate desire   BYBLIS AND CAUNUS
for her own brother, from Apollo's line,
and now serves as a warning to young girls
to love only where they are permitted.
She loved him, but not the way a sister   730

¹Aeacus, son of Jupiter and Aegina, was king of Aegina. Rhadamanthus and Minos were sons of Jupiter and Europa. Minos, as we have seen, was king of Crete.

²Deione was a divine child of Oceanus and Tethys and (in some accounts) mother of Venus.

³Miletus was an important Greek city on the coast of Asia Minor.

⁴The Maeander, as mentioned before, was a river in Asia Minor with a great many large oxbow curves, so that the river repeatedly doubled back on itself.

loves a brother and not the way she should.
At first, of course, she did not understand
the fires inside her and did not believe
that she was doing wrong by kissing him
so many times or by throwing her arms
around her brother's neck. For a long time,
she fooled herself by thinking what she did [460]
stemmed from a form of natural affection.
Gradually, her love grew more perverse,
and when she went searching for her brother, 740
she would dress herself in her finest garments,
too concerned about appearing lovely,
and was jealous of any woman there
if she looked more attractive than herself.

But to this point she has no firm idea
of the feelings welling up inside her,
no explicit sense lurking underneath
the flames of passion. But still, deep inside,
she is on fire. Now she calls him her lord,
hates the name that makes them blood relations, 750
and prefers it when he calls her Byblis,
rather than his sister. Still, while awake
she does not dare to let her mind admit
her illegitimate hope. But at rest,
when she is lying peacefully in bed,
she often dreams about the one she loves
and even sees herself in the embrace [470]
of her own brother. Though she is asleep,
her body even blushes. When she wakes,
for a long time she stays silent, recalling 760
the image of her dream, and then, confused,
talks about her inner doubts as follows:

"I am so unhappy! What do they mean,
these dreams I get during the silent night?
How much I wish they were not true! But then,
why do I see these pictures in my sleep?
He's a handsome man, it's true, even to those
who envy him, and I find him pleasing.
I could love him, were he not my brother,
and he would be a worthy man for me. 770
What frustrates me is that I'm his sister.

Book Nine

But as long as I am never tempted
to do such things when I am wide awake,
I hope that sleep will often come to me [480]
with dreams like these! There are no witnesses
to what we dream, and I can get in dreams
delight from what I am imagining.
O, by winged Cupid and by his mother,
tender Venus, how much joyful pleasure
I have had! How mightily that passion 780
clearly seized me, as I lay melting
to the marrow of every bone. What bliss
that memory gives me, though my delight
did not last long, as night rushed on its way,
resenting what was happening to me.
If only they would let me change my name,
Caunus, and marry you. Then I could be
a fine daughter-in-law to your father.
And you, Caunus, what a fine son-in-law
you would make my father! I wish the gods 790
would let us share everything in common, [490]
except our ancestors! And I would wish
you were by birth more noble than myself!
So now, most beautiful of men, you'll make
some other woman a mother. For me,
who has the evil luck to share your parents,
a brother is the only thing you'll be.
What we have in common stands in our way.
So how am I to comprehend my dreams?
Are they significant? Can dreams, in fact, 800
mean anything at all? The gods forbid!
But still, gods have surely loved their sisters.
Though she was linked to him by blood, Saturn
married Ops, Oceanus married Tethys,
and Jupiter took Juno as his wife.[1]
The gods have their own laws! Why even try
to sort out what humans do by thinking [500]
of the different customs up in heaven.
I will banish this forbidden passion

---

[1] Ops, daughter of Uranus, the first god, was also called Cybele, Rhea, and the Great Mother. She was the wife of her brother Saturn. Oceanus and Tethys were brother and sister. Jupiter and Juno were both children of Saturn and Ops.

>   from my heart or else, if that is something
>   I just cannot do, then I pray I perish
>   before I yield to it! Let my brother
>   kiss me when I am lying there, stretched out
>   on my death bed. Besides, the thing I want
>   would require the consent of both of us.
>   Suppose it pleases me. To my brother
>   it may well seem a crime. And yet the sons
>   of Aeolus had no fear of marriage
>   with their sisters![1] But where did I learn that?
>   Why do I have these examples ready?
>   Where am I being carried? Go away,
>   far away from here, you disgusting fires.
>   Let me have no love for my own brother,
>   except the love a sister ought to have!
>   Still, if he himself were to be seized first
>   and fall in love with me, I could perhaps
>   indulge in these insane desires. And so,
>   if I would not reject him if he asked,
>   should I not seek to court him for myself?
>   But can you speak out? Can you admit it?
>   Love will drive me on, and I can do it!
>   Or if my modesty keeps my lips sealed,
>   my hidden passion I will acknowledge
>   in a secret letter."

Pleased with this idea,
which overcomes the doubts within her mind,
Byblis raises herself up onto her side,
leans on her left elbow, and tells herself:

>   "He will see it. Let me confess to him
>   these crazy feelings! Alas, where am I drifting?
>   What fires are now being kindled in my heart?"

Then, with a trembling grip, she writes the words
she has been thinking of. In her right hand
she holds an iron stylus, in her left
a clean wax tablet. She starts, then hesitates,
writes on the tablet, then rejects the words.
She sets down something and then deletes it,

---

[1] Aeolus, god of the winds, had six sons who were married to their sisters.

changes phrases, approves and disapproves,
puts down the tablet, picks it up again,
not knowing what she wants, dissatisfied
with whatever she seems about to write.   850
The expression on her face shows boldness
mixed with shame. She has written 'Your Sister,'
but chooses to remove those words, smoothes the wax,
and writes the following:

     "One who loves you
sends you this wish for health and happiness,   [530]
which she cannot enjoy unless you grant it.
She is ashamed, too ashamed to tell you
what she is called. If you asked what I want,
then I would wish that I could plead my cause
without stating my name or being known   860
as Byblis, until the hopes I pray for
are fully realized.

     True, you may have seen
signs of my wounded heart in my pale cheeks,
my loss of weight, my expression, my eyes
so often wet with tears, the way I sigh
for no clear reason, all those embraces
and kisses which, as you perhaps have sensed,
might seem as if they were not from a sister.
And yet, though I have been badly wounded   [540]
in my heart and have a savage fire inside,   870
the gods are witnesses that I have done
all I can to make myself more healthy.
In my wretched state, I have been fighting
to escape from Cupid's cruel weapons
for a long time now, and you might well think
the misery I've endured too heavy
for a girl to bear. But in that battle
I have been beaten—that I must concede
and, with these timid words, beg you for help,
the only man who can destroy or save   880
the one who loves you. Choose what you will do.
The girl who asks this is no enemy.
She has the closest links to you and seeks
to make them closer, with even tighter ties   [550]
attaching her to you.

Book Nine

       Let the old men
know what is right and ask what is allowed,
what acts are legal, and which ones are crimes,
preserving points of law. What suits our youth
is love which has no fear of consequence.
We do not yet understand what is allowed
and think all things permitted. We follow
the examples of the powerful gods.
No unforgiving father, no respect
for reputation, no fear will stop us.
And if we have good cause to be afraid,
we will conceal our sweet stolen pleasures
beneath the name of brother and sister.
I am free to talk with you in private,
and we embrace and kiss in front of others.
And how much does what is missing matter?
Pity the one who here admits her love,
who would not speak, if her extreme desire
did not compel her. Do not win the right
to have your name carved into my tombstone
as the reason for my death."

       Her hand wrote out
these ineffectual words and filled the wax,
with the last line just inside the margin.
She quickly sealed her criminal confession
with a jeweled signet, moistening it
with tears (for her tongue was dry). Filled with shame
she summoned one of her servants and said,
in an anxious, coaxing tone:

       "You are one
in whom I have great trust. Take these to my . . ."

For a long while she paused, then added:

       ". . . brother."

As she was passing the tablets to him,
they slipped out of her grasp and struck the floor.
That ominous sign upset her, but still
she sent the message.

    When the servant found
a suitable time, he went to Caunus

309

and delivered her secret words to him.
Maeander's youthful grandson took the tablets,
read part of what they said and, horrified,
hurled them away. Finding it difficult
to control his hands and stop them grabbing
the trembling servant by the throat, he cried:

> "Get yourself out of here, while you still can,
> you wretched agent of forbidden lust.
> I would punish you with death, if your fate
> did not bring with it a loss of honour."

The servant fled in terror, and brought back
those fierce words of Caunus to his mistress.
When Byblis heard he had rejected her,
she turned pale. Her body started trembling,
gripped by an icy chill. But when her mind
recovered, her mad passion came back, too,
and though she found it difficult to speak,
she whispered:

"I deserve it! Why was I
so foolhardy as to confess this wound?
Why did I rush so quickly to write down
on those tablets what should have been concealed?
I should have used ambiguous language
and first of all discovered how he felt.
With one part of my sail I should have seen
which way the wind was blowing, just in case
he would not follow the same course as me.
I could have safely moved across the water.
Now winds I did not test fill up my sail,
and so I am being driven on the rocks,
smashed up, and overwhelmed by the whole sea,
with no escape route where my sails can turn.
Besides, did not those signs of prophecy
instruct me not to follow my desires,
when I was giving orders for that servant
to take the tablets and I let them fall,
thus showing that my hopes would fall, as well.
Should I not have changed the day I acted
or my whole intention—and of the two
preferably the day? A god did warn me
and personally gave me certain signs.

If only I had not been so disturbed!
I should have spoken to him directly
and told him of my passion face to face,
instead of writing how I feel on wax.
He would have seen my tears and seen the face
of one who loves him. And I could have said
more than those tablets hold. I could have thrown
these arms of mine on his reluctant neck,
and, if he pushed me off, I could have looked
as if I were about to die, clutched his feet,
and, lying there, I could have begged for life.
All this I might have done, and if one thing
would not change his willful mind, all of them
combined together might have convinced him.
Perhaps some blame rests with the man I sent.
He did not approach him in the proper way,
I think, and choose an appropriate time,
or find a moment when his mind was free.
All these things have hurt me, for my brother
was not born from a tigress, and his heart
is not rigid flint, or solid iron,
or adamant, and he was not suckled
on lion's milk. He can be won over!
I must try him again. While here inside
I still have breath, I will not grow weary
in my attempts. If I could summon back
what I have done, the finest thing would be
not to have begun, but now I've started,
the next best is to fight on till I win.
If I walk away from my desires now,
it's obvious he never could forget
what I dared to try, and if I give up,
it will look as if my love is shallow,
or else that I was merely testing him,
trying to catch him with deceptive tricks,
or he is bound to think I was not ruled
by the god who, more than any other,
drives and fires up our hearts, but by mere lust.
The point is I cannot now be innocent
of doing wrong—I wrote to him and asked.
I have revealed the way I feel for him,
and even if I added nothing more,

no one could say that I was not at fault.
As for what comes now, I have much to gain
by winning what I want, and little to lose
by being considered a criminal."

She finished. Her mind is so unsettled
and at war, she regrets all her attempts [630]
and yet enjoys them. She goes well beyond
all moderation and, dissatisfied,
keeps trying and is constantly rebuffed. 1010
Finally, when she will not stop, Caunus
flees the country and her crime and founds
a brand new city in a foreign land.[1]

But then, so people say, Miletus' daughter
was so grief-stricken she became insane.
In a frantic state she tore the clothing
off her breasts and beat her arms. Her madness
was obvious to all, and she exposed
her hopes for an incestuous union,
by running away from her own country 1020
and the home she hated and following [640]
the track taken by her fleeing brother.
The women of Bubasus saw Byblis
moving across their spacious fields, howling
like those bacchantes in Ismarus who,
roused by your thyrsus, son of Semele,
celebrate your triennial festivals.[2]
Leaving them behind, Byblis wandered on
through Caria, the warlike Leleges,
and Lycia, travelling past Cragus, 1030
past Lymira, on past Xanthus waters,
and past the ridge which held the Chimaera,
a monster with a lion's chest and face,
a serpent's tail, and fiery breath inside.[3]

---

[1]The city was Caunus in Caria (in Asia Minor).

[2]Bubasus was a region in Caria, Ismarus a city in Thrace. The son of Semele was Bacchus, and the bacchantes were his ecstatic worshippers.

[3]The Leleges were residents of Caria in Asia Minor. Cragus was a mountain in Lycia, Lymira a city in Lycia, in Asia Minor, and Xanthus a river in Asia Minor. The chimaera was a famous fire-breathing monster made of up three different animals—lion, goat, and serpent (Ovid mentions only two).

Then, Byblis, you move beyond the forest
and, exhausted from your pursuit, fall down,
with your hair spread out on the hard ground   [650]
and your face pressed against the fallen leaves.
The Lelegian nymphs try many times
to lift her in their soft arms and often
urge her to curb her passionate desire,
comforting a heart that will not listen.
Byblis lies there saying nothing, clutching
the green turf with her nails and soaking it
in a river of her tears. And, so they say,
for those tears the naiads made a channel
underneath her which never could run dry.
What greater present could they offer her?
Then, just as resin oozes from slashed pines,
or thick bitumen seeps from heavy soil,   [660]
or water which the cold has turned to ice
melts in the sun once West Wind's gentle breath
comes back again, in just that way Byblis,
Apollo's grandchild, dissolved in her own tears
and was transformed into a fountain spring,
which even now flows out from a dark oak
and in those valleys bears its mistress' name.[1]

The fame of this new marvellous event   LIGDUS AND TELETHUSA
might perhaps have filled Crete's hundred cities,
if Crete had not just recently been through
a local miracle, the change in Iphis.
For in the territory of Phaestus,
next to the royal estates of Cnossos,
there once lived a humble man called Ligdus,   [670]
one of the common folk, but freely born.
His wealth was no greater than his station,
but his way of life and sense of honour
were beyond reproach. His wife was pregnant,
and when the time of birth was near at hand,
he addressed these words of warning to her:

"I'm praying for two things—may you give birth
with little pain and may you have a son.

---

[1] As mentioned at the start of this story, Apollo was the father of Mytilene, who was the father of Byblis and Caunus (see 9.712 above).

Book Nine

A girl is a more grievous burden, and fortune
has not given me strength to bring one up.
So—and I hate to say this—if by chance,
when you give birth, a female child is born,
I will, with great reluctance, give orders—
may my lack of natural affection
be forgiven!—that it be put to death."

He finished, and they both started weeping, 1080 [680]
with floods of tears streaming down their faces.
Ligdus, who had issued his instructions,
was weeping just as much as Telethusa,
who had been given the orders. But still,
she begged her husband not to limit her hopes
the way he had. Her prayers were useless,
for Ligdus' resolution did not change.
Then, when Telethusa could hardly bear   IO AND TELETHUSA
the full-grown burden weighing down her womb,
Io, daughter of Inachus, came to her   1090
as a dream in the middle of the night,
while she was sleeping, and stood beside her bed,
or seemed to stand there, with a company
of sacred followers. She was adorned
in majestic splendour. On her forehead
she wore the crescent horns of the moon, wreathed
with yellow ears of corn in shining gold.
Standing with her were barking Anubis,
sacred Bubastis, and dappled Apis,   [690]
together with the god who does not speak   1100
but with his raised finger calls for silence.[1]
The holy rattles—the sistra—were there,
and Osiris, too, the god whom Isis
is always seeking, and that foreign snake
full of sleep-inducing poisons.[2] And then,

---

[1] The gods' names here are those of Egypt. The description of Io would fit the goddess Isis. Anubis had the body of a man and the head of a dog. Bubastis, daughter of Osiris and Isis, was a female attendant on Isis. Apis was a bull god, often identified by Greeks and Romans as Osiris after he had been burned on a funeral pyre. The god who does not speak and advises silence was Harpocrates.

[2] The sistrum was a musical instrument made of metal which, when shaken, made a rattling, metallic sound (something like a tambourine). The god Osiris was killed by his brother Set. Isis (his sister and wife) looked for him for a long time. She found his limbs and put them in a

[Footnote continues]

just as if Telethusa were wide awake
and could see things clearly, the goddess spoke,
as follows:

        "You who are my devotee,
Telethusa, set your grievous worries
to one side, and disregard those orders [1110]
your husband gave you. Do not hesitate,
once Lucina has eased the pangs of birth,
to raise the child, whatever sex it is.[1]
I am a goddess who brings assistance
and, when people call for me, I help them.
You will not complain the god you worship [700]
is ungrateful."

        Io gave this advice
and left the room. Cretan Telethusa,
filled with joy, rose from her bed and, raising
her pure hands up to the stars, humbly prayed [1120]
her vision might come true.

        Her labour pains
grew more intense and, when her burden forced
its way into the air, a girl was born.   IPHIS
Ligdus did not know the child was female,
and so Telethusa, to deceive him,
ordered the child to be raised up a boy.
What she said was accepted as the truth,
and no one knew about the lie she told
except the nurse. The father kept his word
and named the child after its grandfather, [1130]
whose name was Iphis. The mother was pleased,
for that name was common to boys and girls
and would not be misleading anyone. [710]
And from that time on, the fraud, which started
with an affectionate lie, remained concealed.
The child was dressed as a boy, and its face
whether attributed to boy or girl,
people would have considered beautiful.

---

tomb. The gods then resurrected Osiris as god of the underworld. The foreign serpent is the asp (foreign because it is not native to Greece or Italy).

[1]Lucina was goddess of childbirth.

Thirteen years went by. At that time, Iphis,
your father arranged a marriage for you   1140
with golden-haired Iänthe, the daughter   IPHIS AND IÄNTHE
of Telestes from Crete, a virgin girl
so beautiful that she received most praise
among the women of Phaestus. Iphis
was the same age as her, the two of them
were equally attractive, and they both
had received their earliest education
in elements appropriate to their age
from the same instructors. Given all this,
love touched the naïve hearts in both of them   1150   [720]
and wounded each of them in the same way.
But how different their expectations are!
Iänthe is looking forward to the wedding
and to the marriage which has been arranged,
for she assumes that Iphis is a man
and believes that she will be her husband.
Iphis loves Iänthe, but has no hope
she can enjoy her, and this despair itself
makes her passion grow—a young virgin girl
burning with love for another virgin.   1160
Scarcely holding back her tears, she cries out:

  "What will be the end of this love of mine,
a passion no one ever knew before,
a new and unnatural snare of love,
which has me in its grip? For if the gods
desired to spare me, they should have spared me.
If not, if they wanted to destroy me,
they might at least have inflicted on me   [730]
a natural evil, something people know.
Cows do not burn with love for other cows,   1170
or mares for other mares. It is the ram
which rouses passion in the ewe, and hinds
run after their own stags. Birds mate that way.
Among all animals, no passion grips
one female for another. How I wish
I were not like this! But then, to make sure
Crete gave birth to every kind of monster,
the daughter of the Sun, Pasiphaë,
had sex with that bull! Still, she was female,
and the beast was male. If the truth be told,   1180

the love I feel is more extreme than hers.
She, at least, followed a passionate desire
where she had some hope of satisfaction,
and with her tricks and the cow-like structure
she got the bull to mount her.[1] Her lover
was someone capable of being deceived. [740]
But even if all the world's inventiveness
were concentrated here and if Daedalus
were to fly back again on waxen wings,
what could he do? With his artistic skills 1190
could he transform me from a virgin girl
into a boy? Or alter you, Iänthe?
Come on, Iphis, pull yourself together.
Strengthen your resolve, shake off this passion,
these useless, foolish feelings! Consider
what you are by birth, unless you yourself
have been deceived as well. Choose what is right,
and love the way a woman ought to love!
Hope creates love and nourishes desire,
but in your case there is no room for hope. 1200 [750]
No guardian keeps you from her dear embrace,
no watchful husband's care, no stern father,
nor does she herself deny your wishes.
But you cannot possess her or ever know
that great delight, whatever comes about,
not even if gods and men do what they can.
Even now, none of the things I pray for
has been denied. In their kindness to me,
the gods have given whatever they could.
My father, my future father-in-law, 1210
and she herself want just what I want, too.
But Nature, more powerful than all of these,
does not wish that. She alone stands in the way.
See, the moment I long for has arrived,
the wedding day is here, and Iänthe [760]
will now be mine. Yet I cannot have her!
With water all around, I will be thirsty.
Why, Juno, guardian of marriage rites,
and you, too, Hymen, why do you appear

---

[1] Pasiphaë, as noted earlier, concealed herself inside an artificial cow in order to have sex with the bull. Some traditions claim that Daedalus was the artist who made the cow.

at rituals where there is no bridegroom 1220
and where the married couple are both brides?"

Having said these words, Iphis falls silent.
The other virgin is no less on fire
and prays that you, Hymen, will come quickly.
Telethusa, afraid of what Iänthe
so desires, at one point postpones the date,
then causes a delay by feigning illness,
and often talks of omens or her dreams
as an excuse. But now she has used up
all the pretexts she can plausibly invent, 1230
and the time for the marriage she put off
has come—only a single day remains. [770]
She tears the sacred ribbons from her head
and from her daughter's. With dishevelled hair
she grabs the altar and cries out:

"O Isis,
goddess who lives in Paraetonium,
in fields of Mareotis, in Pharos,
and by the Nile with seven branching streams,
I pray to you—bring help and ease our fears.[1]
I saw you once and recognized your signs, 1240
your sacred symbols, and the echoing bronze
of sacred rattles in your company.
I heard your orders and kept them in mind.
Thanks to what you said and gifts you gave us,
this girl now lives and I have not been punished.
Have pity on us both. Give us your help." [780]

When her speech ended, Telethusa wept.
The goddess seemed to make her altars move.
In fact, they trembled, the temple doorways
shuddered, her horns shone out, just like the moon, 1250
and sounds came from her echoing sistrums.
The mother, not yet free from her concern,
but happy about the hopeful omens,
left the temple, and as she walked away,
her companion, Iphis, followed, moving

---

[1]Paraetonium was a city in Libya, Mareotis a lake near Alexandria, and Pharos an island across from Alexandria.

with a longer stride than normal. Her face
had lost its pale complexion, and her strength
had grown. Her features were more sharply drawn,
her hair unstyled and shorter, and she showed
more energy than women do. Iphis, 1260 [790]
you who were a girl a moment ago
are now a boy! Rejoice! Be confident,
and have no fear!

              They take gifts to the shrine
and add a short inscription carved in stone:

What Iphis, as a girl, vowed she would do,
now Iphis, as a boy, is carrying through.

The beams of the next day's sun shine out
across the spacious world, as Venus, Juno,
and Hymen gather by the wedding fires,
and the boy Iphis gains his own Iänthe. 1270

Book Ten

X

[The marriage of Orpheus and Eurydice; Eurydice dies; Orpheus asks Pluto and Persephone if he can have Eurydice back; they send her back on condition Orpheus does not turn around until he reaches the upper world; Orpheus looks behind him, and Eurydice returns to the Underworld; Orpheus refuses to have sex with women; the trees gather to hear Orpheus sing; the story of Cyparissus, Apollo, and the giant stag; Cyparissus is transformed into a cypress tree; Orpheus sings of Jupiter and Ganymede and of Apollo and Hyacinthus; Hyacinthus is mortally wounded and transformed into a flower; Orpheus sings of how Venus turns the Cerastes into bulls, how the daughters of Propoetus become flint, how Pygmalion falls in love with a statue he carved, and how Venus brings the statue to life; Orpheus continues with the story of Cinyras and Myrrha: how Myrrha lusts for her father, how her nurse helps her trick Cinyras, how Myrrha runs away and is transformed to a tree, and how the tree gives birth to Adonis; Orpheus sings of the love of Venus and Adonis and of Venus' story of Atalanta and Hippomenes: how Hippomenes beats Atalanta in a race using golden apples; how Venus punishes Hippomenes; Orpheus tells how Adonis is killed and changed into a flower.]

From Crete, Hymen, dressed in yellow garments,   ORPHEUS AND EURYDICE
flew through vast expanses of the air
and moved to regions of the Cicones,
summoned there by the voice of Orpheus.[1]
His trip was futile. Although he did attend
Orpheus' wedding, he did not speak
his usual words, or have a joyful face,
or bring good luck. Even the torch he held
spluttered with smoke, making his eyes water,
and waving it around produced no flames.   10
What happened afterwards was even worse
than any omen, for Eurydice,
Orpheus' new bride, while wandering
through a meadow with a crowd of naiads,
was bitten on the ankle by a snake.   [10]
She collapsed and died. The Thracian poet,
after he had had enough of mourning   ORPHEUS IN THE UNDERWORLD
in the upper world, dared to travel down
the Taenarian gate to the river Styx,
to see if he could win the sympathy   20
of dead shades down below.[2] He moved through crowds
of insubstantial spirits, the phantoms
of those who had received full burial rites,
and came to Persephone and the god

---

[1] Hymen was the god of marriage, who had just presided over the wedding of Iphis and Iänthe (at the end of Book 9). The region of the Cicones was in Thrace. Orpheus was the son of Apollo and Calliope, one of the nine Muses.

[2] The Taenarian gate in the south Peloponnese was an entrance to the Underworld.

of all the shadows of the dead, who rules
that dismal kingdom. Plucking lyre strings
to accompany his words, Orpheus sang:

"O you gods who live underneath the earth,
where all we created mortal beings
finally descend, if you'll permit me 30
to set aside the uncertain stories
of a deceptive tongue and speak the truth,
then, with your permission, I will tell you
I am not here to see dark Tartarus [20]
or tie up Medusa's monstrous offspring
with its triple throat and snaky hair.[1] No.
The reason I came down here is my wife.
She stepped on a snake, which spread its poison
through her and robbed her of her youthful life.
I wanted to be able to bear her loss, 40
and I can tell you I did try to do that.
But Love prevailed. In the upper regions
he is a well-known god. I'm not aware
if in this place the same is also true,
but I imagine he is known here, too.
If the story of that rape in times gone by
took place, then you were joined by Love, as well.[2]
I beg you by these terrifying spaces,
by this vast Chaos, and by the silence [30]
of this huge realm, weave once again the thread 50
which determined Eurydice's swift fate.
All things, including us, belong to you,
and after we delay a little while,
sooner or later we all hurry down
to this one place. All men come to this spot.
It is our final home, and you possess
the longest rule over the human race.
My wife will also come under your sway,
when, as a mature woman, she has lived
her full span of years. I am asking this 60

---

[1]Medusa's offspring was Cerberus, the dog at the entrance to Hades. Hercules in one of his labours had bound the dog and dragged him away.

[2]Orpheus is here alluding to the abduction of Proserpine (Persephone) by Pluto (for Ovid's version of the story see 5.607 ff above).

> as a favour to me, and if the Fates
> deny my wife this gift, my mind is set—
> I have no wish to journey back. You gods
> can then rejoice that both of us are dead."

As Orpheus sang this, striking his strings
to match his words, the bloodless spirits wept.
Tantalus did not reach for the water
when it flowed out, Ixion's wheel stood still,
as if amazed, and vultures did not gnaw
on Tityus' liver. The Belides,
daughters of Danaüs, put down their jars,
and Sisyphus, you, too, sat on your rock.[1]
And people say that then, for the first time,
the cheeks of the Furies were wet with tears,
overpowered by his singing. The queen
of the lower regions and her husband,
who rules the Underworld, could not refuse
what he had asked. They called Eurydice,
standing there among the spirits of those
who had just arrived. She walked up slowly,
still affected by her wound. Orpheus,
the poet from Thrace, took her back again
and, as he did so, accepted this condition—
he would not turn round and look behind him
until he had moved up from the valleys
of Avernus, and if he did, his gift
would be withdrawn.[2]

          The two of them then climbed
the ascending path through the still silence,
a steep, dark way, enveloped in thick fog.
As they drew near the surface of the earth,
Orpheus feared his wife Eurydice
could not keep up and longed to look at her.
Because he loved her, he glanced behind him.
She instantly fell back. Poor Orpheus
stretched out both his arms, trying to hold her

---

[1] For details of these figures in the underworld see 4.775 ff (and the footnotes), where Ovid describes what Juno sees on her visit there.

[2] Avernus was the name of a crater and a lake in Italy, thought to be near an entrance to the Underworld.

BOOK TEN

and be held. He caught nothing but thin air.
Now dying a second time, Eurydice
made no complaint at all about her husband
(what could she object to except the fact
that she was loved?). She said her last farewell, 100
which scarcely reached his ears, and then turned back
to the region she had come from.

                       Orpheus,   ORPHEUS
numbed by the fact his wife had now died twice,
was like that coward who saw Cerberus,
the triple-headed dog, when he had chains
around his middle neck, the one whose fear
did not leave him until his nature did,
when his body turned to stone, or Olenos
and you, sad Lethaea, so confident
of your own loveliness. You two once had 110
such closely wedded hearts, but Olenos
desired to take your guilt upon himself
and to be seen to take the blame. And now,
you sit on moist Mount Ida, changed to rock.[1]
Orpheus longed to cross the Styx again,
but prayers were useless—the ferryman
pushed him away. He sat down by the shore
for seven days, neglecting his appearance.
He refused all nourishment and fed himself
on his own tears and mental pain. Complaining 120
that the gods of Erebus were heartless,
he moved away to high Mount Rhodope
and windswept Haemus.[2]

                   The Titan sun god
had three times come to watery Pisces,
finishing off the year, and in that time
Orpheus had refused to love a woman,
either because his love had ended badly

---

[1] Hercules descended to Hades and dragged Cerberus away from the Underworld with a chain around one of his three neck. A traditional story said that a man observed this going on and was so terrified he turned to stone. Olenus' wife, Lethaea compared her own beauty to that of a goddess. Olenus volunteered to be punished instead of her. They were both turned to rock.

[2] Rhodope and Haemus were mountains in Thrace.

or because he'd made a promise not to.[1]
But many women, passionate for him,
wished to wed the poet and were upset   130
when he declined. But Orpheus transferred
his love to tender boys and was the first
among the Thracian people to enjoy
their brief spring years and early flowering,
before they were young men.

                   There was a hill   ORPHEUS AND THE TREES
whose summit was an open level plain
with fresh green turf, a place which had no shade.
But when that poet, born of gods, sat down
and struck his lyre strings, the trees moved there.
Chaonian oak and groves of poplar   140   [90]
(Phaëton's sisters), oak trees thick with leaves,
tender lime, beech, and virgin laurel trees
came to the place, with brittle hazels, too,
and ash trees (used for spears), clear firs, holm oaks
weighed down with acorns, delightful plane trees,
maples in all their various colours,
with willows, which grow by banks of rivers,
watery lotus trees, as well as boxwood,
which is always green, slender tamarisks,
twin-coloured myrtle trees, and viburnum   150
with its dark blue berries.[2] You ivy trees
with twisting shoots came, too, and leafy vines,
ivy-covered elm trees and mountain ash,   [100]
spruce, wild strawberry loaded with red fruit,
and bending palms, the prize of victory.
You pines were there, your needles gathered up
into a bushy crest—a pleasing sight
to the mother of gods, for Cybele's Attis
exchanged his human form for such a tree
and hardened in its trunk.[3] Among that throng   160
a cypress was there, too, shaped like a cone

---

[1] Pisces is the last sign of the Zodiac. When the sun reaches it, the year is over.

[2] Phaëton's sisters, daughters of the sun, were changed into poplars. For Ovid's version of the story see above 2.497 ff.

[3] Attis was the lover of the goddess Cybele (the mother of the gods). In a fit of madness he castrated himself and his blood and spirit entered a pine tree.

which on a race course marks the turning point.
Though now a tree, it was a young boy once,
loved by the god who strings the bow and lyre.

There was a huge stag, sacred to the nymphs   CYPARISSUS
who live in Carthaea's fields. This creature
had antlers branching out so far, they cast   [110]
deep shade across its head. Its horns glittered
with gold, and a collar of precious stones
on its glossy neck hung down its shoulders.   170
On its forehead swung a tiny ball of silver,
attached by little straps, and pearls of bronze,
both the same size, shone out from its two ears,
beside its hollow temples. Now, this stag
had no fear at all and would set aside
its natural shyness, visit people's homes,
and, even with strangers, stretch out its neck
for their hands to stroke. Above all others,
it was most dear to you, Cyparissus,
the most beautiful young lad on Cea.[1]   180   [120]
You used to take it to fresh grazing lands
or clear springs with flowing water. Sometimes
you draped different flowers on its horns.
At other times, like a horseman, you rode
on the creature's back and enjoyed yourself
guiding its tender mouth this way and that
with purple reins.
                    One summer day at noon,
when the curved claws of the shore-loving Crab
were blazing in Sun's heat, the weary stag
was resting its limbs on the grassy turf,   190
pleased with the coolness of the shady trees.[2]
The young lad Cyparissus by accident   [130]
threw his sharp javelin and hit the beast.
As he saw it dying from a cruel wound,
the boy resolved to kill himself as well.
Phoebus spoke to Cyparissus, trying
in any way he could to ease his pain.
He counselled him to moderate his grief

[1]Cea is one of the islands in the Cyclades.
[2]The Crab is a reference to the sign of the zodiac.

in proportion to the cause. The young boy
still continued grieving and asked the gods, 200
as a last gift, to let him mourn forever.
By now, as his blood was being consumed
in constant tears, his limbs began to change,
turning a shade of green, and then his hair,
which a moment ago was hanging down
his snow-white forehead, grew bushy and stiff,
pointing upward in a graceful spiky crest [140]
to the starry sky. The god Apollo
groaned and sighed with grief:

            "I will mourn for you.
And you, in your turn, will mourn for others 210
and become a part of people's grieving."[1]

These were the types of trees which Orpheus
attracted to him, and he sat down there,
with crowds of wild beasts and birds around him.
When his thumb had tested his strings enough
and he sensed the various notes they made,
although quite different, were all in tune,
he raised his voice in the following song:

   "My parent Muse, begin my song with Jove,   ORPHEUS' SONG
for all things yield to Jupiter's power, 220
and I have often offered songs before
about the might of Jupiter and sung
more solemn melodies of the Giants [150]
and Jove's victorious bolts of lightning
hurled down upon the plains of Phlegraea.[2]
But now is the time for a lighter song.
I sing of boys the gods have loved and girls
in the grip of forbidden flames who earned
just punishment for carnal love affairs.

The king of the gods once burned with love 230
for Phrygian Ganymede.[3] So he changed   JUPITER AND GANYMEDE
to a bird, feeling that form would better fit

---

[1] Among the Romans, cypress branches were commonly used as a symbol of mourning.

[2] For details of Ovid's treatment of Jupiter's war against the Giants, see above 1.208 ff. Orpheus' parent muse was Calliope.

[3] Ganymede was a beautiful young prince of Troy.

what he had in mind than his normal shape.
He thought most birds beneath his dignity,
so he chose the one with power enough
to bear his lightning bolt. Once in this form,
he did not hold back, but beating the air
with his spurious wings, he flew to Troy
and snatched away the boy, who even now
still brings the mixing cups to Jupiter,
and, flouting Juno's wishes, pours his nectar.

You too, Hyacinthus from Amyclae—   APOLLO AND HYACINTHUS
Phoebus would have settled you in heaven,
if grim fate had given him sufficient time.
Still, as much as things like that are possible,
you are immortal, for every time the spring
drives off the winter and the Ram appears
right after watery Pisces, you rise
and blossom in the fresh green turf once more.
You are the one my father doted on
above all others. His shrine at Delphi,
placed in the centre of the world, lacked
its presiding deity, while the god
remained in Eurotas and unwalled Sparta,
totally neglecting lyre and bow.
Ignoring who he was, he volunteered
to carry hunting nets or hold the dogs,
as he travelled across harsh mountain ridges,
always with his companion Hyacinthus.
In this way, by staying with him, he nursed
his fiery love.

               When the Titan Sun
was almost in the middle of his course
between the previous and the coming night,
an equal distance from each one of them,
Hyacinthus and Apollo stripped down,
rubbed rich olive oil onto their bodies,
until they gleamed, and started to compete
in a discus toss. First Apollo threw,
balancing the discus and hurling it
into the airy breeze. Its weight broke up
the clouds along its path. After some time,
the disc fell back and struck the solid ground,

proof of Apollo's strength and skill combined.
Eager to have his turn, the Spartan lad,
not thinking clearly, quickly ran ahead
to pick the discus up, but the hard earth
made it bounce, and it hit him in the face.
The boy grew pale. So did Apollo, too.
He held your failing limbs, Hyacinthus,
and strove at times to bring your spirit back.
He also tried to stanch the grievous wound
and with his herbs to keep your soul inside,
as it was leaving. But all his expertise
had no effect. The wound could not be cured.
When someone in a garden breaks the stems
of lilies with bushy yellow stamens,
or of violets or poppies, the blooms
no longer stand erect, but quickly droop,
bowing their weakened heads, and their top parts
now gaze upon the ground. In just that way
the dying face of Hyacinthus sagged.
His weakened neck could not support his head,
which sank onto his shoulder. Phoebus said:

   'Son of Oebalus, you are now leaving me,
robbed of your early youth. I see your wound
and stand condemned. Because of you, I feel
both shame and sorrow. This right hand of mine
must be considered guilty of your death.
I am the one who took your life. But still,
how was I to blame, unless playing games
can be called a fault, unless my love for you
can be called a huge mistake? How I wish
that I could die with you or give you back
your life for mine! But I am bound by Fate.
Still, you will remain with me forever,
clinging to my lips as they remember.
The lyre my hand strikes and songs I sing
will ring out for you. And you will become
a brand new form of flower whose markings
imitate my cries of grief. The time will come
when the bravest hero will link himself

to this same flower and on its petals
men will read his name."[1]

                  While Apollo's lips,
which do not lie, were uttering these words,
lo and behold, blood which was pouring out
across the ground, discolouring the grass,   [210]
was no longer blood. A flower sprang up
with a more brilliant tint than Tyrian dye
and a shape like lilies, but where a lily
is silvery white, this bloom was purple.   320
Apollo was the one responsible
for honouring Hyacinthus in this way,
but for the god that was not sufficient.
So he inscribed his own groans on the plant
and put the words *ai ai* on the flower,
and there these mournful letters are inscribed.
Sparta is not ashamed that it gave birth
to Hyacinthus. They still honour him
today, and every year they celebrate
a festival in Hyacinthus' name,   330
based on set rituals from earlier times.

But if, by chance, you were to ask Amathus,   [220]
that mine-rich city, if it was happy   THE CERASTES
to be the home of Propoetus' daughters,
it would renounce them, as it would reject
those people whose rough foreheads bore two horns,
from which they got their name, the Cerastes.[2]
Before the gates of these men's house there stood
Jove's altar, god of hospitality,
stained with blood. If any stranger saw it   340
and did not know their crimes, he would assume
they used that place for offering sacrifice
of suckling calves or Amathusian sheep.
But those men killed their guests! Gentle Venus,

---

[1] The hyacinth allegedly had the letters *ai* depicted on its petals—and this Greek word was commonly used to express a cry of extreme grief. *Aiai* is often translated as "*Alas!*" The greatest of heroes is Ajax of Salamis, whose name in Greek, *Aias*, was often associated with this cry of grief, especially given his tragic story (which Ovid presents in Book 13).

[2] Amathus was a city in Crete. The name Cerastes comes from the Greek word meaning "with horns."

offended by their sacrilegious rites,
was getting ready to reject her cities
and Cretan lands. But then she asked herself:

> 'In what way have my cities or this place,
> which is so dear to me, done any wrong?
> What are their crimes? I should punish instead
> this wicked race with exile, or with death,
> or with some penalty between the two.
> What could that be except a change in shape?
> And so for punishment I will transform them.'

While she is debating how to change these men,
her eyes turn to their horns, which prompts the thought
that she could leave the horns on those men's heads,
and thus she turns their bodies into bulls.

But those obscene daughters of Propoetus   PROPOETUS' DAUGHTERS
dared to deny that Venus was divine.
Because of this and because the goddess
was enraged, those women, so people say,
were the first to sell their reputations
and their bodies as public prostitutes.
But then, once they lost all sense of shame,
blood hardened in their cheeks, and a slight change
was enough to turn them into stony flint.

Pygmalion saw these women's filthy lives   PYGMALION
and was disgusted by the many vices
Nature had placed within the female mind.
So he lived a long time as a single man,
without a wife or partner for his bed.
Meanwhile, with astonishing skill he carved
a statue out of snow-white ivory,
a work of genius. He gave the form
beauty no mortal woman could possess
and fell in love with what he had produced.
She has a face just like a real young girl,
and you might well believe she is alive
and wishes to move, if her modesty
did not prevent her. So much artistry
lies hidden in his art. He is amazed,
and passion for this image of a body
eats at Pygmalion's heart. Often his hands

stroke the work, testing whether it is flesh
or ivory. He still does not concede
that it is stone. He kisses the statue
and imagines those kisses are returned.
He speaks to it, embraces it, and thinks,
when he holds onto a limb, his fingers
make an impression there and is afraid
he may bruise her flesh by pressing on it.
Sometimes he talks to her with flattery
and sometimes brings her presents girls might like—
sea shells and polished pebbles, little birds,
flowers with a thousand colours, painted beads,
and amber tears from Helios' daughters,
which drip from trees.[1] He also clothes her limbs,
puts gemstones on her fingers, and places
long necklaces around her throat. Smooth pearls
hang from her ears and pendants on her chest.
All things suit her, but when she has no clothes,
she seems no less attractive. This statue
Pygmalion places on a couch covered
with fabric dyed in Tyrian purple.
He calls her the companion of his bed
and cushions her reclining neck on pillows,
as if she were alive.

      The day arrived
when throughout all Cyprus they celebrate
the most splendid festival of Venus.
Young heifers with gold on their growing horns
collapsed as axes struck their snow-white necks,
and burning incense smoked. Pygmalion,
having made his offering at the altar,
stood there and timidly spoke out:

     'If you gods
are able to grant anything, I wish
my wife could be . . .'

     He did not dare to say
'my ivory girl,' so he finished with:

---

[1] For Ovid's treatment of how the daughters of the sun god (the Greek god Helios) were turned into trees and weep amber see above 2.497 ff. In Ovid's account the sun god is Apollo.

'... just like my girl carved out of ivory.'

Golden Venus, who was there in person
at her festival, understood his prayer
and what he meant. She gave him a signal
the gods were well disposed—the altar fire
flared up three times, sending a spiky flame
into the air. Pygmalion went home
and hurried to the statue of his girl.
Leaning down over the couch, he kissed her.
She seemed warm, so he kissed her once again
and also felt her breast. Under his touch
the ivory lost its hardness, grew soft,
moved underneath his fingers, and gave way,
just as Hymettus wax softens in the sun
and, once men's fingers work it, can be formed
in many shapes, thus becoming useful
by being used. Pygmalion is amazed,
full of joy but also doubtful, afraid
he may be wrong. The lover's hands caress
the object of his love repeatedly.
It is a living body! When his thumb
presses on a vein, it throbs! Then indeed,
Pygmalion of Paphos in his mind
uttered the most fulsome thanks to Venus,
with his mouth still firmly pressed against those lips
that were no longer stone. The living girl
felt his kisses and blushed. Lifting her eyes
timidly up to the sunlight, she saw
her lover and the heavens both at once.
The goddess was present at the marriage
she had brought about, and when the moon's horns
had nine times formed a perfect circle,
Pygmalion's wife bore a son called Paphos,
from whom the island now derives its name.[1]
This Paphos had a son named Cinyras,
who could have been considered fortunate
if he had had no children.

---

[1] Ovid does not provide a name for Pygmalion's love. In other versions of the story she is called Galatea.

Book Ten

                    I will now sing   CINYRAS AND MYRRHA
of horrifying events. You daughters,
keep far away from here and parents, too.   [300]
Or if my song does captivate your heart,
do not accept my story, and assume
it is not true. Or, if you do believe it,
believe also how the act was punished.
But if nature apparently allows
such things to happen, [I congratulate
the people of Ismarus and my part
of the world]—I am happy that this land
lies at such a distance from those regions
where such appalling wickedness was born.[1]
Let Panchaean land be rich in balsam
and have its cinnamon and costmary,
its incense oozing from the trees and blooms
of different kinds—none of that is worth it,
if it still produces myrrh, for the cost   [310]
of that new tree was much too great.[2]

                              Myrrha,
Cupid himself denies that you were struck
by an arrow from his bow and says his flames
played no part in your crime. It was a Fury,
one of those three sisters with bloated snakes
and firebrands from the Styx, who breathed on you.
To hate one's father is a wicked thing,
but love like yours is a more heinous crime.
Distinguished princes of every country
desire your hand, and from all eastern lands
young men have come competing for your bed.
Pick out a man from all of these, Myrrha,
to be your husband, and make sure one man,
your father, is not included with them.

Myrrha, in fact, senses this and fights back,
trying to conquer her repugnant love.
She tells herself:

---

[1] Line 305 in the Latin is often rejected as spurious. The English text is in square brackets.

[2] Panchaea was a region in Arabia famous for its spices.

'Where is my mind taking me?
What am I trying to do? O you gods,
I pray to you and to the natural ties
and sacred laws of parents, you must stop
this wickedness and keep me from my crime.
If it truly is a crime. One could say
natural affections do not rule out
a love like this, for other animals,
when they have sex, do not discriminate.
When a heifer has her father mount her,
there is no disgrace, and a horse will take
his daughter for a wife, goats will couple
with goats who are their offspring, and birds
with other birds whose seed created them.
How happy they are, that they can do this!
But human worry has imposed harsh laws,
and jealous regulations now forbid
what nature tolerates. Still, people say
races exist where mothers wed their sons
and daughters are married to their fathers,
where natural affection is increased
by double bonds of love. I feel so sad
I was not born there and have to suffer,
because, with my bad luck, I live elsewhere!
But why do I keep going over this?
I must get rid of these forbidden feelings!
He deserves my love, but as a father.
If I were not great Cinyras' daughter,
then I could go to bed with him. But now,
I cannot have him, because he is mine
already—his very closeness to me
is my downfall. If I were a stranger,
I could do more. I would happily leave
and travel a long distance from this place,
if I could just escape this guilty love.
But a malicious passion holds me back.
By staying here I can see Cinyras,
touch him, talk to him, kiss him, even if
those are the only things I am allowed.
You wicked girl, what more can you expect?
Do you have any idea how much
you're mixing up established bonds and names?

Do you wish to be your mother's rival
and your father's whore? Will people call you
your child's sister and your brother's mother?
Are you not terrified of the Furies,
those sisters with black serpents in their hair?
People with wicked hearts see them attack
their eyes and face with savage torches.
But while your body still remains unstained,
do not corrupt your mind or violate
great Nature's laws with such forbidden sex!
Yes, you want to, but your circumstances
rule that out. He is an honorable man
and follows what is right. But how I wish
he felt inside a passion like my own.'

She says this to herself. Meanwhile, Cinyras,
faced with a large crowd of noble suitors,
is not sure what to do. He lists their names
and asks her which one she wants to marry.
Myrrha at first says nothing and just gazes
at her father's face. In her confusion,
her eyes fill with warm tears. So Cinyras,
thinking this a sign of virgin shyness,
tells her to stop crying, dries off her cheeks,
and kisses her. Myrrha is delighted
with his kiss, too much so, and when he asks
what sort of husband she would like to have,
she says:

    'One just like you.'

                    But her father,
not realizing what she means, praises her
and says:

    'Always be this loving to me.'

As he utters that word 'loving,' Myrrha,
aware of her own guilt, stares at the ground.

It was now midnight, and sleep had released
men's bodies from their cares. But the young girl,
Cinyras' daughter, was wide awake,
consumed by passion she could not suppress.
She thought again about her wild desires,

sometimes in despair and sometimes ready
to sound her father out. She was ashamed,
yet keen to try, unable to decide
what she should do. Just as a massive tree 570
struck by an axe, with one last blow to come,
leaves men in doubt where it will fall and causes
fear on every side, so her shifting mind,
struck by contradictory feelings, wavered,
swayed here and there, blown in two directions.
She could see no final end to how she felt,
no rest from her desires, other than death.
She made up her mind to die. So she got up,
resolved to tie a noose and hang herself.
She fixed some clothing above the doorway 580
and said:

        'Farewell, beloved Cinyras. [380]
Understand the reason for my death!'

                      These words
muttered to herself, so people say, reach
the ears of her faithful nurse, keeping watch
at the threshold of the girl she cares for.
The old woman gets up, opens the door,
sees what Myrrha has done to harm herself,
and screams. Then, all in the same instant,
she strikes her breast, tears her robe, removes
the clothes from Myrrha's neck, and rips them up. 590
Only after that does she have time to weep,
embrace the girl, and ask about the noose.
Myrrha stands there without saying a word,
eyes gazing at the ground. She is upset
she was so slow in trying to kill herself [390]
and has been discovered. The old woman
starts questioning her. Baring her white hair
and withered breasts, she keeps begging Myrrha,
by her cradle and her first nourishment,
to tell her what is causing her such grief. 600
Myrrha turns away and groans. But the nurse,
determined to find out, then promises
she will do more than not betray her trust.
She says:

Book Ten

>   'Tell me, and let me be of help.
> I may be old, but I am not useless.
> If it is some fit, I have herbs and charms
> with healing force. If a man has harmed you,
> I can cleanse you with a magic ritual.
> If gods are angry, they can be appeased
> with sacred offerings. I can't imagine   610
> what else it could be. Your house's fortunes   [400]
> are certainly secure and will remain so,
> with your mother and your father still alive.'

When Myrrha heard that word 'father,' she sighed
from the bottom of her heart. Even then,
the old nurse had no notion of the act
she had in mind. But still, she did assume
the young girl's anguish had to do with love.
She kept entreating Myrrha, begging her
to let her know, no matter what it was.   620
Clutching the weeping girl against her breast,
her trembling arms embraced her, and she said:

>   'I know what the matter is—you are in love!
> And in this my readiness to help you
> will be of service. You need have no fear.
> Your father will never know a thing.'

Myrrha was frantic. She pushed herself away   [410]
from the nurse's arms and, pressing her face
into the bed, she cried:

>   'Get out of here.
> I'm begging you. Spare me the wretched shame.'   630

When the nurse insisted, Myrrha shouted:

>   'Either go away or stop asking me
> why I feel such pain. What you want to know
> is an immoral crime.'

>   The old woman

felt a twinge of dread. She stretched out her hands,
shaking with age and fear, and fell down
at Myrrha's feet, just like a suppliant.
She tried coaxing and then frightening her
with what might happen if she did not tell,
threatening to speak out about the noose   640

337

and her attempt to kill herself. She swore
to help, if she would tell her of her love.
Myrrha raised her head. From her weeping eyes
the tears dripped down onto the nurse's breast.
She tried repeatedly to confess her love, [420]
but then would stop herself and hide her face
inside her clothing, too ashamed to speak.
All she said was:

          'Mother is so fortunate
to have the husband she is married to.'

And then she groaned. A cold tremor ran through 650
the nurse's limbs and bones, for now she knew
what Myrrha meant. Across her entire head
the old white hair bristled and stood on end.
She talked at length to Myrrha, telling her
she should get rid of such a fatal love,
if she could do it. The young girl understood
the advice was sound, but was still resolved
to die if she could not have the one she loved.
So the old nurse told her:

              'Go on living,
and enjoy your . . .'

           Not daring to say 'father,' 660
she fell silent. But then she swore an oath [430]
to the gods to validate her promise.

Pious married women were now holding
the annual festival of Ceres,
where they dress their bodies in white robes
and offer as first fruits of harvest time
garlands made from ears of grain. For nine nights
they consider sex and all contact with men
forbidden. Cinyras' wife, Cenchreis,
was a member of that group, participating 670
in the sacred rites, and thus the king's bed
lacked its rightful occupant. When the nurse
noticed Cinyras drunk from too much wine,
she informed him, with misplaced eagerness,
there was a girl truly passionate for him.
She gave a false name and praised her beauty.

When the king asked how old the girl might be, [440]
the nurse replied:

    'The same age as Myrrha.'

Cinyras told her to bring the girl to him.
The nurse returned back home and said to Myrrha: 680

    'Rejoice, my dear child. We have won the day!'

The girl was not completely overjoyed.
Her prophetic heart sensed future sorrow.
But still, there was such conflict in her mind
she did feel thrilled, as well.

                The time has come
when everything is quiet—the Boötes
has turned his wagon with its slanting pole
between the Bears.[1] Myrrha is preparing
to commit her dreadful act. The golden moon
flees from the heavens, and dark clouds conceal 690
the hidden stars. Night lacks its fires. And you, [450]
Icarus, are the first to avert your face,
as does Erigone, your daughter, too,
set in the heavens for the pious love
she showed her father.[2] Three time a signal
makes Myrrha falter, when her foot stumbles,
and three times the funereal screech owl
gives out an ominous shriek of warning.
She still keeps moving. Black night and shadows
lessen her shame. In her left hand she grips 700
the nurse, while with her right she gropes her way
through total darkness. And now she is there,
on the threshold, and opening the door.
Now she is being led into the room.
Her knees threaten to give way beneath her,
her blood and colour disappear, her spirit
fails as she moves on. The closer she gets

---

[1] The Boötes was a constellation in the northern night sky (the Wagoner).

[2] Icarus (or, more commonly, Icarius) was a follower of Bacchus. He helped to introduce the production of wine to human beings. He was killed by a group of drunken peasants. His daughter, Erigone, found the body and, overwhelmed with grief, hanged herself. Bacchus then placed them both in the heavens as constellations (Arcturus and Virgo) and instituted a festival in their honour.

to her great crime, the more she feels afraid.
She regrets what she is doing and wishes
she could return without being recognized.
As she pauses, the old nurse takes her arm,
leads her to the high bed, hands her over,
thus joining two doomed bodies, and then says:

'Take this young girl, Cinyras. She is yours.'

The father welcomes his own flesh and blood
into his incestuous bed, soothing
her virgin fears and encouraging her
when she is frightened. And it may well be
he even calls her 'daughter' to suit her age,
while Myrrha addresses him as 'father,'
two names appropriate to their foul crime.

After having sex with her own father,
Myrrha left the room. In her corrupt womb
full of incestuous seed, she carried
a burden she had criminally conceived.
The next night they once again committed
the guilty act, and they did not stop there.
But after having sex so many times,
Cinyras at length was eager to find out
who his lover was. So he brought in a light,
recognized his daughter and his own guilt,
and, in such pain he could not say a word,
pulled a gleaming sword out of the scabbard
in which it hung. Myrrha fled, saved from death
by the gift of night and pitch-black shadows.
Wandering through wide fields, she moved beyond
the Arabian palm trees and Panchaea
for nine full cycles of the crescent moon
until, at last worn out, she stopped to rest
in Sabaean land.[1] By now, the burden
in her womb was getting difficult to bear.
Weary with life and yet afraid of death,
not knowing what to wish for, she uttered
the following prayer:

---

[1] The phrase Sabaean land refers to a part of Arabia.

BOOK TEN

'O, if any of you gods
listens to those who are truly penitent,
I am not seeking to excuse myself,
for I deserve this cruel punishment.
But in case, by staying alive, I pollute
the living or, by dying, harm the dead,
drive me from both realms by altering me 750
and robbing me of both my life and death.'

Some deity attends to those who pray,
for some god clearly hears her final plea.
While she is speaking, earth covers her legs,
roots shoot out sideways through her breaking nails, [490]
growing a solid base for a tall trunk,
her bones grow stronger and, in the centre,
the blood still in her marrow turns to sap.
Her arms become large branches, her fingers
small ones, and her skin hardens into bark. 760
A tree has grown around her heavy womb,
and covered her breasts, and is preparing
to spread across her neck. She cannot wait
and, leaning down to meet the rising wood,
buries her face in bark. Though she has lost
her body and the senses she once had,
she keeps on weeping still, and the warm drops [500]
drip down the tree. But with these tears of hers
she wins great fame, for the myrrh that trickles
down the bark still bears its mistress' name, 770
which men will hear in every future age.

But underneath the bark, that infant child   ADONIS
her incest had conceived has grown to term
and now is searching for a passageway
where he might crawl out and leave his mother.
Inside the tree, the pregnant womb swells up.
The burden strains the mother, but her pains
have no words of their own. She lacks a voice
to call Lucina in her labour pangs.
But the tree is like a person struggling 780
to be delivered—it groans frequently,
bends over, and is wet with falling tears.
Kind Lucina stands beside the branches, [510]
as they cry in pain, rubs them with her hands,

and murmurs phrases to bring on the birth.
The tree cracks open and through the splitting bark
gives up its living burden, a crying child.
The naiads set him down on the soft grass
and then anoint him with his mother's tears.
Even Envy would have praised his beauty.   790
He looked like one of those naked bodies
of painted Cupids, except to make them
both alike you would have to take away
their quivers or else give him a small one.

Winged time glides past before we notice   VENUS AND ADONIS
and tricks us, for nothing moves more quickly
than the passing years. That young infant child,   [520]
son of his own sister and her father,
not long ago encased inside a tree,
that most beautiful boy born yesterday,   800
is now a youthful lad, and now a man,
even finer looking than he was before,
so much so he wins the love of Venus
and pays her back for his mother's passion.[1]
Young Cupid, while carrying his quiver,
gave his mother a kiss, and, by accident,
one of his arrows which was sticking out
scratched her breast. Venus pushed her son away,
but the wound she had received was deeper
than it looked, more than she first recognized.   810
Now captivated by a human form,
she does not care about Cytherian shores,
or visit Paphos, her sea-girt island,   [530]
or Cnidos, rich in fish, or Amathus,
with its wealthy ores.[2] She even avoids
the heavens, for she prefers Adonis
to the sky. She holds him, remains with him
as his companion, and though her custom
is constantly to linger in the shade

---

[1] In some versions of the story of Myrrha, her passion is brought about by Venus (hence, the suggestion of revenge in these lines). But Ovid has said earlier that that a Fury must have caused Myrrha's incestuous desires, since Cupid has denied that the love associated with him and his mother was involved (see above 10.473 ff).

[2] Cnidos was a city in Asia Minor. Amathus was a city in Crete. The phrase "Cytherian shores" refers to the island of Crete.

and, by cultivating her own beauty,
to enhance it, now she travels with him
over mountain ridges and through forests,
across shrub-covered rocks, with knees exposed
and her clothes hitched up, just like Diana.
She urges on the hounds and even hunts
wild beasts considered safe to chase as prey—
swift-running hares, stags with huge horns, or deer.
But she avoids ferocious boars and shuns
rapacious wolves, bears with claws, and lions,
who gorge themselves on cattle herds they kill.
She warns you to fear these beasts, Adonis,
as if her warnings would have some effect:

   'Be brave against the ones that run away,
for boldness which confronts a bold wild beast
is just not safe. Do not be rash, my boy.
Spare me the danger. Do not chase the brutes
whom nature has fitted out with weapons,
in case your glory comes at my expense.
Your youth and beauty and those other things
which Venus finds delightful will not charm
bristling boars and lions or eyes and minds
of savage beasts. In those curved tusks of theirs
wild boars have lightning, and tawny lions
display a boundless fury when they charge.
How I hate that tribe.'

                    When Adonis asked
the reason why she felt that way, she said:

   'I will tell you, and you will be amazed
at the strange result of a wrongful act
committed long ago. But I am tired.
I am not used to all this exercise.
Look, that poplar tree is beckoning us
with welcoming shade, and the green turf there
will serve us as a bed. I wish to rest
on the ground right here, with you beside me.'

She stretched out, pressing against the grass and him,
her neck reclining on the young man's chest,
and, as she spoke, she mixed her words with kisses:

'You may perhaps have heard about a girl
who in a race could beat the fastest men.
That story was not just a foolish tale—
in any contest she outran them all.
But it was hard to tell if her fast pace
deserved more praise than her great beauty.
Once she asked a god about a husband,
and the god replied:

    'You do not need a man,
 Atalanta. For you, getting married
 is something to avoid. But nonetheless,
 you will not escape it and, while still alive,
 will lose yourself.'

    What the god prophesied
scared Atalanta, so she lived her life
in shady forests and did not get married.
She escaped the crowds of eager suitors
by demanding very harsh conditions:

 'No one will wed me, until a suitor
 beats me in a race. So run against me.
 To the swift will go a wife and wedding.
 For the slow the prize is death. On those terms,
 let the contests start!'

    Yes, she was cruel,
but the power of beauty is so great,
many men agreed to the rule she set
and courted her. At one unequal race
Hippomenes looked on from where he sat
and asked himself:

    'Why would anyone
 seek out a wife at such enormous risk?'

He found the young men's passion foolish
and excessive. But when he saw her face
and her unclothed body—one like my own,
Adonis, or yours, if you were female—
he was amazed. Raising his hands, he said:

 'Those of you I criticized just now,
 forgive me. When I spoke, I did not know
 you were competing for a prize like this.'

Book Ten

By praising her, he lights a fire of love,
and when his jealousy has made him tense,
he prays that none of those young challengers
will beat Atalanta. And then he says:

'But in this contest why not try my luck?
A daring man will get help from the gods.'

While he is reflecting on this question,
Atalanta races past on feet like wings. 890
To the young Boeotian, she seems to fly
with all the speed of a Scythian arrow,
but her beauty astounds him even more.
On her swift feet the facing breeze blows back [590]
her sandal straps, her hair is thrown across
her ivory shoulders, embroidered ribbons
flutter below her knees, and a blush spreads
across the girlish whiteness of her flesh,
just as a purple awning spread across
white hallways colours them a different shade.[1] 900
While the stranger is noticing all this,
the final lap is over. The winner,
Atalanta, receives a festive crown.
The losers groan and pay the penalty,
as they have promised. But Hippomenes,
undeterred by the fate of these young men, [600]
steps forward and, looking right at the girl,
calls out:

'Why seek to win an easy crown
defeating sluggards? Why not race with me?
If fortune gives me strength enough to win, 910
you will not be ashamed to be defeated
by such a worthy man, for my father
was Megareus, son of Onchestius,
whose grandfather was Neptune. So I am
great-grandson of the ruler of the seas.

---

[1] The Latin of line 591 is hard to figure out exactly. I have used the phrase "sandal straps" as a translation of *talaria*, a word which usually means either wings attached to the sandals or a long robe reaching the ankles. The first sense is usually reserved for those who wear winged sandals and seems a bit odd in this context. The image of a long robe seems inappropriate, too, when we have been told that Atalanta races naked or with most of her garments removed and are informed in the next lines that her body is covered with a blush.

Book Ten

My courage is as noble as my race.
And if I lose, you will have overcome
Hippomenes and thus have won yourself
a great and famous name.'

    As he spoke these words,
the daughter of Schoeneus looked at him   920
with a sympathetic face, uncertain
whether she would prefer to win or lose.   [610]
She murmured:

    'What god so despises beauty,
he wishes to destroy this man and tells him
to seek marriage and risk his precious life?
In my own view, I am not worth that much.
It is not his handsome form which moves me
(though I could be influenced by that, as well),
but the fact that the youth is still so young.
It is his age which makes me sensitive,   930
not the man himself. What of his courage
and his heart, which is not afraid of death?
By his descent is he not fourth in line
from the god who rules the seas? And besides,
does he not love me and think our marriage
so important he would die, if harsh fate
denied me to him? While you can, stranger,
go away! Leave these bloody courtship rites!   [620]
A match with me is cruel. No woman
would be reluctant to become your wife.   940
A girl with sense would welcome such a chance.
But why should I concern myself with you,
when many others have already perished?
Let him look to himself! And let him die,
if he will not be deterred by the deaths
of all those suitors and is pushed to it
by weariness with life. Will he die, then,
because he wished to share his life with me,
and suffer death, which he does not deserve,
as a reward for love? If I prevail,   950
people will hate me for my victory.
But that is not my fault! I wish you'd stop,
or, if you are mad to do this, I wish   [630]
you might run faster. Look at that young face,

those boyish features, like a virgin girl!
Alas, poor Hippomenes, how I wish
you had not seen me! You deserved to live!
If I had had more luck, if grievous fate
did not hold me back from marriage, then you
would be the one I'd want to share my bed.' 960

She finished. Like an inexperienced girl
feeling her first twinge of sexual desire
and unaware what she is doing, she loves,
but does not realize she is in love.

Now, as her father and the people cried
to have the usual race, Hippomenes,
Neptune's descendant, prayed to me,
begging for my help:

                   'O Cytherea, [640]
I entreat you to look on me with favour
in this risky contest. Nourish those flames 970
which you yourself have lit.'

                A gentle breeze
carried his flattering request to me.
I admit it moved me. So without delay
I offered him my help. There is a field,
the finest piece of land in all of Cyprus.
The natives call it Tamasus. Long ago,
their elders consecrated it to me
and gave instructions it should be a gift
added to my temples. A tree grows there,
right in the middle of the field. Its leaves 980
are gleaming yellow, and its branches rustle
with golden yellow fruit. As it so chanced,   THE GOLDEN APPLES
I had just left that tree and in my hand
I held three golden apples I had picked.
And so I went up to Hippomenes,
hiding myself from everyone but him, [650]
and told him how he should use the apples.
The trumpets gave the signal. Both runners
leaned out and raced off from the starting line.
Their flying feet skimmed the surface of the sand. 990
You could imagine them speeding over
ocean waves without moistening their feet

or racing over ears of standing grain.
The young man's spirits were stirred up by shouts
and the crowd's support, as they all cried:

> 'Now, now, Hippomenes! This is the time
> to push ahead! Right now with all your strength!
> Don't hold back! You'll win the race!'

                              It was not clear
which one was happier to hear these words,
Hippomenes or Atalanta. How often,
when she could have passed him, did she slow down,
gaze at his face a while, and move on by
against her will! He was gasping for air,
his throat parched, with the end still far away.
At that moment, Hippomenes tossed out
ahead of her one of the three apples
taken from the tree. She was astonished.
Keen to have the shining apple, she swerved,
ran off course, and picked up the rolling gold.
Hippomenes sped past her. Those looking on
applauded wildly. But she raced ahead,
making up for her delay, and once more
left the youth behind. Then she was held up
by a second apple. But she ran on
and passed him yet again. There still remained
the last part of the race. The young man prayed:

> 'O goddess, you who offered me this gift,
> stand by me now!'

                    With all his youthful strength,
he tossed the shining gold off to the side,
far into the field, so Atalanta
would require more time to run and get it.
She was not sure if she should chase the fruit,
but I forced her to pick it up and then,
once she had it, I made it heavier.
So I slowed her down with the apple's weight
and by the time she wasted getting it.
Well, to stop my story lasting longer
than the race itself, Atalanta lost,
and the man who triumphed led away his prize.

Book Ten

Surely I deserved his thanks, Adonis, 1030
and a tribute offering of incense?
But he forgot. I got no thanks from him
or any incense. I felt a sudden rage—
his contempt annoyed me. So to make sure
I would not be slighted in the future,
I took care to make them an example
and stirred myself to move against the pair.
The two of them were going past a shrine
hidden in a forest grove, a temple
which famous Echion built long ago 1040
for the mother of the gods, to fulfill
a promise he had made.[1] Their lengthy trip
convinced them they should stop there for a rest.
My godlike power roused Hippomenes [690]
so he was keen to make love with his wife,
although the time was not appropriate.
Near that temple was shady hollow,
like a cave, with a natural stone roof,
a place sacred to the old religion,
in which the priest had gathered images, 1050
many wooden figures of ancient gods.
Hippomenes went in this holy place
and polluted it with forbidden sex.
The sacred figures turned their eyes away,
and Cybele, great mother of the gods,
in her turreted crown, was wondering
whether she should plunge the guilty couple
deep in the waters of the river Styx.[2]
But that punishment seemed insufficient.
And so a tawny mane covered their necks, 1060
which had been so smooth before, their fingers
bent into claws, their arms turned into legs.
Their entire weight is centered in their chests, [700]
and their tails sweep the surface of the sand.
They have angry faces. Instead of words

---

[1] The Mother of the Gods is the near eastern goddess Cybele, who is often confused with Ops, the mother of Jupiter. Echion was one of the earth-born warriors who grew up when Cadmus sowed the dragon's teeth (see above 3.152 ff.)

[2] Cybele was customarily depicted as crowned with turrets and seated in a chariot drawn by lions.

349

they utter roars, and they roam the forest,
rather than the rooms of their own home.
As lions, they are terrifying to others,
but, once subdued by Cybele, their jaws
bite down quite tamely on her chariot bit.   1070
So Adonis, my love, avoid those beasts
and along with them all savage creatures
which do not flee but stick out their chests
and stand prepared to fight. If you do not,
your courage will be fatal to us both.'

Venus gave this warning to Adonis,
harnessed her swans, and flew off through the air.
But his courage disagreed with her advice.

Now, it happened that his dogs were tracking   [710]
the clear trail of a boar and roused the beast,   1080
which left its den and was getting ready
to charge out from the trees, when Adonis
struck it from the side. Instantly the beast
dislodged the hunting spear stained with its blood
and chased Adonis, who was terrified
and looked for somewhere safe. But the wild beast
sank its sharp tusks deep in the young man's groin
and threw him down onto the yellow sand,
where he lay dying.

                As she moved through the air
in her light chariot drawn by flying swans,   1090
Cythera, still on her way to Cyprus,
heard his dying groans from a long way off,
and turned the white birds back towards him.
When, from high up in the sky, she saw him   [720]
lying dead, body soaked in his own blood,
she jumped down, tore her clothing and her hair,
and with frantic hands pounded on her breast,
as she protested to the Fates, saying:

'But not everything is in your power!
Adonis, memorials of my sorrow   1100
will remain forever, and every year
the image of your death will be performed
and give a re-enactment of my grief.
I will change your blood into a flower.

350

Book Ten

> For if Persephone was once allowed
> to change a woman into fragrant mint, [730]
> will I be begrudged the transformation
> of a courageous son of Cinyras?"[1]

After saying this, she sprinkled the blood
with sweet-scented nectar, which, on contact, 1110
made the blood froth up, the way clear bubbles
rise in yellow mud. Before an hour passed,
a flower grew there, the colour of blood,
a bloom like pomegranates bear, that fruit
which hides its seed beneath a hardened skin.
But one cannot enjoy this flower long,
for its petals are attached so lightly,
in gusts of wind they quickly fly away,
and from those winds the flower gets its name,
for people call it the anemone.[2]

---

[1] Persephone changed a nymph called Mentha into a plant.

[2] The Greek word for wind is *anemos*. I have added the last line to include the name of the flower, which is not included in Ovid's text.

Book Eleven
XI

[Orpheus is attacked and killed by maenads; the world laments his death; Orpheus is reunited with Eurydice; Bacchus punishes the maenads; Bacchus goes to Tmolus; Midas gives Silenus back to Bacchus, who rewards Midas with a wish; Midas wants to turn all things to gold; Midas prays to have the gift revoked; Bacchus complies; Apollo and Pan compete in music; Apollo gives Midas asses' ears; Midas' servant gives his secret away; Apollo and Neptune help Laomedon build Troy; Neptune punishes Laomedon for reneging on his promise; Hercules attacks Troy; Peleus wins Thetis as his wife; Peleus visits Ceyx, who tells the story of Daedalion and Chione, who was seduced by Mercury and Apollo; Peleus' cattle are attacked by a giant wolf sent by Psamathe; Thetis placates Psamathe; the story of Ceyx and Alcyone; a storm at sea kills Ceyx; Juno gets Sleep to send a dream to Alcyone; Morpheus visits Alcyone; the corpse of Ceyx appears; Alcyone and Ceyx are transformed; the story of Aesacus and Hesperië; Aesacus is transformed.]

While with songs like these the Thracian poet   THE DEATH OF ORPHEUS
was making trees, rocks, and wild creature's hearts
all follow him, lo and behold, from a hilltop
the frenzied women of the Cicones,
with skins of savage beasts draped on their breasts,
caught sight of Orpheus playing his lyre,
accompanying his songs with music.
One of them, whose hair was being blown back
by the gentle breezes, screamed:

                        "Look! Down there!
It's him—the man who has rejected us!"[1]   10

She hurled her spear at Apollo's poet,
while he was in the middle of a song.
But the spear had leaves wrapped around the point,
and so it made a mark but left no wound.
Another woman threw a rock at him,   [10]
but while the stone was flying through the air,
it was overpowered by the harmonies
of his voice and lyre and fell at his feet,
as if it were begging his forgiveness
for such a rash assault. But after that   20
the mad attacks increased, and all restraint
was gone—the frenzied Furies took control.
His songs would have made all weapons harmless,
but loud noises from Berecyntian flutes
of curving horn, the din of tambourines,

---

[1] After the death of his wife, Eurydice, Orpheus had rejected the love of women (see above 10.126).

Book Eleven

as well as beating hands and Bacchic chants,
drowned out the music Orpheus was playing,
and finally the rocks turned red with blood,
for now the poet's song could not be heard.[1]

The maenads first rip apart those creatures
still captivated by the singer's voice—
countless birds, snakes, and throngs of savage beasts—
that audience which made the poet famous.[2]
And then they lay their bloody hands on him,
crowding together, like those birds who glimpse
the night owl roaming in the light of day,
or like the dogs in amphitheatre sand
at a morning show in the arena,
when they throng around the body of a stag
who is doomed to become their prey and die.
That's how those women go at Orpheus,
hurling their leafy thyrsus stems, not made
for such a purpose. Some throw lumps of earth,
others toss branches they have torn from trees,
and others flint stones. Their insane attack
does not lack weapons, for it so happens
some oxen have been working on the soil,
hauling a plough, and not far away from there
burly farmers are digging up tough ground,
sweating hard, and getting their fields ready
to plant the grain. But when they see that mob,
they run away and leave their tools behind.
Long mattocks, hoes, and heavy rakes lie there,
scattered across the empty fields. The women,
in their frantic state, get their hands on these,
and, once they have torn apart the oxen,
whose horns are menacing them, hurry back
to kill the poet. Stretching out his arms,
Orpheus speaks, but now, for the first time,
his voice is useless and has no effect.
Those sacrilegious women rip him up,
and through those lips which stones have listened to

---

[1]Berecyntia was a mountain in Phrygia sacred to Cybele, whose worship involved music from flutes.
[2]Maenads were ecstatic female worshippers of Bacchus.

and senses of wild beasts have understood—
O Jupiter!—the soul of Orpheus
slips away and vanishes in the winds.

The grieving birds, the crowds of savage beasts,
the flinty rocks and woods, which so often
followed your songs, wept for you, Orpheus.
Trees shed their leaves and, with their crowns now bare,
grieved at your death, and rivers, too, men say,   70
were swollen with their tears. Naiads and dryads,
their hair unkempt, put on dark mourning clothes.
The poet's scattered limbs lay everywhere.
You, Hebrus, received his head and lyre,   [50]
and (what is amazing!) as they floated
down the middle of the stream, the lyre
sounded some kind of doleful melody,
the lifeless tongue intoned a sad lament,
and river banks echoed the plaintive song.[1]
And then, carried down to the sea, they left   80
their native stream and were tossed up on shore
on Lesbos at Methymna. Here the head,
as it lay on that foreign beach exposed,
with its dishevelled hair still dripping wet,
was assaulted by a ferocious snake.
But as the beast was just about to bite,
Phoebus finally appeared and stopped it.
He froze the striking creature's open jaws
and, in that posture, hardened it to stone.   [60]

The shade of Orpheus moved underground   90
and recognized the places he had seen
on his earlier trip. He set out searching
in fields of the blessed for Eurydice,
his wife, and when he came across her there,
he held her in his eager arms. And now,
they wander side by side together.
Sometimes he follows as she walks in front.
At other times he strolls ahead of her
and, since the action is quite safe, looks back
to watch his own Eurydice.

---

[1] Hebrus was a river in Thrace.

BOOK ELEVEN

                    But Bacchus
does not allow this crime to go unpunished.   BACCHUS AND THE MAENADS
Grief stricken at the loss of Orpheus,
who played his music in the sacred rites,
he quickly ties the Thracian women down
in the woods, using twisted roots, all those
who were there and saw the brutal death.   [70]
On each woman's foot he stretches out the toes
and shoves the tips down into solid ground,
right at the spot where she joined in the chase.
Just as a wild bird, once its leg gets snagged
in a snare crafty hunters have set up,
feels itself held back, beats its wings, flutters,
and with its motion tightens up the noose,
so each of those women, once she is stuck
and rooted in the soil, grows terrified
and tries to run from there. But her attempts
are futile, for the pliant root holds firm
and stops her as she tries to jerk away.
When she looks down for her toes and nails,
to learn where they might be, she sees tree bark
moving up her shapely calf and when, in grief,   [80]
she slaps her leg, her hand hits solid wood.
Her chest and shoulders change to oak, as well.
Her arms are knotted—they look like branches,
and if you said they had been changed to oak,
you would not be mistaken.

                    But Bacchus   MIDAS AND SILENUS
was not satisfied with this. So he left
the land of Thrace, and with a company
of better celebrants went to the vineyards
of his own Mount Tmolus and the waters
of the Pactolus river, which at that time
did not bear gold and were not envied
for their precious sands.[1] The usual throng
went with him, Bacchic worshippers and satyrs,
except for Silenus, who had been seized
by Phrygians, as he staggered along,
tottering from age and wine. Those peasants   [90]

---

[1] Mount Tmolus was in Asia Minor.

chained him in wreaths of flowers and led him
to king Midas, a man who had been taught
the Bacchic mysteries by Orpheus 140
and by Eumolpus, a man from Athens.[1]
Midas recognized him as a comrade,
his associate in the sacred rites,
and was pleased to honour the arrival
of his guest with joyful celebrations
which lasted ten successive days and nights.
On the eleventh day, once Lucifer
had ushered out the distant ranks of stars,
Midas happily set out for Lydia,
where he gave Silenus back to Bacchus, 150
the satyr's youthful foster child. The god, MIDAS AND BACCHUS
pleased to have Silenus returned to him, [100]
gave Midas, as a favour, the chance to ask
for any gift—a fine offer, but wasted,
for Midas made poor use of this reward.
He said:

    "Make all things my body touches
    change to yellow gold."

              Since this was his choice,
Bacchus consented and granted Midas
the harmful gift, sorry he had not asked
for something better. However, the king 160
from Berecyntia was happy as he left,
joyful in his misfortune. He tested MIDAS' GOLDEN TOUCH
his belief in what Bacchus had promised
by touching various things and, when he did,
could hardly comprehend the things he saw.
When on an oak he snaps a green twig off
a lower branch, the twig is changed to gold.
If he picks any rock up from the ground, [110]
it, too, becomes pale gold, and when he grasps
a clod of earth, the power of his touch 170
turns it into a lump of yellow metal.
He gathers in dry ears of Ceres' grain,

---

[1]Silenus was a satyr and a divine patron of drunkenness, who helped to raise Bacchus after he was taken out of Jupiter's thigh. Eumolpus was a disciple of Orpheus and founder of the Eleusinian mysteries.

and they become a harvest of pure gold.
He holds an apple taken from a tree,
and you would think he has received the fruit
of the Hesperides.[1] When his fingers touch
tall pillars by the door, they seem to glow,
and if he dips his hands in running streams,
Danaë herself could well have been seduced
by the liquid gold flowing past his palms.[2] 180
Midas has trouble holding back the dreams
now active in his mind, for he imagines
all things turned to gold. As he rejoices,
his servants set tables out before him
loaded with rich amounts of meat and bread. [120]
But if he puts his hand on Ceres' gift,
the bread grows hard. If his hungry jaws
attempt to chew the meat, when his teeth touch,
a golden yellow plating coats his food.
And when he drinks pure water mixed with wine, 190
a present from the very god who gave him
his new gift, you see a golden liquid
flowing in his mouth. This strange disaster
fills Midas with dismay. For all his wealth,
he is a wretched man. He wants to flee
from all his riches and now despises
the very things he recently desired.
No supply of food relieves his hunger,
his throat is burning with a parching thirst,
and he is plagued, as he deserves to be, 200 [130]
by the gold he now detests. He stretches
his shining hands and arms up to the skies
and cries:

        "Forgive me, father Bacchus.
I have sinned. But pity me, I beg you.
Save me from this gift which seemed so fine!"

The will of the gods is kind. Once Midas
had confessed his fault, Bacchus restored him

---

[1] The Hesperides were three divine nymphs of the evening and western regions. They took care of a tree whose fruit was golden apples.

[2] Danaë was tricked by Jupiter, who had sex with her in the form of a shower of gold.

and took back the present he had given
to fulfill his promise. He told Midas:

> "To make sure you are no longer covered 210
> with gold, as you so foolishly desired,
> go to great Sardis, to the river there,
> and make your way across the shining ridge.
> Keep going upstream to the river's source,
> then plunge your head and body both at once
> right where the spring is frothing up the most, [140]
> and, as you do that, wash away your crime."

Midas went to the spring, as he was told.
When the golden force moved from his human flesh
and passed into the spring, its colour stained 220
the waters of the stream, and even today,
the lands absorbing grains from this old source
gleam and harden in those spots where water
flowing in the river soaks into the soil.

Midas now hated wealth and spent his time
in fields and woods and mountain caves, where Pan
is always present. But his wits remained
as stupid as before, and his foolish mind
was doomed to hurt its owner once again.

Tmolus, a towering, rugged mountain 230 [150]
with panoramic views out to the sea
has one flank extending down to Sardis, APOLLO AND PAN
and another reaching tiny Hypaepe.
Pan is there, boasting to some gentle nymphs
about his songs and playing a modest tune
on a pipe of reeds held in place by wax.
He dares to demean Apollo's music
in comparison with his own. And thus,
it comes to an unequal competition
in which Tmolus will select the winner. 240

The ancient judge sits on his mountainside
and shakes his ears to rid them of their trees.
The only thing he wears in his dark hair
is a wreath of oak, with acorns hanging
by his hollow temples. He looks at Pan,
the god of flocks, and says:

Book Eleven

"No need to wait. [160]
It's time to judge."
          Pan plays his rustic pipes,
and his wild tune fills Midas with delight
(he happens to be there, close by the music).
After that, sacred Tmolus turns his head 250
towards Apollo's face and, as he turns,
his forests follow. Around his golden head
Phoebus wears a wreath of Parnassus laurel.
His garments, dyed with Tyrian purple,
sweep along the ground. In his left hand
he holds his lyre, inlaid with gemstones
and Indian ivory, and in his right
a plectrum. The very way he holds himself
proclaims the artist. Then he plucks the strings
with skilful fingers, and his sweet music 260 [170]
captivates Tmolus, who then orders Pan
to hold his pipes inferior to the lyre.

The verdict of the holy mountain god   APOLLO AND MIDAS
delighted all of them, except for Midas.
He was the only one to disagree
and say it was unfair. The Delian god
could not allow such foolish ears to keep
their human shape, and so he stretched them out,
filled them with white hairs, made them flexible
at the base, and gave them power to move. 270
Midas was human in his other parts,
but in this one feature he was punished,
for he now carried plodding asses' ears.

Midas was anxious to conceal this change
and tried to mitigate his own disgrace [180]
with a purple turban around his head.
But a servant, the one who trimmed his hair
with iron scissors, saw what the god had done.
Though he was keen to tell what he had seen,
he did not dare divulge such shameful news. 280
But still, he could not keep it to himself.
So he went off alone, scooped out the earth,
and in a whisper told the empty pit
the kind of ears he had seen on Midas.
He pushed the soil in place again and buried

the news he had disclosed, then filled the pit
and crept away in silence. But a thick patch
of trembling reeds began to sprout up there,
and in a year, when they were now full grown,
they gave away the man who dug the hole.   290
For when the gentle South Wind stirs those reeds,
they repeat the words the servant buried
and tell the truth about his master's ears.[1]

When Latona's son had punished Midas,   APOLLO AND NEPTUNE AT TROY
he left Tmolus, flew through the limpid air,
and landed in the realm of Laomedon,
on this side of the narrow strait of Helle,
Nephele's daughter.[2] An ancient altar stands
between the western headland of Sigaeum
and high Rhoeteum to the east, a shrine   300
to Jupiter Panomphe, the Thunderer.
Here Apollo noticed Laomedon
building the first walls of his new city,
Troy, a massive project which demanded   [200]
arduous work and immense resources.
And so he and trident-wielding Neptune,
the father of the heaving sea, put on
a human form and built the city walls
for the Phrygian king, who had agreed
to pay them gold to fortify the site.   310
When the task was done, king Laomedon
said he would not pay the gods their wages
and, to complete his treachery, denied
with outright lies what he had guaranteed.
The king of sea cried out:

                "You won't do that
and get away unpunished."

                      So Neptune drove
all the ocean waves against the coastline
of greedy Troy, making the land a sea,

---

[1] The sound coming from the wind blowing in the reeds allegedly resembled the words "Midas has asses' ears."

[2] The land of Laomedon was Troy, and the strait of Helle was the Hellespont, just north of Troy. Helle was a daughter of Athamas and Nephele. She ran away from home (to escape her step mother Ino) and was drowned in the sea which was from then on named after her.

washing away the farmers' property, [210]
and burying their fields beneath his waves. 320
This punishment was not enough for him,
so Neptune said that Laomedon's daughter,
Hesione, must be sacrificed, as well,
to a monster from the sea. She was chained
to a rough boulder but was later saved
by Hercules, who asked for the reward   HERCULES AND LAOMEDON
he had been promised, since Laomedon
had agreed to give him certain horses.
But he refused to pay out the reward,
though Hercules had served him very well. 330
So Hercules attacked and conquered Troy
and seized the walls of the defeated city,
which had broken its word twice. Telamon,
a man who fought alongside Hercules,
did not depart without being honoured,
for he won Hesione as his prize.

Now, Peleus, brother of Telamon,   PELEUS AND THETIS
was already famous, for he had taken
a goddess as his wife. The pride he took
in his father-in-law was no less strong 340
than what he felt about his grandfather,
for Peleus was not, by any means,
the only one whom providence had made
grandson of Jupiter, but only he
had had the luck to wed a goddess, too.[1] [220]
For old Proteus had said to Thetis:

> "Goddess of the waves, get yourself with child!
> For you will be the mother of a youth
> who will achieve more than his father did,
> once he becomes a full-grown warrior, 350
> and will be called a greater man than he."

Once he heard this prophecy, Jupiter—
who did not want anyone in the world

---

[1] Peleus, who was also a part of the Hercules' expedition against Troy, married Thetis, a minor goddess of the sea and a daughter of Proteus (a god of the sea). Peleus' father, Aeacus, was a son of Jupiter. Telamon was also a grandson of Jupiter (he had been one of the Argonauts and had taken part in the Calydonian Boar Hunt with Meleager). Hercules was a son of Jupiter. Peleus is, in effect, claiming double honours from his two connections with divinities.

to be more powerful than he—avoided
having a sexual affair with Thetis,
goddess of the sea, even though he felt
a fierce love for her burning in his heart.
And so, to fulfill a promise he had made,
he commanded Peleus, his grandson,
son of Aeacus, to visit Thetis 360
on his behalf, to hold her in his arms
and make love with that virgin of the sea.

In Thessaly there is a curving bay,
shaped like a sickle, with projecting arms,
where there would be a harbour, if the sea [230]
were deeper there. The surface of the sand
is covered by the waves. The shore is firm.
It holds no footprints, does not slow one down,
and has no seaweed. A grove of myrtle
grows close by, with different coloured berries, 370
and in the centre of it is a cave.
One cannot tell if it was made by nature
or by human art, but probably by art.
This place, Thetis, you would often visit,
riding naked on a bridled dolphin.
And Peleus found you here, lying down,
overcome by sleep. He tried to win you
with his entreaties, but you turned him down.
So Peleus placed both arms around your neck, [240]
ready to use force, and his bold attempt 380
would have prevailed, if with your usual skill
you had not kept changing your appearance.
At one point you became a bird, but Peleus
still kept a firm grip on you in that shape,
and when you turned into a massive tree,
he held on with his arms around the trunk.
But when, in your third change, you turned into
a spotted tigress, that so terrified
the son of Aeacus, his arms let go.
So he poured wine into the ocean waves 390
and, with sheep entrails and smoking incense,
prayed to the sea gods, until Proteus,
the Carpathian prophet, cried out to him
from the ocean waves:

Book Eleven

"Son of Aeacus,
you will obtain the bride you're looking for,   [250]
if you catch her unawares, fast asleep
in that cool cave of hers, and tie her up
with cords she cannot break. Do not let her
deceive you with her hundred tricky shapes.
Hold onto her, no matter how she changes,   400
till she becomes the one she was before."[1]

Proteus said this and then hid his face
down in the sea, letting his own waters
close over his last words.

              The Titan Sun
was low in the sky, with his chariot pole
now slanting down, close to the western sea,
as the beautiful Nereïd left the waves
and went inside her usual resting place.
Once Peleus had seized the young girl's arms,   [260]
she kept on changing shapes, until she saw   410
her limbs were tightly bound and both her arms
pinned down on either side. And so, at last,
she sighed and said:

           "You could not conquer me
without help from some god."

                  Then she changed back
and was Thetis once again. At that point,
when she stood revealed in her true nature,
Peleus held her, got what he desired,
and with her conceived the great Achilles.

Happy with his wife and son, Peleus   PELEUS AND CEYX
was a man fortune blessed in everything,   420
if one excludes the crime of killing Phocus.[2]
But once guilty of his brother's murder,
his native country forced him into exile,
where he was welcomed by the land of Trachis,
which Ceyx ruled, a son of Lucifer,

---

[1] Carpathia was an island in the Aegean Sea.
[2] Peleus had two brothers, Telamon and Phocus (all three were sons of Aeacus). Peleus killed Phocus by accident during a game. Ovid seems to suggest that the killing was deliberate.

a peaceful man who shed no blood. His face [270]
shone with his father's glow, but at the time
he was not his normal self, for he was sad,
mourning his brother's loss.¹ When Peleus
reached there, worn out by worry and his trip, 430
he left the cattle herds and flocks of sheep
he brought with him in a sheltered valley
close to the walls and then approached the town
with few companions. When he got the chance
for an initial meeting with the king,
he went in as a suppliant, holding
a wool-draped olive branch. He told the king
his name and the family he came from,
but did not divulge the killing and lied [280]
about the reason for his flight. He asked 440
if he could stay there, either in the town
or in the countryside. In his response,
the king of Trachis dealt gently with him,
saying:

    "Peleus, our resources here
are open even to the common folk,
and the place I rule is kind to strangers.
As well as these two things, you also bring
the persuasive weight of a famous name—
grandson of Jupiter. So waste no time
in making a petition. All those things 450
you ask for you shall have. What you see here,
no matter what it is, is yours to share.
Think of it as your own. I only wish
the things you see were finer than they are!"

As Ceyx finished, he burst into tears.
Peleus and his companions asked him
what was causing him such heartfelt sorrow. [290]
The king gave this reply:

    "That bird, the hawk—   DAEDALION
the one which lives off prey and terrifies
all other birds—you may perhaps believe 460
it has always had its wings. But, in fact,

---

¹Lucifer was the brightest star in the sky, prominent just before dawn.

the hawk was once a man (and since nature
rarely changes, back then he was already
fierce, an aggressive warrior in battle
and well prepared for violent action.
Daedalion was his name. The two of us
were sons of Lucifer, the star who calls
Aurora forth, the last to leave the sky.
I am a man of peace, and my concern
was to preserve it and to love my wife. 470
My brother got his joy from cruel war.
Kings and nations fell to his fierce power,
that nature which, since he became a hawk,
keeps anxious doves in Thisbe fluttering.[1] [300]
My brother had a daughter called Chione,
fourteen years old and ready to get married.
Because she was so beautiful, she had
a thousand suitors. As it so happened,
Apollo, returning back from Delphi,
and Mercury, Maia's son, travelling 480
from the top of Mount Cyllene, saw her,
both in the same instant, and the two gods,
in that instant, both desired Chione.
Apollo postponed his passionate hopes
until the hours of night, but Mercury
did not delay. He stroked the young girl's face
with the staff which brings on sleep. Chione,
at that potent touch, lay prone and suffered
Mercury's assault. After that, once night
had strewn the sky with stars, Apollo came, 490
disguised as an old woman, and tasted
those delights which Mercury had enjoyed [310]
before he got there. When Chione's womb
was ready to give birth, she bore Autolycus,
a crafty child conceived from Mercury,
wing-footed god, a son so devious,
he was well skilled in every form of theft.
His nature, no less scheming than his father's,
could make black things look white and white things black.
Chione also bore a child to Phoebus 500

---

[1] Thisbe was a town in Boeotia.

(for she had twins), a boy called Philammon,
famed for his melodious voice and lyre.

But what benefits did Chione obtain   DIANA AND CHIONE
from having pleased two gods and given birth
to a pair of boys or from being the child
of a mighty father and the grandchild
of a brilliant star? Is not such glory
also harmful? It has injured many,   [320]
and clearly it harmed her. For she was rash,
thinking she was better than Diana   510
and criticizing how the goddess looked.
Diana, stirred to anger, told herself:

'Let's see if what we do brings her delight.'

She did not wait, but pulled back on her bow
and shot an arrow from the string. The shaft
pierced Chione through her presumptuous tongue,
which then fell silent, for it made no sounds.
Whatever words it formed did not come out,
and as it tried to speak, the young girl's life
drained from her with her blood.

                        Filled with sorrow,   520
I put my arms around her. In my heart   DAEDALION AND APOLLO
I felt a father's grief. With soothing words
I made an effort to console my brother,
but what I said her father did not hear,
any more than cliffs take note of murmurs   [330]
made by the sea. He bitterly lamented
the daughter he had lost. But when he saw
her body burning, he made four attempts
to charge into the middle of the pyre,
and all four times he had to be held back.   530
Then, in a mad escape, he ran away.
Like a young bull tormented by the stings
of hornets on a neck chafed from the yoke,
he charged off to places with no pathways.
And even then it seemed to me he ran
faster than humans do—you could have thought
his feet had wings. So he outran us all,
made swift by his desire for death, and reached
the summit of Parnassus. Apollo

pitied him, and when Daedalion threw himself
from a high cliff, he changed him to a bird
and held him up as he was hovering
on wings he had so suddenly acquired.
He gave him a hooked beak, curving talons
instead of nails, greater physical strength,
and left the courage he possessed before.
And now, as a hawk, he attacks all birds,
is merciful to none, and in his grief
has become a source of grief to others."

While the son of Lucifer was describing
these strange things that happened to his brother,
Antenor, a man from Phocis, who guarded
Peleus' cattle herds, came running up,
out of breath, and yelled:

"Peleus! Peleus!
Let me speak to you! A great disaster!"

Peleus told him to report his news,
whatever it might be, while king Ceyx,
with a worried face, waited in suspense.
Antenor carried on:

"I had just driven
the weary oxen down to the curved bay.
The Sun was at his highest point, halfway
on his daily path, as much behind him
as he could see ahead. Some of the bulls
were kneeling in yellow sand, relaxing
and gazing at the broad expanse of sea.
Others were slowly moving back and forth
or wading in the waves, holding their necks
high above the water. There is a temple
hard by the shore, made from solid timbers,
with no hint of gold or gleaming marble,
and shaded by an ancient stand of trees.
Nereïds and Nereus live around there
(a sailor drying nets on shore informed me
they were the gods of that part of the sea).
Near it is a marsh full of willow trees
in a dense stand, where water from the sea
which does not drain away has made a swamp.

PELEUS AND PSAMATHE

And from that place came fearful crashing sounds
which terrified the neighbourhood, and then,
out of that marsh, a monstrous wolf appeared,   580
its deadly jaws spattered with slime and blood,
a flaming red glare in its eyes. The beast
was ravenous with hunger and with rage,
but it was driven more by savagery
and did not stop, for all its need to eat,   [370]
beside the cattle it had killed and sate
its deadly appetite, but rather slashed
the entire herd and so ferociously
it butchered all of them. A few of us
trying to guard the herd were wounded, too,   590
or else lay dead from fatal bites. The shore
and the sea beside it both turned crimson.
So did the marshland filled with bellowing bulls.
It's dangerous to delay! This business
calls for us to act at once! Let's form a group
and arm ourselves. While something is still left,
we must get weapons and in one large mass
attack the beast with spears."

                      The herdsman finished.
Peleus was not concerned about the loss,
but thinking of his crime, he realized   600   [380]
the goddess Psamathe, still lamenting
her son's death, had brought on these disasters,
as a sacrifice to murdered Phocus.[1]
Ceyx, the Oetaean king, told his men
to put their armour on and pick up weapons
for the coming battle, while he himself
prepared to join them. But Alcyone,
his wife, alarmed by the commotion, ran out—
she had not taken time to fix her hair
and kept pulling at it—clung to Ceyx,   610
her arms around his neck, imploring him
in words and tears to provide assistance
but not go himself, to protect his life
and thus save both of them. So Peleus,
son of Aeacus, said this to her:

---

[1] Psamathe, a Nereïd, was the mother of Phocus.

BOOK ELEVEN

"O queen,
this loving fear of yours is admirable,
but set it to one side. These promises
your husband made fill me with gratitude, [390]
but I do not want weapons to be used
against this strange new monster. Instead, 620
I must placate the goddess of the sea."

A lofty tower with a beacon fire
stood on the summit of the citadel,
a welcome sight for weary ships at sea.
They climbed up there and groaned as they looked out
at cattle lying strewn along the shore
and at that savage beast with blood-stained jaws,
its long fur caked with gore. From that high place,
Peleus stretched his hands out to the beach,
towards the open sea, and prayed to Psamathe, 630
to end her anger and give him her aid.
But the goddess of the sea brushed aside
the pleas made by the son of Aeacus.
Then Thetis, by her intercession, won [400]
Psamathe's forgiveness for her husband.
Though told to stop its murderous carnage,
the wolf kept up the slaughter, driven mad
by the sweet taste of blood, until the goddess
turned it to marble, as it sunk its teeth
deep in the neck of a mangled heifer. 640
Its body stayed the same in every feature
except its colour, and the white stone showed
there was no need to fear the creature now,
for it was a wolf no more. But the Fates
did not permit the exiled Peleus
to settle in that land. Still a fugitive,
he moved on to the Magnetes and there
the king of Thessaly, Acastus, granted
absolution for his crime of murder.[1]

Meanwhile, king Ceyx, whose heart is troubled 650 [410]
by his brother's fate and the strange events
which followed, is making preparations CEYX AND ALCYONE
for a journey to the god at Claros,

---

[1] Magnesia refers to a few different places. The one here is in Thessaly, in northern Greece.

in order to consult the sacred shrine,
which offers grieving mortals consolation.
For evil Phorbys and his Phlegyans
have blocked the route to Delphi's oracle.¹
Before he starts his journey, Ceyx tells
his loyal wife what his intentions are.
Deep in her bones she feels an instant chill, 660
her face turns pale as boxwood, and her cheeks
are moist from weeping. She tries to speak
three times, with tears still streaming down her face,
and as her sobs break up her fond complaints, [420]
she says:

        "My dearest love, what fault of mine
has changed your heart? Where is that care for me
which used to be your first priority?
Can you now go away without concern
and leave Alcyone? Does a long trip
now fill you with delight? And am I now 670
more dear to you when I am far away?
If I thought you were travelling by land,
then I would only grieve, not be afraid.
My worries would be free of dreadful fear.
But oceans and the grim face of the sea
I find so frightening. Just recently
I saw ship timbers lying wrecked on shore,
and on grave markers I have often seen
the names of those whose bodies were not there.²
You must not let your spirit place false trust 680 [430]
in Aeolus, the son of Hippotas,
your father-in-law, who, when he wishes,
locks up the mighty winds and calms the waves.³
For once winds are released and seize the sea,
nothing holds them back. And then they threaten
land and sea alike. They even agitate

---

¹Claros, in Asia Minor, had a well-known shrine to Apollo. The Phelgyans were a group of people in Thessaly. Ceyx would normally go by land to consult Apollo at Delphi, which was closer and more famous than the shrine at Claros.

²A memorial stone was an important way to honour the dead if there was no formal burial because the body was not available (as in the case of people lost at sea).

³Aeolus, god of the winds, was in other accounts the grandson of Hippotas.

Book Eleven

the heavenly clouds with fierce collisions
and make the fiery lighting flash.¹ The more
I learn about them (and I do know the winds,
for when I was a girl I often saw them 690
inside my father's home), the more I think
we ought to be afraid. But if no prayers,
my dear Ceyx, can change what you propose,
if you are all too set on sailing off, [440]
then take me with you, too. At least then
both of us will ride the storms together.
I will fear the things I have to go through,
but nothing else. And whatever happens
we will bear together, and together
we two will sail across the spacious sea." 700

The words and tears of Aeolus' daughter
stirred her husband Ceyx, born of a star,
for the fire of love in him was no less bright.
But he did not wish to scrap the journey
he planned to make across the sea or have
Alcyone share the dangers of the trip.
His answered her with many soothing words,
trying to ease her fearful heart. But still,
for all his effort, she did not agree.
The only part that moved his loving wife 710 [450]
came when he added one more consolation:

"It's true that all delays are long to us,
but I swear to you, by my father's light,
if Fates allow me to return back home,
I will be here again, before the moon
has twice filled in her sphere"

                              By promising this,
he spurred her hopes that he would be back soon.
He quickly ordered men to bring a ship
down from the dock, launch it in the sea,
and fit it out with gear. Alcyone 720
looked on and shuddered, as if foreseeing
what the future held, and then, once again,

---

¹In some scientific theories of Ovid's time (e.g., in Lucretius) the winds were a major cause of all sorts of natural events from lightning to earthquakes.

Book Eleven

shed floods of tears. She hugged her husband
and, still utterly dismayed, said at last
in a mournful voice:

"Farewell."

Then she collapsed,
and all her body sank down to the ground. [460]
While Ceyx was still seeking to delay,
the youthful crew, arranged in double rows,
hauled their oars back against their sturdy chests
and, with equal strokes, cut through the water. 730
Alcyone looked up with weeping eyes
to watch her husband standing in the ship
by the curving stern. When he waved his hand,
she returned the wave. Further out from land,
when she could not observe his features any more,
her eyes kept following the moving ship,
while they still could, and when she found it hard,
as it kept going, to make out the ship,
she kept on looking at the fluttering sails [470]
by the top part of the mast. And later, 740
when her eyes could no longer see those sails,
she went inside, to her empty bedroom,
heart full of grief, and lay down on the bed.
The bed and room brought back her tears again,
for they made Alcyone remember
the part of her that was not there.

By now STORM AT SEA
the ship has cleared the harbour, and the wind
has set the halyards stirring. The captain
boats the sloping oars, raises the topsails
to the masthead, and lets the sails fill out, 750
to catch the coming breeze. But when the ship
has sailed about half way across or less—
no more than half, at most—and both coasts
are far away, as night comes on, the sea [480]
begins to whiten with a heavy chop
and the strong East Wind blows in more fiercely.
The captain cries:

"Quick now! Lower the topsail!
Lash all sails against the yards!"

372

Book Eleven

                       He bellows
his orders, but the wind howls in his face
and drowns out his commands. The roaming sea   760
makes any voice impossible to hear.
But still, some sailors, on their own, move fast
to stow the oars. Some reinforce the sides
or furl the sails. One man bails water out
and throws it back into the sea, another
lashes down the spars. But while they do this,
with no sense of order, the violent storm
grows stronger. Angry winds attack the ship   [490]
from every side and rouse the furious sea.
Even the captain of the ship is fearful,   770
admitting he does not know how matters stand
or what to order or forbid. They face
such mighty perils, much more powerful
than all his skill. The sound is deafening—
men screaming, ship's ropes groaning from the strain,
waves crashing down in heavy seas, and thunder
rolling through the sky. The heaving water
seems to reach the heavens and spray the clouds,
which hover overhead. At times, the seas
turn yellow with the sand the storm churns up   780
from deep below and then, at other times,
are blacker than the river Styx, while waves,   [500]
hissing with white foam, keep surging forward.
Chance blows batter that Trachinian ship,
now lifting it way up, as if it stood
on some high mountain peak and seemed to peer
down in the valleys and the deepest pit
of Acheron, then letting the ship drop
down in a trough, with sea walls all around,
as though the crew were gazing at the sky   790
from the bottom of an infernal gulf.
Waves from the raging sea pound on the hull,
again and again, with massive crashing,
as loud as iron rams or catapults
when they assault a shattered citadel.
Just as savage lions gather their strength   [510]
and charge at hunters armed with lowered spears,
so storm waves surge ahead in rising winds,
as high as the ship, and even higher.

Book Eleven

The wedges slip, and now, as wax is stripped,
seams open up, providing passageways
for the deadly waves. Then, lo and behold,
colossal rainstorms fall from melting clouds.
One might well think all heaven is pelting down
into the sea and all the swollen seas
are rising up to regions of the sky.
The sails are soaked, as water from the clouds
is mixed with ocean waves. The upper air
has lost its fiery stars, and the dark night
is heavy with the blackness of the storm
as well as its own gloom. But lightning bolts
dispel the murk with flashes of their fire
and make the waters glow, as if they burn.
And then the waters breach the hollow hull
and pour into the ship. Just as a soldier
more daring than the rest, who often tries
to scale walls of a city under siege,
at last succeeds, gets what he wants, and then,
inspired by love of glory, takes the wall,
one man among a thousand, in the same way,
once nine waves in a row have crashed against
the ship's steep hull, a tenth wave surges in,
with even greater force, and does not stop
assaulting that exhausted, battered ship,
until it falls inside its captured walls.
So some of the sea keeps trying to get in,
and some of it is now inside the ship.
The whole crew is confused and terrified,
no less afraid than those inside a city
when troops outside are undermining walls,
while other men are now inside, as well,
occupying those walls. Their seamanship
has failed them, and their spirits fall. It seems
that death is charging at them, breaking in
with each successive wave. One man cannot
hold back his tears, another stands there dazed,
while another calls those truly blessed
for whom a proper burial is waiting.
One sailor offers prayers up to the gods,
raising his arms in vain towards the heavens
he cannot see, and pleading for their aid.

Some recall their brothers and their parents,
some their homes and children, or other things,
whatever they have left behind. But Ceyx
is stirred by memories of Alcyone—
nothing but Alcyone is on his lips.
But though she is the only one he longs for,
he is glad she is not there. He would like
to look back at his native shore, as well,
and gaze one final time towards his home, 850
but he has no idea which way to look.
The sea is whirling round him with such force,
and the whole sky is hidden behind sheets
of pitch-black clouds, thus doubling the darkness [550]
on the face of night. The gusting storm winds
snap the mast, and the rudder breaks apart.
And now one final wave, like a conqueror
eyeing spoils with keen delight, arches up,
looks down on other waves, and then, as if
Pindus and Athos had been uprooted 860
and their whole mass hurled out into the sea,
crashes straight down, and with its force and weight
both together, strikes the ship and drives it
to the bottom of the deep.[1] Many sailors
who go down with the ship are overwhelmed
in the swirling water and meet their fate,
without returning to the air. Others
hold onto broken fragments of the wreck.

Ceyx himself clings to a piece of wreckage,
with a hand that used to wield a sceptre, 870 [560]
and calls out to his father, Lucifer,
and to Aeolus, his father-in-law—
alas, with no effect! But as he swims,
his wife's name, Alcyone, is the one
most often on his lips. He thinks of her,
speaks to her, prays the waves will bear his corpse
where she will see it and, when he is dead,
her loving hands will place him in his tomb.
As long as he can open up his mouth
while swimming in the waves, he keeps calling 880

---

[1] Pindus and Athos were large mountains.

to Alcyone, though she is far away,
and even as the waves close over him
he is murmuring her name. Then, behold,
a black arcing wall of water crashes down,
right the middle of the roiling sea,
buries his head below its bursting wave,
and drowns him.

                That day Lucifer was dim
and could not be seen. He was not allowed   [570]
to leave the heavens, so he hid his face
behind a layer of thick cloud.

            Meanwhile,   890
Alcyone, daughter of Aeolus,   ALCYONE
knowing nothing of the great disaster,
kept track of the nights, promising herself
he would be coming home, an empty pledge.
She hurried to make clothes—some for Ceyx,
and some for her to wear when he got back.
She piously gave incense to each god,
but, ahead of all the rest, she worshipped
at Juno's shrine, visiting the altars
for a man who was no more and praying   900
her husband would be safe, return back home,   [580]
and love no other woman more than her.
Of all the prayers she made, this last one
was the only one that could be granted.

But Juno could not bear to hear more pleas
for someone dead, and, to free her altars
from Alcyone's ill-fated hands, she said:

  "Iris, most faithful bearer of my words,
  go quickly to the languid halls of Sleep.
  Tell him to send Alcyone a dream   910
  in the image of Ceyx, who is dead,
  to let her know the truth about his fate."

Juno spoke. Iris put on a garment
with a thousand colours and then, tracing
her curved arc across the heavens, made for   [590]
the home of Sleep, concealed beneath the clouds,
as Juno had commanded.

BOOK ELEVEN

          Near the land   THE CAVE OF SLEEP
of the Cimmerians, there is a cave
carved into the rock, a hollow mountain,
the house and resting place of drowsy Sleep,   920
where the rays of Phoebus can never shine,
not when he is rising, or half way round,
or sinking down, a place where earth exhales
mists mingling with the darkness, in a twilight
of uncertain gloom. Here no crested cock
calls for Aurora with his wakeful cries.
No voices of uneasy hounds or geese
(more vigilant than dogs) break the silence,
no wild animals, or cattle, or branches   [600]
swaying in the wind, or strident noises   930
from human tongues. There quiet silence reigns.
But from the very bottom of the rock
streams of Lethe's waters run, murmuring
as they glide across the whispering stone,
inducing sleep. In front of the cave door,
rich beds of poppies grow, with countless herbs,
and from their juices damp Night gathers sleep
and scatters it across the darkened earth.
In the entire cavern there is no door,
in case some moving hinge should make a noise,   940
nor any watchman by the entranceway.
A bed stands in the middle of the cave,   [610]
raised on black ebony, dark and downy,
covered with black sheets, where the god himself
is lying down, his limbs relaxed in sleep.
Around him everywhere lie unformed Dreams
resembling various shapes, as numerous
as ears of harvest grain, or forest leaves,
or particles of sand cast up on shore.

Iris entered and quickly pushed aside   950
dreams standing in her way. Her splendid clothes   IRIS AND SLEEP
filled the sacred home with light. The god Sleep
had trouble lifting up his heavy eyes.
He kept falling back to sleep again—once more
his chin would droop and strike him in the chest.   [620]
But finally he stirred and roused himself.
Leaning on his elbow, he asked Iris

(for he knew who she was) why she had come,
and she replied:

"O Sleep, gentlest of gods,
in whom all things find rest and minds find peace, 960
who makes cares fly, who eases hearts of men
worn out by heavy work, renewing them
for further labour. Sleep, command a dream,
which in its shape depicts the real man,
to go to Trachis, city of Hercules,
to Alcyone, in the form of Ceyx,
her king, and present to her the image
of a ship destroyed at sea. This order
comes from Juno."[1]

Once she had carried out
what Juno ordered, Iris left the cave, 970 [630]
unable any more to tolerate
the power of Sleep. For once she noticed
that languid force creeping through her body,
she fled and moved across the arcing path
by which she had arrived just moments earlier.

Then, from the huge crowd of his thousand sons,   MORPHEUS
father Sleep roused Morpheus, an artist
expert at imitating human shapes.
No one has more ability than he
at copying someone's way of moving, 980
his face, and speaking voice. To that he adds
the person's clothes and customary words.
Morpheus is the only one who copies
human beings. Another son becomes
a beast, turns into a bird, or changes
to a serpent with a stretched-out body.
Gods call him Icelos. To mortal men   [640]
his name is Phobetor. And a third son
called Phantasos has yet another skill,
for he can easily transform himself 990
to earth and water, to stones and trees,
to anything that has no life. These dreams
are the visions that parade their faces

---

[1]Trachis a city and region in central Greece was associated with and consecrated to Hercules because he and his wife Deïaneira lived there.

to kings and generals at night, while others
appear to citizens and common folk.
Ancient Sleep walked past these dreams and picked out
his son Morpheus from all the brothers,
to carry out what Iris had commanded.
Then he relaxed once more in gentle sleep.
His head drooped, as he collapsed on his high bed.

Morpheus flew through the night on silent wings [650]
and soon reached that city in Haemonia.

MORPHEUS AND ALCYONE

Shedding his wings, he then assumed the form
of Ceyx. As pale as death and naked,
he stood before his wretched wife in bed.
His beard looked soaking wet, and heavy drops
of water dripped down from his sodden head.
With tears flowing from his eyes, he leant down
and said to her:

        "My most unhappy wife,
surely you still recognize your Ceyx,
or has death changed my face? Look up here.
You will know me. But rather than your husband,
you will find your husband's shade! Your prayers, [660]
Alcyone, were of no help to me,
and I have died. Do not deceive yourself
with promises I will be coming back!
The cloud-filled South Wind in the Aegean
caught my ship, tossed it with tremendous force,
and broke it up. I vainly called your name,
until the waves choked off my lips. This news
comes to you from no doubtful messenger,
nor are you hearing some uncertain rumour.
I myself, a victim of that shipwreck,
am telling you my fate. So rouse yourself.
Come, weep for me, put on mourning clothes,
and do not send me off unlamented [670]
to the empty void of Tartarus."

        These words
Morpheus spoke in a voice which she believed
must be her husband's (and the tears he shed
seemed genuine, as well). He also moved
his hands in the same gestures Ceyx used.
Alcyone groaned, shed tears, moved her arms,

and tried to reach his body in her sleep.
But all she held was air. She cried out:

                        "Wait!
Where are you rushing? We'll go together!"

Roused by her own voice and husband's image,
she shook off sleep. First, she looked around her,
to see if the person who had just appeared
was there, for her shout had roused her servants
who brought in a lamp. After she had failed
to find him anywhere, she struck her face
with her own hand, ripped away the clothing
covering her chest, pounded on her breast,
and tore her hair without undoing it.
When her nurse asked why she felt such grief,
she screamed at her:

                        "Alcyone is no more!
She is finished! She has been quite destroyed
together with her Ceyx! Set aside
all soothing words! He perished in a wreck.
I saw him! I recognized him! I stretched
my hand to him as he was leaving here,
eager to hold him back. He was a shade,
but it was clear the shade was really him,
the ghost of my dead husband. If you asked,
it's true he did not have his usual look—
his face was not as bright as earlier.
But in my misery I did see him,
pale and naked, his hair still dripping wet.
The poor man stood here, on this very spot.
Look here!"

            She searched the room, trying to find
some trace of footprints.

                      "This is what I feared.
My mind foresaw it. I kept begging you
not to abandon me and chase the wind.
I truly wish you had taken me as well,
since you were sailing to your death. For me,
going with you would have been much better,
for then none of my life would have been spent
away from you, and death would not have found

the two of us apart. I am not with you, [700]
so now I die. Though I am far away, 1070
the waves are tossing me around, as well.
Without me there, the sea has taken me.
My mind would torture me more savagely
even than the sea, if I attempted
to live on any longer, if I struggled
to subdue such overwhelming sorrow!
But I will not fight. I will not leave you,
my poor Ceyx. At least now I shall come
as your companion. If not in one urn,
one funeral epitaph will join us, 1080
and if your bones will not be mixed with mine,
we will still be there, my name touching yours."

Grief hindered her from saying any more.
Each word was interrupted by a sob,
and groans came from her suffering heart.

Morning came. Alcyone left her house [710]
and went down to the shore, seeking, in her grief,
the place where she had watched her husband leave.
She lingered there a while, saying to herself,

"Here he untied the ropes. This stretch of beach 1090
is where he kissed me when he sailed away."

While she is remembering his actions
from their locations, she gazes out to sea
and, far off in the waves, observes something
which looks as if it is a human body.
At first she is not sure what it could be.
But once waves push it in a little closer,
still some distance out, she can clearly see
it is indeed a corpse. She does not know
who the body is, but, moved by the omen 1100
of a shipwreck, as if she were in mourning
for a total stranger, she says:

"Alas [720]
for you, poor man, whoever you may be,
and, if you have a wife, for her, as well."

The waves bring the body even nearer.
The more Alcyone keeps watching it,

the less and less she can control herself.
Now the body is carried close inshore.
Now she can make out who the person is.
She looks. It is her husband! She screams out,

"It's him!"

    She tears her face, her hair, her clothing—
all at once—stretches out her trembling arms
to Ceyx and says,

      "O my dearest husband,
you poor man, is this how you come back to me?"

A man-made pile of rock along the shore
broke the initial power of the waves,
weakening the water's force. Alcyone
jumped out on it—that she could manage this
was beyond belief—and she kept on flying,
beating the gentle air with new-found wings.
Now a sorrowful bird she skimmed across
the surface of the sea, and while she flew,
from a slender beak her plaintive voice cried
sounds of sorrow, like someone filled with grief.
But when she touched the silent, bloodless corpse,
she clasped the limbs she loved in her new wings
and her hard beak kissed his cold lips in vain.
People wonder whether Ceyx sensed this
or whether it was the motion of the waves
that made him seem to lift his countenance.
But he surely felt it. So in the end,
thanks to the pity of the gods above,
they both were changed to birds. And even then,
though they both met this fate, their love endured.
The change did not dissolve their marriage ties.
They still mate and raise their offspring, and now,
for seven peaceful days in wintertime,
Alcyone broods in her nest, floating
atop the waves, which at that time are calm,
for Aeolus keeps all the winds confined,
prevents their leaving, and makes waters safe
for his descendants.

    Watching these two birds   AESACUS
fly side by side across the spacious sea,

an old man praised the love they had maintained [750]
right to the end. Then someone next to him,
or perhaps it was the same old man, pointed
to a long-necked bird and said:

                    "That bird
you see skimming across the sea, trailing
its thin legs behind, is a child of kings,
and if you seek out his direct descent 1150
in a family line right down to him, he comes
from Ilus, Assaracus, Ganymede
(seized by Jupiter), old Laomedon,
and then Priam, destined by Fate to reign
in Troy's last days.[1] He was Hector's brother,
and if as a young man he had not met
a bizarre fate, he might perhaps have had
a name no less illustrious than Hector's. [760]
Though Hector was the son of Hecuba,
Dymas' daughter, men say that Aesacus 1160
was born in secret, in the shady groves
below Mount Ida, to Alexirhoë,
daughter of the two-horned Granicus.[2]

Aesacus hated cities and spent his days   AESACUS AND HESPERIË
far distant from the glittering palace,
in far-off hills and humble rural places.
He rarely went to crowded Ilium.
But he was not uncouth, nor was his heart
impervious to love. Often he would seek
through all the forest glades to catch the nymph 1170
Hesperië, daughter of Cebrenus.
He had observed her sitting on the banks
beside her father's river, in the sun,
drying the wet hair spread across her shoulders. [770]
But when he looked at her, the nymph ran off,
like a startled deer fleeing a tawny wolf
or water ducks escaping from a hawk,
who catches them far from the pool they left.
The Trojan hero races close behind her,
his feet made swift by love and hers by fear. 1180

---

[1] These are some of the best-known names in the royal family of Troy.
[2] Granicus is a river in Asia Minor.

But then, behold, a sly snake in the grass,
as she races past, bites her in the foot
with its curved fang and leaves its poison
in her body. Her flight and life both end.
The lover hugs the lifeless girl and cries:

> 'It's bad that I chased after you, so bad!
> But I did not expect something like this.
> Winning your love was not worth this to me.
> The two of us have brought about your death,
> unhappy girl. The snake gave you the wound,   1190   [780]
> but I brought it about. And that makes me
> more guilty than the beast, unless I give you
> solace in your death by dying myself.'

Aesacus said this, and then threw himself
from a rock into the sea, where pounding surf
had eaten away the cliff. But as he fell,
Tethys, moved by pity, gently caught him.
While he was in the sea, she covered him
with feathers and would not give him the chance
to die the way he longed to. The lover   1200
was incensed. He was being forced to live
against his will, and his spirit, which yearned
to leave its sad abode, was being blocked.
Once new wings were growing on his shoulders,
he flew up and, once again, hurled his body   [790]
down into the sea. The feathers eased his fall.
Enraged, Aesacus dove headfirst deep down.
He kept on trying—and has never stopped—
to find a route to death. Love made him thin,
with elongated legs between the joints.   1210
His neck remains quite long and holds his head
some distance from his chest. He loves the sea
and still keeps hurling his body into it.
From this he has acquired his name, the diver."

Book Twelve

XII

[Aesacus' family mourn him; the Greek fleet remains at Aulis; a snake kills nine birds; Calchas prophesies; Iphigeneia is almost sacrificed; the home of Rumour; the Greeks reach Troy; Hector kills Protesilaus; Achilles and Cycnus fight; Cycnus is transformed; the Greeks have a banquet; Nestor tells how Caenis was changed from female to male; Nestor tells of the battle between Lapiths and Centaurs, of the achievements in that fight of Pirithoüs, Theseus, and Peleus, of Cyllarus and Hylonome, of Caeneus and Latreus, and of the transformation of Caeneus; Nestor tells Tlepolemus why he does not praise Hercules; Neptune tells Apollo to kill Achilles; Apollo shoots Achilles with the bow of Paris; Achilles dies and is cremated; Ajax and Ulysses claim Achilles' weapons; Agamemnon orders the Greek leaders to adjudicate the quarrel.]

Priam, father to Aesacus, mourned his loss,
not knowing he still lived on as a bird.   THE GREEKS AT AULIS
Hector and his brothers also offered
pointless sacrifices at the burial site
that bore his name.¹ Paris was not present
at this gloomy ceremony, the man
who seized and carried off his wife and thus
brought a long war back to his native land.
A thousand allied ships came after him,
carrying in one united group of men   10
the full force of the Pelasgian race.²
The Greeks would not have waited for revenge,
but fierce winds made the sea impassible,
and so the fleet, which was ready to sail,
lingered in the fishing port of Aulis,   [10]
in Boeotia. After they had prepared,   CALCHAS' PROPHECY
in accordance with their native customs,
a sacrifice to Jove and burning fires
had made the ancient altar glow, the Greeks
observed a dark-blue serpent slithering   20
into a plane tree standing right beside
where they had just begun the ritual.
A nest high in the tree held eight young birds.
The serpent seized these chicks and swallowed them
in its gluttonous jaws—their mother, too,

---

¹The sacrifices are "pointless" because Aesacus is not dead and thus the ritual will not have the desired effect of helping him reach the Underworld.

²Paris abducted Helen, wife of the Greek king Menelaus, and the Trojans refused to return her. Riley notes that different writers have offered different estimates of the size of the Greek fleet: Homer 1186, Dictys Cretensis 1225, and Dares 1140. Pelasgian is a common name for the Greeks (derived from the name for the original inhabitants of the area).

as she fluttered around her helpless brood.
All the men just stood there, stunned. But Calchas,
Thestor's son, who was a soothsayer, foretold
what would, in fact, occur:

      "Rejoice, you Greeks.
We will prevail! Troy will fall. But our task 30 [20]
will be a long one."

     He prophesied those birds—
all nine of them—must mean nine years of war.
The snake, while coiling around green branches
in the tree, was turned to stone, preserving
the image of a serpent carved in rock.

North Wind kept the waters turbulent   SACRIFICE OF IPHIGENEIA
in the Aonian sea and would not let
the war fleet sail. Some believed that Neptune
was sparing Troy because he built its walls.[1]
But not Thestor's son. For he understood— 40
and did not hide the fact—for them to sail
they had to appease an angry goddess,
placate a virgin with a virgin's blood.[2]
But when the demands of the public good
had overpowered all natural feelings
and the king had prevailed against the father,
as Iphigeneia, her retinue in tears,
had taken her place before the altar,
ready to offer her innocent blood, [30]
the goddess changed her mind. She cast a cloud 50
over their eyes in the middle of the rite,
with men crowding in for the sacrifice
and voices praying. Then, so people say,
she made a switch and set a deer in place
of that Mycenean virgin girl.[3] And so,
once a suitable victim had been killed

---

[1] For the story of how Neptune helped build the walls of Troy see above 11.306. The Aeonian sea is a reference to the Aegean sea between Greece and Asia Minor.

[2] Agamemnon, king of Mycenae, the leader of the Greek expedition, had offended the virgin goddess Diana, who sent the winds to hold up the fleet, until the appropriate sacrifice was made. Agamemnon was called upon to sacrifice his daughter, Iphigeneia.

[3] In some other famous versions of this story, Agamemnon does sacrifice his daughter.

and appeased Diana, her rage calmed down,
which eased the anger of the sea. The fleet
of a thousand ships received a tail wind,
sailed away, and after many hazards,
finally reached the coast of Phrygia.

There is a place in the centre of the world,   HOME OF RUMOUR
between earth, sea, and sky, at the limits
of the three-fold universe where all things   [40]
which exist anywhere, even far away,
are seen and where all voices penetrate
attentive ears. In this place Rumour lives.
Here she has chosen herself a dwelling
at the very summit of a citadel
with a thousand doorways and entrances,
but not a single gate to bar the way,
so the place stands open day and night.
Built out of echoing brass, it mutters,
repeating voices and whispering sounds
it has picked up. There is no quiet spot
inside, no silence anywhere. But still,
there is no loud din, only the subdued noise
of voices murmuring, the kind of sound
waves of the ocean often make when heard   [50]
from far away or the rumbling produced
by a final thunder roll when Jupiter
makes the clouds collide. An unruly crowd
fills up the halls, a fickle common throng,
which comes and goes. A thousand rumours,
combining falsehood with the truth, wander
here and there, passing around misleading chat.
Some of these fill empty ears with gossip,
and some bear stories they have heard elsewhere.
The number of made-up tales keeps growing,
as every author alters what he heard
by adding something new. Here one can find
Credulity and hot-headed Error,
empty Joy, alarming Fears, instant Sedition,   [60]
and Whispers whose origin is unknown.
Rumour herself sees everything going on
in heaven, land, and sea, and asks about
events the whole world over.

Book Twelve

                    Since Rumour   THE GREEKS REACH TROY
has already scattered the news that Greeks
are underway with a strong force of men,
when the armed armada sails into sight,
it comes as no surprise. The Trojans there
oppose the landing and defend the shore.
And you, Protesilaus, by Fate's decree,
are the first to fall, killed on Hector's spear.
The fighting starts, at great cost to the Greeks,
who learn of valiant Hector's warlike heart
by the slaughter he inflicts, and the Trojans
come to learn, from the loss of their own men,
what a Greek right hand can do. Already
the shores of Sigaeum are red with blood.
By this time Cycnus, a son of Neptune,   CYCNUS AND ACHILLES
has killed a thousand men. Achilles, too,
has already launched a chariot charge
and overwhelmed whole rows of fighting men
with blows of his ash spear from Pelion,
keen to clash with Hector or with Cycnus.
Achilles' fight with Hector is delayed
until the tenth year of the war, but now,
in this first fight, he does cross paths with Cycnus.
As Achilles urges on his team of horses
and their snow-white necks strain in the yoke,
he aims his chariot right at the Trojans.
With right arm brandishing the quivering spear,
he gives a shout:

           "Young man, whoever you are,
  when you die, take this for consolation—
  you have had your throat cut by Achilles,
  who comes from Thessaly!"

                         Achilles spoke.
His words were followed by his weighty spear.
Though no one could have seen a single flaw
in the way he hurled the spear, the weapon
he threw had no effect. Its sharpened point
left nothing but a bruise on Cycnus' chest,
as if he had been struck by something blunt.
Cycnus shouted:

Book Twelve

          "O son of a goddess—
for we have heard reports of you already—
why are you surprised I am not wounded?"

(For Achilles was, in fact, astonished).

   "This helmet with its tawny horsehair crest,
as you can see, affords me no protection,
nor does this hollow shield on my left arm.   140   [90]
They are mere ornaments, the very reason
Mars himself will often dress in armour.
If you strip me of this protective coat,
I still will walk away without a wound.
There is a benefit to being born,
not from some Nereïd, but from the god
who rules Nereus and his daughters, too,
and all the ocean waves."[1]

          Cycnus spoke these words,
then hurled his spear at Peleus' son.
It lodged itself in his round shield of bronze,   150
passing through metal and the next nine layers
of cattle hide, and stopping at the tenth.
Achilles shook out this spear, and once more
his strong arm hurled a quivering weapon.
But Cycnus' body, once again, remained
unharmed—there was no wound. And a third spear   [100]
could not harm Cycnus, though he left himself
exposed and vulnerable. Achilles
blazed with rage, like a bull in the arena
when its murderous horn strikes purple cloaks   160
men use to make it angry and it sees
the garment has escaped without a wound.
He checked the spear to see if the iron point
had fallen off. It was still fixed in place.
He told himself:

          "Well, then, is my hand weak?
With this one man, has it lost the power
it had before? For it was surely strong enough

---

[1] This is a slur against Achilles, whose mother, Thetis, was a Nereïd, a daughter of Nereus, and a minor sea goddess; whereas, Cycnus' father was Neptune, god of the sea and of everything in it.

when in the foremost ranks I overthrew
Lyrnessus' city walls, or when I soaked
Tenedos and Thebes, Eëtion's city,   170   [110]
in their own blood, or when Caïcus' stream
flowed red from all the men I cut down there,
and Telephus twice felt the way this spear
can do its work.[1] And here, where so many
have been slaughtered—my dead are lying in piles
for everyone to see along the shore—
my hand has proved itself and will stay strong!"

Achilles spoke. As if he had no faith
in what had happened earlier, he hurled
his spear right at Menoetes in a crowd   180
of Lycians standing across from him
and pierced his body armour and his chest
below the breastplate, both in the same blow.
Menoetes, as he lay in his death throes,
hammered his head against the solid ground.
Achilles pulled his spear from the hot wound
and cried:

            "This is the hand and this the spear   [120]
which in this battle helped me win the day.
These same weapons I will use to fight
against that warrior, and I pray with him
the result will be the same."

                            Achilles spoke
and tried to cut down Cycnus once again.
The ash spear did not miss its mark, for Cycnus
made no attempt at all to dodge the blow.
This time the spear struck his left shoulder blade
and bounced away, as if he were a wall
or solid rock. Then Achilles noticed
that where it struck the man was stained with blood,
and he felt great joy. But all for nothing!
There was no wound. It was Menoetes' blood!   200
Achilles, now truly in a rage, jumps

---

[1]Lyrnessus was a city close to Troy. Eëtion, king of Thebes (in Asia Minor, not the Thebes in Boeotia) was a Trojan ally. Achilles and the Greeks attacked and destroyed the city and killed Eëtion. The Caÿcus was a river in Asia Minor. Telephus, a son of Hercules, was wounded by Achilles' spear, but then healed by the spear point.

headlong down from his high chariot, clutching
his bright sword, seeking to battle Cycnus,
his fearless enemy, up close, hand to hand.
He sees his sword slicing shield and helmet,
but Cycnus' body is impervious
and even starts to blunt his iron blade.
Achilles can go on like this no longer,
so he pulls his own shield back and batters
his adversary's face three or four times,
hitting his hollow temples with his sword hilt,
pressing forward as Cycnus moves away,
following close and throwing him off guard,
harrying the man, giving him no rest
from his confusion. Then fear grips Cycnus.
Shadows swim before his eyes. As he moves
backwards in retreat, a boulder standing
in the middle of the field blocks his way.
Achilles drives him back against this rock,
bending his body, and with massive force
turns Cycnus over, hurls him to the ground,
then presses his hard knees and metal shield
into Cycnus' chest, pulls the helmet straps
tight underneath his chin, squeezes his throat,
cuts off his respiration, and chokes him.
But when Achilles goes to strip the corpse
of the man he has defeated, he sees
the armour is quite empty. For Neptune,
god of the sea, has transformed the body
into a white bird, which we call Cycnus,
a man's name only moments earlier.[1]

After this hard fight, there was a truce
for several days. Both forces set aside
their arms and rested. Vigilant sentries
guarded Trojan walls, and alert pickets
kept watch beside the trenches of the Greeks.
Then a day of celebration came, in which
Achilles, the conqueror of Cycnus,
was appeasing Pallas, offering blood

---

[1] The is Ovid's third account of the transformation of a man called Cycnus into a swan. For the other two see 2.530 and 7.599.

from a cow he sacrificed. Once he'd placed
the inner organs on the blazing altars
and that smell gods love had climbed to heaven,
part of the meat was held back for the rite
and the rest served out on dining tables.
The leaders, lying back on couches, filled
their bodies with well-cooked meat and dissolved
their thirst and cares with wine. No cithara
or singing voices or long boxwood flute
with many holes was there to entertain them.
Instead, they spent the night in conversation,
and the subject they discussed was courage.
They talked of their own battles and those fought
by enemies and often got great joy
from recalling, each in turn, the dangers
they had encountered and endured. What else
would Achilles talk about? And what else
would other men prefer to talk about
in the company of great Achilles?
Their discussion focused, first and foremost,
on his recent triumph, the overthrow
of Cycnus. They all found it astounding
that the young man's body could not be sliced
by any weapon, was impervious to wounds,
and made steel blunt. Achilles and the Greeks
were marvelling at this, when Nestor said:

> "Cycnus was the only warrior your age
> who could shrug off a sword and not be cut
> by any blow. But in earlier times
> I myself saw Thessalian Caeneus
> absorb a thousand blows without a wound
> appearing on his body. Yes, Caeneus,
> that Thessalian, famous for his exploits,
> lived on Othrys. What was more amazing
> about the man was this—when he was born,
> he was a female."

All those warriors there,
intrigued with such a strange phenomenon,
entreated Nestor to recount the story.
Along with other men, Achilles said:

CAENEUS AND CAENIS

Book Twelve

"Come now, tell us! You eloquent old man,
the wisdom of our age, all of us here 280
have the same desire to learn the details.
Who was Caeneus? Why was he transformed
to the opposite sex? In what campaign,
in whose battles, did you get to know him? [180]
Who prevailed against him? Did anyone
succeed in a fight with him?"

   Old Nestor said:

"Although my slow old age gets in the way
and many things I saw in earlier years
escape me, I still remember most of them.
I have lived through two centuries and now 290
am living in the third, and a long life
can make one witness numerous events.
But among so many acts in battle
and at home, nothing is more firmly fixed
here in my mind than that.[1]

   Virgin Caenis,
child of Elatus, was celebrated
for her beauty, the loveliest young girl
in Thessaly, and one courted in vain [190]
by jealous hopes of several suitors
in neighbouring towns—in your cities, too, 300
Achilles (for she was of your people).
Perhaps Peleus also might have tried
to win her, but he had already married
your mother, or else by then they were betrothed.
Caenis refused to marry anyone.
But, so people claim, while she was walking   CAENIS AND NEPTUNE
along a lonely shore, the god of the sea
assaulted her, and then (the same story
goes on to say) once Neptune had enjoyed
this new sexual affair, he said to her:

  'You can ask for anything you desire,
  and I will not refuse. Choose what you wish.' 310
               [200]

---

[1] Nestor's old age at the time of the Trojan War was legendary. In Homer's depiction of him, he has ruled over his people for three generations (not for three centuries).

Book Twelve

So Caenis answered:

> 'This attack on me
> makes me really wish I never suffer
> one like it again. So grant me this—
> that I am not a woman. With that gift,
> you'll have given me everything I want.'

She spoke those last words in a harsher tone.
One could have thought the voice came from a man,
as indeed it had. The god of the deep seas   320
had already agreed to grant her wish,
and, in addition, now she was a man,
Neptune ensured that he could not be hurt
by any wound or slain by any sword.
Delighted with this gift, Caeneus left.
He roamed through the Thessalian countryside
and spent his time on things which men enjoy.

Now, Pirithoüs, bold Ixion's son,   [210]
had married Hippodamia and had asked
those savage creatures, the cloud-born centaurs,   330
to sit in proper order at some tables   THE CENTAURS AND LAPITHS
set out in a cave sheltered by the trees.
Thessalian leaders came, and so did I.[1]
Crowds of unruly celebrating guests
filled the royal home with noise. As they sang
the marriage song and fires filled the hall
with smoke, the virgin bride appeared, a girl
more lovely than the others, surrounded
by a group of newly married women
and older wives. We said Pirithoüs   340
was fortunate to have her as his bride,
a prophecy which almost proved a lie.
For your heart, Eurytus, you most savage
of the savage centaurs, was hot with wine,   [220]
as well as from the sight of that young girl,

---

[1] The centaurs had the head, torso, and arms of a human being and the body, legs, and tail of a horse. Both the centaurs and Pirithoüs were descended from Ixion. They had quarreled before over family properties. The phrase "cloud born" refers to the fact that, according to some accounts, the centaurs were born from Ixion and a cloud in the shape of Juno. Jupiter made the cloud to direct Ixion's attention away from Juno, whom he was keen to attack sexually.

and you were ruled by drunkenness and lust.
Suddenly the tables were knocked over,
and the feast became a brawl. The new bride
was hauled away by force, dragged by the hair.
Eurytus snatched Hippodamia, while others   350
seized whichever woman there they fancied
or could lay their hands on. The place looked like
a looted city—sounds of women screaming
echoed through the house. We jumped up quickly—
all of us—and Theseus first cried out:

> 'Eurytus, what mad fit is forcing you
> to injure Pirithoüs with me here,
> still living, and, in your stupidity,
> to cause offense to both of us at once?'

In case what he just said had no effect,   360   [230]
brave Theseus pushed aside the centaurs
who hemmed him in and grabbed the young girl back
from those mad creatures taking her away.
Eurytus said nothing (he could not defend
the sort of thing he'd done by using words).
Instead, his shameless fists attacked the face
of the girl's protector and struck his noble chest.
By chance an ancient mixing bowl was there,
its rough surface covered with embossed designs
in high relief. Theseus raised it up   370
(it was huge, but he was even larger)
and threw it right in the centaur's face.
Eurytus collapsed and lay there on his back,
while gobs of blood, as well as brains and wine,
came pouring from his mouth and wounded face
and his feet kept drumming on the soaking floor.
His brother centaurs, with two sets of limbs,   [240]
incensed at Eurytus' murder, all shouted
with a single voice:

> 'To arms! To arms!'

Wine gave them courage. As the fight began,   380
cups, basins made of bronze, and fragile jars
went flying through the air. Things set down there
to adorn a feast were now being used
to slaughter men in battle.

Book Twelve

The first one
bold enough to strip away the offerings
from the innermost shrine was Amycus,
Ophion's son. He began by taking
from that sanctuary a torch densely packed
with blazing fire. He lifted it high up,
like someone with a sacrificial axe 390
trying to break the white neck on a bull,
and brought it down, fracturing the forehead
of Celadon, a Lapith, and left him [250]
with his facial bones smashed in and shattered
beyond all recognition.[1] His eyes bulged out,
and bones around his mouth, as they were crushed,
had forced his nose back into the centre
of his palate. Pelates from Pellas,
tore off a maple table leg, struck Amycus,
and knocked him to the ground, forcing his chin 400
hard against his chest. Then, while Amycus
was spitting out his teeth and blood, Pelates
hit him once again, and that second blow
dispatched him to the shades of Tartarus.

Next Gryneus stood there with a grim face
staring at the smoking altar. He cried:

'Why don't we use this?'

                              He raised the altar— [260]
it was immense—and threw it, fires and all,
into the middle of the Lapith ranks,
crushing two of them, Broteas and Orius. 410
Orius' mother was Mycale,
whose incantations, people used to say,
had frequently brought down the crescent moon,
despite its struggles.[2] Exadius then cried:

'You'll not get away with that unpunished,
not if I can lay hands on a weapon!'

He had no spear, so he seized the antlers
of a stag hanging on a lofty pine tree

---

[1] The Lapiths were a tribe in Thessaly.

[2] According to popular belief, lunar eclipses were caused by witches stealing the moon.

Book Twelve

as an offering to the gods. Using these,
he drove two points in Gryneus' face, 420
gouging out his eyes—one stuck on the horn,
the other slid onto his beard and hung there, [270]
soaked in blood.

        Then, lo and behold, Rhoetus
snatches up a blazing log of plum wood
burning in the middle of the altar
and, swinging from the right, hits Caraxus
where the yellow hair conceals his temple.[1]
His hair, set alight by the rapid flames,
burns like dry fields of grain, while in the wound
the blood gives off a dreadful hissing noise, 430
as it burns up, the same way iron sounds
when a smith with crooked tongs picks up a piece
still red hot from the fire and plunges it
down in the trough—once immersed in liquid,
it spits and hisses in the lukewarm water.
Caraxus, though hurt, shakes the eager flames [280]
from his tousled hair, tears up a slab of stone
set as a threshold in the ground, and lifts it
shoulder high—it would have filled a wagon—
but its huge weight prevents him tossing it 440
far enough to reach the ones he wants to hit.
But the massive stone does crush Cometes,
a friend of his, standing close beside him.
Rhoetus does not hold back his joy and shouts:

    'I hope that crowd of yours, the other people
    in your camp, are all as strong as he is!'

Then he attacks Caraxus once again
with the half-burned log, battering his head
again and again with damaging blows,
splitting the sutures in the Lapith's skull, 450
till bones sink down inside his oozing brain.

Triumphant Rhoetus now shifts his gaze [290]
to Euagrus and Corythus and Dryas, too.
He first knocks over Corythus, a lad

---

[1] Rhoetus was a centaur.

whose cheeks have their first covering of down.
Euagrus cries:

      'What glory do you win
 by slaughtering a boy?'

       But Rhoetus
stops him saying any more, by shoving
the burning wood right in his open mouth,
as he is speaking, and then driving it   460
viciously through his mouth into his chest.
Then, savage Dryas, he goes after you,
as well, waving the fire around his head.
But with you he does not get the same result,
for, as he is boasting of his success
in killing all those men, you stab at him
with a fire-hardened stake where his neck
and shoulder meet. Rhoetus gives a groan   [300]
and with some difficulty pulls the stake
away from the hard bone, then runs away,   470
soaked in his own blood. Orneus also flees,
along with Lycabas and wounded Medon,
hit in his right shoulder, with Thaumas, too,
and Pisenor, as well as Mermerus,
who recently could conquer anyone
in running, but who moves more slowly now
from the wound he has received. Pholus flees,
with Melaneus and boar-hunting Abas,
and the prophet Asbolus, who has tried,
without success, to keep them from a fight.   480
Nessus, too, is running away, afraid
of being wounded. To him Asbolus cries:

 'Do not run off. For you will be quite safe—
 you're slated for the bow of Hercules.'[1]

But some did not escape their death—Lycidas,
Eurynomus, Areus, and Imbreus—   [310]
all these centaurs were cut down by Dryas
with his right arm, when they confronted him.
You, too, Crenaeus, though you turned to flee,

---

[1]The point here is that Nessus is destined to be killed by Hercules and thus will not die in this fight. For Ovid's story of Hercules and Nessus, see 9.164 ff.

were wounded in the front, for you looked back
and got a heavy spear between the eyes,
right where your nose and lower forehead join.

In the middle of this massive uproar,
Aphidas lay there and did not wake up,
his whole body sunk in a timeless sleep.
His limp left hand still clutched a cup of wine,
and he was stretched out on a shaggy hide
of a bear from Ossa. Seeing him there,
from some distance off, lying motionless
and no use in the fight, Phorbas slipped his hand
inside his javelin thong and shouted:

'Drink your wine with water from the Styx!'

And with no more delay, he hurled his spear
straight at the youthful lad. Now, Aphidas,
as it so happened, was lying on his back,
so the ash shaft tipped with steel was driven
deep into his neck, and he perished there
without feeling a thing. From his full throat
the dark blood poured and dripped onto the couch
and down into the wine cup in his hand.

I myself saw Petraeus trying to lift
an oak tree full of acorns from the earth.
While his arms were round the tree, moving it
back and forth, working on the loosened trunk,
a spear from Pirithoüs pierced his ribs
and pinned his writhing chest to solid wood.
People say that Chromius and Lycus
were slain by valiant Pirithoüs,
but neither of those centaurs gave the victor
as much glory as he got from killing
Helops and Dictys. Helops was transfixed
by a javelin thrown at him from his right.
It drove itself in his left ear and pierced
his temples. Dictys was running away,
afraid of Pirithoüs, Ixion's son,
who was coming after him, but tripped up
on a steep mountain ridge and fell headlong
down the slope. His heavy body split apart

a huge mountain ash and the fractured tree
impaled him in the groin.

                Aphareus
moves up to avenge the death of Dictys.
He takes a rock ripped from the mountainside
and tries to throw it, but as he does this,
Theseus, son of Aegeus, strikes him   THESEUS AND THE CENTAURS
with his oaken club and breaks the huge bones
in his elbow. There is no time to pause,
and Theseus has no desire to slaughter
Aphareus, whose body is now harmless.
So he leaps up on tall Bienor's back,
which is not used to bearing anyone
except Bienor, presses his knees hard
into the creature's ribs, while his left hand
seizes the centaur's hair and holds on tight.
Then using his knotted club, Theseus
batters his face and mouth (still shouting threats)
and hits his solid temples. With this same club
he knocks over spear-throwing Lycopes,
Nedymnus, Hippasus (whose flowing beard
protects his chest), Ripheus (a huge beast
taller than the trees), and Thereus,
who in Thessaly grabs wild mountain bears
and carries them home, alive and kicking.

Demoleon could no longer bear to see
Theseus having such success in battle.
Using all his strength, he tried to rip up
the sturdy trunk of an ancient pine tree.
When that effort failed, he broke off the trunk
and threw it at Theseus, who had moved back
some distance from the approaching missile.
He had been warned by Pallas to withdraw
(that, at least, is what he hoped men would believe).
But the tree trunk did not miss completely.
When it fell, it hit tall Crantor's chest and shoulder,
severing his neck. That man, Achilles,
had once been your father's armour bearer,
given to Peleus by Amyntor,
king of the Dolopes, as surety,
to guarantee the peace. When Peleus,

Book Twelve

from a distance, saw Crantor cut apart
with such a dreadful wound, he cried:

                        'Crantor,   570
the youth I cherish most, at least accept
this tribute to the dead.'

              Then, with all his strength,
his powerful arm threw his ash-wood spear
straight at Demoleon. It pierced his ribs   [370]
and stuck in there, quivering in the bones.
He pulled it out, but could not find the tip
(removing the shaft was difficult enough),
so the point stayed there, stuck inside his lung.
Pain made Demoleon even more enraged.
Though wounded, he went after Peleus,   580
rearing to kick him with his horses' hooves.
Peleus absorbed the echoing blows
on shield and helmet, striving to protect
his upper chest. He held his weapons out
in front of him and with a single blow
through his enemy's shoulder blade he speared
that creature with a double chest.[1] By now,
before this fight, he had already killed
Hyles and Phlegraeus from a distance,
and Clanis and Iphinoüs hand-to-hand.   590
To these he added Dorylas, who wore   [380]
a wolf-skin hat and, rather than a spear,
carried a splendid set of crooked ox horns
dyed red from so much blood.

                  Now, my courage
made my spirit strong, so I shouted out
to Dorylas:

              'See how much your horns
fail to match my steel!'

                  I hurled my spear at him.
He could not avoid the blow, so he raised
his right hand to his forehead to ward off
the wound he would receive. But then his hand   600

---

[1] The centaur has two chests—one of a human being and one of a horse.

was pinned against his head. He screamed in pain,
but Peleus (who stood quite close to him),
seeing him struck like that and overcome
by such a vicious wound, hit Dorylas
with a sword thrust right below his belly.
The furious centaur charged at Peleus,
dragging his guts along the ground, but then, [390]
while trailing his own entrails, stepped on them,
and, as he did that, ripped them all apart
and got his legs entangled. He collapsed
with nothing left inside his abdomen.

And your beauty did not save you, Cyllarus,   CYLLARUS AND HYLONOME
not in that fight, if we, in fact, concede
a nature like your own is beautiful.
His downy yellow beard was just beginning,
and golden hair hung from his shoulder blades
half way down his flanks. His face was pleasing,
young and vigorous. His neck and shoulders,
his hands and chest, and all his human parts
looked like artistic statues men so praise.
Nor was his horse's body down below
flawed or less noble than his human form.
With a horse's head and neck, he would be fit [400]
for Castor. His back deserved a rider,
as did his deep and finely muscled chest.[1]
He was completely black, more so than pitch,
except for his white tail and snowy legs.
Many females of his species courted him,
but one made him her own, Hylonome.
There was no female lovelier than her
among those hybrid beasts in the deep woods.
She was the only one who held his heart
with her endearments, giving him her love
and telling him how much she was in love,
and by taking care of her appearance
(as much as that was possible for her
with those limbs she had). She would use a comb
to smooth her hair and at times deck herself [410]
with rosemary or violets or roses,

---

[1] Castor, son of Helen and Zeus, was famous for his horsemanship.

and sometimes wore white lilies. Twice a day
she washed her face in fountain streams falling
from the high forest ridge of Pagasae
and dipped her body in the flowing water.
On her left flank or shoulders, she would wear
wild creature's hides which she would choose with care
to made her look attractive. Both of them
loved equally. Together they would roam
the mountains and explore the caves. And now
they both had come into that Lapith home
and together both had joined the fighting.
But now a javelin thrown from the left
(just who hurled the missile is uncertain)
hit you, Cyllarus, right below the spot
where your neck and chest both meet. When the weapon
was pulled out, your heart, though slightly wounded,
lost it vital heat, and your whole body froze.
Hylonome quickly held his dying limbs,
placed her hand against the wound to close it,
and moved her mouth to his, in an attempt
to stop his spirit flying away. But then,
when she saw he was gone, she said some words
which the noise prevented me from hearing,
threw herself onto the spear which had killed
her husband, and as she died, embraced him.

Another centaur stands before my eyes—
Phaeocomes, who had knotted together
six lion skins, as a protective cover
for both man and horse. He hurled a huge log
(two teams of oxen would hardly shift it)
and hit Tectaphus, a son of Olenos,
crushing the very top part of his head
[and shattering the broad roof of his skull.
The soft stuff in his brain came oozing out,
through his eyes and ears and hollow nostrils,
just like curdled milk passing through oak twigs
or viscous liquids pressured in a sieve
seeping through dense openings in the mesh.][1]
But as Phaeocomes was getting ready

---

[1] Some editors have cast doubt on the authenticity of these lines.

to strip the armour from dead Tectaphus—
your father knows this story—I plunged my sword
into his lower gut. And my sword killed
Teleboas and Chthonius, as well.
Chthonius was waving a two-forked branch,
and Teleboas had a spear. Look here.
That is the scar from a wound he gave me.
It's still visible, that old mark he made.
Those were the days I should have been sent off
to capture Troy. Back then I had the strength,
if not to take the city, at least to check
great Hector's weapons with my own. But he,
in those days, had not yet been born or else
was just a boy. Now age has made me frail.

Why should I tell you about Periphas,
who overcame the centaur Pyraethus,
or talk of Ampyx, who drove his cornel spear,
without a point, into the opposing face
of four-footed Echeclus? Macareus
slaughtered Erigdupus from Pelethron
by burying a crowbar in his chest.[1]
And I remember how a hunting spear
from the hand of Nessus hit Cymelus
deep in his groin. And you should not believe
that Mopsus, son of Ampycus, was just
a man who prophesied what was to come,
for his throw killed the centaur Hodites,
who tried to speak, but failed, because the spear
went through his tongue, pinned it against his chin,
and fixed his chin against his throat.

                         Caeneus   CAENEUS AND LATREUS
had slaughtered five—Styphelus, Bromus,
Antimachus, Elymus, and Pyracmus
(armed with a battle axe). I don't recall
their wounds, but I kept track of the number
and their names. Then Latreus charged forward,
a centaur with massive limbs and body,
decked out in the armour he had stripped
from a warrior he had killed, Halesus,

---

[1] Pelathron was a region of Thessaly.

who came from Thessaly. He was mature,
between old age and youth, with streaks of gray
across his temples and a young man's strength.
His shield, helmet, and Macedonian spear
made him stand out. He rode around in circles,
facing each battle group in turn, clashing
his weapons and, in his arrogance, shouting
all sorts of gibes into the empty air:

> 'Do I have to put up with you, as well,
> Caenis? Yes, I called you Caenis, because
> to me you will always be a woman.
> That's how I think of you. Does not your birth
> remind you and do you not think about
> the act which brought you this reward, the price
> you paid for this false image of a man?
> Consider what you were when you were born
> or what you suffered, then go and take up
> your spinning wheel and baskets. Use your thumb
> to twist the yarn. Leave warfare to the men.'

While Latreus was taunting him like this,
Caeneus hurled his spear and hit the centaur,
where horse and man were joined, wounding his side
as he was running at full stretch. Latreus,
mad with pain, tried to strike the exposed face
of the Thessalian youth with his long spear.
But the spear just bounced away, like hailstones
from a roof or some small pebble hitting
a hollow drum. Latreus moved in close
and strove to hit Caeneus by thrusting
his sword in his impenetrable side.
But there was no place the sword could enter.
The centaur cried:

> 'You still won't get away!
> Since my point is blunt, I will destroy you
> with the blade.'

Turning his sword blade sideways,
he reached out with his long right arm to slash
Caeneus in the gut. The blow re-echoed,
as if the sword had struck a marble body.

When the blade hit Caeneus' hardened skin
it shattered into pieces.

    Once Caeneus
had exposed his body long enough and,
much to his enemy's astonishment,
received no wound, he shouted:

      'Come on now,   [490]
 let me test your body with my steel!'

He drove his lethal sword up to the hilt   760
in the centaur's flank, twisting and turning
the buried weapon in his flesh, redoubling
Latreus' wounds. Then, lo and behold,
with a huge shout, the furious centaurs
all charged up, hurling and thrusting weapons
against one man. Their spears fell down, blunted,
and Caeneus, son of Elatus, stood there
unhurt. None of their weapons had drawn blood.
The centaurs were astonished at this marvel.
Monychus cried out:

      'What a huge disgrace!   770
We are a whole group of people beaten
by someone who is not a real man.
But now, thanks to our pathetic efforts,   [500]
we are what he used to be. What's the point
of our powerful limbs, our double strength,
our hybrid nature which combines in us
the strongest animals of living things.
I do not think our mother was goddess
or we are Ixion's sons. He was a man
so great he set his hopes on mighty Juno,   780
and we are conquered by an enemy
who is just half a man. Roll rocks and trees
on him, entire mountains, too! And squeeze
the living spirit out by throwing wood.
Let piles of logs press down his throat. Their weight
will end his life instead of wounds.'

      As Monychus finished,
he raised a tree, which, as it so happened,
had been blown down by the furious power   [510]
of the violent South Wind, and hurled it

BOOK TWELVE

at Caeneus, who did not back away.
The entire crowd of centaurs did the same,
and soon Mount Othrys was devoid of trees
and Pelion had no more shade. Caeneus,
overpowered by the enormous heap,
is struggling underneath that weight of wood.
His hardy shoulders hold up the pile of oak,
but once the mound climbs up above his mouth
and higher than his head, he has no air
which he can draw upon to breathe. At times
he tries—without success—to lift himself
into the air and shake off all the trees
heaped there on top of him and sometimes
shifts the pile, just as we see Mount Ida
when, lo and behold, it starts to shudder
and the whole earth shakes. How his story ended
is not clear. Some people claim his body,
crushed by that pile of wood, was driven down
to the void of Tartarus. But Mopsus,
son of Ampycus, denied this. For he observed
a bird with tawny wings fly from the pile
up into the air. I saw it, as well
(that was my first and final sight of it).
When Mopsus saw the bird flying lazily
around his camp, gazing down and making
a loud noise, his eyes and spirit followed it,
and he called:

                'Hail to you, Caeneus,
glory of the Lapith race, a great man once,
but now the one bird of your kind.'

                            We believed
this was the truth, because we trusted Mopsus.
Grief increased our anger. We were incensed
one man had been assaulted by so many,
and we did not stop slashing with our swords
to vent our rage till half our enemies
had been killed and the rest had run away
and scattered under cover of the night."

As Nestor was talking about this fight
between the Lapiths and half-human centaurs,
Tlepolemus, upset because the story

HERCULES AND NESTOR

made no mention of his father, Hercules,
remarked:

    "Old man, it astonishes me   830
that those tales you tell leave out any praise
for Hercules, because I well recall   [540]
my father often used to talk to me
about the cloud-born centaurs he had killed."

Nestor answered sadly:

    "Why force me to remember
sorrowful events, which open once again
those wounds which time has healed, and to reveal
my hatred for your father, whose actions
were so damaging to me? By the gods,
that man accomplished things beyond belief.   840
The world is full of praise for Hercules!
I wish I could deny it. But we Greeks
do not laud Deïphobus or Polydamas
or even Hector, for what man ever praised
his enemies?[1]

    Once that father of yours
destroyed Messene's walls and overwhelmed
two harmless cities—Pylos and Elis—   [550]
demolishing my home with fire and sword.
I will not mention other men he killed,
but Neleus had twelve sons, all of us   850
outstanding younger men, and all twelve,
except myself, fell before the power
of Hercules. Of course, one must accept   PERICLYMENES
that those others could have been defeated,
but Periclymenes' death was really odd.
Neptune, who founded the family line
of Neleus, had given this young lad
the power to take on any shape he liked
and to discard it and change back again.
Well, after Periclymenes had changed   860
into every shape, in a vain attempt
to flee from Hercules, he turned himself

---

[1] Deïphobus, Polydamas, and Hector were important enemies of the Greeks at Troy, especially Hector, the Trojans' leader and their finest warrior.

Book Twelve

into that bird which Jupiter so loves,
the one whose hooked claws usually bear
the lightning bolt. Using that bird's power,
its wings, its crooked beak, and curving talons,
he tore at Hercules' face. But then,
as his wings carried him up to the clouds
and he hovered there, the man from Tiryns
took his bow that never misses and shot.
He hit him where the wing and side are joined.
He was not killed, but the wound had severed
the sinews, which now no longer functioned
and could not move—they lacked the strength to fly.
He fell back to the earth. His injured wings
could not beat the air, and then the arrow,
which was still clinging lightly to his wing,
was driven inward by his body's weight,
straight through his upper chest into his neck
on the left-hand side.

          Now, you most glorious leader
of the fleet from Rhodes, does it seem to you
I ought to sing in praise of Hercules
and his great deeds? But I am not seeking
to avenge my brothers any further
than keeping quiet about those exploits.
You and I, we share a solid friendship."

When Nestor, in that sweet-toned voice of his,
had finished, the warriors turned once again
from telling stories to the gift of Bacchus.
Then they got up, left their couches, and spent
the remainder of the nighttime fast asleep.

But the god who with his trident governs
the waters of the sea was sick at heart,
grieving with a father's sorrow for the son
whose body he had changed into a swan
(like Phaëton's friend, the son of Sthenelus).[1]

NEPTUNE AND APOLLO

---

[1] Ovid is here bringing together two of the three different accounts of the transformation of someone called Cycnus. Neptune is mourning his son Cycnus, whose story is told earlier in this book (see 12.111 ff.). Phaëton's friend, Cycnus, son of Sthenelus, has no relationship to Neptune (for his story see 2.530 ff.). I have added a few words in line 896 of the English, to clarify this point, which is somewhat confusing in the Latin.

Book Twelve

He despised savage Achilles and nursed,
in his memory, a rage against him
which was excessive. So now, when the war
had been dragging on for about ten years,
he spoke to Smintheus, long-haired Apollo,
with the following words:[1]

"O you, who are by far
the dearest to me of my brother's children
and with me built the city walls of Troy,
which will not last, are you not sad to see
that citadel about to be destroyed?[2]
Do you not lament the many thousands
who died defending those same battlements?
I will not name them all, but does your mind [590]
ever think of Hector's shade, that hero
dragged past the walls of his own Pergamum?[3]
And yet that fierce Achilles still survives,
a more destructive man than war itself,
the one who wipes away the work we did.
Let him face me and feel what I can do
with my triple-pointed spear! However,
since we are not permitted to confront
our enemies in combat hand-to-hand,
you should kill him when he is not looking
with a secret arrow!"

The Delian god,
responding to his uncle Neptune's feelings
and his own, as well, nodded his assent.
Concealing himself in clouds, Apollo   APOLLO AND ACHILLES
moved among the ranks of Trojans and there,
in the middle of the men being slaughtered,
saw Paris shooting arrows now and then   [600]
at unimportant Greeks. The god revealed
he was divine and said:

---

[1] Smintheus was an epithet for Apollo. Its precise meaning is unclear ("killer of field mice," perhaps).

[2] For Ovid's account of how Apollo and Neptune built the walls of Troy see 11.294 ff.

[3] The Pergamum was the citadel in Troy, the highest point in the city. When Achilles killed Hector, he dragged him around Troy a number of times.

Book Twelve

"Why waste your arrows
shedding blood of common soldiers? For if
you are concerned about your family,
you should pay attention to Achilles
and avenge your slaughtered brothers."

                       The god said this
and pointed to the son of Peleus
mowing down Trojan bodies with his sword.
Then he turned Paris' bow towards him,
and the god's death-dealing hand directed
the unerring arrow at Achilles.
And now the old man Priam could rejoice
for the first time since his son Hector died.

And so you, Achilles, who have overcome
such powerful men, are finally slain
by a cowardly thief who snatched away
a Grecian wife! If the Fates ordained
a woman's hand would kill you in that war,
you'd prefer to die from a battle axe
in the hands of a warrior Amazon queen.[1]

And now Achilles, grandson of Aeacus,
the man who has terrorized the Trojans,
the great glory of the Greeks, defender
of their Pelasgian name, the leader
who has been invincible in battle,
has been cremated. Vulcan, the same god
who armed him, has consumed him in the flames.[2]
Now he is ashes, and little remains
of the great Achilles, hardly enough
to fill a funeral urn. But his fame lives on
and fills the entire world. The tributes
match the man himself. And with this glory
the son of Peleus remains as mighty
as in earlier days and does not feel
the empty spaces of deep Tartarus.

---

[1] This is probably an allusion to Penthesilea, queen of the Amazons, who was killed by Achilles during the Trojan War. In some accounts, he fell in love with her as soon as he removed the helmet from her corpse. Other accounts say that he sexually violated the body.

[2] Vulcan had made special divine armour for Achilles.

One can tell how glorious Achilles was [620]
by how those warriors fought for his shield. THE ARMS OF ACHILLES
They took up arms to battle for his arms.
But Diomedes, son of Tydeus,
did not dare to claim them, nor did Ajax,
Oïleus' son, or Menelaus,
younger son of Atreus, or his brother,
the greater warrior Agamemnon,
or any of the others. Only Ajax, 1060
son of Telamon, and Laërtes' son,
Ulysses, had the boldness to assert
that they deserved the glory of those arms.
To avoid the burden and bad feeling
involved in the decision, Agamemnon,
blood relative of Tantalus, commanded
the leaders of the Argives to sit down
in the middle of the camp and shifted
the decision in this quarrel to them all.

Book Thirteen

XIII

[The debate over the arms of Achilles; Ajax presents his case, praising himself and attacking Ulysses; Ulysses responds, listing his accomplishments and criticizing Ajax; the Greek leaders award the weapons to Ulysses; Ajax commits suicide; The closing events of the war—the city burned, Priam killed, Astyanax killed, Trojan women led away; Polydorus is killed in Thrace; Achilles' ghost demands a sacrifice; Polyxena is killed at the altar; Hecuba laments Polyxena's death and her own life, then discovers the corpse of Polydorus; Hecuba gets revenge on Polymestor; Hecuba is transformed to a dog; Aurora asks Jupiter to honour Memnon; a flock of birds arises out of Memnon's funeral fire; Aeneas leaves Troy, reaches Delos; Anius tells the story of his daughters; Anius' cup depicts the story of Orion's daughters; Aeneas sails to Crete, then through islands in the Ionian sea; Helenus prophesies their future; the Trojan reach Sicily; Scylla and Galatea; Galatea, Acis, and Polyphemus; Polyphemus in love; Acis is transformed; Scylla and Glaucus; Glaucus tells of his transformation, then leaves for Circe's home.]

Argive leaders sat down in their places,
with common soldiers grouped around them,
standing in a circle. Ajax strode up,   AJAX MAKES HIS CASE
lord of the seven-layered shield, a man
with little patience, quick to grow enraged.
With a fierce look he glanced out at the shore
of Sigaeum and the ships up on the beach.
He stretched his arm and said:

                      "Those ships there—
we are making our case before those ships,
and Ulysses stands here arguing with me!   10
But he did not hesitate to back away
from Hector's flames, when I stood up to them
and drove them from our fleet.[1] And so for him,
it's safer to compete with crafty speeches
than battle on with fists. I am not quick   [10]
at using words, and he is slow to act.
Just as I am powerful in battle
and ferocious warfare, that man excels
in talking. But I do not think I need
to give you an account of my great deeds.   20
You Greeks all saw them. Let Ulysses here
tell us about his exploits, things he did
when there were no witnesses, those actions
which are known only to the night. The prize
I seek is great—that I concede. But then,

---

[1] In the *Iliad*, Hector leads his Trojan forces up to the Greek fleet and sets fire to one ship, defended by Ajax. Ulysses is, at this point, wounded.

my rival here makes it less valuable.
However great a thing may be, for Ajax
there is no reason to take pride in it,
if Ulysses seeks it, too. And in this contest
that fellow has already got his prize,   30
for when he is defeated, he can say   [20]
he fought it out with me. As for myself,
if you had any doubts about my courage,
my noble birth is a strong argument.
My father is Telamon, who captured
the walls of Troy, led by brave Hercules,
and reached the shores of Cochis in that ship
from Pagasae.[1] And my father's father
was Aeacus, who dispenses justice
down there below, among the silent dead,   40
where Sisyphus, the son of Aeolus,
still pushes his huge stone. High Jupiter
has acknowledged Aeacus, admitting
he is his son, and therefore Ajax stands
at three removes from Jupiter himself.
And yet, you Greeks, do not let my descent
speak for me in this quarrel, if those bonds
are not shared by me and great Achilles.   [30]
He was my cousin.[2] What I am seeking
is my cousin's property. As for you,   50
Ulysses, who in thieving and deceit
are just like Sisyphus, your ancestor,
why are you striving to involve the name
of a foreign family in the affairs
of those whose blood links them to Aeacus?

Or am I to be denied those weapons
because I took up arms before he did,
without being tricked by an informant?
Or will he seem to be the better man
because he was the last to take them up   60
and, by pretending to be mad, refused
to serve in war, until Palamedes,

---

[1] This is a reference to the Argonauts, who sailed with Jason in a ship made at Pagasae to Colchis to get back the Golden Fleece. For Ovid's treatment of the story see 7.1 ff.

[2] Ajax's father, Telamon, and Achilles' father, Peleus, were brothers, both sons of Aeacus.

son of Nauplius, a shrewder warrior
(though less alert about his own well being)
exposed the plot his timid mind devised
and dragged him to a war he had avoided.¹
Is this man who declined to take up arms
now to collect the finest arms of all? [40]
Am I, who was the first to face the dangers,
to be dishonoured and denied those gifts 70
from my own cousin?

                How I wish his madness
had been real or we had believed it true
and he had never come as our companion
against the towers of Troy, this fellow
who urges shameful acts on us. For then,
we would not have stranded Philoctetes,
Poeas' son, on Lemnos, to our disgrace!²
Men say that now he hides in forest caves,
shifts stones with his laments, and keeps praying
Laërtes' son will get what he deserves. 80
If there are gods, he does not pray in vain.
So now, alas, a man who swore an oath— [50]
the same one we did—to join the conflict,
one of our leaders, heir to those arrows
left by Hercules, is broken by disease
and hunger, fed and clothed by flying birds,
and uses arrows Fate reserved for Troy
to shoot at fowl. But still, he is not dead,
for he sailed no further with Ulysses.
Wretched Palamedes would have chosen 90
to be left there (he would still be alive
or at least have died without being called
a criminal). That fellow there remembered,

---

¹The Greek leaders had made a promise to the father of Helen, that they would help the man she married. Menelaus married Helen and, when Paris abducted her, called upon the Greeks to honour their promise. Ulysses tried to avoid going to war by pretending to be mad. The warrior Palamedes exposed Ulysses' trick, and so he was forced to join the expedition.

²Philoctetes, one of the leaders in the Greek expedition, had been bitten by a snake, and his cries of pain and the smell of his wound caused so much trouble in the army, that he was abandoned, en route to Troy, on the island of Lemnos. Philoctetes, as we learn a few lines further on, owned the bow of Hercules, which was needed to capture Troy. For Philoctetes' role in Hercules' cremation, see above 9.373.

Book Thirteen

all too vividly, how Palamedes
had exposed his so-called fits of madness
and charged him with betraying the Grecian cause,
something he just made up. He offered proof [60]
by finding gold he had earlier concealed.[1]
So by abandonment or death, he saps
the strength of Greeks. It is Ulysses' way, 100
and that is why he should be feared.

                          And even if
he was more eloquent than faithful Nestor,
I still would not believe that when he left,
abandoning Nestor in that battle,
he did nothing wrong.[2] Nestor was worn out,
and old, and hampered by his horse's wound,
but when he asked Ulysses for his help,
his comrade moved away. Diomedes,
the son of Tydeus, knows very well
I have not made these accusations up. 110
He often shouted out Ulysses' name
and rebuked his craven friend, charging him
with running away. Gods above look down, [70]
with their just eyes, on what we humans do!
For, behold, the man who had refused his help
required help. He had abandoned Nestor,
and now he was to be abandoned, too.
The precedent the man himself had set
was now applied to him. He shouted out,
calling to his companions. I ran up. 120
I saw him trembling, pale with fear, afraid
his death was close at hand. I set my shield
so its enormous size would cover him,
as he lay there, and saved his rotten life
(small reason to get any praise for that!).
If you prolong this contest, why not return
to that location, bring back the enemy,

---

[1] Ulysses forged a letter from king Priam of Troy to Palamedes offering gold for his treasonous services, allowed the letter to be discovered, and bribed Palamedes' servants to hide gold in his camp. Palamedes was stoned to death.

[2] The reference here is to a battle in the *Iliad* in which Nestor is left exposed and needs help. Odysseus does not respond to a shout from Diomedes to help Nestor (in Homer it is clear that Odysseus does not hear the shout, not that he has heard and refuses to respond).

Book Thirteen

the wound you had, and your usual fear,
then crouch behind my shield, and under it
battle it out with me! Once I'd saved him,
the wounded man who did not have the strength
to stand erect just scurried off—no wound
prevented him from running at top speed.
Hector then moved up, bringing gods with him
towards the battle. Wherever he charged,
even brave men were afraid, not just you,
Ulysses. That's how much he terrorized
our ranks. But I picked up a massive rock,
hurled it from far away, and laid him out,
while he was gloating over his success
in bloody slaughter. When he challenged us
to have one man confront him, I was the one
who fought against him, and you men, you Greeks,
prayed my lot would be the one selected.
Your prayers were answered. And if you ask
how that fight turned out, he did not prevail
against me.[1]

    Then, look, Trojans are advancing,
with fire and sword and Jupiter, as well,
against Danaan ships. Where is he now,
the eloquent Ulysses? The truth is this—
I was the one who with this heart of mine
saved a thousand ships, our hope of getting home.
In return for that whole fleet, grant me these arms.
But if you'll now allow me to speak candidly,
those weapons of Achilles are seeking out
a greater honour than I am—they wish
to be united to my glory. Those arms
are seeking Ajax, not Ajax the arms.
Let that Ithacan Ulysses compare
what I have done with slaughtering Rhesus
and that coward Dolon, or capturing
a son of Priam, Helenus, or stealing

---

[1] Hector issued a challenge to the Greeks produce a warrior who would fight him in single combat. A few men volunteered (including Ajax) and the candidate was chosen by a lottery in which each man put a marker in a helmet. The helmet was shaken, and the first lot which fell out determined who would fight Hector. Ajax's token was the first shaken out. The single combat was ended by the heralds of both armies without a clear winner.

Book Thirteen

the image of Minerva.[1] None of these
was done in daylight, and in none of them
was Diomedes absent. If you award
these weapons for such trifling services,
divide them up and give the greater share
to Diomedes. But why offer them
to that man from Ithaca, who always acts
in secret and unarmed and with his tricks
deceives an unsuspecting enemy?
The way that helmet made of gleaming gold
shines out so brilliantly will only show
where he is hiding and reveal his plans.
What's more, that Dulichian head of his,
once he puts on the helmet of Achilles,
will not hold up so great a weight.[2] His arms,
which are not made for war, will find that spear
from Pelion too cumbersome and heavy.
As for the shield embossed with those designs
of the vast universe, how will that suit
the left arm of a coward, born to steal?
Why then, you craven fool, seek out a gift
which will just drain your strength? And if the Greeks
give you Achilles' weapons by mistake,
that will not make your enemies afraid.
They will have a fine excuse to strip you.
Besides, running in flight, the only race
where you surpass all others, you timid wretch,
will be much slower, if you drag with you
so great a load. Then, too, that shield of yours,
which has been used so rarely in a fight,
is still unharmed. Mine has a thousand cracks
from stopping spears, and I need a new one.
But what's the point of talking? Let's end this
by having people look at us in action!
Why not set those arms of brave Achilles

---

[1] Rhesus, a Trojan ally, was slaughtered by Diomedes and Ulysses at night while he had his men were asleep. The two Greek also killed Dolon, a spy they captured and questioned. Helenus, a Trojan prince, was captured by the same two men. Ulysses also stole the statue of Minerva, the Palladium (named after Pallas), inside Troy, on which the security of the city depended (as he mentions in his response to Ajax).

[2] Dulichium was part of Ulysses' kingdom.

right in the centre of the Trojan ranks,
then order them to be retrieved from there.
You can adorn the man who brings them back
with what he has recovered."

      Ajax finished.
After his last words, the common soldiers
murmured among themselves, until Ulysses,
Laërtes' warrior son, rose to his feet.
He paused a moment, gazing at the ground.   ULYSSES MAKES HIS CASE
Then he raised his eyes, looked at the leaders,
and opened up his mouth to start the speech
they were expecting. His style was graceful
and not ineloquent:

      "If my wishes,
along with yours, you Greeks, had any force,
we would not be having this great debate
about the doubtful question of an heir,
for then Achilles would have his weapons,
and we would still have him. But unjust Fate
has taken him from you and me."

      And here
Ulysses dabbed his eyes, as if he wished
to wipe away a tear.

      "What leader
is more suited to succeed the great Achilles
than the one we have to thank for making sure
that mighty warrior joined up with us.
Now, you must not denigrate my rival,
because he seems so blunt, for he is dull.
And do not let it hurt my argument
that my shrewd mind has always helped you Greeks.
As for my eloquence, if that is there,
let no man feel upset, for now it pleads
its master's case—it has often spoken out
on your behalf—and no man should refuse
to use the talents he himself possesses.

Now, as to race and ancestry, those things
we did not do ourselves, it's hard to call
such matters ours. But since Ajax has claimed
he is a great-grandson of Jupiter,

I say my family blood begins with Jove,
and I am just as many steps removed.
Laërtes is my father, his father
was Arcesius, a son of Jupiter,
neither of them guilty of a crime
or condemned to exile.[1] Through my mother,
I can also link myself to Mercury,   240
another noble line.[2] For I have gods
in both my parents' ancestries. But still,
I am not here asking for these weapons
set out before us, because my mother
gives me, on her side, a more splendid birth,
or because my father is quite guiltless
of his brother's blood. You must judge this case   [150]
by our own merits—provided Ajax
gets no credit just because his father,
Telamon, and Peleus were brothers.   250
In dealing with such arms, you should consider,
not bloodlines, but respect for virtuous deeds.
For if what matters is the nearest kin
and closest heir, Peleus is his father,
Pyrrhus is his son. What claim has Ajax?
Let Achilles' arms be taken away
to Phthia or to Scyros.[3] And Teucer
is just as much a cousin of Achilles
as Ajax is.[4] But does he seek these arms?
And if he did, would you offer them to him?   260
So, since this contest is one of actions,
and nothing else, I say that I have done
more than I can easily describe in words,   [160]
but still, I will set them out in order.

Achilles' Nereïd mother Thetis
was aware her son was going to die.

---

[1]This is a reference to the killing of Phocus, a brother of Peleus and Telamon, for which both Peleus and Telamon were considered guilty and exiled.

[2]Ulysses' mother, Anticleia, was the daughter of Autolycus, whose father was Mercury. For the conception of Autolycus, see above 11.478 ff.

[3]Achilles' father, Peleus, lived in Phthia, in Thessaly. Achilles' son, Pyrrhus, was living in Scyros, one of the Cyclades islands, where Achilles had been sent to hide, so that he would not have to go to Troy.

[4]Teucer was Ajax's half-brother. They had a common father, Telamon, but different mothers.

Book Thirteen

So she concealed her child and dressed him up
in women's clothes. The use of this disguise
deceived each one of us, including Ajax.[1]
So among a few things women like to buy
I placed some weapons which would stir the heart
in any man, and when warlike Achilles,
who had not yet thrown off his female clothes,
reached for the spear and shield, I shouted out:

> 'Son of a goddess, that doomed citadel,
> the Pergamum, is waiting there for you!
> Why hesitate to throw down mighty Troy?'

I took him in hand. I sent that brave man
out to do brave deeds. And so his exploits
are my own. It was my spear that wounded
warlike Telephus and, once I'd conquered him,
as he was praying for help, I healed him.[2]
The fall of Thebes was my accomplishment,
and give me credit for seizing Lesbos,
and for Tenedos, Chrysa, and Cylla,
Apollo's cities, and for Scyros, too.[3]
Think of me as the warrior whose hand
knocked down Lyrnessus and its city walls
and razed them to the ground. I will not list
all Achilles' conquests, but there's no doubt
I am the one who brought to you the man
who could kill savage Hector. Thanks to me,
splendid Hector now lies dead! My weapons
found Achilles, and in return for those
I seek his weapons now.[4] I gave him arms

---

[1]Achilles mother, Thetis, did not want Achilles to join the army going to Troy, so she hid him on Scyros and dressed him up as a girl. The people being deceived are the Greek leaders travelling around to muster warriors for the expedition.

[2]Telephus, a son of Hercules, was wounded by Achilles' spear and then cured by the tip. For an earlier reference to this story see 12.173.

[3]Tenedos was an island close to Troy. Chrysa, Cylla, and Scyros were also cities in the vicinity of Troy (the island Scyros, where Achilles was hidden, was a different place). The Thebes mentioned was a city in Asia Minor, not the Thebes in Boeotia.

[4]Ulysses' first reference to weapons here is to those he used to identify Achilles in Scyros. The second is to Achilles' divine weapons made by Vulcan (the object of their debate).

when he was still alive. Now he is dead, [180]
I want them back.

    When Menelaus' grief
had spread to all the Greeks, a thousand ships
near Euboea filled the bay at Aulis.¹
But the winds blew from the wrong direction, 300
or else there was no wind, and so the fleet
for a long time simply waited. But then,
according to a brutal oracle,
king Agamemnon had to sacrifice
his innocent child to cruel Diana.
But he refused to carry out this act
and even grew angry at the gods themselves.
Although a king, he was a father, too.
I used my skill with words to change his mind,
to shift the affections of a parent 310
towards the public good. The case I made
was difficult, and the judge was biased. [190]
That I concede (and, as I confess to this,
may the son of Atreus forgive me).²
But the popular good, his brother's cause,
and his regal responsibilities
at last convinced the king that claims of blood
weighed less than public glory. So I was sent
to Clytaemnestra, the young girl's mother,
not to persuade her by some argument, 320
but to use a trick and get her to agree
[that Iphigeneia should come to Aulis.]³
If Ajax had gone there instead of me,
our sails would still remain without a wind.

Then I was sent as an ambassador
to the Trojan citadel, where I saw
and boldly entered the assembly room
of lofty Troy, still full of warrior men.

---

¹Aulis was a port in Boeotia, Euboea an island facing the port across the bay.

²The son of Atreus is Agamemnon, leader of the Greek army.

³Agamemnon needed Clytaemnestra to agree to let their daughter, Iphigeneia, come to Aulis. Ulysses told the queen that Iphigeneia was to go in order to be married to Achilles. I have added line 322 in the English to clarify what Clytaemnestra was agreeing to (there is no suggestion that she agreed to the sacrifice).

Book Thirteen

I did not flinch but argued for our cause,
as Greece had asked me. I accused Paris,
demanded the Trojans give back Helen,
as well as all the property he seized,
and I won the sympathy of Priam
and Antenor, too, Priam's counsellor.
But Paris and his brothers and those men
under his command who took the plunder
could hardly keep their wicked hands off me.
Menelaus, you know this, for that day
was the first time you and I faced danger
side by side.

            It would be tedious to describe
the useful things I've done with stratagems
and force during the course of this long war.
After those first fights, the hostile Trojans
for a long time stayed inside their city walls,
giving us no chance for open conflict.
But finally, in the tenth year, we fought.
And in that time, Ajax, what did you do,
when the only thing you know is fighting?
What use were you? By contrast, if you ask
what I did then, I was setting ambushes
to kill our enemies, digging ditches
by our defensive wall, encouraging
my companions, so they could tolerate
the tedium of protracted warfare
with patient hearts, and handing out advice
on how the soldiers could be fed and armed.[1]
And I was sent wherever I was needed.

Then, lo and behold, king Agamemnon,
deceived while he was sleeping with a dream
sent to him by command of Jupiter,
ordered us to abandon our concerns
about the war we had begun [and leave—
to get back in our ships and sail for home.][2]
He justified his orders by appealing
to his dream from Jupiter. But Ajax

---

[1] The Greeks erected some fortifications to defend their ships drawn up on the beach.
[2] I have added a line in the English to clarify Agamemnon's order to his troops.

should have stopped him. He should have demanded
the destruction of the Trojan citadel
and fought back—the one thing he is good at!
Why did he not try to stop the soldiers
who were rushing to go home? And why not
pick up his weapons, set an example
which that fickle crowd of men could follow?
This was not too much to ask from someone
who never speaks except to boast aloud.
But what about the fact that he, too, fled?
Yes, I saw you. The sight made me ashamed,
when you turned tail and started to prepare
the sails of our disgrace. I did not wait
but shouted at you:

> 'What are you doing?
> What mad fit, my friends, is pressuring you
> to run from captured Troy? After ten years,
> what will you carry home except your shame?'

Grief made me eloquent. With words like these
and others I brought those stampeding men
back from the fleet. The son of Atreus
summoned an assembly of his allies,
all still in a panic, and, even then,
Ajax, a son of Telamon, did not dare
to utter a word. And yet Thersites
got up the courage to insult the king
(I beat him for his vulgar insolence).[1]
I stood and urged my frightened countrymen
to fight our enemies, and with my voice
I gave them back the courage they had lost.
So from that point on, whatever brave things
you saw that fellow over there achieve
are thanks to me, because I was the one
who dragged him back when he was running home.

Besides, who among the Greeks praises you,
Ajax, or seeks your company? In my case,
Diomedes shares all he does with me.

---

[1] Thersites, a common soldier, was, according to Homer, the ugliest man in the Greek army. He was well known for his scathing insults.

Book Thirteen

He backs me up and has always trusted [240]
Ulysses as a comrade. That is something!
To be picked out of so many thousand Greeks
by Diomedes! I was not compelled
into a fight by any lottery,
and yet, disregarding all the dangers
of the enemy and the night, I went out
and slaughtered Dolon, a Phrygian scout,
whose mission was the very same as ours,   410
but not before I forced him to reveal
all the things he knew. That's how I found out
the plans of the perfidious Trojans.
Once I'd discovered those, there was no need
to keep on looking. I could have come back
to enjoy the promised glory. But no,
not content with that, I searched out the place
where Rhesus pitched his tents and killed him there, [250]
in his own camp, as well as his companions.
Once I had achieved what I was after,   420
I rode back in a chariot I captured,
like the victor in a joyous triumph.
Dolon demanded Achilles' horses
for one night's work, so if you deny me
Achilles' weapons, then Ajax may well be
more generous than you.[1]

            Why should I list
those men Sarpedon led from Lycia
cut down by my sword?[2] In all that bloodshed,
I killed Coeranus, son of Iphitus,
Alastor and Chromius, Alcandor,   430
Halius, Noëmon, and Prytanis.
I brought death to Thoön, Chersidamas,
Charops, and Ennomos (who was urged on [260]
by dreadful Fate). Some others less well known
fell at my hand below their city walls.
I have wounds, my friends, honourable ones,

---

[1] Dolon had agreed to scout out the Greek position at night in return for the gift of Achilles' horses once the Trojans defeated the Greeks. Lines 416-7 may be referring to Ajax's notion that, if he doesn't get the weapons, they should be divided between Ulysses and Diomedes.

[2] Sarpedon was a major ally of the Trojans. Lycia is in Asia Minor.

Book Thirteen

as their location shows.[1] Do not believe
mere empty words. Look!"

                        And here his hand
pulled aside his clothing.

                            "Here is my chest
which has always worked to serve your interests!   440
But the son of Telamon has lost no blood,
in all those many years, for his companions.
His body has no wounds![2]

                    And so what if he claims
he used his weapons to fight the Trojans
and Jupiter, as well, before our ships?
I admit he did, for I do not wish   [270]
to be mean-spirited and criticize
any beneficial deeds. But Ajax
should not get sole credit for those actions
where others played their part. He should give you   450
some of the honour, too. For Patroclus,
from Actor's line, who was well protected
because he was the image of Achilles,
drove back the Trojans from the Grecian ships
which were about to be consumed by fire,
along with Ajax, their defender.[3] He thinks
he was the only one who dared confront
the warlike Hector armed. But he forgets
the king, the other leaders, and myself.
He was the ninth to say he'd fight the man,   460
and he was picked by chance. But then,
most valiant warrior, how did that fight
turn out? Hector walked away uninjured,
without a single wound!

                         And now, alas,   [280]
it grieves me to bring back a memory
so full of sorrow—the day Achilles,

---

[1] An honourable wound is one received in the front, as one is facing the enemy.

[2] According to some traditions, the lion skin Ajax wore made him invulnerable.

[3] Achilles had quarreled with Agamemnon and withdrawn from the fighting. When Hector fired the first ship, Achilles sent Patroclus into battle dressed in Achilles' very distinctive armour. The Trojans thought Achilles was returning to battle and were terrified.

the bulwark of the Greeks, was killed. And yet,
no tears, or pain, or fear prevented me
from picking up his body off the ground.
And on these shoulders, these shoulders of mine,   470
I carried the body of Achilles
and his armour, too, the very weapons
I'm anxious now to carry once again.[1]
I have strength enough for such a burden,
and I have a mind which, you may be sure,
will understand the honour you have done me.
Was it really for this the sea nymph Thetis,
Achilles mother, was so determined
to help her son she brought down from heaven
works of such great artistry, so that Ajax,   480   [290]
a crude soldier with no intelligence
could wear them? For he does not understand
what is sculpted on the shield—Ocean, Earth,
high star-filled skies, the Pleiades, Hyades,
the Bear that never moves down to the sea,
the different cities, Orion's gleaming sword.
He is asking you to give him weapons
[whose meaning he does not even grasp?][2]

And what about how he accuses me
of running from the duties of harsh war   490
and coming late into an enterprise
which others had begun? Does he not see
he is denouncing great Achilles, too?
If you consider it a crime to hide
who one really is, both of us did that.
And if delaying makes me culpable,   [300]
I did join up before Achilles did.
My dear wife detained me—with Achilles
it was his loving mother. We gave them
those early days. The rest we gave to you.   500
If I have no defence against that point,

---

[1] In Homer's *Iliad*, recovering the corpse of a fallen comrade and his armour was considered an act of the greatest bravery. It conferred a very high status on the warrior who did it.

[2] Patroclus was killed wearing the armour of Achilles, which Hector removed. Thetis replaced that armour with divine armour made by Vulcan, god of the forge. Vulcan decorated Achilles' shield with wonderfully comprehensive symbols of the entire warrior universe. Line 295 has been rejected as spurious by some editors.

Book Thirteen

I do not fear a charge which I would share
with that heroic man, who was revealed
thanks to Ulysses' skill. Ajax played no role
in finding out Ulysses.

                          None of us
should be astonished that his foolish tongue
pours insults over me, for he complains
about you, too, and ought to be ashamed.
Was it so wrong for me to falsely charge
the son of Nauplius, yet fine for you   510
to sentence him to death? Palamedes
could not defend himself against a crime   [310]
that was so great and clearly evident.
You not only heard what he was charged with—
you saw his crimes exposed, proved by that bribe!

And I do not deserve to be accused
if Lemnos, Vulcan's island, is still home
to Philoctetes, the son of Poeas
(since you yourselves agreed to leave him there,
defend what you have done). I won't deny   520
I did convince him to withdraw from war
and hardships of our journey and to try
easing his agonizing pain by resting.
He agreed—and is alive! My advice
not only was given in good faith
(and my good faith alone would have sufficed)—
it also proved effective. Now our seers
all say that Poeas' son must be with us   [320]
for Troy to be destroyed. Do not send me!
It would be better if Ajax made the trip   530
and with his eloquence calmed down that man
driven mad with rage and sickness, or else
came up with a sly trick to bring him back!
If my mind ever stopped its work for you,
the stream in Simoïs would reverse its flow,
and Ida's mountain stand there stripped of leaves,
and Achaeans promise help to Trojans,
before the brain in dim-witted Ajax
came up with something useful to the Greeks.
And though you, unyielding Philoctetes,   540
are angry at your friends, the king, and me,

Book Thirteen

and though you never cease pouring curses [330]
on my head and, in excruciating pain,
long for a chance to have me in your power
and drain my blood—to have your way with me,
as I did then with you—I will still go
and try to bring you back with me. What's more,
with Fortune's help, I'll also get your arrows,
just as I brought back that Trojan prophet,
Helenus, whom I captured, and made known 550
what gods had said about the fate of Troy,
just as I stole that statue from the shrine
of Phrygian Minerva, surrounded
by my enemies.[1] And will Ajax now
compare himself with me? We know the Fates
decreed Troy never would be overcome
unless we had that statue. Where was he, [340]
the valiant Ajax? Where were the proud boasts
of that great man? What made him fearful then?
Why did Ulysses dare move through the sentries, 560
commit himself to darkness of the night,
and sneak past the sharp swords of the Trojans,
to make his way inside, not just the city walls,
but even their high citadel, as well,
to snatch the goddess from her temple shrine,
and, once I had her, bear her back again
through enemy lines? If I'd not done that,
the left arm of Ajax would bear his shield—
all seven layers of bull's hide—in vain.
On that night I ensured our victory 570
against the Trojans. On that very night
I conquered their citadels, for my theft
made such a conquest possible.

      Ajax,
you can stop your muttering and those looks, [350]
those attempts to bring up Diomedes.
That deed has earned him his full share of praise!
When you held up your shield before the ships,

---

[1]Helenus, a son of Priam, king of Troy, was a prophet. When Ulysses captured him, he told the Greeks they would not be able to capture Troy unless they brought Achilles' son Pyrrhus (also called Neoptolemus), the bones of Peleus, and Philoctetes (with his weapons) to Troy and, in addition, stole the statue of Minerva (the Palladium) kept in the citadel of Troy.

you were not alone. You had comrades there,
a crowd of them. But I had only one.
If he did not know that a man who fights
is of less value than a man who thinks
and that this prize should not be handed out
merely to a fearless, strong right hand,
he, too, might claim Achilles' weapons.
And lesser Ajax, a more modest man,
would also claim them, and fierce Eurypylus,
and Thoas, illustrious Andraemon's son.
Meriones would surely make a claim,
as would his fellow countryman from Crete
Idomeneus, and so would Menelaus,
Agamemnon's brother. All these leaders
have powerful hands and are my equals
on the battlefield, and yet they follow
my advice. Your right hand gives useful help
in combat, Ajax, but it needs guidance
from my ingenuity. You have strength,
but no intelligence, while I consider
what the future holds. You can fight in war,
but the son of Atreus and I select
the proper time for battle. While you serve
only with your body, I use my mind.
The man who steers a ship is valued more
than the man who rows, and the army chief
is far above the soldier in the ranks.
In just that way—and to the same extent—
I am worth more than you. In my body
the mind has greater power than the hands,
for all my energies are focused there.

So now, you warrior chiefs, award those arms
to the man who has stayed on watch for you,
for all those years I spent with anxious cares.
Grant me this honour as compensation
for all my service. Now my work is done.
I have removed the barriers of Fate,
for I have made it possible to take
high Pergamum, and thus have captured it.
So by our common hopes, by Troy's doomed walls,
by the gods I snatched away so recently
from Troy, and by whatever still remains

which needs a clever mind to carry out, 620
I pray that if there is anything bold
and dangerous still left to undertake,
[if you think, in dealing with Troy's fate,
we still have things to do], remember me!
And if you do not grant these arms to me, [380]
give them to her!"[1]

    With these words, he pointed
to the fatal statue of Minerva.

Ulysses' words swayed the group of leaders— AJAX KILLS HIMSELF
the outcome showed what eloquence can do.
The fluent speaker took the brave man's arms, 630
and Ajax, who fought Hector man to man,
who stood so often against sword and fire
and even Jupiter, for the first time
met an enemy he could not repulse—
his rage. Pulling out his sword, he shouted:

    "At least this sword is mine! Or does Ulysses
want this for himself, as well? I must use it
on myself, and this sword, so often steeped
in Trojan blood will now drip with its master's.
And thus no man could ever conquer Ajax 640 [390]
except Ajax himself."

                  He spoke these words,
then drove his sword into his exposed flesh,
deep inside his chest, which until that time
had never felt a wound.[2] His hand lacked strength
to pull the sword back out, but by itself
his blood expelled the steel. On the green turf
the bloodstained ground produced the purple flower
which earlier had grown out of the wound
of Hyacinthus, the bloom whose petals
in the middle bear those letters common 650

---

[1] Some editors and translators have rejected the words in square brackets.
[2] According to some traditions, the lion's skin Ajax wore (which came from Hercules) made him invulnerable, except in one place, the hole where Hercules's arrow had gone in when he killed the lion. Hence, Ajax's flesh was "exposed" there.

Book Thirteen

to the Spartan lad and to the hero—
a young man's cry of grief, a warrior's name.[1]

Victorious Ulysses then set sail for Lemnos,   THE WAR ENDS
land of Hypsiplye and famous Thoas.
Long ago the place had been notorious,   [400]
for all women there had killed their husbands.[2]
He was going to collect those arrows,
weapons which had once belonged to Hercules.
And when he brought them and Philoctetes,
their owner, back to the Greeks, then, at last,   660
the final acts of that long war took place.
[Troy and Priam fell, and the wife of Priam,
poor Hecuba, when everything was gone,
lost her human form, and in a foreign place,
where the long Hellespont forms a narrow strait,
she fills the air with barking.][3]

                       Troy was on fire,   TROY IS DESTROYED
and the flames had not yet been extinguished.
Jupiter's altar was still soaking up
the meagre streams of ancient Priam's blood.
Apollo's priestess, hauled out by the hair,   670   [410]
was holding up her arms in a vain plea
to heaven, and the victorious Greeks
were dragging away the women of Troy,
an enviable prize, as the women,
while they still could, kept gathering in crowds
inside the burning temples, still clutching
their paternal gods. Infant Astyanax   ASTYANAX
was hurled down to his death from those same towers
where he often watched his father Hector.[4]

---

[1] The letters on the flower, the hyacinth, were *ai ai*, put there by Apollo to indicate his grief over the death of Hyacinthus (for Ovid's treatment of the story, see 10.294 ff. above). The letters are also a close approximation to Ajax's name in Greek (*Aias*).

[2] The women of Lesbos had offended Venus, who then, as punishment, gave them all a nasty smell. When their husbands turned to other women, the wives murdered them. Hypsipyle had saved her father, Thoas, from this slaughter.

[3] Some editors and translators consider these lines spurious. Hecuba's story is told later in this book.

[4] The priestess was Cassandra, a daughter of Priam. Priam was killed by Achilles' son, Pyrrhus (also called Neoptolemus), at the altar in the temple of Zeus, where he had taken sanctuary.

[Footnote continues]

Book Thirteen

Andromache, his mother, would point him out   680
as he was fighting on his child's behalf,
protecting his ancestral realm.

                               And now,
North Wind was urging Greeks to leave for home,
the sails were flapping in a friendly breeze,
and sailors said they had to take advantage
of the winds. The women of Troy all cried:

   "Farewell, Troy. We are being taken away."   [420]

They kissed the Trojan ground and left behind
their smoking homes. The last one to embark—   HECUBA
a wretched sight!—was Hecuba. They found her   690
surrounded by the tombs which held her sons,
clinging to their graves and trying to kiss
her children's bones. Ulysses dragged her off.
But she opened up one grave and carried
Hector's ashes with her, clutched to her breast,
leaving a lock of hair on Hector's stone,
a humble offering, her gray hair and tears.

Now, facing Phrygia and Trojan land,   POLYDORUS AND POLYMESTOR
there was a country where Bistonians lived
and Polymestor had a lavish palace.[1]   700
Your father, Polydorus, sent you to him
to be brought up in secret, a long way
from the war going on in Troy. A wise plan,
if your father, Priam, had not sent you
with such wealth—a tempting prize, rich enough
to turn an avaricious man to crime.
So when the fortunes of the Trojans fell,
the wicked Thracian king picked up a sword
and drove it into Polydorus' throat—
into his foster child!—and after that,   710
as if he could get rid of his own crime
by throwing out the corpse, he climbed a rock
and hurled the lifeless body in the sea.

According to tradition, Ulysses took Hector's baby child Astyanax from his mother and threw him over the walls of Troy.

[1] Bistonians were a people in Thrace, north of the Hellespont.

Book Thirteen

Agamemnon, son of Atreus, moored his fleet
on a beach in Thrace, waiting for calm seas
and more favourable winds. Suddenly
the ground split open, making a wide cleft,
and Achilles' ghost emerged, as massive
as he used to be in life. His face looked
threatening, like the expression he wore
the day he pulled his sword on Agamemnon
in that fierce and lawless confrontation.[1]
He called out:

       "So, you Greeks, you're leaving.
You have forgotten me. Your gratitude
for my courageous acts you buried with me!
Do not let that happen! My funeral mound
must not lack its honours. So to appease
Achilles' shade, you Greeks must sacrifice
Polyxena, Priam's child."[2]

                    His comrades
obeyed the orders of that ruthless ghost.
Though she was almost the only comfort
Hecuba still had, they tore Polyxena
from her mother's arms and led the young girl
to Achilles' burial site. She was strong,
in spite of her misfortune, and kept up
her courage, more than most women do.
But she became a victim, sacrificed
to a pitiless grave. As she stood there,
before the savage altar and witnessed
the harsh rites they were preparing for her,
she remembered she was Priam's daughter.
When she saw Achilles' son standing by,
gripping a sword, and staring at her face,
she said:

ACHILLES AND POLYXENA
[440]

720

730
[450]

740

---

[1]This is a reference to the famous quarrel between Achilles and Agamemnon over captured spoils (the opening scene of the *Iliad*), which led to Achilles' withdrawal from the fighting.

[2]Polyxena was the youngest daughter of Priam and Hecuba. In some accounts, she had been captured and befriended by Achilles, who told her about the one vulnerable spot on his body (his heel). Achilles was killed by a poisoned arrow from Paris. It hit him in the heel in an ambush, when he was on his way to meet Polyxena.

Book Thirteen

>"Now shed this noble blood. You have
no need to wait. So plunge that sword of yours
deep in my throat or chest."

Here she exposed
her neck and breast.

>"You may be sure of this—
Polyxena has no wish to be a slave [460]
to any man, and this kind of ritual
will not appease the gods. I only wish 750
my mother would not hear about my death.
She worries me, diminishing my joy
in dying. And yet she should be mourning,
not my death, but her own life. Move off,
you men, so I may go to Stygian shades
in freedom, and if my prayer is just,
let no man set his hand on virgin flesh.
Whoever you are trying to appease
by killing me will be more satisfied
with blood from someone free. If my last words 760
move any of you—and I am no slave [470]
requesting this, but king Priam's daughter—
return my body with no ransom paid
back to my mother. For the mournful right
to have a tomb, let her pay, not with gold,
but with her tears. Back in earlier days,
when she still could, she used to pay in gold."

Polyxena finished. She shed no tears.
The people did that for her. Even the priest
wept as he reluctantly plunged in the knife 770
and pierced the breast she offered up to him.
As her knees buckled, she fell to the ground,
but to the very end her face remained
quite fearless, and even as she collapsed,
she took great care to hide those parts of her
that should remain concealed and so maintained [480]
the honour of her blameless modesty.

The Trojan women took up the body,
counting all the names of Priam's children
they had mourned and all the bloody killings 780
this one house had suffered. They grieved for you,

435

Book Thirteen

young virgin girl, and you, too, Hecuba.
Not long ago they called you a king's wife
and royal parent, the very image
of rich Asia, and now a worthless part
of captured spoils. Victorious Ulysses
would have refused to take you as his slave,
had you not given birth to noble Hector,
who had great trouble finding anyone
who wished to be his mother's master. 790

Hecuba embraced her daughter's body,   HECUBA LAMENTS
whose spirit, which had been so brave, was gone.
She shed tears over it, the very tears
she had so often wept for her own land,
her children, and her husband, pouring them   [490]
into the young girl's wound. She kissed her lips,
beat her chest, as she had done so frequently,
and trailed her gray hair in congealing blood.
She tore her breasts and cried out many things,
including this:

                "O my child, you are   800
your mother's final grief. What else is left?
My daughter lying here! I see your wound
as my own injury. Look here! This wound
was to make sure I did not lose one child
without some blood being spilled. Still, I thought
you, as a woman, would be spared the steel.
But now, even though you were a woman,
you have fallen to the sword. That same man
who slaughtered so many of your brothers
has killed you, too—Achilles, who ruined Troy   810   [500]
and left me childless. After that man fell
to those arrows of Paris and Apollo,
I said:

         'Now, at least, we no longer need
to fear Achilles.'

                But even in death,
I should have feared him. His very ashes
in his tomb rage against our royal house.
Even from the grave we have felt his hate.
It was for Achilles that I gave birth

to all my children. And now mighty Troy
has fallen. The destruction of our state   820
has reached its bitter end. Still, it's over.
For me alone Troy's citadel yet stands.
My grief will run its course. Not long ago,
I was the greatest lady of them all,
thanks to my husband, my many children,
all those sons-in-law and daughters-in-law.
Now I am helpless, dragged into exile,
torn from my family's burial mounds,
a gift for Ulysses' wife, Penelope,   [510]
who will point me out to married women   830
in Ithaca, as I am spinning wool
she hands to me, and say:

                'This woman here
  is Hector's famous mother, Priam's queen.'

After I had lost so many children,
you, Polyxena, were the only one
who would alleviate a mother's grief.
And now you have been made a sacrifice
at an enemy grave! I bore children
as sacrificial offerings for my foes!
And yet, like iron, I endure. But why?   840
Why am I still here? Why am I preserved
by lingering old age. You cruel gods,
why prolong the life of an old woman
who has lived so long, unless your purpose
is to have me witness still more funerals?
Who could have imagined Priam happy   [520]
once Pergamum fell? But he is happy
in his death! He did not see you butchered,
my child, for he left his life and kingdom
both at the same time. I assumed that you,   850
a royal child, would have rich burial rites,
your body placed in our ancestral tombs.
But that is not the fortune of this house.
Your funeral gifts will be a mother's tears
and a pile of foreign sand! We have lost
everything. The only child remaining
is Polydorus, once the youngest son
of our family line, and now a reason

for me to go on living for a while.
We sent him to these shores, entrusting him
to Polymestor's care, a Thracian king.
But why waste all my time with these laments?
I should rinse your savage wound with water
and wash away those dreadful spots of blood
splashed across your face."

Hecuba said this,
and shuffled off, with an old woman's gait,
down to the sea shore, pulling her white hair.
She cried:

"You Trojan women, fetch a jug!"

The poor woman wanted to draw water
from the sea. But there by the shore she saw
Polydorus' body thrown up on the beach
with gaping cuts from blades of Thracian swords.
The Trojan women screamed, but Hecuba
was dumb with grief. Pain had swallowed her voice
and dried the teardrops welling in her eyes.
She stood still, like impenetrable rock.
At times she fixed her eyes down at the ground,
or raised her haggard face up to the sky.
Then she would look at her son lying there,
at his face and wounds, but mainly at his wounds.
She felt her anger growing deep inside
and made that rage her weapon. She caught fire,
and, as if she were still queen, set her mind
on vengeance, concentrating all her thoughts
on how she could punish Polymestor.
Just as a lioness rages at the theft
of her unweaned cub and looks for footprints
of an adversary she cannot see,
so Hecuba, mixing her grief with rage,
recalled her courage, cast her age aside,
went to Polymestor, who had arranged
the dreadful murder, and asked to see him.
She said she wished to show him stores of gold
she had buried away, so he could give it
to her son. The Thracian king believed her,
and, driven by his usual love of gain,

HECUBA AND POLYMESTOR

came to her in private. He spoke to her
with slyly reassuring words:

                "Come now,
Hecuba, do not wait. Give me that gift
kept hidden for your son. He'll get all of it—   900
what you are giving now and gave before.
I swear by the gods."

                She watched him grimly,
as he uttered this deceitful promise,
and then her simmering rage boiled over.
Calling on her group of captive women   [560]
to seize hold of Polymestor, she sank
her fingers into his treasonous eyes
and gouged his eyeballs out. Rage made her strong.
She plunged her hands, stained with the murderer's blood,
inside the holes and sucked out, not his eyes   910
(for they were gone) but what was in the sockets.

The Thracian folk, angry at the murder
of their king, started to attack the queen,
hurling stones and weapons. But Hecuba
chased after rocks they threw and snapped at them,
growling harshly. And when she set her jaws
and tried to speak, she barked. The place stills stands.
It's called Cynossema, the Bitch's Tomb,
a name derived from things that happened there.
For a long time Hecuba remembered   920   [570]
the ancient evils she had undergone
and still continued howling mournfully
through all the fields of Thrace. Her suffering
moved the Trojans and the enemy Greeks
and all the gods, as well—yes, all of them—
so even Juno, Jove's wife and sister,
affirmed that Hecuba had not deserved
to end her life that way.

                But Aurora,   AURORA AND MEMNON
though a supporter of the Trojan cause,
had no time to grieve at these disasters,   930
the fall of Troy and end of Hecuba.
She was troubled with a private sorrow,
a grief closer to home, her missing son,

Memnon. His rose-coloured goddess mother
had seen him slaughtered by Achilles' spear [580]
on the Phrygian plains, and seeing that,
her rosy tint which dyes the morning light
grew pale, and the sky was hidden in cloud.
When his body was placed above the fire,
his mother could not bear to witness it. 940
Casting her pride aside, she went to Jove
just as she was, with her hair dishevelled,
fell down at his knees in tears, and said:

"I count for less than all divinities
the golden aether holds (in the whole world
my temples are the rarest of them all).
But I come here a goddess, not asking
you to give me shrines or sacrificial days
or altars hot with fires. Still, if you see [590]
how much this female goddess does for you, 950
when with the light of each new dawn I check
the limits of the night, you might well think
I should get some reward. But Aurora
is not concerned about these matters now
and does not intend to seek those honours
she deserves. My reason for being here
is my son Memnon, who is gone from me.
He fought bravely for his uncle Priam,
though in a losing cause, and, while still young,
fell to great Achilles (so you willed it).[1] 960
O supreme ruler of the gods, I beg you—
give him some honour, a consolation
for his death, and relieve his mother's pain."

Jupiter nodded his consent. And then,
as Memnon's high funeral pyre collapsed [600]
in towering flames, columns of dark smoke THE MEMNONIDES
stained the sky, just as a naiad breathes out
thick river mists which do not let the Sun
shine underneath them. The black ash flew up,
merged to a single body, grew more dense, 970
took on a shape, and drew up life and heat

---

[1] Memnon's father was Tithonus, a brother of Priam. Tithonus had been granted immortality by Aurora, but not freedom from growing old. Memnon was a king in Ethiopia.

from flames below. Its lightness gave it wings.
At first the form looked something like a bird,
then like a real bird with whirring wings.
Countless sister shapes, born from the same source,
grew beating wings, as well. Three times this flock
flew past the pyre, and three times they called out [610]
in unison. On the fourth flight, the birds
split up into two different clusters, 980
swooped fiercely in from opposite directions,
and launched a war, with raging claws and beaks,
until the fight wore out their wings and hearts,
and then, recalling they had been produced
from such a valiant man, their bodies fell
as sacrifices to the buried ashes
of their kinsman. The one from whom these birds
were born so suddenly gave them their name,
for people call them the Memnonides
or Memnon's offspring. When the Sun has passed
through his twelve signs, they fight and die again 990
in a ritual tribute to their father.[1]
Thus, while it seemed to others very sad [620]
that Hecuba was barking like dog,
Aurora was concerned with her own grief,
and even now she sheds her loving tears
and scatters them as dew through all the world.

But Fates do not allow Troy's future hopes THE VOYAGES OF AENEAS
to perish with its walls. For Aeneas,
heroic son of Venus, carries off
Troy's sacred images on his shoulders 1000
and his father, too, Anchises, an old
and sacred burden.[2] From all their riches,
his family piety selects that prize,
along with his young son, Ascanius.
From Antandros the fleet of exiles sails
across the sea, leaving far behind them
the polluted homes of Thrace, that region

---

[1] Memnon was worshipped as a god in Egypt, where there was a very famous statue of him.

[2] Aeneas, who was related to the royal family of Troy, was the leader of the Dardanians, allies of the Trojans and closely linked to them (Dardanus was the mythical founder of the Trojan royal family). Aeneas played an important role in the Trojan War.

still soaking in the blood of Polydorus.¹
With following winds and steady currents [630]
he and his group of allies come to Delos, 1010
Apollo's city, where Anius rules,
governing his people, and, as a priest,
managing the rituals of Apollo.
He receives Aeneas in the temple
and in his home and shows him the city,
the celebrated shrine, and the two trees
Latona had once gripped while giving birth.²
The men put incense on the flames, pour wine
onto the incense, slaughter oxen,
and burn the entrails, following their rites. 1020
Then they move off to the royal palace,
where lofty couches have been set for them.
They eat the gifts of Ceres and drink wine.
At that point virtuous Anchises says: [640]

"Chosen priest of Phoebus, I may be wrong,
but the first time I saw your city walls
did you not have four daughters and a son,
if my memory is correct?"

        Anius
shook his head, bound with fillets of white cloth
around his temples, and answered sadly: 1030

"Greatest of heroes, you are not mistaken.   THE DAUGHTERS OF ANIUS
You saw me the father of five children,
and now—given the way fickle fortune
changes things for men—you are seeing me
when I am almost childless. For what help
is my absent son to me? He now lives
and, in his father's name, governs Andros,
an island which derives its name from him.
The Delian god, Apollo, gave him [650]
prophetic powers, and to my daughters 1040
Bacchus gave other gifts, things well beyond
what anyone might hope for or believe.
For everything my daughters touched was changed

---

¹Antandros was a coastal city near Troy.

²For the birth of Apollo and Diana on Delos, see above 6.315.

to grain, or streams of wine, or grey-green olives.
So these girls' touch could serve to make one rich.
When Agamemnon, ravager of Troy,
discovered this, he dragged the girls by force
out of their father's arms and ordered them
to use their heaven-sent gift to furnish
the Argive fleet (for you should not assume   1050
we did not feel, at least to some degree,
the destructive storm you faced). Well, those girls
ran off, each one escaping where she could.   [660]
Two reached Euboea, two went to Andros,
where their brother ruled. Greek soldiers followed
and threatened war unless he gave them up.
Fear overcame his natural affection,
and he handed over his own sisters.
You can forgive their brother's craven act.
He had no Hector or Aeneas there   1060
to fight for Andros, those two warriors
whose courage kept you fighting for ten years.
But as the Greeks were going to chain them,
those daughters raised their arms (which were still free)
towards the heavens and cried:

              'Father Bacchus,
   bring us your aid!'

           The god who gave their gift   [670]
did offer help, if one can call it help
to do away with them in some amazing way.
For I could not tell how they lost their shape,
nor can I tell you now. But I do know   1070
the end of this bad luck—those girls grew wings
and were transformed, changed into snow-white birds,
those doves whom Venus loves, your goddess wife."

After they had feasted and passed the time
with tales like this and other conversation,
they left the table and retired to bed.
They rose at dawn and went off to consult
the oracle of Phoebus and were told
to seek their ancient mother, Italy,

and their ancestral shores.¹ King Anius 1080
escorted them as they prepared to leave
and offered gifts—a sceptre for Anchises, [680]
a cloak and quiver for Ascanius,
and a wine bowl for Aeneas, a gift   ANIUS' WINE BOWL
Anius had been given earlier
by Therses, a Boeotian guest of his,
who lived in Thebes. Therses had sent the bowl,
but Alcon, a man who came from Hyle,
was the artist who produced it. On the surface
he had engraved images depicting 1090
a lengthy story. There was a city.
It was not named, but it had seven gates,
each clearly visible. That detail showed
the place was Thebes. Outside the city walls
were scenes depicting mourning—burial rites,
tombs, fiery funeral pyres, and women
with flowing hair and naked breasts. One could see
nymphs, as well, in tears, weeping for their springs
which had dried up. A bare tree without leaves [690]
stood out, and goats were chewing on dry stones. 1100
And look! In the middle of that city
he has depicted Orion's daughters,
one slitting her bare throat (the sort of wound
a woman does not give herself), and one
plunging a sword in her courageous heart,
each girl dying to protect her people,
and their two bodies being taken off
in a splendid funeral procession
through the city and burned amid a crowd
of mourners.² Then, from the virgin cinders, 1110
to make sure their family does not die,
two young men arise, now celebrated
as the Coroni, and lead the funeral march
that carries back their mothers' ashes.
These were the brilliant pictures he engraved [700]
in the ancient bronze. On the wine bowl's rim

---

¹According to old legends, Dardanus, the founder of the Trojan royal family, originally came from Italy.

²Orion's daughters sacrificed themselves to save their city from a plague. Orion was a king of Thebes.

Book Thirteen

was a raised edge of gold acanthus leaves.
The Trojans offered gifts no less expensive—
for the priest a box to store his incense,
a libation bowl, and a shining crown   1120
fashioned with gold and gemstones.

                      From Delos,   AENEAS' VOYAGE CONTINUES
remembering that, as Trojans, their blood
traced back its origin to Teucer's line,
they made their way to Crete, but did not stay.
They could not bear the climate of the place.[1]
They left the island of a hundred cities,
hoping to reach some Ausonian port
in Italy.[2] But a fierce storm arose
with threatening seas, and so for refuge
they entered the treacherous harbour   1130
of the Strophades, and were terrorized
by winged Aëllo, a harpy.[3] From there   [710]
they sailed past Dulichium's harbour,
past Same, the houses of Neritos,
and the kingdom of devious Ulysses.[4]
They saw Ambracia, a land the gods
once fought about, and the image in stone
of the man who judged their quarrel. The place
is famous now for Apollo's shrine
commemorating Actium.[5] They passed   1140
the land of Dodona which has those oaks
which utter oracles, and the coastal shores

---

[1]Teucer was the name of an early king of Troy. He had originally moved there from Crete (he is not to be confused with Teucer, the half-brother of Ajax, who is mentioned at line 13.257 above). The Trojans are sometimes called the Teucrians (see 13.1189 below). The "climate" of Crete drove them away because of drought and plague.

[2]Ausonia is a name for a region of southern Italy.

[3]A harpy was a flying animal with the face of young girl. The harpies had been chased to the Strophades by two of the Argonauts, Calaïs and Zethes (see above 7.6). The Strophades were islands in the Ionian Sea.

[4]Dulichium, Same, and Neritos were all part of Ulysses' territories.

[5]Three gods (Apollo, Diana, and Hercules) fought over who would be the divine patron of Ambracia. They asked Cragaleus, a man famous for his wisdom, to judge the case. He was persuaded to give the prize to Hercules. Apollo, in anger, turned him to stone. The shrine of Apollo was built by Augustus to commemorate his victory at the Battle of Actium in 31 BC, where he decisively defeated Antony and Cleopatra and consolidated his position of political power in Rome.

of Chaonian land, where the royal sons
of the Molossian king changed into birds
and thus escaped a fire set by thieves.[1]

After that, they headed to Phaeacia,
a region with rich orchards, and from there
sailed to Epirus and to Buthrotos, [720]
a city built like Troy, where Helenus,
the Trojan prophet, ruled.[2] From him they learned 1150
what the future had in store, for Helenus,
a son of Priam, told them everything
he could predict through faithful prophecies.
The Trojans then moved on to Sicily. AENEAS REACHES SICILY
This island has three headlands pushing out
into the sea. Of these three, Pachynus
faces the rainy south, Lilybaeum
confronts the soft west winds, and Peloros
looks to the northern Bear who never dips
into the sea.[3] The Teucrians sailed here, 1160
and, with a helpful current, rowed the fleet
until, as night was coming on, they reached
the sandy shores of Zancle. To their right
loomed Scylla, and on their left, Charybdis,
a restless brute who gobbles down men's ships [730]
and spits them out again. Scylla wears a belt
of savage dogs around her dark-skinned gut.
She has a young girl's face and (if those tales
the poets left are not all just made up)
once long ago she was a virgin girl 1170
whom many suitors courted. But Scylla
rejected all of them. She used to visit
the ocean nymphs—she was their favourite—
and tell them of young men whose love she spurned.

Once when a sea nymph, Galatea, let ACIS AND GALATEA
Scylla comb her hair, Galatea said:

---

[1]Dodona in Epirus was the site of an important shrine to Jupiter. The oak trees there, so people claimed, played an important role in the oracular responses. The children of the Molossian king were changed into birds by Jupiter when thieves set their house on fire.

[2]The Phaeacians lived in Corcyra (Corfu).

[3]For Ovid's account of why the constellation of the Bear does not sink below the level of the sea, see above 2.747 ff. (Juno's request to Oceanus and Tethys).

Book Thirteen

"At least the kind of men who seek you out, [740]
Scylla, are not brutal. You can reject them,
as you do, without fear of getting hurt.
But I, a daughter of Nereus, born   1180
to sea-green Doris, and protected, too,
by a crowd of sisters, could not escape
the love of the cyclops Polyphemus
except through pain and sorrow."

                Here her tears
choked her voice, preventing her from speaking.
With her white fingers, Scylla wiped away
the tears, calmed the goddess down, and said:

"Dearest Galatea, tell me. Do not hide
why you are grieving. You can trust in me."

The Nereïd then replied to Scylla,   1190
daughter of Crataïs:

               "Acis was the son   [750]
of Faunus and Symaethis, a sea nymph,
a great joy to his father and his mother,
but even more to me, for he loved me
and no one else.[1] He was a handsome lad,
sixteen years old, with the first downy hair
starting to grow out on his tender cheeks.
I tried to spend every minute with him,
and Polyphemus did the same with me.
If you were to ask, I could not tell you   1200
which was stronger in me—love of Acis
or hatred for that cyclops, for I felt
strong passion either way. O Gentle Venus
how powerful your rule is over us!   POLYPHEMUS IN LOVE
For that savage creature Polyphemus,
whom the very forest fears and strangers   [760]
cannot look upon without some danger,
who scorns mighty Olympus and its gods,
now has a sense of what love is and, seized
by fervent passion, burns and quite forgets   1210
his flocks and caves. And then, Polyphemus,
you start to worry about how you look

---

[1] Crataïs was a river in southern Italy, Symaethis a river in Sicily.

447

and how to please. You comb your bristling hair
with rakes and love to trim your shaggy beard
with a pruning hook or gaze into a pond
at your wild face and fix how you appear.
Your love of slaughter and your cruelty,
your monstrous thirst for blood—all that is gone.
Ships come and go in safety.

                     In the meantime,   TELEMUS AND POLYPHEMUS
Telemus reached Sicily. He was the son
of Eurymus and had never been deceived
by any omen. He went to Aetna,
met the giant Polyphemus, and said:

  'That one eye in the middle of your forehead
  will be taken from you by Ulysses.'

Polyphemus laughed and said:

                    'You are wrong,
  you stupidest of prophets. Someone else—
  a young girl—has already captured it.'

He spurned the warning. Though it was the truth,
the prophecy was wasted. Polyphemus
strode away with massive, heavy footsteps
along the shore and, when he grew tired,
went back to his dark cave.

                 A wedge-shaped hill
ran a long way out to sea, with ocean waves   POLYPHEMUS' LOVE SONG
lapping along both sides. The wild cyclops
climbed the central ridge, sat down, and took out
his shepherd's pipe made of a hundred reeds.
His woolly flocks, with no one left to tend them,
came up, too. He laid a pine tree at his feet.
It was his walking staff, but large enough
to hold aloft the rigging on a ship.
All the hillside heard his pastoral notes,
as did the sea. I was there, too, hidden
by a rock, lying in my Acis' arms,
and from a distance heard the cyclops' song.
What my ears picked up, my mind remembers.
It went something like this:

Book Thirteen

                     'O Galatea,
whiter than leaves of snow-white columbine,
more flowery than meadows in full bloom,   [790]
more slender than a splendid alder tree,   1250
more bright than glass, more lively than young goats,
more smooth than sea shells worn down by the waves,
more pleasing than the sun in winter time
or shade in summer heat, more beautiful
than apples, a more pleasing sight to see
than lofty plane trees, more dazzling than ice,
sweeter than ripe grapes, softer than swan down
or curdled milk, and, if you do not run from me,
more lovely than well-watered garden parks.

And yet, at the same time, Galatea,   1260
you are wilder than young bulls not yet tamed,
harder than old oak, slyer than the sea,
tougher than willow twigs or branching vines,   [800]
more stubborn than these crags, more violent
than raging streams, more vain than valued peacocks,
more fierce than fire, more prickly than a thorn,
more vicious than a mother bear with cubs,
more hard of hearing than the ocean waves,
more ruthless than a stepped-on water snake,
and, what, above all, I would like to change,   1270
you are not only swifter than a stag
being followed by a pack of baying dogs,
but you run faster even than the winds
and the fleeting breeze.

                    But if you knew me well,
you would feel sorry you keep flying off
and curse yourself for holding back like this.
You'd make more effort to stay close to me.
For I live here, and on these mountain slopes   [810]
I have caves carved out of natural rock
where you'll not feel the cold when winter comes   1280
or the heat in summertime. And I have
fruit-laden branches on my apple trees,
and grapes which look like gold on tailing vines
and purple ones. I save both kinds for you.
You hands will pluck delicious strawberries
born in the shady woods, with autumn plums

and cherries, too—not just the blue-black kind
so full of juice, but full-grown yellow fruit,
the colour of fresh wax. When you are mine,
you will have berries from arbutus trees   1290
and chestnuts. All trees will be your slaves.   [820]
This whole flock is mine, and many others
wandering the valleys, with many more
hiding in the woods or penned up in caves.
If you should ask how many beasts there are
I could not tell you. It's a poor man's job
to keep a tally of the flock he owns.
And you don't need to take my word for it
when I praise them all. Your own eyes can see
how they can hardly move those legs of theirs,   1300
their udders are so full. And there are lambs,
the young ones of the flock, kept in warm folds,
and kids, the same age as the lambs, secure
in other pens. I always have white milk—
some I keep to drink and some to curdle.   [830]

You will have gifts, and not just common ones
anyone can get, like deer or hares or goats
or matching doves or young birds from the trees.
For I picked up a shaggy bear's two cubs
as pets for you to play with, so alike   1310
it's hard to tell which one of them is which.
I saw them on the mountain top and said:

   'I'll keep these for my mistress Galatea.'

Now, Galatea, just raise your shining head
from the dark blue sea. Do not spurn my gifts,
but come here now. You know, I saw myself   [840]
not long ago by gazing at my image
in clear water. And looking at my shape
was a delight. Just see how big I am!
You like to talk about this Jupiter,   1320
whoever he is, who rules in heaven.
His body is no bigger than my own.
And lots of hair hangs down on my stern face
and keeps my shoulders shaded from the sun,
just like a grove of trees. You should not think
this covering of dense and bristling hair
is unattractive. A tree is ugly

Book Thirteen

    when it has no leaves. A horse is ugly,
if it has no tawny mane along its neck.
Feathers cover birds, and a woolly fleece   1330
makes sheep look beautiful. Attractive men
have beards and bodies covered in rough hair.   [850]
And here, on my forehead, in the centre,
I only have one eye. But it is large,
the size of huge shield. And think of this—
does not the mighty Sun see everything
from high up in the sky? And yet the Sun
has but a single eye.

                              And in addition,
my father Neptune rules your ocean waves.
I'll give him to you as a father-in-law.   1340
Just pity me and hear me when I pray!
I am your suppliant. I kneel to you,
and no one else. Yet I spurn Jupiter
and heaven and his piercing thunderbolt.
You are the one I fear, Nereïd. Your rage
is crueler to me than a lightning strike.
I'd find it easier to bear your scorn,
if you were running off from everyone.
But how can you reject a cyclops' love   [860]
and yet love Acis? Why choose his arms   1350
instead of mine? Acis may please himself
and you, as well (I wish that was not true),
but, Galatea, if I could get the chance,
he'd find my strength is every bit as great
as my own body! I'd tear out his guts
while he is still alive, rip his limbs apart,
and throw them in the fields, scatter them there
and in your sea (so he could mix with you).
I burn with love. And when you injure me
my flames get fiercer, till Mount Aetna seems   1360
to have shifted to my heart, for here inside
I carry all its fire. Yet you do not care,
Galatea, you do not care at all."

After these laments—which were quite useless—   [870]
Polyphemus rose (for I could see it all),
and, like a bull who has just lost a cow
and is so furious it can't stand still,

he wandered in familiar mountain glades
and in the woods. Then the savage monster
spied me and Acis—we did not think he could
and so we had not worried. He cried out:

> 'I see you! This is the last time you two
> will be making love—I'll make sure of that!'

His voice was huge. He sounded just the way
an angry cyclops should. His savage shouts
made Aetna shudder. I was terrified
and hurled myself into the neighbouring sea.
But my brave Acis, son of Symaethis,
turned round and ran away, crying:

> 'Help me,
> Galatea, I beg you. Help me out!
> Father, mother—let me in your kingdom!
> I'm about to die!'[1]

The cyclops followed him.
He hurled a rock torn from the mountain side.
Only the furthest tip of stone reached Acis,
but that was still enough to bury him.
I did the one thing Fate would let me do—
made sure that Acis could assert the force
his ancestors once had. Dark red blood seeped out
from underneath the rock. Soon after that,
the redness in the blood began to fade.
At first its colour looked just like a stream
disturbed by rain but slowly growing clear.
And then the boulder Polyphemus threw
split open and a tall and living reed
pushed through the cracks, and from the gaping split
the sound of gushing waters could be heard.
And then, a miracle! All of a sudden,
a youth emerged and rose up to his waist,
with new horns wreathed in waving rushes.
It was Acis, although this youth was larger
and all his face was blue. But even so,

---

[1] Acis is asking to be allowed to hide in the water to escape from Polyphemus. His mother was the daughter of a river god. Or the father and mother in question might be Galatea's parents, Nereus and Doris, gods of the sea.

it was still Acis changed into a stream,
a river that has kept his ancient name.'

After Galatea finished speaking,   SCYLLA AND GLAUCUS
the group of Nereïds broke up and left,
swimming away through tranquil waves. Scylla
did not dare trust herself far out to sea,   [900]
so she swam back to shore and wandered there
on the thirsty sand without her clothes on
or, when she was tired, found a lonely inlet   1410
and cooled herself in its secluded bay.
Then, lo and behold, Glaucus came along,
racing across the surface of the waves.
He had come to live in the ocean deep
not long before, when his limbs were changed
across the sea from Euboea at Anthedon.[1]
When Glaucus caught sight of Scylla, he paused,
his passion roused. He called to her, saying
whatever he thought might stop her running.
But she still sped away—fear made her swift—   1420
and reached a mountain top not far from shore.
It had a huge ridge right beside the sea   [910]
which rose up to a single wooded peak
and leaned out to the water. Here she stopped
and, from a safe location, looked at Glaucus,
not knowing what he was, god or monster.
She marvelled at his colour and his hair,
which concealed his shoulders and clothed his back,
and at his body, which, below the groin,
was a twisting fish. He sensed her watching   1430
and, leaning on a rock that stood close by,
spoke out:

"Young girl, I am not some monster
or ferocious beast, but a god of sea.
Proteus and Triton and Palaemon,
son of Athamas, have no more power
to control the ocean waves than I do.[2]

---

[1] Anthedon was on the mainland of Greece, facing the island Euboea.

[2] Palaemon was a young god of the sea. He had once been Melicertes, the mortal child of Ino and Athamas. For Ovid's account of how the infant Melicertes became Palaemon, see above 4.785 ff.

Book Thirteen

In earlier days I was a mortal, [920]
but still I was devoted to the sea.
Back then I even worked beside it. At times,
I used to haul in nets that trapped the fish   1440
or else I sat down on a rock and used
my rod and line.

              There is a stretch of shore
lying next to pasture land. On one side
is the sea, on the other grassy fields
untouched by two-horned cattle feeding there.
No quiet sheep or shaggy goats had cropped it.
No hard-working bees had ever taken
pollen from the flowers there. No garlands
had been plucked to adorn men's heads at feasts.
No hand had every mown it with a scythe.   1450   [930]
I was the first to sit down on that grass,
drying my soaking nets and setting out
the fish I'd caught. I laid them down in rows,
so I could make a count of those whom chance
had driven to my nets and those whose hopes
had naively landed them on my barbed hook.
What happened next sounds like an untrue story,
but what advantage would I get from lies?
My fish laid on the grass began to stir.
They wriggled around and moved on land,   1460
as if they were now swimming in the sea.
I was surprised, but then, as I waited,
the whole group of them escaped, slipping off
into the sea where they belonged, leaving
their new master and the shore. I was stunned.
What happened had me puzzled for a while.   [940]
I thought about a cause. Was it some god?
Or had some herbal juice brought this about?
I asked myself:

              'What plant has this effect?'

I pulled up some of the grass and my teeth chewed   1470
the blades that I had picked. And once my throat
had swallowed the strange juices down, I felt
a sudden throbbing deep inside my heart,
and my breast was seized with a fierce desire
to be in water. I could not stay there,

454

so I hurled by body down into the sea,
shouting out:

        'Farewell land! Never again
will I be coming back!'

                The gods of the sea
accepted me. They thought me fine enough
to be included in their company.
So they asked Tethys and Oceanus
to take away whatever mortal parts
I might retain, and those two made me pure.
A spell repeated nine times over purged
my wickedness, and I was told to wash
my body in a hundred rivers. Then streams
at once poured out from various sources,
their cleansing waters flowing past my head.
That's all I can describe of those events,
which were amazing, all I can recall.
My mind remembers nothing of the rest.
When I sensed things once again, my body
had completely changed from what it was before,
and my mind was not the same. At that point,
for the first time, I saw this dark green beard,
this hair I sweep along through the wide sea,
these massive shoulders and my azure arms,
and these legs curving into a fish with fins.
But still, what use is it to have this body
or give delight to gods who rule the sea,
what use is it to be a god myself,
if you do not even care about these things?"

Glaucus paused, with still more left to say.
But Scylla ran away. The god was hurt,
angry at being rejected. He moved on
towards the marvellous home of Circe,
a daughter of the Titan Helios.

Book Fourteen

XIV

[Glaucus visits Circe and asks her help; Circe transforms Scylla into a monster; Aeneas continues his voyage; Aeneas abandons Dido, sails on to Italy, and consults the Sybil at Cumae; Aeneas visits the Underworld; the Sibyl tells her story; Achaemenides tells of his escape from Polyphemus; Macareus recounts the adventures he went through with Ulysses: Aeolus and the winds, the Laestrygonians, and Circe; Macareus recounts the story of Picus, Canens, and Circe; the Trojans bury Caiëta; Aeneas reaches Italy, marries Lavinia; Turnus fights the Trojans; Venulus visits Diomedes; Diomedes tells his story; Cybele saves the Trojan ships from fire, then sinks them; the ships change to sea nymphs; Aeneas triumphs over Turnus; Ardea falls, and a heron rises from its ashes; Aeneas becomes a god; the first kings of Alba; Vertumnus courts Pomona; Iphis is rejected by Anaxarete, who is turned to stone; Romulus founds Rome; Sabines war against the Romans; Venus saves Rome from Tarpeia's treachery; peace is declared; Romulus becomes sole king; Romulus and Hersilia enter heaven as gods].

GLAUCUS AND CIRCE

Glaucus, who now lived in the swelling seas
of Euboea, had left Aetna behind,
(a mountain sitting on a Giant's jaws),
moved past Cyclops' fields (where plough and harrow
were unknown and growing crops owed nothing
to straining teams of oxen), past Zancle
and walls of Rhegium across the sea,
and through the narrow ship-destroying strait
between two coasts which mark the boundaries
of Italy and Sicily. He forged ahead,   10
with powerful strokes, across the Tyrrhene sea
and reached the grassy hills and halls of Circe,
daughter of the Sun, whose lands were filled   [10]
with various wild beasts.[1] Once he'd seen her
and the two had greeted one another,
Glaucus cried:

    "Goddess, I'm begging you—
take pity on a god, for you alone
can ease this love of mine, if you believe
I'm worthy of your help. No one understands
more than I do the power herbs possess,   20
for they once changed my shape. O Titan's child,
if you are ignorant of why I feel

---

[1] The Giant under Aetna was Typhoëus, who had fought against Zeus and was imprisoned underground in Sicily, with Mount Aetna above his head. Zancle was a city in Sicily on the Straits of Messina and Rhegium the city in Italy directly across from it. The Tyrrhene Sea is alongside the west coast of Italy. Glaucus is moving around the end of Italy and northward up the coast. Circe, as mentioned previously, was in Greek mythology the daughter of Helios, the Titan god of the sun. She was not a daughter of Apollo, whom Ovid usually identifies as the god of the sun.

such frantic passion, I will tell you.
I saw Scylla on a beach in Italy,
facing Messana's walls. I am ashamed
to talk about my promises, my prayers,
and my entreaties. Scylla scorned them all.
So if your charms have any influence, [20]
then let your sacred lips recite a spell,
or if some herbs would have more potency, 30
apply the proven force of tested plants.
I am not asking you to make me well
or heal these wounds of mine. There is no need
to end my love. But let her have her share
of the heat I feel."

                Now, no one has a heart
more likely to catch fire than Circe does
(the cause of that could be within herself,
or else Venus, upset when Circe's father
talked about what he had seen her doing,
could have placed those urges deep inside her), 40
so she replied:[1]

                        "It would be preferable
to chase someone whose wishes and desires
matched your own, a person captivated
by an equal passion. And you deserved [30]
to be the one pursued (there is no doubt
you could have been), and if you offer hope,
there will be those who court you willingly.
Trust me. If you doubt that and have no faith
in your appearance, then consider me,
a goddess, daughter of the glorious Sun, 50
who has great power with spells and potions,
and yet I promise to be yours. So spurn
the one who spurns you, and reward the one
who now pursues you. In that single act
let your revenge repay the two of us."

The goddess tried to tempt him in this way,
but Glaucus answered:

---

[1] The Sun had observed the adulterous affair of Venus and Mars and had informed Vulcan, Venus' husband. For Ovid's treatment of the story see 4.249 ff. above.

Book Fourteen

"While Scylla is alive,
forest leaves will flourish in the ocean
and sea weed in the hills, before the love
I feel for her will ever change."

         Circe
was annoyed. She could not injure Glaucus
(and, because she loved him, did not wish to),
so she took her anger out on Scylla,
the girl he had preferred to her. Enraged
her love had been rejected, she quickly
ground up some poisonous herbs, whose juices
were well known for their hideous effects,
and, once she had beaten them to powder,
she added certain spells from Hecate.
Wrapped in a dark blue cloak, she left her home,
moved through the pack of fawning animals,
and made for Rhegium, across the strait
from Zancle's rocks. Walking atop the waves
and raging currents, as if setting her feet
on solid ground, and keeping her feet dry,
she skimmed along the surface of the sea.

There was a small bay, shaped like a curved bow,
which Scylla loved for its tranquility.
When the Sun was halfway through his orbit,
at his height, and cast the smallest shadows,
she used to go there to escape the heat
from sky and sea. Knowing she would go there,
Circe spikes the waters, polluting them
with monstrous poisons and sprinkling juices
squeezed from noxious roots. Her magical lips
then mutter a cryptic incantation—
thrice nine times!—a dark, mysterious spell.
When Scylla comes and wades into the sea
up to her waist, she sees around her groin
some hideous barking monsters. At first,
not thinking they are part of her own body,
she tries to run away and drive them off,
fearful of the creatures' slavering mouths.
But what she seeks to flee, she drags with her,
and when she checks her thighs and legs and feet,
she finds, instead of these, the gaping jaws

of Cerberus. She stands there, surrounded
by a raging pack of ferocious dogs,
whose backs below her pelvis hold her up
and out of whom her shortened thighs and belly 100
now emerge.

         Her lover Glaucus wept for her
and ran from Circe's arms. The way she'd used
her power with herbs had been too cruel.
Scylla remained there. The first chance she got, [70]
she acted on the hate she felt for Circe,
by snatching away Ulysses' comrades
and later would have sunk the Trojan ships,
if she had not been earlier transformed
into a reef, whose rocks, even today,
protrude above the surface of the sea, 110
a hazard sailors still avoid.

         The oarsmen   AENEAS AND DIDO
in the Trojan ships rowed on past Scylla
and ravenous Charybdis.[1] As they approached
the shores of Italy, winds drove their ships
back to the Libyan coast, where the queen,
Sidonian Dido, welcomed Aeneas
to her home and heart. But when they parted
and her new Trojan husband went away,
she found the loss impossible to bear.[2]
Pretending to offer up a sacrifice, 120 [80]
she had a pyre built, then took a sword
and killed herself, deceiving everyone,
just as she had been deceived.

         Aeneas
moved off once more, fleeing the brand new walls
of Dido's city in the sand. Carried back   AENEAS CONTINUES HIS VOYAGE
to the land of Eryx and loyal Acestes,
he made a sacrifice and offered presents

---

[1] Charybdis was a monster in the form of a whirlpool on the side of the strait opposite Scylla.

[2] Aeneas married Dido, who was building the city of Carthage in North Africa, but then left her in order to fulfill his destiny of founding his own city in Italy.

at his father's tomb.[1] Then, after Iris,
on Juno's orders, almost burned his ships,
Aeneas set sail, moving past the realm   130
of Aeolus, grandson of Hippotas,
and lands with clouds of boiling sulphur fumes,
past those island rocks where the Sirens dwell,
the daughters of Acheloüs.[2] His ship
had lost its pilot, but kept sailing on
past Inarime, Prochyte, and Pithecusae,   [90]
built on a barren hill, a place whose name
is taken from the tiny apes that live there.[3]
Once long ago, the father of the gods,   THE CERCOPES
disgusted with the frauds and perjuries   140
of the Cercopes and the criminal acts
of that deceitful people, changed them all
into misshapen beasts, making them look
like human beings and yet unlike them, too.
He shrunk their limbs and made their noses flat,
bent up towards the forehead, scarred their cheeks
with furrows and the wrinkles of old age,
and then, after covering their bodies
with yellow hair, he sent them to this place,
but not before he took away their speech,   150
the power of those tongues born for deceit,
thus leaving them unable to complain   [100]
except with strident shrieks.

                   When Aeneas   AENEAS AND THE SIBYL
had passed these places and left behind him
on his right the walls of Parthenope
and on his left the tomb of Misenus,
a trumpeter and son of Aeolus,
he moved on to the swampy shores of Cumae,
full of marshy sedge, and then into the cave
of the long-lived Sibyl, entreating her   160
to let him venture through Avernus to find

---

[1] The land of Eryx was Sicily, and Acestes was a king there. Aeneas' father, Anchises, had died on the journey.

[2] For the story of how the daughters of Acheloüs became the Sirens, see above 5.859.

[3] These names refer to islands off the west coast of Italy.

his father's shade below.[1] For a long time,
the Sibyl kept her eyes fixed on the ground,
but then, inspired by the god within her,
she finally replied:

                        "You are a man
who has done great things, whose right hand has stood
the test of war, whose faith was proved in fire.
What you are seeking is a mighty gift!
But, Trojan, do not fear, for you will have   [110]
what you desire and, with me to guide you,
will see the dwellings of Elysium,
the strangest kingdom in the universe,
and the shade of your beloved father.[2]
There is no path which virtue cannot tread."

As the Sibyl said this, she pointed out   AENEAS IN THE UNDERWORLD
a branch of shining gold among the trees
sacred to Avernian Juno, telling him
to break it from the trunk.[3] Aeneas did so
and beheld the power of dread Pluto.
He saw his ancestors and the old ghost
of Anchises, his great-hearted father.
He also learned about that region's laws
and all the dangers he would have to face
in future wars.

                  On his way back from there,   [120]
as with weary steps he trudged along the trail,
Aeneas tried to ease the tiring effort
by conversing with his guide from Cumae,
and, while moving up the daunting pathway
through the darkening twilight, said to her:

"Whether you are actually divine
or someone truly favoured by the gods,
you will always be just like a goddess

---

[1] Sibyls were prophetesses who could read the will of the gods. Avernus was a region in Italy where people believed there was access to the Underworld. Parthenope was the name of the city that later became Naples.

[2] Elysium was a special place for those shades of the dead who had been given an afterlife much happier than the one in Hades.

[3] Avernian Juno is a title sometimes given to Proserpine, goddess of the Underworld.

in my eyes, and I will confess my life
comes as a gift from you, for you let me
observe the places of the dead and then,
when I had seen them, led me back again.
To repay your kindness, when I return
and reach the upper air, I will construct
a temple in your honour and offer
gifts of frankincense to you."

                              The priestess
looked at him and, with a heavy sigh, replied:

"I am not a goddess. And you should not
honour a human being with a gift
of holy frankincense. Just to make sure
you do not, in your ignorance, do wrong,
I will tell my story. Phoebus Apollo
was in love with me and made an offer—
I could have eternal, never-ending life,
if I surrendered my virginity.
While he was still hoping to persuade me
and before I had agreed to his request,
he wished to bribe me with some gift and said:

    'Virgin of Cumae, choose what you want.
    You will have whatever you desire.'

                              I pointed
to a heaped-up pile of dust and asked him
if he would give me as many birthdays
as those particles of dust, but like a fool,
I did not ask that all those years should come
with ageless youth, as well. Still, he offered me
the years and eternal youth, provided
I would have sex with him. I spurned his gift
and stayed unmarried. Now my happier years
have passed me by and, on tottering steps,
a sick old age comes on, which I must bear
a long time yet. I have already lived
through seven generations and still must see
three hundred harvests, three hundred vintages,
to match the number of those bits of dust.
The day will come when that long stretch of time
will shrink my body from its present shape

APOLLO AND THE SYBIL

and my appendages, worn out with age,
will shrivel to a trifling size. And then,
it will not seem that I was ever loved
or that I pleased a god. Phoebus himself [150]
may well not recognize me or perhaps
he will deny he was my lover once.
I will be changed so much that men will say
they cannot see me. But they will know me
by my words, for the Fates will leave my voice."

As the Sibyl said this, climbing along 240
the rising path, Trojan Aeneas moved
from the Stygian realm up into Cumae,
a city men from Euboea had built.
When, following his usual practices,
he had offered sacrifice, he went out
along the shore, which later on was named
after the nurse who once had cared for him.

Here, too, Macareus from Neritos, ACHAEMENIDES
a comrade of adventurous Ulysses,
had settled after long and weary travels. 250
He saw the Trojan group and recognized
Achaemenides, who he thought was dead,
abandoned years before on Aetna's rocks. [160]
Amazed to see him so unexpectedly—
and still alive—Macareus shouted:

"Achaemenides! What god or chance
saved you from death? Why are you, a Greek,
on board a boat of barbarous Trojans?
And that ship of yours, where is it heading?"

Achaemenides, no longer wearing rags 260
and bits of clothing held in place by thorns,
was now the man he used to be. He said:

"May I look on Polyphemus once again
and those jaws of his dripping human blood,
if this ship is not a finer place to me
than home and Ithaca and if I honour
Aeneas any less than my own father.[1] [170]

[1]Achaemenides was one of Ulysses' comrades sailing back from Troy. He and a few others were captured by Polyphemus, the cyclops. In Homer's *Odyssey* Polyphemus eats a number

[Footnote continues]

If I did everything I could for him,
there is no way I'd ever demonstrate
sufficient gratitude. Could I forget 270
or not give thanks that I can speak and breathe
and gaze upon the sky and glorious sun?
Aeneas saw to it that this soul of mine
did not pass through the cyclops' gaping mouth.
Even now, if I were to lose my life,
I know I would be buried in a tomb
and not that monster's belly. How did I feel,
when you left me behind and I saw you
sailing out to sea? Well, my fear wiped out
all sense and feeling. I wanted to call out, 280
but was afraid I'd give myself away [180]
to Polyphemus. Even Ulysses,
when he gave those shouts, almost sunk your ship.[1]
I saw the cyclops tear a colossal rock
away from the mountainside and toss it
far out into the middle of the sea.
I watched again as his gigantic arms
hurled massive stones, just like a catapult.
Forgetting I was not aboard the ship,
I was terrified the waves and boulders 290
might sink us all. But when you got away,
escaping certain death, Polyphemus
wandered all across Mount Aetna, groaning,
groping with his hands among the trees,
and, without his eye, stumbling on the rocks.
He stretched his bloodstained arms towards the sea,
cursed the race of Greeks, and cried:

    'O if some chance
would only bring Ulysses back to me
or one of his companions, then I would
vent my rage on him and eat his innards. 300
My hands would rip apart his living flesh,

---

of the men he has trapped in his cave. Ulysses tricks Polyphemus, blinds him, and leads his men back to their ship.

[1] As Ulysses was sailing away from the island, he shouted taunts at the blind cyclops on the shore. Polyphemus hurled two rocks in the directions of the sound and almost swamped the Greek ship.

and I would fill my gullet with his blood.
His torn-off limbs would quiver in my teeth.
And then losing my eye and going blind
would be no loss, or else a trivial one.'

He was so enraged, he kept on shouting
things like this and more. A ghastly terror
gripped me, as I saw his face still soaked in gore, [200]
his savage hands, his eye ball's gaping socket,
his limbs and beard still caked with human blood. 310
Death was there, right before my eyes, and yet
of all my troubles that mattered least of all.
I thought that any moment he would seize me
and then stuff his stomach with my innards.
My mind kept seeing a picture of the day
I watched the bodies of my two companions
being smashed repeatedly against the ground
and Polyphemus, like a shaggy lion,
jumping on them, swallowing their organs
and their flesh, with bones and marrow, too, 320
cramming their trembling limbs, still half alive,
in his voracious gut. I shook with fear [210]
and stood there shocked, blood draining from my face,
as I observed him at his bloody feast,
chewing and belching and vomiting up
pieces of human bodies mixed with wine.
I thought he was preparing a fate like that
for me, as well, and so for several days
I hid myself, startled by every sound,
afraid of death, but longing to be dead, 330
relieving my hunger pangs with acorns
and a mix of grass and leaves—all alone,
without hope or help, left abandoned there
to my afflictions and my death. But then,
after some time, I saw a ship far off.
I ran down to the shore and by waving
begged them to rescue me. And they were moved—
that Trojan ship welcomed a Greek on board! [220]
And now, my dearest comrade, you tell me
what you've experienced with Ulysses 340
and that group of men, who, along with you,
risked life and limb to sail the open sea."

Macareus then spoke about how Aeolus,   ULYSSES AND AEOLUS
grandson of Hippotas, ruled the Tuscan sea,
and how that god had shut up all the winds
in an ox-hide bag, which Aeolus then gave
to the man from Ithaca, their leader,
an amazing gift. Sailing on from there
with favourable breezes for nine days,
Ulysses and his men could see the land   350
they wished to reach. But when the tenth day dawned,
Ulysses' crew were overcome with greed
and a desire for plunder, so the men,
thinking the leather bag contained some gold,
untied the strings which kept the winds confined.   [230]
These winds then blew the ship away from land,
back through the seas it had just sailed across,
until it once more sailed into the port
of Aeolus, their king.
                Macareus
continued with his story:

                      "From there,   360
we went to the ancient town of Lamus,
a Laestrygonian, where Antiphates ruled.   LAESTRYGONIANS
I was sent to him with two companions.
We had to run away. I only just escaped,
with a single comrade. The other man,
the third one in our group, was eaten
by the Laestrygonians—their evil jaws
turned red with his dark blood—and as we fled,
Antiphates came after us, urging
his people to attack. They charged at us,   370
hurling rocks and tree trunks, destroying ships   [240]
and drowning men. But one ship got away,
with Ulysses and the two of us on board.
Full of grief and mourning our lost comrades,
we reached that land which you can see out there,
in the distance (and trust me when I say
that island is best seen from far away).
You are a goddess' son and the finest
of the Trojans—for now the war is over,
I cannot hold you as an enemy—   380

but, Aeneas, I warn you—stay away
from Circe's coast!

         We dragged our boat ashore   CIRCE AND ULYSSES
on Circe's island, but, remembering
Antiphates and the savage cyclops,
we too refused to move on any further.   [250]
Not knowing anything about the place,
we held a lottery to choose some men
to go and check the house. My name was drawn,
so I was sent to enter Circe's walls
with Eurylochus, faithful Polites,   390
Elpenor (who was much too fond of wine),
and eighteen comrades.[1] But when we got there
and stood right by the entrance to her home,
a thousand wolves, with bears and lions, too,
rushed up to us. We were all terrified.
But there was no need for us to be afraid.
The beasts had no desire to injure us.
They fawned on us, wagging their friendly tails,
and followed our tracks, until some servant girls
received us and led us through a hallway   400   [260]
roofed in marble to their mistress, Circe,
who was sitting in her lovely chamber
on a stately throne, dressed in a fine robe,
with a golden cloak around her shoulders.
Nereïds and nymphs are there together.
Their deft fingers are not working fleeces
or spinning slender thread, but setting herbs
in proper order, sorting out in baskets
flowers and variously coloured grasses
lying strewn in piles. Circe oversees   410
the work they do, for Circe understands
the power of each leaf and the effects
herbs have when they are properly combined.
She watches closely and inspects each batch   [270]
as it is weighed.

         When Circe saw us
and we had greeted one another, her face

---

[1] In Homer's *Odyssey*, Elpenor has too much to drink and, as a result, falls off the roof of Circe's house, killing himself.

looked pleased and seemed to us to indicate
our prayers were answered. Without delay
she gave orders for a drink to be prepared
from toasted barley grains, honey, strong wine, 420
and curdled milk, all combined together.
Secretly she added special juices,
whose taste the sweetness of the drink would hide.
Her divine right hand offered us some cups,
and we accepted them and had a drink,
for we were thirsty, and our lips were parched.
Then that fearful goddess picked up her wand
and with it quickly tapped us on the head.
And then—I am ashamed to tell this part,
but I'll continue—hair began to grow 430
all over me, I could no longer speak, [280]
but gave out raucous grunts instead of words.
I began to bend, till my entire face
was staring at the ground. I felt my mouth
harden into a turned-up snout, my neck
grew strong and fat, and these hands of mine,
which, a minute before, had raised the cup,
now were leaving footprints in the ground.
I was shut up in a sty with others,
all in the same state (that's how powerful 440
those magic drugs can be!). But we noticed
Eurylochus was the only one of us
whom Circe had not changed into a pig,
the only one who had declined the cup
when it was offered. If he'd not done that,
I'd still be there, one of those bristly swine,
even today, for he would not have run
and told Ulysses of the great disaster,
and Ulysses would not have come to Circe [290]
to pay her back. Peace-bearing Mercury 450
gave him a whitish flower growing out
from a dark black root (gods call it moly).
Protected by that plant and heaven's warnings,
he entered Circe's home, where she asked him
to take the poisoned cup. But when she tried
to stroke his hair, he knocked away her wand,
drew his sword, and terrified the goddess.
She backed away. But then the two of them

pledged their good faith by shaking their right hands,
and Circe took Ulysses as her husband, 460
welcoming him in bed. There he asked her,
as a wedding gift, to give his comrades
their old bodies back. So she sprinkled us
with more wholesome juices of unknown herbs,
reversed her wand, and tapped us on the head, [300]
while muttering some charms to neutralize
the ones she used before. The more she spoke,
the more we stood erect, moving upward
from the ground. The bristles on our bodies
all dropped off, in our cloven feet the split 470
soon went away, our shoulders reappeared,
with arms and forearms properly in place.
With tears of joy, we embraced our leader,
hanging on his neck (and he had tears, as well).
We told him nothing of what we'd been through,
until we had expressed our gratitude.

We stayed on Circe's island one whole year,
and in that time I witnessed many things
with my own eyes and ears. Among them all,
there is a story one of the servant girls 480 [310]
who used to take part in the sacred rites
told me in secret. While Circe was away,
spending time with Ulysses on her own,
this servant took me to a young man's statue, PICUS AND CANENS
a figure carved from marble white as snow,
and on his head he had a woodpecker.
It stood in a sacred shrine and was wreathed
with many garlands. Well, I wished to know
who the young man was, why he was worshipped
in a temple, and why the bird was there. 490
So I asked the servant girl, and she replied:

'Listen, Macareus. Pay attention
to what I say, and you, too, will find out
the powers of my mistress, Circe.
Picus, a son of Saturn, was a king [320]
 who ruled Ausonia.[1] He loved horses
trained for use in warfare. This hero looked

---

[1]Ausonia was the name of a region in southern Italy and sometimes refers to Italy generally.

the way you see him here. You get a sense
of how good looking he was and, from this,
a statue of him, you can recognize   500
his true appearance. And his character
matched his good looks. As for how old he was,
he could not yet have seen four times those games
they hold in Grecian Elis each fifth year.¹
His handsome looks made him enticing
to dryads born on Latium's mountain hills.
Nymphs of the fountains sought his company,
and naiads, too, the ones Albula bore,
those born in waters of Numicius,
and in Anio's stream and flowing Almo   510
(whose stretch of water is so very short),
and from the rushing Nar and Farfarus,   [330]
with its dark shade, and those who haunt the pool
of Scythian Diana in the woods
and nearby lakes.² But Picus spurned them all
and fixed his heart on just a single nymph,
the daughter of a god, two-faced Janus.
They say Venilia gave birth to her
on Palatine hill.³ When she was mature
and ready to get married, she was given   520
to Picus of Laurentum, whom she preferred
to all her other suitors. Her beauty
was exceptional, but her skill in singing
even rarer still and, given that gift,
they called her Canens.⁴ That sweet voice of hers
could attract the trees and rocks, tame wild beasts,
hold back the flowing streams of lengthy rivers,
and arrest birds in their wandering flight.   [340]
One day, when she was singing melodies
in her delightful voice, Picus left home   530

---

¹This reference is to the games held at Olympia, in the Peloponnese.

²Albula was an old name for the Tiber river, running through the site of Rome. The Numicius was a river in central Italy. The Anio was a tributary of the Tiber, as were the Almo, a very short stream, and the Nar. The Farfarus was a river in Umbria. Diana is called Scythian because her worship is said to have come into Italy from Scythia.

³Janus was an Italian god with two faces looking in opposite directions. The Palatine was one of the hills in Rome.

⁴Canens, from the verb *cano*, means *singing*.

Book Fourteen

astride a lively horse, to hunt wild boar
who roamed around the lands of Laurentum.
He wore a purple cloak pinned with a clasp
of yellow gold. His left hand held two spears.

Now, Circe, daughter of the Sun, had left Circe and Picus
Circaean fields (which get their name from her)
and come to those same woods, wishing to pick
fresh herbs from fertile hills. Hidden by trees,
she glimpsed the youth and right away was stunned.
Her hand let go the herbs she had collected,   540   [350]
and she felt as if a burning flame had seared
her bones right to the marrow. When the shock
had passed and Circe had regained her wits,
she was about to say what she desired,
but could not come up close enough to him,
for his horse moved fast and his companions
formed a group around him. So Circe cried:

'Although the wind may carry you away,
you will not escape, if I know my skill,
if my herbs have not lost all their power,   550
and if I am not wrong about my spells.'

After she said this, Circe conjured up
an insubstantial image of a boar
and ordered it to run out past the king,
right before his eyes, and then seem to go   [360]
into a thick clump of forest, where the trees
were really dense and no horse could enter.
Without a moment's pause, Picus instantly
followed the image of his prey, not knowing
it was false, quickly jumping off the back   560
of his sweat-soaked horse, to move ahead on foot,
proceeding through the deep part of the wood,
in pursuit of a vain hope. Meanwhile, Circe
muttered prayers and magic incantations,
worshipping unknown gods with unknown chants,
the ones she used for darkening the face
of the snowy Moon and drawing thirsty clouds
across her father's head.[1] So back then, too,

---

[1] Circe's father, as mentioned before, was in Greek mythology, the Titan god of the Sun.

as Circe sang her spells, the sky grew dark
and the ground breathed mist. The king's companions
wandered along blind trails, and Picus lost
the escort guarding him. Having prepared
the time and place, Circe said:

'By your eyes
which have captivated mine, by your form,
you most beautiful of men, which makes me,
though I am a goddess, your suppliant,
accept this love of mine, and take the Sun,
who sees all things, as your father-in-law.
Do not treat Circe harshly and reject
a Titan's daughter.'

Circe's plea ended.
Picus fiercely spurned her and her appeals,
crying out:

'I am not the one for you,
no matter who you are. Another woman
holds me captive, and I pray she holds me
for a long, long time. As long as the Fates
keep Janus' daughter Canens safe for me,
I will never break the vows that bind us
by having an affair with any stranger.'

Circe kept repeating her entreaties,
but in vain. So she said:

'You will not leave here
without being punished. Nor will you return
to Canens. Now you are going to learn
what a woman slighted in her love can do,
for Circe is a woman who's in love,
and you have spurned her!'

Circe turned around,
twice towards the west, twice towards the east,
then touched young Picus with her wand three times
and three times uttered spells. Picus ran away
but was amazed to find that he could run
more quickly than before. On his body
he saw wings appear. Then he grew annoyed
that he had so suddenly been added

BOOK FOURTEEN

to the strange new birds of Latium's woods [390]
and pecked hard oak trees with his solid beak
and, in his rage, inflicted injuries
on their long branches. Feathers on his wings
took on the purple colour of his cloak,
and the golden brooch holding it in place
turned into feathers, so around his neck
there was a ring of gold. Nothing remained 610
of what Picus had been, except his name.[1]

Meanwhile, his comrades call out repeatedly,
shouting for Picus throughout the countryside,
without success. Then they come on Circe
(by this time she has cleared away the mists
and let the sun and wind disperse the clouds). [400]
They badger her with charges (which are true),
demand their king, make threats they will use force,
and are prepared to fight her with their spears.
She starts to sprinkle venomous juices 620
and harmful potions, calling on the Night
and gods of Night from Erebus and Chaos,
and prays to Hecate in long wailing cries.
Then (amazingly!) the trees spring upward
from their places, the ground begins to groan,
the neighbouring woods turn pale, and the grass
where Circe sprinkled is soaked with drops of blood.
It seems as if the rocks are groaning harshly,
dogs are barking, black snakes are slithering [410]
along the ground, and thin shades of the dead 630
are flitting about. The men all shake with fear,
astonished at these marvellous events.
As they watch in terrified amazement,
Circe taps their faces with her magic wand,
and, at its touch, those youthful men are changed
into wild animals of various kinds.
Not one retains the human form he had.

The setting Sun had bathed Tartessian shores, CANENS
while Canens' eyes and heart waited in vain
for her husband to return.[2] The people 640

---

[1] *Picus* is the Latin for *woodpecker*.

[2] The name Tartessus is a reference to the western coast of Europe.

and her servants carried lamps and rushed around
all through the forest, trying to find him.
Although the nymph wept and tore her hair
and beat her breast, all that was not enough.
She forced herself outside and moved around
in a frantic state through the Latian fields.
Six nights and six returns of the sun's light
saw her going over hills and valleys,
as chance might lead. She did not eat or sleep.
River Tiber was the last to see her,
as she laid her body down on his wide banks,
worn out by grief and wandering. And there
she wept and, as she mourned, sang quietly,
pouring out her sorrow, just as a swan
on the point of death sings its funeral song.
At last her grief dissolved her very bones,
down to the tender marrow. Gradually
she pined away and vanished in thin air.
But where she died still recalls her story,
for ancient muses rightly called the place
after the nymph and named it Canens.'

In that long year at Circe's home, I heard
many tales like that and witnessed many things.
But when we had grown lazy and lethargic
from relaxing for so long, we were ordered
to hoist sails again and set out to sea.
When Circe, the Titan's daughter, told us
our voyage would be long and perilous,
with many dangers from the raging sea
lying in wait for us, I must admit
I was afraid, so when I reached these shores,
I went no further with them and stayed here."

Macareus ended. Then they buried
Aeneas' nurse in an urn of marble.
On it the Trojans carved this brief inscription:

> *The man I nursed, whose piety men praise,*
> *saved me, Caïeta, from the Argive blaze*
> *and here cremated me in righteous ways.*

Loosening cables from the grassy shore,
they left that treacherous island far behind,

Book Fourteen

where the notorious goddess had her home,
and sailed on towards those wooded regions
where the river Tiber, covered in shade,
pours out his yellow sands into the sea.
And there Aeneas seized the royal house   AENEAS IN ITALY
and married the daughter of Latinus,
son of Faunus, though not without a fight.   [450]
He had to war against a hostile people,
and Turnus fought hard for his promised bride.[1]
All Etruria clashed with Latium,   690
an anxious, drawn-out struggle, with both sides
seeking hard-won victory.

                        The two armies   DIOMEDES
tried to increase their ranks with foreign help.
Many men supported the Rutulians,
and many helped defend the Trojan camp.
Aeneas was successful seeking help
from Evander's walls, but Venulus
made a futile trip to Diomedes,
who was now an exile, but had founded
a great city in the realm of Daunus,   700
in Iapygia, and held land there
awarded to him as a marriage gift.[2]
Venulus carried out what Turnus ordered   [460]
and requested aid, but Diomedes,
an Aetolian hero, declined to help.
He was unwilling to commit himself
or the forces of his father-in-law
in such a fight. He claimed he had no men
of his own race whom he could arm for war.
He said to Venulus:

                     "In case you think   710
these are excuses, I will force myself

---

[1] The daughter's name was Lavinia. She had already been promised to Turnus, king of the Rutulians, a people in Latium.

[2] Evander had founded a town on the future site of Rome. Venulus was an ambassador sent by Turnus. Diomedes was an important warrior chief in the Achaean forces at Troy (as we learn in Book 13). He had been forced out of his own city in Greece (as he explains below). Daunus was a king in Iapygia, a region in south-east Italy.

to tell my story, though to talk of it
rekindles painful grief.

              After high Ilium
was on fire and its citadel had fed
the Grecian flames and Locrian Ajax
had seized a virgin in a virgin's shrine,
bringing to all of us the punishment
which he alone deserved, the Argive fleet
was scattered, its ships driven by the wind
across unfriendly seas.[1] We Greeks on board
had to cope with rain, thunderbolts, darkness,
raging skies and waves, and, last but not least,
the Caphereus rocks.[2] I won't detain you
with every detail of these sad events,
but back then even Priam might have thought
Greece deserved some pity. Still, in my case,
warrior Minerva took good care of me,
kept me alive, and saved me from the deep.
But then I was forced out of my homeland
once again, for that gentle goddess Venus,
remembering the old wound I gave her,
demanded punishment.[3] I had to face
such mighty hazards on the open sea
and such great challenges in war on land,
that many times I called those soldiers happy
who perished in that storm we all went through
and in the restless Caphereus waves.
I often wished I had been one of them.
By now my comrades had experienced
the utmost miseries of war and sea
and had lost their courage. So they begged me
to put an end to all our wandering.
But Acmon, who had a fiery temper

---

[1] Locrian Ajax (the Lesser Ajax) was the son of Oïleus. During the sack of Troy, Ajax assaulted Cassandra, a daughter of Priam, in the temple of Minerva, thus bringing divine anger down on the Greek forces during their return home. Ajax, along with a number of others, was drowned in a shipwreck.

[2] Caphereus was a headland on the island of Euboea where several of the ships returning from Troy were wrecked.

[3] In Homer's *Iliad*, Diomedes wounds Aphrodite/Venus on the battlefield (scratching her wrist). In Homer's account of the war, Venus consistently supports the Trojans.

and at that time was even more incensed
at our disasters, shouted:

       'At this point, men,
what is there still left which your endurance
would refuse to bear? What more can Venus do,
beyond all this, assuming she might wish to?
While there are still more dreadful things to fear
there is room for prayer, but when men's lot
is as bad as it can get, they trample fear
beneath their feet, and the most grievous ills
do not concern them. Let Venus herself
hear what I say. Let her despise the men
Diomedes leads—and she does despise us—
we still scorn her hatred. Her great power
is hardly great to us.'

    These words of Acmon,
who came from Pleuron, insulted Venus
and stirred her ancient rage.[1] Few of the men
approved of what he'd said, and most of us,
who were his friends, told Acmon he was wrong.
But when he tried to speak, his voice grew thin,
as did his throat, his hair turned into feathers,
his shrivelled neck, his chest and back had plumage,
with larger feathers covering his arms.
His elbows bent around to form light wings,
his feet were mostly toes, his mouth grew stiff
and hardened to a horny pointed beak.
Lycus, Idas, Abas, and Nycteus
watched in amazement, with Rhetenor, too,
and, as they stared, they took on the same form.
Most of my crew flew up on beating wings
and circled round the oarsmen. If you ask
what these birds formed so suddenly looked like,
they were quite similar to snowy swans,
although they were not swans. As for myself,
though I'm a son-in-law of royal Daunus,
Iapygia's king, I find it difficult
to hold this home as well as these dry fields
with the small group of comrades who remain."

[1] Pleuron was a city in Aetolia, near Epirus.

Diomedes, grandson of Oeneus,
had nothing more to say. So Venulus left
the realm of Calydon, then travelled on
past Peucetia's gulf and reached Messapia,
where in the fields he saw a hidden cave
concealed in reeds, with many trees for shade.[1]
At that time goat-god Pan lived in the cave,
but it had once been occupied by nymphs.
A shepherd from that region of Apulia
had scared these nymphs and sent them running off   790
in sudden fear. They soon regained their wits
and, ignoring the man pursuing them,
resumed their choral dance, moving their feet   [520]
to match the rhythm. The shepherd mocked them,
mimicking their dance with ungainly jumps
and adding foul abuse and filthy insults.
He did not shut his mouth until his throat
was wrapped in wood, for he became a tree,
and from its juice you sense his character,
for bitter berries of wild olive trees   800
bear traces of that man's insulting tongue.
The harshness of his words moved into them.

When the ambassadors returned from there
and reported Diomedes had refused
to assist them with Aetolian troops,
the Rutulians still carried on the war   TURNUS BURNS THE SHIPS
they had prepared for, without that help.
Plenty of blood was shed on either side.
Turnus attacked, bringing his hungry flames   [530]
against the pinewood fleet, and Trojans feared   810
those ships the waves had spared would sink in fire.
Already Vulcan's flames had set alight
pitch and wax and whatever else would burn
and were moving up the high masts to the sails.
In the curving ships the benches smouldered.
But then the sacred mother of the gods,
remembering these pines had been cut down
on Ida's summit, filled the air with sounds

---

[1]The land controlled by Diomedes, given to him as a wedding gift, was called Calydon after the Greek city. Peucetia and Messapia were regions in southern Italy.

of beating cymbals and shrill boxwood pipes.[1]
As her tame lions drew her through thin air,
the goddess cried:

    "Turnus! Your profane hands
are hurling fire in vain. I will save the ships!
I will not allow your ravenous flames
to burn what once was part of my own grove.
Their bodies are my own."

     Once Cybele spoke,

CYBELE AND THE SHIPS

there was at first a growl of thunder and then
a heavy rainstorm fell, with pelting hail.
The four fraternal winds, Astraeus' sons,
rushed into battle and with sudden gales
whipped up the air and swollen heavy seas.[2]
Then all-nourishing mother Cybele,
using one wind's force, snapped the hempen ropes
on the Trojan fleet, swept the ships away
headlong out towards the sea and sank them.
As the drowned wood softened, it turned to flesh,
and curving stern posts changed to heads with faces.
Oars were transformed to toes and swimming legs.
What used to be a hull became a flank.
The central keel, running below the ship,
changed to a spine, the rigging and the ropes
were now soft hair, and yardarms turned to limbs.
Their colour stayed the same, a dark blue green.
As naiads of the sea, with young girls' games
they splash around in waves they used fear,
and though they come from rocky mountainsides,
they dwell in gentle seas, quite unconcerned
about their origin. But those naiad nymphs
do not forget the numerous dangers
they had to face so often from the sea,
and frequently they place their helping hands
on ships tossed by a storm, except for those
which have had Greeks on board. For to this day,
they still remember the collapse of Troy
and hate the Greeks. They watched with happy smiles

---

[1] The sacred mother of the gods is Cybele.

[2] Astraeus was a Titan who fathered the four major winds.

when Ulysses' ship was wrecked and felt great joy
to see that boat of Alcinoüs transformed
into a rock, as stone replaced its wood.[1]

When the fleet turned into living sea nymphs,   THE FALL OF ARDEA
there was some hope the Rutulian force,
through fear of this amazing miracle,   860
might end the fight. But Turnus would not stop.
Each side had its gods, and each had courage,
which matters just as much in war as gods.
But now they were no longer waging war
to obtain a dowry or a kingdom,
or the sceptre of a father-in-law,
or even you, virgin Lavinia.   [570]
They fought because each wanted victory
and would have felt disgraced if he had stopped.
Finally Venus saw her son prevail,   870
and Turnus fell, as did Ardea, too,
a city which, while Turnus was alive,
was thought to be so strong. When savage fires
had consumed the place and all its houses
were buried in hot ash, a bird flew out,
a kind no one had ever seen before.
It rose up from the middle of the ruins,
beating the embers with its flapping wings.
Everything that fits a captured city
was in that bird—in its cry, its leanness,   880
and its pallor. In it the city's name
lives on, for people call it *ardea,*
or *heron,* and every time it beats its wings,
the people of Ardea mourn their fate.[2]   [580]

The virtues of Aeneas had now forced   AENEAS BECOMES A GOD
all the gods, including even Juno,
to bring their ancient quarrels to an end.[3]

---

[1]Alcinoüs, king of Phaeacia, organized a ship to take Ulysses back home to Ithaca. Neptune was outraged and turned the boat on its return journey into a rock in the sea.

[2]I have added the English and Latin names of the bird to clarify the meaning of these lines.

[3]The ancient anger of the gods goes back to the Judgment of Paris, when the Trojan prince gave the apple "for the fairest" to Venus, rather than to Juno or Minerva, an action which led to the abduction of Helen, the Trojan War, and the animosities among various gods who took sides in that human conflict.

And since the fortunes of young Iülus,
his growing son, had been firmly secured,
it was time for the heroic son of Venus   890
to enter heaven. Venus had petitioned
gods above on her son's behalf and now,
throwing her arms around her father's neck,
she said:

        "You've never been unkind to me,
but now I'm begging for a special favour.
Please grant my Aeneas, who, through my blood,
is your grandson, a touch of the divine,
however small, so long as you give some.   [590]
He has already crossed the river Styx
and seen the hateful kingdom of the dead.   900
One visit is enough!"[1]

                The gods agreed.
Even Jupiter's wife did not look unmoved
and nodded her consent, and her face showed
that she was satisfied. Then Jupiter spoke:

   "You are worthy of this gift from heaven,
both you who ask and he for whom you ask.
My daughter, you may have what you desire."

Jupiter spoke. Venus was overjoyed.
She thanked her father and then, borne away
through light air by her harnessed pair of doves,   910
reached Laurentum's shore, where the reedy stream
of the Numicius winds its way down
to the nearby sea. Venus told the stream   [600]
to cleanse Aeneas of all those part of him
which could be harmed by death and carry them
in his silent currents deep into the sea.
The river god with horns performed the task
that Venus had assigned, and his waters
purged Aeneas of what was mortal in him,
washing it away. His best parts remained.   920
Once his body had been purified, his mother
anointed it with heavenly perfume,
wiped a special ointment on his lips,

---

[1] For Aeneas' trip to the Underworld, see 14.153 ff.

a mixture of ambrosia and sweet nectar,
and transformed Aeneas into a god.
The Roman people called him Indiges
and welcomed him with altars and a shrine.

After that, Alba and the Latin realm　　　　　　　THE KINGS OF ALBA
were under the rule of Aeneas' son
who had two names, Ascanius and Iülus.　　　　　930
Silvius succeeded him, and his son,　　　　　　　　[610]
Latinus, took the name and ancient sceptre
of his ancestor. After Latinus
famous Alba reigned, and then Epytus.
The first king following him was Capys,
then Capetus. After them, Tiberinus
inherited the realm and, when he drowned
in a Tuscan stream, it acquired his name,
the Tiber. He had two sons—Remulus
and fierce Acrota. Remulus was older,　　　　　　940
but was wiped out by a strike of lightning
while trying to imitate its fiery flash.[1]
More moderate Acrota passed the sceptre
to valiant Aventinus, who was buried　　　　　　　[620]
on the very hill where he had once been king,
a hill to which he gave his name. After him,
Proca ruled the people of the Palatine.[2]

Pomona lived during king Proca's reign.　　　　　POMONA AND VERTUMNUS
In Latium no other hamadryad
had more skill than she did in her garden　　　　950
or was more attentive to the fruit trees
from which she got her name.[3] Streams and forests
did not interest her. She loved the countryside
and branches bearing ripening apples.
In her right hand she did not clutch a spear,
but held a pruning knife she used sometimes
to cut back plants whose growth became too lush,
or slice off branches spreading here and there.
Sometimes she slit the bark to graft a stem,　　　[630]

---

[1] Apparently, in order to impress his subjects, Remulus constructed machines to imitate the noise of thunder and the flash of lightning.

[2] The Aventine Hill was one of Rome's seven hills. Palatine was another.

[3] *Pomum* is the Latin for *fruit*. A hamadryad is a wood nymph.

providing nourishment for different stock. 960
She never let her plants get dry and thirsty,
but trickled water on the winding tendrils
of the roots to let them drink. Pomona
loved her orchard. It was her great delight.
She did not want the love which Venus brings,
but still, afraid of some uncouth attack,
she built a wall around her orchard grounds,
to stop men, whom she shunned, from reaching her.
What did those men not do in their attempts
to get their hands on her—the youthful satyrs, 970
whose age made them well suited for a dance,
the Pans with wreaths of pine around their horns,
Sylvanus, always younger than his years,
and Priapus, the god whose pruning hook [640]
and massive penis frighten thieves away?[1]

Now, Vertumnus adored this nymph, as well.
He loved her more than any of the rest.[2]
But he had no more luck than other men.
O how many times did he disguise himself
as a simple reaper and bring her baskets 980
filled with ears of grain, the very image
of a farmer who has just brought in his crop!
He frequently showed up with fresh-cut hay
around his head, as if he could have come
from turning new-mown grass, and many times
he clutched an ox goad in his solid fist,
so one could take an oath he had just finished
unharnessing his weary team of bulls.
If given a knife, he was a pruner
who dressed and tended vines, if a ladder 990
lay across his shoulder, you could well think [650]
he was setting out to pick some apples,
if he held a sword, he was a soldier,
and with a rod, he was a fisherman.
In fact, with these numerous disguises
he often was allowed inside the garden,

---

[1]Sylvanus was a Roman god of the fields, wood, and flocks. Priapus was a minor rural deity noted for his huge penis. The Pans were deities of the woods.

[2]Vertumnus was an Italian god of the changing seasons.

where he could enjoy himself by gazing
at Pomona's beauty. Once he even came
as an old woman leaning on a stick,
wearing a coloured scarf, with graying hair
around his temples. He gained admittance,
walked in the beautifully tended garden,
admired the fruit trees there, and said to her:

"It makes you seem even more attractive!"

And to emphasize his praise, he kissed her
a few times in a way no real old woman
ever would have done. Then, stooping over,
he sat down on the grass and gazed upward
at branches loaded down with autumn fruit.
There was a splendid elm tree facing him
holding clumps of shining grapes. Vertumnus
stared at the tree and its companion vine,
and said:

"But if this tree stood by itself
and was not wedded to the vine, it would
have nothing anyone would want to take
except its leaves. And the vine now resting
on the elm and joined to it would lie there
on the ground, if not wedded to the tree
and leaning on it. And yet you are not moved
by this example of the tree and vine,
for you shun marriage and have no desire
to join with anyone. O I wish you did!
You would have more suitors pestering you
than Helen did or Hippodamia
who made the Lapiths fight the centaurs,
more than Penelope, Ulysses' wife,
when he spent all that time away from home.
Even now, when you reject all suitors
and run from them, a thousand men want you,
along with gods, demi-gods, and spirits,
all those deities who haunt the Alban hills.[1]
But if you are wise and want a good man
for your husband and wish to hear the words

---

[1] The Alban hills were a few miles south of Rome.

of a woman who is older and loves you
more than all the others, more than you think,
then decline all common offers and choose
Vertumnus as a partner for your bed.
I can vouch for him, for I know him well,
just as well, in fact, as he knows himself.
He is not one to wander round the world,   1040   [680]
roaming everywhere. He remains right here
and farms the land. And unlike most of those
pursuing you, he does not fall in love
with some young girl he's only just now seen.
No. You will be his first and final love.
To you alone he will devote his life.
Besides, he is young with natural charm.
He can also quickly disguise himself
in any shape. And if you order him
to go through all of them, he will become   1050
whatever you command. What's more, you both
like similar things. He is the first to get
the apples which you grow and is so happy
when his hands are holding gifts from you.
But this time he does not desire the fruit
from your orchard trees or those garden herbs   [690]
with their sweet juice. The only thing he wants
is you. Take pity on his flaming love,
and imagine that the one who loves you
is here in person pleading through my lips.   1060
You should fear the avenging deities
(for Idalian Venus hates unfeeling hearts)
and the wrathful memory of Nemesis.[1]
To make you fear them more, I will recount
a tale from Cyprus, a well-known story
(for my old age has taught me many things).
It may make you easier to persuade
and help you change your mind.

               Once, long ago,   IPHIS AND ANAXARETE
Iphis, a man of humble parentage,
saw noble Anaxarete, a girl   1070

---

[1] Here, as before, Ovid refers to the goddess of retribution by the name of Rhamnus (see 3.623). The phrase Idalian Venus refers to Idalium, a mountain in Cyprus.

descended from the blood of ancient Teucer.[1]
When he saw her, he felt the flames of love [700]
in every bone. He fought against that fire
for quite some time, but once he realized
his reason could not overcome his passion,
he went as a suppliant to her door,
where he talked about his aching feelings
to the young girl's nurse and appealed to her,
by the hopes she had for Anaxarete,
not to be too hard on him. At other times, 1080
he spoke to each of the servant women,
complimenting them and trying very hard
to win goodwill and ask for favours.
Often he gave them tablets to deliver,
full of his flattering words. And sometimes
he hung garlands damp with dewy tears
up on the doorpost and would lie down there,
across her threshold, with his tender ribs
resting on hard stone, cursing the harsh bolts [710]
that barred his way.
                        But Anaxarete, 1090
crueler than the surging sea when the stars
of those Young Goats sink down, harder than iron
refined in fires at Noricum or rock
in its natural state, still fixed in place,
spurned and mocked him.[2] And to these spiteful acts,
she added proud, insulting words, as well,
robbing the man who loved her of all hope.
Iphis could not endure the agony
of his long torment, and before her door
he cried out these last words:
                        'Anaxarete, 1100
you win! You will no longer have to bear
my pleas to you, which you find tedious.

---

[1] Teucer, the Greek warrior leader at Troy, survived the war and arrived home, but was banished by his father Telamon for not avenging the death of Ajax. Teucer went to live in Cyprus, where he founded the city of Salamis.

[2] The Haedi or Young Goats were two stars in the constellation Auriga. Their setting was associated with severe storms. Noricum, a region between the Alps and the Danube, was famous for its iron.

Prepare your joyous triumph and call on
Paean, god of victory! Crown your brows
with splendid laurel! For you have conquered,
and I am glad to die! Your iron heart
should start rejoicing, for surely you must now
find something you can praise about my love,
an action I have done to make you happy,
and admit I had some worth. Remember
that the love I feel for you did not end
before my death. Now, in the same instant,
I lose the lights of life and love together.
No rumour will announce my death to you,
for I will come in person. Do not doubt that.
I will be there. You will see me present,
and you can feast those cruel eyes of yours
on my lifeless corpse. But, you gods above,
if you see what mortals do, remember me
(my tongue can pray for nothing more than that).
In times to come let people tell my story,
and to my fame add on those extra years
you've taken from my life.'

       Iphis finished.
He raised his weeping eyes up to the doorposts
where he had often hung his wreaths of flowers.
Then, lifting his pale arms up to the lintel
he attached a rope, made a noose, and cried:

 'Here's a garland you will find delightful,
you mean and vicious girl!'

       He thrust his head
inside the noose and hung there, his throat crushed,
a mournful, heavy sight. And even then
he was still facing her. His twitching feet
kept kicking at the door, making a sound
which seemed to be demanding to come in,
and when the door was opened, people saw
what he had done. The servants gave a shout
and cut him down, but it was now too late.
They took the body to his mother's home
(for his father had passed on). She hugged him
to her breast, embracing the icy limbs
of her own son. When she had said the words

a mourning parent says and done those things
a grieving mother does, she walked, in tears,
and led the mourners in a funeral march
through the centre of the city, bearing
the pale corpse on a bier toward the fire.
As it so happened, the sad procession
made its way down a street close to the home
of Anaxarete, and their laments
came to the ears of that hard-hearted girl, 1150
whom now some god of vengeance forced to act. [750]
For all her stony heart, the sounds of mourning
moved her, and she said:

      'Let us take a look
at this sad funeral.'

     She went upstairs
to a rooftop room with open windows
and, looking down, saw Iphis lying there,
stretched out on his bier, and in that instant
her eyes froze, the warm blood left her body,
and she turned pale. She tried to step away
but both her feet were rooted to the floor, 1160
and when she strove to turn her face aside,
she found that was impossible, as well.
Little by little, the stone which had lived
so long in her hard heart gained possession
of her body. And if you think this tale
is just a story, there is a statue
of that lady still kept in Salamis,
a place which also has a temple shrine
which people call *Venus Prospiciens*, [760]
the Venus who looks on.

      Remember this, 1170
my nymph. I beg you put aside your pride,
which has gone on too long, and join yourself
to the man who loves you. Then cold weather
will not hurt your budding fruit in springtime,
and gusting winds will not remove your flowers."

The god Vertumnus, in old woman's clothes,
told the story, but it had no effect.
So he took off his costume and returned

to being a young man once again. To her
he seemed just like an image of the Sun   1180
when his most brilliant light breaks through the clouds
that hide his face and shines out unopposed.
Vertumnus is ready to use force with her,
but there's no need. The beauty of the god   [770]
has seized the nymph, and she feels a passion
equal to his own.

               Unjust Amulius   THE SABINE WAR
was the next king to rule Ausonia,
relying on military force. But then,
old Numitor, who had lost the kingdom,
got it back—a present from his grandson—   1190
and on the day of Pales' festival,
they marked the founding of their city, Rome.¹

The Sabine chieftains, led by Tatius,
waged war against them, and when Tarpeia
showed them the way to take the citadel,
she received the punishment she deserved—
being crushed beneath a pile of weapons.²
Then some men from Cures, their voices hushed   VENUS SAVES ROME
like silent wolves, attacked the Roman guards
while they were fast asleep and charged the gates   1200   [780]
which Romulus, son of Ilia and Mars,
had closed and firmly barred.³ But then Juno,
Saturn's daughter, opened one of the gates,
which swung back on its hinges silently.⁴
Venus was the only one to notice
that bars holding the gate had fallen off.
She would have pushed them back, except no god

---

¹Numitor had been removed from the throne by his younger brother Amulius. Numitor's grandson, Romulus, killed Amulius and restored Numitor to the throne. Pales was a goddess of flocks and herds. The walls of Rome were built by Romulus.

²The Sabines were a people living near Rome. Tarpeia was the daughter of the Roman commander of the citadel. She let the enemy in, demanding some payment. Tatius ordered his soldiers to give her, as her reward, their shields, telling his troops to throw them at her, all at once, so that she was killed.

³Ilia was the daughter of Numitor.

⁴Juno would here seem to be continuing her hostility to the descendants of Trojan Aeneas, even though Ovid tells us the gods' quarrels were concluded earlier (see 14.885 above).

ever is permitted to reverse the acts
of other gods.

               The naiads of Ausonia
lived close to Janus' temple, in a spot
kept moist by waters from an ice-cold spring.
Venus went to these naiad nymphs for help.
They did not refuse, for what the goddess
asked of them was just. So they called upon
the streams and rivers which supplied their spring.
But not even they could block the Janus gate.
It was still open. The flowing water
had not barred the way. And so those nymphs
placed yellow sulphur deep in the bubbling spring
and warmed its hollow veins with burning pitch.
By this and other forceful means, the heat
moved down the spring, to the very bottom,
and those waters which, a moment ago,
could dare to rival freezing Alpine cold,
were now so hot they matched the heat of fire!
Both doorposts by the entranceway now smoked
from fiery spray, and the gate which promised
to let tough Sabines through the city walls
was now, thanks to these new waters, blocked,
until the warlike Romans armed themselves.
After that, Romulus led his armies
outside the walls, and Roman ground was strewn
with Sabine bodies and with Rome's own sons.
The blood of son-in-law and father-in-law
was mixed by evil swords, until at last
they all resolved they would not fight it out
to the bitter end but let peace end the war
and Tatius have a share in ruling Rome.

When Tatius died, then you, Romulus,   ROMULUS IS MADE A GOD
ruled both people equally. At that point,
Mars removed his helmet and spoke these words
to the father of both gods and men:

                       "Father,
now the Roman state has firm foundations
and does not depend on just one champion.
It is time for you to hand out that reward
you promised me and your worthy grandson.

Book Fourteen

Raise Romulus from the earth, and set him
here in heaven. For you once said to me
when we were in a council of the gods
(I well recall the gracious words you spoke   1250
and made a note of them):

> 'There will be a man
> whom you will raise to the azure heavens.'

That's what you said. So let those words of yours
be carried out in full."

                    Jupiter nodded.
Then the all-powerful father of the gods
hid the sky behind dark clouds and terrified
the world with thunder rolls and lightning strikes.
Mars knew this was a sign allowing him
to carry off his son, as he'd been promised.
Leaning on his spear he boldly vaulted   1260   [820]
into his chariot. The horses were in place,
straining underneath the blood-stained pole.
With a flick of his whip he urged them on,
and, driving his team headlong through the air,
landed on the top of wooded Palatine.
There he swept up the son of Ilia,
who was administering royal laws
to his own people. The mortal body
of the king disappeared into thin air,
just as, in mid flight, a lead ball often melts   1270
when the broad strap of a catapult sends it
hurtling through the sky. After that, his form
was beautiful and more appropriate
for the lofty couches of the heavenly gods,
like Quirinus in ceremonial robes.[1]

Romulus' wife, Hersilia, mourned him   HERSILIA
when he was gone. But then royal Juno
ordered Iris to go down her curving path   [830]
and tell the widowed queen of her commands:

  "O queen and chief glory of your people,   1280
  the Latin and the Sabine race, worthy

---

[1] Quirinus was a Sabine deity, identified with Romulus.

in earlier days to have been the wife
of such a mighty hero, you now deserve
to be with Quirinus as his consort.
So end these tears of yours. If you desire
to see your husband, follow where I lead,
to that lush grove on the Quirinal hill,
which shades the temple of the Roman king."

Iris obeyed and, gliding down to earth
on her coloured rainbow, spoke to the queen,   1290
as Juno had commanded. Hersilia
found it difficult to look at Iris   [840]
and, in all modesty, replied:

                    "O goddess,
(for though I cannot tell who you might be
you clearly are divine), lead the way, then.
Lead on and let me see my husband's face.
If Fates will give me just one glimpse of him,
I will declare that I have entered heaven."

They did not linger. With Thaumas' daughter
Hersilia climbed the hill of Romulus.   1300
There a star fell, gliding from sky to earth.
Its fiery light set the queen's hair ablaze,
and with that star she rose up in the sky.
The founder of the Roman city held her
with the hands she knew so well and changed her,
both her name and the way she looked before.   [850]
Now he calls her Hora. She is a goddess,
united with her partner Quirinus.

Book Fifteen

XV

[Numa succeeds Romulus; Numa goes to Crotona; Hercules visits Croton; Myscelus founds a new Greek city in Italy; Pythagoras moves to Crotona; Pythagoras proclaims his philosophy: vegetarianism, as in the Golden Age, immortality of the soul, doctrine of metempsychosis; constant changes in nature and human bodies, the four elements, geological changes, different effects of different waters, Mount Aetna's fire, spontaneous generation, the phoenix, strange animals, the rise and fall of civilizations, the destiny of Rome (Helenus' prophecy to Aeneas), immorality of eating meat; Numa becomes king, educates the Romans in arts of peace; Numa dies; Egeria mourns him; Hippolytus tells her the story of his death and return; Egeria is transformed; the story of Romulus' spear; Cipus grows horns and refuses to enter Rome; Aesculapius comes to Rome; Julius Caesar is made a god; Venus tries to prevent his assassination; the gods send omens to warn of the disaster; Jupiter reveals the future triumphs of Augustus; Julius Caesar becomes a star; the poet celebrates the achievements of Augustus; Ovid's final words.]

NUMA

Meanwhile Rome was looking for a leader
who could succeed great Romulus as king
and bear the weight of such a heavy burden.
Then Fame, prophetic messenger of truth,
selected famous Numa for the throne.
He was not satisfied merely to know
the rituals of the Sabine people,
for his wide-ranging mind was keen to think
about much grander schemes and to explore
the nature of things. This passion of his
led him to leave Cures, his native town,
and travel to Crotona, where Hercules
had once been well received.[1] When Numa asked
who could have been the very first to found
a Grecian city in Italian land,
one of the citizens, an older man
with knowledge of the past, gave this reply:

HERCULES AND CROTON

"They say that Hercules, Jupiter's son,
coming back by sea with a splendid herd
of cattle he had taken in Iberia,
after a prosperous voyage landed
at Lacinium on the coast.[2] And then,
while his cattle grazed on tender grasses,
he went in person to the friendly home
of mighty Croton, to renew his strength

---

[1] Cures was a city near Rome, and Crotona a Greek city in southern Italy.

[2] Lacinium was a coastal promontory near Crotona.

by resting after his extended labour.
As he was leaving, he remarked

'In future,
when your grandsons are alive, this place
will be a city.'

And what he promised
did come true. An Argive man called Alemon
had a son Myscelus, whom the gods loved
more than anyone his age. Hercules,
the club-wielding god, went to Myscelus
when he was fast asleep, leaned over him,
and said:

'Come, leave your father's land and seek
the pebbled streams of the distant Aesar!'[1]

And Hercules made many fearful threats
if he did not obey. Then the god and sleep
both disappeared together. Myscelus
got up and, saying nothing, thought about
the vision he had only just received,
going through a lengthy struggle with himself.
The god was telling him he had to go,
but the law prevented him from leaving.
The punishment for anyone who wished
to change his native land was death. By now,
the shining Sun had hidden his bright face
beneath the Ocean, and the darkest Night
had raised her starry head, when Hercules
seemed to appear again, threatening him
in the same way and warning Myscelus
his punishment would be much more severe
if he did not carry out his orders.
Myscelus was afraid and at once began
preparing to move his paternal goods
into a foreign land. But in the city
people talked, and he was brought to trial
for disobeying the law. His accusers
presented their case first. When it was clear
the charges had been proved without the need

HERCULES AND MYSCELUS

[20]

[30]

[1] The Aesar was a river in southern Italy.

for witnesses, the wretched prisoner
raised his face and hands to the gods above
and shouted out:

      'O you, whose twelve labours
gave you the right to a place in heaven,
I'm begging for your help! You are the one   [40]
who drove me to this crime.'

                Now, long ago
it was the custom to vote with pebbles,
black ones to declare the person guilty,
white ones to acquit, and in this case, too,
the harsh result was rendered in this way.   70
Every pebble placed in the cruel urn
was black, but then, when they tipped it over
and poured the pebbles out to tally them,
their colour had been changed from black to white.
So, through the sacred power of Hercules,
Alemon's son was favoured in the verdict
and set free.

              Myscelus thanked his patron,
Amphitryon's son, and with following winds
sailed across the Ionian Sea, passing   [50]
Neretum, a city where Sallentines lived,   80
Sybaris, Tarentum (a Spartan settlement),
the bay of Siris, Crimisa, and fields
of Iapygia.[1] Once he had he passed
these lands that overlook the sea, he found
the Aesar estuary, his destined home,
and close beside it a burial mound
which covered Croton's sacred bones. So here,
Myscelus built his city, naming it
after the man who had been buried there."

This was the way the city first began,   90
according to the best-received traditions,
and the reason it was built in Italy.

---

[1] Amphitryon was king of Thebes and married to Alcmena, the mother of Hercules. However, the real father of Hercules was Jupiter. The Ionian Sea is between Greece and southern Italy. Myscelus is moving around the heel of Italy and up the west coast towards Latium. The series of names refers to people and places near or on the coast of southern Italy.

Book Fifteen

There was a man living in Crotona [60]
called Pythagoras, who was born in Samos   PYTHAGORAS
but had fled that island and its rulers
and gone into exile of his own free will,
because he hated tyranny. In his thoughts
he visited the gods, although they lived
far off in distant regions of the sky,
and what nature has denied to human sight   100
his mind could see. Once he had scrutinized
all things with his inner eye and studied
them with care, he made his knowledge public
and taught his silent audience, who heard
and were amazed by what he had to say
about how the vast universe began,
about how things are caused, what Nature is,
what gods are, where the snows originate,
where lightning comes from, whether Jupiter
or wind makes thunder when clouds split apart,   110 [70]
what forces make Earth shake, what laws control
the motions of the stars, and everything
that lies hidden away from human sight.
He was the first one to complain about   VEGETARIANISM
wild beasts being killed and served for dinner,
the first to say things like the following
(judicious words, indeed, but not believed):

> "O you mortal beings, stop corrupting
> your own bodies with such defiling food.
> We have grain, apples weighing branches down,   120
> along with grapes which ripen on the vine.
> You can use fire to cook sweet-tasting plants
> and make them tender. There is no lack of milk
> or honey smelling of the fragrant thyme.   [80]
> Munificent Earth offers you her wealth,
> producing feasts of harmless things to eat,
> without the need for blood and slaughter.
> Some beasts feed on meat, but many do not,
> for horses, sheep, and cattle live on grass.
> Those whose temperament is wild and savage—   130
> Armenian tigers, raging lions, bears,
> as well as wolves—delight in blood-soaked meat.
> How wrong it is to feed our flesh with flesh,
> to fatten up our gluttonous bodies

by eating bodies, to let one creature live
by bringing death to other living things.   [90]
Is it really true that, with all this wealth
the Earth, the best of mothers, offers us,
nothing pleases you unless your savage teeth
can bring back the habits of the cyclops   140
and gnaw on pitiful wounds? Can you men
not satisfy the ravenous hunger pangs
inside your greedy and intemperate gut
unless you butcher other living things?

That earlier time, which we call Golden,
was happy with its harvests plucked from trees
and crops the earth produced. Men did not stain
their mouths with blood. Birds winged their way
in safety through the air, hares roamed unafraid   [100]
in open fields, and fish were not hauled up   150
on hooks because they were so credulous.
There was no treachery in anyone,
no fear of fraud. All things were filled with peace.
Then someone, whoever he was, acting
against the common good, was envious
of what the lions ate, and stuffed raw meat
into his greedy stomach, thus opening
the road to crime. It may well be the case
that at the start men's gory swords grew hot
from slaying animals, but that's all right,   160
for I concede that men may kill those beasts
intent on killing them. That is no sin.
But while such creatures may be put to death,   [110]
it is not right for men to eat them, too.

From that time on the wickedness spread further.
The pig is thought to be the first wild beast
men felt deserved to die, for its broad snout
dug up the seeds and killed the hoped-for harvest.
And then men led the goat away to die
on Bacchus' altars, as a punishment   170
for chewing on his vines. And so the harm
these animals went through was their own fault.
But what have sheep done to deserve the same?
O you peaceful flocks, born to serve mankind,
you bear sweet milk for us in your full udders

and grow the wool from which we make soft clothes.
Your life serves us so well, more than your death.
What have oxen done, simple, harmless beasts, [120]
without fraud or deceit, and born for toil?
That man is truly an ungrateful wretch, 180
unworthy of the gift of harvest grain,
who, after he has just relieved his ox
by freeing it from the heavy, curving plough,
can kill the creature who has tilled his fields,
hacking its worn down neck with his sharp axe,
when with its help he has so many times
worked hard to open up hard earth and sow
so many harvests. Even crimes like this
are not enough, for men involve the gods
in their own wickedness when they believe 190
that killing toiling cattle brings delight
to higher powers in heaven! A victim
of outstanding beauty, without a flaw [130]
(its pleasing looks make it a sacrifice),
adorned with gold and garlands, is led out
before the altars. In its ignorance,
it hears the praying priest and sees him shake
the grain it helped produce across its forehead,
between the horns. And when the beast is struck,
its blood then stains the knives which earlier 200
it may have seen reflected in still water.
Next, while the animal is still alive,
its lungs are quickly ripped out from its chest,
and priests probe into them to ascertain
what gods may be intending . And after this,
(the human craving for forbidden food
has so much force) you dare to eat that meat,
you race of mortal men! Do not do this,
I beg you, and keep my admonitions [140]
in your mind! Know and understand this well: 210
when you put the meat of slaughtered cattle
in your mouths, the food you are devouring
is flesh from those who labour on your land.

And since a god is urging me to speak,
I will follow, as I should, the deity
who moves my lips and tell you what I know
of Delphi and of very heaven itself.

Book Fifteen

The oracles of a majestic mind
I will unlock and sing of mighty things
left unexplored by previous intellects
and long concealed. It pleases me to move
among the lofty stars, and I delight
in leaving earth and this dull home behind
to ride up on the clouds and stand up there
on mighty Atlas' shoulders looking down
on men from far away, as they scurry
everywhere, with no good sense or reason,
and to unfurl for them the scroll of fate
and comfort them in their anxiety
and fear of death, by speaking words like these:

> 'O race of men, so stricken by your dread   IMMORTALITY OF THE SOUL
> of icy death, why do you fear the Styx,
> and shadows of the dead and empty names,
> the stuff of poets, the terrors of a world
> which is not there? For you should not believe
> these bodies of ours, whether destroyed
> by funeral fires or ravages of age,
> can suffer any further injuries.
> For souls do not die. Once they depart   METEMPSYCHOSIS
> an earlier dwelling place they always find
> new homes, and, once received in there, live on.
> I myself at the time of the Trojan war
> (and I remember this) was Euphorbus,
> a son of Panthous, whose chest was pierced
> by a heavy spear from Menelaus,
> a son of Atreus. Not long ago,
> in Argos, that city ruled by Abas,
> I recognized in Juno's holy shrine
> the shield I used to hold on my left arm!
> Each thing changes, but nothing ever dies.
> The spirit wanders, roaming here and there,
> and takes possession of a creature's limbs,
> whatever body it desires, passing
> from savage animals to human beings,
> from human beings to beasts, but spirits
> never are destroyed. Just as pliant wax
> shaped in a new form does not stay the same
> as what it was before or keep its shape,
> and yet in essence does remain the same,

so, according to the principles I teach, 260
our souls always continue on unchanged,
passing into various body shapes.
And thus, in case your stomach's appetite
overwhelms your natural affections,
I warn you: stop this wicked butchery
which drives the souls of your own relatives
out of their homes. Do not feed blood with blood.'

And now that I am being transported   CHANGES IN NATURE
over the great sea and have spread my sails
and filled them with the wind, I will go on. 270
Nothing in the whole universe persists.
Matter is always changing. Particular things
arise as transitory images,
and even time itself, like a river,
keeps flowing on with never-ending motion.
For like the running stream, the fleeting hour   [180]
can never stop. As one wave drives another,
chasing the one in front, while being pursued
by one behind, in just that way time's moments
run ahead and follow and are always new. 280
For what was once ahead is left behind,
what did not exist comes into being,
and every passing instant must give way
to some fresh instant. You observe how night
completes its course and passes into day,
how the light of dawn replaces darkness.
The colour of the sky is not the same
at midnight with all weary things at rest
and when bright Lucifer on his white horse
emerges. Its colour changes once again 290   [190]
when the herald of the day, Aurora,
paints the world she must hand on to Phoebus.
The Sun god's shield is red when it is rising
from underneath the earth and red once more
when sinking down below, but at its height
the shield is brilliant white, because up there
the aether is more pure and far removed
from earth's contagion. And Moon at night
cannot remain the same, keeping her shape
the way she was before—if on the wane 300

tomorrow she will be smaller than today,
and if her orb is waxing, she will grow.

Besides, have you not noticed how the year
travels through a sequence of four seasons,
and in this imitates the way we live? [200]
For early spring, with its new life, is tender
and full of juice, and very like a child.
Then the plants spring up, fresh but delicate,
not yet robust, and kindle farmers' hopes.
It is the time when all things are in flower. 310
In fertile fields the coloured blossoms dance,
but there is still no strength in any leaves.
As summer follows on the spring, the year,
now sturdier, displays his youthful strength.
No season is more vigorous or rich,
none glows with greater heat. Next Autumn comes,
all youthful passion spent, ripe and mellow,
in temperament halfway between our youth [210]
and our old age, his temples flecked with gray.
And then comes aged, trembling wintertime, 320
with tottering steps. He has lost his hair,
or else the hair he has is now quite white.

And our bodies, too, are always changing.
They never stop. Tomorrow we will not be
what we have been or what we are today.
There was a time when, early in our lives,
we lived inside our mother's womb as seeds,
mere hopes of mortal beings. Then Nature
put her skilful hands to work, refusing
to let our twisted bodies stay concealed 330
inside the belly of our swollen mother,
and sent us out into the empty air. [220]
Brought out into the light, the infant lies there,
helpless, but soon, just like a quadruped,
he moves his limbs the way wild creatures do,
and gradually, with something for support
to help his trembling sinews, he stands up
on shaky knees, not yet quite firm enough.
Then he grows strong and swift, passing through
his youthful stage, and soldiers on through years 340
of middle age, then glides along the path

of his old age, where life declines, a time
which undermines and saps the strength he had
in earlier years. Old man Milon weeps
to see his arms, once strong and muscular,
like those on Hercules, hang limp and scrawny.[1]
And Tyndarus' daughter Helen cries
to see an old crone's wrinkles in the glass
and wants to know why she's been ravished twice.
Devouring Time and you, hateful Old Age,   350
destroy all things. The teeth of passing years
gnaw everything to shreds, and gradually
you two swallow them all in a drawn-out death.

Even those things we call the elements   THE ELEMENTS
do not remain the same. Focus your minds,
for I will show the changes they go through.
The everlasting universe contains
four substances which generate all things.
Two of these, earth and water, are heavy   [240]
and sink down from the force of their own weight.   360
The other two, air and fire (which is
more rarefied than air) lack any weight.
If nothing holds them back, they try to move
up to the heights. Though these four elements
are distinct in space, all of them arise
from one another and resolve themselves
back into one another. When earth breaks down,
it liquefies and turns into clear water,
water, once it becomes less dense, changes
into wind and air, and when air loses weight   370
and turns into the subtlest element,
it flashes out as high aetherial fire.
Then in reverse order, they all go back,
traversing the same stages as before—
fire grows more dense, turns into heavy air,   [250]
air changes into water, and water,
as it grows more dense, changes into earth.

And nothing retains its shape. For Nature,
who renews all things, keeps recreating
one form from another. And, believe me,   380

---

[1] Milon was a citizen of Crotona famous for his great strength.

nothing in the entire universe can die,
but things do alter, changing how they look.
What men call 'being born' is just the start
of turning into something different
from what was there before, and 'dying'
means ceasing to remain in the same form.
Though this thing may perhaps change into that,
and that to this, the total sum of things
remains unchanged.

                  For my part, I believe   GEOLOGICAL CHANGES
nothing retains the same appearance long.   390
Thus, the ages passed from Gold to Iron,   [260]
and many times the fortunes of a place
have been upended. I myself have seen
what once was solid earth turn into sea
and looked at land created from the waves.
We notice sea shells lying far from shore,
and on a mountain summit men have found
an ancient anchor. A flow of water
creates a valley where there was a plain,
floods have carried off and flattened mountains,   400
swampy areas have changed to arid sand,
and thirsty lands to stagnant marshy pools.
In one place nature opens up fresh springs,   [270]
while in another closing off their flow.
Rivers may burst forth, disturbed by tremors
deep inside the earth, or they may dry up
and disappear. Thus, the river Lycus,
once swallowed by a chasm in the earth,
is reborn from a new source and flows on
far away. The mighty Erasinus   410
in one place is pulled down, flows underground,
and emerges once again in Argos.[1]
They say the river Mysus grew ashamed
of his first source and his original banks
and now, as the Caïcus, flows elsewhere.
The Amenanus, too, in Sicily,
can sometimes flow so fast it churns up sand,

---

[1]Lycus was the name of a river in Lydia. Erasinus was a river in Arcadia which disappeared and then re-emerged.

but then at other times its sources stop,
and it dries up. The river Anigrus,
which in earlier days was fit to drink,
now flows with water you would never touch,
not since the time the centaurs used that stream
to wash the wounds inflicted by the bow
and club of Hercules (unless, of course,
we stop believing all tales poets tell).
Is it not true the river Hypanis,
born in the Scythian hills, once tasted sweet,
but has been ruined now with acrid salt?[1]

Antissa, Pharos, and Phoenician Tyre
at one time were surrounded by the sea.
None of these cities is an island now.[2]
Inhabitants of Leucas long ago
worked in fields connected to the mainland.
The place is now encircled by the sea.
Zancle, too, they say, was linked to Italy,
until the sea destroyed the boundary
and waves flowed in to carry off the land.[3]
If you look now for Helice and Buris,
once Achaean cities, you will find them
buried in the waves, and sailors, even now,
like to point out these inundated towns
with walls beneath the sea.[4]

      Near Troezen,
where Pittheus was king, there is a mound,
steep and bare of trees, which some time ago
was the most level part of the whole plain.
Now it is a hill. How this came to be
is a strange tale. Fierce and powerful winds

---

[1] The Hypanis river flowed into the Black Sea.

[2] Antissa was an island in the Aegean, thought to have once been a part of Lesbos. Pharos had been an island off the Egyptian coast, until soil deposited by the Nile joined it to the mainland. Tyre, a city in Asia Minor, had been built on an island. Now it was part of the mainland.

[3] Leucas had been a peninsula on the coast of Acarnania. Zancle was a coastal city in Sicily on the strait separating Italy and Sicily.

[4] Helice and Buris, cities on the coast near Corinth, were destroyed by an earthquake and flooded by the sea. Their ruins could be seen under the water.

shut up in hidden caverns wished to find
some outlet for their gales and vainly fought
to enjoy the open sky. But their blasts
had no way out, for in their prison cell
there were no cracks at all. And so those winds
put pressure on the ground and made it swell,
the way our human breath inflates a bladder
or the skin of a horned goat. After that,
the swelling stayed and, as the years went by,
it hardened, so it looks like a steep hill.

Though many more examples of such things   PROPERTIES OF WATER
occur to me from what I have been told
or learned about myself, I will list here
just one or two. Think of water. Does it not
take on and generate new forms, as well?
At noon the waters of horned Ammon's spring
are freezing cold, but when Sun is rising
or declining they grow warm.[1] People say
the Athamanians set fire to wood
by pouring water from this spring on it
when Moon has shrunk down to her smallest size.[2]
The Cicones live by a stream whose water,
once drunk, turns inner organs into stone
and, when it touches things, spreads over them
a layer of marble. The Crathis river
and the Sybaris (which is close to here,
near our own lands) can change a person's hair
and make it look like amber or like gold.[3]
Even more amazing are those rivers
capable of changing not just bodies
but even minds, as well. Who has not heard
of Salmacis, with its disgusting pools,
or of those lakes in Ethiopia
where anyone who drinks becomes insane
or falls into a deep and wondrous sleep?[4]
Whoever drinks from the Clitorian spring

---

[1] Ammon was a spring and lake in Libya.
[2] Athamanis was in Dodona, where Jupiter had an important shrine.
[3] Crathis was a river in Arcadia, and Sybaris a river near Crotona.
[4] For Ovid's account of why the Salmacis has disgusting waters, see above 4.418 ff.

avoids all wine and in his sober state
enjoys pure water. This may well take place
because there is some power in the water
which works against the warm effects of wine.¹
Those who live there give another reason—
after Melampus, Amythaon's son,
had with his spells and herbal potions saved   490
Proetus' raving daughters from the Furies,
he threw the medicines which purged their minds
into the spring, and that is why its waters
generate a strong distaste for wine.²
The flowing stream of the Lyncestius
has an opposite effect. Whoever
swallows some of it, even a small amount,
stumbles around, as if he had been drinking   [330]
unmixed wine.³ Arcadia has a place
(Pheneus was its name in earlier days)   500
whose waters are mistrusted, for they have
two different effects. During the night
you must beware, for then a drink does harm,
but in the day its water is quite safe.
Thus, various lakes and rivers can possess
quite different properties.

                       Ortygia,
once a floating island, is now fixed in place.⁴
Men on the Argo feared those clashing rocks,
the Symplegades, and the spray tossed up
by crashing waves. And now they do not move,   510
but stand fixed in place, defying the winds.
Mount Aetna, glowing with its furnaces   [340]
of blazing sulphur, will not always burn   MOUNT AETNA
and was not always burning in the past.
For if Earth is a living animal
with many passages that breathe out flames,

---

¹Clitorium was a town in the Peloponnese.

²Proetus was king of Argos. His daughters were driven mad by Venus for boasting of their beauty.

³Lyncestius was a river in Epirus.

⁴Ortygia is another name for the island of Delos. For Ovid's story of it as a floating island see Book 6.

then, every time she moves, she can remake
those breathing holes. She can seal some up
and open others. Or if rapid winds
imprisoned in deep caves hurl rocks together 520
with matter which contains the seeds of flame,
and friction causes Aetna to catch fire,
the caves will cool off once the winds calm down.
Or if the fires are blazing bitumen [350]
and yellow sulphur burning with less smoke,
surely, after many ages have gone by,
that rich supply of food the earth provides
will be used up and it will have no fuel
to feed the flames. Without the nourishment
their greedy nature craves, the flames will starve, 530
and, as they die, will starve Mount Aetna's fire.

They say that in Pallene, in those lands
beyond the northern winds, there are some men
who cover their skin with downy feathers
by plunging in Minerva's pool nine times.[1]
As far as I'm concerned, this is not true,
but people claim that Scythian women [360]
have spells to do this, too, by sprinkling limbs
with magic potions.

        But if what you believe   SPONTANEOUS GENERATION
relies on what experience can prove, 540
you must have seen that corpses when they rot,
because of time or melting heat, are changed
to tiny animals. We know full well
that if you take a sacrificial bull
and bury the tossed-out carcass in a ditch,
from every portion of the putrid entrails
flower-sipping bees will rise. And these bees,
just like the animal from which they spring,
live in the fields, love toil, and work with hope.
A war horse buried in the ground becomes 550
a source of hornets, and if you remove
a land crab's hollow claws and put the rest [370]
below the ground, from that buried part
a scorpion will emerge and threaten you

---

[1] Pallene was a mountain in Thrace.

with its hooked tail. As farmers have observed,
those grubs which cover leaves in country fields
with their white thread change into butterflies,
their shape transformed to emblems of the dead.¹
And mud contains the seeds that generate
green frogs, which, when they first appear, lack feet. 560
Soon it gives them legs well formed for swimming
and makes the back ones longer than in front,
adapting them to jump huge distances.
When she gives birth to young, a mother bear
does not produce a cub but a mere lump
of living flesh, barely alive. But then,
by licking it, she gives that lump its limbs [380]
and turns it into something with a shape
just like her own. And have you not observed
how grubs from honey bees which lie contained 570
in their hexagonal cells have bodies
but no limbs and how their legs come later
and then, even later still, their wings?

Who could imagine, if he did not know,
that Juno's bird, whose tail plumes carry stars,
and Jupiter's eagle with the lightning bolt,
and Venus' doves, and every race of birds
come into being from inside an egg?²

Some people claim that when the human spine
is buried in a tomb and rots, its marrow 580 [390]
is transformed into a snake.

              The elements   THE PHOENIX
of all these animals originate
from other species. But there is one bird
which reproduces and renews itself
all on its own. Those in Assyria
call it the phoenix. It does not live on grain
or grasses, but eats drops of frankincense
and balsam sap. And when this bird has lived
five centuries, it builds itself a nest

---

¹The butterfly was an emblem of the dead because its transformation from a worm into a flying creature reminded people of the escape of the soul from the body at death.

²Juno's bird was the peacock.

in a swaying palm tree, in the branches
at the very top, using its chaste beak
and claws. Then, after it has lined the nest
with bits of cassia, smooth ears of nard,
pieces of cinnamon, and yellow myrrh,
it sits down on the top and ends its life
in the perfumed air. And, so people say,
from the father's body a small phoenix
is reborn, destined to remain alive
for just as many years. When this bird's age
has made it strong enough to bear the weight,
it lifts the heavy nest from the high branches
and piously removes its father's tomb
and its own cradle, flying through the air
towards the city of the Sun, and there,
inside the temple of Hyperion,
it puts it down before the sacred doors.

If there is anything astonishing   STRANGE ANIMALS
in these strange events, we might well wonder
how hyenas can alternate their sex,
with a female who has just been mounted
by a male now becoming male herself.
Then, too, there is an animal which feeds
on winds and air. When it touches something
it at once takes on that object's colour.
Conquered India once gave its lynxes
to Bacchus, god of the grape-bearing vine.
Every time these beasts discharge their bladders,
so men report, the liquid turns to stone
which hardens from its contact with the air.
And coral, which, while underneath the waves,
remains a tender plant, grows hard, as well,
in just this way, when it is touched by air.

The day will end and Phoebus' weary horses   CIVILIZATIONS
will plunge into the sea before my words
can mention all those things that have been changed
into new forms. So with revolving time
we see some nations growing powerful
and others in decline. Troy, for instance,
which was so great in wealth and citizens
and for ten years could squander so much blood,

is now a humble ruin. Ancient stones
are all it has to show, and all its wealth
lies in ancestral tombs. And Sparta, too,
was famous once, great Mycenae flourished,
as did Athens, king Cecrops' citadel,
and Amphion's city, Thebes. But Sparta now
consists of worthless land, and proud Mycenae
has collapsed. What is Oedipus' Thebes
except a story? And Pandion's Athens—
what remains of that except its name? 640 [430]
Today the story goes Dardanian Rome ROME'S DESTINY
is growing and, close beside the Tiber,
which rises in the Apennines, building
an immense foundation to provide support
for mighty things. And with this kind of growth
the city's shape is changing. The day will come
when Rome will be the head of the whole world!
That, they say, is what the seers predict,
and those oracles which foretell our fate.
As I remember, when the Trojan state 650
was facing ruin and Aeneas was in tears,
anxious about the safety of his race,
Helenus, a son of Priam, said to him:

'Child of Venus, if you will take good note
of what I prophesy, while you are safe [440]
Troy will not fall completely! Fire and sword
will offer you a path, and you will go,
taking with you our plundered Pergamum,
until you reach a foreign place kinder
to you than your own native land of Troy. 660
Even now I see a city destined
for Phrygian posterity, a town
so mighty nothing like it now exists
or will exist, or has been seen before,
in earlier years. Through long centuries
other leading men will make it powerful,
but one man born from blood of Iülus
will make that city mistress of the world.
And when that leader's time on earth is done,
aetherial realms will welcome him with joy 670
and heaven will be his final dwelling place.'

My mind recalls how Helenus prophesied [450]
these matters to Aeneas, who carried
ancestral gods away from Troy. My heart
rejoices that city walls are rising
for his posterity, and I am pleased
the Greek defeat of Troy has led to this,
such a benefit to Trojans.

                               But now,
I must not wander too far off my course
and let my horses lose sight of the goal. 680
The heavens and everything below them
change their form. So does the earth, as well,
and all things it contains. We mortals, too,
part of the universe, are not mere flesh,
but souls with wings, and thus we can create
a home inside the bodies of wild beasts
or settle in the hearts of our own cattle.
And therefore, we should allow those bodies
which could well contain the souls of parents,
brothers, or others linked to us somehow, 690 [460]
or human beings, at least, to rest safe
and undisturbed and not cram our stomachs
with food fit for Thyestes' dinner feast.[1]
How those men get used to evil actions
and, in their impiety, prepare themselves
for spilling human blood, when with their knives
they slit a young calf's throat and, quite unmoved,
hear its mournful bleats, or slaughter a young goat,
which cries out like a child, or feed on birds
which they themselves have fed. When they do this, 700
how close are they to acting out real crimes?
Where do such actions lead?

                             Let oxen plough
or perish from old age. Let sheep provide [470]
protection from the freezing northern winds,
let well-fed she goats offer us their udders
for our hands to milk. Throw your nets away,
your traps and snares and your deceptive tricks.

---

[1] Atreus, father of Agamemnon, invited his brother, Thyestes, to a banquet of reconciliation, where he served Thyestes the cooked flesh of his own children.

BOOK FIFTEEN

Do not use twigs and lime to fool the birds,
or scare deer into nets with feathered rope,
or hide barbed hooks inside deceiving bait. [710]
Destroy what injures you, but even then
do nothing more than kill. Make sure your mouths
abstain from blood and eat more wholesome food!"

The story goes that when his mind had learned   NUMA AS KING
these and other teachings of Pythagoras,
Numa went back to his native city,
and there, by popular request, took up
the reins of power and ruled in Latium.   [480]
Blessed with his wife Egeria, a nymph,
and guided by the Muses, he brought in   720
sacrificial rites and trained his people,
who were familiar with ferocious war,
in the arts of peace. When, in ripe old age,
his life and reign were over, everyone—
Latian matrons, senators, and citizens—
all mourned the death of Numa. But his wife   EGERIA
moved from the city and hid herself away
in the dense valley forests of Aricia,
and there, with her groans and lamentations,
kept interfering with the sacred rites   730
worshipping Diana, which Orestes
first introduced into those wooded groves.[1]
O, how often the nymphs of lakes and trees   [490]
advised her to be quiet and spoke words
of consolation! And Hippolytus,   HIPPOLYTUS
brave son of Theseus, would say to her,
as she continued weeping:

                "You must stop.
You are not the only one whose fortunes
are a cause for grief. Consider others
who have gone through similar disasters,   740
and you will find yours easier to bear.
I wish I knew examples of such sorrow,
apart from mine, which could relieve your pain.
But even mine can help.

---

[1] According to some Greek and Latin traditions, Orestes, Agamemnon's son, had brought the worship of Diana/Artemis from Taurus into Italy and set up a shrine in Aricia.

BOOK FIFTEEN

               Perhaps your ears
have picked up stories of Hippolytus—
how he met his death because his father
was so credulous and his stepmother
so evil and deceitful. You will find
my words astonishing—it will be hard
for me to prove the things I say. But still,   750
I am Hippolytus. Some time ago,   [500]
Phaedra, the daughter of Pasiphaë,
tried to seduce me into dishonouring
my father's bed.[1] When she did not succeed,
she accused me of the criminal act
she herself desired (she may have done that
more through fear of being found out herself
than through her rage at being rejected).
So I was charged. Though I was innocent,
my father ordered me to leave the city   760
and, as I left, rained down hostile curses
on my head. I went off into exile
in my chariot, intending to reside
in Troezen, a city ruled by Pittheus.
While I moving past the shore near Corinth,
the sea rose up. A huge amount of water
seemed to curl and grow into a mountain
which bellowed and, at the very summit,   [510]
shot up spray. Then that seething mass of sea
spat out a bull with horns. It just stood there, 770
in the gentle breezes, chest above the waves,
its gaping mouth and nostrils vomiting
great quantities of sea. My companions
felt terror fill their hearts, but I remained
quite unafraid, my mind preoccupied
with thoughts of exile. But my fierce horses
turned their necks towards the sea and trembled,
ears erect. Frightened by that monstrous bull,
they panicked and dragged the chariot down the rocks.
My hands tried hard to gain control but failed. 780
I pulled the reins, now white with flecks of foam,
and leaned out backwards to take up the slack.   [520]

---

[1] Pasiphaë was the wife of Minos, king of Crete. She was notorious for having sex with a bull and giving birth to the Minotaur. See above 8.212 ff.

Book Fifteen

I might have reined those maddened horses in,
but one of the wheels collided with a stump,
right on the axle hub where it spins round.
The wheel broke off and shattered. I was tossed
clear of the chariot, my arms entangled
in the reins. My living flesh was torn away,
while my body was still skewered on the wood.
Some of my limbs were pulled right out, and some
stayed on the stump. With a loud snapping noise,
my bones broke off. You could have seen me there,
totally done in, breathing out my life,
with no part left which you could recognize,
and every part a single giant wound.
Now, nymph, can you or dare you still compare
your tragedy with mine?

                              I also saw
that kingdom where there is no light and bathed
my mangled body in Phlegethon's stream.
My life would not have been restored to me
without the power of healing potions
from Aesculapius, Apollo's son.
Thanks to his potent herbs and Paean's help,
I came alive once more, although this act
made Pluto angry. So Diana cast
dense fog around me, in case my presence
increased the rage he felt about my gift.[1]
To keep me safe and away from danger
when I was visible, the goddess added
years to my age and changed the way I look,
so I would not be known to anyone.
Then, for a long time Diana wondered
whether she should make my home in Delos
or in Crete but in the end rejected both
and placed me here. She also ordered me
to cast aside my name, which could arouse
ideas about the horses I had owned.

790

[530]

800

HIPPOLYTUS AND DIANA

810

[540]

---

[1] Paean is a common name for Apollo.

BOOK FIFTEEN

'You, who used to be Hippolytus once,
must now be Virbius!'[1]

                From that time on,
I have lived as one of the minor gods   820
within this grove, where I remain concealed
under the sacred power of Diana,
my mistress, to whom I am now linked."

But disasters other people suffered
could not relieve Egeria's discontent.
At the foot of a mountain she lay down,
dissolving in her tears, until Diana,
moved by Egeria's loyal sorrow,
transformed her body to an icy spring   [550]
and made her limbs an ever-flowing stream.   830

This remarkable event amazed the nymphs.   TAGES
Hippolytus, too, an Amazon's son,
was no less astonished than that ploughman
in Tyrrhenian fields when he first saw
a fateful lump of earth begin to move,
all on its own, with no one touching it.
The clod soon lost its earth-like form and changed
so it looked like a man. Its new-formed mouth
then opened to reveal man's future fate.
The natives called him Tages, the first one   840
to teach Etruscan people to foresee
what was to come.

                And Romulus, as well,   ROMULUS' SPEAR
was equally surprised when he once saw
his spear sticking in the Palatine hill   [560]
suddenly sprout leaves and stand fixed in place,
held there by new roots, not by its iron point
which he had driven in the ground, for now
his weapon had become a hardy willow,
offering those who looked on in amazement
its unexpected shade.

                Praetor Cipus   850
was astonished, too, when he saw his face   CIPUS

---

[1] The first part of Hippolytus' name comes from the Greek word for *horse*.

515

reflected in the waters of a stream,
for he saw he had grown horns.¹ At first,
thinking the image was a mere illusion,
he touched his forehead, then touched it again.
His fingers felt the horns which he had seen.
Now he could no longer blame his eyesight.
At that moment, he was on the march back home,
having prevailed against his enemies.²
So he stopped, raised his eyes up to the sky,   860   [570]
stretched his arms out in the same direction,
and cried:

        "O you gods in heaven above,
no matter what this omen indicates,
if it is auspicious, may it benefit
my native land and Quirinus' people,
but if disaster threatens, let that be
for me alone."

              He built a grassy altar
of green turf and sought to appease the gods
with burning fires of incense. He offered
bowls of wine and had the trembling organs   870
of slaughtered sheep inspected to find out
what they might indicate about his future.
Once the Etruscan seer peered into them,
he saw at once the signs of something great,
though not yet clear. But when his watchful eyes
glanced upward from the entrails of the sheep   [580]
and saw the horns on Cipus, he cried out:

   "Hail to you, O king! For to you, Cipus,
and your horns this place and every citadel
in Latium will pledge obedience.   880
But you must not delay. With all speed
you must go in the open city gates.
So Fate commands. For once the people there

---

¹The Praetors were important civic officials and military leaders in Rome.

²In Ovid's time the Roman state was still nominally a republic and the notion of a having a king was repugnant. Although Augustus was de facto emperor, he was careful to maintain many of the outward trappings of republican Rome.

have welcomed you, you will become their king
and safely hold the everlasting throne."

Cipus stepped back. Turning his stern features
from the city walls, he said:

> "May the gods
> drive all such prophecies a long way off—
> far, far away! It would be much better
> to spend my life in exile than to have
> the Capitol see me enthroned as king."

He said this and immediately summoned
the people and distinguished senators
to an assembly. But first he wrapped his horns
with laurel symbolizing peace, then stood
upon a mound raised by his brave soldiers,
offered up prayers to the ancient gods,
as was their custom, and said:

> "With us here
> there is a man who will become our king,
> unless you expel him from the city.
> I will not name him, but I will tell you
> a sign that indicates just who he is.
> On his forehead he has horns! The seer
> predicts that if this man comes into Rome
> the laws he makes will turn you into slaves.
> He could have entered through the open gates,
> but I prevented him, despite the fact
> that no one is more closely linked to him
> than me. Romans, you must make sure this man
> stays outside the city. If he deserves it,
> bind him in heavy chains or end all fear
> by sending the destined tyrant to his death."

There was a murmur from the crowd, like the sound
of lofty pines trees when raging East Wind
whistles through their leaves or like ocean waves
when heard from far away. Amid the sounds
of that confused and noisy crowd, one voice
cried out:

> "Which one is he?"

Book Fifteen

                    Those in the crowd
looked at each other's foreheads, trying to find
the horns he had predicted would be there. 920
Then Cipus addressed the crowd once more:

"That man you're looking for—you'll find him here."

Then he removed the wreath around his head, [610]
though some men tried to stop him, and displayed
the two horns clearly growing from his head.
The whole crowd groaned and lowered its eyes.
Who could believe that people would not wish
to gaze at such a famous and deserving head?
No longer able to watch him standing there
without a tribute to his honour, they placed 930
a festive garland on his head. And then,
Cipus, since you were not allowed to pass
inside the city walls, they honoured you
with land, as much as you could move around
from dawn to sunset, with a team of oxen
harnessed to the plough, and on bronze pillars
by the city gates they carved a pair of horns, [620]
a lasting symbol of that miracle
which would remain through ages yet to come.

And now, you Muses, divine presences 940
who attend on poets, since you know the past   AESCULAPIUS
and vast extents of time cannot mislead you,
reveal to us where Aesculapius,
the son of Coronis, came from and why
that island which deep Tiber flows around
made him a part of sacred rituals
in Romulus' Rome.

                    Once, long ago,
a foul disease infected Latian air,
and people's pallid bodies were destroyed
by a sickness which siphoned off their blood. 950
When they realized, after so much death,
that human efforts were of no avail
and their healing skills were ineffectual,
they looked to the heavenly gods for help, [630]
travelling to the centre of the world,
the oracle of Phoebus built in Delphi,

praying to the god for his assistance
in their distress, asking for some remedy
to make them healthy once again and end
the evils plaguing so great a city. 960
The ground, the laurel tree, and the quivers
belonging to the god himself, trembled,
all together, and from the deepest place
within the shrine, the tripod spoke these words
and shook their fearful hearts:[1]

                "What you seek here,
Roman, you might have looked for in a place
nearer where you live. Now go and seek it
closer to your home. The help you ask for
will not come from Apollo but his son.
The omens are propitious, so go now 970
and summon Aesculapius to help."[2] [640]

The prudent Senate heard the god's command,
then, in their deliberations, enquired
about Apollo's youthful son, to learn
the city where he lived, and sent out men
to follow the winds to Epidaurus.[3]
As soon as their curved ship had touched the shore,
the men who had been sent at once approached
the elder statesmen in the Grecian council
and urged the Greeks to let them have the god 980
who by his presence might end the disease
which was destroying people in Ausonia,
for that was what Apollo's oracle,
the voice of truth, had said. Among the Greeks,
the various opinions were divided.
Some believed they should not withhold their help,
but most men argued they should keep the god
and not give up what now belonged to them, [650]
or let other men sail off with their own gods.
While this debate wore on, as the evening 990
pushed away the waning light and darkness

---

[1] The priestess who uttered the response sat on a tripod deep inside the shrine of Apollo.

[2] Aesculapius was the son of Apollo and Coronis. For details of his birth, see 2.929 above.

[3] Epidaurus is a city in the Peloponnese.

covered earth in shadows, the Roman envoy,
fast asleep, seemed to see the healing god
standing beside his bed. In his left hand
he gripped a rustic staff, while with his right
he stroked his lengthy beard, the way he looks
in his own temple. The words he uttered
were full of reassurance:

      "Do not fear.
I will leave my images here and come.
Gaze upon this serpent folding itself   1000
around my staff and note the features well,   [660]
so you can recognize it. I will change
into this serpent, but in a larger form
and look as huge as celestial bodies
should be when they change their shape."

      His voice stopped,
and, when it did, the vision disappeared.
With them sleep fled, as well, and, as it went,
the gentle light of day arrived. Once dawn
had scattered fiery stars, the civic leaders,
still unsure what they should do, assembled   1010
at the splendid temple of the very god
the Romans wished to take, prayed to him,
and asked him for some heavenly signal
to indicate where he might wish to live.
They had barely finished praying when the god,
a golden serpent with its crest erect,
gave out a hiss to announce his presence,   [670]
and, as he entered, made his statue shake,
as well as altars, doors, marble paving stones,
and gilded pediments in the temple roof.   1020
He halted in the middle of the shrine,
reared up chest high and gazed around the crowd,
eyes flashing fire. The people gathered there
were paralyzed with terror, but the priest,
a white band holding down his sacred locks,
recognized the presence of the god
and cried:

      "It is the god! Behold the god!
Let all those present keep pure tongues and minds.
Most beautiful one, may we look on you

and prosper, and may you help all people
who observe your sacred rites!"

                    Those in the shrine
adored the god as the priest had ordered,
echoing his words. And the Romans there
with voice and heart showed reverent respect.
The god nodded and, as he moved his crest,
confirmed his favour with a triple hiss
and a flickering tongue, then glided down
the gleaming stairs. About to move away,
he turned his head for one last final look
at his ancient altars and nodded farewell
to the familiar sanctuary and shrine
which had been his home. Then the huge serpent
moved away, slithering across the ground
now strewn with flowers, winding his coils,
gliding through the middle of the city,
to the crescent spit around the harbour.
Here he stopped and with a calm expression
seemed to dismiss the crowd of worshippers
who dutifully followed in his train.
Then his body moved into the Roman ship,
which felt the heavenly load, as his weight
forced it to settle further in the sea.
Aeneas' descendants were overjoyed.
They sacrificed a bull beside the shore,
then loosed the twisted cables on their ship,
all wreathed in garlands, and gentle breezes
pushed the vessel through the sea. Arching up,
the god placed his neck on the curving stern,
pressing it down, and gazed at the azure waves.
Fair winds blew him across the Ionian Sea
and, as Aurora rose on the sixth day,
the god arrived in Italy, passing
Lacinium's coast, with Juno's famous shrine,
and Scylaceum's coast, then sailing on
past Iapygia, rowing around
the rocks of Amphrisia on his left,
while passing steep Cocinthia on the right,
then moving by Romethium, Caulon,
and Narycia, through Pelorus' strait
in Sicily, then past the dwelling place

Book Fifteen

of Aeolus and mines of Temese,
moving by Leucosia and Paestum,
with fields of roses.¹ He sailed past Capri,
Minerva's headland, the fertile vineyards
on Surrentum's hills, Herculaneum, [710]
Stabiae, and Parthenope, a place
created for idleness and leisure,
past the Sibyl's shrine at Cumae, and from there
to Baiae's thermal pools and Liternum,
with rows of mastic trees, Volturnus' stream, 1080
whose waters bear huge quantities of sand,
and Sinuessa, where the white doves fly,
Minturnae's marshes, full of pestilence,
Caïeta, whose name comes from the nurse
Aeneas buried there, and then the home
of Antiphates, and swampy Trachas,
to Circe's land and Antium's firm shore.
The sailors steered their ship, still under sail,
towards the beach, for the sea was restless. [720]
The god unwound his coils, fold after fold, 1090
and his huge arching body glided away
towards his father's temple close to shore.
Then, once the seas grew calm again, the god
from Epidaurus left Apollo's shrine,
where his own father's hospitality
had brought him joy, dragging his raspy scales
and ploughing furrows in the level sand,
climbed on board by sliding up the rudder,
and settled his head on the lofty stern.
There he stayed until the ship reached Castrum 1100
and Lavinium's sacred shrines and sailed
to where the Tiber's waters meet the sea.
All the people from every side rushed down
to meet the god, hordes of men and women,
along with those who tend your sacred fires,
O Trojan Vesta.² Every person there [730]

¹The names here refer to coastal towns in southern Italy. Ovid is again describing a voyage around the toe of Italy, through the Strait of Messina, and up the west coast towards Rome.

²The Vestal Virgins were important traditional religious figures in Rome, in charge of tending a sacred fire which was not allowed to go out and of looking after ancestral relics thought to have been brought to Rome from Troy.

hailed the god with shouts of joy. As the swift ship
made its way upstream, crackling incense burned
on rows of altars on both riverbanks,
filling the scented air with perfumed smoke,   1110
while sacrificial knives grew hot with blood
of slaughtered victims.

                    The god now entered Rome,
capital of the world. The snake reared up,
set his head on the summit of the mast,
and turned his neck, searching out a place
suitable for him to live. Where Tiber
splits into two streams flowing past a spot
they call the Island, with both arms branching   [740]
equally on either side, surrounding
dry land in the middle, the serpent god,   1120
a child of Phoebus, left the Latian ship,
resumed the form of his divinity,
and ended all their grief, for he came there
as one who would restore the city's health.

The god Asclepius was a foreigner   JULIUS CAESAR
who came into our shrines from far away.
But Caesar is a god in his own city,
a man preeminent in peace and war.
Still, it was not the battles that he fought
and finished with triumphant victories,   1130
or his achievements in affairs at home,
or the speed with which he won such glory,
that changed him to a brand new heavenly star
with a fiery tail, but rather his own son,   [750]
for of all great Caesar's deeds, the greatest one
was that he was the father of this man,
Augustus Caesar.[1] Yes, he overcame
that British race surrounded by the sea,
steered his victorious ships up seven mouths
of the papyrus-bearing river Nile,   1140
compelled those rebels in Numidia

---

[1] Julius Caesar was not the biological father of Octavius (later called Augustus), but his great uncle. In his will he adopted Octavius and made him his heir. Octavius fought on Caesar's behalf during the civil wars and, after Caesar's assassination, continued the struggle, finally emerging victorious in 31 BC. He went to become the first of the Roman emperors and changed his name to Augustus.

Book Fifteen

to follow Rome, along with Juba, too,
from Cinyps, and Pontus, swollen with pride
to hear the very name of Mithridates,
earned many triumphs, and enjoyed a few.[1]
But surely all these feats cannot compare
with being the father of a man so great?
With him in charge of our affairs, you gods
have shown great favour to the human race!
Thus, to make sure Augustus was not born
from mortal seed, Caesar had to be divine.
When the golden mother of Aeneas
thought of this and saw men were preparing
an armed conspiracy to bring about
the tragic death of Caesar, she grew pale
and kept repeating to every god she met:

> "Look at how they hatch their plots against me,
> using every kind of fraud to take the life
> of the only man who is still left for me
> of those who come from Trojan Iülus.[2]
> Am I to be the only one who cares
> about these troubles, which are all too real
> and come up all the time? I was the one
> wounded by that Calydonian spear
> of Diomedes. Then the walls of Troy
> and the wretched way they were defended
> brought me grief. I saw my son Aeneas
> driven out to wander far and wide, tossed
> by the sea, moving to the silent realm
> of shadows, and waging war with Turnus,
> or rather, if I speak the truth, with Juno.
> Why remember now the ancient sufferings
> my family went through? This present fear
> inhibits all my thoughts of earlier days.
> You see those lethal knives being sharpened!
> Stop those men, I beg you. Prevent their crime.

---

[1] Juba was king of Mauritania, in northwest Africa. He and the Numidians had supported Caesar's political opponents in Rome and were conquered. Caesar defeated the son of Mithridates, a famous king of Pontus, beside the Black Sea. A triumph was a large celebratory procession in Rome to mark an important military victory and was considered a rare honour.

[2] Iülus (also called Ascanius) was the son of Aeneas. The mother of Aeneas is Venus.

Book Fifteen

Do not let them extinguish Vesta's flame
with the blood of her own priest."[1]

                    With words like these,
Venus spoke about her anxious worries
throughout the heavens, but without success.
Gods were sympathetic, but could not break
the ancient sisters' iron rules of Fate.[2]
Still, they did give unambiguous signs

OMENS OF CAESAR'S DEATH

of future sorrow. Men talk of weapons
clashing high among black clouds, fearful blasts
from horns and trumpets pealing in the sky,
warnings in advance of the disaster.
The visage of the sun grew dark, as well,
and cast a pale light down on troubled earth.
People could often see torches blazing
in the middle of the stars, and often
drops of blood fell from the clouds. Lucifer
grew dim with rusty dark spots on his face,
the chariot of the moon had flecks of blood.
The Stygian screech owl shrieked mournful cries
in a thousand spots, an ominous warning.
In a thousand places, ivory busts
wept tears of sorrow, and, so men maintain,
chants were heard in sacred groves and with them
words of caution, No sacrifice revealed
a welcome omen. The inner organs warned
a major conflict was in store. They found,
among the entrails, livers with the top part
sliced away. In the forum, by men's homes,
and near the temples of the gods, dogs howled
all night and, so they say, the silent dead
roamed everywhere, while tremors shook the city.
But still, no omens from the gods could halt
the treacherous act or what Fate had in store.
Drawn swords were carried to the sacred house,
for no place in the city pleased those men
for their foul murder except the Senate.
Then Venus struck her breast with both her hands

---

[1] Julius Caesar, at the time of his death, held an important position as a priest in Rome.

[2] The ancient sisters are the three Fates.

and tried to hide that offspring of Aeneas
in a cloud which earlier had hidden Paris,
when she snatched him away from Menelaus,
the warlike son of Atreus, the same cloud
which covered Aeneas when he escaped
the sword of Diomedes.[1]

                      Jupiter,   JUPITER AND VENUS
her father, then said to Venus:

                        "My child,   1220
are you attempting on your own to change
immutable Fate? You are permitted,
as a goddess, to go inside the house
where those three sisters live. There you will see
huge tablets made of solid brass and iron   [810]
where everything is clearly written down.
These have no fear of heavenly thunder,
or lightning's rage, or any form of harm,
for they are safe throughout eternity.
You will find the fates of your descendants   1230
inscribed in everlasting adamant.
I myself have read them and remember.
And to ensure that you no longer stay
quite ignorant of what the future holds,
I will repeat them now.

                    This man Caesar,
for whom you are so anxious, Cytherea,
has lived out his time. The years allotted
to his life on earth are over. Now you,
together with his son, heir to his name,
will make sure great Caesar reaches heaven   1240
as a god and his people worship him.
And Caesar's son, all by himself, will bear
the heavy burden placed upon his back.   [820]
We will be with him when he goes to war
and seeks with utmost courage to avenge   ACHIEVEMENTS OF AUGUSTUS
his father's death. Under his leadership,
the walls of Mutina will be besieged,

---

[1] These two moments, when Venus rescues Trojan warriors from their battlefield opponents by hiding them in a cloud, are part of Homer's *Iliad*.

BOOK FIFTEEN

and fall, and sue for peace. Pharsalia
will come to know him well, and Philippi
will twice be soaked in Macedonian blood.   1250
Pompey's famous name will be defeated
in Sicilian seas, and Cleopatra,
a Roman general's Egyptian wife,
will place mistaken trust in marriage ties,
and fall, and render empty all her threats
that our own Capitol would be enslaved
by her Canopus.[1] But there is no need
for me to list barbarian races
and nations placed beside both ocean shores.
He will control all habitable lands   1260 [830]
and will be master even of the sea.
Once countries are at peace, his mind will turn
to civil affairs, and he will prove himself
a most just legislator through the laws
he will enact. By his own example
he will guide our morals, and with an eye
on future ages and generations
as yet unborn, he will order a child
born from his blessed consort, to take up
his own name and, with it, all his duties.[2]   1270
He will not come to his celestial home
and kindred stars, until, in his old age,
his years will rival those of ancient Nestor.[3]
In the meantime, take out Caesar's spirit   [840]
from his murdered corpse. Change it to a star,
so from his seat high in the sky, Julius,

---

[1] Mutina was a place in Gaul where Octavius won a battle against his major rival, Antony. Pharsalia in Thessaly was the site of a battle where Julius Caesar defeated his main rival, Pompey, and Philippi in Thrace was the site of a battle where Antony and Octavius defeated Brutus and Cassius, the main conspirators in the plot to murder Julius Caesar. Ovid treats the two famous battle sites as the same place. Pompey's son was defeated at sea near Sicily. The Roman general who married Cleopatra was Antony, who had been married to Octavius' sister. Canopus was a city in Egypt. Octavius defeated Antony and Cleopatra at the Battle of Actium in 31 BC, a victory which brought the civil wars to an end and left him in complete control of political affairs in Rome.

[2] Augustus took Livia Drusilla as his wife (she was married and pregnant at the time), and later adopted her son, Tiberius, and made him his successor.

[3] Nestor, king of Pylos, was famous for living a long time. There are some editorial difficulties with the Latin in this line.

now transformed into a god, may gaze down
upon our forum and our Capitol."

Jupiter had hardly finished speaking   VENUS AND JULIUS CAESAR
when gentle Venus, invisible to all,
stood in the centre of the Senate house,
snatched away the soul from Caesar's body,
now it had been freed, thus preventing it
from scattering in the air, and took it
up to the heavenly stars. As she moved,
she felt the soul catch fire and start to blaze.
She hurled it from her bosom, and it flew
high above the moon, dragging in its train
a tail of fire. Now a glittering star,   [850]
Caesar looks down at his son's splendid deeds,
confesses they are greater than his own,
and derives great joy from being surpassed.
And though the son forbids men to maintain   GLORY OF AUGUSTUS
his exploits should be praised more than his father's,
nevertheless, when people talk, his fame,
which in its freedom follows no commands,
prefers the son, even against his will,
and in this one matter disobeys him.
In the same way, mighty Atreus yields
his claim to glory to Agamemnon,
Theseus is greater than Aegeus,
Achilles so much more than Peleus,
and finally, to offer an example
worthy of both Caesars, father Saturn
is a lesser god than Jupiter, his son.
For Jupiter commands the citadels
high in celestial space and every realm
of the three-fold universe. Augustus
governs lands below. Each is a ruler   [860]
and a father, too. I pray to you gods
who accompanied Aeneas, for whom
sword and fire gave way, to our native gods,
to Quirinus, founder of our city,
to Mars, father of unconquered Romulus,
to Vesta, worshipped with the household gods
of Caesar, and along with Caesar's Vesta,
you too, Phoebus, living here among us,
and Jupiter, who from on high occupies

the fortress of Tarpeia, and other gods,
all the ones a poet is permitted
with piety and justice to invoke,
I beg you—let that day be slow to come,
postponed to well beyond our generation,
when Augustus will leave the world he rules
and move up to the heavens and, once gone,
will grant his favours to all those who pray.

My task is now complete. Here I end my work,
which neither Jupiter's rage, nor fire, nor sword,
nor gnawing time can ever wipe away.
Let that day which brings my tenuous life
to its allotted end come when it will,
its power will only kill my body.
The finer part of me will be borne up,
as an immortal, beyond the lofty stars,
and my name will never be forgotten.
Wherever the power of Rome extends
throughout the nations it has overcome,
I will be read. Men will celebrate my fame
for all the ages, and, if there is truth
in poet's prophecies, I will live on.

1320

[870]

OVID'S IMMORTALITY

1330

1340

Glossary and Index

The following list contains the more important names in Ovid's text. The numbers refer to the relevant book and line in the English text. The list normally includes only those references where we learn something about the name. Material in the footnotes or chapter summaries is not listed in the index. Where a name is mentioned several times in a short space, the reference indicates that with the letters ff. (e.g., 2.342 ff.), rather than listing each separate occurrence of the name.

As a guide to pronunciation, the spelling of each name includes spaces to indicate the syllabification and an accent to show where the stress falls. Opinions about pronunciation of Classical names sometimes differ. The following comments should clarify some of the practices I have followed.[1]

The letters *-eus* at the end of a name are almost always two syllables: (e.g., *Orpheus* is pronounced *Ór·phe·us*, *Pentheus* is pronounced *Pén·the·us*, and so on). The same rule holds for those names ending in *-aus* (e.g., *Menelaus—Me·ne·lá·us*).

Final vowels are pronounced by themselves, as in *Calliope* and *Penelope* (each four syllables) or *Achaea*, *Hecate*, and *Cybele* (each three syllables), although there are several exceptions, usually when the name has become quite familiar in English (e.g., *Crete, Palatine, Rome, Ganymede, Nile, Palestine, Sabine*, and so on). Where these exceptions occur I have placed (E) after the name, to indicate that the name is pronounced as it is in English.

In the text, a vowel with a diaeresis placed above it is pronounced in a separate syllable (for example, *Caïcus, Danaë,* and *Phaëton* all have three syllables). The names in the list do not include the dieresis, since the syllables are indicated with spaces.

---

[1] My guide to pronunciation in most cases has been John Walker, *A Key to the Classical Pronunciation of Greek, Latin, and Scripture Proper Names* (London 1830).

GLOSSARY AND INDEX

A·CHAÉ·A: a region in the northern Peloponnese, also used for Greece generally—(*Teiresias*) 3.780; (*worships Bacchus*) 4.900; 5.487; (*Arethusa*) 5.900; (*Achaeans cheer Jason*) 7.234; (*Minos*) 7.790; (*Theseus*) 8.428; (*drowned cities*) 15.439.

ACH·AE·MÉN·I·DES: one of Ulysses' comrades—(*his story*) 14.252 ff.

ACH·E·LÓ·US: a river god and river northwest of Corinth—(*daughters transformed*) 5.862; (*Theseus*) 8.860 ff.; (*Echinades*) 8.903 ff.; (*Perimele*) 8.927 ff.; (*story of Erysichthon*) 8.1139 ff.; 8.1364; (*Theseus*) 9.2 ff.; (*fights Hercules*) 9.12 ff.; (*loses horn*) 9.139 ff.; 9.157; 9.659.

A·CHÍL·LES: son of Peleus and Thetis—8.490; (*conceived*) 11.418; (*fights Cycnus*) 12.112 ff.; (*Menoetes*) 12.178 ff.; (*sacrifices to Pallas and feasts*) 12.238 ff.; (*Nestor*) 12.278; (*Neptune and Apollo*) 12.897 ff.; (*killed*) 12.1021 ff.; (*fame*) 12.1030 ff.; (*fight for his weapons*) 12.1052 ff., 13.1 ff.; (*links to Ajax*) 13.48; (*hidden on Scyros, tricked by Ulysses*) 13.265 ff.; (*conquests*) 13.279; (*body recovered*) 13.466 ff.; (*delay in joining the army*) 13.492 ff., 13.493; (*ghost appears*) 13.718 ff.; (*Hecuba's children*) 13.808 ff.; (*Memnon*) 13.935, 13.960; 15.1302.

Á·CIS: son of Faunus and Symaethis—(*Galatea*) 13.1191 ff.; (*transformed*) 13.1370 ff.

A·COÉ·TES: a Tyrrhenian worshipper of Bacchus: (*his story*) 3.878 ff.

A·CRÍS·I·US: king of Argos, father of Danaë, grandfather of Perseus—(*denies Bacchus*) 3.852, 4.901; 4.911; (*Perseus*) 5.376.

AC·TAÉ·ON: son of Autonoë, grandson of Cadmus—(*sees Diana*) 3.210 ff.; (*killed*) 3.342 ff.; 3.1095.

A·DÓ·NIS: son of Myrrha and Cinyras—(*birth*) 10.772 ff.; (*Venus*) 10.795 ff.; (*dies*) 10.1086; (*transformed*) 10.1109.

AE·A·CUS: son of Jupiter and Aegina, king of Aegina, father of Telamon and Peleus—7.743; (*Minos*) 7.749 ff.; (*Cephalus*) 7.793 ff.; (*describes the plague*) 7.810 ff.; 7.1356; (*in old age*) 9.698, 706; 13.39.

AE·É·TES: king of Colchis, father of Medea—(*Jason*) 7.12 ff., 7.172; 7.281.

AE·GÉ·US: king of Athens, father of Theseus—(*Medea*) 7.637; (*Theseus*) 7.663 ff.; (*Minos*) 7.713; 15.1301.

AE·GÍ·NA: a nymph, daughter of Asopus, also an island in the Saronic Gulf—(*in Arachne's tapestry*) 6.183; (*Minos*) 7.744 ff.; (*Cephalus*) 7.769; (*plague*) 7.811 ff.; (*Jupiter*) 7.958.

AE·NÉ·AS: mortal son of Venus and Anchises, prominent Trojan warrior—(*leaves Troy*) 13.998 ff.; (*Anius*) 13.1009 ff.; (*moves to Crete and through Ionian islands*) 13.1121 ff.; (*reaches Sicily*) 13.1154 ff.; (*Dido*) 14.111 ff.; (*continues voyage*) 14.123 ff.; (*Sibyl and Underworld*) 14.153 ff.; (*Achaemenides*) 14.267; (*Macareus*) 14.378; (*Caïeta*) 14.676; (*war in Latium*) 14.685 ff.; (*Evander*) 14.696; (*deified*) 14.885 ff.; (*Helenus*) 15.651; 15.1085; 15.1167; 15.1214; 15.1311.

AÉ·O·LUS: god of the winds—(*confines Boreas*) 1.384; (*Tisiphone*) 4.718; (*confines winds*) 4.981; (*incest of children*) 9.818; 11.681; (*Ceyx*) 11.872; 11.1140; (*Aeneas*) 14.131; (*Macareus*) 14.343 ff.; (*Aesculapius*) 15.1071.

AÉS·A·CUS: son of Priam and Alexirhoë—(*his story*) 11.1146 ff.; (*birth*) 11.1160; (*Hesperië*) 11.1164 ff.; (*transformed*) 11.1196 ff.; (*mourned*) 12.1.

AES·CU·LÁ·PI·US: son of Coronis and Apollo—(*birth*) 2.929; (*Ocyrhoë*) 2.950 ff.; (*Hippolytus*) 15.802; (*journey to Rome as a god*) 15.943 ff.

AÉ·SON: a Thessalian, father of Jason—(*Medea*) 7.265 ff., (*restored*) 7.403 ff.; 7.478.

GLOSSARY AND INDEX

AËT·NA: a volcano in Sicily—(*on fire*) 2.319; (*prison of the winds*) 4.982; (*holds down Typhoëus*) 5.559; (*Ceres*) 5.688; (*Daedalus*) 8.416; (*Telemus*) 13.1222; (*Polyphemus*) 13.1360, 13.1376; 14.2; 14.253; (*Polyphemus*) 14.293; (*Pythagoras*) 15.512 ff.

AG·A·MÉM·NON: king of Mycenae, leader of the Greeks at Troy—(*at Aulis*) 12.46; (*arms of Achilles*) 12.1059, 12.1065; (*at Aulis*) 13.304 ff.; (*dream from Zeus*) 13.358 ff.; 13.590; (*in Thrace*) 13.714; 13.721; (*Anius' daughters*) 13.1046; 15.1300.

A·GÉ·NOR: father of Europa and Cadmus—2.1274; 3.4; (*Juno's hatred*) 3.383; 3.471.

AG·LAÚ·ROS: daughter of Cecrops—(*Erichthonius and Pallas*) 2.826; (*Mercury*) 2.1102 ff.; 2.1171; (*Envy*) 2.1187 ff.; (*transformed*) 2.1218.

Á·JAX (1): son of Telamon—(*Hyacinthus*) 10.311; (*arms of Achilles*) 12.1060; (*presents his case*) 13.3 ff.; (*his ancestry*) 13.34; (*saves Ulysses*) 13.120 ff.; (*exploits against the Trojans*) 13.134 ff.; (*insulted by Ulysses*) 13.221 ff.; (*invulnerable*) 13.441; (*kills himself*) 13.631 ff.

Á·JAX (2): son of Oïleus, the "lesser" Ajax, from Locris—13.585; 14.715.

AL·CÍTH·O·Ë: daughter of Minyas—(*denies Bacchus*) 4.1 ff.; (*tells story*) 4.401 ff.; (*transformed*) 4.595.

ALC·MÉ·NE: daughter of Electryon, wife of Amphitryon, mother of Hercules—(*in Arachne's tapestry*) 6.181; 8.851; (*with Iole*) 9.443 ff.; (*giving birth*) 9.460 ff.; 9.625 ff.

AL·CÝ·O·NE: daughter of Aeolus, wife of Ceyx—7.635; 11.607; (*Ceyx*) 11.659 ff.; 11.845; 11.874; 11.881; 11.891; (*Juno*) 11.907; (*with Morpheus*) 11.1005 ff.; (*laments*) 11.1036 ff.; (*finds Ceyx's corpse and is transformed*) 11.1092 ff.; 11.1138.

AL·PHÉ·US: a river god and river near Elis in the Peloponnese—(*boils*) 2.361; (*Arethusa*) 5.758, 5.934 ff., 5.968 ff.

AL·THAÉ·A: daughter of Thestius, wife of Oeneus, mother of Meleager—(*revenge against Meleager*) 8.699 ff.; (*kills herself*) 8.831.

AM·PHÍ·ON: son of Jupiter, husband of Niobe, king of Thebes—(*music*) 6.298; (*sons*) 6.370 ff.; (*kills himself*) 6.444; 15.636.

AN·AX·ÁR·E·TE: a well-born girl in Cyprus—(*Iphis*) 14.1070 ff.; (*transformed*) 14.1149 ff.

AN·CHÍ·SES: father of Aeneas—9.680; 13.1001; (*Anius*) 13.1024; 13.1082; (*ghost*) 14.181.

AN·DRÓM·E·DA: daughter of Cepheus and Cassiope—(*saved by Perseus*) 4.994 ff.; 4.1127.

ÁN·DROS: son of Anius, also an island ruled by him—(*Minos*) 7.738; 13.1037 ff.; (*gives in to Greeks*) 13.1054; 13.1061.

Á·NI·US: king of Delos—(*Aeneas*) 13.1011; (*children*) 13.1028 ff.; (*gifts, wine bowl*) 13.1080 ff.

A·Ó·NI·A: a region in Boeotia, in central Greece—1.456; 3.523; 6.2; 7.1200; 12.37.

A·PÓL·LO: divine son of Jupiter and Latona, twin brother of Diana, also called Phoebus and Paean, god of the sun—(*kills Pytho*) 1.643 ff.; (*loves Daphne*) 1.659 ff.; (*Cupid*) 1.661 ff,; (*chases Daphne*) 1.706 ff.; (*laurel tree*) 1.813 ff.; (*Phaëton's concerns*) 1.1108 ff.; (*palace of the Sun*) 2.1 ff.; (*Phaëton's request*) 2.31 ff.; (*grieves*) 2.477 ff., 2.550 ff.; (*Raven and Coronis*) 2.801, 2.889 ff.; (*Aesculapius and Chiron*) 2.929; (*cattle stolen*) 2.1006 ff.; (*Cadmus*) 3.15; (*Venus and Mars*) 4.246 ff.; (*Leucothoë*) 4.280 ff.; (*Typhoëus*) 5.523; (*in Arachne's weaving*) 6.200; 6.269; (*Latona*) 6.344 ff.; (*Niobe's sons*) 6.365 ff.; (*Marsyas*) 6.626 ff.; 7.617; (*Rhodes*) 7.578; (*Cephisus*) 7.617; (*walls of Megara*) 8.24; 8.48; (*Mopsus*) 8.556; (*Dryope*) 9.532; (*Cyparissus*) 10.196 ff.; (*Hyacinthus*) 10.243 ff.; (*Orpheus' head*) 11.87; (*Pan*) 11.237 ff.; (*punishes Midas*) 11.266 ff.; (*with Laomedon at Troy*) 11.294 ff.; (*Chione*) 11.479 ff.; (*Daedalion*)

GLOSSARY AND INDEX

11.539; 11.921; (*kills Achilles*) 12.901 ff.; 13.670; 13.812; (*Delos*) 13.1011; (*Andros*) 13.1039; (*Ambracia*) 13.1139; (*Sibyl*) 14.206 ff.; 15.803; 15.969; 15.983; 15.1094.

A·RÁCH·NE: a girl from Lydia—(*her weaving*) 6.9 ff.; (*Minerva*) 6.37 ff.; (*tapestry*) 6.166 ff.; (*transformed*) 6.214 ff.; (*Niobe*) 6.247.

AR·CÁ·DI·A: region in the central Peloponnese—(*Lycaon*) 1.312; (*Syrinx*) 1.1018; (*Callisto*) 2.590; (*dogs*) 3.313; (*Ancaeus*) 8.616; (*the boar*) 9.312; (*Pythagoras*) 15.499.

ÁR·CAS: son of Callisto and Jupiter—(*birth*) 2.689; (*Callisto*) 2.729 ff.; (*transformed*) 2. 741.

ÁR·DE·A: city in Latium—(*falls, burns, bird appears*) 14.871 ff.

AR·E·THÚ·SA: a nymph from Elis living Sicily—5.640; (*Ceres*) 5.757 ff.; (*her story*) 5.892 ff.; (*transformed*) 5.961 ff.

ÁR·GO·NAUTS: heroic crew of the Argo—6.1165; (*voyage*) 7.2; 7.17; (*Jason*) 7.189, 7.197; 15.508.

ÁR·GOS: city and region in the Peloponnese—(*Juno*) 1.887; (*dries out*) 2.347;. (*shuts out Bacchus*) 3.854; (*Perseus enters*) 5.374; (*meeting of cities*) 6.676; (*fame of Theseus*) 8.427; 15.247; (*Erasinus*) 15.412.

ÁR·GUS: a monster with a hundred eyes—(*Juno and Io*) 1.923 ff.; (*Jupiter*) 1.991 (*Mercury*) 1.1002 ff.; (*killed*) 1.1056 ff.; 2.788.

A·RI·ÁD·NE: daughter of Minos—(*Theseus*) 8.278 ff.; (*Bacchus*) 8.286.

AS·CÁL·A·PHUS: son of Orphne and Acheron—(*Proserpine*) 5.841; (*transformed*) 5.849.

AS·CÁ·NI·US: son of Aeneas (also called IÚLUS)—(*leaves Troy*) 13.1004; (*gift*) 13.1083; (*king*) 14.930.

AT·A·LÁN·TA (1): a girl from Tegea—(*Boar Hunt*) 8.502; (*Meleager*) 8.513 ff.; 8.600; (*boar's head*) 8.674.

AT·A·LÁN·TA (2): daughter of Schoeneus—10.848 ff.; (*Hippomenes and the golden apples*) 10.872 ff.; (*transformed*) 10.1060.

ÁTH·A·MAS: son of Aeolus, husband of Ino—(*Pentheus*) 3.861; (*Niobe*) 4.621; 4.692; 4.697; (*Tisiphone*) 4.722 ff.; (*goes mad*) 4.756 ff.

ÁTHENS: city in Attica—2.1064; (*Envy*) 2.1182; (*Ceres*) 5.1004; (*Triptolemus*) 5.1018; (*in Minerva's weaving*) 6.117; (*at war*) 6.688, 6.699; (*Tereus visits*) 6.731; (*Erectheus*) 6.1103; 6.1153; (*Medea*) 7.632; (*Theseus*) 7.642; 7.762; (*Cephalus*) 7.770 ff.; 7.1131; (*no tribute*) 8.421; (*Theseus*) 8.858; (*Eumolpus*) 11.141; 15.635; 15.639.

ÁT·LAS: giant son of Iapetus—2.429; (*Perseus*) 4.932 ff.; (*transformed*) 4.972; (*daughters of Phorcys*) 4.1150; (*Niobe*) 6.292; (*Hercules*) 9.439; (*Pythagoras*) 15.225.

AU·GÚS·TUS: Roman emperor in Ovid's time—1.286; 1.290; (*gates*) 1.827; (*his greatness*) 15.667; 15.1137 ff.; 15.1150; (*achievements*) 15.1242 ff.; 15.1293.

AU·RÓ·RA: goddess of the dawn—1.87; (*Phaëton*) 2.165; 2.210; 3.916; 4.933; 5.684; 6.82; 7.169; 7.339; (*Cephalus*) 7.1095 ff.; 7.1128; 7.1308; (*complains*) 9.672; 11.468; 11.926; (*Memnon*) 13.928 ff.; (*Jupiter*) 13.941 ff.; 13.994; 15.291; 15.1061.

AU·SÓ·NI·A—a region in southern Italy, also Italy generally—13.1127; 14.496; 14.1187; 14.1209; 15.982.

AU·TÓ·NO·E: daughter of Cadmus, mother of Actaeon—3.295; (*Pentheus*) 3.1094.

A·VÉR·NUS: place in Italy with access to the Underworld, also the Underworld generally—5.843; (*Orpheus*) 10.86; (*Aeneas*) 14.161 ff.

GLOSSARY AND INDEX

BÁC·CHUS: divine son of Jupiter and Semele, god of wine—(*birth*) 3.474; 3.485; (*Thebes*) 3.793 ff., 3.807 ff.; 3.874; (*with Acoetes*) 3.925 ff.; 3.1071; 3.1114; (*Alcithoë*) 4.4; (*tribute to*) 4.17 ff.; 4.399; 4.576; (*fame in Thebes*) 4.612; 4.633; (*Ino*) 4.773; (*fame*) 4.898; (*Acrisius*) 4.904; 4.913; 4.1140; (*Typhoëus*) 5.524; (*in Arachne's tapestry*) 6.206; (*Procne*) 6.975; (*Medea*) 7.413, 7.462; (*stolen bullock*) 7.568; (*Ariadne*) 8.286; (*Oeneus*) 7.439; (*avenges Orpheus*) 11.100 ff.; (*Tmolus and Silenus*) 11.126 ff.; (*Midas*) 11.151 ff., 11.203 ff.; (*Anius' daughters*) 13.1041, 13.1065 ff.; (*Pythagoras*) 15.170, 15.616.

BAÚ·CIS: wife of Philemon—(*her story*) 8.994 ff.; (*transformed*) 8.1119.

BEAR/BEARS: constellation in the northern sky—2.193; 2.250; (*Juno's anger*) 2.777; 3.70; 3.910; 4.926; 8.334; 10.688; (*on shield*) 13.485; 13.1159.

BOE·Ó·TI·A: region of central Greece—(*dries up*) 2.346; 3.23; 5.497; (*Iolaüs*) 8.492; (*Hercules*) 9.181; (*Hippomenes*) 10.891; (*Aulis*) 12.16; (*Therses*) 13.1086.

BÓ·RE·AS: the North Wind—(*moves north*) 1.91; (*locked*) 1.383; (*helps end the Flood*) 1.478; 2.270; 5.453; (*Orithyïa*) 6.1112 ff.; (*holds Greek fleet*) 12.36; (*urges fleet home*) 13.683.

BRONZE AGE: 1.173.

BÝB·LIS: daughter of Cyane and Miletus, sister of Caunus—(*born*) 9.726; (*her story*) 9.727 ff.; (*goes mad*) 9.1014; (*transformed*) 9.1053.

CÁD·MUS: king of Thebes, son of Agenor—(*founds Thebes*) 3.5 ff.; (*fights Serpent*) 3.40 ff.; (*sows Serpent's teeth*) 3.140 ff.; (*family troubles*) 3.199 ff.; (*Pentheus*) 3.861; (*Juno's hatred*) 4.696; 4.809; (*in exile*) 4.835 ff.; (*transformed*) 4.857 ff.; (*Niobe*) 6.298.

CAÉ·NE·US: son of Elatus—(*Great Boar Hunt*) 8.484; (*once a woman*) 12.269 ff.; (*made invulnerable*) 12.323; (*centaurs*) 12.708 ff.; (*Latreus*) 12.737 ff.; (*attacked by centaurs*) 12.763 ff.; (*transformed*) 12.809.

CAÉ·NIS: daughter of Elatus—(*raped by Neptune, changed to a man*) 12.295 ff.; 12.726.

CAÉ·SAR: (*Julius Caesar*) a prominent Roman politician and general—1.286; (*made a god*) 15.1127 ff., (*Jupiter*) 15.1235 ff.; (*star*) 15.1282 ff.; 15.1304; 15.1316.

CAI·É·TA: nurse of Aeneas and a place named after her—14.247; (*buried*) 14.674; 15.1084.

CAL·LÍ·O·PE: one of the nine Muses, mother of Orpheus—(*sings of Ceres*) 5.538 ff.; 5.1034.

CAL·LÍR·HO·E: daughter of Acheloüs, wife of Alcmaeon—(*asks for necklace*) 9.653; (*Jupiter*) 9.659; 9.692.

CAL·LÍS·TO: a nymph, daughter of Lycaon—(*Jupiter*) 2.595 ff.; (*Diana*) 2.648 ff.; (*Arcas*) 2.687; (*transformed*) 2.700 ff.; (*sees Arcas*) 2.735; (*a constellation*) 2.741; (*Juno's anger*) 2.777.

CÁL·Y·DON: a city in Aetolia—6.678; (*Theseus*) 8.430; (*Great Boar Hunt*) 8.433 ff.; 8.776; (*mourns Meleager*) 8.823; 8.1140; 9.4; (*Deïanira*) 9.241; (*city in Italy*) 14.783.

CÁ·NENS: wife of Picus—14.525 ff.; 14.586; (*transformation*) 14.639 ff.

CÁ·PI·TOL: important hill in Rome—1.825; 2.795; 15.891; 15.1256; 15.1278.

CAS·SI·O·PE: mother of Andromeda, wife of Cepheus—4.996; 4.1025 ff.; 4.1095.

CÁS·TOR: son of Tyndareus and Leda, twin brother of Pollux—(*Boar Hunt*) 8.480, 8.587; 12.624.

CAÚ·CA·SUS: a mountain and a region around the Black Sea—(*burns*) 2.327; (*Abaris*) 5.138; (*Hunger*) 8.1239.

CAÚ·NUS: son of Miletus and Cyane—9.725 ff.; (*Byblis*) 9.919 ff.; (*flees*) 9.1011.

GLOSSARY AND INDEX

CEN·TAURS: sons of Ixion, monsters with the head, arms, and torso of a human being and the body of a horse—(*Chiron*) 2.933 ff., 2.942; (*Nessus*) 9.164 ff.; 9.310; (*Lapiths*) 12.330 ff.; (*Hercules*) 12.835; 14.1025; 15.422.

CÉPH·A·LUS: husband of Procris—6.1110; (*Aeacus*) 7.773 ff.; 7.1038; (*spear*) 7.1047; (*Procris*) 7.1071 ff.; (*Aurora*) 7.1094 ff.; 7.1359; (*Athens*) 8.4.

CE·PHE·US: father of Andromeda—(*Perseus*) 4.993 ff.; 4.1095; (*at feast*) 5.20, 5.53, 5.73, 5.156.

CE·PHÍ·SUS: river in Phocis, father of Narcissus—(*Deucalion*) 1.536; (*Cadmus*) 3.31; (*Lirope*) 3.527; 7.616; (*Theseus*) 7.691.

CÉR·BE·RUS: three-headed dog guarding Hades—(*Juno*) 4.667; 4.739; (*venom*) 7.648; (*taken by Hercules*) 7.652; (*Hercules*) 9.302; 10.35; 10.104; 14.97.

CÉ·RES: sister of Jupiter, mother of Proserpine, goddess of the harvest and food generally—(*Calliope*) 5.543 ff.; 5.649; (*Proserpine*) 5.681 ff.; (*transforms a boy*) 5.704; (*Cyane*) 5.724 ff.; (*punishes Sicily*) 5.742 ff.; (*Arethusa*) 5.760 ff.; (*Jupiter*) 5.792 ff.; (*Arethusa*) 5.891 ff.; (*Triptolemus*) 5.1003; (*Lyncus*) 5.1031; (*Neptune*) 6.194; (*Eleusis*) 7.693; (*Oeneus*) 8.438; (*Erysichthon*) 8.1159 ff.; (*Hunger*) 8.1209 ff.; (*Iasion*) 9.675; (*festival*) 10.664.

CÉ·YX: son of Lucifer, husband of Alcyone, king of Trachis—(*Peleus*) 11.425 ff.; (*Daedalion*) 11.458 ff.; (*Chione*) 11.520; 11.557; 11.604; 11.610; (*his voyage*) 11.650 ff.; (*storm at sea*) 11.746 ff.; (*drowns*) 11.883; 11.895; 11.911; (*Morpheus*) 11.1004 ff.; (*his corpse*) 11.1110 ff.; (*transformed*) 11.1128.

CHA·RYB·DIS: a whirlpool between Sicily and Italy—7.109; 8.193; (*Aeneas*) 13.1164; 14.113.

CHI·MAÉ·RA: a monster made of up different animals—6.554; 9.1032.

CHÍ·O·NE: daughter of Daedalion—(*with Mercury and Apollo*) 11.475 ff.; (*Autolycus*) 11.493; (*Philammon*) 11.501; (*Diana*) 11.503 ff.

CHÍ·RON: son of Saturn and Philyra, the most famous of the centaurs—(*Aesculapius*) 2.933; (*Ocyrhoë*) 2.938; (*future life prophesied*) 2.964; 2.1004; (*Saturn*) 6.209; 7.559.

CIC·ON·ES: a people of Thrace—6.1152; 10.3; (*women attack Orpheus*) 11.4 ff.; (*punished by Bacchus*) 11.104 ff.; (*Pythagoras*) 15.469.

CÍP·US: a Roman general—(*his story*) 15.850 ff.

CÍR·CE: divine daughter of Helios and Perse—4.299; (*Glaucus*) 13.1506, 14.12 ff.; (*Scylla*) 14.60 ff.; (*Ulysses*) 14.382 ff.; (*Macareus*) 14.477 ff.; (*Picus*) 14.535 ff.; 14.667; 15.1087.

CLÝM·E·NE: mother of Phaëton, wife of Merops—1.1117, 1130; 2.49, 2.58; (*grieves for Phaëton*) 2.482; (*Heliades*) 2.514 ff.; 4.298.

CLÝT·I·E: daughter of Oceanus—4.300; (*her jealousy*) 4.344; (*transformed*) 4.375 ff.

CÓR·INTH: city in the Isthmus between the Peloponnese and mainland Greece, also called Ephyre—2.348; 5.638; 6.680; (*Medea*) 7.621; (*Hippolytus*) 15.765.

CO·RÓ·NIS: a girl from Larissa, mother of Aesculapius—(*Apollo*) 2.800 ff.; (*killed*) 2.887 ff.

CRETE (E): large island in the Mediterranean—(*Jupiter*) 3.3; (*dog*) 3.309; (*bull*) 7.685; (*Jupiter's birthplace*) 8.157; (*Scylla*) 8.188; (*Minos*) 8.243; (*Daedalus*) 8.297; (*Cretan bull*) 9.304; 9.1059; 9.1142; 91177; (*Hymen*) 10.1; 13.589; (*Aeneas*) 13.1124; 15.814.

CRÓ·TONA: city in southern Italy—(*Numa*) 15.12; (*Hercules*) 15.12 ff.; (*founded*) 15.88; (*Pythagoras*) 15.93.

CROW: daughter of Coroneus—(*Raven*) 2.807 ff.; (*Minerva*) 2.815 ff.; (*transformed*) 2.842 ff.

GLOSSARY AND INDEX

CÚ·MAE: a shrine on the coast of Italy—(*Aeneas*) 14.158, 14.242; 15.1078.

CÚ·PID: son of Venus, god of love—(*Apollo and Daphne*) 1.662 ff., 1.689; 4.469; (*Pluto*) 5.578 ff.; (*Medea*) 7.126; 9.874; (*Myrrha*) 10.474; (*Adonis*) 10.792; (*Venus*) 10.805.

CY·A·NE: a nymph—(*Pluto*) 5.641 ff.; (*transformed*) 5.664; (*Ceres*) 5.724; (*Miletus*) 9.720.

CỲB·E·LE: Near Eastern mother of the gods—(*Attis*) 10.158; 10.1041; 10.1055; 10.1069; (*Aeneas' ships*) 14.816 ff..

CY·CLOPS/CY·CLÓ·PES: one-eyed giants who make Jupiter's thunderbolts—1.379; 3.467; 13.1202; 13.1235 ff.; 14.4; (*Achaemenides*) 14.274 ff.; 14.384; 15.140.

CỲC·NUS (1): son of Sthenelus—(*grieves for Phaëton, is transformed*) 2.530 ff.; 12.896.

CỲC·NUS (2): son of Hyrië and Apollo—(*Philius*) 7.589 ff.; (*transformed*) 7.601.

CỲC·NUS (3): son of Canace and Neptune—(*fights Achilles*) 12.111 ff.; (*transformed*) 12.228; 12,261; 12.894.

CYL·LA·RUS: a centaur—(*his beauty*) 12.612 ff.; (*Hylonome*) 12.629; (*killed*) 12.653 ff.

CYL·LÉ·NE: mountain in Arcadia, associated with Mercury—1.310; 2.1075; 5.946; 7.612; 11.481.

CYP·A·RÍS·SUS: young boy of Cea—(*the stag*) 10.179 ff.; (*transformed*) 10.202.

CỲ·PRUS: island in the eastern Mediterranean—10.409; 10.812; 10.975; 10.1091; 14.1065.

CYTH·E·RÉ·A: another name for VENUS

DAE·DÁ·LI·ON: son of Lucifer, brother of Ceyx—(*his story*) 11.466 ff.; (*transformed*) 11.540 ff.

DAÉ·DA·LUS: an Athenian—(*labyrinth*) 8.255 ff.; (*Icarus*) 8.296 ff.; (*Perdix*) 8.379 ff.; (*in Sicily*) 8.415; 9.1188.

DÁ·NA·Ë: daughter of Acrisius, mother of Perseus—(*Perseus*) 4.908; (*Jupiter*) 4.1033; (*in Arachne's tapestry*) 6.182; 11.179.

DÁPH·NE: daughter of Peneus—(*Apollo*) 1.660 ff.; (*Peneus*) 1.705; (*transformed*) 1.806 ff.

DEI·A·NÍ·RA: daughter of Oeneus, sister of Meleager, wife of Hercules—8.850; (*fight over her*) 9.13 ff.; (*Nessus*) 9.169 ff.; (*Iole*) 9.229 ff.; (*sends shirt to Hercules*) 9.250.

DÉ·LOS: an island in the Cyclades—3.912; (*Latona*) 6.316, 6.543; 8.357; 9.533; (*Aeneas*) 13.1010; 13.1121; 15.813.

DÉL·PHI: important oracle in central Greece—1.758; 9.533; 10.251; 11.479; 11.657; 15.217; 15.956.

DEU·CÁ·LI·ON: son of Prometheus, husband of Pyrrha: (*survives the Flood*) 1.463 ff.; (*Themis*) 1.532 ff.; (*restores human life*) 1.582 ff.

DI·Á·NA: divine daughter of Jupiter and Latona, twin sister of Apollo, also called PHOEBE—1.697; 1.711; 1.1027; (*Callisto*) 2.605; 2.621; 2.645 ff.; (*Actaeon*) 3.238 ff.; 3.372; 4.446; (*fears Typhoëus*) 5.525; 5.593; (*Arethusa*) 5.963 ff., 5.993; (*Latona*) 6.269, 6.344 ff.; (*Niobe*) 6.472 ff.; 6.679; 7.1171; (*Calydonian Boar*) 8.434 ff.; 8.559; (*Meleager's sisters*) 8.847; 8.907; 9.147; 10.824; (*Chione*) 11.510; (*at Aulis*) 12.42 ff., 13.305; 14.514; 15.731; (*Hippolytus*) 15.805 ff.; (*Egeria*) 15.827.

DI·O·MÉ·DES: Greek warrior leader—(*arms of Achilles*) 12.1055; (*chides Ulysses*) 13.108; 13.165, 13.167; (*closeness to Ulysses*) 13.401; 13.575; (*Venulus*) 14.698 ff.; 14.755; 15.1165; 15.1219.

DIS: an alternative name for PLUTO—4.648; 4.754; (*shot by Cupid*) 5.606; 5.887.

DÓ·RIS: wife of Nereus, mother of the Nereïds—2.13; 2.387; 13.1181.

GLOSSARY AND INDEX

DRÝ·OP·E: daughter of Eurytus, sister of Iole—(*her story*) 9.529 ff.; (*transformed*) 9.561 ff.

EARTH: 1.16; (*formation*) 1.40 ff.; (*creation of human beings*) 1.113; (*abandoned by Astraea*) 1.207; (*produces new human life*) 1.218; (*the Furies*) 1.346; 1.358; (*the Flood*) 1.414; (*life after the Flood*) 1.606; 1.632; (*Pytho*) 1.638; 2.9; 2.18; (*Phaëton*); (*complains to Jupiter*) 2.392 ff.; (*in darkness*) 4.293; (*Pluto*) 5.661; (*Arethusa*) 5.765, 5.780; (*Niobe*) 6.311; (*produces armed men*) 7.212; (*Medea*) 7.320; (*Antaeus*) 9.299; (*on shield*) 13.483; 15.111; 15.125; 15.138; 15.515.

ÉCH·O: a nymph—3.546; (*Juno*) 3.556; (*Narcissus*) 3.568 ff., 3.754 ff.; 3.774.

E·GÉ·RI·A: a nymph, wife of Numa—15.719; (*mourns*) 15.726; (*transformed*) 15.825.

É·LIS: a city and region in the western Peloponnese—(*Apollo*) 2.1010; (*Arethusa*) 5.757, 5.769; 5.948; 8.489; (*Hercules*) 9.305; 12.847; (*games*) 14.504.

E·NÍ·PE·US: a river in Thessaly—1.849; (*Neptune*) 6.189; (*Medea*) 7.369.

ÉPH·Y·RE: old name for the city of CORINTH on the Isthmus—2.348; (*Medea*) 7.621.

ÉR·E·BUS: another name for the Underworld—5.847; 10.121; 14.622.

E·RÉC·THE·US: king of Athens—6.1105; 7. 680; 7.1088; 8.859.

ER·ICH·THÓ·NI·US: son of Vulcan—(*Pallas*) 2.816; 2.1131; (*age*) 9.677.

ER·Y·MÁN·THUS: a mountain and river in Arcadia—(*overheats*) 2.353; (*Arcas*) 2.734; (*Arethusa*) 5.948.

ER·Y·SÍCH·THON: (*daughter*) 8.1156; (*insults Ceres*) 8.1157 ff.; (*punished by Hunger*) 8.1263 ff.; (*eats himself*) 8.1359.

ETHIOPIA/ETHIOPIANS (E): region in northern Africa—(*Phaëton*) 1.1152; (*turn black*) 2.340; (*Perseus*) 4.991; (*royal feast*) 4.1136, 5.3 ff.; 15.480.

EU·BOÉ·A: island off east coast of mainland Greece—7.373; (*Lichas*) 9.354, 9.365; (*Greek fleet*) 13.299; (*Anius' daughters*) 13.1054; (*Glaucus*) 13.1416, 14.2; 14.243.

EU·RÓ·PA: daughter of Agenor, mother of Minos—(*Jupiter*) 2.1253 ff.; (*Juno*) 3.385; (*on Arachne's tapestry*) 6.166; (*Minos*) 8.37; 8.191.

EU·RÝD·I·CE: wife of Orpheus—(*Orpheus*) 10.12 ff.; (*dies again*) 10.78 ff.; (*reunited with Orpheus*) 11.93.

EU·RÝS·THE·US: king of Mycenae, son of Sthenelus—(*Hercules*) 9.328; 9.440.

FATES (E): daughters of Night, three goddesses who determine length of life—(*Ocyrhoë*) 2.949; 2.973 ff.; (*Actaeon*) 3.266; 3.837; (*Proserpine*) 5.831; (*Cephalus*) 7.1077; (*Meleager*) 8.711; 8.1219; (*Dryope*) 9.541; (*Orpheus*) 10.61; (*Venus*) 10.1098; (*Peleus*) 11.644; (*Ceyx*) 11.714; (*Achilles*) 12.1033; (*Troy*) 13.555; (*Aeneas*) 13.997; (*Sibyl*) 14.239; (*Picus*) 14.585; (*Hersilia*) 15.1297; (*home*) 15.1224 ff.

FURIES (E): goddesses of blood revenge—1.346; (*Juno*) 1.1069; (*Underworld*) 4.670 ff.; 6.703; (*Tereus*) 6.1080; (*Althaea*) 8.754; (*Alcmaeon*) 9.653; (*weep*) 10.74; (*Myrrha*) 10.476, 10534; (*Orpheus*) 11.22; (*Melampus*) 15.491.

GA·LÁN·THIS: servant of Alcmene—(*tricks Lucina*) 9.490 ff.; (*transformed*) 9.510.

GAL·A·TÉA: a Nereïd—(*Scylla*) 13.1175 ff.; (*Acis and Polyphemus*) 13.1190 ff.

GÁN·Y·MEDE (E): young prince of Troy—(*Jupiter*) 10.231 ff.; 11.1152.

GIANTS: divine monsters—(*war on heaven*) 1.209 ff.; 1.258; 5.509; 10.223.

GLOSSARY AND INDEX

GLAÚ·CUS: fisherman and later a sea god—7.375; (*Scylla*) 13.1412 ff.; (*his story*) 13.1432 ff.; (*leaves for Circe*) 13.1503; (*Circe*) 14.1 ff.; (*rejects Circe*) 14.101.

GOLDEN AGE: 1.126 ff.; 15.145; 15.391.

GOLDEN FLEECE: 6.1167; 7.13; (*Jason takes it*) 7.249, 7.256.

HAR·MÓ·NI·A: daughter of Venus and Mars, wife of Cadmus—3.202; (*an exile*) 4.844 ff.; (*transformed*) 4.876 ff.

HÉC·A·TE: goddess of witchcraft and magic—6.233; (*Medea*) 7.129; 7.286; 7.292; 7.316; 7.387; (*Circe*) 14.69; 14.623.

HÉC·TOR: son of Hecuba and Priam, a prince of Troy—11.1155 ff.; (*mourns Aesacus*) 12.3; (*kills Protesilaüs*) 12.104; 12.116; 12.690; 12.844; 12.1000; 12.1029; 13.12; (*attacks Greeks*) 13.134; 13.292; 13.458 ff.; 13.631; (*Astyanax*) 13.677; (*ashes*) 13.695; 13.788; 13.833; 13.1060.

HÉC·U·BA: wife of Priam (king of Troy)—11.1159; 13.663; (*hauled away*) 13.690 ff.; (*Hector's ashes*) 13.694; (*Polyxena*) 13.732 ff.; 13.782; (*laments*) 13.791 ff.; (*Penelope*) 13.832; (*Polydorus' corpse*) 13.870 ff.; (*her revenge and transformation*) 13.881 ff.; 13.920; 13.927; 13.930; 13.993.

HÉLEN: mortal daughter of Jupiter and Leda, wife of Menelaus—13.331; 14.1024; 15.347.

HÉL·E·NUS: son of Priam, a prophet—13.162; (*captured*) 13.550; (*Aeneas*) 13.1149 ff.; (*Aeneas*) 15.653; 15.672.

HE·LÍ·A·DES: daughters of the Sun (Apollo)—(*grieve for Phaëton, are transformed*) 2.491 ff.; (*Orpheus*) 10.141; 10.397;

HÉ·LI·OS: son of Hyperion, Greek god of the Sun. See APOLLO. (*love for Leucothoë*) 4.280 ff.; 13.1507.

HÉR·CU·LES: son of Jupiter and Alcmene, husband of Deïanira— (*Cos*) 7.576; (*Cerberus*) 7.651; (*constellation*) 8.294; (*fight with Acheloüs*) 9.19 ff.; (*Nessus*) 9.167 ff.; (*his fame*) 9.220; 9.230; (*Nessus' shirt*) 9.258 ff.; (*achievements*) 9.296 ff.; (*suffering*) 9.330 ff.; (*Lichas*) 9.341 ff.; (*pyre and death*) 9.370 ff.; (*deified*) 9.390 ff.; 9.441; 9.451; (*birth*) 9.462 ff.; (*Iolaus and Hebe*) 9.635; (*saves Hesione, attacks Troy*) 11.326 ff.; (*Trachis*) 11.965; 12.484; (*kills Nestor's family*) 12.829 ff.; (*kills Periclymenes*) 12.862 ff.; 12.882; 13.36; (*arrows*) 13.85, 13.658; (*Croton*) 15.12 ff.; (*Myscelus*) 15.32 ff.; 15.346; 15.424.

HER·MAPH·RO·DÍ·TUS: son of Hermes (Mercury) and Aphrodite (Venus)—(*his story*) 4.423 ff.; (*is transformed and drowns*) 4.542 ff.

HÉR·SE: daughter of Cecrops—(*Erichthonius and Pallas*) 2.824; (*Mercury*) 2.1080 ff.

HE·SÍ·O·NE: daughter of Laomedon—(*saved by Hercules*) 11.322; (*Telamon*) 11.336.

HES·PÉ·RI·E: daughter of Cebrenus—(*Aesacus*) 11.1171 ff.; (*killed by snake*) 11.1181 ff.

HIP·POD·Á·MIA: bride of Pirithoüs—12.329; (*abducted and rescued*) 12.350 ff.; 14.1024.

HIP·PÓL·Y·TUS: son of Theseus—(*his story*) 15.735 ff.; (changes name) 15.818; 15.832.

HIP·PÓM·E·NES: son of Megareus—(*Atalanta*) 10.872 ff.; (*transformed*) 10.1060.

HUNGER (E): (*Ceres*) 8.1217 ff.; (*her home*) 8.1241; (*obeys Ceres*) 8.1263 ff.

HY·A·CÍN·THUS: a lad from Amyclae—(*Apollo*) 10.242 ff.; (*transformed*) 10.315 ff.; 13.649.

HÝ·DRA: a monster with many heads—(*poison blood*) 2.969; (*heads*) 9.113, 9.121; (*Nessus' shirt*) 9.210; 9.261; 9.312.

HY·LÓN·O·ME: a female centaur—(*Cyllarus*) 12.629 ff.; (*kills herself*) 12.660.

GLOSSARY AND INDEX

HÝ·MEN: god of marriage—1.702; 4.1130; 6.701; 9.1219; 9.1224; 9.1269; (*Orpheus*) 10.1.

HÝR·I·Ë: mother of Cyncus (2), also a lake in Boeotia—(*Medea*) 7.586; (*transformed*) 7.603 ff.

I·ÁN·THE: daughter of Telestes—(*Iphis*) 9.1141 ff.

I·A·PYG·I·A: region in southern Italy—(*Diomedes*) 14.701; 14.778; 15.83; 15.1065.

ÍC·A·RUS: son of Daedalus—(*with Daedalus*) 8.315 ff.; (*drowns*) 8.360.

ÍDA: mountain near Troy—(*on fire*) 2.316; 4.405; 4.424; 4.30; 7.568; (*Laethea*) 10.114; 11.1162; 12.803; 13.536; 14.818.

ÍN·A·CHUS: a river in Argolis, father of Io—(*grieving*) 1.856; (*with transformed Io*) 1.945 ff.

Í·NO: daughter of Cadmus, wife of Athamas—(*Bacchus*) 3.481; (*Pentheus*) 3.1098; (*Juno*) 4.614 ff.; (*Tisiphone*) 4.721 ff.; (*jumps in the sea*) 4.780; (*transformed*) 4.799; (*companions changed*) 4.804 ff.

Í·O: daughter of Inachus—(*Jupiter*) 1.859 ff.; (*transformed and suffers*) 1.900 ff.; (*at the Nile, transformed back*) 1.1072 ff.; (*son with Jupiter*) 1.1100; 2.773; (*as Isis*) 9.1090.

I·O·LÁ·US: son of Iphicles—(*Great Boar Hunt*) 8.491; (*made young*) 9.629, 9.690.

Í·O·LE: daughter of Eurytus—(*Hercules*) 9.230; 9.248; (*Alcmene*) 9.445 ff.; (*story of Dryope*) 9.522 ff.; 9.623.

IÓNIAN SEA: part of the Mediterranean between Greece and Italy—(*Myscelus*) 15.79; 15.1060.

IPH·I·GE·NEÍ·A: daughter of Agamemnon—(*at Aulis*) 12.47; 13.305; 13.322.

Í·PHIS (1): daughter of Telethusa and Ligdus—(*her story*) 9.1061 ff.; (*transformed*) 9.1255.

Í·PHIS (2): a man from Cyprus—(*his story*) 14.1069; (*kills himself*) 14.1098 ff.

Í·RIS: daughter of Thaumas, divine messenger—(*in the Flood*) 1.393; (*purifies Juno*) 4.709; (*Juno*) 11.908 ff.; (*Sleep*) 11.950 ff.; 14.128; (*Hersilia*) 14.1278 ff.

IRON AGE: 1.176 ff.; 15.391.

Í·TYS: son of Procne and Tereus—(*birth*) 6.710; 6.716; (*killed*) 6.1014 ff.

I·Ú·LUS: another name for ASCANIUS—14.888; 14.930; 15.667; 15.1160.

IX·Í·ON: father of Nessus and Pirithoüs and the centaurs—(*in the Underworld*) 4.682, 4.688; 9.202; (*Orpheus*) 10.68.

JÁ·SON: son of Aeson—(*leads Argonauts*) 7.9; (*Aeëtes*) 7.12 ff.; (*Medea*) 7.19 ff.; 7.132 ff.; (*tested by Aeetes*) 7.184 ff.; (*Golden Fleece*) 7.244 ff.; (*Iolchos*) 7.259; (*Medea and Aeson*) 7.269 ff.; 7.407; (*Medea's revenge*) 7.625; (*Great Boar Hunt*) 8.481, 8.549; 8.646.

JOVE (E): another name for JUPITER.

JÚ·NO: sister and wife of Jupiter—(*Iris*) 1.394; (*suspicious of Jupiter and Io*) 1.887 ff.; (*Argus*) 1.923; (*Argus' eyes*) 1.1063; (*torments Io*) 1.1068; (*forgives Io*) 1.1080 ff.; 2.635; (*Callisto*) 2.683 ff.; (*Tethys and Oceanus*) 2.747 ff.; (*Semele*) 3.379 ff.; (*Teiresias*) 3.490 ff.; (*Echo*) 3.556; 3.788; (*Ino*) 4.619 ff.; (*Underworld*) 4.662 ff.; 4.774; (*Ino's companions*) 4.812; (*Typhoëus*) 5.526; (*Pygmy queen*) 6.148; (*Antigone*) 6.153; 6.347; (*Latona*) 6.551; 6.702; (*plague*) 7.821; 8.356; 9.27; (*hatred for Hercules*) 9.36, 9.221 ff.; 9.417; (*delays Hercules' birth*) 9.460 ff.; (*incest*) 9.805; 9.1218; 9.1268; (*Ganymede*) 10.241; 11.899; (*sends Iris to Sleep*) 11.905 ff.; (*Ixion*) 12.780; (*Hecuba*) 13.926; 14.129; 14.886; 14.902; (*opens gates of Rome*) 14.1202; (*Hersilia*) 14.1277; 15.248; 15.575; 15.1063; 15.1171.

GLOSSARY AND INDEX

JÚ·PI·TER: son of Saturn, husband of Juno, chief Olympian god—1.150; *(rules after Saturn)* 1.159; *(creates seasons)* 1.162; *(Giants)* 1.212; *(summons gods)* 1.233 ff.; *(Lycaon)* 1.297 ff.; *(sends the Flood)* 1.367 ff.; *(ends the Flood)* 1.472; *(Io)* 1.865 ff.; *(Mercury)* 1.987 ff.; *(Juno and Io)* 1.1079 ff.; 2.88; *(Phaëton)* 2.440 ff.; *(Cycnus)* 2.546; 2.565; *(calms Apollo)* 2.576; *(Callisto)* 2.596 ff.; 2.696; 2.705; 2.717; *(Callisto and Arcas)* 2.741; *(Mercury and Europa)* 2.1240 ff.; 3.1; 3.12; *(Semele)* 3.437 ff.; *(Bacchus)* 3.478; *(Teiresias)* 3.487 ff.; 3.788; *(Celmis)* 4.412; *(Perseus)* 4.947 ff.; *(J. Ammon)* 4.993; *(Danaë)* 4.1033; 4.1123; 5.30; *(Typhoëus)* 5.520; *(Ceres)* 5.798 ff.; *(Ceres and Pluto)* 5.878; *(in Minerva's tapestry)* 6.121; *(in Arachne's tapestry)* 6.167 ff.; *(Telchines)* 7.581; *(Aegina)* 7.914; 7.956 ff.; *(Crete)* 8.157; *(Minos)* 8.245; *(visits Philemon and Baucis)* 8.984 ff.; *(Hercules)* 9.388 ff.; *(Capaneus)* 9.641; *(Callirhoë)* 9.660; *(calms gods)* 9.685 ff.; *(incest)* 9.805; *(Ganymede)* 10.230 ff.; *(J. Panomphe)* 11.301; *(Thetis)* 11.352; 11.1153; *(ancestor of Ajax)* 13.42; *(Hector)* 13.147; *(ancestor of Ulysses)* 13.233 ff.; *(Agamemnon's dream)* 13.360; 13.445; 13.633; *(Aurora)* 13.964 ff.; *(Polyphemus)* 13.1320, 13.1343; *(Cercopes)* 14.139; *(Aeneas)* 14.904 ff.; *(Romulus)* 14.1254; *(Venus)* 15.1219; *(greater than Saturn)* 15.1305; 15.1306; 15.1318.

LAM·PÉ·TI·E: sister of Phaëton, one of the Heliades: *(transformed)* 2.503.

LA·ÓM·E·DON: founder of Troy—6.154; 11.296; *(Apollo, Neptune, Hercules)* 11.302 ff.; 11.1153.

LÁ·PITHS: a tribe in Thessaly—*(fight with Centaurs)* 12.347 ff.; 14.1025.

LÁ·TI·UM: region of central Italy where Rome was built—*(brides)* 2.529; 14.506; 14.603; 14.690; *(Pomona)* 14.949; *(Numa)* 15.718; *(Cipus)* 15.880; *(disease)* 15.948.

LA·TÓ·NA: daughter of Coeus, divine mother of Apollo and Diana—*(call to worship)* 6.268 ff.; *(insulted by Niobe)* 6.287 ff.; *(anger at Niobe)* 6.342 ff.; *(Lycian peasants)* 6.516 ff.; *(gives birth)* 6.540 ff.; *(Calaurea)* 7.611; *(birth tree)* 13.1017.

LÉL·E·GES: original inhabitants of parts of Greece and Asia Minor—7.699; *(Minos)* 8.9; *(Byblis)* 9.1029.

LÉ·LEX: a warrior from Troezen—*(Boar Hunt)* 8.493; *(with Acheloüs)* 8.888, *(Baucis and Philemon)* 8.970 ff.; 8.1135.

LÉM·NOS: an island in the Aegean Sea—2.1132; *(Vulcan)* 4.269; *(Philoctetes)* 13.77; 13.517; *(Ulysses)* 13.653.

LÉ·THE: river of the underworld—7.251; *(in Cave of Sleep)* 11.933.

LEU·CÓN·O·Ë: one of the daughters of Minyas—4.244 ff.; 4.395; *(transformed)* 4.595 ff.

LEU·CÓTH·O·Ë: daughter of Orchamus—*(Apollo)* 4.285 ff.; *(buried alive and transformed)* 4.348 ff.

LÍ·CHAS: servant of Hercules—*(Nessus' shirt)* 9.255; *(killed and transformed)* 9.341 ff.

LÚ·CI·FER: morning star, father of Ceyx—2.168; 2.1078; 4.932; 4.983; 8.1; 11.147; *(Ceyx)* 11.425; 11.467; 11.871; *(mourns)* 11.887; 15.289; 15.1192.

LU·CÍ·NA: goddess of childbirth—*(Evippe)* 5.482; *(delays birth of Hercules)* 9.473 ff.; 9.1112; *(Myrrha)* 10.779 ff.

LY·CAÉ·US: mountain in Arcadia: 1.309; *(Pan and Syrinx)* 1.1033; 2.1060; *(Atalanta)* 8.504.

LY·CÁ·ON: king of Arcadia, father of Callisto—*(Jupiter)* 1.230, 1.279; 1.297 ff.; *(transformed)* 1.331 ff.; 2,728; 2.776.

LÝ·CI·A: coastal region of Asia Minor—4.435 ff.; 6.516; *(Latona)* 6.554 ff.; *(Byblis)* 9.1030; 12.181; 12.427.

GLOSSARY AND INDEX

LÝ·DI·A: an inland country in Asia Minor—(*Arachne*) 6.22; 6.242; (*Midas*) 11.149.

MA·CÁ·RE·US: a comrade of Ulysses:—14.248 ff.; (*his story*) 14.343 ff.

MAE·ÁN·DER: a river in Asia Minor—(*overheats*) 2.355; 8.260; (*Cyane*) 9.720.

MAÉN·A·LUS: a mountain in Arcadia—1.307; 2.606; 2.646; 5.947.

MAE·Ó·NIA: an alternative name for LYDIA—2.364; 3.892; (*Arachne*) 6.8; (*Niobe*) 6.248.

MAÉ·STRA: daughter of Erisichthon—8.1315 ff.; (*transformed*) 8.1326 ff.

MÁRS: son of Juno and Jupiter, god of war—(*sacred Serpent*) 3.50; (*Cadmus*) 3.200; (*Venus*) 4.250 ff.; (*his rock*) 6.116; (*Tereus*) 6.698; 12.142; (*Romulus*) 14.1201; (*petitions Jupiter*) 14.1241; (*brings Romulus to heaven*) 14.1258 ff.; 15.1314.

MÁR·SY·AS: a satyr—(*Apollo*) 6.625 ff.; (*river*) 6.654.

ME·DÉ·A: daughter of Aeëtes—(*Jason*) 7.18 ff.; (*Hecate*) 7.128 ff.; (*Iolchos*) 7.259; (*Aeson*) 7.269 ff.; (*Incantation*) 7.313 ff,; (*Bacchus*) 7.464; (*daughters of Pelias*) 7.467 ff.; (*stabs Pelias*) 7.553; (*flies over islands*) 7.556 ff.; (*revenge*) 7.625; (*Aegeus*) 7.632 ff.; (*Theseus*) 7.644 ff.

ME·DÚ·SA: one of the Gorgons—(*her head*) 4.918; (*transforms Atlas*) 4.972; (*transforms sea weed*) 4.1106; (*killed by Perseus*) 4.1164 ff.; (*birth of Pegasus*) 4.1168; (*seduced by Neptune*) 4.1177 ff.; 5.114; (*head used by Perseus*) 5.286 ff.; 5.383; 5.392 ff.; 6.195.

MEL·E·Á·GER: king of Calydon, son of Oeneus and Althaea—(*Great Boar Hunt*) 8.433 ff.; 8.476 ff.; (*Atalanta*) 8.513 ff., 8.606; (*kills boar*) 8.650 ff.; (*Atalanta*) 8.667; (*kills uncles*) 8.690 ff.; (*fatal log*) 8.711 ff.; (*dies*) 8.807 ff.; (*mourned*) 8.823; (*sisters transformed*) 8.838 ff.; (*Deïanira*) 9.245.

MÉM·NON: son of Aurora and Tithonus—(*death*) 13.934; (*transformation of his ashes*) 13.965 ff.; (*Memnonides*) 13.988 ff.

MEN·E·LÁ·US: king of Sparta, husband of Helen, brother of Agamemnon—(*arms of Achilles*) 12.1057; 13.297; 13.338; 13.590; (*Euphorbus*) 15.245; 15.1216.

MÉR·CU·RY: divine son of Jupiter and Maia—(*Argus*) 1.990 ff.; (*Syrinx*) 1.1017 ff.; (*Argus*) 1.1057; (*Battus*) 2.1018 ff.; (*Herse*) 2.1055 ff.; (*helps Jupiter*) 2.1236 ff.; (*Hermes*) 4.425; (*grants Hermaphroditus' request*) 4.570; 4.1121 ff.; (*fears Typhoëus*) 5.528; (*Philemon and Baucis*) 8.986 ff.; (*Chione*) 11.480 ff.; (*links to Ulysses*) 13.240; (*helps Ulysses*) 14.450.

MÍ·DAS: a Phrygian king—(*Silenus and Bacchus*) 11.139 ff.; (*golden touch*) 11.153 ff.; (*gets asses' ears*) 11.225 ff.; (*his secret and the servant*) 11.274 ff.

MI·LÉ·TUS: son of Deione and Apollo, father of Caunus and Byblis—(*Minos*) 9.710 ff.; (*Cyane*) 9.720

MI·NÉR·VA: goddess of wisdom, divine daughter of Jupiter, also called PALLAS—(*Erichthonius and Raven*) 2.816 ff.; 2.870; (*Aglauros and Envy*) 2.1118 ff.; (*Cadmus and dragon's teeth*) 3.145 ff.; 4.1122; (*Medusa*) 4.1188 ff.; (*protects Perseus*) 5.78; (*visits Muses*) 5.397 ff.; (*Pierus' daughters*) 5.469 ff.; 5.594; (*Muses*) 6.1 ff.; (*Arachne*) 6.7, 6.43 ff.; (*weaving*) 6.116 ff.; (*reed pipe*) 6.629; (*Perdix*) 8.402 ff.; (*Athens*) 8.424; (*Oeneus*) 8.440; (*Theseus*) 12.560; (*image stolen*) 13.163, 13.553; 13.627; (*Diomedes*) 14.727; 15.535; 15.1074.

MÍ·NOS: son of Jupiter and Europa, king of Crete—(*threatens war*) 7.716 ff.; (*visits Aeacus*) 7.740 ff.; 7.789; (*at war*) 8.9; (*Scylla*) 8.37 ff.; (*labyrinth*) 8.243 ff.; (*imprisons Minotaur*) 8.251 ff.; 8.299; *old and weak*) 9.701 ff.; (*Miletus*) 9.709.

MÍN·O·TAUR: monster child of Pasiphaë—8.212; 8.251; (*imprisoned*) 8.272 ff.; (*killed*) 8.276.

GLOSSARY AND INDEX

MÍN·Y·AS: a king in Boeotia—(*his daughters*) 4.1 ff.; 4.48 ff.; (*daughters transformed*) 4.595 ff.; 4.628.

MO·LÓS·SI·ANS:—a people of Epirus in Greece—(*Lycaon*) 1.325; (*royal sons changed*) 13.1144.

MÓP·SUS: son of Ampycus, a Lapith—(*Great Boar Hunt*) 8.499, 8.553; (*kills Hodites*) 12.703; (*see Caeneus transformed*) 12.808 ff.;

MÓR·PHE·US: son of Sleep—11.977 ff.; (*Alcyone*) 11.1001 ff.

MÚLC·I·BER: an alternative name for VULCAN. 2.7; 9.676.

MÚSES (E): daughters of Jupiter and Mnemosyne—2.318; (*Minerva visits*) 5.404 ff.; (*Pyreneus*) 5.435 ff.; (*daughters of Pierus*) 5.467 ff.; 6.2; (*Orpheus*) 10.219; 15.720; 15.940.

MÝR·MI·DONS: people from northern Greece—(*appear from ants*) 7.994 ff.

MÝR·RHA: daughter of Cinyras—(*her story*) 10.473 ff.; (*transformed*) 10.754.

MY·SCEL·US: son of Alemon—(*Hercules and Crotona*) 15.31 ff.

NAÍ·ADS: fresh water nymphs—1.948; 2.472; 6.536; 6.743; 9.142; 9.1046; 10.14; 10.788; 11.71; 14.508; 14.843; 14.1209.

NAR·CÍS·SUS: son of Lirope and Cephisus—(*birth*) 3.532; (*Echo*) 3.549 ff.; (*in love*) 3.634 ff.; (*dies and is transformed*) 3.737; (*sisters' lament*) 3.771.

NÁX·OS: island in the Cyclades—3.970, 3.975; 3.991; 3.1048.

NÉ·LE·US: king of Pylos, father of Nestor—2.1025; 6.682; (*family killed*) 12.850 ff.

NÉM·E·SIS: goddess of retribution—3.623; 14.1063.

NÉP·TUNE: divine brother of Jupiter, god of the sea—(*aids the Flood*) 1.400 ff.; (*helps end the Flood*) 1.482; (*complains about Phaëton*) 2.389; 2.421; (*transforms Ino*) 4.788 ff.; (*seduces Medusa*) 4.1186; (*in Minerva's tapestry*) 6.124; (*in Arachne's tapestry*) 6.186; (*transforms Perimele*) 8.934 ff.; (*saves Maestra*) 8.1323 ff.; (*Hippomenes*) 10.914; (*with Laomedon and Apollo at Troy*) 11.306 ff.; 12.38; (*Cycnus*) 12.228; (*Caenis*) 12.308 ff.; (*Neleus*) 12.856; (*asks Apollo to kill Achilles*) 12.892 ff.; 13.1339.

NÉ·RE·IDS: daughters of Doris and Nereus, nymphs of the sea—1.438; 5.29; 11.572; 13.1405; 14.405.

NÉ·RE·US: a god of the sea, father of the Nereïds—1.265; 2.387; 11.572; 12.147; 13.1180.

NÉS·SUS: son of Ixion, a centaur—(*with Hercules*) 9.164 ff.; (*dies*) 9.208 ff.; 9.252; (*Lapiths*) 12.481; (*kills Cymelus*) 12.701.

NÉS·TOR: king of Pylos, son of Neleus—(*Boar Hunt*) 8.495, 8.576; (*Caenis/Caeneus*) 12.265 ff.; (*Centaurs and Lapiths*) 12.238 ff.; (*Dorylas*) 12.593 ff.; (*Centaurs*) 12.680 ff.; (*Hercules*) 12.826 ff.; (*alone in battle*) 13.102 ff.; 15.1273.

NÍLE (E): main river of Egypt—1.615; (*Io*) 1.1072; (*overheats*) 2.366; (*Nileus*) 5.299; 5.515; (*Isis*) 9.1238; (*Caesar*) 15.1140.

NÍ·O·BE: daughter of Tantalus, wife of Amphion, king of Thebes—(*her pride*) 6.246 ff.; (*children killed*) 6.365 ff.; (*transformed*) 6.493 ff.

NÍS·US: king of Megara, father of Scylla (1)—(*purple hair*) 8.12 ff.; (*hair stolen*) 8.132; (*transformed*) 8.231 ff.

NO·NÁC·RIS: mountain in Arcadia—(*Syrinx*) 1.1019; (*Callisto*) 2.596.

GLOSSARY AND INDEX

NÚ·MA: king of Rome—15.5 ff.; (*king*) 15.716; (*death*) 15.723.

NYMPHS: semi divine young women living in nature—1.273; 1.466; 1.845; 1.1021; 2.19; 2.344; 2.652 ff.; 3.250 ff.; 3.482; 3.557 ff.; 3.700; 4.424; 4.1110; 5.499 ff.; 5.643; 5.843; 5.1035; 6.23; 6.75; 6.645; 7.465; 7.563; 8.894; 8.908 ff.; 9.544 ff.; 9.1041; 10.165; 11.234; 13.1098; 13.1173; 14.405; 14.507; 14.788 ff.; (*ships transformed*) 14.835 ff.; 14.1212 ff.; 15.733; 15.831.

O·CÉ·A·NUS: a sea god, husband of Tethys—(*Juno visits*) 2.750 ff.; (*incest*) 9.804; (*Glaucus*) 13.1481.

O·CÝRH·O·Ë: daughter of Chiron and Chariclo—(*prophecy*) 2.945 ff.; (*transformed*) 2.989.

OÉ·NE·US: king of Calydon, father of Meleager and Deïanira—(*Diana*) 8.436 ff.; 8.761; (*mourns Meleager*) 8.828; (*Acheloüs*) 9.18.

OÉ·TA: mountain range in northern Greece—1.457; (*burns*) 2.316; (*Hercules*) 9.272, 9.331; (*Hercules' death*) 9.372; 9.400.

OLÝMPIAN GODS: the major divine figures—(*meet with Jupiter*) 1.234 ff.; (*calm Apollo*) 2.573; (*run from Typhoeus*) 5.510 ff.; (*on Minerva's tapestry*) 6.119.

O·LÝM·PUS: mountain in northern Greece—(*smashed by Jupiter*) 1.214; 1.302; 2.85; (*on fire*) 2.328; (*Medea*) 7.363; 13.1208.

O·RITH·Y·Í·A: daughter of Erectheus—(*Boreas*) 6.1111 ff.; 7.1083.

ÓR·PHE·US: son of Oeagrus and Calliope—(*Euridice*) 10.4 ff.; (*Underworld*) 10.16 ff.; (*loses Eurydice again*) 10.91 ff.; (*love of boys*) 10.131; (*sings to trees*) 10.138 ff.; (*attacked and killed*) 11.1 ff.; (*mourned*) 11.66 ff.; (*his head*) 11.74 ff.; (*finds Eurydice*) 11.90; 11.140.

OR·TÝG·I·A (1): another name for the island of DELOS. 1.1025; 15.506.

OR·TÝG·I·A (2): an island off Syracuse—5.776; 5.995.

ÓS·SA: mountain in northern Greece—(*smashed by Jupiter*) 1.215; (*on fire*) 2.327; (*Medea*) 7.362; 12.498.

Ó·THRYS: mountain in northern Greece—(*burns*) 2.322; (*Medea*) 7.363, 7.560; (*Caeneus*) 12.272; (*stripped of trees*) 12.792.

PA·CHÝ·NUS: a cape in Sicily—5.557; 13.1156.

PÁG·A·SAE: town in Thessaly where the Argonauts' boat was built—7.1; 12.642; 13.38.

PA·LAÉ·MON: god of the sea—(*once Melicertes*) 4.803; 13.1434.

PAL·A·MÉ·DES: son of Nauplius, Greek warrior leader—(*exposes Ulysses*) 13.62; 13.90, 13.94; 13.511.

PÁL·A·TINE (E): one of Rome's hills—14.519; 14.947; 14.1265; 15.844.

PAL·LÁ·DI·UM: statue of Minerva in Troy—(*stolen*) 13.552 ff.; 13.627.

PÁL·LAS: an alternative name for Minerva. (See MINERVA)

PAN: god of woods and shepherds—(*Syrinx*) 1.1031 ff.; 11.226; (*Apollo*) 11.234 ff.; 14.787; 14.972.

PAN·CHAÉ·A: island region of Arabia—10.468; (*Myrrha*) 10.737.

PAN·DÍON: king of Athens, father of Philomela and Procne—(*with Tereus*) 6.698, 6.733 ff.; 6.793 ff.; (*dies*) 6.1100.

PÁN·DRO·SUS: daughter of Cecrops—(*Erichthonius*) 2.824; 2.1102.

GLOSSARY AND INDEX

PÁ·PHOS: city in Cyprus and boy born there—(*Pygmalion*) 10.441; 10.451 ff.; 10.813.

PÁR·IS: son of Priam and Hecuba—(*burial site*) 7.571; 12.5; (*Apollo*) 12.1016 ff.; 13.330; 13.335; 13.812; 15.1215.

PAR·NÁS·SUS: mountain near Delphi—(*Deucalion*) 1.460; (*Cupid*) 1.682; (*on fire*) 2.321; (*Themis*) 4.951; (*Muses*) 5.441; 11.253; (*Daedalion*) 11.539.

PÁ·ROS: island in the Cyclades: 3.642; (*Minos*) 7.731; (*Daedalus*) 8.357.

PA·SÍPH·A·E: wife of Minos, mother of the Minotaur—8.210, 8.217; 8.249; 9.1178.

PÉG·A·SUS: winged horse—(*birth*) 4.1168; (*makes new spring*) 5.409 ff.

PÉ·LE·US: son of Aeacus, husband of Thetis, father of Achilles—(*Minos*) 7.747; 7.1042, 8.4; (*Great Boar Hunt*) 8.490, 8.599; (*Thetis*) 11.337 ff.; (*in exile, with Ceyx*) 11.419 ff.; (*cattle and Psamathe*) 11.553 ff.; (*absolved of murder*) 11.645; 12.302; (*Crantor*) 12.566 ff.; (*Centaurs*) 12.591, 12.602 ff.; 13.250 ff.; 15.1302.

PÉ·LI·AS: half-brother of Aeson—(*his daughters and Medea*) 7.471 ff.; 7.519; (*killed*) 7.537 ff.

PÉ·LI·ON: mountain in northern Greece—(*smashed by Jupiter*) 1.215; (*Medea*) 7.362, 7.559; (*Achilles' spear*) 12.115; (*stripped of trees*) 12.793; 13.179.

PÉ·LOPS: son of Tantalus, brother of Niobe—(*his ivory shoulder*) 6.660 ff.; 8.980.

PE·LÓ·RUS: a cape in Sicily—5.557; 13.1158; 15.1069.

PE·NÉ·US: river in Thessaly, father of Daphne—1.660; (*Daphne*) 1.703 ff.; 1.802; (*his home*) 1.837; (*overheats*) 2.352; (*Medea*) 7.370.

PÉN·THE·US: son of Echion and Agave, king of Thebes—(*Teiresias*) 3.784 ff.; (*Bacchus and Acoetes*) 3.811 ff.; 3.1051; (*killed*) 3.1065 ff.; 4.33; 4.635.

PÉR·DIX: nephew of Daedalus—(*with Daedalus*) 8.381 ff.; (*transformed*) 8.403.

PÉR·GA·MUM: the citadel of Troy—12.1001; 13.276; 13.616; 13.847; 15.658.

PER·I·CLÝM·E·NES: a son of Neleus, brother of Nestor—(*transformed, killed*) 12.855 ff.

PER·I·MÉ·LE: daughter of Hippodamas—(*transformed*) 8.927 ff.

PER·SÉPH·O·NE: see PROSERPINE.

PÉR·SE·US: son of Jupiter and Danaë—4.908; (*visits Atlas*) 4.913 ff.; (*transforms Atlas*) 4.968 ff.; (*saves Andromeda*) 4.985 ff.; 4.1119 ff.; (*daughters of Phorcys*) 4.1148; (*cuts off Medusa's head*) 4.1164; 5.1; 5. 53; (*fights at the feast*) 5.58 ff.; (*uses Medusa's head*) 5.281 ff., 5.373 ff., 5.392.

PHÁ·E·TON: son of Apollo and Clymene: (*wonders about his father*) 1.1106 ff.; (*Apollo and the horses of the Sun*) 2.24 ff.; (*killed by Jupiter*) 2.450 ff.; 2.462 ff.; (*epitaph*) 2.474; 2.532; 4.362; 12.896.

PHA·E·THÚ·SA: eldest sister of Phaëton, one of the Heliades—(*transformed*) 2.501.

PHI·LÉ·MON: husband of Baucis—(*his story*) 8.994 ff.; (*transformed*) 8.1119 ff.

PHIL·OC·TÉ·TES: son of Poeas—(*Hercules*) 9.373; (*abandoned*) 13.76 ff.; 13.518 ff.; (*rejoins Greeks*) 13.659.

PHIL·O·MÉ·LA: daughter of Pandion, sister of Procne—6.727; (*with Tereus*) 6.739 ff.; (*transformed*) 6.1088.

PHÍ·NE·US: brother of Cepheus—(*feast*) 5.12 ff.; (*begs*) 5.333 ff.; (*transformed*) 5.367.

GLOSSARY AND INDEX

PHLÉG·E·THON: a river of the Underworld—5.850; 15.799.

PHÓ·CIS: region in central Greece—1.455; 2.843; 5.438; 11.552.

PHÓ·CUS: son of Aeacus—(*with Minos*) 7.749; 7.1041 ff.; 7.1248; (*killed by Peleus*) 11.421; 11.603.

PHOÉ·BE (1): a Titan, the moon—1.15; 2.1079.

PHOÉ·BE (2): an alternative name for DIANA—1.697; 2.605.

PHOÉ·BUS: another name for APOLLO.

PHOÉ·NIX: a fabulous bird—15.586 ff..

PHRÝ·GI·A: region in Asia Minor around Troy—6.244; 6.278; 6.296; 6.654; 8.262; 8.976; 10.231; 11.136; 11.309; 12.61; 13.409; 13.553; 13.698; 13.936; 15.662.

PÍC·US: son of Saturn—(*statue*) 14.483; (*his story*) 14.495 ff.; (*transformed*) 14.595; (*companions transformed*) 14.612 ff.

PÍ·E·RUS: king of Emathia—(*his daughters and the Muses*) 5.467 ff.; (*story of Typhoëus*) 5.511 ff.; (*daughters transformed*) 5.1044.

PÍN·DUS: a mountain in Thessaly—1.838; (*on fire*) 2.328; (*Medea*) 7.363; 11.860.

PI·RÍTH·O·US: son of Ixion—(*Great Boar Hunt*) 8.482; 8.634; (*with Acheloüs*) 8.886; (*ridicules Acheloüs*) 8.961; (*wedding feast, fight with Centaurs*) 12.328 ff.; (*kills Centaurs*) 12.515 ff.

PÍT·THE·US: son of Pelops, king of Troezen—6.683; 8.979; 15.443; 15.764.

PLEÍ·A·DES: daughters of Atlas and Pleione, now a constellation—(*Maia*) 1.990; (*Niobe*) 6.291; (*on shield*) 13.484.

PLÚ·TO: brother of Jupiter and Neptune, god of the Underworld, also called DIS—(*alarmed by earth opening up*) 2.376; 3.441; 5.565; (*shot by Cupid*) 5.569 ff.; (*Proserpine*) 5.620 ff.; (*Cyane*) 5.645 ff.; 5.790; (*Jupiter defends him*) 5.819 ff.; 5.880 ff.; (*Medea*) 7.398; (*Orpheus*) 10.24, 10.76; (*Aeneas*) 14.179; (*Hippolytus*) 15.805.

PÓL·LUX: son of Tyndareus and Leda—(*Great Boar Hunt*) 8.479, 8.587.

POL·Y·DÓ·RUS: son of Priam and Hecuba—(*sent to Thrace, killed*) 13.701 ff.; (*Hecuba*) 13.857; 13.871; 13.1008.

POL·YM·ÉS·TOR: a king in Thrace—(*Polydorus*) 13.700 ff.; 13.861; 13.885 ff.; (*Hecuba's revenge*) 13.906 ff.

POL·Y·PHÉ·MUS: a cyclops—(*Galatea*) 13.1183; 13.1199 ff.; (*Telemus*) 13.1223 ff.; (*love song*) 13.1235 ff.; (*Acis*) 13.1370 ff.; 14.4; (*Achaemenides*) 14.263 ff.

PO·LÝX·E·NA: daughter of Priam and Hecuba—(*sacrificed*) 13.729 ff.; (*Hecuba laments her death*) 13.800 ff.

PO·MÓ·NA: a hamadryad in Latium—(*her story*) 14.948 ff.

PRÍ·AM: king of Troy, husband of Hecuba—11.1154; (*mourns Aesacus*) 12.1; 12.1028; (*Ulysses*) 13.333; (*killed*) 13.662 ff.; (*Polydorus*) 13.704; 13.779; 13.846; 13.958; 14.725.

PRI·Á·PUS: rustic fertility god—(*Lotis*) 9.557; 14.974.

PRÓ·CNE: daughter of Pandion, wife of Tereus—(*Tereus*) 6.699 ff.; (*transformed*) 6.1088.

PRÓ·CRIS: daughter of Erechtheus, wife of Cephalus—6.1109; (*with Cephalus*) 7.1082 ff.; (*killed*) 7.1318 ff.

PROÉ·TUS: brother of Acrisius—(*turned to stone*) 5.378; 15.491.

GLOSSARY AND INDEX

PRO·POÉ·TUS: (his daughters)—10.334, 10.359 ff.

PRÓ·SER·PINE (E): daughter of Ceres and Jupiter, also called PERSEPHONE—(*alarmed at earth opening up*) 2.377; (*abducted by Pluto*) 5.615 ff.; (*her belt*) 5.731; 5.786; 5.828; (*and pomegranate seeds*) 5.835 (*transforms Ascalaphus*) 5.847; (*companions transformed*) 5.866; (*divides her year*) 5.881; (*seduced by Jupiter*) 6.185; (*Medea*) 7.399; (*Orpheus visits*) 10.24, 10.75; 10.1105; (*Avernian Juno*) 14.177.

PRÓ·TE·US: a sea god—2.11; (*changes shape*) 8.1144 ff.; (*with Thetis*) 11.346; (*Peleus*) 11.392 ff.; 13.1464.

PYG·MÁ·LI·ON: a young man of Cyprus—(*his story*) 10.368 ff.

PÝ·LOS: city in the southwest Peloponnese—(*Apollo*) 2.1017; 6.681; 8.576; 12.847.

PÝ·RA·MUS: a young lad of Babylon—(*Thisbe*) 4.85 ff.; (*kills himself*) 4.178 ff.

PYR·E·NÉ·US: king of Thrace—(*Muses*) 5.435 ff.; (*kills himself*) 5.458.

PÝR·RHA: daughter of Epimetheus, wife of Deucalion—(*survives the Flood*) 1.464; (*restores human life*) 1.508 ff.

PY·THÁG·O·RAS: a Greek philosopher—15.94 ff.; (*teachings*) 15.101 ff.; (*vegetarianism*) 15.114 ff.; (*immortality and migration of souls*) 15.231 ff.; (*geological changes*) 15.389 ff.; (*Aetna*) 15.512 ff.; (*spontaneous generation*) 15.541 ff.; (*phoenix*) 15.583; (*strange animals*) 15.607 ff.; (*civilizations*) 15.626; (*Rome's destiny*) 15.641 ff.

QUI·RÍ·NUS: Romulus' name once he becomes a god—14.1275; 15.1284; 15.1308.

RAVEN: a bird associated with Apollo—(*changes colour*) 2.789; (*Crow*) 2.803 ff.; (*informs on Coronis*) 2.882 ff.; (*punished with change of colour*) 2.934.

RHAD·A·MÁN·THUS: son of Jupiter and Europa—(*in old age*) 9.699, 9.706.

RHÉG·I·UM: city in Italy across the sea from Sicily—14.7; 14.72.

RHÓ·DO·PE: mountain in Thrace—(*burns*) 2.322; (*once a mortal*) 6.143; 6.965; (*Orpheus*) 10.122.

ROME (E): (*founded*) 14.1192; (*Venus saves the city*) 14.1198; (*Tatius*) 14.1238; (*Numa*) 15.1; (*Pythagoras*) 15.641 ff.; (*Cipus*) 15.904; (*Aesculapius*) 15.947 ff.; 15.1142; 15.1336.

RÓM·U·LUS: son of Ilia and Mars, founder of Rome—14.1190 ff.; 14.1231; (*deified*) 14.1239 ff.; 15.2; (*spear transformed*) 15.842 ff.; 15.947; 15.1314.

RUMOUR:--(*Deïanira*) 9.225; (*home*) 12.62 ff.; 12.97.

RU·TÚ·LI·ANS: a people of central Italy—14.694; (*continue fighting*) 14.805, 14.859.

SÁ·BINES (E): people of central Italy—(*war on Rome*) 14.1193 ff.; 14.1281; 15.7.

SÁL·MA·CIS: a nymph and a pool—(*her story*) 4.418 ff.; (*drowns*) 4.544 ff.; 15.479.

SÁ·MOS: island off Asia Minor—(*Daedalus*) 8.355; (*Pythagoras*) 15.94.

SÁ·TURN: father of Jupiter, Juno, and others—(*in Tartarus*) 1.158; (*in Arachne's weaving*) 6.207; (*incest*) 9.803; 15.1304.

SCÝL·LA (1): daughter of Nisus—(*Minos*) 8.27 ff.; (*Nisus' hair*) 8.127 ff.; (*transformed*) 8.236.

SCÝL·LA (2): daughter of Crataeis—7.111; (*Aeneas*) 13.1164 ff.; (*Galatea*) 13.1175 ff.; (*Glaucus*) 13.1406 ff.; 14.24 ff.; (*transformed*) 14.78 ff.; (*Ulysses*) 14.106; (*Aeneas*) 14.112.

GLOSSARY AND INDEX

SCÝ·THI·A: northern regions generally—1.92; (*on fire*) 2.325; 5.1012; 7.646; (*Hunger*) 8.1223; 8.1237; 10.892; (*Diana*) 14.514; 15.427; 15.537.

SÉM·E·LE: daughter of Cadmus, mother of Bacchus—(*Juno and Jupiter*) 3.388 ff.; (*killed*) 3.471.

SÍB·YL: a priestess at Cumae—(*Aeneas*) 14.160 ff.; (*her story*) 14.200 ff.; 15.1078.

SÍCILY: 5.550; (*Ceres punishes the island*) 5.722 ff.; (Arethusa) 5.770; 7.112; 8.455; (*Aeneas*) 13.1154; (*Telemus*) 13.1220; (*Glaucus*) 14.10; (*Aeneas*) 14.126; 15.416; (*Aesculapius*) 15.1070; (*Pompey*) 15.1252.

SI·GAÉ·UM: a headland near Troy—11.299; 12.110; 13.7.

SI·LÉN·US: a satyr and companion of Bacchus—4.40; (*Midas and Bacchus*) 11.135, 11.150 ff.

SILVER AGE: 1.159 ff.

SÍRENS (E): transformed daughters of Acheloüs—(*transformation*) 5.865 ff; (*Aeneas*) 14.133.

SÍS·Y·PHUS: son of Aeolus—(*Underworld*) 4.680 ff.; (*Orpheus*) 10.72; 13.41, 13.52.

SLEEP: god of sleep—11.909; (*his home*) 11.917 ff.; (*Iris*) 11.952 ff.; (*with Morpheus*) 11.977 ff.

SPÁR·TA: city in central Peloponnese—(*dog*) 3.310; 3.329; 6.677; (*Apollo*) 10.254; 10.274; 10.327; 13.651; 15.81; 15.633 ff.

SPER·CHÉ·US: a river in Thessaly—1.850; (*overheats*) 2.361; 5.139; (*Medea*) 7.370.

STYX: (also STYGIAN SHADES) a river of the Underworld—1.194; 1.267; 1.1085; 2.62; 2.149; 3.409; 3.441; (*Narcissus*) 3.771; 3.1057; 4.642 ff.; 5.185; (*Arethusa*) 5.784; 6.1082; (*Orpheus visits*) 10.19; 10.115; 10.478; 10.1058; 11.782; 12.502; 13.755; 14.242; 14.899; 15.232; 15.1195.

SUN: see APOLLO.[1]

SÝ·RINX: a hamadryad—1.1021 ff.; (*Pan*) 1.1031 ff.; (*transformed*) 1.1041.

TÁN·TA·LUS: son of Jupiter, father of Pelops and Niobe—(*in the Underworld*) 4.678; (*Niobe*) 6.289; 6.397; (*cuts up his son*) 6.666; (*Orpheus*) 10.67; 12.1066.

TAR·PÉ·I·A: Roman girl who betrayed the citadel—14.1194 ff.; 15.1319.

TÁR·TA·RUS: deepest pit in the Underworld or the Underworld generally—(*Saturn*) 1.158; (*cracks open*) 2.375; 5.587; 5.662; 6.1101; 10.34; 11.1027; 12.404; 12.808; 12.1051.

TÁ·TI·US: king of the Sabines—14.1193; (*shared rule of Rome*) 14.1238 ff.

TEI·RÉ·SI·AS: a prophet in Thebes—(*Jupiter and Juno*) 3.494 ff.; (*Lirope and Narcissus*) 3.521 ff.; (*his fame*) 3.781; (*Pentheus*) 3.781 ff.

TÉL·A·MON: son of Aeacus, brother of Peleus—(*with Minos*) 7.746 ff.; (*Myrmidons*) 7.1007 ff.; 7.1042, 8.4; (*Great Boar Hunt*) 8.489, 8.596 ff.; (*Hesione*) 11.333; 11.337; 13.35; 13.250.

TE·LE·THÚ·SA: wife of Ligdus, mother of Iphis—9.1068 ff.

TÉM·PE: a valley in Thessaly—1.836; 7.358; (*Cycnus*) 7.587.

TÉN·E·DOS: island near Troy—(*Apollo*) 1.758; (*Achilles*) 12.170; 13.285.

---

[1] Ovid normally identifies the Sun with Apollo (or Phoebus) but at times, following Greek traditions, he will refer to the Sun as a Titan or the son of Hyperion. In this index almost all references to the Sun and the god of the Sun are listed under Apollo.

GLOSSARY AND INDEX

TÉ·RE·US; king of Thrace, husband of Procne—(*Athens*) 6.693; (*Procne*) 6.696 ff.; (*Philomela*) 6.746 ff.; (*transformed*) 6.1094; 6.1115.

TÉ·THYS: a sea goddess, wife of Oceanus—2.96; (*Phaëton*) 2.227; (*Juno visits*) 2.750 ff.; (*incest*) 9.804; (*Aesacus*) 11.1197; (*Glaucus*) 13.1481.

TEÚ·CER (1): early king of Troy—(*founder of Aeneas' line*) 13.1123.

TEÚ·CER (2): son of Telamon, half-brother of Ajax (1), Greek warrior—13.257.

THÉBES: main city of Boeotia—(*building*) 3.198; 3.838; 3.844; 3.864; (*Bacchus*) 4.613; (*Cadmus leaves*) 4.841; (*Minerva*) 5.403; 6.265; (*Niobe*) 6.299, 6.365; 6.673 ff.; (*monstrous fox*) 7.1200; (*Alcmene*) 9.488; (*war prophesied*) 9.640; 13.1087; (*Anius' bowl*) 13.1094 ff.; 15.636 ff.

THÉ·MIS: goddess of justice—(*Deucalion and Pyrrha*) 1.467, 1.546 ff.; (*prophecy to Atlas*) 4.952; (*the fox*) 7.1197; (*prophesies*) 9.638 ff.

THÉ·SE·US: son of Aegeus—(*reaches Athens*) 7.640; (*Medea*) 7.644 ff.; (*almost poisoned*) 7.665 ff.; (*his fame*) 7.679 ff.; (*kills Minotaur*) 8.276; (*Ariadne*) 8.276 ff.; (*fame in Athens*) 8.420 ff.; (*Boar Hunt*) 8.430; 8.481; 8.636 ff.; (*Acheloüs*) 8.856 ff., 8.885 ff., 9.1 ff.; (*fights Centaurs*) 12.355 ff., 12.533 ff.; (*Demoleon*) 12.554 ff.; 15.1301.

THÉS·SALY: a region of northern Greece—2.888; 7.260; 7.359; 7.422; 8.1262; (*Thetis*) 11.363; 11.648; 12.127; (*Caenis*) 12.298; (*Caeneus*) 12.326; 12.333; 12.551; (*Halesus*) 12.717.

THÉ·TIS: daughter of Proteus, a sea goddess, mother of Achilles—11.337; (*Proteus and Peleus*) 11.346 ff.; (*Jupiter*) 11.355; (*Psamathe*) 11.634; (*hides Achilles*) 13.265; 13.477.

THÍS·BE: a young girl of Babylon—(*Pyramus*) 4.85 ff.; (*kills herself*) 4.236.

THRÁCE (E): region to the northeast of Greece—6.143; (*Tereus*) 6.693; 6.711; 10.82; 11.128; 13.715; (Hecuba) 13.923; (*Polydorus*) 13.1007.

TÍ·BER: river through Rome—(*overheats*) 2.372; 14.650; 14.683; (*name*) 14.939; 15.642; (*home for Aesculapius*) 15.945, 15.1102, 15.1116.

TI·SÍPH·O·NE or TI·SÍPH·ONE (E): one of the Furies—(*obeys Juno*) 4.701 ff.; (*Ino and Athamas*) 4.711 ff.

TÍT·Y·OS: monstrous son of Jupiter—(*Underworld*) 4.676; (*Orpheus*) 10.70.

TLE·PÓL·E·MUS: son of Hercules—(*with Nestor*) 12.828 ff.

TMÓ·LUS: a mountain in Lydia—(*burns*) 2.316; 6.25; (*Bacchus*) 11.130; (*Pan and Apollo*) 11.230 ff.; 11.295.

TÓX·E·US: son of Thestius, uncle of Meleager—(*Great Boar Hunt*) 8.482; (*killed*) 8.678 ff.

TRÁ·CHIS: a city in Thessaly—(*Ceyx*) 11.424; 11.784; 11.965.

TRIP·TÓL·E·MUS: son of Celeus—(*Ceres sends him away*) 5.1005 ff.; (*Lyncus*) 5.1013 ff.

TRÍ·TON: a sea god—(*helps end the Flood*) 1.483 ff.; 2.11; 13.1434.

TROÉ·ZEN: town in the Peloponnese—6.682; (*Lelex*) 8.888; 15.442; 15.764.

TROJANS (E): citizens of Troy, also applied to Aeneas and his comrades—12.101; 12.107 ff.; 12.1014; 12.1038; 13.147; 13.331; 13.343; 13.413; 13.444; 13.454; 13.537; 13.562; 13.571; 13.707; 13.924; 13.1118; 13.1123; 13.1184; 13.1154; 14.258; 14.379; 14.675; 14.810; 15.658.

TROY (E): city by the Hellespont—9.376; 10.238; (*Laomedon*) 11.304 ff.; (*Hercules*) 11.331; 11.1155; 12.30; 12.39; 12.688; 12.994; 13.36; 13.74; 13.87; 13.277; (*Ulysses' visit*) 13.328; 13.381; (*Fate revealed*) 13.529 ff.; (*falls*) 13.662 ff.; 13.997; 13.1149; 15.628; 15.656 ff.; 15.1165.

548

GLOSSARY AND INDEX

TÚR·NUS: king of the Rutulians—(*war*) 14.689 ff.; (*burns ships*) 14.809 ff.; 14.861; (*killed*) 14.871; 15.1170.

TY·PHÓ·E·US: a monstrous giant—3.464; (*fights gods*) 5.511 ff.; (*held underground*) 5.552 ff.

TÝRE (E): city in Asia Minor—2.1255; 3.55; 3.822; 6.103; 15.429.

TYR·RHÉN·I·AN: a name applied to certain non-Greek people from Asia Minor who moved into Italy—3.880; 3.1058; 4.36; 15.834.

U·LÝS·SES: king of Ithaca—(*arms of Achilles*) 12.1061; (*verbally attacked by Ajax*) 13.21 ff.; (*Palamedes*) 13.62, 13.90; (*leaves Nestor*) 13.101; (*saved by Ajax*) 13.119 ff.; (*responds to Ajax*) 13.203 ff.; (*his ancestry*) 13.230 ff.; (*discovers Achilles*) 13.265 ff.; (*his accomplishments in war*) 13.278 ff.; (*at Aulis*) 13.309 ff.; (*in Troy*) 13.325; (*Thersites*) 13.389; (*Diomedes*) 13.401; (*Dolon and Rhesus*) 13.409 ff.; (*Trojans killed*) 13.426; (*Achilles' body*) 13.466 ff.; (*Palamedes*) 13.509; (*Philoctetes*) 13.516 ff.; (*Helenus*) 13.550; (*Palladium*) 13.552 ff.; (*wins debate*) 13.628; (*brings Philoctetes back*) 13.653 ff.; (*Hecuba*) 13.693, 13.786, 13.829; 13.1135; (*Telemus*) 13.1225; 14.106; 14.249; (*Polyphemus*) 14.282 ff.; 14.340; (*Aeolus, Antiphates*) 14.343 ff.; (*Circe*) 14.448 ff.; 14.855; 14.1026.

UNDERWORLD: 2.376; (*Juno visits*) 4.639 ff.; (*Orpheus*) 10.16 ff.; (*Aeneas*) 14.178.

U·RÁ·NI·A: one of the Muses—5.413 ff.; (*daughters of Pierus*) 5.1039 ff.

VEN·Ú·LUS: a messenger from Turnus—(*Diomedes*) 14.697 ff.; (*returns*) 14.782 ff.

VÉ·NUS: goddess of love, wife of Mars, mother of Aeneas—(*Cadmus*) 3.200; (*Mars*) 4.250 ff.; (*Aphrodite*) 4.425; *(Hermaphroditus)* 4.570; (*Ino*) 4.785 ff.; (*fears Typhoëus*) 5.527; (*Cupid*) 5.576 ff.; (*Anchises*) 9.678; 9.1268; (*Cerastes and daughters of Propoetus*) 10.344 ff.; (*Pygmalion*) 10.410 ff.; (*Adonis*) 10.803 ff.; 10.968; (*Hippomenes*) 10.974 ff.; (*Adonis*) 10.1089 ff.; (*Circe*) 14.38; (*Diomedes*) 14.730 ff.; (*transforms crew*) 14.758 ff.; 14.870; (*petitions gods*) 14.891 ff.; (*Idalian Venus*) 14.1062; (*Venus Prospiciens*) 14.1169; (*saves Rome*) 14.1205 ff.; (*Caesar*) 15.1152 ff.; (Jupiter) 15.1219 ff.

VER·TÚM·NUS: god of the seasons—(*Pomona*) 14.976 ff.

VÉS·TA/VÉS·TAL VIRGINS: priestesses of Vesta, goddess of fire—15.1106; 15.1177; 15.1315.

VÚL·CAN: god of fire and the forge, husband of Venus, also called MULCIBER—2.7; 2.157; (*Mars and Venus*) 4.253 ff.; (*Erichthonius*) 9.678; (*Achilles*) 12.1042.

XÁN·THUS: river near Troy—(*overheats*) 2.354; (*Byblis*) 9.1031.

ZÁN·CLE: another name for Messana in Sicily—13.1163; 14.6; 14.73; 15.435.

THE TRANSFORMATIONS

[This list does not include the changes which occur when gods disguise themselves as human individuals or as animals or temporarily alter their shape. Nor does it include physical or temporal changes to the existing landscape where no human or divine character is transformed into something else. The information here confines itself to what is mentioned in Ovid's poem. The references are to the lines in the English translation.]

ACONTEUS—changed to stone by Medusa's head (5.320).

ACHELOUS' DAUGHTERS—changed into Sirens (5.872).

ACIS—changed into a stream (13.1388).

ACTAEON—changed into a stag by Diana (3.288).

ADONIS—changed into a flower (the anemone) by Venus (10.1109).

AENEAS—changed into a god (14.909).

AENEAS' SHIPS—changed into sea nymphs by Cybele (14.835).

AESACUS—changed into a bird (the diver) by Tethys (11.1198).

AESON—rejuvenated by Medea (7.452).

AGLAUROS—changed to dark stone by Mercury (2.1218).

AJAX'S BLOOD—changed to a flower (the hyacinth) (13.646).

ALCIDAMAS' DAUGHTER—gives birth to a dove (7.583).

ALCINOUS SHIP—changed to stone (14.856).

ALCYONE—changed into a bird (11.1119).

AMPYX—changed to stone by Medusa's head (5.292).

ANAXARETE—changed to stone (14.1154).

ANIMALS—change to other animals (15.539).

ANTIGONE—changed into a stork by Juno (6.151).

ANIUS' DAUGHTERS—changed to birds (doves) by Bacchus (13.1066).

ANTS—changed into human beings (Myrmidons) by Jupiter (7.994).

ARACHNE—changed into a spider by Minerva (6.241).

ARCAS—changed into a constellation by Jupiter (2.741).

ARDEA'S ASHES—changed into a heron (14.873).

ARETHUSA—changed into a river by Diana (5.985).

ARGUS—eyes are changed into designs on a peacock's tail by Juno (1.1063).

ARIADNE'S CROWN—changed into a constellation by Bacchus (8.287).

ARNE—changed into a jackdaw (7.734).

ASCALAPHUS—changed into a screech owl by Proserpine (5.849).

ASTYAGES—changed to stone by Medusa's head (5.324).

ATALANTA—changed into a lioness by Cybele (10.1060).

ATLAS—changed to rock by Medusa's head (4.970).

ATTIS—changed to a pine tree (10.158).

The Transformations

BATTUS—changed into flint by Mercury (2.1051)
BAUCIS—changed into a tree by Jupiter (8.1119).
BOY—changed into a spotted lizard by Ceres (5.707).
BYBLIS—changed into a fountain spring (9.1049).
CADMUS—changed into a snake (4.857).
CAENEUS—changed into a bird (12.809).
CAENIS—changed into a man by Neptune (12.318).
CALAUREA'S KING AND QUEEN—changed into birds (7.609).
CALLIRHOË'S SONS—made older by Jupiter (9.658).
CALLISTO: changed into a bear by Juno (2.700) and into a constellation by Jupiter (2.741).
CANENS—changed into air (14.657).
CASTOR—changed into a star (8.587).
CELMIS—changed into a rock (4.411).
CEPHISUS' GRANDSON—changed into a seal by Apollo (7.615).
CERAMBUS—changed into a flying creature by nymphs (7.561).
CERASTES—changed into cattle by Venus (10.355).
CERCOPES—changed into monkeys by Jupiter (14.139).
CEYX—changed into a bird (11.1131).
CINYRAS' DAUGHTERS—changed into stone steps (6.158).
CIPUS—grows horns (15.850).
CLYTIË—changed into a heliotrope plant (4.388).
COMBE—grows wings and flies (7.607).
CORAL—changes to stone in the air (15.617).
CORONEUS' DAUGHTER—changed into a Crow (by Diana?) (2.859).
CRAGALEUS—turned to stone (13.1137).[1]
CROCUS—changed into a flower (4.415).
CYANE—changed into a spring (5.668).
CYCNUS (1)—turned into a swan (2.540); CYCNUS (2)—turned into a swan (7.600); CYCNUS (3)—turned into a swan by Neptune (12.228).
CYPARISSUS—changed into a cypress tree (10.202).
DAEDALION—changed into a hawk by Apollo (11.539).
DAPHNE—changed into a laurel tree by Peneus (1.806).
DAPHNIS—changed into a stone by a nymph (4.404).

---

[1] Ovid's text does not provide this character's name.

The Transformations

Diomedes' Men (Acmon, Lycus, Idas, Abas, Nycteus, Rhetenor)—changed into swan-like birds by Venus (14.762).

Dryope—changed into a tree (9.561).

Earth—turned into human beings by Prometheus (1.113), produces other animals, including monsters (1.606); rejuvenated by Medea (7.447); changes into prophet Tages (15.837).

Echo—voice changed by Juno (3.552), loses her body (3.609).

Egeria—changed into a stream by Diana (15.826).

Eryx—changed to stone by Medusa's head (5.315).

Galanthis—changed into a weasel by Lucina (9.506).

Giants—dead forms turned into new life by Earth (1.216).

Glaucus—changed into a god of the sea (7.375; 13.1471).

Haemus—changed into a mountain (6.1430).

Harmonia—changed to a snake (4.857).

Hecuba—changed to a dog (13.662; 13.914).

Heliades (Daughters of the Sun)—changed into trees (2.498).

Hercules—changed to a god (9.422) and to a constellation (9.436) by Jupiter.

Hermaphroditus—merges with Salmacis to form one person (4.550).

Hersilia—changed into a goddess (14.1301).

Hippolytus—brought back to life, appearance changed (15.803).

Hippomenes—changed into a lion by Cybele (10.1060).

Hyacinthus—changed into a flower by Apollo (10.317).

Hyenas—change sex (15.609).

Hyrië—changed into a lake (7.603).

Ino—changed into a sea god by Neptune (4.799).

Ino's Companions—changed into rocks and birds by Juno (4.819).

Io—changed into a cow by Jupiter (1.899), then back to a nymph (1.1085).

Iolaüs—rejuvenated by Hebe (9.629).

Iphis—changed from a girl into a man by Io (9.1252).

Julius Caesar—changed into a star and a god (15.1279).

Lampetie—changed into a tree (2.498).

Lethaea—changed to rock (10.108).

Leucothoë—changed into a frankincense plant by the Sun (4.371).

Lichas—changed into a stony reef (9.354).

Lotis—changed into a lotus plant (9.554).

Lycaon—turned into a wolf by Jupiter (1.332).

LYCIAN PEASANTS—changed into frogs by Latona (6.603).
LYNCUS—changed into a lynx by Ceres (5.1031).
LYNX URINE—changes to stone, as does coral (15.617).
MAN (who saw Cerberus dragged away)—changed to stone (10.104).
MACAREUS AND HIS COMPANIONS—changed into pigs by Circe (14.429), then back again into human beings (14.463).
MAENADS—changed to oak trees by Bacchus (11.102).
MAESTRA—changed into a man and then back again a number of times by Neptune (8.1323).
MEDUSA—her blood drops change to snakes (4.919); her hair changed to snakes by Minerva (4.1190).
MELEAGER'S SISTERS—changed into birds by Diana (8.847).
MELICERTES—changed into a sea god by Neptune (4.799).
MEMNON'S FUNERAL SMOKE—changes to birds (the Memnonides) (13.969).
MIDAS—given asses' ears by Apollo (11.266).
MINDS AND BODIES—changed by spring water (15.476)
MINYAS' DAUGHTERS—changed into bats by Bacchus (4.598).
MOLOSSIAN KING'S SONS—changed into birds (13.1143).
MULBERRY TREE—fruit changes colour from Pyramus' blood (4.186)
MUSHROOMS—change into human beings (7.622).
MYRRHA—changed into a tree (10.754).
NAIAD—changes young men into fish and is changed into a fish herself (4.74).
NARCISSUS—changes into a flower (3.739).
NILEUS—changed to stone by Medusa's head (5.307).
NIOBE—changed into rock (6.439).
NISUS—changed into a sea eagle (8.231).
NYCTIMENE—changed into an owl by Minerva (2.873).
NYSEAN NYMPHS—rejuvenated by Medea (7.466).
OCYRHOË—changed into a horse (2.989).
OLENOS—changed to rock (10.108).
OLIVE BRANCH—rejuvenated by Medea (7.441).
ORGANS—changed to stone by water (15.469).
ORION'S DAUGHTERS' ASHES—change into two young men (the Coroni) (13.1110).
PEBBLES—changed from black to white by Hercules (15.71).
PEGASUS—born (with his brother) from Medusa's blood (4.1168).

The Transformations

PEOPLE—changed to stone by Medusa's head (4.1159); two hundred turned to stone by Medusa's head (5.332); grow feathers (15.532).

PERDIX—changed into a partridge by Minerva (8.403).

PERICLYMENES—changes himself into an eagle (12.860).

PERIMELE—changed into an island by Neptune (8.950).

PERIPHAS—changed into a bird (7.633).

PHAËTHUSA—turned into a tree (2.498).

PHENE—changed into a bird (7.633).

PHILEMON—changed into a tree by Jupiter (8.1119).

PHILOMELA—changed into a bird (6.1088).

PHINEUS—changed to stone by Medusa's head (5.638).

PHOENIX—changes into its own young (15.583).

PICUS—changed to a woodpecker by Circe (14.595).

PICUS' COMPANIONS—changed into various wild beasts by Circe (14.634).

PIERUS' DAUGHTERS—changed into magpies by Urania (5.1044).

PIGMY QUEEN—changed into a crane by Juno (6.147).

POLLUX—changed into a star (8.587).

POLYDECTES—changed to stone by Medusa's head (5.395).

POLYPEMON'S GRANDDAUGHTER—changed into a bird (7.635).

PROCNE—changed into a bird (6.1088).

PROETUS—changed to stone by Medusa's head (5.381).

PROPOETUS' DAUGHTERS—changed into flint by Venus (10.365).

PYGMALION'S STATUE—changed into a living girl by Venus (10.427).

RAIN—changes into the Curetes (4.414).

RAM—rejuvenated by Medea (7.501).

RAVEN:—changed from white to black by Apollo (2.934).

RHODOPE—changed into a mountain (6.1430).

ROCKS—thrown by Deucalion and Pyrrha become human beings (1.585).

ROMULUS—changed into a god (14.1254); his spear is changed into a willow tree (15.842).

SALMACIS—merges into one person with Hermaphroditus (4.550).

SCYLLA (1)—changed into a bird (the Ciris) (8.239). SCYLLA (2)—changed into a sea monster by Circe (14.83), then into a reef (14.108).

SCYRON'S BONES—changed into rocks (7.703).

SEAWEED—changed into rock by Medusa's head (4.1107).

SEMIRAMIS—grows wings to live with doves (4.72).

SERPENT'S TEETH—grow up into armed warriors (3.159) and again (7.204).

SHEPHERD—changed into a wild olive tree (14.797).

SITHON—becomes male and female (4.409).

SMILAX—changed into a flower (4.415).

SNAKE (1)—changed to stone by Apollo (11.88). SNAKE (2) changed to stone (12.33).

SYRINX—changed into marsh reeds by nymphs (1.1035).

TEARS (shed for Marsyas)—changed into a stream (6.648).

TEIRESIAS—changed to a woman and then back to a man (3.496). His sight is taken away by Juno, but Jupiter gives him the power to see (3.513).

TEREUS—changed into a hoopoe bird (6.1094).

THESCULUS—changed to stone by Medusa's head (5.289).

WILD BEASTS—changed to stone by Medusa's head (4.1159).

WOLF—changed into marble by Thetis of Psamathe (11.636).

WOMAN—changed by Persephone to mint (10.1105).

WOMEN OF COS—grow horns (7.574).

ACKNOWLEDGMENTS

Among the many translations and commentaries I consulted in preparing this text, the following have been particularly useful:

Innes, Mary M., translator. *The Metamorphoses of Ovid*. London, 1955.

Kline, Anthony S., translator and editor. *Ovid's Metamorphoses*. Available online at http://etext.virginia.edu/latin/ovid/trans/Ovhome.htm.

Melville, A. D. translator. Introduction and Notes by E. J. Kenney, *Ovid, Metamorphoses*. Oxford and London, 1986.

Riley, Henry T., translator and editor. *The Metamorphoses of Ovid*. London, 1893. Available online at http://www.gutenberg.org/files/26073/26073-h/main.html.

A Note on the Translator

Ian Johnston is a retired instructor (now a Research Associate) at Vancouver Island University, Nanaimo, British Columbia, Canada. His translations include the following titles:

Aeschylus, *Oresteia*
Aeschylus, *Seven Against Thebes*
Aeschylus, *The Persians*
Aristophanes, *Birds*
Aristophanes, *Clouds*
Aristophanes, *Frogs*
Aristophanes, *Knights*
Aristophanes, *Lysistrata*
Aristophanes, *Peace*
Cuvier, *On Revolutionary Upheavals on the Surface of the Earth*
Descartes, *Discourse on Method*
Euripides, *Bacchae*
Euripides, *Medea*
Euripides, *Orestes*
Homer, *Iliad* (Complete and Abridged)
Homer, *Odyssey* (Complete and Abridged)
Kant, *Universal Natural History and Theory of the Heavens*
Kant, *On Perpetual Peace*
Lucretius, *The Nature of Things*
Nietzsche, *Beyond Good and Evil*
Nietzsche, *Birth of Tragedy*
Nietzsche, *Genealogy of Morals*
Nietzsche, *Uses and Abuses of History*
Ovid, *Metamorphoses*
Sophocles, *Ajax*
Sophocles, *Antigone*
Sophocles, *Oedipus the King*
Sophocles, *Philoctetes*

These translations have been published by Richer Resources Publications, and some of these titles are available as recordings from Naxos Audiobooks.

Ian Johnston maintains a website at the following address: records.viu.ca/~johnstoi/index.htm.